The
Wrong Grief

ANDREA LANDY

PAGE PUBLISHING
Conneaut Lake, PA

First originally published by Page Publishing 2024

ISBN 979-8-88793-668-0 (pbk)
ISBN 979-8-88793-680-2 (digital)

Printed in the United States of America

For Stevie

Acknowledgments

I would like to thank Kimberly Littrell, APRN, for giving me the wonderful opportunity to work with persons with schizophrenia, and Dr. Steven Littrell for educating me on how to be the best co-facilitator as possible. I would also like to thank my teachers and professors—Sheila Murphy, Helen Landfear, and Dr. Ben Howard—for giving me the love of literature and poetry and teaching me how to write. I thank my incredible friends and family for all their encouragement, and most of all, I thank my husband, Steve Landy, and my father, Ron Nuzzo, for their constant love and support throughout this entire process. They made this novel a reality.

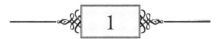

1

My sister and I had very special talks, but as we grew up, we grew apart a little, and Marisa didn't live long enough for us to really share important memories. I think my mother thought the rest of us were all liars anyway, even though I believed somewhere, she had to know the truth.

My first memory was when I was two years old. I was in Marisa's green bedroom upstairs, watching my mother lift Marisa's tiny legs as she lay on her back on the bed while my mother spanked the shit out of her little butt. My mother had this awful snarl on her face. The year was 1965.

I don't remember my parents wanting to move out of the Buchner home behind Boochie's Fish Store so that they could build a new home in Crescent Hills. Knowing Dad the way I did, that seemed impossible and more like something my mother would have wanted.

My father was the third-generation proprietor of Boochie's Fish Store, and he lived in the house directly behind it his entire life. His parents lived there, his grandparents lived there, and although I don't remember, it would have been my mother Lavinia who would have wanted to break the cycle, pack up, and move out of South Wellton. I suppose I could see how other people could want to do the same, just not Rudy Buchner.

What I do remember were the fights, the arguments, and as I recall, it was mainly my mother's squawking that rocked the house. Dad wasn't a yeller. He just shrugged his shoulders, waved his hands, and tried his best to ignore her. That wasn't easy because she could get really loud. One time he put cotton balls in his ears, and that really pissed her off. But for reasons unknown, I felt this need to cling to my mother at times. She was my mother after all.

One summer morning that I remember particularly well was when my parents were still married. It was unusually hot, and the sun was high in the sky. The four of us prowled around this big parking lot in our blue Plymouth station wagon with the wooden side panels. My mother fidgeted and squirmed in the front seat and kept muttering to herself. I heard a couple of words and phrases like "embarrassed" and "sell this thing" while my father, with the windows down, his shoulder-length black hair flipping around his ears in wisps, sang to the music on the radio.

"I'm having lunch with Penelope," she declared as she snapped her head back to look at Marisa and me in the back seat. "Are you listening to me, Marisa?"

I answered yes for the both of us. Marisa was busy giggling at my father's singing as she waved her arms out the window.

My mother swatted Marisa on the thigh. "If you continue to stick your arms out the window, young lady, another car is going to come along and rip them right off your body."

"Will she die, Mom?" I asked, horrified at the thought.

My mother shrugged her shoulders. "I don't know."

My father pulled up beside the Wellton Savings Bank, which was a tiny outparcel at the far end of the parking lot where my mother was supposed to meet her friend. I could feel the heat of the engine and the smell of the exhaust as my mother, forgetting to say goodbye and give my father a kiss, hurriedly grabbed her white patent leather pocketbook and escaped from the car as if it were about to explode. Her thick auburn hair remained perfect as her large white faux pearls bounced over her chest and her white polka-dot sundress swayed softly just above her knees.

"You look beautiful, Mom," I said to her as she disappeared into the bank. I climbed over the back seat and peered out the back window. Once my father turned the corner, both the bank and my mother were gone. I was sad and worried. She had forgotten to say goodbye to us; she never touched my arm or leg, never turned around once. She was running away from us, and I wondered if she would ever come back.

"Rudy, can we get a cat?" Marisa bounced up and down in her seat.

My father let out a quick robust laugh. "Cat? You want a cat? I'm not really a fan of cats. It's not that I don't like them. I don't know much about them." He paused for a second. "Now, wait a minute, there's that one cat that hangs around the store. That's bad enough. A cat that hangs around a fish store."

"Don't say you don't know about cats. You know everything about stuff," Marisa said.

My father put his hand on his chest and tossed his head back. He was all puffed up and proud of himself. The two of them continued to discuss cats, singing, and hair, all of which I found boring. I continued to sit in the way back, which was what I called the long beige carpeted area of our station wagon.

"Want me to roll down the big window for you back there?" my father called back to me, ignoring my mother's rules.

I shook my head as I pressed my nose up against the side window.

"All right. We're gonna be home soon anyway."

We turned onto the Boulevard or what I always called the pretty road when I was little. The brilliant green and endless mediums wove through the concrete in perfect little strips hidden under maple trees one after the other. At night, the Boulevard would sparkle with ordinary streetlights until you drove around the old firehouse and the Roman Catholic church my grandmother always admired. There you could see the vintage gas lamps in forest green, fire flickering within.

It was so hot in the way back, even though I could feel a little bit of a breeze coming from Marisa's open window. It was the same window that she continued to hang out of, challenging other drivers and pedestrians alike to "go ahead take my arms off!"

I remained isolated in the back, face pressed up to the window, wondering who Penelope was and why my mother had to have lunch with her. We had lots of things to eat for lunch at home. That's exactly where we were going and what we were planning to do, go home to eat lunch. My mother, who was always so beautiful to me, looked like a princess back at the bank with her white handbag and matching shoes, her long shimmering strand of make-believe pearls; she looked like she was about to board an airplane. Her white dress with the red polka dots was my favorite. The way it swung and lay so quietly, you couldn't even tell she was wearing a slip and a girdle underneath. I knew she was because I spied on her that morning and watched as she slowly pasted her undergarments to her smooth pale body. Had she known I was on the other side of that door, she would have yelled and slapped me. My mother got angry at things like that. Why did she have to get so dressed up to eat lunch?

Unlike my father's fine jet-black mane that fell untamed, every strand of hair on my mother's head was perfectly planned. It was an organized lush of a deep redwood. That day she swooped it back on both sides behind each ear and fastened a handful with a shiny white barrette. Her red hair was just a little darker than the red polka dots.

As I sat in the hot car, the front windows still all rolled down, I wished that I could spend more time with my mother in her polka-dot dress and that she didn't want to run to Penelope. I never remembered her running to Marisa, Dad, or me like that, and I was sure neither Dad nor Marisa had any recollections either. I could ask, but no, never mind.

"Hey, Alice, are you still out here?" Marisa was hanging off the car door. "Come on inside. Rudy's got us some of that homemade bread with the rest of the leftover borscht." She fidgeted with the door handle. "And gumballs."

As soon as I heard *gum*, my head snapped around. "He doesn't have gumballs for us." I shook my head and sneered, missing my mother again and suddenly noticing the overcast sky.

"He does!" she insisted. "If you come right now, I'll show you. I *promise* you. Rudy's giving us gumballs with lunch. He said he got them at the bank the other day."

"Mom isn't going to like that," I said darkly.

She put her foot up into the car as she swayed back and forth. "Mom's not here, is she? She's gone to have lunch with her friend, so we can do anything we want, and Rudy's not going to tell. It was his idea anyway."

As my sister chattered about wanting a cat, I used the opportunity to cram myself all the way back at the end of the car. I lay sideways like a log, attempting to roll toward the front, with each roll saying, "I don't want any borscht, I want—"

"You're never going to make it over that seat," she said, shaking her head and curling her lips in disgust.

"Gumballs." I plopped over the back of the seat and landed belly down. "Yes, I just did!" I rolled over on my back and started to get up.

"You're a dummy. Come on." Marisa galloped up the stone walkway and then up the steps to the Victorian-style house behind Boochie's Fish Store. Victorian style was what my mother called our house. She said it wasn't really a Victorian house; it was a Victorian-style house. I wasn't sure what the difference was.

Boochie's Fish Store is where Dad's employee and best friend Frank and sister Aunt Nancy were, as my dad would say, "holding down the fort." My mother referred to my father's younger sister and my aunt Nancy as crazy. Aunt Nancy had paranoid schizophrenia for as long as I can remember, and that would be my whole life. As long as she stayed on her medication, she was okay—well, pretty much okay. I didn't think it was very nice of my mother to call Aunt Nancy names behind her back, but I didn't dare tell my mother that. I just pretended not to listen, and I always hoped that Aunt Nancy didn't hear her because it would probably really hurt her.

When I turned around from the car, I noticed that Aunt Nancy didn't look like she was "holding down the fort" like she was sup-posed to, but I think Dad was used to that. She was standing in the shade on the side of the building smoking what was probably her two hundredth cigarette. She looked very thin. Aunt Nancy's weight went up and down and up and down. She seemed to always talk about it. She stood up against the gray concrete wall, one knee up, wearing a white T-shirt with blue jeans and some sort of white towel wrapped around her head. Normally, she wore the regular hairnet that looked like a white shower cap. I had no idea what she was doing with that towel.

Noticing that I was watching her, she smiled and waved.

I waved back. "Hi, Aunt Nancy." I probably said it too quietly for her to hear, and then I made my way up to the house.

Marisa liked my aunt Nancy a lot. The two of them played the piano together, picked flowers, drew pictures, and pressed those wax paper maple leaf things. Marisa liked to do all that arts and crafts stuff, and Aunt Nancy liked to tag along with her. A lot of the time Aunt Nancy would forget Marisa's name and end up calling her Elizabeth or Melissa. I loved Aunt Nancy, but she could be very annoying because she would squeeze my fat cheeks and kiss me really hard. At least she could remember my name. Who wouldn't remember the name Alice? I thought that Alice was one of the most ordinary names on earth. Marisa's name was lovely and beautiful and unique, just like her.

Dad set our little wooden table in the kitchen. Marisa was already sitting at one end, waiting for my father to bring her borscht and bread. She reminded me of a beautiful petite princess, all magnificent and regal as she slowly caressed her long, thick, shiny, auburn ponytail. And she sort of reminded me of Mom.

"Dad, is it true?" I asked. "Did you really get us gumballs for lunch?"

He had a dish towel tossed over his left shoulder, and in his right hand, he held a ladle as he slumped over the countertop, stirring a big stainless steel pot of borscht. "See for yourself." He nodded toward the table.

My father had evenly divided ten gumballs between us, but Marisa took it upon herself to take all the pink and red ones, leaving me all the yellow and green.

"Now, you girls might want to wait until you're finished with your lunch. You can't eat borscht and chew gum at the same time," he joked.

I looked across my bowl at my sister. "You took all the red and pink ones."

"Marisa?" My father was at the sink, his back to us. Then he walked out of the kitchen on his way upstairs. "I divided those colors evenly between the two of you. Alice likes the red ones too, you know."

She shook her head as if I had inconvenienced her. "Alice, why do you have to be such a baby? Come on."

The room went dark. I didn't really care about gumballs or what color they were. I was wondering what was so special about this Penelope person that made my mother want to dress up and run away? Suddenly, an eerie feeling crept over me. It was still hot out, but the sun was gone as the clouds moved in and swallowed up the sky. "Where's Mom?"

Marisa was shoveling beets into her mouth. "What?" There was sour cream on her lips. "You know where she is. We dropped her off at the bank, you know, to meet her friend."

"Penelope."

"Yeah." Another mouthful.

"I want Mom to come back."

"She's coming back."

"When?"

"I don't know. Later."

"I don't want to wait until later. I want her back now. I want my mother back now!" I yelled and slapped my palm down into my borscht, causing some of the thick pink liquid to spill onto the table. Then I dropped a yellow gumball into my bowl.

"What's wrong with you, Alice? Mom's coming back, and you *know* she's coming back. She lives here, stupid! Why all of a sudden do you miss her so much? Why did you just—is it because of the red and pink gumballs? Isn't that kind of dumb? God."

I was sobbing quietly as my father, having just changed into a T-shirt and boxer shorts, walked toward me. I looked up at his chest area, too afraid to meet his eyes. I thought I was in trouble for making a mess or that Marisa would make it sound worse than it really was. Had my mother seen my behavior, she would have slapped me so hard on the side of my head, my ears would have been ringing for the rest of the afternoon.

"Okay," he said quietly as he wiped down the leg of the wooden table with a green sponge, "let's take the yellow gumball out of the borscht."

"I don't know what's wrong with her, Rudy. One minute she's fine, the next minute she goes ape. Now she's worried that Mom's never coming back."

"You're a thief," I said.

"Ladies, come on. That's enough. You're sisters, you're supposed to love each other, share and be kind."

Neither one of us said anything to that. My reason was because I had the B-word on the launching pad and ready to go, and I knew that would really disappoint Dad. But Marisa had no control over herself, and I watched her. She just gave me a smug look and returned the red and pink gumballs she stole from me.

"Ew. They have borscht all over them. I don't want them anymore. You can have them," I said.

"Good. Thanks." She took the rest of her bread and gumballs and headed for the kitchen door. "I'm going outside to see if I can find Shelly."

"Who's Shelly?" my father asked, tossing the sponge in the sink from across the room. "Two points."

"He's that stray cat we were talking about today that comes around sometimes. He's gray and he likes shellfish, so I named him Shelly." She was excited as she looked around for the cat.

"You better not be feeding him!"

"I'm not!" she insisted, her face up in the screen door.

"Watch he doesn't bite you."

"He's not gonna bite me. He won't even let me get close to him." She was gone.

I sat still at the table as my father turned to me. "Do you want some more soup?"

I shook my head.

"Well, wipe your nose. You got snot running down your face."

I blew my nose into a clean napkin my father put in front of me. He looked tired.

"Dad."

"Hmm?"

"I'm sorry."

"Aw, don't be."

"How come Mom always has to go places?" Why was this so hard for everyone to understand? I was ten years old, and I could understand that mothers were not supposed to get all dolled up and run off to meet a friend that nobody seemed to know while leaving their families at home. "Like today, she was wearing a beautiful dress, the kind she only puts on when we go over to Bunic and Bunica's for the holidays, and she hates doing that and going over there. But today she was all happy to go and see Penelope in her dress. It must be Penelope."

My father chuckled. I didn't know what was funny. "Oh, you're a smart one, Alice." He pulled up a wooden chair from the side of the table and sat. It was too small for him. "I don't know where you got it from, but it sure as hell wasn't from me."

"You're smart, Dad," I objected.

He raised a finger. "I can put on a good show when I need to." Then he got up and started puttering around the kitchen. My father didn't like to sit in one place for very long unless he was exhausted and had a book in his hands. He shrugged his shoulders. "She just wants to spend a little time with her friends. You know, get away from us every once in a while."

"Get away from us?" *I knew it.*

"Okay, get away from me." He threw his hands out in front of him as if he was trying to stop something from running him over.

"Why does Mom want to get away from you? You're married!"

He let out this loud laugh and shook his head. He walked over to the sink, stood there for several seconds, and started tinkering with something while his back was toward me. He was annoying me.

"She's always going out places, Dad. Why can't she invite her friends like Penelope over here? Does she hate us or something? Do you love Mom, Dad?"

"Of course I love her."

"Then why doesn't she want to be with us or with *you*?"

"I…I don't know, Alice." He turned to me and threw his hands up again. "Sometimes adults—women—like to go out to lunch with their friends. You wait until you get older, you're gonna want to go out to lunch with the ladies too."

"You don't go out to lunch."

"I don't eat lunch. And I'm not a lady."

I giggled. "Everybody in the world eats lunch, Dad."

"I gotta tell you, Alice, if I had known that I was going to have a kid who was going to stump me and ask me all these hard questions, I would have sold you a long time ago."

"Sell me?" I asked. "Where? At the store?"

He raised his eyebrows and did a little dance with his head. "The store sounds good. I could have sold you to the sideshow at the state fair."

"The sideshow?"

It must have been the way I said *sideshow* because suddenly, my father was laughing hard, not the way he had been laughing earlier when we were talking about Mom. This was real laughter, when something was really funny, when there was something to actually laugh about. In the backyard, I could hear Marisa talking sweetly to Shelly the cat.

For that moment, I remember everything was perfect.

Except Mom was gone.

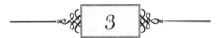

3

At dinnertime, my mother had still not arrived home. When I asked my father again where she was, he said that she had called earlier and announced that she would be spending the rest of the afternoon with Penelope and that Penelope would be driving her home later.

The house was beginning to cool down a little. Dad opened the windows in the kitchen, the library, and the living room, and a slight breeze crossed through the downstairs, giving us some relief. The sun disappeared again except for a small silver shimmer that made its way through the grayish clouds. Off in the distance were slight streaks of pink shown over someone else's part of Wellton. I couldn't see the moon, but the early signs of evening had a clarity about them. I wondered if my mother would be home before the clock struck the late hours.

Dad brought us back fish sticks, homemade sauce, and "World Famous" fries from the store. As soon as I saw the amount of fries Dad had in the bag—or chips as he referred to them in a really bad English accent—I knew for sure that Mom would not be joining us for dinner. Dad prepared us two whole packages of frozen baby peas and then squashed them up like mashed potatoes, explaining that "this is how the Brits do it—more or less." Marisa smothered her food with ketchup, tartar sauce, and malt vinegar while Dad and I discussed sixteenth century England. Marisa thought Dad and I were boring. We probably were to most people.

My father always liked to talk about different places, about the world's cultures and religions. He loved to read. When he wasn't at the store or driving my mother around to meet strange people for lunch dates, he would spend hours pacing the library with a book in

11

his hands. Sometimes we would just sit on the sofa and read together. It could be a book about anything. My father claimed that the world was so full of things to learn that we could spend the rest of our lives reading and learning, and we wouldn't have even begun to make a dent in the knowledge that was available to us. He knew everything he needed to know about running a fish store, but he always said that just picking one thing to learn and to master was a bore. He even said once there were more things to learn about running a fish store. He said we never really knew *everything* even if we were masters. "Expand your mind," he would say. "Your brain needs to be active, so keep it active." My mother always told him that he was full of shit, but he didn't care. He would just laugh, shake his head, and keep reading everything he found interesting. I would be his partner.

It was dark when my mother came home, and I may have been asleep for some time. My bedroom window, which faced the front of the house, was open, and a soft breeze must have sent me off. I had been fighting sleep just so I could see my mother in her dress before I climbed into bed. Gone were the regular sounds of the evening: familiar honking on the South Wellton strip, which was the south side Boulevard but nowhere near as nice, the occasional screeching whoosh of an airbrake as Frank stood on the loading dock, smoking a cigarette and chatting away with a truck driver, a distant bounce of a basketball. Now, the house was crowded with the booming sounds of impatience, anger, and fury, all of which came from my mother.

I couldn't actually hear what they were arguing about, but tonight, it sounded as if my mother was a burglar lost in the dark, a burglar who was clumsy and very mad. My sister wasn't a chicken clutching her stuffed whatever under the covers, however. She would always brazenly stand at the top of the staircase in her pajamas, listening like a bad spy, eager to report back to me. The bright yellow overhead light in the hallway flicked on, and as I gingerly allowed one eye to creep over the sheets, I saw a slither of Marisa's face in the cracked bedroom door.

"Mom's home."

4

"What do you think you're doing?" It was my mother's slow voice, low like a cat watching a bird's every move, holding back, drawing out for as long as it could until it decided on the perfect time to pounce.

"Nothing. I just had to go to the bathroom." Marisa retreated to her bedroom. I knew she was scared.

"Don't lie to me."

Through the crack of the door, I saw a whiz of white as my mother flew into Marisa's bedroom.

"I didn't do anything!" Then a loud crack. "Ow! Mom!" There was another crack and a third that sounded more like a thump. Then crying.

"Shut up!" My mother's two favorite words when talking to the two of us. "Where is your sister?" she demanded. "Did you hear me? I asked you a question. Where is your sister?"

"In her room, sleeping. I just checked on her." Marisa's answer was just above a whisper. I had to strain to hear it.

I turned my head to the wall. I knew if I stayed under the covers, my mother would know that I was hiding. I froze as I could see the slight pink of light behind my eyelids. I could smell the faintness of her perfume mixed with the staleness of afternoon cigarettes, and I wondered where Dad was. Probably hiding too. She was only there for a second, then the door slammed behind her, and she was gone. I still hadn't seen her all day, not since we dropped her off at the bank to meet Penelope to eat lunch, smoke cigarettes, drink alcohol, and do other adult things. It would be so much better to wait until morning.

* * * * *

I woke up, and there was a freezing silence in my bedroom. My window was still open, and I looked out and saw that the floodlights at the back of the tiny warehouse were still on and the same truck I had seen the night before still backed into the loading dock. Shelly the cat was wandering along the sidewalk, most likely looking for scraps of trash. I thought I would giggle, but before I could utter a sound, I closed my mouth quickly and tightly. If I woke my mother, there would be a bar of green soap in my trap whether I had said a dirty word or not.

When I looked out the window again, Shelly was gone. How was he so fast? Cats were pretty fast animals, I knew that. Much faster than dogs. Most dogs, I guess. I made a mental note to look that fact up in the library at school in the fall.

I thought about sneaking into my sister's room. My father was snoring, and my mother wasn't. I knew they were both asleep, and when I looked up…

"Hey!"

Marisa put her fingers up to her lips. "Get back into bed," she whispered. "Why is your window open so far? I think it's going to rain."

"I was afraid to shut it. I didn't want Mom to hear."

She pulled the window down, leaving a couple of inches. I cringed at the sound of the low gnawing squeak, but there was no stirring from my parents' room, so I knew we were safe.

"Come on, lie down."

We both got under the covers, and my sister put her arm around me. Her pajamas smelled really nice.

"What are you doing?"

"Why are you wearing slippers, Alice?"

"I'm cold."

"It's August, dummy."

Then she got up and went back to her room.

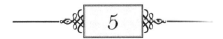

5

The smell from Boochie's deep fryer filled me with comfort, and I noticed that people were beginning to line up around the corner for Dad's salmon. Or was it the steel-headed trout? I always got those two confused, and Dad would have put ice cubes down the back of my shirt if he thought I would have ever gotten the two mixed up. Aunt Nancy was at the back of the building with a towel on her head, smoking a cigarette and quietly talking with someone I couldn't see. Frank was rolling a hand truck filled with boxes before he disappeared into the warehouse. I still hadn't seen my mother since we dropped her off at the bank the day before, but I wasn't nearly as upset about it as I had been. I thought it best to stay out of her way as much as I could since it was obvious that she had been in a terrible mood after her day out with Penelope. Penelope probably only saw my mother when she was in a good mood.

Marisa was nowhere to be found on that summer morning. I figured she was probably up the road playing with her friends. She had so many friends. I didn't have many friends at all, definitely not during the summer like she had. Marisa had her friends at school and her friends in the summer. Friends everywhere. None of that mattered much to me. I had Dad, Marisa, Aunt Nancy, and it looked like I was making a new friend in Shelly the cat. I suppose he was a friend whenever he was around, which was really only when he could smell fish. Shelly came around anytime he smelled any food, and I knew that Marisa was lying to Dad. She fed him. Even though I hadn't caught her, I knew she did. She was sneaky.

Mom threatened to ditch us at our grandparents' house for the day while she went out with a real estate agent. I knew that Dad wouldn't be selling our house. It had been in the family forever. His

15

grandfather built the house when he came to America from Germany. I wasn't sure if we were going to buy another house; after all, that would be silly, and who needs two houses? Our house was right behind the store. Dad could walk to work. I could throw a baseball and hit Aunt Nancy's towel on her head, that's how close we were, but doing that would be a bad idea. It would make things much worse for her than they already were. Even though my mother had no use for Aunt Nancy, she was still my aunt and my father's younger sister, and throwing a baseball at the towel on her head would hurt my father's feelings. I would not be able to tolerate that.

And so there would be no new houses, nor would there be the selling of the old one, but as I would later learn that evening when Dad and Mom actually sat down at the big table together, my mother would be taking Marisa and me to live with her in a new apartment. That surprised and terrified me as I eavesdropped—not really the part about the new apartment, but the fact that my mother wanted my sister and me to go with her. I thought we would just get in the way when she wanted to go out to lunch. It didn't make any sense. I guess she could have ditched us with our grandparents. Now, here's the funny thing. I remember exactly what happened next, but I had absolutely no recollection of the events leading up to it. And I don't know why Marisa was late for dinner.

"Rudy, what are you doing?" Marisa suddenly exclaimed, her mouth wide-open with astonishment.

It was my father's eyes that I would never forget. They always had a remarkable warmth to them. They were beautiful and brown, like chocolate. Now, they were a dry blackish-gray stare, predatory, like a wild animal. Maybe he didn't want us to move. I didn't want to move either. He had shaken up a can of beer and popped the top when the rich foamy liquid elegantly squirted about three feet in the air, arcing onto my mother's perfectly laid table.

My mother's roar crashed through the room like a lioness fighting off a male lion she found threatening her cubs. But it wasn't the lioness protecting her cubs; it was the male protecting the cubs. And the cub he was protecting wasn't even his own.

My mother threw both her arms back and, with full force, leveled the table of all its contents. Hot dogs, buns, and baked beans were strewn all over the kitchen, and the glass mustard jar in the middle of the table that was the size of a bowling ball was the only thing that remained, but with a huge jagged chunk missing. There must have been sixty-four ounces of bright yellow mustard cascading onto the table as my mother screamed and cried. "You know I don't like a mess!"

She screamed so loud, I thought for sure the neighbors could hear, and they didn't even live close by.

"You did that on purpose! Goddamn you!"

Marisa stood speechless with her back against the refrigerator, her face frozen with a mixture of awe and glee. If my mother had turned around, she would have killed her had she seen that face. I said nothing. I did nothing. I just stared.

"I'm going to take her to the doctor, Lavinia," my father said to my mother in a direct and threatening manner that sounded unusual for him. He was furious, but he didn't yell or lose his temper. He was holding me with his right arm, but I was lopsided with my head facing the gray speckled linoleum floor. I wondered if he had forgotten about me.

"Dad, can I get down?"

"She's not even your kid, Rudy. Don't pretend that you give a shit!" my mother hollered.

He put me down first and bolted out of the kitchen. Marisa followed behind, and my mother continued to holler through her wet red face. I couldn't understand what she was saying through all her crying and shouting.

"Okay. Fine. I'm going now." My father walked powerfully to the front door.

"No, Daddy!" I shouted. "Don't go!"

He ignored me and was gone.

I spiraled around and sat down on the sofa when Marisa yanked my arm, and we ran upstairs to my bedroom.

"Let's just stay here," she said quietly. "She'll find me in my room, but she won't come in here."

"Yes, she will."

"No, she won't. Just stay."

"It's Dad! He's back."

"He is?"

"Yes! I just heard him downstairs!"

"He can't be so soon." She was whispering, but it could have been yelling; it felt and sounded so loud. Marisa seemed calm as she opened the door farther. I was scared to death.

"Mom isn't yelling anymore."

I managed to stop and listen for a second.

"No, I think she's just crying now." Marisa was motionless.

It sounded like she was cleaning up the war zone she had created in the kitchen as she continued to sniffle and cry. All the while she kept saying things like *asshole* and *cheap son of a bitch*.

"Just stay quiet, please, Marisa?"

She nodded, but I could see this little smile starting up at the corner of her mouth, and I knew we were going to be in the worst trouble if she didn't crush that smile immediately.

"Marisa."

"That was so funny. Did you see Rudy squirt that beer at Mom?"

See it? How could you not *see it?* I smiled. "Yeah."

"I'm gonna tell everyone."

"You are?" *God, please don't.*

"All my friends."

"Girls?" My father was down at the bottom of the stairs. "You up there?"

I felt more relaxed the minute my sister made the beer can incident just a big funny joke, even though I knew that there was nothing funny about it. But once I heard my father calling for us, my stomach immediately untwisted, and I wasn't as frightened.

"Yeah, we're up here, Daddy." I poked my head farther out of the bedroom doorway. I didn't like to call my father Daddy this much because it made me sound like a baby, and Marisa teased me for it. But I was still a little scared, and it just slipped out.

"Come on, we're going to Jodie's."

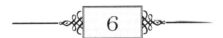

6

I turned my head to the open window as we drove farther down the Wellton Strip, and as I closed my eyes, I tried to drink in the happiness of what summertime was supposed to be. It was the smell of diesel and the flapping sound of an old Opel with a bad muffler that calmed me. It was nice to just be outside in the air.

The parking lot at Jodie's was full of families. Real families, like families that had kids with both their parents who weren't arguing and fighting all the time. Everybody liked each other, and they all piled into their cars afterward and headed to the drive-in or went home and watched something funny on TV, and everyone would laugh at the same time. Home would be that place where you could be with the people who loved you and who you loved back, the people who really loved you, no questions asked. You could just be quiet, feel safe, and relax.

We didn't have that in our home. My parents didn't just argue—they really fought. My mother screamed, and my father left. My mother didn't like Marisa or me to get in her way. My father read his books, sometimes with me, or have his conversations with his customers that I didn't always understand, and my mother became jealous and annoyed. My mother went out and ate lunch with Penelope, and she smiled and looked forward to it. Later that same day, she would walk into the house and, within seconds, be hollering, red-faced with snot and tears, and swatting Marisa for eavesdropping on a fight with Dad. Now we were moving out.

My mother constantly reminded my father that Marisa was not his real daughter, and so he shouldn't pretend to care about another man's child. Now, that was something I didn't get. You either cared about someone or you didn't. You could also think that person was okay, and you weren't totally crazy about him *or* her, but who cares who that person's father is? Dad and Marisa got along well, and he loved her like she was his own girl.

Dad always remarked on how smart I was for my age. Well, if I was so smart, I would have been able to get my family to look like the family in the car next to us. It was all very hopeless as I looked around the parking lot at Jodie's and all the nice families. Mom said these strange things that made everyone feel bad.

I was an expert at counting. Counting was something I did most every day, but I didn't talk about it. Because I liked to count, I counted three different places at Jodie's where you could eat. One was the dark green concrete tables with the yellow and white super hard plastic umbrellas at the far side of the parking lot. I had already counted one couple sitting with their cute fat baby who reminded me of a huge ball of dough. Another were the big orange booths inside where lots of kids a few years younger than I would have their birthday parties, and the third were in the way backs of the station wagons where we were tonight. We never ever sat at the dark green concrete tables outside. My mother refused to sit at those tables. She said there were flies everywhere, and it was dirty. She also hated sitting inside because she said there were too many children, so we just always ate in the car, which was rare anyway because my mother didn't like Jodie's much. So we never went to Jodie's when we were with Mom.

Dad opened the back door. I carried the sodas while Marisa handed the bags to my father.

"Okay, you two," he said, catching his breath after crawling all the way down into the way back. "Who gets the cheeseburger, who gets the other cheeseburger, and who gets all the cherry pies? I think that's me!"

"No!" I protested. "You can't eat all the cherry pies, Dad."

"That's right, Rudy. You start eating too many cherry pies, even *you're* going to get fat."

"I don't care about being fat," I said, taking a bite out of my food.

"That's obvious," Marisa said.

I ignored her and looked over at my father. He was sprawled out sideways, faded white sneakers dangling out of the back of the car. He wore faded blue jeans and a navy-blue T-shirt. He was staring at me.

"Dad, what's that white thing on your forehead?"

He reached up and knocked away what looked like a tiny piece of a napkin. "Your mother must have thrown something at me back there." He continued to look me square in the eyes.

"That was so funny, Rudy, what you did. You know, when you squirted that beer all over Mom?" Marisa's eyes rolled up into two comical little slits as she pulled her body into a laughing ball.

"Careful, you're gonna choke on your cheeseburger."

I nodded and smiled. "I don't think it reached that far, did it?"

Marisa nodded, her mouth full. "Yeah, it did. Must have gotten her right in the face 'cause she was really mad."

"I'll tell you, these french fries are not nearly as good as whose?" my father asked the two of us.

"Boochie's," we responded in bored unison.

I wasn't ready to stop talking about the beer can. I wanted to know more. I also wanted to know when we were moving out and if Mom and Dad were getting a divorce. Then I remembered that Marisa hadn't heard that part of the conversation. I was the one who heard it, and maybe I shouldn't say anything.

"Why was Mom so mad at you, Dad?" I felt like I was asking the same question over and over, just in different ways.

He didn't reply with his usual shrug and get up and walk around the room. Instead, he continued to stare at me as we ate. "Your mother and I don't get along that much these days."

"But why did you squirt her?"

"I squirted the table, not her."

"Were we supposed to eat all the food she pushed off the table?"

Marisa looked at me. "That was our dinner, Alice. What do you think we were supposed to do with it?"

"Supposed to," Dad agreed. Then he asked, "Are you two girls okay?"

We both nodded as Marisa continued to eat her fries, and I took a bite out of my cherry pie.

"Where did you go before, Dad?"

"When?" He chewed and stared.

"When you left the house."

He shrugged. "I went out to look at the car. I wanted to make sure I had enough gas to get us here."

* * * * *

Later that night, Marisa and I sat on the bed in my room. My mother didn't like it when we sat on a made-up bed, and after everything that happened, we still didn't seem to learn a lesson. Marisa wanted to be with me in my room. She didn't always like her bedroom. She said it scared her. We sat across my twin bed, legs out, watching the white drapes on my windows sadly stir to the silence of the river breeze. We compared our legs. Although Marisa was three years older than I, my legs looked nearly as long as hers.

"You're going to grow up to be a big girl someday, Alice. See?" She pushed her left thigh into my right and lifted her rear end a little. "I'm older than you are, and you're nearly the same size as I am. It's like my dad wasn't such a big guy, maybe?"

"You never met him."

She shook her head slowly. "And Mom doesn't like to talk about him much. But she did say that he was very rich—an Indian prince."

I looked at her. "An Indian prince? Like A Navajo? I remember Dad giving me a lecture on the indigenous peoples of America."

"No, an *Indian* Indian, you know, a person from the country of India."

"Wow," I said quietly and adjusted myself so that I was sitting with my back against the wall.

"Yeah. An Indian prince from India. It's a subcontinent."

"What's a subcontinent?" She would never know the answer to that.

"I don't know." She twisted her brow and looked up in my direction. "I think it's a continent that's not quite a continent yet."

Good try.

"It's in Asia too. Even farther away from Africa. It's on the other side of the world."

"Would you like to meet him one day?"

"Who?"

"Your father."

"Yes. For sure."

"Do you think one day Mom will tell you where he lives?"

Her eyes widened as she raised her brow and shrugged slowly. "I don't know." She had a cautious look in her eye. "Hopefully some day when she's in a good mood, and I can ask her about him again. She gets mad a lot though."

"Is that ever the truth. Do Bunic and Bunica know about him?"

She shook her head.

"How about Dad?"

"Nope."

I was instantly intrigued by that. My father would have been fascinated by India. An Indian prince? That would have been something that he and I would have talked about for days. But I never heard my father talk about Marisa's father, let alone the fact that he was an Indian prince. That would have made Marisa a princess.

Suddenly, I thought my big sister was spinning a tall tale. It certainly wouldn't have been the first time. The funny thing was that she didn't sound like she was fibbing. She looked like she was telling the truth.

"Now listen, Alice," she said, lowering her voice as she pulled my chin up to her face with her fingers. "Don't ever, *ever* tell anyone about this—not your weirdo friends at school, not Rudy, and *especially* not Mom. Do you understand me?"

I swallowed hard, never losing eye contact.

"Because if Mom found out we were talking about my father, she would hit me hard, and I would probably die."

Horror gripped the back of my throat. "No, Marisa," I whispered, feeling panicked and helpless. "Please don't say that. You're scaring me. I promise. I won't tell anyone!"

She let go of my face with a little push. "It's a secret. I have to be able to trust you."

I nodded quickly and crossed my heart.

We didn't talk for what seemed like a long time. I kept thinking about what she said about my mother hitting her hard enough that she would probably die. Die? I was so frightened, and I wondered what to do next. I guess there was nothing I could do except worry about it. But I did know one thing. I wouldn't just sit back and let my mother hit Marisa hard enough to make her die. I would jump on her and start scratching and punching. I would pull her hair out of her head and bite her. Maybe both Marisa and I would die together.

"I know why Rudy shook his beer can and opened it."

Her words jarred me.

"You do?" I was astonished, even though I probably should have seen this coming.

Marisa looked toward the door and its hopeful silence beyond. There was no creaking sound from my mother, and my father's voice was faint out front. He was either going to the warehouse or coming back toward the walkway. It didn't matter with Dad though. He didn't care about Marisa and me having our routine clandestine discussions.

She turned to me as if she were about to say something very important, then tucked one leg under her. I sat up to attention. "Do you remember, I don't know, I guess a couple of weeks ago or maybe longer than that, when you got sick with that stomach flu or bug or something?"

I nodded. "Dad and I went to the department store on the boulevard and ate too many malt balls."

She rolled her eyes and shook her head. "That's not *why*. But anyway, you were really sick, and Rudy and Frank had a huge delivery, and Mom was going to drop us off at Bunica's, and she made me put on that ugly lavender dress, and the three of us were downstairs in the doorway to the kitchen." She lowered her voice and moved her face closer to mine. "And I stepped in it."

"Stepped in what?"

"Don't tell me you can't remember."

My lips suddenly twisted in slow disgusted recall. "*Ew.* I threw up on the floor."

"No, not throw-up, little piggy. Worse. Number 2! You pooped on the floor. You did diarrhea all over the floor. What do you mean you don't remember?"

Now I knew she was lying.

"Oh yes," she answered me before I could even get my question out. "And I stepped in it with my white patent leather shoes. Mom was *the maddest* I think I had ever seen her all summer."

I looked down at my lap and played with the fabric of my lime green shorts. First she tells me about her real father, the Indian prince, and swears me to secrecy; otherwise, she may face certain death. Then she says that I did diarrhea all over the floor, and she steps in it, and Mom gets really mad, and that's why Dad squirts his beer all over the place. I wasn't buying any of it. Now she was making *me* mad, but still I was smart enough to remain as calm as I could without smacking her on her forehead that was practically pressed into mine.

"You'd better stop lying, Marisa," I demanded. "Don't you think I would have remembered if I pooped all over the floor and you stepped in it? Mom would have beaten the two of us to a pulp!"

"Oh, you got a spanking, all right, but she really got me good."

And then I saw the same fear but strange honesty in her eyes when she insisted on the Indian prince story. She turned away from me and lifted her pink shirt. On her back were fading purple and yellow sausage-looking marks.

I gasped. "Does that hurt?"

She shook her head and pulled her top back down. "Not so much now. She hit me with a spatula. Then she took my ponytail and used my head as a paddleball." She smiled and pretended to play with an imaginary paddleball. "Boing, boing, boing!"

My nose started to tickle, and I felt myself beginning to cry. But my sister put her arm around me, and I buried my face in her warm shoulder. "I'm sorry, Alice. I shouldn't have told you. Here"— she threw over my pajama bottoms—"you better wipe your face too. And stop crying. You don't want Mom to see you."

A bird flapped near my open window. It was as if it was eavesdropping on us and flew off with our lives' secrets forever.

"I don't remember any of this, Marisa, I'm sorry. I don't even know where I was. I feel so guilty. Where was I?"

She shook her head and sat back against the wall. There were a few birds on the maple tree out in front of my window now as darkness enveloped what little I could see of the sky. "I don't know, maybe you went into the other room? Or"—her face brightened with an idea—"maybe you were hiding." She sat back again. "You were really sick, Alice. I think you had a really high fever. Did you go to the store that day?"

"I don't know," I whined.

She hugged me again. We were beginning to have a lot of secrets between the two of us. "It's okay. Now, don't start crying again."

"Do I hear voices up there?" It was my mother on the landing; a tiny waft of cigarette smoke floated upward. "Marisa, get into your room right now. It's late!"

My sister got up and casually walked over to the door. She didn't seem frightened at all, but I sure was.

"Marisa, wait."

"I can't, I gotta go." Then she turned around and pointed a finger at me. "Remember what I said."

I nodded in terror. Mom could have been right outside that door.

"Good night."

She was gone.

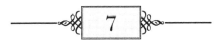

7

For most of the night, I kept turning my pillow over to get the cold side, facing the wall, then facing the door. I remember once I heard one of my grandmother's friends suggest to her to count sheep, and that would help her sleep. This did not help Bunica, so she went to the doctor, who gave her a bottle of pills. I pictured a crowded pasture full of fluffy beige sheep, and I began to count them in my mind. I tried counting these sheep several times, and it didn't work for me either. I remained wide-awake. I thought about asking Bunica for some pills, but something told me she would start crying, so I decided not to ask.

I could not stop thinking about Marisa and her Indian prince story, and I couldn't understand why wanting to know about her real father would make our mother so mad. Mom got mad really easy these days, and if Marisa was smart enough to know what triggered this, then it was probably best that no one ever talked about the Indian prince. What I couldn't stop thinking about was my sister's fear that my mother would beat her to death and that she trusted *me* with her innermost thoughts. I suppose that meant all I had to do was say the two words *Indian prince*, and my sister would be dead? God help me. Indian prince. Indian prince. What if I said it by accident? What if I shouted it out loud while I was having a bad dream? My father did that on occasion, and he's even told me that I have done it once or twice as well. He said it was probably in the Buchner genes, but I kind of doubted *that*. And so I just prayed to God really, really hard and asked him to please remove the words *Indian* and *prince* from my brain.

If all that wasn't enough for me to think about, I had to also seriously consider how I could have pooped all over the floor and not remember doing it. I don't care how sick you are with a stomach bug; you don't poop on the floor, and if you *do* poop on the floor, you sure as hell know you've done it.

I tucked my head under my pillow and begged myself to remember where I was when my sister was being beaten on the back with a spatula because of something I did. I'm sure she didn't mean to step in it. It just had to be something that didn't happen. But *something* happened. I saw the sausage-like marks. Why would Marisa lie to me? She didn't sound like she was lying. But what if she was? I wished I could find out. No, I *was* going to find out. But how? Dad was at the store. Bunic probably didn't care. Well, he would, wouldn't he? Did Bunica know? Should I just ask my mother? No, that would be a fatal mistake.

I squeezed my eyes shut. My sister was torturing me, tormenting my mind from her bedroom. I wanted to loudly walk in there and rip the covers off her and punish her for causing me so much anguish, making me responsible for her secrets, burdening me with such fear. If I made enough noise, my mother would wake up, and the fury of my sleepless head would be splashed like blood all over the walls. It would be my suicide mission. But I was a chicken, a coward. I couldn't betray Marisa, no matter how infuriated I was with her. She could take as many gumballs in as many different colors as she wanted the next time. That meant nothing to me anymore. And I wouldn't be able to leave my poor father alone. With us girls gone and Mom in jail forever, he would have this big old house all to himself. I guess if you look on the bright side, Frank would keep him company along with his millions of customers. Maybe Aunt Nancy would move out of her efficiency on Ludlum Street and move back into the family home.

* * * * *

"Why is she still sleeping? Alice? Alice! Come on. Time to get up. We've got things to do today."

"Oh…" I stirred under my covers, just barely blocking out the morning sun.

My mother burst through the door like a locomotive. "Come on, let's go." She clapped her hands, pulled the covers off me, and tapped my bottom. Why did she have to make so much noise? All she had to do was open the door and poke her head inside. She had to get agitated about everything.

I brushed my teeth and washed my face with the cleansing bar Bunica gave to Marisa and me and pulled on some clothes. There was a staleness in the air as I walked down the old hardwood staircase; the scent of fighting and anger that lived with us hit me hard. I knew why there was such a rush to leave. I wished *I* could have left, but I had nowhere to go. And it would be just another hot summer morning on the south side of Wellton where the smell of fish, the clanking of trucks, and a display of some of the most interesting people in town ruled. The usual routine played out—Marisa in the yard looking for Shelly the cat, my father in his library reading a book, and my mother hollering at everyone and everything, including the cabinet next to the refrigerator.

"Lavinia, just let 'em have a bowl of cereal first for Christ's sake," Dad said as he put his cigarette out in the ashtray I made him in my first-grade art class. He put his book down. "I gotta get to the store."

"I am taking them to the Stanhope Cafeteria for pancakes, Rudy, or do I need your permission to do that too?"

"Yeah, good." He waved at her dismissively and left the room.

Pancakes, I thought. Marisa loved pancakes. I preferred frozen waffles toasted with enough butter to fill all the little squares and lots of maple syrup. Of course, I dare not mention this to Mom. After all, it was pancake morning, *not* frozen waffle morning. In addition, we were finally going to have the privilege and honor of meeting Ms. Penelope Pantaliano, the woman whom my mother was so eager to spend her time with.

Penelope Pantaliano was a real estate agent who, according to my mother, "specialized in relocating her clients to the most exclusive properties in Wellton." She had the blackest hair I had ever seen. It was long and black like my dad's, but absent of the friendly sleekness and shine. Instead, it was dull and powdery and lay in waves that looked like they were glued to her head. Her skin was as white as paper, and her heavily made up eyelashes looked like a spider's legs. Her pink lips were as lifeless as her demon black hair, and she wore a dark forest green blouse and matching skirt that clung to her bones. I noticed that she had no breasts, and I wondered how she could hold a pencil in her hand with those long pink fingernails. Even her black pumps had an ugly dull finish.

The big thing about Penelope Pantaliano was she sucked in any light that was in that empty bedroom she stood in with my mother. It only took a hello to Penelope Pantaliano to make me like her less than I thought I already had. But then she clinched it when Marisa and I started arguing about blue jays versus bluebirds.

"Mom!" Marisa walked down the hall to where my mother and Penelope Pantaliano were talking. I followed her, having this deadly feeling in my stomach that this wasn't going to end well. "Mom?" she repeated loudly when my mother's head whipped around like a snapping turtle.

"What. Do. You. Want. God. Damn. It."

"Oh, come on, Marisa!" Penelope Pantaliano contributed with exasperation, her made-up nose crinkling like a road map.

I was stunned. Marisa just nonchalantly turned around and walked out of the room, pinching my flabby stomach on her way out. Who was this Penelope Pantaliano real estate woman? And what right did she have to scold my sister? She wasn't her mother. She didn't even know Marisa, and yet she spoke to her as if she *did* know her and didn't like her. And my mother just stood there and let her snap at her. Maybe it was my mother who told Penelope Pantaliano bad things about Marisa and made her not like her. After all, Mom didn't seem to like either of us very much, but it was Marisa who made her the angriest—even more so than Dad.

One time Mom was braiding Marisa's hair, and I heard her tell her, "I love you because I have to love you. You are my daughter. But I don't like you." Marisa didn't even care that our mother said she didn't like her. I was devastated when Holly Munn told me she didn't like me, and I was one of two in the whole class who didn't get invited to her birthday party. I couldn't imagine what that would be like hearing it from my own mother.

My mother decided to take the apartment. I decided not to say anything to Marisa, who was outside doing something she probably wasn't supposed to be doing. I should have told her, but I was way too scared. Mom bid farewell to Penelope Pantaliano, who promised a phone call and a follow-up appointment, and she shoved a pile of papers at my mother.

After we stopped off to pick up some groceries, my mother said it was time that the three of us discuss what was about to happen. "Your father is a no-good son of a bitch," she began while taking a right turn up a hill, which toppled over the brown paper bags in the way back of the station wagon. "This damned car. This car is a piece of junk. Garbage! Complete garbage!"

I didn't think it was the car's fault that we took a sharp turn up a hill, and the groceries just happened to fall all over the place, but I was not about to argue with my mother by giving her my opinion. I waited for her to continue, which she inevitably did.

"As you may already know, your father and, uh, Rudy, and I are separating."

"Separating?" Marisa asked from the back seat. "You mean like getting a divorce?"

I didn't look over at her. She couldn't have been that dumb, but then again, she sometimes had the common sense of a fruit fly. What did she think we were doing looking at an apartment? The thing was, I didn't tell her what I had overheard before that fateful dinner. I didn't tell her anything. Not only were they separating, we were going to live in that apartment with Mom. I should have told her that. But she didn't ask. And I was always a coward. She was off outside and then talking about some cute guy on television and in some magazine, and I was pretending to listen like I normally did.

"Possibly. But we're going to take one thing at a time, and for now, that thing is a separation. That's what I was just discussing with Ms. Pantaliano. We'll be moving into that lovely new apartment."

"Mom," I protested, throwing caution right out the window at thirty-five miles an hour. I couldn't help it. Suddenly I had the chance, and I took it. I knew it was stupid, but I didn't want to go. "I...I don't want to move. I like living with Dad."

"Alice, you have no choice." She looked in the rearview mirror and lifted a finger. "You are a child—both of you are coming with me."

"But what about Dad? He's going to be lonely in that big house all by—"

"That big house!" she snapped. "That big house has needed repairs and redecorating for nearly fifty years. The place is a dump. The neighborhood has become run-down, the school system is atrocious, and I am tired of living with a grown man who acts like a goddamned teenager."

"Teenagers are messy, and they listen to loud music and take drugs like pills," Marisa chimed in.

I looked over at her. I wondered what she was talking about.

"And as far as loneliness is concerned, your father, or Rudolph, of course to you, Marisa"—she was the only one to ever call my father Rudolph—"doesn't have the slightest problem with loneliness. He has his harem of young blonds. You don't have to worry about that."

My mother looked in the rearview mirror again and waved her hand.

"Oh, who cares? Your father, Rudy, is a cheap, self-centered, insecure baby. Of course, lots of men fit that description, but Rudy takes the cake. The only one he cares about is himself."

The groceries fell over again, and my mother went on a brief tirade about how cheap and selfish Dad was. Then she started to cry.

"I married your father for one reason and one reason only. I wanted security for me and Marisa. Maybe two reasons." She wiped her nose with the top of her finger. "Getting out of my parents' house was of *utmost* importance at the time. He had a successful business, your father. He had that once somewhat beautiful Victorian that had been passed down—"

"Did you love Rudy, Mom?" Marisa interrupted.

My mother let out a cackle. I was surprised. I thought for sure she would scream, "*No, never!*" as loud as she could.

"Love." She shook her head. "Let me tell you about love, girly. It means nothing. Love *is* nothing when it comes to men and marriage.

The two of you will find that out soon enough. Oh, and before I forget, both of you will be starting a new school in the fall."

"Oh no, Mom!" Marisa protested after a moment of shock and silence. "But what about my friends?"

"You can see your friends when you go to visit Rudy on the weekends," my mother said evenly.

I noticed her flickering green eyes in the rearview mirror. They became darker, and the light faded from them before they looked dead.

"I don't want to change schools, Mom. Please."

My mother slammed her fist into the steering wheel, causing the car to swerve a little. Then looking in the rearview mirror again, she pointed a ferocious finger at my sister and said, "You will do exactly as you are told. We are moving out of Rudolph Buchner's home."

It sounded so poisonous—Rudolph Buchner. As she said his name, the venom shot from her teeth. It was blinding. She clearly hated him, and I felt tears trying to push their way out of my eyes. I did everything I could to stop them. Marisa was openly crying.

"You are coming with me to this beautiful apartment in an upscale part of this dead-end town—an apartment that I just spent a goddamned fortune on in deposit money. That son of a bitch doesn't care about you!"

By that, I assumed she was talking about Dad. And that wasn't true.

"I am your mother, and you will do what *I* say."

Marisa's crying was out of control. I tried as hard as I could to hide my tears, although it was pretty much impossible. Marisa, on the other hand, shook with each hard sob. She howled like a sick animal that couldn't catch its breath. I looked down at her white sneakers with Peds socks with the pink ball at her ankle so that I wouldn't have to see what was really happening. She continued to scratch the top of her thigh with her thumbnail when her crying began to sound like a little baby's. If I had a rattle to shake in front of her wet face, maybe she would stop crying or maybe even start to giggle. In my mind, I pleaded for her to stop, but she wouldn't, so I had no choice but to comfort her.

"Come on, Marisa, it's gonna be okay. We'll get to see Dad on the weekends, and now we get to share a room—"

She pushed me hard. "Get off me, Alice! I hate you!"

At first I was stunned. Then I wanted to push her back, but I knew that would only anger my mother if angering her further was possible. Marisa didn't seem to care, however, and suddenly, I felt cornered, alone, and very frightened.

The car swerved into the other lane. My mother jerked the steering wheel back, causing the two of us to abruptly slide down the back seat. I was positive she did that on purpose.

"Look what you made me do!" my mother roared as tears sped down her face, which twisted into a picture of such despair that, for a second, I actually felt sorry for her. She banged the side of her fist against the steering wheel so hard that the plastic top of the horn fell into her lap. She screamed so loud, I covered my ears. Marisa's face lost its color as her mouth hung wide-open.

My mother pulled the station wagon over into an empty church parking lot and slammed the car into a screeching halt. I looked around quickly, hoping there was someone who could help us, but there wasn't a soul. Not even a car went by.

My mother dragged Marisa by her thick long auburn ponytail out of the car. She was clinging to me for safety.

"No, Mommy! Please!" Marisa cried as I tried to get out of the car on the other side.

"Move one more inch, Alice Buchner, and you'll get it too."

I froze.

She lifted my tiny sister by her ponytail again and shook her like a rag doll. "If I had a pair of scissors, I would cut this goddamned thing right off your head."

But then what would she use to drag Marisa around with?

"Oh god, no!" Marisa screamed breathlessly.

My mother slapped my sister so hard on the left side of the face, the cracking sound made me bolt upright. Then she took an umbrella from the back seat and, using my sister's butt as a baseball, slugged it three times as hard as she could. But the worst was when she took the end of that umbrella and rammed it with what looked like all her strength into her butt crack. I looked over with one horrified eye and thanked God Marisa still had her shorts on.

My sister let out this weird sound and fell face-first on the back seat. I turned an eye to look at my mother through the driver's side window. She was smiling and a lot calmer.

"Don't you move a muscle, Alice." She pointed a finger at me. She pushed my sister's floppy legs onto the back floor and slammed the door.

We drove the rest of the way in silence, my mother's cigarette smoke the last perpetrator.

* * * * *

I snuck out of my bedroom late at night. I couldn't find one star in the sky, and the moon was hiding in the blackness so thick and quiet. I wondered for a moment if God was even there. I was disconnected without my father's snoring, and then I noticed their bedroom door was wide-open, and no one was inside. The bed was perfectly made with the green ruffles and the frilly shams and throws, the way my mother did it every morning. I heard the TV downstairs, and when I poked my head down around the staircase, I saw Aunt Nancy sitting in the dark with a cigarette between her fingers, gazing at the bright gray and white light. I heard laughter from the TV, and then I turned back up the steps. She didn't see me, or if she did, she wasn't paying attention to me, and I was glad. I had some unfinished business I needed to tend to.

I hadn't seen Marisa for most of the day after my mother had tried to shove an umbrella up her clothed rear end. I think I was avoiding her. I wasn't being a very good sister, but she didn't appear to want me around either. She ran off with a friend and then disappeared into the dog day looking for Shelly. For me, the best alternative was to get as far away from my mother as I was allowed. That meant spending the afternoon at the store chatting with Dad and Frank as Pick Hudson's *All Soul All the Time* radio show blared, entertaining the customers with my supposed cuteness and bidding a final farewell and giving one last pep talk to the doomed lobsters in the tank by the register. And I wondered. Why would I miss my mother so much during those times she wasn't around?

I opened Marisa's bedroom door. She was sleeping with her back toward me and her head buried under a pillow. I was hoping by now she would have forgiven me and didn't hate me anymore. "Marisa?" I treaded very lightly as I put on my sweetest, most apologetic voice.

"I'm awake, Alice." She startled me, and I stopped dead.

The only light was coming from the cracked door from my bedroom down the hall. I was going to ask her where Mom and Dad were, but I decided I really didn't care. I proceeded gently. "Do you remember when Dad squirted his beer?"

"Yup," she answered quietly. She sounded so tired and sad. Of course she remembered. It was a stupid question.

"I remember him saying that he was going to take you to see the doctor."

No response.

"I know he was talking about you because, um…" I fidgeted around in the dark for the right words, but I was so lost, so I put a smile in my voice and said quickly, "Well, because Mom was saying that he really didn't care because you weren't really his, and you know." I stopped talking for a second. Then I started again. "Did… did Dad ever take you to see the doctor?"

"Uh-huh."

"What did he say? The doctor, I mean."

"He told Rudy to get me out of that house."

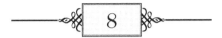

8

"Don't get attached to them, Allie. We've been getting so many big fellas, they're just flying out the door."

I stood in front of the lobster tank looking at my poor rubber-banded clawed friends as the radio crooned sixties soul. My mood darkened when a beautiful voice was suddenly replaced by Frank's. Frank always said that because he was black, he could sing soul better than any white guy—including and especially Dad. Frank thought he had a great voice, but really, it was downright awful, and on that day, I just didn't feel like joking about it. He was ruining everything.

"Aw, you gonna be fine, girl. You be here on the weekends, right?" Frank wiped the counter as he winked and smiled. It was his eyes that weren't smiling at the same time. When Frank was smiling, his face lit up—everything smiled, and that didn't happen, so I knew he was pretending.

"He told Rudy to get me out of that house." We were out of the house, but when the doctor told my father to get Marisa out of that house, I don't think that's exactly what he had in mind.

I was angry with Dad. I also missed him a lot. Spending the weekends with him was not enough. Now that Marisa was making all kinds of new friends in our new school, she rarely bothered to come with me to see "Dad" or "Rudy" or *whoever* in South Wellton. Did that ever piss off Mom, but her lawyer said there was nothing she could do about it because guess why? Dad wasn't her real father.

I was disparaged. I ran my fingertips across the lobster tank, hoping for a visit. My father slapped a large shimmering salmon down on the long wooden block. I felt sorry for its dead and indifferent eyes. I hung off the counter and watched my dad. I wished he knew what I was thinking. I thought maybe we could go out back

37

where he could smoke a cigarette, and I could sit in the green and yellow yard chair, and we could talk and joke around. Instead, he took out a knife and began to bone or filet or do whatever it was he did with the poor fellow on the chopping block in front of him. I was so sad too. At first I was worried about my father. I didn't want him to be lonely, rattling around that big old empty house all by himself. He and my mother were separated now, and he seemed the same to me. It didn't appear as if he was the least bit lonely.

"Will Aunt Nancy be moving back in with you?"

"Oh god, no. Your aunt likes to be as independent as she possibly can. She likes that little efficiency of hers. She's got everything she needs right there, you know? Kitchen, bathroom, all her junk…" His voice trailed off.

I turned to look out the front double doors, hoping we wouldn't be interrupted by customers, but it was still pretty early on a Saturday morning. "Dad, I miss you. I want to come home."

"Aw, Al." His tone was patronizing. He didn't look up from his salmon. "I miss you too, kid. But you're a young girl, and you should be with your mother and sister."

He told Rudy to get me out of that house.

"But you must be lonely, Dad, without us?"

"Don't you worry about me, I'm busy with the—hey, you're here every weekend. We'll spend lots of time doing things, reading and you know."

I nodded and focused on one large lobster.

Dad shook his head. "You just have to live with your mother, that's all."

That's all.

"No judge in the world is gonna let a young girl live with her old man who keeps the kind of hours we do around here. A girl is supposed to be raised by her mother. Besides, when you're eighteen, or maybe even a little younger, you can start making your own decisions about where you want to go and what you want to do—who you want to go live with."

Turning eighteen was a lifetime away.

My father disappeared into the back.

9

My father said that our apartment complex, the Stanhope Ridge, was like a holiday camp. He told me that in England, families would vacation at these resort-type compounds by the sea where they would engage in activities like swimming and tennis, maybe golf and nightlife for adults after the kids were put to bed. We never took a vacation like that.

Wellton had nothing that closely resembled a holiday camp. We had the Maidenhead River that had a pretty beach up near Harbins, but there was no "seaside" as Dad referred to it in his fake English accent. He also said the English called a vacation a *holiday*, not a *vacation*. Of course, we had a pretty good state fair that came to Wellton every year and an amusement park in Seagramsville about a half hour or so outside the city, but other than that, if you wanted a nice vacation or a *holiday* as the English called it, you really needed to escape Wellton, which we rarely did.

We went to Niagara Falls once and visited Bunica's brother, Great-Uncle Nick, in Orlando. It rained nonstop at Disney World, and Mom and Dad fought the entire time. Great vacation. Dad was usually too busy at the store to go on holiday. My mother only wanted to go to fancy places we could never afford for extended periods of time, preferably without my father and us, so vacations, holidays, whatever were not part of our family routine. I guess that was one of the many reasons why we ended up at the Stanhope Ridge. And once I started to think about those reasons, my head began to swim, and my stomach began to churn. It was best to just try to stop thinking about things, but that was very hard for me to do. My mind didn't shut off easily.

Dad said one thing missing from the Stanhope Ridge was a bar or pub like they called it in England. I thought the Stanhope was missing more than that. It was not home. Every building was stucco and painted pale yellow with a terra-cotta roof. At the far end of the property was the office and clubhouse. The superintendent owned a trampoline that he rented out, but children had to have a parent supervise them while they jumped.

When Marisa found out there was a trampoline on the property, I thought she would die of happiness; she was so excited. It was kind of exciting, but it was not meant to be. My mother smashed our dreams into a million tiny pieces when she refused to allow Marisa and me to jump on the trampoline mainly because she did not want to pay the four dollars per hour fee *and* she didn't want to stand there and watch us jump. I was disappointed. I had never been on a trampoline before, and it looked like so much fun when we watched the other kids from the window. Marisa was completely crushed. The thing about my sister, though, was that she was never able to get used to be being crushed, to being disappointed by our mother. She needed to learn because it wasn't going to change—not in any circumstance.

There was a swimming pool that officially closed after Labor Day and a tennis court that I had no idea what to do with. The best part was the huge playground and sand pit. Still, none of any of it felt like what Dad referred to in his silly accent as a holiday.

Marisa may have disagreed with me though. She and some of the other kids would go to the playground after dinner while it was still light and talk about things I knew nothing about. I tried to get her to go down the slides with me belly first, or jump ten feet down into the sand pit, or mess around on the wooden planks with the big springs underneath. They were probably not as much fun as the trampoline, but maybe a close second. She would just laugh at me and say no way was she going to do stupid kid stuff when her friends were around. Then I met a boy named Bruce who was my age and liked to hang around with me. He didn't seem to mind that I was a girl either. His parents bought him a calculator for Christmas, and he wore it on his belt, except when we were belly sliding, he had to leave it in his room. It was a really nice one too. He was lucky to have it.

I was a little jealous of Marisa. I had to hide it as much as possible because my mother would notice my jealousy and not only make fun of me but bring it up again and again. The only thing that would accomplish would be to puff up Marisa's head like a snobby little girl and make me feel embarrassed and foolish. The one positive thing was that I could see how happy Marisa felt when she received the tiniest bit of favorable attention from my mother, even though it was completely false.

My sister was turning into a real beauty. She was a petite girl, small for her age, like my mother had been when she was young. I was three years younger, and I was taller, which wouldn't have been so bad if I hadn't been such a fat slob of a kid. My mother's new friends in the neighborhood were always commenting on how I looked like the older sister because I was "so much bigger" than Marisa. My mother found those comments very funny. It was one of those few times I would see her laugh herself into near hysteria when her friends made comments about my weight.

I'll admit, I liked to eat a lot. When Dad combined his home-made Boochie's Crab Dip with his World-Famous Boochie's Fries and maybe some cherry pie, it was impossible for me to turn my nose up to these things. Luckily for Marisa, she didn't have this problem. She didn't have my enormous appetite, and she could eat as much as she wanted and always look pretty and skinny, "like a girl was sup-posed to look," my mother would say. Marisa had begun to resemble my mother: the glowing velvety skin, thick and shiny auburn hair, emerald green eyes that were as deep as a well. The difference was that Marisa's gaze twinkled with her soft uniqueness while my moth-er's eyes were hard angry rocks. There was a whirling stiffness and hopelessness that followed my mother all the time. Her beauty was invariably noticeable, but when a person is mean, people don't care what that person looks like after a while.

Mom started to go out on dates with lots of different men. There was this one guy, Arthur, who was really friendly, and I liked him a lot. He was always smiling, kind of like Frank at the store. My mother stopped dating him because he was a basketball coach for a Catholic school in Crescent Hills, and he didn't make enough money. My mother said that she was thinking long-term, and this was one of the things she had to consider.

The other guy I liked was Dale. Dale was really tall and skinny and worked at a local television affiliate. He also drove a silver Cadillac, which really impressed my mother, but their relationship went down in flames when Dale found out she was married to Rudy Buchner. Dale was an occasional customer of my dad's, and he had a couple of old stories about my grandfather that made Marisa and me laugh. When my mother heard this, she told him to haul his skinny ass out of her house and yelled at us for laughing at his jokes and listening to his stories.

Our grandmother, or Bunica as we had called her our whole lives, came over to the apartment to babysit us a lot. Sometimes my mother would drop us off at her house on a Friday night, and my dad would pick us up in the morning for our weekend visits. My grandparents were Romanian immigrants who fled Eastern Europe with my mother and her little brother Anton, who died of pneumonia when he was a baby. I think it was pneumonia. It may have been leukemia. But no one ever talked about it, and I dared never ask. I had never even seen a picture of the little boy who would have been my uncle. It was sad, but I was never very interested in learning about him either. I should have been.

Bunica was always cooking for us. She made us homemade soups, stuffed cabbage, sausages in the pan, breaded meatballs, all kinds of desserts and bread, and her square kitchen was always filled with the warmth of food. This was another reason I was a fat kid. I loved visiting most of the time, when Bunica was in a good mood. She reprimanded us frequently for not making our parents take us to church every Sunday. She and Bunic could win a medal each for bickering and picking at each other like a couple of monkeys. Their arguments, however, were far different than the knock-down-drag-outs my parents had.

My grandparents' house was usually filled with the humming of needling and banter in which they spoke in their native tongue. They both assumed we didn't understand. My mother could speak fluently but didn't speak much anymore. Marisa had no idea of what they were talking about. However, the assistant librarian at the public library within walking distance from the store, Mrs. Ban, just *happened* to be from Bucharest, *and* she had a Romanian dictionary at the reference desk. I had been phonetically writing down words for as long as I could remember, words that sometimes made Mrs. Ban's eyebrows raise, but nevertheless, I was teaching myself a minimal amount of Romanian, and with Mrs. Ban's help, I would learn enough to get by until she told me that she would no longer be a part of my conspiracy. My grandparents seemed to be getting along fine one evening until I messed everything up. It was me who was so depressed that I didn't know what to do with myself.

"Oh no, Alice," my grandmother said, grimacing as I started to cry over my plate of meatballs. It was an uncontrollable faucet I couldn't stop. My grandmother started to raise her voice, which made me nervous and angry. "I do not like this, Alice. Why are you crying?"

My grandmother did not tolerate negative emotion. She and my mother were similar in that way. Sort of. I was happy yet surprised once when she cuddled me and poured me a bowl of cereal when one of the neighborhood boys pulled me across the lawn by my hair. That was one of the rare times she was sympathetic to my tears. But not on this night.

"I know what you're crying about." Marisa looked at me from across the table and then scanned the kitchen doorway to the dining room. "Why, Alice? Just be happy she's going somewhere—God!"

"Marisa," Bunica warned.

"I don't want Mom to go." But Marisa was right. I should have been thrilled to see the back side of my mother climbing into some man's elegant car, but again, for some reason I did not know and could not explain, I wasn't. Even Bunica was glad to get rid of her daughter. No one understood me. They thought I was a kook, and maybe I was. Maybe I was going to grow up to be just like Aunt Nancy. My father had already told me that mental illness was what he called genetic—that it ran in the family. I panicked all the time, and that was a simple way to tell whether or not you were a kook. I was just so scared, but there was nothing in particular that I was frightened of. I was just…scared. And every night before I went to bed, I knew that I wouldn't be able to fall asleep because I was too afraid. My father told me that I used to have nightmares a lot when I was a little girl. I shared a large bedroom with Marisa now, but even that wasn't enough to comfort me.

"What's the matter with her?" Bunic asked, grabbing a beer from the refrigerator.

My grandmother ignored him. She stood over me like a prison guard, a threatening tower. "Do you want me to get your mother?" Bunica asked.

"You make sure you eat all your dinner," Bunic demanded.

"Radu, enough."

Then they started up again, squabbling, talking over one another. I had no idea what they were saying.

Marisa rolled her eyes. "Look what you've done, Alice. We're both gonna get it now. Thanks a lot, you little brat!"

"That's enough, Marisa." Bunica snapped as Bunic wisely left the room.

I cried harder when suddenly, I smelled my mother's perfume. As she entered the kitchen, her black stilettos clicked with a dull tiny thud on the ancient linoleum. "What is going on in here?" Her voice of death was measured.

Marisa went back to shoveling meatballs into her mouth. At least *that* would make my grandparents happy during this tense and awkward situation that was heading toward an explosion.

My grandmother stood firm in front of her daughter, eyeing her up and down. "You talk to your daughter, Lavinia."

My mother shifted her balance from one foot to the other and twirled her shiny auburn hair in exasperation. She reminded me of Marisa for that split second I glanced up at her with one eye. "Talk to my daughter about what exactly?"

"She's upset."

"She is always upset, Mother. They both are."

Bunica didn't back down one bit. She had both working hands placed on her wide hips as she looked at my high-heeled mother. "And why do you think this is?" She tossed her head back, never losing eye contact with her only daughter. "You—all dolled up like this, meeting men. The ink is still wet on your divorce papers."

"Mother, I do not need a lecture from you."

"Oh, but it looks like you might, my dear."

"I'm an adult, Mother. I've been one for a long time." I heard tears mixing up in my mother's voice, and I prayed they didn't fall from her eyes. She looked so beautiful with all that blue shadow and mascara painted on so perfectly.

Bunica shook her head and turned to me. "Stop playing with your food. Look at your sister, how good she eats. I usually have to say these things to her, not you."

I didn't look at Marisa, but I could feel that smile creeping across her face.

"All right. We'll have a little discussion right now," my mother announced brightly.

My grandmother put a strong hand on my shoulder.

"What, Mother?"

"She is eating her dinner, Lavinia."

"You're the one who just said that I needed to speak to my own child. So let's do it." She took a deep breath as if she were trying to calm herself. "Alice, what's the matter? Why are you upset? Why are you crying?" She placed her hand on the back of the kitchen chair and leaned toward me.

I looked up at her, but I couldn't tell if she was mad. "I don't want you to go."

Marisa started to say something, and Bunica's fingers flew up to her lips.

"Well, what do you want? What would you have me do, stay here?"

I nodded as I gazed at her metallic gold belt with the hoops and circles with stones.

"Well, I have to go, Alice. I'm seeing a gentleman tonight." Her eyes became rounded and focused, and I didn't want to mess things up for her. She was happy to be away from my father, and she liked to go out on dates a lot. She and that awful Penelope would sometimes go out together to the Japanese restaurant. I wanted my mother to be happy, and yet, I couldn't help myself from stirring it all up.

"I know, Mom."

"So you don't cry anymore tonight?" Bunica looked down at me, her heavy hand still on my shoulder.

I shook my head.

"Very good." My mother thudded off, looking for her jacket.

She was gone. I decided not to watch her leave from Bunica's picture window. If I didn't see her leave, then maybe she would be back sooner. She might not even like the guy, and she would be home a lot sooner. That's happened a couple of times. Look what happened to poor Dale.

Bunic wandered in and out of the kitchen a few times as Bunica finished the dishes. They talked about the news as Marisa and I continued to sit at the kitchen table and go through the funny pages from an old morning paper. It was dark, and the sky was heavy and low with a fast and relentless thunderstorm approaching. The wind whipped the branches of the maples, and the huge weeping willow twisted and danced slowly then wildly as the sky spit on Bunic's lush grass.

I knew I wouldn't sleep that night. I knew I would be too scared that bedtime would be a chore, but I didn't tell my grandparents or Marisa. I had already caused enough trouble. I looked around at different things in the rooms of my grandparents' house. With each gaze at each item, I rhythmically said to myself, *I am going to be scared tonight. I*—the chair, the grandfather clock—*am*—the window shade—*going*—then the doorway—*to be*—the door handle, Bunic's head—*scared tonight*—the picture above the fireplace mantle. Over and over again. *I am going to be scared tonight.*

I still counted a lot. I liked to count because it relaxed me. It kept me focused. The only problem was that I was focused on being scared. That was because I knew I would be. I had been every other night, and there was no reason that this night should be any different. The rain didn't help. It only made it worse.

The world outside was dark and violent. The battered lawn was unusually green as the wind flitted through tiny blades of grass, back and forth and in every possible direction. I watched as cars splashed by, each with their headlights on, taillights following blindly, thinking that if I could drive, I would go a lot slower than these fearless people ripping through the waters of these saturated streets. I wondered where my mother was. Was she scared too? I thought about calling my father at the store to see if he, Frank, and Aunt Nancy were scared, but my grandmother said it wasn't safe to use the telephone during a thunderstorm. Lightning could zap me in the ear. That was enough for me, and I doubted Frank and Dad were scared anyway. Aunt Nancy was probably in the cellar cleaning something with her music turned up full blast unless she was at her apartment, where there was no telling what she was up to. She hated thunderstorms.

My grandparents didn't seem to be affected by anything, including the devilish weather, as they continued with their usual evening routines in the brightened house. I thought the power would go out. Bunic watched a boring baseball game on television, Bunica folded laundry, and Marisa had a drawing pad out with colored pencils. I was the one who was walking around, ready to peel off my skin. I was the only one who was scared.

I am going to be scared tonight.

And then finally, yet with almost some strange relief, the dreaded bedtime hour was upon me. Bunica tucked Marisa and me into the warm double bed. Everything was fine when the lights were still on as Bunica arranged our covers.

"Bunica, do you think you could please leave the bathroom light on?"

Marisa turned over. "Alice, what's the matter with you again? Why are you acting like such a little punk?"

"Marisa Ionescu, I will not hear you call your sister names." My grandmother pointed her rough finger at my sister. "Apologize, now."

"I'm sorry," she said with faint sarcasm, quietly snorted, then rolled over.

My grandmother smoothed her worn apron and gave us each a hard kiss on the cheek. "I have an idea," she said and walked over to the old wooden bureau, opened a drawer, and took something out to show me. "I'll plug in this night-light for you. See?" She bent down next to the bedroom door and pushed the little white fixture into the socket. The light flickered and then brightened. "Oh." She held the small of her back as she pushed herself up. "This is good?"

"Thanks." I was relieved.

She nodded slowly. "You two girls have good dreams tonight." When she turned out the overhead light and closed the door, the little night-light shone bright. I listened as her footsteps faded down the hallway. She said a few inaudible words to my grandfather and then headed down the stairs.

"Alice?"

"Yeah?"

"What is it that you're so scared of?"

"I don't know."

"You didn't use to be scared when we lived at Rudy's all the time."

"Dad said sometimes I would have nightmares." She had no idea.

"Maybe sometimes, but it's not like *this*. I don't understand. You've *got* to know."

"But I don't." I started to feel my nose itch, and I knew that at any minute, I would start to cry. Again.

She rolled over on her side and faced me. She put her skinny arm across my chest. "Okay, okay, I believe you. You don't know why you're scared. Just…you don't have to cry now, okay?"

I nodded my head and sniffled.

She lay on her back and pulled the covers up to her chin, even though it wasn't cold. I didn't worry about the two of us chattering away like we normally did when we could. Bunica didn't care about things like that unless it interfered with Bunic's TV shows.

"Alice," she began, and then paused, trying to sound clever. "It's just that you've got to *pretend* everything is fine. You can't go around being scared to go to bed at night, crying like you do, wondering when Mom is coming home."

"Well, you did." I interrupted her with a stern look that she could barely see in the darkened room if it weren't for Bunica's night-light.

"What are you talking about? I didn't do—"

"Yes, you did, Marisa. Remember when Mom told us we had to move out of Dad's? You were all upset because you were going to have to go to a new school. You couldn't stop crying when we were in the car. I prayed in my mind that you would stop. The only thing you did was make Mom really pissed off."

She opened her mouth, and her eyes got wide. Then she smiled. "Where did you learn that word?"

"And that's not the only time, you know. How about all those times when you were listening—"

"Where did you learn that word, Alice?"

"What word?"

She looked at the closed bedroom door and then whispered, "Pissed?"

I looked up at the ceiling and shrugged. "I don't know." I thought for a second. "School, I guess, maybe. No—maybe Dad. Could have been you."

She settled back down into her pillow. "No wonder we're both in so much trouble all the time."

We lay in silence for a while like we sometimes did.

Then she said, "I know I do these dumb things too. That's why I'm warning you not to do them. Because they're dumb." She looked at me for a second. "Like cry and disagree and talk loud, I guess. You know, stuff like that. It's just that sometimes, I can't help it. I get so angry, so incredibly angry, that sometimes, I want to scream. It *is* like that time when we were going home after looking at the apartment—Mom telling us we had to move out of Rudy's and change schools whether we liked it or not. I was so mad. I...I couldn't help myself. I didn't want to cry. I didn't want to get so pissed off that... that I was begging. I just couldn't help it, you know what I'm talking about?"

"I know. You can't control yourself."

"Yes!" she exclaimed as quietly she could and smiled broadly. She turned back toward me and propped herself up on one elbow. "But see, you're smart, and you *can when you have to*. And I...I'm your big sister, and I should be protecting you from bad things, you know."

I threw her a hurt-filled look. "You know, you get mad at me sometimes. Even when I didn't do anything wrong."

"I'm sorry."

She actually sounded like she meant it that time, so I pressed harder. "And you don't let me hang around you and your friends at the sand pit. I have to hang by myself and sometimes with Bruce. He—"

She started to giggle.

"Don't laugh at Bruce. He's a nice boy, and he's my friend."

"So why would you want to hang around with us?"

She sounded so logical. I could have given her all my birthday money I had saved from last year, and she still wouldn't have let me hang around with her and her friends. But she *said* she should be protecting me as if it were her duty because she was older. That was nice.

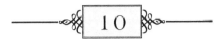

I liked to watch reruns after I finished my dinner and completed my homework. Now every night, the only thing that was on were people talking about President Nixon and the Watergate hearings. I sat on our blue striped sofa and watched them anyway, even though I found them boring. Most times I had no idea of what they were talking about. It was like listening to Bunica and Bunic argue about lettuce in Romanian, but it was better than nothing. I also made the stupid mistake of promising my father that I would watch all week and maybe learn something that the two of us could discuss on Saturday.

On this night, I had a little headache, and I was not just a little bored, I was just tired of it. I was sick of the hearings and decided to see if Marisa needed any help with her homework. My math skills were advanced for my age, and Marisa's were at a disadvantage.

As I walked down the hall, I passed my mother's bedroom, and I heard her crying. Marisa was sitting next to her on the bed, comforting her. "What's the matter, Mom?"

Marisa's back was to me. Her lustrous auburn hair cascaded in thick waves. "Mom's a little sad right now."

I slowly walked into the bedroom.

"You come right over here, sweetheart, and you sit down with us." My mother reached out a soft pale arm past my sister. She was wearing her Indian sari–type satin nightgown. I was with her when she bought it, so I knew it wasn't a gift from the Indian prince. *Indian prince.*

I stuck my finger in my ear in an effort to delete that thought, and I went and joined my mother and sister on the bed.

She pulled the side of my fat head into her breast. "I'm so glad you're both here," she declared, sniffling. "I thought you were watching the hearings." Then all of a sudden, she cried harder.

"Oh no, Mom, no. I don't like watching them. They're boring. I would prefer to watch my reruns. I'm more of the science fiction type." I knew my sister's eyeballs were rolling.

She laughed through her tears. "I'm so proud of you, Alice. You're a brilliant little girl, do you know that? Now you tell me, what fifth grader would sit in front of the Watergate hearings on television?" She stroked Marisa's smooth forehead with the perfectly plunging widow's peak. "And look at you, my little beauty. I looked a lot like you when I was your age, just not nearly as gorgeous." She shook her head and started to cry again. She wiped her nose and dabbed her eye with a tissue. She looked up at the wall. "I'm sorry, girls, I'm really, really sorry. I know I haven't been the best mother to either of you. I understand that I'm not exactly warm or patient. I never liked having tea parties with you when you were little. I can be cold. I can be downright mean."

I glanced at Marisa. She didn't notice. If she did, she was ignoring me. I was alone.

My mother gave us each a squeeze. "I just want what's best for you children. I don't want you living in South Wellton, where crime is lurking around every corner."

I never noticed any crime. We always kept the windows and the doors locked at the house, and Dad locked the store.

"I didn't want the two of you growing up behind a fish store, for Christ's sake! I want you girls to grow up in a good neighborhood, go to good schools, college. I want you to do all the things that I never did. I want you to meet nice men from good families, with money in the bank. You should have these things. All beautiful women are entitled to these things."

I would have agreed that my mother was beautiful, but today, as the three of us sat at the end of her bed, she was anything but. Her dark red nail polish was chipped, and her hair was dull and flattened from sleep. She stank of cigarettes, and as she cried, I noticed a puffy darkness around her eyes. But that was not all. There was something else. There were other things too, and if this was what beautiful was supposed to be, I was glad that I wasn't. I would live with my chubbiness, accept the fact that not only was I the tallest girl in the class, I was the tallest kid. I'd go ahead and take my frizzy black hair and nose from Dad's side of the family. If beauty made you reek of cigarettes, feel awful, scream all the time, and then cry like that, I would rather be homely, live with my father, listen to soul music, and teach customers how to braise mussels. It would have been a lot better than this. Who cared about hair and eyes and schools and families when it felt like the sky was raining down on you, even when it could have been a perfectly sunny day?

And when a man named Barton Withers entered our lives, I never thought I would see my mother cry like that again, cuddling her daughters and apologizing for being a bad mother.

I was right.

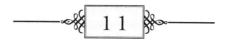

11

Barton Withers was the most handsome man I had ever seen in my life. He reminded me of one of those TV stars I would watch on the Friday night movies, but even better by about five hundred times. He had thick wavy salt-and-pepper hair that looked like it was about two inches deep all around his head. His jaw was square, and he had just enough lines at his mouth and eyes that made him look like he was tough and manly, but he was also not afraid to smile and laugh. His eyes were sparkling gray with just enough black to offset the gray, and they actually twinkled like perfectly cut diamonds. He was well over six feet tall, and there wasn't one extra pound of fat on him, unlike the potbelly my father had developed. Barton Withers was perfect. I wondered why someone like him would live in some boring little sleepy town like Wellton.

"That cuz he own the damned town." Frank put my curiosity to rest one weekend when I was visiting my father. "He own jus' about everything 'cept this square acre we standin' on. Hell, he even own the radio station we listenin' to." He looked up at the ragged tan speaker. "These rich folks? They got everything, baby, every *thang.*" He started to sing along with the music, failing miserably, but still managing to make everyone in the store laugh. I was so embarrassed, I wanted to leave.

"He doesn't own the radio station, Frankie. That's Stern, but I'm telling you"—my father turned to me and shook his head slowly—"I'll bet your mother is thrilled. Finally caught that big fish she's been waiting for her whole life. Big fish!" He laughed uncontrollably.

Frank put a long cardboard box down on the floor and pulled some white paper out of it. "I read his name in the paper some time. He done some DWI. A drinkin' man."

A customer laughed. Then the three of them started arguing over who actually owned the radio station. Was it Withers, or was it Stern? It used to be Withers, but he sold out to Stern or vice versa. Who cared?

Then Frank said, "I heard one time they had to rescue his drunk ass from an elevator shaf' at that ol' swanky hotel downtown. Can you believe that? An *elevator shaf'!* What he doin' in an elevator shaf'?"

"What *was* he doing in an elevator shaft? He would have died!"

"*What?*"

"Who?"

"He musta fallen."

"When he was drunk."

"That's not true."

"An elevator shaft, man. An elevator shaft."

"That's impossible."

"Dat cat lucky he alive."

"He couldn't a' been that high up."

It went on and on. Everyone had an opinion. Frank, Dad, the customers, even Bump the truck driver from Pensacola, who barely said a word. There was more laughter to accompany more stories about Barton Withers than I'm sure Barton Withers even knew he had. He probably wanted to keep each one of those embarrassing stories private too. My father had been around for a long time, Frank even longer, and they knew everything there was to know about Wellton and its notoriety. Of course, Dad knew my mother very well. He was right. She didn't want a working man like Rudy Buchner, who happened to run a local business. She wanted someone like Barton Withers, heir to the Withers-Chambliss Construction fortune. A handsome multimillionaire, she would never have to lift a finger again.

I looked over at my dad, whose glasses lay lopsided on his face. Normally, that would have made me giggle. That day, I wasn't giggling. The whole thing felt so shameful—everyone making fun of Barton Withers and my mom. I was embarrassed picturing my mother in my mind.

After getting to know Barton, who insisted we never call him Bart or Mr. Withers, I found Dad and Frank's tales hard to believe.

He liked to drink, but he was never drunk, or if he was, he didn't act like he was drunk, not that I've been around a lot of drunk people. He liked to drink that brown stuff. My parents would occasionally have a glass of wine, of course Dad liked beer and gin or vodka, whatever that clear stuff was that looked like water, so when Barton Withers came to our apartment, we didn't have the right kind of glasses for his drinks. He had to bring over his own. They were nice too—crystal highballs, my mother called them, and he placed them in the cabinet over the sink.

Since she was going out on dates with a rich guy, she seemed so blissful. She was even happier than the day we were finally unpacked and were living in our new apartment. And so I was surprised at her response when Marisa, who never seemed to learn a lesson, opened her big mouth one night at the kitchen table when Mom and Penelope the real estate agent were playing cards.

"Rudy and Frank said that Barton Withers was a drunk who was always getting into trouble, not real trouble because his rich parents are always bailing him out. Oh, and what does bailing mean?" she said.

I flinched as I waited for my mother's tiny but powerful hand to shoot across the table and smack my sister's perfectly sculpted cheekbone. But in my hushed amazement, that didn't happen.

"Oh, give me a break," Penelope said as she studied her cards, spider eyes squinting, extra long cigarette dangling from bright red lips.

My mother shook her head. "You know, Frank Watson is a black man from the poorest possible section of South Wellton. The only thing he has ever done in his life is work for the Buchners, cleaning fish for Christ's sake. As for your father"—she stubbed out her cigarette—"he is jealous. He sees that I am moving on with my life and no longer have any use for him."

Except to pay for this nice apartment.

"You two girls will understand someday that there will be people in this world, the have-nots, who will want what other people *have* or possess, like money, beauty, an education. Barton is a wonderful man who comes from a good family and has all of the things that your father, Rudy, will never attain. And he can't stand it. It is driving him insane."

Penelope nodded in full agreement.

"So what does *bailing* mean?" Marisa asked again.

My mother ignored her. "And furthermore, young lady."

God help me, here it comes.

"Rudy is not even your real father."

No, that would be the Indian prince. I stuck my finger in my ear. Thankfully, nobody saw it.

"And Frank should mean nothing to you. He's right up there— no, excuse me, I meant to say, *down there* with that awful Nancy."

"That's Rudy's sister, right?" Penelope asked. "Isn't she the one who's been in and out of the loony bin?"

I wanted to put that cigarette out in her eye—that was if I could find her eye under all that makeup.

My mother nodded. "That's the one. Crazy, crazy. I can't even begin to tell you how glad I—*we* are to be out of there and away from all that unwashed."

I wasn't glad. I wasn't glad at all.

"It's taken some getting used to, we know that." She looked at both of us. "Oh, but this is going to be so much better for the girls. Right, girls? Hey?" She tapped Marisa's arm as she played with the corner of a place mat.

"Sure, Mom." I nodded for the both of us even though *I* didn't agree with her. It just seemed a lot easier. In a way, I felt like I was betraying my father, but I knew that he and Frank, even Aunt Nancy, would understand, maybe in her own way.

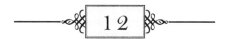

"What's bailing?" Marisa whispered to me the next morning as each of us lay in our twin beds.

I was awake, but my entire body except my nose was under the covers. It was freezing, and the wicked weather was upon us. "It's like when you're in trouble, and someone comes to your rescue." I raised one eye above my blanket, only to see a confused look on my sister's face.

"Like if you're in a burning building, and a fireman saves you by dragging you out?"

"Well, in the true sense of the word, I would say—"

"English."

"Not really. That's not really *bailing*, I guess, it's more like if you get *arrested*, you go to jail, then someone you know comes to the jail and pays a bunch of money so you don't have to stay there."

"Where?"

"Jail. You get bailed out of jail."

"Oh, right," she said.

"Why?"

"Do you think Barton Withers has ever been in jail?" she said.

"I don't know. Maybe." I knew he might have after listening to Frank and Dad talk about him.

"Do you think we should ask him?"

"No, I don't think we should ask him, Marisa. He's been so nice to us. I don't want to hurt his feelings." I hadn't slept all night. I was worried that Marisa was going to get in trouble again, and there wouldn't be anything I could do for her. She kept jumping. She never checked to see if there was ever any water underneath. She always did what she told me not to do, and I didn't care if she was protecting me or if she couldn't control herself. Somehow she had to learn how. And I had no idea what to do. I just prayed she would stop forgetting her own advice. *Indian prince.*

"Rudy probably knows. Or Frank." She interrupted my thoughts, and I focused my gaze on her once again.

"I don't think he's been in jail," I said. I hoped she would just change the subject.

I could hear my mother in the kitchen banging pans around. She had just turned on the television. I bit my lip, wondering how much of our conversation she heard. I was always careful to be quiet, but this place was a lot smaller and less creaky than Dad's house, and Mom was smart. She was really, really smart.

"All right, you two! Up!" My mother flew open the bedroom door and crash-landed into the freezing cold room.

Marisa moaned.

"Come on, both of you, get up. Get ready for school. I have a lot of things to do today. Let's go."

It was so early and cold, and I was so tired. I could have stayed under those covers in total quiet all day. Darkness still shone between a crack in the drapes. The light in the post on the sidewalk was fading down into morning as a chill clung to the window like a wet cloud. I could smell the lovely aroma of bacon as I watched my mother crack eggs over a frying pan in her peach-colored bathrobe. The toaster popped, and Marisa opened the door to our brown refrigerator.

"There's nothing in there. Come on." My mother pushed my sister toward the kitchen table.

"How come we're having eggs today, Mom?" I asked.

"Because there's no milk in the house for cereal, and you have to eat, so here it is. We have to get going. I want to have this cleaned up before you leave for school."

Now I understood why we were literally up and out of bed at the crack of dawn. "Where do you have to go today, Mom?"

"I have things to do today, Alice."

Marisa looked over at my plate. "Mom! Her eggs are bigger than mine! Alice is too fat. She shouldn't have bigger egg yolks. I'm the older—"

My mother interrupted her with a whirling roar that cracked the universe. She grabbed Marisa's right ear and beat her on the side of her stomach, underarm, and shoulder as my sister tried to twist away. Marisa shrieked, and they both cried loudly at the same time. Her arms flailed as I tried to back away and run out of the room, but I found myself trapped between the table and the wall and couldn't get out fast enough. I gagged, and tears exploded from my eyes.

As I tried in vain to move the table off and away from my chest, my mother backed away, hunched over, toward my sister. Her robe was open, and her white bra and girdle were exposed. She held a greasy butter knife in her hand. "Do you know what I just did?" she cried in anguish. "I could have stabbed you in the back! Do you know that? All because of a goddamned egg. An egg, goddamn it!"

Marisa held her arms up in front of her head and coiled far back into herself, as if she was trying to escape through the back of her chair. She let out a little shriek again, and I thought of my father, who was supposed to get her out of "that house," but he was very busy with other things. My mother backed up against the countertop. The three of us were crying, but there was no one there to offer comfort. My tears were silent, and my eggs were cold.

There was a sudden knock on the door. My mother dried her face with the kitchen towel and headed for the hallway. She tied her robe back together and smoothed back her sweaty hair.

I heard an older woman's voice. It sounded kind and patient and so peaceful. "Is everything all right?"

"Yes, yes, everything is fine," my mother lied to the concerned voice.

"I heard shouting and it sounded like banging on the wall," the concerned voice said.

"I'm very sorry. It's—it was my girls. They were fighting over something silly and ridiculous. You know how young girls can be. I'm sorry. I'm very, very sorry." My mother sounded normal and calm. She was a totally different person than who she had been five minutes before.

"Oh?" The concerned voice was unsure.

My mother said a few more things that I couldn't make out because Marisa started coughing, and I heard the concerned voice mumbling something as it shuffled away down the corridor.

My mother walked back toward where we were seated in the kitchen. The stillness was thick, and as I looked down at what was left of my breakfast, I prayed that neither one of them would say another word. Instead, my mother looked at Marisa, walked over to her, bent over, and calmly stuck a finger in her face. "If we get kicked out of here because of you, there will not be anywhere else for you to live. You will not live with Rudy, you will not live with my parents, and you will not come with me. You will not eat, sleep, be clothed, or attend school. You will be gone. Do you hear me?" She lowered her voice and moved in closer. I couldn't see my sister's face. "Gone."

She took our book bags and my coat and threw them into the hallway. A couple of my perfectly sharpened pencils and my protractor were strewn all over the plush avocado green carpet in front of the door. I scrambled to pick them up. We had to get out of her way fast.

"Now, both of you, out," she hissed quietly, eyes closed. "Get to that goddamned bus stop right now before I do something I just *might* regret later on!"

I was still on the floor putting my book bag back together when I turned toward her voice. My nose steered directly into the hem of her peach-colored robe. I could smell the flowery detergent she must have used in the wash. The door slammed. The desolate corridor where the concerned voice trailed off was cold as streaks of early winter sunlight painfully made their way through the large windows in the back of the building.

Marisa knocked on the door.

I turned. "What? Don't!"

"I forgot my jacket."

I looked at the sinister closed door. I waited for it to fly open in fury as I stood at the top of the stairs, ready to flee.

"Mom?" She bravely put her forehead against the beige metal. She went to knock one more time, but then stopped. I noticed the side of her small hand was very red, and I had a feeling that by the end of the day or the next, it might be bruised.

"Here, you can wear mine. I know it will fit."

She turned toward me looking hopeless as I handed her my jacket with the fluffy gray lining. She pushed past me and headed down the stairs. "I don't need it, Alice. Come on, let's just go."

I followed. "But wait. It's cold out, what are you going to do? No, really, what are you going to do? I have a sweater on. You're just wearing that thin turtleneck."

She turned to me at the front door, just before the two of us were enveloped into the freezing November air. "What kind of big sister would I be if I took your jacket?" Her face froze with determination, and her voice was focused. "I'll be fine. Thanks for offering, but no. Let's go."

A blast of early winter air accompanied the whoosh of the building's front door. Thankfully, there was no snow on the ground, but it was just a matter of days if not hours before the gray corners of the sky exploded into a freezing wet blanket.

We were early for the bus, and I could feel tears of anger caged all the way down in the back of my throat. Barton Withers could have bought my sister a whole truckload of winter coats, but the only way to him was through my mother. I wondered if Barton Withers had any idea of what he was getting himself into. She was really good at fooling the innocent. I'll bet so many people saw Lavinia Ionescu as just a beautiful, graceful, newly divorced mother of two. She didn't have a job; she struggled to put food on the table. She had two ungrateful daughters who didn't give her a moment's peace. Things were tough for her. She was so lonely. I was sure by the next day, I would love her again, would miss her when she was away, and would try to understand and get to know her. I would probably feel tremendous guilt. I would be afraid to think, afraid to sleep. But on this day, I hated her. I hated what she was doing to Marisa.

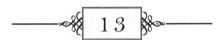

13

We were nearly fifteen minutes early for the bus. I kept asking Marisa if she wanted to put my coat on, but she refused. Once she said she wasn't even cold, but I knew that was a lie. You couldn't even talk without seeing your breath in the air, and she kept hopping from one foot to the other. I noticed that she was sniffling a lot. Still, she refused to take my jacket.

Slowly the bus stop began to populate, and everyone hovered around my hopping sister to keep her warm. I stood away with Bruce and this girl, Aubrey. Her parents were from France, and she had this infection on her skin and had to wear a patch that looked like a big square bandage on her face.

"Wow, really? Can I see?" I heard someone say, and then I felt Bruce touch my arm, which made me jump.

"Alice? Is that true?"

"Is what true?"

"Your sister. She's telling everyone she was stabbed."

I was confused, but only for a second. "What? Stabbed?"

"Yeah! Stabbed with a knife. What happened? Did your mom really stab her?"

Suddenly, I needed a place to hide. I didn't want to talk about this with Bruce. I didn't want to talk about this with anyone. I shook my head. Damn her! "She wasn't stabbed," I said.

Bruce looked so worried. "But she said it happened a little while ago. She said your mom did it with a butter knife." He moved closer to me, a flash of horror in his eyes.

"I'm telling you, Bruce, she wasn't stabbed. My mother didn't stab her."

"Well then, why would she say something like that?"

Thank God the bus was coming. "You know what she's like."
"Umm. No."

And he was right. I don't think Marisa ever said three words to Bruce. "She just likes to get attention, and she likes to tell tall tales."

I felt so guilty about saying those things to Bruce about my sister. After everything that happened to us that morning, Marisa wanted me to wear my own jacket because she was the big sister trying to protect me, and there I was betraying her.

I wanted to ask Bruce if Marisa and I could come live with him and his nice mom and dad. I also thought about telling the bus driver Pricilla about my mother and my sister fighting that morning, but I didn't know how. I was scared, and I didn't know where to begin. No one was going to believe that my mother stabbed Marisa because she didn't, not really. She almost did, but that didn't count. Who was going to listen to anything I had to say? My father was so busy all the time, and my mother would know if I placed a call to my grandparents. Who was going to help us? Bruce? Aubrey? No one could help us. Maybe Barton Withers, but he was on Mom's side. It was hopeless, and I figured that there wasn't any point in thinking about it anymore, much less talk about it.

But Marisa wouldn't let it go. She sat in the back of the bus with all her friends, gleefully bouncing in her seat, telling everyone that our mother stabbed her in the back with a butter knife while making our eggs and bacon. I knew Pricilla could hear every word, but she just ignored Marisa like I thought she would. I decided it would be best to just sit as far away from my sister as possible, so the three of us—Bruce, Aubrey, and I—filed into the front seats right behind the bus driver. Marisa showed her friends with her fingers how far the knife went into her back.

I thought it was funny that no one even asked to look under her shirt so they could see an actual stab wound, and it was then that I swear Bruce read my mind.

"If your sister was really stabbed, there would be a lot of blood. I mean, we would be able to see it. The blood would be soaked right through her shirt." He looked behind him. "And if you look at where she's pointing"—he nudged me, but I wasn't interested in looking at her—"that's where her kidney is. She couldn't have been stabbed there, Alice! That could have been a fatal wound!"

I nodded, never taking my eyes off my notebook. *Fatal wounds. What does he know about fatal wounds?* "That's because she wasn't stabbed. Do you want to look at this?"

Bruce finally turned his attention to our task at hand. Both of us were on the tutor team at school, and every Wednesday, we were assigned a student who needed help with math. We would work with them for forty-five minutes on their problems. On this day, I was grateful to get to school for two reasons: first, I was tired of listening to my sister weave her tale about her stabbing adventure, and second, I knew that once she was inside the building, she would no longer be cold.

Of course, there was no stopping Mrs. Madge Cranston from noticing Marisa almost immediately, and within the first ten minutes of arriving at the front door, it seemed like everyone knew that my mother stabbed my sister in the back with a butter knife.

"Ms. Ionescu, where is your coat this morning?" Mrs. Cranston's voice boomed with authority throughout the hallway.

"I forgot it at home."

"How could you forget your coat on a morning like this? Sounds a bit unlikely to me." She towered over Marisa, her back at the hinge of her door, large arms crossed.

"She didn't forget it."

I heard an unknown voice and turned around.

"She had to leave! Her own mother knifed her *this* morning. Stabbed in the back!"

"It only went in about *this much*." She showed Mrs. Cranston about an inch between her thumb and forefinger. I looked around for Bruce, but he and Aubrey were lost in the crowd all the way at the other end of the hallway.

Mrs. Cranston opened her mouth, then closed it. She looked at me, her face very serious. "Alice, what is this all about?"

I tried to speak, but my lips were fumbling around with each other, and I couldn't think of the right words to say.

Mrs. Cranston gave me a disappointed look, took her large hand, and guided my sister between the shoulders into her classroom and then into the bathroom in the front far corner of the room and shut the door. I could hear the two of them talking, but I couldn't hear what they were saying. Later, Marisa told me that Mrs. Cranston pulled up her shirt and examined her back.

Throughout the day, several of the kids, even ones I didn't know, asked me about the attack. I said that it was a misunderstanding or that it wasn't that bad. What I should have told everyone was that Marisa was definitely not stabbed and that there was no knife wound on her back. They should see for themselves if they were so curious, but I didn't because I couldn't put those words together. All I wanted to do was hide, but there was nowhere to go. The only one I could talk to was Bruce, but even then, I didn't want to talk about this.

From the little bits and pieces that I learned from my sister throughout the day, she was also telling people that the "stabbing" wasn't so bad, that the knife didn't go in that far, it was really nothing, and no, she wouldn't be showing anybody her "wounds." Oh, so it was *wounds* now. Plural.

On the bus home from school, I sat silently behind Pricilla, looking out the window at the cloudy sky, wondering what would happen to us when my mother found out about this day. I thought it would be best if we went back to live with my dad. I don't even know why Mom wanted us to live with her in the first place. All the two of us ever seemed to do when we were around our mother was cause her grief. She went as far as telling Barton Withers and some of the neighbors like Bruce's mom and Penelope the spider-eyed witch how difficult and expensive and tiresome it was to cope with the two of us.

I didn't mind going home to my father's. Not one bit. After all, he was supposed to get Marisa "out of that house" anyway, and after some pretty careful thinking, I came to the conclusion that what the doctor meant was that my father needed to get Marisa *away from that mother*.

The thing was, my father wasn't Marisa's father, and my mother always went out of her way to make that clear to *everyone* now. I never understood what difference it made and why it was such a big deal.

Indian prince.

My mother even made Marisa's last name her maiden name, Ionescu, when the rest of us were Buchners. Moving back to Dad's wouldn't be a problem for me at all. I didn't care about changing schools or friends or any of that stuff like Marisa did. It didn't mean a thing to me. I wanted my mother to be happy, and now that Barton Withers was coming over most of the time, she was happy. Or happier, maybe. I was hoping she would be happier still.

Marisa sat all the way in the back of the bus, giggling with her friends and insisting this time that "the stabbing was really nothing" and was "no big deal." I wondered about the phone call my mother would receive from school and what she would do next. Mrs. Cranston was very smart, and she didn't put up with any nonsense. I knew that she had to have seen bruises on my sister when she yanked her into the bathroom and examined her back. I figured a phone call was sure to follow, and when Mrs. Cranston didn't find that stab wound, I thought she would definitely call my mother to tell her that Marisa was going around school lying to anyone who would listen that my mother stabbed her in the back with a butter knife during breakfast.

Why did she tell everyone she forgot her coat on a freezing-cold morning? I thought about asking her but decided not to, and just when I was about to get the nerve up, I chickened out. I was always too scared, and lately, all I wanted to do was bury myself under some object. Half of me wanted Mrs. Cranston or the vice principal, anyone, to make that fatal call to my mother. Maybe we would be rescued, and Marisa would be "out of that house" like the doctor prescribed. I also knew that a deadly phone call would mean that Marisa would learn her lesson for good, and I would have probably died in battle to protect her. She wanted to protect me? I was going to protect her too.

Marisa bounced off the bus with an absent-minded goodbye to Pricilla and quickly forged ahead away from me. She must have been cold even though the afternoon sun began to filter through. She looked silly as she ran down the sidewalk with the coordination of a six-year-old. Her arms and book bag fought the frigid air as her little brown boat shoes toddled about the smooth pavement. I decided that I needed to catch up with her fast. I was, after all, preparing for battle.

"Marisa! Wait up!" When I finally caught up with her, I was out of breath. I was far too much of an ox to be running that hard. "Where are you going in such a hurry?" I watched her steam through the double doors and up the green-carpeted stairwell.

"Home. Where do you think I'm going? It's freezing!" She plowed ahead.

"Marisa, wait. Marisa, please!" I was breathless and panicking. I had that same nervous knot in my stomach that I had when I sat down with my first pupil after I was chosen for Tutor Team.

She stopped at the top of the stairs about ten feet from our door. She too was out of breath, but not nearly to the degree that I was. "What's the matter?"

I put my hand on my chest. "I'm scared."

"Of what *now*?"

My top teeth slid behind my bottom teeth. *Of you walking into that apartment and getting yourself beaten for lying at school, getting blamed for not taking your coat, for just being who you are.* "Can we just walk in together?"

She shrugged and looked around the hallway. "Fine."

"Wait," I demanded.

"What?" She turned around.

"Aren't you afraid?"

She walked back to me. We were nearly nose to nose. My confronting her surprised me, and suddenly, my heart jumped around on pins, but I didn't want to back down.

"Afraid of what? Afraid of what?"

I was incredulous. "You went around school all morning telling everyone that Mom stabbed you in the back with a kitchen knife. Mrs. Cranston knows it's not true, but I'll bet she's seen this bruise." I grabbed her arm. The reddening on the side of her arm was bruising just like I knew it would.

"Ow! Damn!" She yanked her arm away. "What is wrong with you?"

"With me? What is wrong with me?" I couldn't believe her.

"Yes! With you. You sound like a broken record." She shifted her weight and crossed her arms. She was trying to bully me, and I was not about to let her do it.

"Do you need to have your head examined?" I simply asked.

She laughed. "Oh, Alice, you and your big words."

I was amazed, but I knew I shouldn't have been. "Don't you remember anything we talked about? How about all that stuff you said at Bunica's?"

"I don't care right now. It doesn't ma—"

"There are my two lovelies! I knew I heard you out here." My mother was standing in the doorway wearing a tight white cashmere sweater with red flowers and dark denim jeans. She held a cigarette in one hand and a short fat glass in the other half full of Barton Withers's yellowy-brownish Scottish stuff that she had grown to love so much. Her blazing green eyes drooped. Her pupils looked like two pinpricks. "What are you doing out here in the hallway? It's cold. Marisa, where is your coat?"

She didn't wait for an answer as she motioned for us to come inside.

"Barton has a surprise for us." Then she pulled me toward her and kissed me hard, the way Aunt Nancy did. I figured there was no phone call from school. Yet.

Marisa went straight to the kitchen while I hung up my coat and put my book bag aside. I followed my sister into the kitchen and saw Barton Withers standing by the doorway holding two bags of live lobsters. I didn't know where they came from, but I knew they didn't come from Boochie's just by looking at the bag. "Those didn't come from Dad."

My mother put her hands on my shoulders. "That's right, darling. Your father is not the only one on the planet who sells seafood. His crap isn't even fresh."

Barton Withers looked at me from across the room. I could smell his cologne. He smiled at me, and his smile stuck. It wasn't like it was frozen, it was more like he was watching me with this sympathetic look on his face. I think he thought I was crazy. I didn't care where the lobster came from; no way was I eating it.

"Barton, I don't like lobster."

As soon as the words fell out of my mouth, I felt as though I was being rude.

"You don't? Since when?" My mother stubbed out her cigarette in the full ashtray in the middle of the kitchen table.

"I don't know." I felt stupid standing alone, quietly protesting in the middle of the kitchen.

My mother emptied out the ashtray as Barton Withers, still smiling, placed the lobster down on the countertop. Marisa was examining his bottle of scotch.

"You used to love it when you were little," my mother called over her shoulder as the water ran.

I didn't want to discuss the fact that I had made friends with some lobsters along the way, and I didn't care for the fact that one minute they were alive in front of me, and the next minute, they were dead.

"Now don't you worry about a thing, little one," Barton Withers said.

Little one?

Barton Withers knelt down so that he was closer to my face. His teeth were so white, they didn't look real. "Now that I'm here, the world is your oyster. No pun intended." He looked over at my mother, who giggled. His smile never left his face. "If you don't like lobster, then you don't have to eat it. Do you like steak?"

I nodded. "Sure."

He stood up and snapped his fingers. "Then I will order you a perfectly cooked fillet—sweet and tender, just like you." He patted me on the head and nodded to my mother, who came over and put her arms around me and kissed me again. I knew that when I went into the bathroom and looked in the mirror, I would have blobs of red lipstick all over my face.

"I like lobster, Barton!" Marisa called out cheerfully.

"Careful with that bottle, Marisa," my mother warned, but she was laughing and didn't seem to care about it.

Barton Withers walked over to Marisa, his powerful stature commanding the room. "She's fine, Lavinia. Anyone want to try a little?"

My mother let out a giggle that didn't sound like her. "Barton, are you about to give my children booze?"

He looked over his shoulder, his sparkly eyes soft and innocent like a puppy's. "Just a little white wine, babe?"

My mother, sitting at the very end of the kitchen table, let out another squeal while pulling her knees up to her chest. I noticed she was wearing silvery sequined ballet-like slippers. I had never seen them before. They looked brand-new. Barton Withers must have bought them for her.

"I'll try some." Marisa was the first to volunteer, raising the glass to her lips. "*Ew.*" Her face twisted into something sour. "That's awful. Do you want to try some, Alice? I don't think you'll like it either."

She was right. I didn't like the taste of white wine, but I did like the little feeling of warmth it gave me deep in my belly. I could have taken another gulp, but I didn't want to push it.

"That's a thirty-five-dollar bottle. Barton has impeccable taste!" my mother exclaimed.

"Anything for my girls," he said.

Barton Withers was still smiling. He spread out a white linen tablecloth over our kitchen table and lit long lavender-colored candles that he brought with him. His gold lighter flickered so quickly in his hand that I knew he was a professional. He prepared a big salad, and just as those poor lobster were ready to be eaten, there was a knock on the door. It was some man delivering my steak. Barton Withers met him with cash as he carried a brown paper bag back in the kitchen and put my steak on a plate with some roasted potatoes and salad. Then he placed the plate in front of me.

Our little kitchen looked so pretty. It felt like the holidays at my father's house. Barton Withers told us jokes and stories that made us laugh, and he talked about his parents' two dogs, Ruby and Pearl. I don't think I had ever eaten a steak that was quite as delicious as the filet mignon Barton Withers ordered for me. It was so filling that I knew that even I would have some leftovers.

Our lives were not the same since our mother met Barton Withers. When he was around, our mother was so happy. She was giddy and silly, just like Marisa's friends. When he wasn't there, she was her normal self—sometimes she was in a pretty good mood, and other times she would turn on us like a rabid dog. I got thrown around my share of times, but it was nothing compared to Marisa. She got it the worst. My mother just had it in for her, and so I was always relieved when Barton Withers came around, or the two of them went out and stayed out late.

A girl from the neighborhood named Nina who was about three years older than Marisa would come over and watch us when my mother and Barton Withers went out. I didn't think we needed anyone to babysit us, but my mother claimed Marisa had to be at least fourteen years old to be left alone with me, or else Mom would go to jail. It sounded like a stupid law to me, but having Nina around was a lot of fun. She would paint our nails in sparkles and play her favorite albums. When Nina was there, I found that I didn't miss my mother as much as I had in times past. I knew that wherever she was, she was safe and happy with Barton Withers.

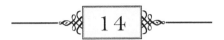

14

"Now, the only thing this does is confuse me." My father pushed his black glasses back up the bridge of his nose and slowly shook his head. "There's a god for this and a god for that." He tapped the page with the back of his hand. "You have a god for water, a god for wind, a goddess for—or if one particular god doesn't suit your thinking, then you can chose your own? Is that right? Let's say there are no real definitions, and this religion is, ah, well, all-inclusive, I would say. I just don't get any of this. And I'm thinking that's good, and—oh, and then here. There are volumes and volumes of ancient writings. They're called Vedas. I-I just don't think that I'm, well, okay. No, kiddo, go ahead and tell me more about Big Bucks and your mother."

My father was engrossed in a book on comparative religion and seemed stuck on Hinduism, but he chose the wrong person to talk to about it. I had no idea of what he was talking about, and I wasn't interested in learning on that day either. Eventually, he would figure it out. We sat on the old red velvet couch in the library in front of the fire.

"They're engaged."

He slapped his book shut and looked over at me. "Engaged? Ha! Engaged? *Engaged?* Are you shittin' me? Engaged! Oh, Jesus Christ."

I nodded.

"So Lavinia is finally getting everything she wanted. The rich guy with the fast car." He smiled, shook his head, and opened his book again. "So I guess this means that I don't have to pay for that apartment anymore."

"I don't know. I guess not." I hadn't thought about it, and I wondered. "He gave her a ring too."

Dad chuckled this time and tipped his head back. "Well, of course he did. What's it look like, the diamond from—"

"It's an emerald."

"A big one, no less."

"Yeah, but it's not shiny, it's dull, and it's light in color. I didn't know what it was when I first saw it. Mom said it was 'opaque.' She said it was very rare and very expensive." Saying that to Dad felt strange.

He rolled his eyes. "For the love of all that is holy."

I managed a giggle. "And it's got two diamonds, one on each side. She said one was for me, and one was for Marisa. I'm sure you'll get to see it."

He raised his eyebrows as he continued to scan the pages of his book. "Oh, no doubt. She'll be flashing that thing all over town."

Suddenly, it felt good to be in my pajamas in front of Dad's smoldering fire, listening to him read to me about religion. "You know, there's just one thing though." I didn't want to hurt my father's feelings by bringing up the subject, but I had been frustrated by it, and I couldn't contain myself any longer. "Barton Withers keeps bringing us shellfish for dinner."

I waited.

"And…and it's not from here."

I should have known that Dad would seem unfazed and more focused on his book than on what I was saying. That wasn't unusual behavior.

"I won't eat it, Dad. And you *know* I won't ever eat the lobster."

"I know that. But you can eat. You have to eat what he brings home, kiddo. You know he sure as hell isn't going to come down here shopping in the ghetto. Could you imagine your mother's face if he brought home one of my big bags?" His laughter made me laugh too. "He's probably going up to that swanky little market up in Harbins. It's all right. It's way overpriced. He has to do things like that. Again, you'll understand this adult nonsense one day."

"He always smiles at me, this Barton Withers, but he looks at me like I have three eyes."

He rubbed me hard on the top of the head. Then he got up to poke the fire. "Listen, don't let it get to you. And another thing, I'll give you a bigger lecture on free enterprise when we're done with religion. This is what makes America the greatest country on earth. Competition." He sat back down on the comfortable red couch and pointed his finger upward. "Competition is good because it makes you work harder to be the best. So what? There's another seafood market in the neighborhood. People like Big Bucks might want to spend their money there. That's perfectly fine. All that does is make me work harder to make my store better than the swanky store. And of course, he's doing all this on purpose. He has to please your mother. Really, don't let it get under your skin."

The fire popped. It smelled so good. I wished I could have sat there forever. My father always acted as if he never worried about anything at all, as if he wasn't scared of anything. I wished I could be like that, but it was impossible. I worried about everything, just not at that very moment.

Then I heard a faint scratching noise coming from upstairs. "Do you hear that noise? What is that?"

My father looked in the direction of the sound. "Oh, that's just your aunt."

I didn't even hear her before. I had no idea she was even in the house. But she could be really quiet when she wanted to be. She had a way of weaving herself in, out, and around people like a bird that could fly for a long time without having to flap its wings. "What is she doing up there? It smells clean." Of course it smelled clean.

Dad looked down at his book then turned another page. "She's painting Marisa's old room."

Marisa hadn't been with me to visit my father on the weekends for months. I thought she would have missed her old friends in the neighborhood, but she seemed to have moved on to a new and better phase in her life. She didn't talk about the cat she named Shelly anymore, who now hung around the front porch and was a lot friendlier.

"Actually, I think she's—Nance?" My father called from the couch when he saw her shadow sweep by the door.

"What!"

"Are you painting yet?"

"Still scrubbing."

"That's right. She said she was going to scrub the baseboards and the walls and all that first before she was going to paint the room. That kind of activity keeps her busy, you know. She's enjoying herself."

I didn't realize you had to scrub a wall before you painted it. But then I didn't know anything about painting walls. Aunt Nancy was very specific about the way she liked to proceed with a project. "What color is she painting the room?"

"Same color," he said. "Just going to freshen it up a little, that's all."

"Do you think she'll paint my room?"

He shook his head, never taking his eyes off his book. "Nah, your room doesn't need it."

When I returned to my mother's, I was going to tell Marisa that Aunt Nancy was not only scrubbing out her room, she was also giving it a fresh coat of paint. Marisa probably wouldn't care. She was spending a lot of time with Barton Withers, her soon-to-be stepfather.

He lived with his parents in Harbins, which was a small wealthy suburb on the nice part of the Maidenhead River. Mr. and Mrs. Withers's home was built in all gray stone and dark brown, almost black glass. As you drove up to it, it actually looked as if one side of it was built into a cliff directly behind it. The rocky cliff looked exactly like the house. Barton Withers explained to us that the cliff was carved out from a glacier during the Ice Age. This state had a lot of glacial formations, and it wouldn't have been uncommon. It was just so convenient that a rare and natural piece of beauty would just happen to present itself on his parents' land. It was so spectacular that I wondered if that's what led them to buy the property in the first place. I could have asked, but I didn't. Mom and Marissa lapped it up, and everyone, *everyone*, had to hear about it. It was so embarrassing, I wanted to cover my ears most of the time when I was around the two of them.

I did have to admit though that I had never seen a house quite like this. Maybe on television. The grand entrance was surrounded by hand-carved smooth marble, and the eaves met in Tudor-style

arches one after another. In the middle of the house was a huge structure of apparently Italian marble with a rounded dome-like roof and
floor-to-ceiling dark brownish-black windows. This was where Mrs.
Eloise "Sunny" Withers hosted her galas, luncheons, parties, and
charity events. It wouldn't be until my mother's wedding to Barton
Withers would we actually see the inside of that room. It seemed like
such a waste to have a huge room like that and not use it for your
family and your books.

The Witherses also had a stable full of horses. Good ones. My
mother told us that when Barton Withers turned twenty-one, his
father bought him some kind of racehorse that cost a half a million
dollars. My father said that he remembered the newspaper article.
Marisa was becoming very interested in horses, and Barton Withers
promised to set her up with riding lessons as soon as the weather was
better. I had no idea what the big deal was when it came to horses.
I had no interest in learning how to ride one. I thought they were
dumb, ugly, smelly, and they attracted flies.

It was cold and dark. Wellton had just been blanketed with
fresh snow that reflected in the sky, so there wouldn't be that starry
blackness above that Marisa and I could silently gaze upon and sometimes have our discussions under. Not that we even did much of
that anymore. She and Barton Withers were exploring all kinds of
father-daughter type adventures, and she had little time for me these
days. Far less for Dad, so I guess my father's obligation to "get Marisa
out of that house" wasn't such a priority anymore. I don't think it
even mattered at all. I seemed to be the only one to be thinking about
it. I know I didn't know what other people were thinking about, but
if I had to bet money on it? I'm pretty sure that I was the only one
thinking about it.

I watched the fire travel around and up the logs, and the occasional crackle brought peace to my mind. I looked over at my father,
who was now deeply engrossed in his book. Then suddenly, my
peacefulness escaped me, and so many different thoughts clouded
my head. I felt like telling my father that I had many things to discuss
with him, but that I would do it at a later time. I've done that before
with Bruce, Marisa, my mother, my teachers at school, and each of

them looked at me like I was weird. My mother told me that if I had something to say that I was to go ahead and say it. She would not be waiting around until later, and she would not be tolerating this behavior. So I didn't say anything because I thought it was probably better that way. Maybe I would be lucky and forget. Sometimes I did, but rarely.

My father finally looked up from his book.

"Dad, I think Marisa and I should move back in with you."

He was annoyed. "I told you, Alice, you don't have to worry about me. We're all fine here. I promise you, I can take care of myself."

I sat up. This was serious business, and no matter how much it would panic me, I intended to make my father listen and understand. "No, Dad, I'm not worried about you. Not right now, anyway. I'm worried about us—Marisa and me. I don't want to live with Mom anymore."

He held up a hand. "Alice—"

I decided it was best to keep my voice as low as I could, although I could feel the anger and frustration creeping up my throat. The last thing I wanted to do was upset Aunt Nancy. "I don't even know where we're going to go. We're looking at these…these real estate books right now." I fought to find the right words. "We won't be living in the apartment anymore. I'm sure I'll end up in another school."

That was an afterthought. I wondered if Marisa would go ape again.

My father looked at me carefully as if he was actually listening. If I were to keep this up, I might, for once, go somewhere.

He let out a long breath as if he had been holding it. "You might stay there for a while until he builds your mother her palace, or you might go to his pad."

"He doesn't have a pad. He lives with his mom and dad in Harbins. And I'm scared of that house. It's way too big and creepy. What if it's haunted?"

"Are you kidding me?"

I had my father's full attention. "No, Dad. It's huge. There aren't enough people to fill it up. It's like—"

"He lives with his parents? He *lives with* his parents? Jesus Christ, am I ever getting an education today." He let out a cackle that completely deflated me. Then he smiled like one of the boys at my school when they were acting silly. "What is he, forty?"

I shrugged. "I don't know. Something like that."

He shook his head slowly. "My father, your grandfather, Berndt, God rest his soul, wouldn't even let me come back for the night. I waited until *after* he was dead and buried before I moved one stick of furniture into this old place."

He looked around the room with pride, and I knew this conversation wasn't going anywhere. Then suddenly, a spark of hope.

He turned to me and scratched my head. His eyes were narrow and beckoned me closer to him. "Listen to me, little girl, and this is serious now."

Of course it was serious.

"First of all, as much as I wish I did, I have absolutely no claim to Marisa."

"Who is her father?" It just slipped out.

He just shrugged. "And besides, I don't think she would agree with you right now. She's having too much fun playing Princess Withers."

He had a point. He made a gesture that looked like he wanted me to sit really close to him so that I could put my head on his shoulder, but I didn't want to do that.

"Your mother has custody of you, Alice," he continued. "You're a minor child, and right now, the court mandates you to live with her, wherever she goes, for the time being. The only thing she can't do is take you out of state. Come on, we've talked about all this."

I felt tears sting my eyes.

"You keep coming down on the weekends. We have that, and…" His voice just sort of faded away, but I wasn't finished.

"How about this summer? It's not like I'm in school."

He crushed me with another casual shake of the head. "You'll still be a minor then. You won't be able to do anything until you're eighteen."

That was it. He had reached in and pulled my throat out. How could this possibly be?

"Eighteen!" I cried. "Eighteen? That's seven more years!"

"It's a lifetime to you, I know. But I was just thinking about Teddy Rickerman's kid, you know, Matthew."

Yes, I knew fat Matthew and his fat father. Teddy owned a catering company, and they were always in the store buying food. I didn't care about them either.

"Now that kid—um, Matthew, moved in with Teddy when he was about fifteen or sixteen. I guess it could happen if the kid really has a preference as to which parent he wants to live with, and, well, in Teddy's case, he had a fairly easygoing ex wife. By the way, your mother is *not* a fairly easygoing ex-wife, not by a long shot."

Why was he taking this so lightly? This was my life we were talking about. Mine and Marisa's.

"And," he continued, "a sympathetic judge—"

I didn't want to listen to my father continue to ramble on about different cases, other people, judges, and everyone else. None of this was helping me, and I was beginning to feel like my father didn't even want me to come home and live with him. Since he wasn't the Indian prince and had no claim to my sister, he didn't have to worry about making decisions about her. Not that any of that was going to make a difference anyway. I guessed Marisa would never give up Barton Withers and his horses, sweets, pocket money, and sips of beer to come back here and live with my father. She barely ever came to visit "Rudy" anymore, and I couldn't remember the last time she spent the night. Maybe that's why Aunt Nancy was so freely scrubbing and painting Marisa's room when most people were getting ready for bed.

"You said this was the greatest country on the planet." I looked hypnotically into the fire. I was defeated.

He smiled and shook my shoulder. "Ah, but it is, kid. The justice system is too. You just wait and see. Someday you'll understand. You got it good right now. I know you don't think so, but someday, you'll understand. You'll get it."

I didn't know how he could say these things. I wished I wasn't so afraid to ask him, but now I was. I think I had irritated him enough.

Why did people think that just because you were young, you were automatically fine? That you would bounce back like a little rubber ball, unharmed and untouched? Just because I didn't have any bills to pay like he said once didn't mean I didn't understand. Just because I was a kid who was supposed to be resilient and forgiving didn't mean I didn't *get it*. I wasn't forgiving, and I wasn't a rubber ball. As far as resilient went, I decided I would figure out that word on my own. The only time I had ever even heard that word was on a commercial for makeup. And what about my father always yammering on and on about how smart I was for my age? He obviously didn't think I was smart enough. Maybe he didn't care to know how smart I really was or how smart I would be when I grew up.

Aunt Nancy suddenly came galloping into the library with an empty bucket in one hand and a green sponge in the other. She was smiling. "Do you want to see what I just did?"

"Sure, let's take a look." My father dog-eared his page and put his book down. I figured our conversation was dead, so why *not* take a look at my aunt's laboring?

My father climbed the dimly lit staircase as I followed behind. I knew where every creak in every step was, and the thought filled me with warmth. But I made myself try to think of Aunt Nancy's new project immediately since it would probably be another seven years since these stairs would be a part of my home again. By then there would most likely be new sounds and creaks, ones that I wouldn't recognize.

Marisa's room, empty of all her belongings, was lit up and clean, but lonely. She hadn't even left a sock in the drawer. I left a bunch of my things at Dad's. She didn't even *pretend* to want to be there. I thought there was something wrong with Marisa. Dad didn't seem to mind at all. It didn't look as if he noticed the barren starkness that used to be her bedroom. Aunt Nancy had washed it all away.

"Well?" She beamed. "What do you think?"

My father ran his hand along the smooth seafoam green wall. "You haven't painted yet?"

She rolled her eyes. "No, Rudy. I'm talking about my *scrubbing*." She put the sponge and the bucket down and, with enthusiasm, went over to inspect her work. "I cleaned everything. Years of grime on these walls and the baseboards? Blech! Oh, and I used a wood polish to brighten up the floor. *Might* have to do *that* again though. Phil, the man who does the work in my building, told me that painting is 90 percent preparation and 10 percent paint. That took me the longest time to remember." She spun around and pointed to the ceiling. "I cleaned the ceiling."

My father looked up. "You *scrubbed* the ceiling? How? You gotta be careful, Nance."

She looked at her brother like he should have known that. "Of course, Rudy. I scrubbed it with this broom and that stepladder. I'm careful. Did you know this used to be my room when we were kids? I'll bet you don't remember that, Rudy. Did you know that?"

My dad's face softened into a smile. "Of course I remember, Nance. How could I forget?"

"Aunt Nancy, I think it looks really great," I said.

She walked toward me. "Thank you. Are you really telling me the truth? Do you really think so?"

"Yes, I do really mean it."

She put her arm around my shoulders.

I walked around the room, marveling at how much she did. "I think you've done a great job. I mean, it seems like it was awfully hard work."

"Well?" She drew out the *well* for a long time. "You know it was, but it will all be worth it. I hope I can find the same green paint. If not, I'll have to find another color that I'm sure I'm not going to like as much, and I'm going to have to say so what? It'll be good anyway." She suddenly lunged for me, wrapped her arms around me, and hugged me hard.

"Nancy, I don't want you staying up here all night doing this," my father called from across the room.

She ignored him and put her palms on my fat cheeks as she looked straight into my eyes. "I've been meaning to tell you this for a very, very long time, Alice." Her breath stank of cigarettes. "You are a very special girl, and I love you very, very much. You will never forget that?"

I nodded as my smooshed face lay captive in her hands. "I promise."

My eyes sought out my father, who had been inspecting a windowsill.

"Don't pay any attention to him," she whispered. "Wanna soda?"

"Sure. Thanks."

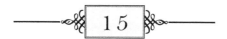

15

When the warmth of spring arrived in Wellton, the scent of the air was more like a taste. It was an entirety that lifted me, an intense light when I looked into the faces of regular people I saw anywhere. Still, I always preferred to be alone. I liked the company of myself. Both my parents, each from their separate corners of the ring, didn't think it was normal for a twelve-year-old to be without dozens of friends at all times of every day. I believed it was important for my mother that I have friends because she wanted me out of her hair when I wasn't in school. My father *should* have realized that my books provided me with plenty of company, but he didn't.

Anyway, I liked going over to Aubrey's house, particularly when her mother was baking. Also, Bruce and I had been working to put together his latest invention, and so it wasn't like I was lonely. Marisa would always be my best friend even though we didn't have as many clandestine discussions as we used to. She had so many friends, but it seemed like all they ever did was talk about each other behind each other's back.

So I asked myself, *Is this what a friend is supposed to do? Would I rather spend time with Aubrey, Bruce, and his cats and inventions, or would I rather be among a gaggle of backstabbing girls?* It's not like I had or wanted a whole lot of free time for friends anyway. I spent a lot of my time going over and over things in my head, and I liked to sit on the bench in front of our apartment and watch black squirrels and robins.

The clamorous sound of birds every morning before the sun rose was another indication of spring. The noise didn't wake me as I was usually lying in bed with a pillow over my open eyes at that time of the morning. I had no idea of what kinds of birds they were, maybe a combination of sparrows and robins, if they happened to be outside my window at that exact time of day. I made a mental note to look in Dad's library or in the library at school.

There was another bench directly across from where I sat. I studied it and focused on it as I thought of a pretty song I had heard on the radio earlier that day. I wondered how Aunt Nancy was coming along with her cleaning project. And with all this, I was perfectly content.

Then I saw him. Bob. He was staring down at me from a giant hallway window in the building across the lush grass. I didn't like his staring, so I gave him a dirty look. Bob or Bobby, as the swooning girls called him, was the neighborhood paperboy and had a younger sister in Marisa's class named Hilary. Marisa thought that Hilary was the luckiest girl alive to share a kitchen, bathroom, last name, and just about everything else with Bobby. This Bobby guy was Hilary's brother, so *of course* she shared these things with him. She *lived* in the same *house* naturally. There were times that I thought my sister's brain was the size of a potato chip when it came to boys.

Bob or Bobby (I wondered if he even liked being called that? Probably, just as long as it was a female doing the calling) was tall and thin with a soft and silky face and not a pimple in sight. He had deep-set dark blue eyes and thick straight sandy blond hair that fell halfway down his back that he tied in a ponytail. Of course Marissa thought he was gorgeous. I thought he looked like a girl.

Suddenly, I saw a green car pull up and heard the deafening but familiar sound of a song I knew. I only knew that because I liked to go through Dad's album collection every now and then. What looked like college students got out of the car with a cooler and disappeared into Bruce's building. I decided to amble up there to tell him that my mother would be marrying Barton Withers, and we would be moving to a ridiculous-sized house in Crescent Hills. Bruce hadn't been in school that day.

I walked up the grassy hill and knelt in front of his basement living room window. I was surprised to see that the curtains weren't pulled back; they were gone altogether, and the room was dark. Normally, Bruce's big friendly orange cats, Nathan and Ringo, would pop up like two fat pieces of toast, arch their backs, stretch, bump into each other, and then jump down upon the first sight of a visitor. But the cats were gone too.

"Looking for something?"

I whipped around at the voice of Bob or Bobby. His army green canvas sack was draped over his shoulder and across his bony chest and was still brimming with newspapers.

"Yeah," I answered, even though it was hardly any of his concern. "I'm looking for Bruce."

"Is he your boyfriend?"

"No!" I protested. "He's my friend."

"All right, take it easy, chubby cheeks." Bob or Bobby was a little too sure of himself.

I crossed my arms in front of my chest and twisted my feet around in my sandals as best as I could. I didn't need for him to be noticing my plumpish toes peeking out the front either.

He turned his blond head and spit about five feet over the sidewalk and onto the mowed lawn. "Looks like they lan out on their rent to me."

I was confused. "What's a 'lan out'?"

"Not *lan* out. *Ran* out."

"Oh," I said quietly.

As Bob or Bobby stood in front of me gassing about Bruce's family leaving town and the probable reasons why, I looked at him and wondered why Marisa and her friends thought he was so handsome. Maybe if he would just shut up for long enough, stop spitting, and cut his hair to a decent length, he would look normal. Maybe. Besides, Dad always said that it was *women* who had a habit of nattering on and on like broken records, not men. This guy was obviously weird, but then again, my sister was weird sometimes too.

"Huh?" I scratched my forehead. "What about the cats?"

"The cats?"

"What did you just say about the cats?"

"They probably took the cats with them. Come over here."

I followed Bob or Bobby down a small incline, and we looked into the living room window, both of us cupping our eyes. The apartment was vacant. There were a few wires and cables sticking out of the wall in one of the bottom corners, and there was a plastic sandwich bag and a paper coffee cup lying where Bruce's father's recliner used to be. The overhead light was ripped out of the ceiling, and on the side to the left where the kitchen was lay open a big space where the refrigerator once covered in photographs and magnets used to be. The little chalkboard that hung on the pantry door was also gone. What was once someone's comfortable little home now looked dirty, barren, and angry, as if someone or something had snatched away its life without warning. Bruce Collins was gone, and he didn't even say goodbye. Maybe he couldn't say goodbye.

"Hey, kid."

I looked up. Bob or Bobby was now standing over me.

"Kneeling in front of that window for the rest of the afternoon isn't going to make your friend come back. Come on, it's just like I said. His old man probably owed money. You seem to be a good kid." He turned and spit again. "You'll make some new friends."

I slowly picked myself up and brushed the grass off my knees.

He pumped himself up again as he tossed his head quickly from side to side. "I would be your friend, but I don't hang around girls your age. Although, you *are* kind of big, aren't you?" With a quick turn, he spotted his thin yellow ten-speed and popped on. He was gone quickly with his canvas sack of papers.

I looked around. It seemed like I was the only person within miles. The huge grassy courtyard of the Stanhope Ridge was suddenly a vacuum, as if all the clean spring twilight air had been sucked out of it, and I stood alone, trying to figure out which direction to walk, where I should start to find my way out of this tunnel, how I could find my way back home.

I looked at the building across from where I lingered, and I focused on one of the windows. I thought for a very long time, but even so, there wasn't anything concrete snaking its way through my mind. My stomach roiled with sickness and more fear until finally, it all imploded.

Slowly I moved away from what was once my best friend's living room window and made my way back up to the sidewalk. I didn't look back; I just kept walking back down the hill, passing the bench I had sat on a little while ago. I didn't want to sit back down on it again. What if the whole process started all over again?

It was dusk now. The sun was fading into streaks of pink, finding their solace in purple. The sky was warm and gray, and somewhere off in the distance, I could hear a police siren, a man talking, and someone hosing off the wheels of a car. I knew I wasn't alone, but as I continued to the front door of our building, I knew that no matter what was going on around me, I would be lost inside my own head for a very long time.

I continued to replay the song I had just heard over and over in my head as a numbing dreamlike sensation crushed me. I didn't know if I was angry or sad, and I wondered if Bruce had told anyone *anything at all* about this sudden departure. I hadn't even realized I was at the front door of our apartment until I put my hand on it. *Maybe I should ask the superintendent? They won't tell you anything. Would* they *even—they won't even let you jump on the trampoline without your* mother *there, you idiot! I mean, come on!*

My mother sat alone at the kitchen table. I could hear the TV turned on in the other room, but I knew Marisa was at a friend's house, and I never knew Barton Withers to sit in front of the television unless it was to watch a baseball game or some other type of sporting event. The ashtray was overflowing with butts as my mother smoked and cried, "Where is your goddamned sister, Alice?"

"She's having dinner at Karen's." Karen, the girl with hundreds of shoes. "What's the matter, Mom? Why are you crying?"

She looked up at me. Her mascara was running down her painted cheeks, imprisoning them in pink. She had been wearing too much makeup lately. It looked as though she had been getting pointers from Penelope, the spider-eyed witch. She shook her head and started to cry harder. The look in her eyes made me feel so sorry for her. She looked sad, not angry or irritated like she normally did, but genuinely sad.

I lightly touched her shoulder, but she pushed me away. I thought about sitting down, but I decided that remaining stationary was probably safest.

She drew hard on her cigarette, then blew the gray smoke across the table as she wiped her nose with the back of her hand. "We have a problem."

I was worried if this problem had anything to do with my sister. I wanted to take a deep breath, but I didn't dare. "What's the problem?"

"Well…" She flicked her ash in irritation and cocked her head. "It would seem like Mr. and Mrs. Withers, Barton's parents, are less than impressed with my parents."

"What, Bunic and Bunica?" I sat down hard.

"That would be correct."

"But why?" I already had the answer.

"First of all, Barton II, or Mr. Withers and Sunny, are so, you know, the perfect picture of class. Sunny doesn't have a hair out of place, and—" She slapped the table, and I jumped a little. "They are wanting us to get married on the Boulevard. My mother goes to that…that shit cathedral down on Wysocki—"

She heard me gasp. There was no turning back now.

"What?" she said as she blew out smoke like a dragon.

"Mom, that cathedral is the oldest building in Wellton." I felt as if I was floating. I knew my mother agreed with me. I also knew I was in trouble.

"Oh, Alice, it's not the building, it's the people who go *into the building*. Every immigrant from every walk of life! That place is open twenty-four hours a day. It's a wonder it's still standing! People with walkers, people who haven't changed clothes in days, hobos, they smell, they stink, those Catholics will let anyone through those doors, Alice, anyone and anything. Jesus Christ Almighty God! And hear this: your grandfather, who hasn't darkened the doorway of a church since 1948, for god's sake, has made it *clear to all* that he would not be able to give his only daughter away on the most important day of her life. *So sorry, Lavinia.*"

I suppose marrying Dad was her second most important day?

My grandfather, Radu Ionescu, or Rod, which was what his American friends called him, had not been in a church since he and my grandmother fled Romania after the Second World War. He and my grandmother were attending Mass when the church was massacred by Russian soldiers aimed to convert Orthodox followers to the Stalinist state religion of communism. Only about a quarter of the people in the church survived, which Bunica claimed was miraculous. Bunica also said they didn't care about converting anyone as they hid under a pew all the way in the front of the church and pretended to be dead. All they wanted to do was harm and kill.

That would be the last visit to church for my grandfather. He had a gruesome scar on the back of his neck, and although he never spoke of the horrific day, he never made any apologies as to why he wouldn't attend a funeral or a wedding inside *any* house of worship. My mother marrying the town's rich and handsome prince and the whole event being photographed and having its own little home in the corner of the Society Page of the *Wellton Morning News* did not make one bit of difference to Bunic.

"It has been thirty years, for Christ's sake," my mother whined. *She had disdain for people who needed walkers.*

"His wife got over the whole thing!"

"So I guess Bunic won't be at the ceremony." That would be correct, Alice, you perfectly round imbecile.

She nodded as fresh tears washed away what was left of her very black mascara. "Not unless you drug him *very* heavily, and even then, what would be the point of that?" She grimaced, got up, and poured herself some of that scotch that Barton Withers introduced her to. I was dying for a sip as I watched her lean against the countertop. "Can you imagine drugging my father just to get him to attend his only child's wedding? Can't even give his only daughter away. God forbid!"

The more she talked about Bunic, the more her voice dripped with venom. It was as if she wanted to kill him for what he was doing to her. She took another sip of the alcohol that made my insides feel so warm.

"Heh! Drugging that old fool would certainly make him more of an embarrassment than he already is."

I looked down at my finger as I listened to her. I could feel her watching me.

"My god, Alice, my future in-laws are sophisticated, educated, cultured people. I could just tell by the way Sunny looked at them the other day that she was repulsed. I don't think Dad had changed his pants all week, and Jesus Christ, do you think your grandmother could do something, *anything*, with that hair?"

I wasn't sure if she was waiting for a reaction. I had no idea how to respond to any of this.

"They look old. They are poor immigrants from the west side. No wonder Barton's parents don't think I'm good enough for their only son!"

I looked up at her. "Did they say any of that?"

She waved her hand in the air as she continued to sip her drink. "Oh lord, no. Those people have far too much grace to openly make a statement like that. But they think it. I know they think it. They view me as a poor dirty immigrant, just like my parents. Dad runs a newsstand, and Mom barely leaves the fucking kitchen! How can I marry into this family?"

"Maybe you shouldn't." And as soon as I said it, I regretted it and cringed.

That was definitely not the response my mother was looking for. I didn't think she was interested in my opinion at all. I felt a whoosh of tingly warmth as she slithered in behind me and sat back down, drink in hand. "What do you mean, 'Maybe I shouldn't?' What are you talking about, Alice Buchner?"

She was interested after all, wasn't she? What had I done? And I was always lambasting Marisa for having such a big mouth.

"I just want you to be a happy and beautiful bride, Mom," I said. "And right now, you don't seem happy at all."

She moved her face closer to me in urgency. I could smell the scotch on her breath. Her eye makeup was gone, and she looked tired, and her face was puffy. "And whose fault do you think that is?"

I squinted and retreated into my chair like I was about to be ripped apart. "Um, mine?"

"No, you stupid kid! The Ionescus! Your good-for-nothing grandparents!"

We both said nothing for about a half second.

"I have done nothing but try my whole life to escape from that filthy image those two portray!" She was crying again, but louder this time, and I wondered which neighbor would be knocking on our door. What would happen if we got kicked out of here before the wedding and before the palace would be ready?

"So what do I do? What does your fool mother do?" She persisted. "Marry into a German-Jewish-God knows what else type of arrangement with your idiot father." She lit another cigarette and muttered while exhaling smoke. "Smart, Lavinia, real fucking smart. Common as dog shit."

I didn't understand my mother's reasoning. She was angry at Bunic for not coming to the wedding ceremony. He would most likely be at the reception, but I didn't think Mom wanted him there at all. I didn't understand how she could feel this way about her parents and then be angry at one of them for not wanting to be at her wedding. If she truly felt this way deep in her heart, why then did she care whether either of them showed up?

"Mom, who gave you away at your wedding to Dad?"

"Your father's father. Your grandfather Berndt. Nice, huh? Everyone used to call him Bernie. Oh, they were very sympathetic to Dad. Those people knew all about troubles and persecution, for Christ's sake." She usually accentuated her sarcasm by using her fingers for quotations. She blew out dirty smoke again and wiped snot off her face with the back of her hand. "Bernie was a nice-enough man. He died when the two of you were very young."

I remembered my grandfather. Vaguely. Apparently, he had been very sick. Something was wrong with his brain. Nobody ever told me what, and I never thought to find out. "Was Bunica there?"

"Oh, sure"—she flicked her ash—"she was there. Mother of the bride wearing her hair in the same gray bun that she wears it in now."

"How about Aunt Nancy?" I knew that all these people were there, but I still felt this need to ask.

My mother swallowed and nodded. "Loony as a bird. In hindsight, it was probably a good thing for Grandpa Buchner to walk me down the aisle in a church he didn't even belong to. He was a Jew, you know, widowed for a long time."

She looked at me and moved the flop of hair out of my eyes.

"You definitely have his blood running through your veins, that's for sure—the eyes, the hair, that nose. Good Christ."

She continued to examine me with her red puffy eyes.

"I still don't know where you got the height from."

Maybe I had a mysterious father too?

I looked at her, and by the way she was looking back at me made me think that somehow she was reading my thoughts. I stuck my finger in my ear and pretended to wipe my nose.

It had been a long time since my grandfather and my grandmother had been attacked, but it must have seemed like it may have well been yesterday to my grandfather. Bunic obviously still felt scared, and I was sorry for him. Mom didn't care about any of that. Knowing Bunic, he would probably think I was foolish and silly had I ever put my arms around him and vowed to protect him. After all this time, he was still deeply haunted by the event. Bunica may have been too, but it clearly didn't stop her from going to church, and she was good not to force Bunic.

On the exterior, however, my grandfather was built of iron. He ran a little stand on Bean Street, the bustling center of the Eastern European section of Wellton. Marisa and I loved going over there. Marisa especially, when she was younger, because she was way too cool for us as she blossomed into her teenaged years. Bunica would walk up with us because it wasn't far from their home. Bean Street was lined with the warm smell of ethnic bakeries and delicatessens, peppered with family-owned pubs and thrift stores.

My father told me once when he was a boy, he fell in love with a girl from Poland, and they had a hard time communicating because her English was so broken, so he took the bus over to Bean Street and sat on the side of the road. He held up a sign that read "If you teach me Polish, I will teach you English." After some laughs from passersby and some drunken takers, two police officers came by, slapped my father around a little bit, and broke up the party.

Bunic's stand sold everything, from fruit to cigarettes to magazines, to even the occasional television set. Bunica also told me that he could get the occasional state-run Romanian newspaper. It may have not been that day, but it was pretty current. Bunica had no idea how he was able to do that, and she said she didn't want to know. She said they had a roof over their heads, warm clothing, good food on the table, beautiful granddaughters, and freedom (until Bunic was "hauled away to the Great American Dream of a penitentiary" as Dad remarked a time or two). They paid the bills. "What more could you ask for?" Bunica would say.

That was not a fraction of what was required to satisfy my mother, and as she got up to pour herself another drink, I wondered what that was. She placed her drink down on the table in front of me as if she knew I had been eyeing it. I hoped she knew what she was doing. I knew full well that drinking that stuff wasn't exactly like ordering another root beer. The amount of things I have learned outside the classroom. Would they make a difference?

"You know, Alice." She cleared her throat. "I can tell you this because if anyone would understand, of course it would be you. Penelope said that no matter what the situation is between Sunny and Big Barton and Rod and Ana—"

I was surprised to hear her call her parents by their first names. Had I referred to her as Lavinia in conversation, she would have called me a disrespectful little brat and knocked me on the back of the head.

"That my marrying Barton is going to be the best thing I have ever done for myself. And for you and Marisa, by the way." She put her drink down again and continued in a new and refreshed voice, "I'm sure your father will continue to whine like the baby he is about paying your child support, but that will just be too damned bad because you are, after all, his flesh and blood, and he is still responsible for you no matter who I'm marrying. *But* I am getting off topic."

Suddenly, she looked over at me like I was one of her girlfriends. I wanted to back away, but I didn't dare.

"A whole new world is available to us, Alice. Shopping, travel, beautiful homes, cars, clothing, culture, you name it! And you"—she squinted at me like I was a piece of chocolate cake she was about to devour—"you are so bright, Alice, so smart and so clever. I brag about you to everyone. You know that."

Actually, I didn't know that.

She moved her drink and ashtray away and moved her chair closer to mine. "Come closer." She motioned to me, smiling brightly like a great idea just dawned on her.

I obeyed as she took both my hands in hers. I thought of Bruce.

"What do you want to be when you grow up?" she asked.

I had never seen her eyes look so twinkly and interested. I knew I needed to say something that would make an impression on her. But I shrugged instead. "I don't know. Dad said I should be a cardiac surgeon or a librarian."

She threw my hands down and swatted the air. "Oh, your goddamned father!" She pulled another cigarette out of the pack. She had to be working on pack number two now. Maybe three.

"I like math," I said, and she turned back to face me, all thoughts of my goddamned father quite likely forgotten.

"That's right, you do!" It was as if she had learned something new. "You could be an astronaut!" She pointed to me and moved the cigarettes on the table. "Do you remember when we watched the moon landing about six years ago? It was a rerun. You were only what, six then? You could be an astronaut, Alice!"

An astronaut?

"I-is there any such thing as a female astronaut?"

"Is there any such thing as a female cardiologist whatever kind of surgeon? What I am saying is this: every door on the planet is going to open for you, my dear, especially because you're so brilliant. You'll go to college anywhere you want to go, any school anywhere, my darling. *Anywhere.*"

I noticed she hadn't mentioned going to State.

"You can study math, even though that's a subject I think the boys excel in more than the girls, and *you*, my cherub, can do anything you want, and do you want to know why?"

I bit my lip.

She thrust her thumb into her chest. "Because *I* am *finally* marrying Barton Withers III, that's why."

She seemed so delighted with herself, so I nodded. "What about Marisa?"

"What about Marisa?"

"Will she be able to go anywhere and do anything she wants too?" I felt compelled to ask first out loud, then again and again, over and over, in my head.

"Not the same." My mother shook her head quickly, and it irritated me. "She'll marry a wealthy man too, and the cycle will start all over again, *and* she might have a gifted child of her own, but I very much doubt that. You, Alice. You are a special girl, and you will grow up to be one of those women who will rule the world and put men right in their places."

My head was facing my lap, but my eyes remained focused on my mother. I guess I was going to have some very big shoes to fill.

Thank you, Bruce. Thanks a whole lot for leaving me here all alone. Without you.

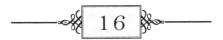

16

My mother's wedding was far more than a dream or a fairy tale. There were photographers and makeup artists and hairstylists and caterers and waitstaff and what looked like hundreds of people. I had never in my life seen anything like it, not even in the movies. It was pure fantasy.

And then there was Bunic. He had shown up at my mother's wedding after all. My mother had been so distraught over her parents causing her so much embarrassment that Barton Withers swooped in like a giant white dove and brokered a deal between his parents and my grandparents. While acting as the family diplomat, Barton Withers suggested that instead of having the ceremony at a church, why not bring the church to them and have it right there at Sun Chance, the Witherses' estate in Harbins? Weather permitting, the exchange of vows could be done among the lovely gardens right in front of the minister, and the reception would remain where it was originally planned—in the grand ballroom that no one ever used. Barton and Mom decided to forget about the Catholic Church, despite futile protests from Bunica.

Sunny and Barton II thought that was a fabulous idea, and so the dispute had been settled, and my mother's filthy immigrant parents would both be attending her wedding. Her father would even be giving her away, although I thought my father would have been the more appropriate person in that role. He was so happy to be rid of her. It was a solid win for all involved, but I wasn't surprised that it took so long and required so much turmoil. My mother ended up wasting a lot of energy and tears.

Sunny Withers hired a wedding dresser out of New York to organize matching tuxedos for all the men in the wedding party except for Bunic's. His was going to look a little different—more elegant if that was possible. His was going to be gray and the others would be black, so Bunic wouldn't be wearing his week-old pants after all.

There was also no need to be ashamed of Bunica's bun that had been spun into a perfect nest of baby robins for the last twenty years, according to my mother, since Sunny also hired a New York City hairdresser to do all our hair exactly the same. A makeup artist designed each of our faces with enough paint to choke me. He was probably from New York too, even though he spoke with a British accent. I immediately thought of Dad when I heard the makeup person speak. Dad would have loved to be there just for that.

English makeup man took a sponge of what looked like beige paint and rubbed it all over my face. Then he took two different-sized brushes and applied two different colored powders that made me sneeze. "I was thinking that you would just a-*dore* this, do you not?" he asked me as he brought out what he introduced as lash curlers. "Teenage girls just *love* makeup."

The horrible-looking torture device scared me, and I automatically went to put out my hand in protest, but I knew that if I didn't cooperate with English makeup man, I would hear about it later. "I'm actually not quite a teenager yet," I said, trying to distract myself with his relaxing instructions. "I'm still twelve."

"Really?" He looked surprised as he rubbed my forehead and chin. "You're such a big gal for your age. Very tall." He examined my face as he held my chin in his long delicate hand. "Maybe someday you'll do some modelling."

"*Modelling?*" I almost fell off my highchair. "You must be kidding me! Fashion models are pretty. Look at my older sister over there." I pointed to Marisa, who was giggling with some of the other style people. "She is so much prettier than I am. Everyone says she'll grow up to be a movie star or"—I lowered my voice—"marry a rich guy like my new stepfather who can take care of her and her looks."

He looked at Marisa and smiled at me. He seemed nonplussed. "She's a cutie. She looks like a younger version of your mom. But *you*, my kitten"—he softly tapped the end of my nose—"you are different. I've seen all of that. Don't let me ever hear you say that you're not pretty again."

I thought English makeup man was going out of his way to be especially nice. He kept using that British word *lovely*. No one had ever told me before that I was pretty or lovely. That's because I wasn't. But he kept going on, and I was interested in hearing what he had to say.

"You have what we call *raven black hair.*"

"I thought it was just black."

He shook his head quickly, "Oh, no, my dear, and it is so natural. Don't color it. *Ever.* Well, someday you will, I shouldn't say *ever*, but you are only a child, so you shouldn't be experimenting with those things anyway right now. Your mother would kill me for even talking to you about these things!"

Probably.

"And it's thick and naturally curly." He took a fistful of my hair. "Perfectly gorgeous. Your skin. Porcelain. Don't ever—and *this* is an order—lie out in the sun with those awful tinfoil boards and baby oil."

"My aunt loves to do that in the summertime."

"You'll end up looking fifty when you're really twenty-five. And I mean that, young lady."

"I promise."

"You have lovely eyes, so dark, almost black! Those must have come from your father's side of the family because I don't see that from Mother. And it took me nearly a tube of mascara to cover those mile-long lashes."

"Thank you." I smiled.

"You're the one who needs to see these things, lovie. You need to look in the mirror every morning." He looked through his lipsticks. "And do you know what I think is the best thing about your face? Mind you, I know faces."

"Hmm?"

"Your nose. Very ethnic."

"My nose? It's huge!" He had been lying to me the whole time.

"So is Catherine Merchant's, and look where she is! And her voice! Breathtaking."

"Who?" The name sounded familiar.

He waved his hand. "I keep telling you, kitten, I have seen plenty of faces. There is *nothing* wrong with yours. But it is *you* who must believe it. No one can tell you. I can't tell you. You're very young. Someday, hopefully you'll grow and have confidence in yourself. I do hope so."

That was irritating, but I didn't tell him how I felt.

He finished painting my lips a pretty pink.

"What's your name?"

"Bruce."

"I'm Alice."

"It has been a pleasure working with you, Alice."

"I had a very close friend named Bruce, but he and his family moved away."

"The good ones always get away, lovie. You'll find yours someday. It might not be the next one or the next, but he's out there, you can count on it."

I wondered if all Bruces were so wonderful and complimented so much.

·No, probably not.

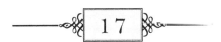

17

Getting prepared for this wedding took hours, and it was so boring. I took a look at my made-up face in one of the powder room mirrors. Bruce was full of it, but makeup was really something. I was a palette of blended purples and blues, black and ruby, pink and gray. It was like art. But I was too tall, too fat, and I still thought my nose was too big. As I examined my heavily curled and painted eyes, I thought of my mother's maid of honor, Penelope. I thought makeup was supposed to make a girl beautiful. I wanted to wash it all off, but I didn't dare. That would only hurt Bruce's feelings. He had said nice things to me in that room with all the hot lights, and I was scared to think what my mother would do to me.

As I examined my new face, I caught a glimpse of Bunic loading some bottles and cartons of cigarettes behind a wet bar. "What are you doing, Bunic?"

"This," he stated breathlessly as he bent over a shelf behind the bar, "is my contribution." He stood back up and looked down at me, but only slightly since I was becoming closer to eye level with him with each day. He lifted his craggy hands. "My contribution to all this fanciness. Enough alcohol to put the party on the head and tobacco too." He walked away.

"Dad said you were at the store last week."

He waved as he continued across the loud room, his back toward me.

* * * * *

"You know, I saw your grandfather in here the other day," my father said as Aunt Nancy and I sat at the loading dock trying to get a suntan. Dad, Frank, and Frank's son, Scotty, counted boxes. "He said something about making a contribution to your mother's wedding, you know, as father of the bride."

"Huh. I wonder what he meant by that?" I said without looking up from my tinfoiled piece of cardboard.

"At first, I didn't know what he meant. I mean, after all, who the hell can afford to throw a prince and princess of who's who kind of bash that Lavinia's going to require?"

I ignored his tone. When Dad and Frank got together and decided to cause trouble, there was no stopping them. They reminded me of the boys who sat in the back of class when a substitute teacher was in charge.

"Come on, you would have to own, let's see, a stable full of horses, an island, maybe a medium-sized mountain to put on a bash like that. Wouldn't you say that's about right, Frank?"

"That abou' right, Rudy."

"What are you guys talking about?" Scotty asked.

My father lifted his pen in the air as if he had this amazing idea. "So *then* I thought maybe ol' Roddy wanted *us* to cater the whole thing!"

"Uh-uh, Rudy!"

"But *then* I said, 'Whoa! How many people are gonna be at Big Bucks's and Lavinia's wedding? Five hundred? A thousand?"

"Dat many?"

"I would *have* to give ol' Rod a break. Don't let the old man fool you, he's a sneaky old hustler, he's doin' *just fine,* your pops, but he's no Big Bucks Withers. I would give him a break. I would have to."

"Ha' to, Rudy, ha' to."

"Now"—my dad lowered his voice—"can you imagine the look on your mother's face if Nancy and I showed up with Teddy Rickerman and 255 pounds of lox? Holy shit!"

There was the eruption of laughter and inaudible words.

"Das' a lot a lox."

I tried not to laugh, but my father knew I would as I looked over and saw Frank's bright white grin and my dad's goofy expression as they both howled like boys. It was inevitable.

Frank looked down at me and nodded. He was laughing. "You okay, girl. It all goot. Dat mama a' yours. It all goot. You know we teasin' you."

Even Scotty was cracking up with his fist up to his face. He had no idea what he was laughing about either, but once Dad and Frank got going, Scotty was just a regular sheep.

The only person who was unimpressed was Aunt Nancy. "Rudy!" she admonished. "Does everything have to be a joke to you? That's her mother. Alice and Marisa are going to be flower girls."

"It's okay, Aunt Nancy, I'm not mad." I touched her bony reddish-brown finger.

"Oh, Nance, come on." My father tried unsuccessfully to be serious for a moment. "If we don't laugh around here, what are we going to do? We're going to cry, that's what we're going to do. We're just going to double over and"—he continued to laugh—"you know how that goes. Isn't it better just to laugh? Get all that pent-up frustration with life out of your belly?"

I looked over at him. He should have known better, but he seemed unfazed. Not the best choice of words. Aunt Nancy and stomachs weren't a good mix. Years back, Aunt Nancy thought there was a demon intertwined in her intestines, squeezing the life out of her. It had entered through her bedroom window at night.

What was *he* frustrated about? *Mom* was gone; *I* was gone. He had the whole place all to himself. I opened one eye and saw Aunt Nancy looking down at her skinny stomach.

"What do you think?" my father prodded.

"You're right, Rudy. I guess. Just promise me you won't pick on Alice."

I exhaled.

"I promise. You have my word."

I wondered when that silly smile would crack wide-open.

Nancy still didn't seem convinced.

"That's my girl, Nance! Those are *my* girls. Both my girls getting a suntan over there. I'm proud of them."

18

"What do you think you're doing behind that bar, little lady?"

I looked up and saw Barton Withers, my soon-to-be stepfather, beaming down at me with his perfectly white teeth.

"I was just talking to my grandfather."

"Oh, I see. You know…" He paused and looked off. "Your grandparents are very interesting and wonderful people."

I nodded. He made me feel very uncomfortable. He was so tall and handsome, he could have been a movie star. I didn't want to stare, but it was so hard, and there wasn't a flaw to be found. I wondered if he was even a real person—nobody could be that perfect, but I quickly pushed that question out of my head. Of course he was real.

"Alice, did you hear me?"

"What?"

"Where is your sister? Where is the lovely Marisa?"

"I'm right here, Barton!" Marisa came bouncing over in a dress that was supposedly identical to mine. On her dress, however, the lilac chiffon and cream satin made her look like a princess. Her auburn hair was twisted up into a chignon, like mine (well, sort of), with little cream-colored pearls twinkling within and all around it. Her makeup made her look so beautiful; she was an angel. I looked like a potato head with too much rouge. Bruce lied. I know he did. Barton Withers was stunned into silence when he looked at my sister. He acted the same way I did when I looked at him.

"Well, aren't you a vision, enchanting, my dear," he said.

"Thank you." Marisa smiled sweetly and curtsied.

Oh, for the love of god.

"I would like for the two of you to meet my two sisters. They're going to be your new aunts, and they have children, so the two of you will finally have cousins. Won't that be great?"

Marisa and I looked at each other. "Yeah, sure," I said.

Barton Withers had one older and one younger sister. The older sister was named after their mother, Eloise, but like Mrs. Withers, she didn't use her real name; instead, everyone called her Lil. Lil and her husband, John, lived way up in a mountain town called Northrington with their two daughters, Kay and Robin. Kay, according to my mother, "was supposed to go to medical school someday and was even smarter than you, Alice."

Barton Withers's younger sister, Mary Jo, had a normal name and lived in Denver with her husband Steve. They seemed to be nice people, the kind of people who stood in line at Boochie's, not the type who attended fancy weddings at mansions in Harbins. Mary Jo and Steve had two boys, Josh, who was fifteen and seemed to hate being at this place, and little Danny. Danny was seven years old with a shock of blond hair that was so bright, it was almost white. According to my mother again, Danny had "motor problems." Marisa eventually told me that the little boy was "mildly retarded."

"Your dad owns the fish store on the south side, Alice. I remember. How's business?" Mary Jo sweetly commented.

I quickly scanned the scene. If my mother was within earshot of *anything* said about Dad on her day, I would be in the worst trouble, and Marisa would really end up paying for it. But she was safely tucked away with her ladies-in-waiting. I nodded and attempted to keep my voice as low as possible. "Everything's going well. H-have you been there before?"

"Oh, sure, lots of times." She waved her hand. "Your dad has a younger sister, Nancy."

My breath caught in my throat as I looked to the right and saw Marisa flirting with her new stepcousin. "You know my aunt Nancy?" I prayed my mother would remain exactly where she was.

Mary Jo Withers McLaughlin nodded and lifted a small crystal glass to her pretty pink lips. "Sure. We went to the old convent together. You know, the one that closed down years ago and converted into a Catholic school for girls. It's not far from where you live."

"St. Mary?"

"That's the one. Nancy was a great gal. *Is* a great gal, I'm sure she still is, of course. Smart and artistic. It's funny, one is either really adept in subjects like math and science, or the other, for example, eh, poetry and literature."

She fought to find the right words as I wished I could be anywhere else than standing in front of this very nice woman dressed in powder blue silk.

"But your aunt, God help me, she was good at everything—artistic, athletic. She was an excellent swimmer, sprinter. She could complete a fifty-yard dash in under seven seconds."

Really? I was over nine with the other fat girls.

"Civics, music."

She played the piano, but blasting classic rock while cleaning the attic of invisible cobwebs is not exactly mastering music unless we're talking about a long time ago. That's the only type of music I had ever known my aunt to enjoy.

"And that snappy little golden finger–waved pixie. She was a real beauty."

I wondered what Aunt Nancy would have thought of this old friend saying all these really nice things about her. "She's grown it out down to her shoulders now. It's still really pretty. Thick and wavy. A lot of blonde still with a tiny bit of gray on the top. I help her color it though. She's in pretty good shape. She likes to walk when she's in the mood."

"Grays," she said disparagingly. "Oh, we're all getting there eventually. Thank the good lord for the beauty parlor every six months or so." Mary Jo Withers McLaughlin stopped rambling on about gray hair. "Are you all right, Alice?"

I didn't know what gave her the impression that anything was wrong, but I was so frightened that I couldn't move. I felt paralyzed, and my chest felt so tight. It was hard for me to breathe, and when I sipped my soda at Mary Jo's suggestion, I could only take in a small amount.

I shook my head. "I'm sorry." I spoke, but my voice didn't sound the same. It was as if only air was escaping my mouth, no sound.

"Come on, sweetheart." She put her warm arm on my shoulder and led me to a window seat out of the way. It was large and comfortable and lined with bookshelves. She probably sat there a lot when she was a girl. Maybe with Aunt Nancy?

I started to feel grateful that my mother was getting married in such a huge place. Regardless of all the people, there were still plenty of places to hide.

"Mommy?" Danny trotted up behind us and tugged at his mother. "Where you going?"

"Alice and I are going to sit down over by the window. Would you like to join us?"

"Yeah!" His smile was big. "I like Alice! She's nice!"

I tried to force a smile because of the little boy, but I couldn't. It was too hard as I tried to focus on that cushion I was supposed to sit on. The more I looked at it, the farther away it got.

"Come on, sit down. Are you drinking soda? Would you like some water instead?" Mary Jo asked with a look of incredible concern as she smoothed the cushions for the three of us.

I said a thank-you and sat down.

"It's fairly comfortable, don't you think?"

I nodded, keeping my eyes down.

She collected her son in her arms. He was sprawled over her lap, and she gave him a kiss. He grinned and waved at me. He was such a cute little kid that I wanted to pinch his cheek. But I didn't—I knew what it was like to have fat cheeks that some people liked to squeeze and kiss. I felt a little more relaxed, but it was only for a short while.

"Feeling a bit better?" she implored.

I nodded. She seemed like a very nice person, but I didn't know her, and I didn't meet a whole lot of new people much, and now she had me trapped like a cat backed into a corner. But now I felt like I had no choice.

I quickly scanned the room again, looking for anyone who could hurt me. Then I thought I was fairly safe.

"What is it, Alice?" This woman was too perceptive.

"My mother doesn't like my aunt Nancy."

What are you doing?

Mary Jo shrugged and looked a little surprised. "Well, that's okay, lots of people don't get along with each other, it's nat—"

"No, you don't understand." I couldn't stop myself. "Sometimes Aunt Nancy is a little less, well, sometimes she's not well. She's not well always. I know that doesn't make any sense."

She blinked twice. "Yes, I'm aware of that. She's had mental illness for many years. That isn't her fault, and…" As she searched for words, Danny suddenly bolted from her lap and ran for his brother, who was still sitting with Marisa.

"He won't say anything?"

"Who? Danny? No, honey! He's not even paying attention to our conversation. He's a little boy with Down syndrome. What on this earth has you so frightened, Alice?"

I was deflated. I wanted to cry. Thank God I didn't with all that color around my eyes. "My mother doesn't like it when we…" I shifted on the window seat cushion. "Talk about things."

Now you're crazy. Are you crazy?

"What things?"

"Any things. Any stuff. Anything at all, really. Anything that has to do with her, our family, you know, anything at all. And…Aunt Nancy…is, well…" I didn't know what else to say.

"I don't understand why she would care," she said. "We're going to be family soon." She looked at her watch. "In just a couple of hours, as a matter of fact. We're having a normal conversation. I can't see why your mom would be bothered by that."

This lady was in for a big surprise. I didn't want to be rude and laugh. "She would be bothered. *Believe me*, she would care."

"But *why?*" She leaned forward and frowned. She didn't believe me. "What would happen? Would you get a spanking?"

I laughed, and it was loud, but none of the headhunters were around to notice. "I would get it. Marisa would get it more."

You better shut up.

"Marisa? Your sister?"

Now you've done it.

"Sometimes when my mother gets angry with me, she'll hit me or say something mean, but that only makes her get madder, and then she starts to hit Marissa. Only a lot harder."

That's it. You said it. You told her, and she's one of them. It's over now, and you can't take it back. The only thing your stupid squishy little brain would like to know is why? Why did you think you could trust this woman? You don't even know her, and you don't trust anyone. And so? Now what?

I felt as if I hadn't eaten in days, and my head pounded.

As if reading my thoughts, Mary Jo reached out and touched my arm with her soft and light warm hand. "Alice, I want you to do everything you possibly can to relax and enjoy this beautiful day. I am honored that you would feel so comfortable talking to me, and I don't want you to worry about a thing. I'll keep our conversation in confidence. Your secrets are always safe with me."

Mary Jo Withers McLaughlin seemed concerned when I got up and left her at our little meeting place. I couldn't be worried about one more thing, or I would implode. The damage was done. I had just negotiated with the enemy, and I was going to pay for it. I wasn't thinking. I had not used my head. I was listening to my heart, and for some reason, I had tampered with a floodgate that was supposed to be secure, sealed shut, and suddenly everything—gallons of murky poisonous water, dying sea life, and garbage—came gushing forth like death. There was nothing I could do to stop it because it had been me who had caused it, and I couldn't have it both ways.

My heart tickled with fear. I knew that I wouldn't be able to sleep again. I wouldn't be able to eat. I couldn't even breathe, and I couldn't get close or reach for anything as people and objects continued to keep getting farther away as I shook my way through the giant room.

God, if you're real and you're out there somewhere, can you help me? Can you forgive me? Can you protect me and my sister?

What gave me the impression that she was safe? I didn't care that she was nice, or that she had kind eyes, or she was sweet. She was Barton Withers's sister, and Barton Withers was about to marry my mother. And my mother, with her tiny, little hands, could grab me and crush me in her palms like a common housefly. It would happen because I brought it on myself. My sister wasn't safe. She had enough problems keeping her own floodgates closed.

I thought of how I harmed my best friend, my beautiful sister, as I made my way through mazes of people whom I didn't know or hadn't met. They were mostly friends of the Withers family. There were men and women in cream-colored satin vests weaving throughout the masses with silver trays filled with libations. I was told they were supposed to wear the cream color *before* the ceremony. There were bottles and half-full glasses of scotch. I eyed them and thought of the comforting warmth when I stole a mouthful—but that would have to wait.

"Alice? You look lost." It was my grandmother sitting next to a piano. She had a clear-colored drink in her hand with a cocktail napkin underneath. "Come. You're walking around. What is it?"

I wasn't in the mood for more discussion. "Nothing, I was just going to look for Mom."

She waved her hand in disgust. "Here I am the mother of the bride, and I couldn't even get close to her, not that she wanted me to. She is having her hair done, her makeup done, they help her into her dress. My god, it's white, and the train must be nearly fifteen feet long." She shook her head and mumbled something in Romanian.

It was then that I knew I wanted to leave her alone with whatever she had in that glass. Her mumbling was annoying.

"Where's Bunic? I asked blindly.

"Outside smoking," she snarled.

I walked away. I wasn't really looking for my grandfather. I wasn't looking for anyone. I just needed to plan, and I didn't want to be distracted by idle people.

A woman in a lime green sparkly gown began to usher out nameless faces onto the sprawling gardens of the glorious Withers estate. There wasn't a cloud in the sky. We took our places. Marisa and I wouldn't be walking behind my mother throwing petals at her. Instead, we would stand silently together with our huge wicker baskets filled with white roses. My mother burst onto her white satin walkway with her gigantic white dress, cascades of endless white flowers, and a train so long I thought for sure it would get caught on something.

I licked my dry lips and realized I still had on my war paint.

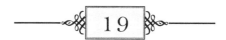

19

"We're rich!" Marisa said, and we both gasped when we walked into the new house in Crescent Hills. My mother and Barton Withers had just returned from their honeymoon in Barcelona and the Greek Isles.

"That's not exactly true, Marisa. *We* aren't rich. We don't have any money. We don't have any jobs—" I said before she cut me off.

"It looks like we don't need jobs, does it?"

The two of us surveyed the huge family room with the stone fireplace that was almost large enough for Barton Withers himself to stand in.

"Do we get to pick out our rooms?"

"I think Mom has already done that for us."

She rolled her eyes. "That figures. Hey, what's in here?"

We walked through two heavy wooden doors to an open entrance foyer.

"Wow, Alice, would you look at this?"

"I know, it's just… Wow. It's huge. That's the slate tile on the floor Mom was talking about."

"And look at all this wood stuff around the doors and the ceilings and these handles. I think they're like…*glass.*"

I stood in the middle of the enormous entrance looking up at the pristine crystal chandelier. *What a mess that would make if it happened to fall.* The front staircase with its thick highly polished reddish-colored wooden bannister and plush blue carpet, swept and twisted upward and away, like a snake.

"It's not quite Sun Chance, but it's really pretty." I tried to show Marisa how positive I was about our most recent move, but really, I was growing tired of the whole thing. Hopefully this would be the last stop for a while. Thank God we didn't have to change schools again. I just wished I could go back and live with Dad in my old room, even though I still couldn't convince him to take me back.

Hurry up, eighteenth birthday.

"It's like Sun Chance is the mommy, and this place is the baby," she said.

"What?"

"The house, idiot. God, you're off staring into space again. You're the one who brought it up. I mean, of course the palace where the king and queen live is going to be *way* bigger and *much* fancier than the palace, or is it the castle where the prince and his princess live?"

I crossed my arms. "A palace or a castle."

She looked up the stairway. "What's the difference again?" She slowly began to climb. "I would say this is pretty much a palace, Alice. Hey, that rhymes! Alice lives in a palace! Do you want to take a look at our new rooms?"

"Mom said we have to stay downstairs." It sounded as stupid as it felt when I said it. But I didn't want to face my mother's wrath. I looked at her cautiously.

She let out a snort. "Oh Jesus, Alice, you have to follow every single rule all the time, don't you?"

"Oh god," I said.

"What?"

"You can't just say that."

"Say what?"

"Jesus."

"You just said god."

"That's different."

"How?"

"Mom says *Jesus* and *Christ* all the time. That's really bad."

"That's different too."

"How is any of it different?" I said. I was sick of this conversation. It was going nowhere.

"Who cares?" she said. "Do we go to church every Sunday?"

"You know we don't," I said.

113

"Do we even *have* a religion?" she said.

"Not really, I guess," I said.

"All right, Alice, so who cares? Jesus, Jesus, Jesus, Jesus."

I shook my head as I casually peered around the doorway to see if my mother was anywhere within earshot. I decided it best to change the subject.

"Are you scared?" she asked.

I jumped. "Of *what?*"

She sat down on a step and tried to look at me through the chunky banister.

"Don't get your head caught in between those rungs! I'll have to call the fire department if you don't strangle yourself first. Don't think I'll break them just to get YOU out!" I remember Mom telling me that once. I was about five years old.

"Mom hearing me say *Jesus?*"

"No." I shook my head quickly, trying to rid the room of that last conversation. "How about you? Are you worried about school? About starting your sophomore year?"

"Ah, no. What's there to be afraid of? It's not like I'm losing any of my friends. We're all going to the same school. It was worse when we moved from Rudy's."

She made a place for me to sit next to her on the step.

I plopped myself down, remembering how she had cried, and I tried to comfort her before she had been beaten with an umbrella. "I would be scared. I'll probably be really scared when I get to the tenth grade. You know, high school and everything."

She tugged on my ponytail. "Alice, that's your problem. You're scared of *everything.*"

"I am?" I knew she was right. We've had conversations similar to this one.

"Yes! You know you are. How long has it been since you've been able to just lie down at night and go to sleep?"

It had been a long time. "I can't remember. It's the dark though, I don't like it. And the sounds. There are always creaking and foot-steps and strange noises. It's worse at night, I don't know why."

"But it's not always at night. You are afraid all the time. Even when you don't say anything. I know."

That wasn't a good sign. "Do you think Mom knows?"

"I don't know. But I'll tell you this—you are scared of your own shadow, and if you don't stop being so jumpy, you're going to end up all kooky like Aunt Nancy."

"No, no, I won't," I protested, and then I thought of my aunt Nancy, who had been nothing but kind to me and Marisa when we were living at my father's. "And besides, you shouldn't be talking about her. She loves you, Marisa."

She gave me one of those looks that told me I was being ridiculous. "I know she loves me. But she's nuts. Remember when we saw her putting all that lipstick on at the kitchen sink, and she was swearing at the window? It might run in the family."

I was annoyed. I wanted to slap her perfectly chiseled face so hard. It was amazing how much she sounded like our mother. I stood up and looked at her. "What?"

She was smiling. She was being cruel.

"Don't talk about her like that. She's a good person, and she's our aunt. She's dad's sister just like you're my sister, and I would never let anyone talk bad about you either."

She looked down at the space between her feet. Her voice sounded like she was still smiling as she stated quietly, "It's not like he's *my* dad."

"Oh yeah, I forgot," I snapped. "He's no Indian prince, is he?"

The room suddenly became quiet, as if all the air had been sucked out.

Marisa's green eyes went dark, and there was a look of fear on her face that I never recognized before. "You said you would never say anything about that." Her voice was just above a whisper.

I realized why I was scared all the time. This was the reason. This was why—I couldn't say anything. I couldn't speak. I cupped my mouth with both hands. I wouldn't look at her.

She sprung up quickly and glared around the corner. Still no sign of our mother. The last time either of us saw her, she had been out in the garage. Marisa walked over to where I stood and looked at me. Her eyes had partly turned to their normal color.

"Do you want me to go?"

I removed my hands from my mouth. "Go where?"

"I don't know. Away. Far away, forever."

"Of course not." I looked down at the slate floor.

She knocked me hard against the wall. Her rage gave her incredible strength. "Then keep your fucking mouth shut." She stood very close to me.

"I'm so sorry, Marisa. It will never happen again. You're swearing a lot lately."

"I don't care."

We looked at each other carefully for a minute, and then I stepped beyond her and peeked around the corner to look for our mother. I turned back to my sister, who was at the bottom of the staircase with her back to me. She was still angry. I continued to stand at the double doorway, keeping one eye on the lookout. Because both of us were frustrated, it was tempting to yell.

"Your mouth is just as big as mine," I said first. "How many times have you done or said something stupid that got us into trouble? You say I'm frightened of my own shadow? Well, maybe some days I am, but I know one thing—it's hard living around here."

She looked up at the crystal chandelier. "Around here?"

"Yeah. Around here. Around everywhere. I'm always wondering if I'm going to say the wrong thing or, I don't know, maybe act badly or something, or…or do something and get caught. Maybe piss off Mom."

She turned to me. "Well, listen to you! Why don't you just be yourself? I remember Rudy telling us how important that was a long time ago."

I remembered that discussion. It was one of Dad's pep talks. I scratched my scalp. "What if you don't like yourself?"

She shrugged her shoulders and went to look out the window next to the huge front door. "I don't know. It doesn't matter. You still have to do it. And you have to stop worrying about Mom. There's nothing you can do about Mom."

"But you worry about her too, Marisa. You worry about the other thing too. Like who your father is."

"I do not. Will you just keep your voice down, please?"

"You see?"

"That is different, Alice," she hissed.

"Different."

We both froze at the sound of our mother's voice.

"The two of you!"

We heard the warning from afar.

"You had better not be going up those goddamned stairs!"

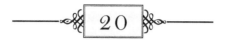

20

Just like my former math teacher, Mrs. Cranston, and the incident involving my sister's "stabbing," Mary Jo Withers McLaughlin never got around to reporting my gossip or whatever it was to my mother. I still wasn't free though, and I wondered if I ever would be.

When our mother wasn't home in the afternoons, she made each of us take a school bus to Karen DeSantis's house because no one was allowed in the new house in Crescent Hills unless either she or Barton Withers was present. I don't think Barton Withers really cared, but my mother was really particular about these things, and her new husband went along with it.

Karen was a divorced mother of three and an old high school friend of my mother's. She ran a babysitting service in her home. Marisa was content because Karen had two big dogs and a little black cat named Whitey. She also loved to play with and entertain the children in Karen's charge. I would have liked the little kids a lot better if they didn't stick to everything, and so I usually just hung around in Karen's daughter Maggie's room, playing cards or doing my homework.

When I asked my mother why we couldn't go to Dad's or even Bunica's where the snacks were much better than at Karen's, she told me that I was an idiot for even thinking up a question like that. None of the school busses travelled out of their district. She never called me an idiot before. Normally, she reserved *idiot* for Marisa. My mother's moods were becoming worse all the time.

Sometimes she would be really, *really* angry at what appeared to be nothing at all. She would scream and yell at the three of us— Barton Withers included, Marisa especially—and then other times she would be so sad she would cry. She would sob so hard that I felt sorry for her, often forgetting how badly she behaved that day, sometimes just minutes before.

Then everything began to make sense, at least to Karen DeSantis and a few of the other moms who ditched their kids at her house.

My mother exploded through Karen's front door one afternoon, leaving behind a trail of jubilation I didn't think existed in her world. She announced to all of us that she was pregnant. I was shocked and also a little baffled. I didn't understand why my mother was so happy to be expecting another baby. She had a hard-enough time dealing with Marisa and me, and we didn't cry all the time for our diapers to be changed and a bottle to be shoved in our mouths. And some of these babies at Karen's just cried for no reason at all, or at least they seemed to. But seeing my mother so happy meant a lot to me. I wanted more than anything else for her to be happy.

Marisa was thrilled. And when that fat little redhead they named Helena Eloise Withers was born, she told me that she had a new favorite sister. I was shocked and saddened by her remarks, but I wasn't totally surprised. Marisa liked all things cute: babies, puppies, cats with the smooshed-in faces. And I knew that when Helena grew up, she wouldn't be quite as cute anymore, and then Marisa and I could go back to being best friends again.

But day after day, I was lonelier without her. Marisa moved on and forgot about people in her past. This included old friends, my father, Aunt Nancy, Frank, and now with our new baby sister in the picture, she did the same thing to me. Dumped me like a smelly bag of trash. My father just laughed at me and called her fickle. But I was angry. And I was sad. And I was tired of feeling so left out of my sister's and Barton Withers's little relationship and my sister's overvalued love for some dumb little baby. I was tired of her fun adventures and outings and trips to the movies and roller skating parties with her new high school friends.

Everyone seemed to love Marisa. Everyone thought she was petite and beautiful and creative and artistic. She was everything I wasn't. While she would have a different friend over just about every day in the summer to visit Helena, then go to the mall, I would go through my reading list and teach myself how to freestyle swim in the backyard pool. I missed living with my father, and I was sick of Marisa's attitude.

By the following winter, something was different. Marisa and my mother continued to fight constantly, but Marisa didn't plead anymore. Marisa had a mouth on her now, and it was big and crude and nasty. She always had a big mouth, but she was less and less afraid to use it. My mother was constantly comparing Marisa with her friends and the children of the people whom she and Barton Withers socialized with. She would build Marisa up just so she could tear her down. Once she had one of her friend's sons come over to the house to take snapshots of Marisa in various modeling poses so that she could supposedly send them off to a modeling agency in New York City. A week later when the pictures came back, my mother looked down at them and frowned.

"You're a beautiful girl, Marisa Ionescu. That hair, those eyes, that face. You have the most beautiful skin. Just like me, by the way." Then she would shake her head slowly. "It's the height. You don't have the height to be a model. You're too short. If you and Alice could just change your heights, god! This is typical, isn't it?"

Marisa never measured up to my mother's expectations no matter how hard she tried or how much my mother fluctuated them. She was constantly dangling a poor wiggling mouse by the tail in front of the cat's mouth. Then she would rip the mouse away at the very last minute while always blaming the cat. My mother threatened to cut off all of Marisa's hair, but in the end, she didn't because she found her hair to be her accomplishment. She also warned Marisa lots of times that if she didn't shut her trap, she would put her fist right through her perfect mouth. But Marisa's beautiful teeth that never needed a jacket of metal like mine were what my mother considered her creation. Lavinia Ionescu suddenly never wanted to cause any damage to anything she felt was hers or about her. The thing was, though, my mother killed a part of everyone she should have loved and cared for. Nobody would ever believe me or understand, so I just continued to tuck myself away and nestle in the confines of my mind.

My sister liked to paint, she could draw, she wrote poetry—the real interesting artistic kind that didn't rhyme—she could sing pretty well, she played the piano by ear when we went to visit Sun Chance, but these were things that my mother hated about Marisa. Marisa was an individual who was liked by many, and that wasn't my mother's plan for her. I often wondered what that plan really was, but I was never able to figure it out, no matter how hard I pondered. I approached it with the same vigor that I would any advanced algebra problem, but I soon found out that advanced algebra was a sunny stroll compared to my mother's and sister's relationship.

My mother was always comparing Marisa. Marisa was beautiful. Just not as beautiful as friend number 1. Her style was not as classy or as unique as friend number 3. Friend number 2's figure was better, and of course, friend number 10 was much smarter. At times, I was thrilled to be a fat shadow on the wall. My mother could have cared less about the fact that I was two math, science, and history classes ahead of my schoolmates, and that was perfectly fine with me. Her attention was rarely good attention, and when the five of us went to visit Barton Withers's older sister Lil Schuester at the chalet in Northrington, it would have looked like a horror story had it not been 100 percent real.

On the morning we left, Marisa came into my room. The room was twice the size of the room at my father's house. We could have shared the space, and I wish that we had.

"The mountains are a six-hour drive from here, Alice, did you know that? I'm scared."

"It's not that far. I would say closer to about four or five. What are you scared of? Hey, did I tell you Dad's got a new girlfriend? Her name is Jennifer—"

"Did you not hear me? I said I'm scared. I'm really frightened."

I looked at my sister carefully. She was pale, and there was worry in her eyes. "Why? What are you scared of?"

"It's a six-hour drive to the mountains from here, Alice, did you know that? I'm scared," she said again.

"It's not that far. Why are you repeating yourself? Who cares how far the drive is?"

"Remember a long time ago when you, me, and Rudy went to New York City, and we had to pull over a whole bunch of times because I was so carsick? I was throwing up, do you remember?"

"We were in a seafood van."

"I don't want to go on this trip."

"Don't they have those little pills you can take for motion sickness now?" I asked.

"Yes! They do!" She was almost frantic. Her voice was full of desperation. "But we don't have any, and when I asked Mom if we could pick some up, she said they were a waste of money."

That sounded like something my mother would say. *But that closet full of clothes wasn't, was it? A couple of bucks so your kid doesn't puke all over Barton Withers's leather interior Lincoln Continental.*

"Marisa, wait!"

Her eyes got big with what looked like the fascination that I had a bombshell of an idea. "You can get some pills?" she asked.

"No," I said as I watched her soft pale face deflate. "But when we drove to New York City, we were in Dad's old straight refrigeration truck. You remember what that was like. It was like driving on the moon!"

Her shoulders sunk in defeat as she walked over and sat next to me at the end of the bed. She put a tiny hand on my knee and patted lightly. "You're probably right. I hope you're right."

But I was anything but right. Barton Withers's sleek black sedan was worse than Dad's little reefer because it drove so smoothly, it almost felt as though we were gliding above the road. We were barely out of the county when Marisa, who was sitting behind Barton Withers, began to cry. My chin sank to my chest. I was so worried because she was so sick and worried that she would get in trouble by stirring things up.

"Here, eat a pretzel," my mother commanded, shoving the can in front of my sister's nose.

She gagged. "Can't we just pull over for a minute?" she pleaded.

"No, we cannot just pull over for a minute!" My mother was becoming more exasperated with each mile marker, and she wasn't hiding it from Barton Withers, whose strong tanned hands gripped the steering wheel and his regular painted-on smile disappeared.

Marisa continued to cry. It wasn't loud, but she groaned and rocked and wrapped her arms around her stomach as if she were dying. Barton Withers's snotty niece Kay sat in the front passenger seat. She had no trouble chatting with her uncle, but she was quieter around my mother, and I don't think she completed one sentence when it came to my sister or me. She didn't even say hello to either of us when we picked her up at Sun Chance that morning. She barely moved her shoulders when she shot a look of disapproval out of one bluish-green eye at Marisa as she was close to death from car sickness. I wanted to scratch that big eye right out of her stuck-up little head.

"Do you want me to open a window for you?" I asked her quietly.

"It's the middle of February, Alice, you jerk!" she shouted, tears and snot marring her red angry face.

I didn't have time to feel the horror that was brewing in my chest as my mother shot an arm across the back seat and, with a closed fist, back-handed her jeweled fingers directly into my sister's face. "Shut up!"

Barton Withers swerved and pulled over to the side of the road and stopped. There were no other cars around, and thick unrelenting snow fell onto the brown slushy road. The sky was an evil gray. I stuck my fingers in my ears and held my breath, but when I saw Barton Withers turn around and look at my sister, I pulled them out and listened. His voice had a tone that I never heard before.

"We have another several hours in this car, so you had better get used to that. I don't want to hear one more word out of your mouth, you got that? If I hear another one of your tirades, I will pull this car over and let you out."

My mother nodded.

He couldn't do that, could he?

"Then the police will pick you up, and you'll be on your own. Do you understand me?"

Marisa sniffed, wiped her nose with the back of her hand, and nodded.

Suddenly, he thrust a long finger directly into her face. *"Do you understand me?"* He shouted so loud that we all jumped, even Big-Eye Kay. Even my mother.

Marisa nodded fast. "Yes, I understand you," she half whispered, half crackled, and put her head down.

"Now, you apologize to everyone in this car," he demanded, pointing to each one of us, beginning with himself. I don't think there had ever been a father figure male type who had ever spoken to her like that before. Certainly not my father. Usually free-spirited and independent, my sister looked more terrified than ever, and I could see she was stunned. She and Barton Withers enjoyed a relationship that was beyond stepfather-daughter. They were buddies, friends. It annoyed me a lot. It could be sickening. I was jealous. But I saw something in my sister now that said "There is no turning back. This is over."

Barton Withers then took it upon himself to rap the side of my sister's head with his fingers. My mother raised an eyebrow, but not at him—at Marisa. "Go on, apologize."

It didn't appear as if he wanted to repeat himself.

"I'm sorry, B-Barton." She was so quiet. "I'm sorry, Kay and Mom and Alice."

"It's okay," I spurted out abruptly and without thinking. "You don't have to apologize, Marisa. I know you don't like long drives."

"Oh yes. Oh yes, she does have to apologize, Alice. She's rude and childish, and she's not going to yell in my car." Barton Withers looked at me pointedly. I guess the only person who was allowed to be rude, raise her voice, and lose her temper was our mother.

"All right. I forgive her." I smiled and looked him right in the eye. It was the least I could do. I didn't care. Throw *me* out of the car. I didn't care very much about being there anyway. So what if I'm picked up by the police? They'll just drive me to my dad's. That's where I wanted to be anyway. They can't throw me in jail if I haven't committed a crime. Barton Withers was what Bruce would say "full of a four-letter word."

"It's a damned good thing Helena isn't in this car," my mother said as Barton Withers started the car and eased back onto the road. "If you had caused my baby to cry because of your bitchy behavior, you would have *really* been in trouble, girl."

Marisa didn't respond. She was hurting. She was tormented both physically and emotionally, and it exhausted her. I put my head on her small shoulder. She seemed to like that, and we fell asleep for what felt like several hours.

When I awoke, we were passing through the bleakness of the upstate. Barton Withers pulled over so we could eat and go to the bathroom. We staggered into this smoky, dark, saloon-like place that reminded me of those cowboy movies on TV during Sunday afternoons. The place was called the Alpine Grille with the *e* on the end. It felt good to be inside, and the warmth, smell of beer, and background music was comforting after sitting in a car all morning.

The bartender had a long gray beard and a red T-shirt with tattoos covering his massive arms. He immediately recognized Barton Withers, who left the four of us standing in the middle of the room. He went to pump the man's hand and talked to him as if they hadn't seen each other in years.

"That's Dean," Kay quipped as she examined her perfect long red nails. "He owns the place. My family has known him for years."

Your family? Really? You mean your family actually associates with fat guys with tattoos who look like they slept in the same clothing for a week? Does the local society page know about that? What would the Harbins Country Club people say? Is there a society page in this neck of the woods, no pun intended?

"Are you ladies waitin' for a table?" A very tanned cheerful blonde with a very tight T-shirt and enormous boobs skirted past us holding a tray loaded with food.

My mother nodded sweetly. "Yes, miss, five please. Preferably a large booth if you have one."

Big Boobs nodded. "You got it, sister. Follow me."

"Isn't this wonderful, girls?" My mother was elated as she passed around menus.

"Are we allowed in here, Mom?"

"Of course you're allowed in here, Alice. Why wouldn't you be?"

"I don't know." I looked around. I could hear people playing pool beyond a wooden door propped open with a barstool and the jukebox blasting classic rock. Another recognition from Dad's elaborate album collection. "Because there's a bar. I've never been in a real bar before."

"You are perfectly fine here," she lectured, putting her palm up, "as long as we're eating our lunch and you're here with an adult, there isn't a problem."

"Just as long as *you*, a *minor*, aren't drinking the alcohol," Kay snothead opined as my mother looked around for Barton Withers.

"That was Alice's entire point, *Kay*," Marisa sneered.

I stifled a laugh, and thankfully, my mother was concentrating on Barton Withers's push to make the earth move a little faster as he strode from the bar to our table. "He's a great guy, Lavinia, that Dean Anderson—been sole proprietor of this place for the past twenty-six years."

"Oh, how nice, honey. How do you know him? Just by the drive up?"

He took a sip of his giant mug of beer while no one else had a drink yet. "Yep. Had a problem this past fall with a bear completely cleaning off his apple tree. Apple tree or pear tree. Plum tree. I don' know."

"A bear?" Marisa looked up, startled.

Barton Withers nodded. "Black bear. Ate all the fruit off one of his trees, so what does he do? Goes to the store, buys a full bag of fruit, and puts it down on the ground near the tree. His wife Cheryl was less than pleased!" He smiled and nodded toward our waitress.

I guessed that Big Boobs was Dean's wife Cheryl. I turned to look at Stuck-Up-Face Kay, who was looking down at her fingernails again. "Why was she unhappy?"

"Well…" Barton Withers opened his menu, looked at it for about half a second, and closed it again. "Know what you want? Ah, Alice, well, because you don't ever want to feed a bear—or any wild animal for that matter."

Marisa caught her breath. I could feel her body suddenly tense up as she sat beside me. I looked at her. The color had washed out of her skin. "What's the matter?" I whispered. She didn't respond. Instead, she looked straight ahead at Barton Withers, a stony glare.

"Why don't you want to feed a bear?" I asked, still watching my sister. "I would think that would make them happy, make them friendlier."

"Are you guys ready to order?" Big Boobs interrupted. She took everyone's order and then bounced off to someone else's table.

"Are you going to eat all that, Marisa?" My mother immediately honed in on my sister's menu selection.

"So why not, Barton?"

"Why not what?" Another sip of beer.

"Why don't you want to feed a bear?" I knew my father would be able to answer that question just as easily as Barton Withers could. *I* should have known the answer to that question.

"The reason you don't want to feed a bear is because he becomes dependent on you, and the next thing you know, he's around your property all the time. Then when you don't feed him, he expects it. He starts going through your trash, and if you happen to corner him in your garage, well, he could attack you. Just like your little cat your father shouldn't be feeding. Shelby."

Shelly. Shithead.

"Just bigger and deadlier. If you leave a wild animal to his own devices and let him do his own hunting, chances are he'll remain more frightened of you than you are of him."

"And feeding him means that you are trying to domesticate a wild animal," I said.

"That's exactly right, young lady." He bowed his head. "The bear and his bear friends lose respect for your human superiority, and the outcome could be dangerous."

When our food came to the table, Marisa, still silent, just stared at her cheeseburger with all the trimmings. "I didn't know there were bears up here," she said finally.

"Of course there are bears up here," my mother said, eyes fixed on my sister's plate. "We're in the mountains, for Christ's sake. Don't you pay attention in that school? You had better eat all that. It cost money."

Snooty Kay darted a look at my mother, who was trying to pick up a large sandwich from her plate. "Well, not *now*. It's snowing. Bears hibernate in the winter."

"They hibernate," my sister repeated quietly.

"That's right, they hibernate."

"Alice, don't talk with your mouth full."

"Sorry, Mom, I'll swallow it."

"Jesus Christ."

"Bears hibernate in the wintertime. They go into their dens and go into a deep sleep until spring. I think it's back to the den or maybe they build a snow cave, something like that."

Marisa left her lunch untouched.

"There are still hundreds of bears around here," Barton Withers said gleefully, "*and* you never know which one of them is going to come out of hibernation first."

My mother pointed an open hand at him and spoke slowly and loudly. Other people at nearby tables could hear her embarrassing voice. "Barton, that is enough. I do not want to have to listen to that little bitch anymore today. Please." Then she pointed a mayonnaise-smeared finger at Marisa. She was even louder because more people in the restaurant turned around to look. "I am tired of hearing about bears. Now eat that goddamned hamburger, or we will be taking it with us for you to eat for your dinner."

My sister started to nibble at some food.

"Don't worry about it, Lavinia. It's a four-dollar hamburger. I don't want to think about any of that later."

"No, Barton!" my mother snapped, and the same people looked over.

Kay looked over at my mother like she was a piece of old chewing gum stuck to the bottom of her snazzy leather boot.

"She's going to eat whether she likes it or not!"

"I'll help her out, Mom."

"Don't help her out too much. You don't exactly need to be eating any more than you actually are."

Kay winced, and I was so embarrassed. I knew I was fat, but what was I supposed to do, throw away a perfectly good cheeseburger? Suddenly, I was wishing we could just get back into the car and drive. It was so much better when we were all asleep.

I could tell that Kay Schuester had no use for my mother. She sat there with her expensive ski jacket placed perfectly on the back of her chair, trying to move her way closer to her uncle as if he would somehow protect her from the crude bog scum that clearly infiltrated her classy quiet family. There was a tiny flash of dismay that shot from her big bluish-green eyes when she heard our mother insult us. I wondered what she thought when Barton Withers threatened to throw Marisa out of the car. She had her back toward us, and she remained silent like a mannequin in a department store window. I wasn't going to ask her about her thoughts.

Marisa took a couple of bites here and there of her food and gave some to me as if I was a stray dog scrounging at her feet. I got tired of the cold fries, and no amount of salt and ketchup made them taste any better.

Finally we were back on the road. I quietly thanked God that Marisa was no longer carsick. The snow fell like fresh white puffs from the low gray sky. The maple trees were bare and solemn against the scant pine that loomed over the road on each side, like the high cliffs of old filed down mountains. Occasionally, we would pass another car or two. The roads could become treacherous in the wintertime, and most people didn't want to brave the winding drive. I wondered why we were. From the start, it just seemed like an awful idea.

As we continued on our journey, I noticed a cluster of cabins down a slope that reached out to a frozen lake. There was smoke escaping from a gray stone chimney. At one small cedarwood-and-stone house was an older man with what looked like his son. They were carrying blankets to a station wagon, and both were smiling. They looked like they liked life and liked each other. I wondered how often they became afraid of things, if they spoke quietly when they talked to each other. Did they get embarrassed? Did the air clench at their chests like sparks that made them want to hit each other? Hurt the people they supposedly loved and those who were there to take care of them? I doubted all of that. It didn't happen that way with other people. I couldn't bear other people. They were just too happy.

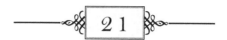

21

I wanted to cry when we got to the bridge that elegantly cascaded over this big lake. I wanted to beat my fists on the inside
windows of Barton Withers's fancy car until they bled. Marisa, who
was the one who was always so adventurous, so outspoken and full
of charm and energy, was nearly lying on my lap, weak and pale.
She was once again suffering from motion sickness, even though I
thought that had subsided a little before our lunch stop.

I was told it was normally me who was obsessed with the "unim-
portant." I was the one who was frightened of what might happen
and the one who couldn't get to sleep most nights because I was
afraid of something, and I didn't ever really know what that something might be. Marisa was the one who would giggle herself into a
frenzy, teasing me over anything she knew would disturb me, and I
hated her for it.

But it wasn't that way this time. With my mother sitting up front
engaged in a loud and strenuous conversation with Barton Withers
and Kay shoved up against her side of the car like the ill-mannered
unsociable twit that she was, it was up to me to take care of Marisa
and make sure she would live the next hour before we got to Chalet
Schuester.

"We're getting close to Northrington!" My mother turned
around and smiled at us. "And am I glad we made that bridge! *Whew!*"

"What do you mean?" I asked and then regretted it.

"That bridge closes at a certain time of day," Barton Withers
answered matter-of-factly.

"What happens if you need to get over it though?" I asked.

"I guess you would be out of luck," he answered.

"I would just beg the man in that little house back there to let me over. I would tell him that I would pay him double," I said.

"You wouldn't be able to bribe the attendant, Alice." My mother looked at me like I was foolish.

"Why not?"

"Well, for one thing, it's not up to him. The bridge automatically closes, isn't that right?" She looked over at Barton Withers, who nodded deeply. "It's like a drawbridge, only it closes up into a little package about the size of a suitcase."

I looked over at Kay Schuester, who looked like her bunny fur forehead was glued to the car window. She exhaled, shook her head, and looked out at the cluster of pine.

"I know you're joking, Mom." I tried to sound innocent and agreeable.

"Nope."

Barton Withers, Kay, and Marisa continued in silence, and I wondered if she was trying to be funny with me or trying to frighten Marisa, just like Barton Withers had done with the bears. I couldn't help but pursue.

"Wait, you mean to tell me that if you're on that bridge back there when it's time to close, you and your car are going to get closed up into a little suitcase?"

Barton Withers and Kay said nothing.

"Yes, Alice, I would say so." My mother smiled, had Kay crack her window, and lit a cigarette.

This is ridiculous. Come on.

"That would kill a person. Sounds like murder to me," I said.

Marisa looked up at me.

Barton Withers and his niece began talking about colleges as my mother tried to interject her opinion.

I looked down at my sister, made a face, and shook my head. "She's just kidding. None of that would ever happen. You know that. You're just not feeling well."

She sat up, her red hair slightly matted against the deep sleep lines on her face. She wiped the small amount of drool from the side of her mouth. "I saw it in a movie once. It could happen. It was like

131

a drawbridge or something, and this alarm went off, and the road or bridge or whatever split, and her car went straight down into the black water. It was freezing cold. She tried to get out of the car, but she couldn't, and she drowned."

"Was that a movie where there was one of those police chases?" I asked. "Where one guy jumps the bridge with his car and the other one doesn't make it?"

She nodded. "It was really scary. The lady died."

"It's only a movie. She didn't die in real life."

"But it could happen."

"I doubt it. Think how many people would get smooshed up into a suitcase!" I joked.

"This is going to be an awful vacation," she said quietly, her voice trailing off between black bears and collapsed bridges.

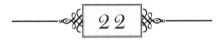

2 2

Kay Schuester's parents' "chalet" was just one more unbelievable property owned by someone in the Withers family. I was thinking we would stay in a ski lodge with a pointed roof, but this was a huge, immense home that was on huge stilts that were made of metal or concrete.

Marisa made a beeline to the door at the garage area without taking any of her stuff out of the car, which immediately infuriated my mother.

"Hey, Marisa, where do you think you're going?" Barton Withers called out after her in the still cold twilight, his voice banging off trees in a motionless echo.

Kay Schuester turned to me. "I hope she's not afraid of any bears, Alice," she said as she pulled a small case out of the trunk. "They're all hibernating. Even in the summertime they don't bother anyone unless you threaten the cubs. You just stay away and observe from a distance."

I was stunned. Not only did Kay Schuester actually utter a word to me, but she addressed me by name. More importantly, she seemed genuinely concerned about Marisa.

"I know. I'll talk to her. Thanks."

She nodded, and suddenly, I felt guilty about thinking of her as Kay Snooty Lips.

I felt as if I were a stick of butter over an open flame when I walked into Mr. and Mrs. Schuester's home, or now, Aunt Lil's and Uncle John's. It was dark and warm, and the scent of cedar and fire logs spread with just a little bacon fat filled the stone-and-wood entrance way. To the left was a large but cozy room with a plush beige carpet and a couple of big maroon fabric chairs and love seats with pillows everywhere. In one corner stood a huge stone fireplace and in the other an organ with the tiered keyboards. It looked so comfortable and inviting that I just wanted to throw myself on one of those beautiful sofas and fall asleep.

"Look who's finally here!" The very tall, slender, and elegant woman with very short salt-and-pepper hair whooshed her way through the room to her younger brother Barton Withers and, with delicate hands on each of his shoulders, kissed him on each cheek.

I immediately recognized Lil from my mother's wedding.

"Hello, Lavinia," she addressed my mother, and they air-kissed each other, again on both cheeks.

"And where is my girl?" She eagerly began looking around for Kay.

"She's out getting more of her things from the car." Barton Withers motioned toward the ajar heavy wooden door.

Lil Schuester threw her palms up and shook her head, smiling, suddenly spotting Marisa and me. "My daughter! She has a black belt in packing. And you two girls—"

"Mom!" Kay Schuester squealed as she nearly ran through her parents' elaborate stone foyer with a designer case in each hand.

"I think I hear my child." John Schuester appeared wearing a red crew neck sweater, beige pants, and very shiny shoes. After exchanging what felt like hours of formalities, he finally finished his wife's thought. "Look at you two ladies, bedraggled and what not." His smile was similar to Barton Withers's—white, wide, and had the appearance of being pasted on.

I smiled back.

"Can I show you your room? You must be really exhausted. I'll bet you have never been in a car that long, have you?"

"No, sir," I said, counting the hours from Wellton in my head as fast as I could while Marisa shook her head.

John Schuester looked around for his wife, who had already scampered off somewhere arm in arm with their daughter.

My mother held up her hand, which seemed to throw John Schuester off guard. "No, John!" she practically shouted at the nice man. "There's no reason the girls can't stick around for a little while and visit."

I've got a reason. How about the fact that I've got to pee, Mom?

"It isn't a problem, Lavinia," Barton Withers said calmly. "We're here all week. There will be plenty of time for catching up." Then with his large hand, he gently pushed Marisa toward our room. I followed.

Once our small amount of luggage was inside the bedroom, Barton Withers turned and walked away, and Marisa shut the door hard.

"What did you do that for?" I asked, worried that our mother would burst into the room demanding to know the same answer.

"Because I don't feel like getting undressed in front of a whole bunch of people, is that all right with you?" she snapped.

I nodded and made my way to the large bathroom and talked to my sister while I peed. "You've been having a really hard day, haven't you?"

"Well, yeah. Really hard. I mean, I don't want to be here, and I'm forced to. I want to go home. I would have stayed at Sun Chance with little Helena."

I stood in the doorway. "That doesn't sound like much fun."

She threw her hands in the air. "And this does? Are you kidding me? I don't know anyone up here—all my friends are home. I don't want to learn how to ski, but Barton and Mom are *making* me! I hate snow, I hate mountains, I hate the outdoors! I don't want to get eaten by a bear—I hate everything about this trip!"

I cringed as I listened to her tired voice escalate with rage. I put my hands out, glanced at the closed door, and gently walked over to her. "Marisa, I promise you, no one's going to get eaten by a bear. Bears don't wake up in the wintertime."

"And the bridge?" she continued red-faced, tears welling up. "What about the bridge? Huh? What about the goddamned bridge? If it closes at five and we're on it at five oh one, it will crumple up our car and kill us all! Don't you remember what Mom said? It closes into a little suitcase!"

I thought I heard something or someone, and once again, I turned to look at the heavy wooden door. "She was only trying to scare us," I said calmly.

"Why?" Her tears were heartbreaking, and I felt the pain hard as she cried. "Why would she do that?"

I shook my head slowly as I opened my mouth, but no words came out at first. "I…I don't know why."

But I was beginning to know why, or at least I thought I did. My mother wasn't a *real* mother. She didn't like us—she *really* didn't like Marisa. "I don't know what's happening with you lately, but you're not yourself. You've got to just calm down. I know what you're gon—"

"Don't you tell me to calm down, you cunt!"

My jaw fell as I tried to catch my breath.

"Hey, what's going on in there?" Barton Withers called out and twisted the door handle, which had locked when Marisa closed the door. "Open this door right now, Marisa Ionescu, do you hear me? Right now!"

"Hold on!" I called back to him. "I'm not sure how it got locked, but—"

Just as I absentmindedly unlocked the door, my sister's hand grabbed the back of my collar, and she pulled me down to the floor. The door swung open, and Barton Withers and my mother half sprung, half fell into the room as Lil, John, and Kay stood beyond, watching with mixed expressions of horror and bewilderment.

"What have you done to Alice?" Barton Withers demanded of his once-favorite little friend.

"I'm fine," I insisted. "There's nothing wrong."

Without a word, my mother marched over to where Marisa stood by the window, grabbed her face, and tried to smash it into the glass. But Marisa was able to back away first, and she slipped sideways and fell between the bed and wall.

"God, Lavinia!" Aunt Lil, still in the doorway, threw her perfectly manicured hands up to the side of her skinny face.

"You have been a bitch since before we set off on this trip!" my mother wailed, pointing that finger. "You are *not* going to ruin my vacation! Do you hear me? You are *not* going to ruin my life!"

"Lavinia, that's enough." Barton Withers finally decided to pull his wife off her daughter.

I looked in the doorway. The Schuesters were gone. My mother was bawling with her head buried in Barton Withers's huge chest. As Marisa lay on the floor, he stroked my mother's hair as she sobbed. It looked as though she had been the one who needed the comfort, not Marisa, and Barton Withers gave it to her freely and willingly. Poor Lavinia. She did so much and had such wretches as daughters.

I stood in the same place where Marisa pulled me over. *Pretty strong for a skinny little shrimp.* I looked at Barton Withers, and he looked at me. Our eyes locked. The smile and supreme confidence that normally radiated from his face was gone. Instead, he looked cold and contemplative. Neither he nor my mother bothered to check on Marisa, who was still on the far side of the bed. I was dying to get to her, but I was a chicken.

As if reading my thoughts, Barton Withers gently led my mother, still crying, out of the room. Poor Lavinia. The absolute grief we caused that woman.

"No more bickering, okay, Alice?" he warned, quietly but firmly.

I nodded just as my mother cuffed me hard on the ear. My head flew to the side in surprise.

"Now, darling, it's okay," he whispered to my mother, who now looked like a disabled old woman being led out to the hallway. Without looking again, they left the room, and Barton Withers quietly closed the door behind him.

I rushed over to Marisa. "Oh my god, are you okay?"

"Oh, yeah," she answered, her face still buried in the plush carpet. "I don't even feel it anymore. If I just cover my face, it's not so bad. She's not as strong as she used to be, and I'm bigger, sort of."

I helped her up from the crevice on the floor.

"I apologize for calling you a cunt," she said.

"Where did you *hear* that word? It's supposed to be the worst swear word on earth. It sounds awful."

"Arthur Dwoskin," she answered matter-of-factly. "He pushed me up against the wall in elementary school once and told me he wanted to stick his finger up mine."

"Stick his finger up where?" I asked, joining her at the end of the bed, feeling stupid.

She pointed to the area between her legs. I decided not to press any further. I knew where the conversation was heading, and I found it disgusting. We sat at the end of the bed together for a long time.

"Do you remember that time at Bunica's when you told me that I had to be smart, think really hard, and not do stupid things?"

"Sort of remember, I guess. Why?"

"Because you said you couldn't always help it, and well, you better start learning how to help it. If you keep getting angry like this, if you keep having these outbursts…" I looked at the door, listened for movement, and lowered my voice. "Mom is really going to hurt you one day."

She shook her head nonchalantly. "I don't care."

"What do you mean you don't care?"

"I don't care. Just like I said. She can do whatever the hell she wants. She's going to do it anyway. And she can't make me hate her any more than I already do. I hate both of them—her and Barton."

I sat quietly and examined the huge mahogany bureau in front of us. The beveled mirror on top looked like it weighed a ton and gave off a yellowy sheen. Then I remembered that Lil Schuester owned an antique shop, so it was most likely pretty old. "You and Barton seemed so close at one time, a lot closer than you and my dad were."

"Not anymore." She was quiet and resolute. "I thought he was a good guy, a lot of fun and everything, but really he isn't. He's a bad guy. He laughs. He makes fun of me. Mom took us to the store that one time when you got the coat with the belt that ties in the front, remember? She bought me a training bra. I didn't even need one. I hated it, it itched all the time. One night at the dinner table when it was just the two of us sitting there, he whispered, 'Got your bra on?' Just today he told me to run for Aunt Lil's front door because 'you never know when a bear with insomnia might come along.'"

"Oh my god, Marisa, there are no bears with *insomnia*." I shook my head. Why would Barton Withers torture Marisa about something she was so frightened by? It sounded like Mom and her rantings about that damned bridge back there.

"I hate him," she said simply.

"But you don't hate me?"

She looked at me and furrowed her brow. "No, you know I don't hate you."

"And you love baby Helena."

Her whole face softened into a childlike smile. "How could anyone *not* love that smooshy little angel face? I wish she was mine."

I wasn't sure how I would categorize our fairly new little half sister. My mother thought Marisa was bad? Helena Eloise cried at nothing and pooped at least a hundred times a day, but Marisa adored that baby, and Helena adored her. Marisa's face just brightened when I mentioned little Helena's name.

Suddenly, the bedroom door opened, and an authoritative Barton Withers appeared. "Let's go, Alice. The adults are getting ready to go out for dinner at John's restaurant. Lil's making some pizzas." We both headed for the door. I could smell tomato sauce, and my mouth was beginning to get a taste for a lot of food.

"No, not you." Barton Withers stuck his hand up to block Marisa from taking another step.

I looked at her, then at him, and then back at her.

"You have upset your mother, and I don't want any more shenanigans in my sister's house. You can stay here for the night."

"The night?" I protested. "But she's gonna get hungry. You guys are going out anyway. You're not even going to see us. We'll be good, I prom—"

Barton Withers put a palm up to his tanned forehead. I thought for a minute he might come around to my way of thinking, but he didn't. "Alice are you going to argue with me?"

"Barton? What's the matter?" my mother hollered from another room.

I didn't answer him. I just glared at him.

He ignored my mother. He looked down, and I saw his large hands in front of him as if he were about to calmly beg, but again, he said something different. "I'm not asking you, Alice, I'm telling you. Go out to the kitchen now. Right now."

I was confused and I was worried, but I did as he said. I hurriedly looked around. Marisa was sitting on the end of the bed, silently looking down at her socks.

"Now," he repeated, putting his hand firmly between my shoulders and leading me from the room. Then he closed the door behind us.

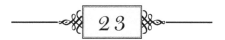

23

Kay gave me a lopsided smile as I slowly found my way into the giant rustic kitchen. I smiled back, but it was tentative. "Don't worry," she said quietly, her mother Lil Schuester standing beside her, ripping apart lettuce. "We've got another one to pop on the oven. We'll make sure she gets dinner."

Lil Schuester looked up, winked, and smiled, then went back to preparing salad. I didn't know what to say to them about any of this. I suddenly felt very tired. Lil Schuester shook her hands off in a large stainless steel sink. I wondered how much she knew about us, particularly from her sister, Mary Jo. A tinge of embarrassment combined with sadness bolted through me as I focused on the large brown grout lines in the terra-cotta floor.

"You gals have a seat and eat your pizza. I've got salad here, Alice. Do you like Thousand Island? I'm going to go and freshen up, and we'll see the two of you later. Oh, and I've got fudge bars for dessert. Fudge bars are mine and Kay's favorite, Alice, and I'll just bet you love them too!"

"Of course." I smiled, a little more relaxed, although I still wondered what Marisa was doing back in that room all by herself.

"See you later." She gave Kay a big kiss on the forehead. "I love you, babe. Have a good night, we won't be long."

"Bye, Mom!" Kay called out after her mother as she disappeared with a wave from the kitchen. I watched an even-tempered Lil Schuester leave the room. This was a relationship between two people that I had seen before and watched from the sidelines.

The pizza would be ready in three minutes. I was starved, and pizza was one of my favorites. "Do you want to go get Marisa?"

"My mother will see me, won't she?"

"They're leaving. Nobody's going to come back here, and besides, my mother will make sure of it. She's ushered everyone out the door."

"Are you sure?" There was no way.

"I am positive. Really, don't worry. Come on, I'll go with you."

I followed Kay back to the bedroom where I left my sister. She was lying on her back now, looking up at the ceiling. She didn't seem interested to see either one of us, but she did agree to come out to the kitchen and eat dinner.

It ended up being such a nice evening. Kay showed us her yearbooks and her older sister Robin's tennis trophies. We talked about skiing, horses, boys, Dad's fish store, and then Kay came up with the idea to do our hair. She had a drawer full of clips and bands and barrettes, and she even had these black wooden chopstick things that she said she could use for "the Ming Dynasty look." We started with Marisa when the phone rang.

Kay jumped up from the plush salmon-colored sofa and reached for the phone in her bedroom next to her own color television set. "Hello? Hi, Mom!"

I could hear the sounds of the public and Lil Schuester's voice cheerfully beeping.

"Oh, okay. That sounds good. We'll probably be asleep by the time you get home? Well, maybe not! Okay! Have a great time! I love you too, Mom." She walked back over to the salmon sofa and continued to brush Marisa's lush auburn hair. "They're going to see a movie, and then if they're not too tired, they're going to this new club that my dad's friend just opened for a nightcap."

"I can't see my mother in a disco," Marisa muttered as she flipped through one of Kay's fashion magazines.

"Maybe they'll have some fun dancing." I was hoping that spending an evening out in new surroundings would cheer my mother up a little—anything to get us out of her sight might make her happy.

Kay had an incredible talent for hairdressing, even though she wanted to be a doctor. She rolled, twisted, and braided Marisa's hair, then piled it high on top of her head to make it look like a crown. Then to make it look even more elaborate, she pulled the top of it up even higher and secured these thick plastic pins near the center so that the hair actually stood up off my sister's head. Then she sprayed it. I had never seen anyone do anything like that before. It was truly a work of art, and Marisa looked like royalty. I was in awe of Kay's skills. I also couldn't wait to see what Kay was going to attempt with my out-of-control mess of a mop.

When she was through twisting, pulling, twirling, and spraying, I looked like a cross between a princess and a rat, although it was far better than before, and I was grateful. Kay proceeded to teach us the technique for french braids. I was all thumbs, but Marisa was able to braid Kay's hair in these small braids from her forehead, down behind her ears, and down her shoulders. Then she placed glittery little beads on the ends.

We ate potato chips and drank tonic water from Uncle John's bar and watched a detective movie on TV. Before bed, I managed to get myself a healthy swig of vodka. In one of my father's lectures on booze, he said that scotch leaves a smell behind on your breath, as does many of the spirits. He said vodka didn't. I made sure to remember this little tidbit. My mother smelling scotch on my breath would have been a disaster.

I slept well that night and was so warm and comfortable in the morning that I didn't want to get out of bed. Maybe it was the quiet stillness of the mountain air, or maybe it was the vodka. It felt like the first time in my whole life that I slept through an entire night without being frightened of something.

Kay, Marisa, and I all went to sleep the night before with our hairdos in place, aside from the little sticks on top of Marisa's head, and in the morning, we took turns taking each other's hair down. I looked like I had a giant Afro that went slightly past my shoulders. My sister looked like a movie star who liked to go disco dancing with soft auburn curls that fell back over her ears and down her back. Her widow's peak looked even more dramatic. Kay told us that Marisa didn't exactly have a widow's peak, as my mother had always called it, but a softer, more swirly cowlick instead.

Marisa must have forgotten that my mother was angry with her. But that was typical of Marisa, who then claimed to be immune to my mother's exploding wrath. When she flitted into their bedroom, my mother was aghast. Apparently, Barton Withers, the private and reserved gentleman unfolding before our eyes, didn't want Marisa or me walking into his room while he and his wife were dressing. From where I stood, they were both fully dressed, so I didn't know what the problem was. He never seemed to have a problem walking around the house—*his house*, as we were always reminded—in his boxer shorts and a white undershirt.

My mother quickly studied my sister's hair. "You look like a hooker," she said matter-of-factly, "and with the way you are and your behavior lately, I would be surprised if you amounted to even *that* in society."

"You're a baby, Marisa," Barton Withers quipped from across the fresh cedar-smelling room. That wasn't supposed to be affectionate or complimentary.

My mother turned to him as she puttered through a top drawer. "That's right, Barton." Then she turned back to Marisa as Barton nodded. "You are very babyish. A good-for-nothing. You're emotionally disturbed. And Alice! Jesus Christ! Must you make yourself any homelier than you already are? You look like your father's yearbook picture! For god's sake, the two of you go fix yourselves up. Otherwise, you won't be going into town with the ladies."

"It's the mountain air, Mom," I muttered, my back to her.

"What did you just say to me?" she demanded, her voice already rising, and we hadn't even eaten breakfast.

"It's the mountain air. It makes your hair frizzier than normal."

"Go away!" She closed the door on us.

I looked at Marisa, and I saw a look on her face and in her eyes that was becoming more familiar to me. It looked as though she was thinking, remotely processing the words our mother used when she talked to her. She was far away, maybe a little numb, maybe somewhat in shock. She didn't seem angry or vengeful, but I could tell, somewhere in her heart, was a deep sadness. Under the beautiful smile, the tough individual adaptability, my sister was very, very sad, and there was nothing I could do to make it better for her.

Marisa's sadness would be there as long as our mother was so direct with her obvious hatred. Maybe if she ignored Marisa like she did with me, it would be much easier. But I didn't know how to bring that about. It wasn't just about Marisa; it was about my mother too. She was obsessed with Marisa. It wasn't the kind of relationship that Kay Schuester enjoyed with her mother Lil. It wasn't unconditional, an underlying blood bond, an ineffable force that binds beyond reason. All of it was breached by conditions. And two people couldn't get beyond the smallest complications of a relationship when there were conditions in place, and there should have never been conditions between a mother and a daughter. Unless all you have to hold on to is hatred. Then everything else just falls out the window to its death. Everything.

And my mother didn't have to remind me I was homely. I already knew that.

* * * * *

Barton Withers and our new uncle John hit the slopes that day while the ladies would go into town for some shopping and lunch. It was a beautiful morning. There was lots of thick, clean, fresh fallen snow on the ground, and the sun shone through the blue sky, winding its way through the heavy pine, creating a relaxing warmth. I hoped the four of us could really take advantage of and enjoy the perfect day that I felt as if God had specifically given only to us.

But that wouldn't happen. My mother refused to speak to Marisa. I knew it was frustrating for Marisa—it was frustrating for me. I saw my mother as being very childish. She had no trouble whatsoever reminding my sister that she acted, most of the time, like a spoiled toddler, yet it was Marisa who brushed out our hair, pulled back and braided it, went out and braved the bears, and seemed to try to forget that she had been humiliated in front of near strangers the night before.

Lil and Kay didn't seem to mind the tension much, or if they did, they didn't let on. The two of them were so close. It almost seemed as if they were best friends in addition to being mother and daughter. They laughed and linked arms occasionally. When we were in a tiny antiques shop, Lil wanted Kay's opinion on a couple of knickknacks she thought would look cute in one of the bathrooms. Lil had pretended to be annoyed because Kay had "stolen" a pair of her blue jeans. They talked to each other. Their voices were low. They listened to what each other said. They had conversations with one another. Kay was the center of Lil's universe, her whole reason, but it wasn't tangible, it was a given, and as I grew into my teenage years, I was seeing this so often with people outside of us.

It was almost as if it was a revelation, and I watched from the outside. I didn't experience this with my parents. I experienced something similar with Marisa, maybe, but it wasn't the same. It was fleeting, and Marisa was changing all the time. Maybe we both were. The one thing I did notice was the way Lil spoke to my mother. It was like she was talking to a child, but she sounded as though she felt sorry for her, or that there was something wrong somewhere, and this was the only thing she could do to ease away the pain.

My mother went out of her way to compliment and praise Lil. And she put Kay on such a perverse pedestal that it was embarrassing. Kay was ravishingly beautiful. It was always about physical appearance with my mother. Why? Marisa was much prettier.

Kay was so smart! She does so well in school.

How do you know that, Mom? I could take her on any quiz.

Kay is so lovely and tall.

I'm almost as tall as she is, and I'm what, four years younger?

Kay will achieve great things in life.

What happened to being an astronaut, Mom?

Kay is so thin!

Marisa is a toothpick, for god's sake!

And on and on.

Lil drove us to a tiny historical restaurant in town. Apparently, it used to be a post office at the turn of the century. It was a cozy little place, with a small bar and some tables on the first floor, and about six tables up a flight of rickety old stairs, where the four of us sat. Its specialties were deep-fried turkey BLT sandwiches, and as usual, I was ravenous at this time of day.

My mother was absolutely enthralled with the place. She was so enamored that I was positive that the whole place could hear her loudly coo how quaint it was, how old it was, how historic it was, the BLTs that were served. Hadn't she ever heard of a turkey BLT?

Lil was so patient with the embarrassing scene my mother made when she walked into the otherwise quiet establishment. My mother was a Withers now; she was supposed to carry herself in such a way as to show the world that she was the pinnacle of society. We have the perfect manners, the demure, charm, grace, and all the other crap that went along with these people and their stupid money, but she was very overcharged that day. And she was constantly criticizing her parents. Maybe she tried too hard to be something she was not.

The amount of times she put Marisa and me down, I couldn't begin to imagine what the new Aunt Lil was thinking. I didn't even look at her or at Kay for the longest time. I was ashamed to let these thoughts even enter my head. And when I wasn't mortified, I was downright scared, once again, only this time, it was about what I might do. I was terrified of what I might do.

My mother still wouldn't speak to Marisa, who had been very quiet all morning. She was even being quiet to me, which wasn't out of the ordinary, but when my mother wanted something passed at the table that happened to be closest to my sister, she asked *me* to ask Marisa, who was sitting only a few feet away. This happened three times. Once I passed the cream and twice Marisa passed the salt, but I never did as my mother requested because it was just so… ridiculous.

I continued to avoid Kay's and Lil's gazes as the temperature rose in my skin. As I looked over at my mother and listened to her mindless drivel, I wanted to grab her and press whatever fingernails I had into her pale flesh. I wanted my mother to feel the pain she inflicted on me and my sister, especially on my sister. I wanted to push her from her chair and hold her down. I was that angry with her for what she did to my sister, but I just as quickly tried to push those terrible thoughts from my mind.

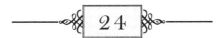

24

My mother and Barton Withers insisted skiing would be the activity for the remainder of the week. Everyone had these really nice skis and boots, even my mother, who, like Marisa and me, was a beginner. But the two of us instead had ski boots that looked like something Bunica would have worn back when she was a little girl in Romania. Not only were they ugly, but they were really difficult to put on and buckle into place. I had a hard-enough time getting my foot into the first boot, but Marisa was devastated by the whole process. This was partly because it *was* hard getting into the boots and because this place seemed to be the last place my sister wanted to be.

The once-close relationship she shared with Barton Withers was definitely over. Marisa alienated him, and he alienated her, and the one thing I knew about my sister was once she was alienated, the perpetrator would be frozen out for good. When she insisted she *could not, would not* get her ski boots on, and I attempted to stuff her foot into the boot, repeatedly saying over and over again, "You can do it, you know you can do it." It was a disaster.

Like most people from Northrington, the Schuesters were pros when it came to the slopes. Mom, with her brand-new bunny fur that covered her head like a lion's mane, bought herself a day pass while signing up Marisa and me for a full morning of ski lessons. The pros teaching the class were a husband and wife team from Norway. They had a small Norwegian flag sewn into their elaborate ski suits. Marisa was probably the oldest of about twelve kids, all of whom were way better at skiing than either of us. It wasn't so bad, even though I would have preferred to be reading a book in front of the fireplace. I kept trying to sidestep my way up a bunny slope, which looked to be at least twenty miles away from the summit, and then snowplow my way back down to the rest of the group.

Marisa was barely able to stand up on the skis. She couldn't do any sidestepping up hills. Her obvious behavior made me think. I knew she wasn't athletic, but I also knew she wasn't as uncoordinated as she was pretending to be. I had the feeling she was trying to get herself excused from class so she could go into one of the lodges and get warm. When that didn't work, she cried. Then crying turned into sobbing and then hysteria. I was angry. Some of the kids kept asking and reminding me that she was my sister. It was as if they were asking, "Isn't she too old to be crying and throwing temper tantrums?" I tried to reason with her, but she ignored me. She told the husband, Mr. Norway, that there was no one there to take care of her. That annoyed me since the two of us were there to take care of each other. That was the way it had always been, or at least I had thought it was. When Mr. Norway told my sister that he was there to take care of her, she cried harder.

I was finished. I was through with her. I couldn't talk to her or console her. She treated me like a dirty dish rag that was hopelessly thrown over the sink. I didn't think any of this was so bad. I actually *liked* learning to ski, even though I was pretty terrible at it. I didn't mind if it was cold—I had on layers of sweaters and, at last count, three pairs of socks, including the thick red ones Kay let me have. Besides, the sun was bright and warm and high in the sky, or so it seemed, and there wasn't a cloud within miles. Even though you could see your breath escape and the area around your nose was wet and mushy, I was learning something I had never tried before. My father had always stressed to me the importance of learning, regardless of what it was—a new sport, a different religion, a different language.

Marisa had a way of bleeding me to death even though I didn't really die; I just felt like I did. It wasn't the same anymore. And so I kept it up—sidestepping, snowplowing, turning, and when I finally looked up, Marisa was gone. I scanned the suddenly overcast horizon, and I spotted her navigating her way over large rocky mounds of snow by the parking lot. I don't know what she thought she would do or if she was trying to get to the car, but she didn't have the keys, and even if she did, she would freeze. My mind wandered as I took in more of the air that suddenly felt so much colder and sharper as it filled my lungs.

As if reading my mind, Mr. Norway told me in a gentle but authoritative voice to "let her go" and that she didn't want to be there in the first place. He was right, but he had no idea that the events in our lives were not brought about by our own decisions. He didn't know that Marisa would most likely have to give her Christmas presents back to my mother and Barton Withers in order to pay for this ski lesson.

And what about me? I could just imagine the consequences *I* faced for allowing her to wander away from her mandated ski lesson. *Why, Marisa? Why did this have to happen again? Again!* You could have slapped me across the face or pulled me down by the collar and dragged me across the damned floor if you had wanted. All that would have been a lot less painful than the strangling worry I had at that moment. I was tired of caring how selfish I sounded as I silently argued with my mind until the Norwegians dismissed the group from class.

Damn you, Marisa. What was going to happen to me if I lost you?

After class, I quickly set off to find my sister, who vanished into the frozen wilderness.

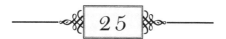

25

I wasn't sure which way to go. First I had seen her, and then she was gone. My joy of learning something new was quickly stolen by thick clouds that ripped the sun from the sky. It began to snow, and I began to panic. Everyone dispersed. Mr. and Mrs. Norway were long gone, and I found myself at the bottom of the hill watching people in their colorful ski outfits and pompom hats sitting on the perpetually moving chair lift in an easy attempt to get back up the mountain. I thought I spotted my mother, but then I quickly realized there were several women wearing fluffy round rabbit and lion's manes.

I took off my skis and walked the short distance to the long rack behind a small two-story log cabin called the Sea Dew Lodge. The warm air blasted me with a mixture of cedar and french fries as I made my way through a huge group of people speaking a foreign language. I pulled myself up the steps and followed the wooden arrows that were supposed to lead to the café, lounge, and restrooms. I couldn't find her anywhere. There were a few women in the ladies' room talking loudly to each other over the noise of the wall hand dryers. I called out her name and looked beneath each of the stalls, hoping I could recognize her boots, but she wasn't there.

The restaurant was packed with happy families drinking hot chocolate with big dollops of whipped cream, eating lunch, chatting, laughing, spending time together, but there was no sign of my sister. I didn't see anyone from our group—no mother, no Barton Withers, no Schuesters.

It began to snow harder. Large innocent white puffs doggedly fell to the ground. On any other day, I would have quickly found a piece of dark construction paper and caught the flakes, examining the flower tops that looked like they were sculpted but were instead designed by

God. I thought about asking an adult to help me page her, but then I remembered how huge this resort was, and unless she was hiding from me in the men's room, I had covered every inch of the building.

A bright yellow snowmobile whizzed by like a giant bumblebee, and there were people all around me ski-walking toward wherever they were going. I tried to ski-walk as it could have helped me pick up the pace, but I was unable to coordinate my legs to do what they needed to do. I started to cry as I used my poles to ease my sliding self toward the parking lot where I last saw my sister. Why had I listened to that dumb Mr. Norway? I should have gone after my sister when I had the chance, before the snow. Now she was gone, and where was he? Probably drinking hot chocolate with his wife and family, certainly not out there helping me track down my missing sister whom he let wander off in the first place.

I continued to slide until I found myself at the bottom of another slope right across from the parking lot. I didn't have a pass, so I couldn't get on a chair lift, not that I would know what to do when I was on one anyway, so I began to sidestep my way up the mountain. One step, two steps, farther and farther until I was too tired to go another step. I was nowhere near even a quarter of the way up the hill. I was still in a white field where everyone was getting ready to skid to a halt, ready to get in line for the next chair.

Then I saw her. I recognized the pointy wool red hat. She was dragging her yellow skis alongside, and she was walking with two people I didn't recognize. One was an older man who was helping her lift her skis onto her shoulder, and the other was a girl who looked like she was college aged.

"Marisa!" I cried, suddenly feeling a swarming sense of urgency and an overwhelming wash of relief both at the same time. "Marisa! Marisa!"

Thank God the three of them looked up at me as I half slid, half snowplowed down the hill and eventually landed on my butt about ten feet in front of them.

The old man looked startled. "You must be Alice, young lady." He smiled kindly and helped me to my feet. "Marisa here has had a little fall."

My sister's face was as white as the snow, and her green eyes that regularly danced faded into a distant gray. Her jacket was torn, and she was missing a mitten. She had been crying again. "What happened? I've been looking for you."

"She fell into a small ravine over there next to that run where they held the ski class this morning." The lady pointed to a collection of trees. "Thank God it wasn't very deep. My dad and I both saw her stumble over, so we were able to pull her up right away. She'll be fine. She's just a little shaken and banged up."

The old man turned to me with a voice filled with warmth. "Where are your parents, dear? You two ladies shouldn't be alone out here. It's not safe."

The four of us walked toward the Sea Dew Lodge. Arthur and his daughter Rachel slowed down so that both Marisa and I could keep up.

"I looked all over that Sea Dew place, and I couldn't find Marisa or anyone. Our new stepaunt, stepuncle, and stepcousin live up here, and they're all really good skiers, so they probably went on the hard slopes."

I could see out of the corner of my eye Marisa rolling hers.

"Our mother bought herself a lift ticket when she signed us up for lessons this morning." I put my hand on Marisa's arm. She looked at me and gave me a weak but sarcastic smile. I noticed the huge main lodge about a football field or so away along the side of the mountain. "I didn't go in there."

"That's the Gable Resort Lodge," Arthur said.

"I figured I would look for Marisa in the last place I saw her, over by the parking lot."

"You did the right thing, Alice," Arthur said and nodded deeply. He looked a little tired. My sister and I had this way of wearing out the adults around us.

"You sure did the right thing, Alice! Have you ever thought of being a police detective when you grow up?" Rachel asked.

I thought maybe she was joking. I smiled. I could feel myself getting red. She was talking to me like I was a little kid.

"She would be a great policewoman," Marisa finally spoke, the color finding its way back to her sullen face. "She's really good at puzzles, and you can't get a whole lot past her."

It was as if there was nothing else in the universe other than the song of the four of us trekking through the snow. We placed our skis on the racks behind the Sea Dew Lodge and went inside. Rachel got a blue piece of paper from a man behind the desk as Arthur led us to a pay phone. Suddenly, I heard the man behind the desk repeatedly page the Withers-Schuester party. We waited to see if someone would come to the front desk, but no one did.

"It doesn't look like anyone's here, but we'll keep trying. Meanwhile, we can try Gable Lodge. They have a couple of restaurants up there, but I think they have a central paging system."

"There's one more place too, Dad."

Arthur looked at his daughter and nodded.

Rachel closed her eyes and snapped her fingers, "That a—you know. Events Lounge. It's up the slope. You either have to drive up to it or ski down to it."

"Are they open during the day?"

"I think for lunch, yes."

Rachel looked at a plastic clock mounted to the wall above the front desk. "And that's about now."

The four of us huddled around the payphone. Marisa had an accident, and even though I knew my mother would be annoyed that we were going through desperate measures trying to use the resort PA systems to try to locate her, I wasn't very worried. This was important. Arthur and Rachel thought so, and they were a normal father and daughter who seemed to love each other the way a normal family was supposed to, so I trusted their judgment.

"Oh great, they're there! We found your mom, Marisa!" Rachel bounced around to face us. "They're coming back down now. Marisa, here—your mom wants to talk to you."

Marisa gingerly took the phone from Rachel, who then quickly reached out and stroked my sister's long ponytail. She turned to me and whispered, "I have to use the ladies' room. Be right back."

"Okay." I nodded and looked over at Arthur, who was talking to the same man behind the desk. I couldn't make out what they were saying, but Arthur's words were kind and unassuming. He was gentle, and his voice was low. The man behind the desk laughed.

I didn't have to look at my sister's face to know that whatever was happening on the other end of that phone line wasn't pleasant.

Suddenly, a damp blanket of fear slithered around my shoulders and down my back, leaving a shivering sensation on my skin. I felt like I did when I was a little girl, and Marisa and I would play hide-and-seek in my father's house. She was always one step ahead of me. She knew all my best places, and she always found me crouched and cowering in the dark. The middle of my chest tickled and tightened with horror as I looked at the light screeching through the crack between the door and the floor, her feet thumping ominously toward me, cutting off my only supply of light. Standing, taunting, waiting.

Marisa hung up the phone.

"Are they coming?" I asked. "Did you talk to—"

"Mom."

"Okay."

"I'm not making up any of this. I fell. It hurt. I got scared."

"What did she say to you?"

"She said that I just made a complete fool out of myself."

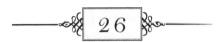

26

"Wait a minute. Wait." My father, looking like he hadn't slept in days, put his hand up and squinted. "What happened now?"

I tried not to let out a sigh of frustration as I slowly repeated myself. "I think Mom tried to kill Marisa."

The music filled the room. It was too loud.

"You think your mother tried to kill your sister."

"Yes. In the mountains. Yes."

"Alice—"

"I saw it, Dad. I know what I saw."

"Now, say that again?"

"They were coming down the hill from this big ski lodge. They hadn't been getting along all week. Marisa did something, said something, you know, and Mom just couldn't forgive her no matter what." I watched my father carefully as he sliced potatoes.

"And that's unusual?" The water ran fast and hard in the steel sink.

"No!" I raised my voice with frustration. "It's not, but—" I drew a breath and collected my thoughts. I wanted to at least get this right. "We were behind them, me, Barton Withers, and his brother-in-law John. I kept hearing Mom tell Marisa to move over, 'move over to the right.' Only she couldn't move over to the right because we were on this road that was sort of like a *bridge*. It went over this concrete wall. There was this tunnel underneath with a black part in the snow where there was this tiny stream."

"Culvert." He threw a pile of potato strips into the deep fryer. The sound of splashing oil annoyed me. I didn't want noise.

"I guess. Anyway, Marisa couldn't move any farther to the right, Dad. If she had, she would have fallen off the side. Mom was trying to push her, Dad, I know it. I saw it."

155

Ignoring my accusations, he scratched the side of his head with the eraser end of a pencil. "Aw, well, surely there was a guard rail, right?"

"Yes. Yeah, there was a guard rail." I tried to draw a diagram in the air with my hands. "But it wasn't until you actually went over the road, and it wasn't very long. But Mom and Marisa were up a ways back where there wasn't one. If Marisa had slipped—and she was awful with those skis—she would have fallen over the side. It was a long, long way down. She would have died."

My father watched me for a long time. Then Scotty walked in with a question, and I wanted to throw something at him. My father answered him and turned his attention back to me.

"Sorry, Alice." Scotty looked at me with a streak of fear in his eyes and slipped away.

"It's okay." I liked Scotty. None of this was his fault.

My father began to peel another potato from his large pile. He drew a deep breath and raised his heavy black eyebrows. "I'm sure if someone fell off a-there, they wouldn't die. Probably wasn't very steep, and I'm sure it wasn't that high up."

I'm sure you are correct, Dad. That's because you were there and saw the same thing I did.

He had to listen to me and believe me. I had to make him believe me. I took another breath and I tried to remain calm. "It was high up, Dad. I promise you. I'm not lying. I'm not exaggerating. Mom was trying to push Marisa over the edge!"

"She didn't though, Alice, did she?" I heard his voice over the racing cold water, indifferent to our conversation. He stopped chopping his potatoes and looked up at the big pink clock shaped like a crab that had hung on the wall for as long as I could remember. "Listen to me, that Ross Allen or Russ Allen Gables whatever place is one of the most exclusive resorts in the country. These people are not going to have some gaping hole for some rich guy's teenaged daughter to fall through—"

He stopped suddenly.

"Rich guy's teenaged daughter? Dad!"

The water stopped.

"She isn't some rich guy's teenaged daughter." My voice lowered with the silence. "She was your stepdaughter before she was that jerk's—"

"Look, I'm not going to argue with you about this. I've got customers coming in here in less than twenty minutes."

"Why are you doing fries at six in the morning?"

"Buy one get one free fries by six thirty. People have actually been eating Boochie's fries for breakfast, can you believe that? This is why I am up to my eyeballs in potatoes."

Anything he could do to occupy his time with work.

"Alice, I was married to your mother. I know her very well. She's shallow, she's materialistic, she's an alarmist, she's got a temper. But you know."

No, I don't know.

"She has done some good things too. She only wants the best for you girls. The best education, the best neighborhood, the best this, the best that. Christmas comes around, and you got more cash than you can fit into that ceramic hotel bank I bought you for your birthday when you were a kid. And Marisa, Jesus! She's been wearing those lace-up horse-rider boots and those earth shoes with the three-inch rubber heel. Those things were advertised as thirty-six bucks a pair! I *know* what she's like, Alice, really I do, but she loves you girls in her own strange way. She's no murderer, for Christ's sake."

Who is the Indian prince? Remember when you were going to take Marisa to the doctor?

"I wish I could come back home, Dad, Marisa and me. All I ever do is remember the past, you know? I miss living with you."

"Alice, come on." His voice darkened as he threw his towel down on the table and looked up again at the pink crab clock. "We've been over this so many times. Come on, I shouldn't have to keep repeating myself. The court's got you with your mother. You're a young girl now, you belong with your mother. You come down on the weekends, Wednesdays, whatever."

I decided to use my silver bullet. "We may have to move back anyway, Dad."

"What? Why?"

I suddenly felt the confidence to pop off my stool. "Well, Marisa was already home from school when I saw her hovering at the top of the staircase. She told me that she overheard Mom and Barton Withers talking about kicking her out of the house."

The pause was brief, but I had made a kill shot.

"Oh, really?"

Or so I thought.

"Well, I don't have to tell you that your sister has a way of making things up."

"Not everyone is making things up today, Dad. This is something else that isn't just my imagination. It makes perfect sense. Barton Withers *hates* Marisa, Dad. They hate each other now. They haven't spoken in weeks unless it's an argument."

My father nodded. He knew it was true.

I continued. "They each find ways to pick on each other, you know, get under each other's skin. Marisa is really stubborn, but he's just mean."

"And what does your mother do?" Of course he knew the answer to that.

"Blames Marisa. She blames Marisa for everything."

He silently nodded his resignation.

"If lightning struck the house, you could be sure she would blame Marisa. If one of their dumb friends dropped dead of a heart attack at one of their dinner parties? Guess whose fault it would be?"

He gave me a look. "You think that's an exaggeration?"

"I'll just bet you it wouldn't be. And the funny thing is, she's scared! But she doesn't *want* to move, can you believe that? She says she likes her room, she's got her friends, and she's got a boyfriend, Mark. He's a senior."

His interest peaked. "Your mother lets Marisa date?"

"She does it anyway. He's a rich boy, so of course Mom is thrilled about that. But he's half Japanese, his mother is from Tokyo, and Mom really isn't happy about that." I came here to tell my father that my mother was an attempted murderer, and I softened. I did exactly what I knew he would make me do.

He shook his head. "Are they Buddhists?"

I shrugged. "I have no idea. If I were her, I would jump at the opportunity to move, but she doesn't want to change her life again. I mean, why?"

My father raised his hands, looked at the clock again, and began chopping at double speed. He was so good at chopping. "Well, where the hell do they think she's going to go? She's a minor, for god's sake! She's not even seventeen years old!"

I looked beyond my father as I heard something metal fall in the back of the store. "Bunic and Bunica's, here."

"Here?"

"Yeah."

"Here?"

"I guess. That is if Mom doesn't push her over something first—"

"She can't live here!" He was yelling now.

Frank poked his head around the corner for a split second.

"She's not my kid!"

"Maybe you should have adopted her?" I was stunned at my own bravery.

He looked at the ceiling and sounded as if he might cry. "Oh, god, Alice! Barton Withers! Barton Withers does not dictate to me who does and does not live in my house! *I* own this property, the house, the store, the land it sits on, not him or his fucking family! Who the fuck does Big Bucks think he is?"

And then Dad was saved. A customer walked in, and my father went from exasperated at the prospect of Marisa moving in with him to the chatty lovable Rudy that people had known for years. That was one of the things that made my father an institution. He was a great businessman. He could turn it on. He could turn it off. No one knew. No one ever knew us.

I left the store and walked back to the house. Shelly was at my feet.

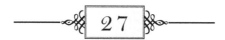

27

The one thing my mother and father had in common was that neither of them was a lover of animals. Dad even admitted to being scared of cats once. We never owned a pet. Ever. But through Marisa, my father had grown to love this handsome gray fellow appropriately named Shelly because he loved shellfish so much. He looked up at me with pleading golden eyes and his prolonged meow. I reached down and tickled his head. He now wore a blue sporty collar with a bell so you could hear tinkling when he was close by. My father even took him to the vet to have him neutered and to have his annual checkup and vaccines.

"Don't be fooled by him," my father would often say, constantly pretending to dislike the cat. "The only reason why he even likes me is because I own a fish store. But watch this, lately I've noticed he likes grilled chicken even more than fish. Damned cat."

Grilled chicken. Lucky cat.

"I don't have anything for you, Shelly," I told him as I petted his face, and he bumped his ears into my leg and rubbed. "All you ever do is eat."

He continued to happily whine as he followed me up the stairs and into my room. He jumped onto the bed and turned around slowly again and again until he found the perfect place to rest.

I heard someone in the hallway and figured it was Aunt Nancy. "Oh, there you are." She stood in the doorway. She wore a beige turtleneck with what looked like a black T-shirt over it that had her name in sequins across the front and an overstuffed down jacket over her shoulders that she started to put on. "Can I come into your room?"

"Of course you can."

She pulled out the old wooden chair that was once my grandfather's and sat down, facing me. "I thought you were down at the store talking to your dad."

I quickly sighed as I was about to answer.

"I know, I know. You can't talk to people." She smiled widely; her giggle was loud and fast. "People don't understand things."

I didn't respond to that. It was barely past sunrise, and I was already exhausted. I didn't feel like doing any more discussing or rehashing. It also didn't help that I was up most of the night trying to make my pillow comfortable and staring up at an old roof leak in the form of a brown spot on my ceiling. "So what are you planning to do today?"

She looked at the cat and smiled, then with a serious look back at me. She counted the tasks on her fingers. "Well, first I'm going to make some lemonade, *then* I have to go in and work at the store, later I have to go to the drugstore, and then, I don't know, I can't remember, but I'll probably have to do something else, let me see. Oh! I'll watch some TV or something like that." She nodded.

Suddenly, I was curious. Marisa's old room only contained her old mattress and box spring, lying without sheets on the perfectly polished hardwoods. Aunt Nancy had done all that, from cleaning to painting the trim an oil glossy bright white and the walls and the ceiling nearly the exact seafoam green.

"Aunt Nancy, why did you do all that work in Marisa's room?" I looked around my faded pink walls. "Wanna do something in here?"

She looked at me blankly for a second, then followed my gaze to Marisa's old room down the hallway. "Oh! Ah, you don't need to do anything in here." She smiled and looked around the room brightly but tentatively. The sound of air brakes made Shelly's head pop up. "This is your room. Everything is okay here."

"Everything is okay?" I was confused.

"Yes. Everything is okay," she said.

"But in Marisa's room, everything wasn't okay?"

Her face darkened, and she looked at me with a foreboding stare. She closed her eyes and tucked her chin into her neck. "No." She shook her head back and forth quickly. "Bad things, you know?

Just bad. Bad feelings. It was time to clean everything up and make it all nice and bright again."

I knew I had never heard this before. "Bad things? Was Marisa bad? Did she do bad things, Aunt Nancy?"

She put her arms out in front of her as if she were pushing me back. I was worried that somehow I had upset her. Shelly lazily opened his eyes. "No! Oh no. She isn't bad. Just a lot of hollering. Oh no. Melissa, Mel—I mean *Marisa* hasn't done anything wrong, nothing bad, nothing bad. No, no, she's a good girl. I…I don't know how to say these things, Alice. Are you mad at me?"

"Of course not," I said. "Never." I shook my head. "I could never be mad at you. You are the best aunt anyone could ever ask for. You're my favorite."

She nodded, and a blush of pride smeared her face. "And you're the best niece in the whole wide world! *My* favorite!" She stood up and, in one step, had her hands on my face and her lips on my forehead. "Wanna take a walk?"

I nodded. "But aren't you going to the store?"

She waved both hands and started to walk out of the room. "Rudy. Don't even think about him."

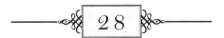

28

Don't even think about him. Aunt Nancy was lucky. She didn't remember things like I did. If thoughts nagged at her, she kept it all in, and she didn't hold grudges no matter how annoyed she got at my father. I never heard her say a bad word about anyone. Except when she was delusional about my father.

My mother. Aunt Nancy always spoke kindly to my mother, even though my mother made it sparkling clear if by nothing but her mannerisms, she thought Aunt Nancy was a nut and didn't want to have a thing to do with her. Aunt Nancy was always complimenting my mother, even when she wasn't around to hear it.

Aunt Nancy had some fine qualities. Sometimes I wished I could have been more like her in those ways. My father told me that I was too sensitive. I was beginning to believe that being sensitive was a bad thing, that the word *sensitive* was a swear word. Dad thought I should be a duck and just let it all roll off my back. I couldn't do that. That was impossible for me, and if my father knew what it was like to live my life, he would understand.

I felt pure anger when my mother would haul off and smack the back of my head in the dressing room in a department store, in front of everyone, just because I didn't like the pair of jeans she chose for me to try on.

Marisa and Barton Withers were constantly at a tension-churning standoff until one of them decided to draw. It was so confusing to me, unbelievable, frightening, that two people could have at one point been so close, had such a friendly relationship, and allow it to deteriorate to where they hated each other with such furor.

Weeks would go by before one of them would spit their venom at the other. Marisa would deliberately come to the dinner table wearing a bathrobe and her wet hair wrapped in a towel, knowing full well that it made Barton Withers crazy with anger. He would systematically accuse her of using his toothbrush and even once accused her of stealing a rare gold coin from him. Marisa screamed so hard in denial that she lost her voice, and my mother made me take Helena with me to the neighbors before the palace crumbled to its foundation. I fell asleep in front of the television one night only to be awoken by Barton Withers and Marisa arguing upstairs. She ran so fast down the staircase that it looked as though she had jumped all the way down or had been pushed. I was too frightened to ever find out. Once at the bottom of the staircase, she turned around and called Barton Withers a useless bastard and a good-for-nothing drunk. Shortly after that, I found out again that Marisa would be moving out. I didn't know where, and I'm certain that no one cared except for me. Marisa didn't want to go. She didn't want to leave her friends, her school, her boyfriend, Helena, maybe me, although I think I was pretty low on her list.

Then one day, our mother took us out for a drive. It was the last thing I wanted to do—go for a drive with my mother. Marisa finally passed her driving test after the second attempt, but it was futile since Mom said we didn't have any cars suitable for teenage drivers. Barton Withers could have easily helped Marisa purchase her first little run around, as my dad called it, but with the way things were going, that was not going to happen.

The three of us headed toward a tiny historical area of Wellton called Pennington. Way back years ago, collectors and residents actually found buttons, buckles, jewelry, and a myriad of memorabilia from the Revolutionary War. There was no sign, but everyone knew the little area behind the elementary school was aptly called Pennington after one of the winding little roads that ran through the wooded area. With its statuesque pine, abundance of maple, cherry, and green apple trees, there was a realness to the area and a small town classic feel that didn't exist in the extravagance of Harbins or the new suburban-type neighborhoods like Crescent Hills.

My mother loved it there; she always had. Driving slowly through the neighborhood, especially in the early spring when forgotten buds began to bloom like thousands of quiet but bright windows, brought my mother a measure of solace and lifted her spirit. That made me happy. The houses were mostly built in the twenties and early thirties, some during the forties. Some were built as early as the 1800s and were what I envisioned witches' houses would look like in the fairy tales. Lots were nestled, and houses were stone and brick with funny little roofs and rounded doorways. I never knew anyone who lived back there.

My mother said the detached-garage bungalows were much bigger than they looked on the outside. Some residents liked to renovate and build additions, trying not to interfere with the original charm. I wondered if we had moved here, would we have been happy? But Mom said that it was very rare that a house came up for sale in Pennington, and the same people had lived there for years.

We drove around for several minutes as my mother and Marisa talked about which house she would live in. I wondered why Helena stayed behind with Barton Withers. Marisa loved having that little girl around so much, and even though she couldn't wipe her own snotty nose and her face always required cleaning, her fat cheeks and her giggle were always the comical barrier that my mother and sister needed between them.

When my mother pulled the big silver-and-black Chrysler to a stop behind the elementary school, I was worried. Marisa rolled down her window and tapped her fingers on the frame. She stared defiantly outward, refusing to look at my mother. It was different, but somehow, it was the same as that drive a few years ago when my mother told us we would be moving out of my father's house, changing schools, and moving to Stanhope Ridge. Everything changed then, but nothing ever got better. It just got worse.

Marisa seemed to know what my mother was going to say before anything was even said. "Mom, I don't want to go—"

"Marisa. Please." My mother was calm. "We're going to arrange things with Rudy, and you'll have to move in with him."

"We're moving in with Dad?" Finally, I was elated. What had she said to him?

My mother turned around and pointed her finger at me. Her eyes were a warning, but there was a sadness beyond the fierce glare. "You're not going anywhere, Alice. Now, please. Shut. Up. This has nothing to do with you."

I knew I wasn't moving back to Dad's, and I wondered why I was even there in the car. I could have stayed home. Then Marisa began to cry, and my mother began to cry. But it wasn't their angry, screaming, fighting crying; it was sorrow and defeat, and finally, the three of us were in tears. I tried to be as quiet as possible, using the back of my hand and my T-shirt to wipe my eyes and nose.

"My friends, Mom." Marisa pleaded to a useless end. "I'll have to go to a whole new school again—I won't even graduate with my class."

"Your friends? You mean Mark, don't you?" My mother wiped her nose.

Marisa shook her head. She sounded so reasonable, so grown-up, that she didn't even sound like the sister I had known for almost fourteen years.

"No, not Mark. He has a car. He can drive to wherever I am if he wants. It's not even that. Helena, what about Helena? I love that little baby girl, Mom, you know that. When am I gonna get to see her?"

"Barton doesn't want you around her, Marisa." Her tone was even and patronizing.

My sister just stared at my mother in disbelief, as if she had just plunged a knife into her stomach.

I was amazed.

"You're unruly, you're a troublemaker, and you can't stay. It is his house, he bought it with his money. He makes the rules. He's afraid—"

"I would never hurt that baby! She's my angel, I love her so much! So, so much." My poor sister's voice trailed off into low, howling, desperate sobs.

My stomach roiled in sickness and regret. I put my palms over my eyelids, but tears marched right through.

"Mom, please—"

"Marisa, listen to me. Listen to me closely because this is very important: You have to go. You have to. Because if you don't, he will. *He will go.* Barton will leave me. And I will lose. Everything." Fresh tears bathed my mother's face as she turned and looked at my sister, who was slumped against the car door. "Don't you understand?" My mother was whining loudly now. "He will take everything away from me. Everything. My home. My pool. My cars. He will take Helena away. You have to do this. Please. Please."

"Okay." Marisa's voice was sad, whispery, and filled with guilt. "Okay." She nodded as her hands covered her face.

When I was a little girl, my father slowly read one of his books with me. It was the one about the Asiatic lion. According the book, these lions, who had some different features than the African lions, were the ones that were referenced in the Bible. They were only found in this one area of southwest India called Gir, and conservationists worked day and night to preserve the home of these rare animals. I remembered a part in the book that talked about the lonely life of the wandering male lion. He was always trying to find his territory and constantly fighting with other males who were trying to do the same exact thing. But even worse was if he happened upon a group of females and some cubs, those of which were probably not his own babies. The situation could have been very dangerous for all those involved; after all, the male lion was strong enough to tear those cubs apart if he wanted to, but "not so fast," as my father would say. The lioness mother and the other females would rip the male to shreds in a combined effort to protect those babies from that male. I understood why the female lions would kill to protect their young. It's a maternal instinct in the wild to fight to the death to keep an intruding male away.

Human beings are *supposed* to be a higher form of life. A human mother was supposed to *know* that a human male is coming into *her* territory to destroy her child. Fight that male to the death. Take your children and go somewhere else. Unless there were those conditions. I wondered what type of fight Lil Schuester would put up for Kay? How far would Mary Jo McLaughlin go to keep her little son Danny safe? Aren't children supposed to be treasured by their parents?

I thought about my old friend from school, Bruce, whom I still hadn't seen. I thought about Aubrey from the old bus stop. I wondered about Marisa's friends and Mark the boyfriend, whom she liked to talk to for hours on that telephone. Flesh and blood. The lion has instinct. The mother should reason.

* * * * *

My father had to commit Aunt Nancy. She had not been taking her medications and went running up and down the street near her efficiency threatening to beat her neighbors to death with a broom and then fly off with their bodies to the Temple of the Seagull, wherever that was.

Marisa was still in the throes of being kicked out of the house, but no one seemed to have a plan as to where she would go. My father came over for an impromptu meeting with my mother and told her and her husband that in no uncertain terms would Marisa be moving back to her childhood home. He said that he was very busy running a business, he was currently dealing with Nancy's medical issues, and more to the point, Marisa was Lavinia's daughter and not his and was completely and totally her responsibility. Period. Then he was gone.

Bunic and Bunica would be the next dump site, but Marisa definitely did not want to move in with them. They were old. Bunica was a devout Catholic with very particular rules and expectations (i.e., no Mark the boyfriend). The only school in the district where Marisa could attend if she lived with Bunic and Bunica was Strong High. The kids from Strong were from poorer inner-city families, smoked a lot of cigarettes, and got into more than the occasional knife fight. Strong was notorious for drugs and violence and was worse than South Wellton, where my sister and I would have been educated had my parents kept their marriage together.

The only things that were remotely of any relief were my school activities. I liked my trigonometry class and my teacher, and I was still tutoring in math. I found trig to be one of those challenges where I had to push myself, and it helped a little bit to keep my mind off things that were happening at home. My tutoring job was still on a volunteer basis, but I received a little slip of paper along with a merit certificate saying that I would be receiving minimum wage as soon as I turned sixteen. That was less than three years away, but it still seemed like a lifetime, so I filed that slip of paper away in my top desk drawer inside my important folder.

Somehow, I became president of the Humanities Club. I don't know how it happened, except that I was first nominated by a very overweight, quiet, but really nice boy named Greg Egglestein. I took the post. It helped me, and Dad was beyond thrilled. Also in hopes of staying away from the house for at least another hour or two during the week, I tried out for the girls' freshman volleyball team and made first pick. Coach Haddad told me that I was quite possibly the tallest thirteen-year-old girl she had ever coached, and that was a great thing for volleyball. And some days were pure heaven. Away games meant we didn't get home until after 9:00 p.m., and Coach was always nice enough to give me a ride home. Sometimes if I allowed myself to forget if only for a little while, or if I tried to occupy my time with other things to do, certain parts of life would just go away.

It was close to the Easter holidays. Marisa was still waiting for someone to take her in. Barton Withers and my mother were not pleased with my father's resounding no to their request. My mother should have known that Dad could be very hardheaded when he felt like a cat trapped in a corner and did not like being pushed around. But it was Barton Withers who acted very angrily and like a spoiled child when he threw a small television set across their bedroom and threatened to put Boochie's out of business.

At first, I worried about my father, but then something told me that Barton Withers would not be able to destroy him. And so, without having any information at all, Marisa and I waited and wondered. I supposed the negotiations would resume with Bunic and Bunica if there were any in the first place. I didn't know, and I pretended that I didn't care. I also pretended that none of it was real.

But the times the three of us—Marisa, baby Helena, and me—had in front of the television set were some of the most fun I ever had. We made popcorn and drank soda. We had burping contests and bubblegum-blowing contests, which made Helena smile and shriek. Marisa and I would stay up really late and make prank phone calls to her "friends," the ones she hated. Some nights we would fall asleep in front of the TV.

All of our fun would be short-lived when once again, Marisa would make one of her mistakes. It was very late. My mother and Barton Withers were at a dinner party, and Helena was still sleeping in her peanut seat, as my mother liked to call it, when she should have been upstairs in her crib. I kept looking at the clock on the wall. Marisa had been on the phone with Mark the boyfriend for over an hour, and I knew that my mother and Barton Withers would be livid if they were trying to get through.

"Mark's coming over, and we're going out." She hung up the phone.

"What do you mean you're going out? Now?" I looked at the clock. It was almost one in the morning.

"I'm going *out* out." She casually pointed behind her. "I'm just going outside. Mark's coming by, so just sit there and watch Helena. I won't be long."

"Do you think she should—"

"No, Alice. Just stay there. I won't be long! God." She walked out of the darkened family room, down the hallway, and out through the garage.

I looked down at Helena, who sounded as if she were baby snoring. She should have been upstairs asleep. Normally at this time, we would have turned off the TV and taken Helena to her room before we said our good nights or maybe had a good long chat before we turned the lights out. There was no telling when my mother and Barton Withers would be home. Sometimes I would see the dawn crack through the night when the faint sound of the garage door entered my last-minute dreams.

An unfamiliar foreign station identification appeared on the television set, and I sat and watched a comedy program from the Netherlands. It was neat watching a television show from a foreign country. It was kind of funny, I guess, with a lot of ladies dancing, and I kept looking down, hoping Helena was still asleep. I was starting to see that the show was more for adults, yet I was still intrigued.

Then suddenly, I heard the sound of the garage door open as Marisa ran into the family room. "Shit!" she hissed, and I noticed she was wearing one clog while holding the second one in her hand.

I wondered what she was doing, and then I saw that her orange shirt was inside out. Helena groggily woke up and started to cry a little, and before I could even reach for the television knob, my mother and Barton Withers were standing in the family room. There was the warm smell of cigarettes and alcohol as my mother swooshed past me and turned off the television. Barton Withers stood like a stone statue, his hands clenched into meaty fists at his side.

"What the hell do you think you're doing?" My mother's voice cut through the silence with a deadly calm.

"There was something on my shoe! I had to go out—" Marisa scrambled for the perfect explanation.

"You were outside with that boy."

"No! I mean, I had to get something—"

"You're a liar. You're supposed to be watching your sisters."

"We were fine, Mom—"

"Shut up, Alice!" My mother thrust a finger at my nose. I worried that Helena would start to cry. As my mother berated my protesting sister for neglecting her responsibilities, I saw Barton Withers's eyes. They were dull and black. He carefully watched Marisa with a steaming hatred. It scared me, and I looked away. I took Helena upstairs to her room and put her in her crib, blindly promising the baby that her mother would be up to tuck her in shortly. I overheard Barton Withers tell my mother that Marisa will be gone by next weekend. Gone? But where was she going? Bunic and Bunica were stalling. They loved Marisa, but they just couldn't take in their wildly beautiful, lively teenage granddaughter. Not Marisa, no way.

Barton Withers made my sister pack up enormous amounts of belongings and told her that she had to stay away from the house until 9:00 p.m. every night. Marisa appeared to be completely fine with that. She and Mark the boyfriend zipped around in his black Pontiac T-top, and that first Monday night, they went to the mall so Marisa could find a part-time job. She wanted to save up some money and eventually find an apartment. She told me she and Mark were planning to move in together. I had the feeling that Mark's very traditional parents had far grander plans for him, none of which included moving into some cheap apartment somewhere in Wellton with my sister.

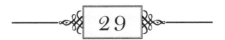

29

In my mother's kitchen were a bunch of hanging baskets of plants, lots of ferns, and a few of those lightweight metal containers that you filled with onions and potatoes. When you took the onions and potatoes out, the containers just collapsed onto each other. My mother never put onions and potatoes in these containers, and so I was always collapsing them. She hated that, and she was always yelling at me for it. I couldn't stop myself. One, two, three, collapse. One, two, three, collapse. Three, two, one, collapse.

Barton Withers bobbed and weaved into the dark room among the ferns like a soldier in some war movie. He was wearing an undershirt and a pair of rust-colored corduroys. He looked dirty, unshaven, and sweaty, as if he had been mowing the lawn or working on his car. But Barton Withers didn't mow lawns or fix cars. The only thing he did was drink, go to parties, and go on vacations with my mother and their friends. Really *his* friends. She didn't seem to like any of them.

"What are you doing here? Huh?" he asked Marisa, poison dripping from his tongue.

Marisa had just pulled some orange juice out of the refrigerator and was about the pour me a glass. She ignored him as if he wasn't in the room. My forehead had become furnace-hot, and my stomach started to close in on itself, pushing acid upward and causing my mouth to fill with saliva. Orange juice was no good unless I swallowed some toast.

As if reading my thoughts, Marisa pushed a plate of dry toast in front of me. "Eat that slowly, Alice. You'll feel better right away. Go ahead."

"Maybe we should go upstairs." I watched him in front of the refrigerator, blocking my sister's tiny body with his gargantuan frame. She turned her back on him, then swiveled past him and put the glass of orange juice down hard in front of me. I drank it up in seven gulps.

"I'm sick," she said, looking at me.

"You're not sick." He followed her around the kitchen. "I mean you're sick—sick in the head. I asked you a question, you druggie, you…you drug-addled cunt!"

She faced him directly. "Please leave me alone!"

I felt my nose burn, and I looked around for my mother and the baby, and then I remembered she took Helena to have brunch with Sunny Withers so the baby wouldn't catch my illness. At that very moment, I looked at the knife set on the counter. I started to cry. I thanked God there was no sound.

"Leave you alone? Leave you alone?" he taunted as he staggered around the kitchen.

I tried not to watch, but he absolutely hovered over my sister. Moving away and coming back. Taunting her. But then I pushed away a smile that was fighting its way onto my lips. Marisa didn't seem to be the least bit frightened by him. I wondered what kind of man bullied a teenage girl in this way.

He shoved a long perfectly manicured finger into her face, poking her in the nose. Her head popped back in surprise. "You'll be outta here! Oh, I'll leave you alone all right. All alone. Lock, stock, and barrel." He hissed and puffed like a viper as she looked away from him. Her ignoring his glare made him angrier. He followed her out into the hallway, which led to the garage.

I was tired, and my throat felt like a pocket of broken glass. It would have been nice if I could have gone upstairs to bed, but I knew that no matter how big the house was, nothing was going to drown out Barton Withers's hollering and Marisa's caustic rebuffs. She was at the point where she hated him so much. She couldn't just completely ignore him anymore. It would have been impossible for *anyone* to live under the circumstances she was living under. I felt a reason to be with her at that moment, and suddenly, that very large hallway became very crowded.

"What do you *want*, Alice?" Barton Withers turned around to look at me with that wrinkled defeat around his eyes. He was standing between Marisa and me, and his frame continued to hide her tininess.

"Just leave her alone!" my sister hollered. "Is that all you're good for? Bullying little girls?"

He quickly turned back to her like a grizzly claiming its prey. I caught a whiff of cigarettes and alcohol. He couldn't *possibly* be drinking his scotch at *this* time of the day, could he?

"You little pig!" he roared.

I tried to say or do something, but the only thing I could do was open my mouth and then close it again. Something was wrong.

Barton Withers kept yelling. "You are leaving *this house today if I have to throw your swine ass out in the street*!"

My arms and chest froze. I thought I stopped breathing.

Marisa spit a big wad of saliva upward and directly into his face. She backed up and hit the wall. I felt my head lower, and then I saw pure horror. Barton Withers wiped the spittle from his face with the same hand, and in what seemed like an effortless motion that lasted forever, he lifted my sister off the floor by her throat and slammed her high into the wall. She struggled hard, kicking and clawing away at the air, trying to catch his dodging head. Her mouth looked like it was saying "gaga" like a baby, but nothing came out. Then gurgling sounds. Then both hands around her neck. Her once-green eyes bulged, and her head moved outward and to the side, and then she stared at me as if begging me to run, run away before his ugly head snapped back again like a poisonous snake with a frozen bottomless glare.

Then I heard the sound of glass breaking.

The knife set. The. Knife. Set. Get to the knife. Get a knife. Go now. I. Passing. Get past him. Go. Knife.

He shrieked. Just shrieked. No words. Just screamed. "*Get the hell out of here*!"

He screamed again. I didn't look at him. He sounded like a woman. He shrieked again. "*Get out of here*!"

My legs didn't move anymore as Marisa lay on the floor in a puddle of blood, facing me. Her eyes were open, but I wasn't sure if she was looking at me. There was water soaking through the wallpaper and pouring down onto the floor. Lots of water. I tried to sit down on the chair behind me, but I fell over. He screamed another time. My knees crashed onto the tile floor, smashing one by one. If I could have just turned around, maybe I could have pushed him over out of the way somehow and pulled my sister up and away from him. We could have run together. But I remembered her eyes, and I didn't look back. I was angry with her for making me go and angrier with myself for leaving her.

For an instant, the regret that would mark the rest of my days overtook me as I sprinted through my mother's immaculate and stained kitchen and her inviting and tarnished family room. She would have been so annoyed with me had she seen me sliding around on her clean slate floor as I rounded the corner in Marisa's old beige gym socks that were always too big for her.

I didn't know where I was heading, although I knew it was in the opposite direction, and I knew that I should have been trying to get back to my sister.

When I found myself in my bedroom, I suddenly slipped on the deep wooden burgundy floor and fell straight forward. My palms and chin smashed down on the hard surface. I felt no pain. I breathed in a tiny bit of dust, and it startled me as I tasted the bitter wispy salt on my tongue. I found my way to the bed, crawling and awkwardly cramming myself beneath it. I hit my head on something metal, but I never stopped trying to run, trying to hide. I lay my cheek on the floor and breathed in more dust. I listened intently. I wondered when his footsteps would be upon me. I could hear nothing. There was no other noise but the confusion in my head. There was nothing. My eyes didn't blink. I was focused on the candy apple red alarm clock that fell off the end table and into my line of sight. There was no time. I was freezing cold.

Where was my sister? I already knew the answer. It was in her eyes. Her once-beautiful emeralds. I felt myself scream her name. There was no sound. I realized in horror what I had done, and I waited and waited forever. I was a coward enveloped in that terror. I listened closely. I could hear her. "Why did you run? Why did you go? You thought I was *looking* at you? I'm dead, you fucking idiot. How can I be *looking* at anything?"

I shivered with cold. I choked in just enough air to breathe. I couldn't hear him anywhere in the house as I lay crippled in silence. Everything was dead now. I strained as hard as I could to hear a killer quietly creep, waiting to pounce on his next victim. I would keep running. The monster would never get me because it was in her eyes that I saw the direction. I would run and I would hide, and I would stay alive.

I smacked my head against the black metal bar as fresh warm fluid seeped from every hole in my face. Suddenly I heard a loud but comforting purring sound, and to the right of my forehead, the neighbor's cat Pinkie curiously questioned my face with his leathery nose. His large wondering blue eyes and sandy pink tongue comforted me.

I tried to find my voice without the killer hearing. I whispered as the cat's head bumped my chin. "Pinkie. Who let you in here?" I had never heard this cat meow. I wanted to lift my arm up to pet him, but I was too frightened to move. His purring became louder and louder as he nudged the side of my nose with the top of his ear.

I whispered again, and I worried that my movement made too much noise. "I'm scared. I'm so scared. Can you stay with me, please?" I asked the cat. I wondered again how he had gotten into the house. Somewhere a door must have been left open. I knew it would have been impossible for my racing mind to figure out which door at that moment as every bit of energy that once formed my strange thoughts had drained away.

My mother hated cats. Hopefully, she would never spot him in her house. He knew I was thinking about him because he nuzzled up to my wet eyes. I blinked fast. "I don't know where Marisa is," I whispered into his smooshed vibrating face. "She would have come and found me by now. I would have heard her. I think she's dead. I think Marisa's dead. I saw him. I saw him kill her."

I couldn't believe I was saying the words now.

"What are we going to do? He'll be coming for us next. You should run home."

I smelled the air. A snap of eventual summer with memories of large giant fans in the windows and softball games with girls wearing heavy long nylon and polyester T-shirts with matching caps. Some were red and white, some were gold and blue, others were maroon and gold. The light shifted. I heard a horrible scream again, but it seemed as if I felt it first. My skin was cold again, and my pajamas were wet. I felt relaxed just beneath my stomach, as if I had been squeezing tightly for a long time, and I faintly smelled urine. I peered at the candy apple alarm clock still lying uselessly on its side when a hot knife shot through my heart. I noticed a face. It was a face I didn't know.

"Alice?" the face asked softly.

I screamed. "*You stay away from me! who are you! you go away! help! help!*"

"You're safe now, honey," the face said.

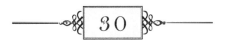

30

It was different than what I had feared death would be. I always thought that only good people went to heaven, that they would lie on their backs and levitate gracefully upward into the white puffy clouds and beyond to a peaceful blue paradise. In order to be considered a good person, you had to believe in God, pray, go to church, things like that. I thought that upon my death, I would be sucked down through a huge dirty pipe into the bowels of hell where some evil creature would welcome me with a caustic smile. All around me would be insects and caves of fire.

Maybe God was trying to figure out what to do with me. Maybe I *had* been good and didn't know it. Maybe I had a shot at heaven. I dreamt that I had been loaded into a screaming ambulance—a nurse with pretty long blond hair injected me in the butt with a serum in a big white room. Bunic carried me for miles across this huge room. I recognized him by the smell of the cherry tobacco he stuffed in his pipe. He looked handsome in his light-colored pants and his black turtleneck sweater as he hummed a song to me and said every couple of seconds, "You're going to be all right, you're going to be all right." He spoke to me in Romanian, but I couldn't understand him this time. My leg kept sliding down out of his arms, but he just kept swooping it back up with ease. "Don't try to walk," I heard him say. "Don't try to walk."

I had no idea where anyone was. I thought someone would be at the door to let me in and show me what to do, where to go, how things worked. I looked around for Marisa, but I couldn't find her. Then darkness. Then I saw Frank. He was sitting in a chair up against the wall by a door. Then it was dark again, and suddenly, I felt as if I had awoken from a terrible dream I couldn't remember. My head pounded. I saw a huge insect on top of a chest of drawers, and I screamed for my father.

"Don't worry, you'll be okay, you'll be okay." It was Bunic again. This time I noticed the perfect crease down the front of his pants, his shiny black shoes, and his salt-and-pepper hair that gleamed in deep thick curls. I had never seen him sit at that desk before, the one with the wooden swivel chair. He kept swiveling around to look at me. He smiled and nodded, and then he waved. "You'll be okay. You'll be okay."

Then darkness again.

Then Dad. He was carrying a small paper bag filled with something red. Did he even look at himself in the mirror? His long black hair was dirty and unruly.

"I want to talk to Marisa." My voice was croaky, and speaking was difficult. I couldn't remember speaking before.

"She's still in the hospital, kiddo, had an episode at her efficiency the week before."

"No, not—I'm talking about Marisa."

"You looked really pretty at the wedding. I saw some of the pictures."

"What?"

"Your grandparents think you should go with them, but I think you should come with me now."

"Marisa, where is she?"

"You're my kid, after all. Everything is going to be okay, sweetheart. Try to not talk. You need your rest."

"She's dead, isn't she, Dad? I saw him murder her! Dad!"

"Honey. Alice, you have to lie back and calm down. Please."

"Dad, please—"

"Yes, honey, Alice. We'll get to the bottom of this."

I didn't want to hear anything else after that. I was so tired, and I thought maybe I could still be dead. Or dreaming. I wanted to be dreaming, and I would make myself dream. "There was blood everywhere, Dad. Is Marisa dead?"

"I want you to try and get some rest. Can you try?"

"No. It was soaking wet, Dad. Water. All over the wall."

"If you can get some rest, then maybe later you can have a little soup."

"I want Marisa."

"No one is going to talk to you. No one is going to bother you until you can talk to them. I'm going to protect you, I promise. No one is going to talk to you until you're ready."

"It's my fault."

"Do you want to talk to your mother?"

"She saved my life."

"Your mother did?"

"No! Marisa did."

"Your cat's worried about you."

"Pinkie."

"Shelly. I didn't know cats could worry, but I think this one has been wondering where the hell you've been. Can you drink a little water?"

"He killed her!"

"Alice, you have to stay calm, or they will pump you full of more shit. Come on, Allie. We will get him, okay, come on. The investigators know what they're doing. Let the police do their jobs. Come on, Allie, rest for me, please. Please. Rest."

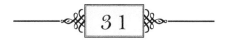

31

I didn't want to get out of my sweaty, worn, day-in, day-out pajamas. I couldn't get out of bed anymore, and I didn't want to either, but I knew that in order to get justice for Marisa's murder, I had no choice but to talk to the district attorney. It felt like it took hours to wash myself in the shower. I couldn't wait to get out of there, but it was an odyssey washing every inch of my body, and I couldn't make myself go any faster. The water was so hot, no matter how cold I tried to make it. Everything was so slow, and it just took so long.

I put on an ugly teal-colored dress with a childlike collar that I owned forever and quietly followed my father to the blue Plymouth station wagon that Marisa and I rode in so many times.

"You look nice, Allie," my father said as I struggled into the passenger seat.

"Thanks." I watched the house and yard move as we backed out of the long driveway. A cluster of gray clouds moved toward the center of the sky.

Sometimes there was nothing worse than the stillness of a dark rainy afternoon without her. I would look around the room and focus on an object, like a lamp, as the dark rain beat the roof with insensitive ease, and I would think about my sister and cry alone. My stomach would feel nervous, but not in anticipation of something—only nervous that nothing was coming at all. I missed her. I longed for her. I couldn't let myself think. But to me, that was nearly impossible.

My father kept both hands on the wheel. "Don't be nervous or scared, anything like that. Just tell—tell the DA everything you know, everything you remember." His eyes reminded me of a puppy hound dog. I could see how tired he was too. I had to look away. "It'll be easier for you now, you look a little better. I'm glad you had a little water for me."

I hated water. I only drank it to force down the medicine. When Marisa was alive, my father and I had a discussion about how you could go for days without food, but not nearly as long without water. I could have just spit out the water. I didn't want it. Water meant nourishment and life, and I wasn't interested in nourishing myself. I didn't look in the mirror. I didn't want to see my life on the other side and be reminded that I was still there. I would remain empty and breathing until I could figure out my next step. I still needed air for that.

"I promise, Dad, I'll tell the truth about everything."

"Aw, now you don't have to make any promises to me. I have no doubt in my mind that you'll tell the truth. I just don't want you to worry about a thing, that's all. You…you need to be as relaxed as you can."

"Dad?"

"Yeah?"

I was quiet. I was embarrassed.

"Really. Did I *really* tell my mother to go to hell?"

His reaction shocked me as his face cracked into a smile. It had been the first time in a long while I had seen my father's smile. "No, god, no, Alice." He was adamant.

Maybe I had been dreaming.

"No, no, she called last week because she wanted to see you, but you were in no shape for visitors. Oh, no."

"You're smiling again, Dad." I knew he was lying.

He just shook his head and kept his eyes on the road.

My stomach hurt, and I was nervous. I wasn't going to banter with him. And I wasn't going to smile.

The district attorney's office or police station or wherever we were looked empty.

"You want a soda? I'm gonna' have one."

"Sure," I said, looking at the bottom of the vending machine. I could just sip a little bit at a time or pretend to sip it if it made me feel worse.

"Wait, Mr. Buchner, please." The man with a big face came barreling over, his pants a little short, his feet huge, his tie a little lopsided. He was a giant man. "Please, sir, take this change, it's all quarters here. Let me pay for that for you, please, sir."

"Thanks, Detective," my father said.

Detective Kenneth Holloway of the Maidenhead County Sheriff's Department moved in closer to me, but I didn't move back. I was glad I didn't. I didn't want to be *that* rude, but I could have just as easily been if I wanted to be. He smelled kind of nice, like soap, but a manly soap, not a flowery soap. He smelled clean. He was so large.

"My sister is dead."

He nodded. He looked sad. "I know that, Alice. And I want both you and your dad to know"—he looked right at my father—"that we are very, very sorry for your loss." His voice was rich and seemed sincere. He wore a very short Afro. There was something soothing about his presence, which I fantasized could break every bone in Barton Withers' body. He spoke gently to me. I didn't want Detective Holloway to know that I felt the urge to climb up onto his lap and cry into his huge chest.

"Hello, y'all." A wiry-looking kind of man with short, straight, greasy strawberry-blond hair and very pointed and chiseled features made an unusual entrance. After brief introductions, the man placed his shiny black briefcase next to him as he joined the three of us at the round fake wooden table.

"This is deputy district attorney for Maidenhead County, Martin Giles. And if you happen to be wondering why he talks funny, that's because he's from way down south in Georgia."

DA Giles nodded and briefly but firmly grasped our hands. My father smiled. I did not.

My mouth felt numb, and I held back tears, but I continued. "Mr. Deputy District Attorney, I would like you to know that my seventeen-year-old sister, Marisa Ionescu, was murdered by our step-father, Barton Withers. I saw the whole thing with my own two eyes."

Mr. Giles didn't blink. Then he told me that we would just have a conversation. He would ask me questions, and I would answer them as best as I could.

"All right, Alice," he began as he casually motioned for us to sit. "On the morning of April 27, you stayed home from school because you said *you* were sick, or was it your sister Marisa the one who was sick? Which one of you was sick?"

That's the way the questions went. Monotonous and tedious. He questioned me about what I ate that morning, what Marisa ate, could it have been possible that we were *both* running a fever? What was the monster wearing? Where was my mother? At what time did she leave the house? How far is Sun Chance from our house by car? How do I know? How old is Helena? When was she born? On and on.

I knew he was doing his job. I *wanted* him to do his job. I wanted to wave my arms in the air and scream, but I didn't dare. I didn't ask anyone why we needed all this background. Even though it all appeared to be nonsense, I knew that it all *had* to make sense because this was what investigating my sister's murder would be all about.

I was relieved when after what seemed like forever, Deputy District Attorney Giles finally decided to talk about the whole reason why I was sitting in this police station kitchen-like room wearing this ugly dress.

"Okay, Alice."

"Yes?"

"What made you decide to follow Withers and Marisa out into the hallway?"

I looked at my dad for several seconds. I shook my head back and forth. "I had a feeling that she needed me."

"Did you have anything in your hand?"

"What? In my hand?"

"Yes. You said your sister poured you a glass of orange juice."

"Yeah. That's right, but I finished it and left the glass on the kitchen table."

Giles's eyes were downward. Then he closed them and looked back up at me. "Okay, you said you had a feeling that she needed you. Explain that to me." He put his pen up to his mouth and waited. And he stared.

My nose began to feel heavy again. I pinched it, and it was all wet.

Detective Holloway passed me a little square box of pink tissues. "Take your time, Alice."

I knew that I was about to cry hard. It was amazing to me that my eyes hadn't run out of their last tear. I shook my head slowly and lifted my hands. "I don't know. I was afraid something was going to happen—something was going to happen to her."

My eyes felt like two hot wells.

"He wasn't right that morning. He was wearing those clothes. I had never seen him dress like that. Ever. He was dirty, like he had been working on an engine or fixing a car or something greasy. But he never did those things. And he smelled like body odor and cigarettes, and I smelled alcohol. You could have smelled it a mile away. He grabbed her by the throat, and he threw her up high. She was looking at me. She was trying to get down, and then I heard something like…like…glass breaking. There was blood everywhere, Dad." I looked at my father.

Detective Holloway rubbed the area above his eyes as my dad's head lowered like a dying swan. He looked at me closely. "Blood, Allie?"

"Blood, did you say, Alice?" Giles asked.

"Yes. Blood. These things are important, Dad. I've already told you this. You have to remember this. And the wall was wet too. I don't know if there was a broken pipe or something, I don't know. Maybe he slammed her so hard, a pipe broke. Do you know what I mean? It was wet like water mixed with blood. It was so, so—and he was screaming like a woman. I let her die, and I couldn't help her. Dad, why are looking at me like that?"

My father slid his chair as close to me as he could. "No, Allie, no. No one is looking at you in any way. Come on, don't cry, come on, have another tissue. Guys, do we have to keep doing this?"

"Yes, we can still do this, Dad. You see, this is what I'm talking about—"

"What are you talking about, Alice?" Giles was calm.

"This, right here." I took a sip of soda and pointed a finger at my father and then looked directly at Giles, then at Holloway. "I told him. I told you, Dad, about the time Mom tried to push Marisa over the side of that, you know, whatever hill thing into that culvert when we were up in Northrington." I looked back at the two lawmen. "I told him, but he didn't believe me."

"Aw, come on, Allie, relax. You have to calm down a little."

"Dad, you are once again failing to see the importance in anything. And Deputy District Attorney Giles and Detective Holloway here are going to continue to ask me the same questions over and over again, backward and forward and in different directions all day today until—"

"Alice, but we don't have to continue with this right now. I understand this can be very traumatizing for people, and you? You are barely a fourteen-year-old girl."

Giles's drawl was making me want to vomit. He was being so syrupy nice, and I hated him. He was supposed to be putting my sister's killer in jail forever, and his sweet tone sounded accusatory.

"If this is too hard, we can do it at another time. I mean that, really and truly."

"Do you want some water or another soda?" Detective Holloway looked like he had just struck out and was desperate. "If you need to stretch your legs or use the restroom, anything like that, it's just down the hall."

"You just let us know," Giles concurred before continuing with an even *bigger* drawl. "And how 'bout takin' a coupla big ol' deep breaths."

I sat in silence for a minute. Then I slowly placed my palms down on the table and spoke quietly. "I don't want to do this later. I want to tell you everything I know right now. I owe this to Marisa."

"All right." Detective Holloway nodded his head once.

"I…I remember stumbling backward just a little. He, Barton Withers, I hate even saying his name, kept yelling at me to 'get the hell out of here.' And it was like I was trying to, but I—I couldn't, you know? I remember I fell on the tile floor. I was trying to move, but my legs weren't working or something. I hope that makes sense. It was like this dream I had once about my old friend Bruce. He was in a house on a street somewhere, and I was trying to find him, but the more I tried to find him, the harder it was to move forward. I knew that I was trying to run, but I was on an escalator going backward."

I felt a strong desire to make Detective Holloway and DA Giles understand.

"Dad and I read a book together once about being lost. It was like that—I couldn't find my way home, and Marisa's—" I started to cry, but only a little. I was determined. "Her eyes were so pretty and green, but I looked at her. They weren't green like they once were. They were bulge—they were putrid, far away, and the light had disappeared from them."

The room was silent. Even the bustle in the hallway with slashes of people, color, and hair passing swiftly by the skinny rectangular window in the door stopped. Maybe this was just the beginning of my punishment for not saving my sister's life.

The knives. Why didn't I at least try? I know that she wanted me to run, but why did I pay attention to her at that exact moment? I should have tried to take him down. Maybe we would have made it out or maybe we wouldn't have, but if I had done something, at least we would have been together. I kept wishing with such strength and regret that I had gone back and not left her to die. I fantasized and pretended, but no amount of my arguing with myself was going to change the fact that Marisa was dead. Murdered. Within feet of my uselessness.

I looked over at Detective Holloway's hands. They were folded neatly, one over the other. He wore a shiny gold wedding band and a gold watch. His huge brown hands had a soft gracefulness about them, a powerful yet childlike quality. They were nothing like the enormous spider-like claws of the monster that effortlessly clamped around my sister's neck in violation of her right to live.

"You were able to get away, Alice. That's the reason why you're here today." Detective Holloway gently interrupted my thoughts.

My father covered his eyes with one of his hands.

"I shouldn't be here. I don't want to be here." I was tired and beginning to feel like there were few words left. But I had to find them. I looked at Detective Holloway's calming face. His eyes were as black as a lake. They sparkled when he smiled, and I'll bet they looked intimidating when he was angry.

"You said you were having a hard time getting to wherever it was you were trying to get to, but you were able to get away from him. He kept yelling for you to leave," Holloway remarked.

"I ran up the stairs to my room. I fell again." I showed everyone the fading scrape on my knee. "Thank God Pinkie came along when he did. He was trying to help me, you know? And it made me feel safer, if only for a little bit."

"Pinkie?" My father looked up. Again. I *knew* I told him about this too.

"Pinkie. Mrs. Goldstein's cat. You know, the neighbor. You can see the top of her house from my bedroom window."

"She was in the bedroom," DA Giles stated.

"No, not Mrs. Goldstein. Her cat."

"Right."

"Oh, I see what you're saying, yeah, no, Pinkie's a boy. I don't know why he's named that, he's always wearing a pink collar. Maybe she thought he was a girl before she brought him to the vet's office. Or maybe she always wanted a girl cat. I don't know. He *looks* like a girl. He's fluffy and soft. He's very pretty. I can understand why someone would think he's a girl, but he's a boy. He's neutered, so he doesn't…you know. I don't know."

I waited for my next question.

"Do you know how the cat got into the house?" DA Giles took notes.

I shook my head. "I wondered the same thing. Through an open door or window, I suppose. How else would he get into the house?"

"How long did the cat stay?"

I shrugged. "I guess it was for longer than a few minutes. I don't really know exactly for how long. He just purred a lot and rubbed his head on my face. Then he bumped me and turned around and around until he could find a comfortable spot. He didn't seem frightened at all."

"Did anyone else come into your room? Before you saw the officer?"

"No, no one."

"Did you hear anything, a noise or a struggle?"

189

"No, nothing."

"And you don't remember when the cat left?" he asked again.

"Well, see, that's the thing, I don't know. I think I must have fallen asleep because when I woke up, Pinkie was gone. All I remember was the policeman looking at me while I was under the bed. I remember being so scared. I didn't know who he was, and I thought he had done something to Pinkie."

My father was quiet. His eyes were dark with warmth and approval, but his smile was full of sorrow.

"DA Giles," I said, "before you ask me any more questions, could I ask one of you? I know I've already asked you a bunch already, but this one's kind of important. No, this one is *really* important."

"Of course, Alice." He put his pen down. His straight hair was combed perfectly and parted to the side.

"Where is he now? The man who murdered Marisa?" I still got a sick feeling even when I thought of his name. "He is in jail, right?"

Giles eyes flickered in Holloway's direction. "Not at this time, Alice." He looked at me. "He was arrested. He was in jail for a very short time. But the judge set bail, a high one, and the Withers family were able to pay it. We suspected they would be able to, but we didn't think that the judge would set bail."

"You two must have fucked something up. What was it?" my Dad asked, his mouth coming to rest on his knuckles.

"Wait, Mr. Buchner, now just hold on—"

I held my breath.

Dad got up and started to pace the room, his arms flailing like streamers in the wind. "I hope you took that cat's passport, that's all I got to say, because that Big Bucks can go *an-nee-where* in the whole wide world he wants if that son of a bitch fat fuck of a father of his wants to send him somewhere. Hell, what makes you think they can't get him a fake passport? What the hell is goin' *on* here? We are talking about the murder of a seventeen-year-old girl, fellas."

"Mr. Buchner, sit down. Now," Detective Holloway ordered.

"He's *had* to surrender his passport. I can assure you he's *not* going to leave the country. There will be no fake passports," Giles said.

"How do you know that?"

Giles didn't answer my father.

"Right. You got people. Is that what you're telling me?"

"Mr. Buchner, calm down. Your daughter."

"I'm perfectly calm. You don't think she's heard all of this before? This fool needs to be locked up! Where the hell is he?"

I smelled hot anger pouring out of those slightly wet chiseled pale cheeks.

DA Giles looked hard at my father. "You need to really remain calm, Mr. Buchner."

"Indeed," My father said with a smack of sarcasm.

"We will get him. We *will* lock him up in due time."

I saw my father's facetiousness. I yawned. Every color in that room was amplified by a thousand percent, and it stunk of some kind of stale food. Barton Withers was not in jail, and I was in hell. I felt as if I was sleeping, but my eyes were wide-open. "Where is he, Mr. Giles?"

"At his parents' house."

Dad tapped his fingers lightly on the table while shaking his head from side to side. Then he crossed his arms in front of him tightly. "Back at Mommy and Daddy's."

The stale room was silent again.

"This was a seventeen-year-old girl, Mr. Giles," my father repeated, but he wasn't getting anywhere. I saw that now.

"No one knows that more than us, Mr. Buchner." Detective Holloway's voice was low and gentle.

No, you don't. You don't know anything.

My father's face was in his hands, and he continued to slowly shake it back and forth. But he backed down from his original accusation. I guess he just didn't want to get arrested. I should have asked him, but I never did. I was afraid to ask him. I was always so afraid.

"Rudy, please."

"Beg your pardon, sir?"

"Call me Rudy, please." He sat up for a second and regained his composure. No one was paying any attention to me. Suddenly, Dad looked over at Giles. "You know, Mr. Giles, I'm stunned at this whole bail thing. Just who is this nutjob judge?"

Giles looked down quickly at his papers. "Her name is Baeza. Fairly new, two years on the bench. I don't know her that well."

"Means nothing to me," my father mumbled. In other words, she was some stupid woman who wasn't a customer.

"So he's not in jail," I said out loud. I knew the answer to that, but I was begging for this to be a dream. My nose fought that burning twitch again. I wanted to whine, then scream, throw something, anything. I didn't care if Giles put me in a cell for the rest of the week. I wanted to cry until I was dead.

"No, Allie, Big Bucks is out of the cooler. Instead he will be eagerly awaiting trial at the family castle on the hill. For now anyway."

What's the difference between a castle and a palace?

"You two gotta go after this punk," my dad said as he looked at them sideways and slumped in his chair. "You know his record. Hell, what does any of that mean when you can buy your way out of shit."

"You have my word, Mr. Buchner. Rudy," Detective Holloway said.

"Of course we're going to go after him, Mr.—Rudy. *I'm* going to go after him with absolutely everything I have and everything I can obtain." DDA Giles turned his cool professionalism once again into his Southern warmth as if it were all one big faucet. "But it is imperative that both you and Alice know that just because Barton Withers isn't in the county lockup right at this very minute does not necessarily mean that he won't be spending the rest of his life in prison for murder."

I noticed my finger in my ear. I hoped he was right, but I saw something in Detective Holloway's face that made me wonder. Maybe it was something in Giles's face that I *didn't* see. It was as if they were avoiding being honest with us. Maybe it was because I was a fourteen-year-old girl, and they felt more comfortable discussing this crime with adults, like my father. But I was the one who was there. I saw my sister being murdered by someone who should have loved and protected her. I was there. I was the one who could help the police and the DDA. I just wanted to get it over with.

My father held up his hands and slumped back in his seat. "All right. All right. I got it. Fine, fine, fine."

We were almost finished.

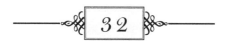

32

It rained a steady drizzle all the way home from the police station. The sky was a whitish gray, and the windows on Dad's Plymouth kept steaming up as the constant sound of the wipers thumped in sorrow. The longing for Marisa was more than I could bear as I sat in the passenger seat with my head back, gazing out the window and hoping for silence. I couldn't even cry.

We passed a muffler store that we must have passed a million times before. The blue plastic sign was falling off the poles and draping downward at a slant. A skinny man walked by with shoulder-length scraggly brown hair and a blue ball cap. He was wearing a red T-shirt with jeans and blue sneakers. He had no umbrella. I closed my eyes. I thought about packing my clothes and running.

"Want some music?" my father asked.

I shook my head.

"Kiki's invited us to dinner at her house this weekend. She's a great cook, you know. She's making Italian."

Kiki. She was my father's latest girlfriend. She seemed to like kids. She was very thin, but she had gigantic boobs, and her pixie-cut hair was so blond, it almost looked white. She wore a lot of makeup. When I looked at her eyelashes, they made mine hurt. She met Marisa once. "I'm probably not going to be hungry this weekend."

Dad let out his normal chuckle. "How do you know whether or not you're going to be hungry this weekend? You only know when you're hungry when you're hungry."

I wished he would just stop talking. "I really haven't been that hungry lately."

"I know, kid, but I've said this, and I understand you've heard this a hundred times, but you *have* to eat. *Got* to. You need your fuel."

I pulled the material of my dress up around my stomach. "Lost a couple of pounds, I think. Mom was always telling me that I needed to."

My father waved a hand at me while looking out his window. "Your mother, Alice. Jesus, don't listen to that, come on."

I didn't care. I wasn't hungry.

The house was warm and dark, which was exactly what I wanted. I turned to my father as he closed the door. "When is Aunt Nancy coming home?"

He shook his head. "Ah, I don't know. Soon, I hope. She's doing better."

I felt my neck weaken as my head lowered, but my eyes remained on my father's forehead. "She doesn't know about Marisa, does she?"

He rubbed his eyes and adjusted his shoulders. "No, she doesn't. And her doctors think she needs to stabilize on her medication and take some more time first."

"Hmm. So what do you think's gonna happen when she finds out?"

Just shut up, Alice. Go to bed.

Dad thoughtfully walked to the large windows and opened the drapes. I wished he hadn't. Even though the rain had slowed a little and it was still dark, he had let in far too much light. I felt like a vampire as I covered my eyes and pushed back the light. He began to quickly brush off the couch with his hand and clear away some newspapers that were sitting there—all of which had Marisa's Ionescu's name printed in them. We had a couple of reporters milling around, but the story lingered in the more upscale parts of town. I could hear the exhaustion in his voice. "I don't know. Nancy is a tough girl. Sometimes I think she can handle things better than we give her credit."

"Are you going to go back to the store?"

"I'm afraid I'm gonna have to for a while. Wanna come?"

I shook my head.

"What are you gonna do?" He was suddenly standing up straight, and I didn't think he cared what my answer was.

I looked to the staircase for a response. "I'm going to just go up to my room and put on some music. Is that okay?"

"Of course." He shrugged, furrowed his brow, and belched, all at the same time. "Still not hungry?"

"Nope."

"You gonna be okay here alone?"

"Yes, Dad. I'll be fine, I promise."

His face opened into a faint smile as he pushed his black glasses up his nose. "That's what I like to hear." He gave me a double thumbs-up, grabbed a ball cap from the hook by the door, and bolted through the breezeway and out the front door.

I was glad he was gone, and the house was its rickety silent self. I suppose I hadn't realized how much I wanted to be totally alone. No cops, no fathers, no deputy district attorneys from Georgia, very little sound, very little light.

When I looked down, Shelly was looking up at me with perfectly round huge green eyes. He meowed loudly and then bumped and rubbed my legs. He turned around and arched his back and flung his pluming gray tail into the air and shook it in this quick, quiver-like way. I reached down and scratched his head and rubbed his jowls and neck. I felt a fresh hot tear fall from my right eye. Shelly reached up and stretched and kneaded my ugly dress. His claws hurt my legs underneath, but the pain wasn't bad, sort of like little needles.

"I'm so glad you're here," I whispered to the cat, knowing I sounded ridiculous. "You're the only thing that makes me happy. Do you know that?" I scratched and rubbed him as he purred. Then he sneezed. "Oh! God bless you! Do you want to come upstairs with me and listen to some music?" I caught myself smiling as the cat made a little sound and flung his way up the stairs. I ascended the old staircase.

I was glad to finally be home with my father, but this was not the way I wanted things to turn out. I was so tired. I yawned when I sat and when I walked, even though my father always said yawning was a sign of boredom, not fatigue. I felt as though I was sleepwalking. All the time. I thought that maybe had I not complained so much about wanting to move back that Marisa might have been alive today. Then I quickly pushed that idea out of my head as quickly as it smashed into it. I blamed myself for everything, and I never forgave myself.

You are stupid, and you don't make any sense.

I could hear her tormenting me.

You're an idiot, Alice. He did this. Not you. Come on, stop. You were standing right there.

I felt her in my mind.

Oh my god, I know.

My drapes had already been closed from when we went to the police station. I also had two old beige shades with the ropey-looking pull rings that I never pulled down before. Dark. Darker. Just the way I wanted it. If I didn't have light, I wouldn't be able to see. I left the door open a crack in case Shelly wanted to leave, but for the minimal amount of light that filtered in across and down the hallway, it was good. Dark. I had a little transistor radio that my grandfather gave me from his stand with a cloth strap that hung from my bedpost. I decided to turn on 14WEL AM. Marisa hated that channel, so I thought I could listen to all those "stupid songs" and not have too many images in my mind that would make me think of any part of her. I didn't want to think about her, even though I knew that was impossible.

I flipped the little switch and stroked Shelly, who was now curled up next to my side, tucked into my stomach, and a poppy song made me think of Bruce. I immediately turned the radio down. Bruce and I used to listen to this song when it came on the radio. We usually sat in the hallway on the green carpeted steps outside his parents' apartment while attempting to fashion a top secret listening device out of tinfoil and caulk.

Just go to sleep. Stop thinking.

Then I suddenly started to think about our neighbor in Crescent Hills, Mrs. Cruikshank. Maura Cruikshank. Marisa told me something very bizarre about Mrs. Cruikshank once. Marisa was very upset about it. She was walking to the school bus stop with her friend when they, as they normally did each morning, passed the Cruikshanks' house. Mrs. Cruikshank appeared to be cleaning a french door to a veranda and was standing outside in the morning sunshine. Marisa said she was wearing a long blue terry cloth robe. Marisa and her friend waved to Mrs. Cruikshank and continued to walk to the bus stop.

"What's the matter?" I found Marisa sitting at the end of the drive by the elaborate wrought iron mailbox with the monster's full name and address painted on it. Thank God my mother didn't see her sitting there like some sort of hobo, she would say. She had her knapsack with her, and she looked as though she hadn't been inside the house yet. She looked up at me. Her auburn hair was pulled back, but the wind had caused it to tousle and fall a little. Her beautiful face looked worn and tired, and her eyes were red and confused, and she had been crying and blowing her nose.

I sat down on the ground next to her. "Marisa, what's wrong?"

"I'm so glad you're here. I've been waiting for you. I saw you coming up the road and—"

"What? What happened?"

"I got called out of class this morning, right before lunch. The principal's secretary announced my name on the loudspeaker—I got called down to the office to take a fucking *phone call* from Mom!"

"Why would Mom be calling you at school?"

She looked confused and shocked. Then she spoke slowly, as if trying to explain something to a child. "She said she just got off the phone with Mrs. Cruikshank and that *she*, Maura, was *crying*. She told Mom that I laughed at her."

"What? Why?"

"You have to believe me, Alice. I don't know why. She told Mom that she saw me and Suzanne walking to the bus stop, which *was* true, and that because she was outside cleaning her doors and windows in her bathrobe, I *laughed* at her."

I tried to examine my sister as best as I could without her noticing. I knew when she was lying. She wasn't. She was adamant. I couldn't see much of her eyes as she looked down, but I could tell how sad and frustrated she was through her long lashes as tears slid off their ends. She was dying for someone to hear her, to believe her. I wondered if anyone would besides me, and I wondered how that made her insides feel like. I couldn't imagine the fury.

"Alice, I didn't laugh at Mrs. Cruikshank! I didn't laugh at anyone. Yeah, I noticed she was wearing her bathrobe, but so what? I *waved* at her. Both of us did, but no one laughed!"

"Did Mom yell at you on the phone?"

She said nothing.

"What did the secretary say?"

She shook her head. "She didn't yell, Mom, she asked me, but it didn't sound like she believed me, you know?"

"Yeah."

"And I was crying too, you know? I begged her."

I nodded with my head down.

"I mean, not a lot, but just a little because I was kind of like, like—"

"Frustrated because you were trying to convince her that you were telling the truth. I know, I—"

"Yes!" She put her arms around me. "That's it! That's right. Then she said that I had to be very careful with Mrs. Cruikshank because she is going through some problems right now, marital problems, problems with her kids—" Her voice trailed off as she explained to me the problems that Maura Cruikshank supposedly had. She stopped crying; she seemed to feel better and was glad that I believed her, but I was really thinking that we needed to get up off the lawn. Although I did wonder to myself, *Why the hell would Mrs. Cruikshank be having any marital problems?* Mr. Cruikshank, Eddie, always suntanned from his constant travel to Fort Lauderdale, was such a nice man. He was always smiling, he was always friendly. He seemed to like Marisa and me. Originally from Pittsburgh, he was a huge Steelers fan. All she had to do was stay home and wait for that nice man to come home. He was nice, and she was *nothing* like my mother, although what happened with my sister was one of the weirdest things that I had ever heard in my life—and I could think of very weird things.

I wondered suddenly if Marisa had ever done it with Mark the boyfriend. She certainly knew an awful lot about it because she was the one who explained the mechanics to me. I got sick to my stomach, but she said it was supposed to be the most fun a person could ever have in their lives. Of course, I would never ask her. Never in a million years would I ask her. I was way too afraid to ask her, even though I was dying to ask her.

"And that bitch Lisa," she continued.

"We should go in."

He puts that whole thing in you? He pees out of it! Oh my god, Marisa! No!

"I hate Lisa. But I never laughed at her mother."

Lisa was the Cruikshanks' youngest of four daughters.

I smiled. "I never liked her much either."

"Why are *you* smiling?"

"What? When? Oh. Hey, after you got the call from Mom, did they see you crying?"

She shook her head again, eyes focused somewhere across the road by the woods. "No, I don't think they saw me. The secretary was talking to someone else. There were some other people around too. When I hung up, I just left." She looked down at her shoes and wiggled her toes, still shaking her head back and forth.

I looked at my sister carefully. I knew we should not have been sitting there, but the longer we sat, the lazier I felt, and it was going to be hard to get up. It was nice and comfortable in the grass. She didn't seem to notice my staring at her as she dug her fingers through the grass, looking for the one perfect blade to pull up from the root and stick in her mouth.

* * * * *

The rain was coming down heavy again from an angry sky. Detective Holloway promised my father and me that every angle of Marisa's murder investigation would be examined, and that included my mother and Marisa near that snowy culvert at the resort. But I had a feeling it was my word against hers. There was no proof. She would win.

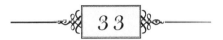

33

Detective Holloway and his partner, Sheriff's Investigator Archer, showed up one morning. Dad told me that Aunt Nancy was supposed to be discharged by the end of the week. He was mumbling in the very early morning as the sun struggled to wake. The smell of his sizzling bacon warmed the large cluttered kitchen and the sound of banging cabinets meant home. The only thing missing was Marisa. I noticed the newspaper, but I ignored it.

"Don't get your hopes up about Nancy. And she doesn't know anything about Marisa."

"Dad, I won't say *anything* about Marisa to Aunt Nancy. Promise." I didn't care about Aunt Nancy at that moment in time.

As if reading my thoughts, he swung a dish towel over his shoulder. "All I was saying was that—never mind."

I sat back in my chair. "I wish the medical examiner would hurry up and release her body. You know how my grandmother wants a proper Catholic funeral. Marisa deserves that—to be laid to rest. Properly. The way Bunica would arrange it."

The memorial service at the high school was so sad, yet joyous and celebratory of my sister's short life. Marisa was so loved. Crying teenagers were everywhere; her friends and Mark the boyfriend in particular were a mess. His mother was there dabbing her eyes. People had written things about her, prose, poetry. There were three blown-up photographs of her that Dad and Bunica gave her guidance counselor, who organized the occasion. There was a huge wreath of flowers, and her favorite art teacher, Mr. Hoffman, other teachers, the principal—everyone was so nice to Dad, Frank, and me. Bunic and Bunica were there.

Dad had a reception at the house, and Bunica brought her homemade plum dumplings, carrot cake, and chocolate cake, which were three of Marisa's favorites. I felt like I was sleepwalking again, and I hadn't slept for the next two days after that. My mother didn't even show up with the baby, and everyone said they *totally* understood. They understood? She was so fragile and on some sort of sedative. She was under a doctor's care. Bunica was so disappointed.

"And I agree with that. We just have to give them their room, I guess. They'll release her when it's exactly the right time. They have their job to do. Everyone's got a job." Dad shook his frying pan around. "Feel like going back to school anytime soon?"

I shrugged. "Not particularly. Not *that* school anyway."

"Well, you won't be able to go back there, not unless I take up residence in Crescent Hills, which sure as hell ain't gonna happen." Using an oven mitt, he carefully placed a hot plate of what looked like two pounds of bacon and sausage links in the middle of the table.

"I heard bacon causes cancer," I said.

"Everything causes cancer."

"You must be hungry," I said, motioning to the plate.

"Starved. You're not?"

"No."

"You gotta eat, Allie."

I carefully put a couple of strips of bacon on my plate. "It smells good. I'll have a little."

"I remember not too long ago when you could eat almost as much bacon as I could," he said, his mouth full of buttered rye toast.

I couldn't swallow the bacon, so I left it in my mouth as long as possible until it was a watery mush and would go down easier. It was so hard. All of this. I just wanted to sleep.

Shelly silently padded into the room and sat at my father's feet as I thought about how I would do anything to have my sister back. My stomach was nervous, as if I were about to go on stage or speak in front of class. I couldn't believe she was gone—she was dead. God, how was I going to get through this pain?

I yawned again. I hated when he saw me do that because he would ask questions most of the time, or make remarks, and I couldn't handle it. I didn't want to talk about it. It hurt so much, and I just wanted to go to my room.

"You're the most spoiled cat I have ever known in my entire life. Here." He threw Shelly a little piece of sausage. "That's all you're getting from me, now get lost." My father looked back across the table at me, eyes still smiling from the exchange he just had with the cat. "How are your eggs? Yolk hard enough?"

I nodded. Both of us knew I was picking at my plate. "They're fine."

"What about your mother? Don't you want to see her? She's been calling here and at the store. You haven't been picking up the phone, I noticed."

My eyes shot up across the table. "I don't really want to *see* her, Dad. I don't want to speak with her either."

My father swallowed some hot coffee with a loud gulp and helped himself to some more bacon. "Well, if you're not going to eat this, I will. Um, I believe she took the kid and is staying with her friend, what's her name? Melanie? Penelope."

Perfect. Penelope the Dragon Lady.

"You're not going to be able to avoid her forever. She is your mother, after all."

"I'm not trying to avoid her." I was matter-of-fact. I was trying to avoid her, and I was trying to avoid myself. And I was tired of reading or at least trying to read books that I knew my sister would hate. Concentrating on reading was the hardest thing. I was tired of listening to pop music that I knew would make her laugh at me. Anything I set my mind to was something that I did to keep from remembering her.

The rawness and panic that swept through me and sometimes startled me awake in the middle of the night was another hanging mirror I couldn't look into. I hated clothes, I hated makeup; I couldn't even look at a fashion magazine. The only thing I wanted to do was be naked in bed under the covers or wear my pajamas in my room with the curtains drawn. But hearing their names from the department—Detective Holloway, Archer, DDA Giles—any *one* of their names made me jump into action because they could provide information that could put the monster behind bars for life. Just knowing they were working on her case made me feel as if I had a reason to go on.

There were others that contacted me and Dad. I received a big card signed by Coach and the entire volleyball team from school. They missed me, and they wanted me to come back. I was never going back. My old bus stop friend Aubrey, from our life at the Stanhope before the monster when my sister was alive, came by to check on me one day with her mother. They brought two huge trays of pastries, and Mrs. Meslier made coffee for Frank and my father with lots of milk and just a little bit of coffee. Aubrey hugged me for a long time, and Mrs. Meslier smiled a lot and kissed me hard the way Aunt Nancy did. I wanted to cry again with graciousness this time because there were people in my tiny miserable world who actually cared. I was still terrified and depressed. And suddenly I couldn't cry, and I didn't want to see anyone anymore. But then I *did* want to see the people who were investigating Marisa's murder. I didn't even know what they were investigating. But it all seemed hopeful.

I must have changed clothes at least twice. I would try to find something suitable to wear for Detective Holloway, who showed up at the door. I had not looked at my hair in days and decided the only thing I could do with the overwhelming mop of frizz was to pull it back into a tight bun. I didn't want to look at the body in front of me that wore only a white bra, white cotton briefs, and black knee socks, but it was hard not to notice the droopiness that used to be fat. I saw I was losing a lot of weight, although it didn't mean anything anymore. I wasn't eating much, and that was fine. So what? When I thought about it, eating was a disgusting habit anyway. I wondered how many people had actually *sat* and *watched* someone eat. I had. It was an awful practice.

I finally settled on a pair of brown fatigue pants and a really old beige shirt with brown stripes that used to belong to my father. I wanted to see Detective Holloway so badly that I could hardly stand it.

When I saw the unfamiliar car with Holloway in the driver's seat pull into the driveway, I hurried up the stairs and started frantically changing clothes. I waited for the knock. My father beat them to it and opened the door as Detectives Holloway and Archer barreled through along with a trail of fresh morning air.

Detective Holloway spotted me immediately. "Hello, Alice." He looked tentative as he turned to me. Holloway was a giant in the giant room. "How are you holdin' up today?"

I glanced around the room quickly. "Fine."

"Would you gents like to sit down? Can I get you some coffee?" my father asked.

There was a brief awkward moment.

"No, no, no, thank you, Mr. Buchner, we're fine," each agreed as the men sat, and I continued to stand apart.

"I'm glad to see you, Alice," Detective Holloway said.

I thought he was going to arrest me for truancy. "Thanks," I said.

"Alice, come sit over here. You remember Detective Archer."

"Oh, yeah, sure." My father, smiling, reached over to pump Archer's hand.

Then their focus was on me. Detective Holloway took a deep breath but just as quickly leaned forward and watched me with an unfamiliar intensity. "I'm going to need you to do something for me that's real important, all right?"

He didn't wait for me to acknowledge him, and there was a tone in his rich and gentle voice that made me wonder how frightened I should be.

"I want you to tell me again, and of course, Detective Archer here, in your own words, everything that happened between the time you followed Barton Withers and your sister Marisa into the front hallway next to the garage and when you first saw the officer. Can you do that for me without the questions and the interruptions?"

"Why?" I asked.

His eyes quickly locked into mine like two puzzle pieces.

"Because it's important to the investigation that Detective Archer here hears this from you, in your own words. Now go ahead," he commanded.

I didn't want to do this *again*, but I knew that if Detective Holloway said it was important, then it meant putting Barton Withers behind bars for the rest of his life. We were going to have to do it at some point. Again.

I rubbed my forehead. "Okay. Hmm. Marisa walked out of the kitchen, and our stepfath—Barton Withers followed her into the hallway that leads to the garage. He wouldn't leave her alone. He kept screaming at her and calling her names. She kept yelling back at him to leave her alone, but he wouldn't. He just kept yelling and calling her disgusting names and egging her on. He kept walking toward her. He backed her up against the wall. He screamed that he would be kicking her out of the house that day. Then she just…she just…spit in his face. I was standing behind him near a chair, and I got so scared. I was scared because I thought that he would get even angrier than he already was, if that was even possible. And then…then he grabbed her by the neck and lifted her up against the wall. He held her by the throat. Didn't he know that would hurt her? And, and then she tried to get down, away from him, but she couldn't. She grabbed at his arm I know once, and she kept trying to grab his face and kick him. I—I can't. I just heard something like—I can't do this, please."

I knew I wasn't going to go over this again or go over it with any clarity that day. There were some places in my memory that I tried so hard to bury, and that wasn't helpful to them, but we had gone over and over it so many times. I never wanted to be reminded of my failure. The pain was sickening. I wished I had died instead.

Marisa could have had a better life than me. She had so much to offer, and maybe she would have been able to talk to people like DDA Giles, Holloway, and Archer with ease.

The room was rife with silence.

As my father looked down at his hands, Detective Holloway once again edged forward with encouragement. They said it was important, and that equaled locking Barton Withers in a hole forever. I was able to get through all the way up to when I saw the face peering down at me as I lay beneath my bed. I did it. Again. It was exhausting and brought me so much guilt and anguish. I was ready to go back upstairs.

"Alice, do you know how Marisa died?" Detective Archer's clean face focused on me, and his voice revealed a hardened matter-of-fact tone that shot through me like a dart.

"Of course." I moved awkwardly in the old soft chair. I had ideas about how Marisa died, none of which I could bring myself to think about. I didn't want to think. I wanted to go back to my room and pray for nightfall.

"He snapped her neck."

My father made a noise.

"Come on, Cal!" Holloway said. "This is a kid."

I looked over at my father, and I shook my head and searched for words that wouldn't come. My nose burned, and I gulped for air. I pictured my mother.

"There was no blood, Alice." Detective Holloway gently continued what Archer began. "There was no blood, no water, no leaking pipe from behind the wall, no water or blood on the floor."

"So what now, Detective?" my father asked, rubbing his face.

"Wait a minute," I said.

Archer didn't seem to care. "And the cat. There was no cat—"

"Okay," my father said.

I was breathing in pins, and my heart beat fast.

Archer burst through the confusion in the room, but not before he shot a quick scowl at Holloway. "There was no blood on the wall nor was there water. Anywhere. Marisa Ionescu died from severe trauma to the neck. Her neck was snapped, broken, and she died very quickly thereafter." He went on to read exactly what happened to the bone and tissue in Marisa's neck, throat, and eyes. It was all a very long and drawn-out scientific explanation, and I thought that I had heard it at another time, I just couldn't remember from who or when. Maybe I dreamt it. I was sinking in grief, and I knew she suffered. There was so much anger in that room. I could feel my forehead crinkle up like a little old woman, and I opened my mouth but closed it again. My head started to tip until it touched the side of the chair. I lifted it.

Archer continued as he thumbed through what seemed like reams of data. "Mrs. Goldstein, Goldstein, Mrs. Goldstein, Mona

Goldstein's cat is a seventeen-year-old Persian that never leaves the house unless he is penned and is going to and from the vet."

He was talking, whispering, mumbling to himself, but quickly. Why was he being so cruel? Why was he doing this?

"On the morning of April 27, a Thursday the day Marisa was killed, Mrs. Goldstein was in her sewing room on the phone with her sister. The cat was sleeping on the love seat in the sewing room. The cat remained in the sewing room with Mrs. Goldstein until the early afternoon." He continued to thumb through his binder. "Mrs. Goldstein is a widow who lives alone and, according to her, 'always' has her windows and doors closed and locked. The cat was not with you under the bed that day, Alice. Mrs. Goldstein can testify to the whereabouts of her cat that day."

"I'm so sorry. I'm so very, very sorry. But we'll—" Holloway said.

"Wait. Wait." I carefully placed my hands out in front of me as if that would stop Archer's mouth. Dad taught me not to point at people, and so I made sure my right arm was stretched out in front of me as far as possible with my hand pointed at Archer's head. My top row of teeth were tucked under the bottom row. I was shaking. "Don't tell me!" I shouted to the two men in dark clothes sitting on my father's sofa.

"Alice—" Detective Holloway reasoned.

"No. Don't tell me!" I yelled. "I saw blood! Pinkie was under the bed with me. I saw blood! The wall was *wet*. It was *streaming* water!"

I stood up, but Dad stopped me. I tried in panic to break free from his arms, but he was too strong as I pushed down as hard as I could on his biceps. Archer and Holloway stood up and moved to the side.

"Dad!"

"It's okay, Allie, come on. You're okay."

My father held me to his chest as I sobbed like a child. My face remained buried there as my father stroked the back of my burning head. My nose was blocked and runny, and my throat was on fire. I just wanted to sleep forever and never wake up again.

"We're gonna have to do this another day, guys. Sorry," my father said.

No. No more days. No more of this. They continued to talk, but I couldn't make out what they were saying. I didn't want to know. I hated them all.

As my father walked me toward the stairway, I heard a shuffling of people, keys, and papers and then the quiet closing of the front door. Dad helped me onto my bed and carefully placed an old quilt over me. I lay curled up in a ball. I never wanted to be anywhere else again. I just wished it had been me who had died that morning.

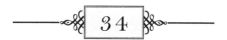

34

I had a dry acidic taste in my mouth, and my head and teeth were mildly pulsating with pain. I had dozed off. My nose was running as a tiny tingling sensation filled the back of my throat. That usually happened when Shelly slept on top of my head. I turned to the cat and scratched behind his ears. "I suppose they're going to tell me next that you're not really here either."

Waking up was an awful thing. I never had an easy time falling asleep, but since Marisa's murder, waking up had only brought me to the worst depths of despair, and I didn't know what to do with myself. The shifting of twilight into my room was the gray color of evil itself. I should not have been there. I was the one who shouldn't have had the opportunity of life. I had always promised myself that I would be right there fighting alongside my sister to the death. Instead, I watched Marisa get murdered.

I should have never run from her. I heard the murderer yelling, hollering at me to leave, to get the hell out of there. It went on and on in my mind like a prisoner who would never be free, a permanent fixture, worse than a song repeating in my head, but more like two large conch shells glued to my ears forever, making me listen to the phony sound of the ocean.

What I should have done was run back into the kitchen and grab one of his precious solid silver knives and stab him with it over and over again until there was nothing left. Then there would have been plenty of blood for the police to find.

Dad left a couple of lights on for me. I heard a truck out front, and I knew there was some activity at the small warehouse. I found his note on the olive-green countertop that my mother always hated.

Went to the store then to pick up Kiki. Please feed the spoiled, overweight cat. See you in the morning. I love you, Dad.

I looked around the stillness of the room. I spotted one of the throw pillows from the living room propped up on the kitchen table chair, and as I stared at the out-of-place accessory. I suddenly wished that my father had stayed home with me. Dad's work was number one in his life, and now that he was with Kiki, another top priority kicked me down a rung. I saw his bottles on top of the refrigerator.

"A little liquor, Shelly?" The first time I had ever had a mixed drink was when Mark the boyfriend fixed Marisa and me a seven and seven. My father didn't have the exact ingredients, so I filled a highball with gin and a splash of ginger ale and sat in front of the television with my drink. I smelled how strong it was when I raised the glass to my lips. Poor Mark, I felt so sorry for him. He came over to the house with a box of candy and a face that looked like it had been crying nearly as long as mine. He too wanted to know when the coroner's office would be releasing Marisa's body so she could have a proper burial. We had nothing to tell him. Instead, we just stood around like idiots looking at each other with little to say.

I took a gulp of my gin concoction and wondered what my father would do if he caught me drinking his booze. I wasn't really sure how he would react, and I guess I didn't care. Nothing really mattered anymore. Come kill me if you wanted to—I welcomed it.

The next day, I borrowed Scotty's bike that was locked to a pole near the loading dock and sped off for a clear ride. I pulled my hair down and let the wind whip through me and cleanse me as much as it could. I would always be dirty with grief and anger, and I couldn't tap into the memories that made it any easier, but at least I could give myself to nature as it was bigger than any of this. I had never known much about God, but maybe if I had set my mind to it, if I learned to pray, maybe God could help me, tell me how to do this right.

My father's family on the Buchner side were Jews. Dad told me that his mother, my grandmother Rosalie, was a nonobservant Catholic. Bunica was a very religious Roman Catholic. Everyone who knew her knew that. There was no cohesiveness whatsoever when it came to my place with God. I had no idea where I was. But I did believe in God. That much I knew. I knew God was out there somewhere. I just hoped that he was taking good care of Marisa.

I crossed over the river at the top of the hill from South Wellton. It was the steamy humidity right off the water that pushed my world from my mind and helped calm and settle me into understanding for just the briefest moments that I did not have control over everything. I raced as hard and as fast as I could up the industrial path standing up as I pedaled upward, pumping my legs as hard as I could, as if the face of the murderer lay below my hard leather soles. I pumped and crushed, then let up just a little as the monster hollered in pain.

I passed a row of run-down houses where the paint had chipped away over the years; dead-looking gray vines appeared to be keeping a roof from crashing with its building to the ground. A couple of boys hovered around a car engine lying on dead grass. The huge quarry speckled with giant yellow dump trucks that were harmless from a distance, with their enormous childlike wheels, were terrifying and loud up close. The main office sat way up in the air like Dracula's castle above the massive mountains of stone and blue sand, and Jodie's Burgers was next on the left, nestled in the corner and recently painted a bright blue. There was one employee's car parked out in front. Too early for the lunch crowd.

I suddenly remembered the last time I was there—sitting in the car with Dad and Marisa. It had been such a long time ago. I had a feeling of urgency, and I couldn't allow myself to think as I wound my way down and down, noticing the large and undeveloped parcels of dirt and gravel sprinkled with young pine trees, wondering why no one ever walked there. I pumped ferociously again, plowing the monster into pieces, with my face in the wind. I knew I would get him one way or another. I would make him pay not only his debt to society, but his debt to us. Maybe I was late, but I was prepared to die trying *this* time to make the future as difficult as I could for my ex-stepfather. The next breath didn't matter anymore.

I wound through the wooded hills past some ranches until I was there, in front of the white building with the picket fence and hearty yellow flowers giving off the feel of something built back in the 1800s, but with a much slicker, cleaner, more modern look. The police station stood before me. Crescent Hills, where crime never happens, violent crime anyway—murders. I didn't know what to expect this time when I climbed the green and white steps.

Then a light went off in my head. I realized that Detective Holloway wasn't a Crescent Hills police officer; he was a Maidenhead County sheriff's investigator. How could I get this so *wrong*? Why didn't I just go back downtown? Why didn't I just go to Giles's office? What was I *thinking*? I was only thinking about my sister that morning, and all that other awful stuff that became nothing but a wad of string rolling around my head, tangling up, and getting bigger and bigger.

I walked backed down the steps and took the bike back across the street from the charming little police station and hid in the trees. I knew what I saw. But they didn't believe me. Realizing that I might not ever see Detective Holloway again, I turned around and pedaled home, killing the monster all the way back.

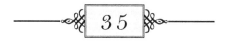

35

"Mom! Oh my god!" It must have been loud. *"Mom!"*

Still no answer.

"Alice? What's wrong?"

I heard Marisa through the door, and although her voice provided some relief, I was still panicking. "I'm having a problem. I don't know what to do."

"Did you get your period?"

Terror ripped through me. "How did you *know?*"

"I could just tell." She sounded old. "Just hold on, I'll get some pads and safety pins. It's about time!"

I sat on the toilet looking down at my cotton underwear and the big roundish blood mark in horror. I owned these underpants for a couple of years at least. They were thick, faded, blue, and big. I knew what was supposed to happen, but I was still terrified.

When I heard Marisa coming back, I hobbled over to the door, my pajama bottoms down around my ankles. Marisa quickly explained to me that if Mom had seen me hobbling to the door like that, she would have thrown a fit. Mom didn't understand that menstrual blood stopped. It wasn't a constant flow like a faucet that was turned on indefinitely. Later, I wondered why a woman didn't understand that. But I never asked, and I never found out.

"I brought you some clean undies," she said. "Take the old ones off, fold them up so the blood is on the inside, and lay them aside for now. I'll show you how to pin this pad in."

I looked at her in dismay. "I don't want to stick one of those things in my hole. Do I have to do that?"

Her head slowly flopped to one side. "No, you dingbat. Here, sit back down and relax. I'll show you what to do, it's really easy."

214

Then I stood up to face her. The bathroom felt very small, and it was beginning to get hot in there.

"Do you have any pains? You know, like cramps? Down there?" She pointed to the area below my stomach and to the side.

I shook my head.

"That's good, but you will, so we'll have to talk about it. Now, come on, we have to go down cellar."

"Why?" I was confused, but only a little. I had seen Marisa and my mother do the "down cellar" thing with the underwear before, and although I didn't pay much attention to it, I knew they were up to something that would eventually include me.

"Mom's going to make you soak your underwear and hang them to dry. She won't let you just throw them in the laundry bin. She says that blood gets all over the rest of the clothes." She turned and walked away. I followed after her.

"*Ew*, really? If that were true, it couldn't be *that* much. And… and, well now, wait. It's a washing machine. It's blood. It washes blood out, it doesn't *spread it around*." That didn't sound right. Was Marisa messing with me?

"Alice, have you *ever* known me to make the rules around here? How many times have you seen me come up and down those cellar stairs with my underpants? I don't know why, I don't know if it's true or not, but I know we *have* to do it. And if she finds out that you had your period, and I knew about it and I covered for you—"

I stopped arguing with her and followed her downstairs. I turned the required cold water on over the basin. "Thank you for helping me with all of this, Marisa. I felt a little embarrassed."

"It's all right," she answered me quietly. "I'm your big sister. It's my job to take care of these things."

36

I locked up Scotty's bike exactly where it had been that morning. I glanced at him through an open door and saw that he was busy with Frank filling cases. I knew I had the bike back in plenty of time.

The front door to the house swung open. It was Aunt Nancy waiting for me. She was smiling, and her bright green eyes and streaked blond hair gave the impression of a golden glow against the dark wooden backdrop of the large foyer and hallway.

"There's the princess of the Buchner Realm!" she exclaimed, and I fell into her usual secure embrace. I didn't want to start sobbing again. I didn't want to upset her, but as I buried my face in her shoulder, the tears came unabashed. "Oh, poor Alice, it's okay," she cooed quietly as if she were talking to a baby. "It's okay, everything's going to be fine. Don't cry, dear, don't cry, Alice." Then suddenly she stopped. "Hey," she said, "who's the big colored man that dropped by the store this morning? He looked so sad. He has no one."

37

It was still dark when I woke up the morning of Marisa's memorial service. There was a slow breeze that swished through the trees, my hair, and the back of my sweaty neck as I paced back and forth and up and down the driveway. The weather people were seldom good at determining the forecast, and I was surprised to see the orange and purple break in the distant sky. But it was still the bleak reality of a young beautiful girl whose life was brutally snatched from her.

I sat on the top step of the porch and smoked the cigarette I stole out of my father's pack and watched, as far as I could see, the blurry mounds of life waking up and becoming sharper. It would only be a minute before the old Boochie's sign and floodlights at the warehouse would snap on as the morning rose to the sky. Maybe they wouldn't. I looked down to the right at a little square disarranged patch of concrete that lay near the gutter in front of the house.

When we were little, Marisa dared me to pull my pants down in broad daylight, pee on my thumb, and lick it clean. She said it would bring me good luck and promised not to tell on me. She was always able to get me to show my bare butt to all who would notice back in those days, and despite her increasingly convincing promises not to tell, she always did. She was the perfect con artist, and I was the perfect sucker as each and every time, our mother would throw me over her knee and clobber my little soft cheeks with a two-pound wooden salad spoon.

That was one memory of Marisa that made me giggle. I tried unsuccessfully a lot of the time to wrench my mind away from her suffering in the last moments of her life when I should have helped her, could have helped her, but instead ran. It was so easy not to care about little things anymore.

I didn't care if my father caught me smoking or helping myself to his gin. I was a coward. I just shut myself up, and I deserved what came to me.

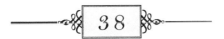

I'll never forget the day they finally released Marisa's body. They released her to her next of kin, who was my mother. I wanted a lock of her hair, but my mother thought *that* was gruesome. I thought it was gruesome for her to take it upon herself, against my grandmother's pleas and religious beliefs, to have my sister's body burnt to a crisp, turned into ash, and scattered in places *she* found appropriate. When my mother was gone, I simply scooped out some ashes from the plastic bag placed inside the ugly pewter urn. I laughed and then I cried at how easy it was. It was as if Marisa was right there opening a door and ushering me through.

Go on, dingbat, don't be a chicken! Take some of my ashes. Do it now!

I could feel her presence fill the room with a soft heavy glow, and I knew I would never tell anyone I knew she was still there. Miraculously, I had an old envelope from the South Wellton Library inside my knapsack, and I quickly but carefully put a teaspoon of what used to be my sister into the small envelope, making sure that every bit of dust either fell in or disintegrated into the air. I rearranged the contents and folded the envelope into a square as neatly as I could. Then I placed it inside a zippered pocket of my knapsack. I fixed the plastic inside the ugly pewter urn exactly as it was and put the top back on. Finished.

It was the first time after my sister's murder that I actually felt calm and happy. It was as if a warm euphoric wind ripped through me, reached my contented heart, and encased it. I couldn't help but smile at my deception and subsequent triumph, and it felt strange and new on my face.

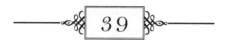

39

My mother was somber without makeup or nail polish. She had this weird look of worry and fear on her face all the time. She entertained that look I always disliked on her, and that annoyed me—that washed hair that she let air dry, that unstyled, tangled, unshapely red heap. She was suffering even though she would never admit it. I imagined that her turmoil had a lot to do with being married to a male who turned out to be a killer, and his victim was her own daughter. Guilt, maybe?

She allowed me to go through only some of Marisa's things and keep the personal items I wanted. I took her little jewelry box, her wool socks, her diaries that she insisted upon writing because she had no memory of day-to-day events, her sketchbooks, and her favorite Icelandic fisherman's sweater, which really looked like a dress on her when she wore it.

I quickly exited Penelope Pantaliano's chic townhouse, kissing little Helena on the way out to my father's Plymouth. I felt sorry for the little child with the reddish-brown hair molded to her big head, parted to the side. She smiled and waved, but she didn't understand what was going on around her, even though I'm sure somewhere in that tiny brain of hers, she felt fear and confusion. There was nothing I could do at that moment though, nothing. Helena was my half sister just like Marisa was, but Helena did not belong to me. I couldn't stay there with her. I needed to be away from that townhouse. I knew how much Marisa loved that child, so Helena had to miss her. When she got older, she would understand, but I just needed to get into the car and go and not spend too much time allowing her to look at me.

40

I looked over and noticed my father's shiny black shoes. "There you are," he said.

I nodded a few times and looked straight ahead again into the hills, my cigarette long discarded. "You look really handsome, Dad." I was quiet.

His long jet-black hair was tied into a ponytail at the nape of his neck and fell down over his black jacket. He wore what he called his after-hours wire-rimmed glasses that actually fit his face properly. "Aw, thanks, kid. I haven't darkened the doorway of a church in God knows how long. Of course, I'm not looking forward to it either."

"Where is everyone?"

"They're on their way. We'll pick up Kiki on the way to the service."

Neither of us had a tear in our eyes.

"Is Aunt Nancy up yet?" I moved over a bit so my father could sit next to me on the porch. He could have opted for one of the chairs, but he didn't. He sat next to me on the step and lit a cigarette. "Oh yeah, she's up, but she's not coming."

"No? Why not? She adored Marisa."

He nodded deeply and exhaled smoke. "I know she did, I know, but her doctor doesn't think her attending her teenage niece's funeral is a good idea *at all*. He thinks it could send her right over the edge again, and it could even be worse, particularly because she was murdered by her own father."

"Stepfather."

"Right. Stepfather. She wasn't doing well last night. You didn't hear her, did you?"

I shook my head.

221

"Thank God for that. She was talking all about how frightened she was about family members being carried away by evil ghosts at funerals." He used his fingers for quotation marks. "That's all I needed to convince me that the doc was right. And then she said she wanted to remember Marisa when she was alive. By the time she had taken her medication and had gone to sleep, she was feeling a lot better, and now she's up folding some laundry. She's fine. She might even fall back to sleep for a little while. Tommy's going to hang around with her today and keep her company."

"Okay. I don't think Mom should've had her cremated."

He flicked an ash. Now I was dying for a cigarette. "Well, there's hardly anything we can do about that now."

I wasn't ever going to tell Dad about the ashes I transferred from the envelope in my knapsack to a sandwich baggie, which I carefully placed in a dark bluish-purple velvet jewelry pouch that my grand-mother gave to me years ago.

"We didn't have control over it in the first place, Allie."

We both sat watching the morning sun back away enough to grace the coolness of the early hour, and I just decided it was time. What could possibly happen that could be any worse than Marisa's murder? "Dad, who was Marisa's father? Her biological father?"

He stared back at me for a second. I noticed nothing different in his face. He shook his head. Then he looked down. "You know." He exhaled the last of that second cigarette and then flicked the butt away. "I have no idea, to be perfectly honest with you."

I looked at him, partly confused, partly stunned. "You *don't?*"

He casually shrugged. "No, I don't know who her father is. I'm not even sure your mother even knows who Marisa's father is. It was something Lavinia never wanted to talk about. I never pushed her because when your mother didn't want to talk about something, your mother did *not* want to talk about something."

"Oh my god," I whispered, rubbing my ear, trying not to put my finger in it. "You have got to be kidding me, Dad. How could she not know who the father of her firstborn daughter was?"

He looked at me. "Now, maybe she did. She just didn't want to tell me about anything, and believe me, she wanted to be as quiet as possible about the *whole thing*. Look, this is the day of Marisa's—"

"Dad, please."

"Look"—he lowered his voice to barely above a whisper—"this was 1959. Your grandmother was about to send Lavinia off to a convent. I was good for something, and I came around just in time. But even still, I would always be that little girl's stepfather. And we did not discuss the father."

I could tell that he was ready to change the subject. It was incredulous. "Do you think Bunic and Bunica know who he is?"

"I don't know, Alice."

"You're my father, aren't you?"

"Am I your father? Just go look in the mirror. Of course I'm your father, I can promise you that. But Marisa's?" His voice was eerily strange. He shook his head. "It's too bad. A day like this. Maybe it would have been nice if he knew, whoever he was."

He wasn't not letting it go, so it was fair game, right until Frank and Scotty were within earshot. "She told me he was an Indian prince."

"A what? Who told you what?" His expression was twisted.

"Marisa. Yes. She's dead now, and she was afraid that revealing this would cause Mom to kill her anyway, so what difference does it make now? Not a Native American, no. An Indian, like from the country of India. A prince like royalty. An Indian prince. She said that Mom told her that a long time ago. It was a secret, and she was scared, Dad. She didn't even like the fact that she had revealed it to me. She regretted it because I had brought it up again a couple of times to her, even though I never told anyone else."

"Oh, for Christ's sake," he muttered and placed a third cigarette to his lips. I didn't want one anymore.

I felt exhilaration, as if I had the upper hand. I knew something because I had been there. It hadn't done any good because I had been pegged a traumatized teenager and stressed from seeing my sister die and then hallucinated to keep myself safe and all that bullshit. But then? I felt empowered. I wondered what Marisa thought of all this because I believed spirits were alive and were watching. "I'm just telling you what she told me, Dad."

"First of all," he began as if he was going to give me the lecture of a lifetime, "Marisa had very fair skin. She burned easily."

I squirmed, knowing I had a chunk of her ashes upstairs in my bedroom.

My father waved a hand at me. "I'm sorry, poor choice of words, I know. What I'm trying to say is that people from Asia, India to be specific, have lovely brown skin. Their hair is very dark, sometimes very black. If your sister was part Indian, I am positive we would see it in her, but come on, really, you don't, do you? See it?" He shook his head again, but this time, I think he rolled his eyes.

"I'm not disagreeing with you, Dad. I just don't know where Marisa would come up with a story like that. I thought she was lying too, and I was only, like, ten years old then."

"I'll tell you where she got that story from." He pointed a finger at me.

"But she seemed really scared," I interrupted, but he ignored me.

"She got it from her own head—that wild imagination of hers, and she wanted to frighten her little sister, that's all. I don't mean to speak ill of Marisa, especially on the day of her memorial, but she could be a real pain in the ass in that way, and she sucked you right in, Alice."

Marisa was good at pretending, but she had this deep-rooted fear when it came to her relationship with her mother and her non-existent father. "Mom always had to drive that point home, that you were not Marisa's father. I don't know what that all meant Dad."

Before he could answer, Frank's car pulled in the driveway, then Tommy's, as if they orchestrated the timing perfectly. I wanted to get through this memorial service and come home as quickly as possible and curl up in bed. Living this way in constant pain, frustration, and loneliness was just never going away.

We piled into the blue Plymouth—Frank, Scotty, Dad, me— and headed over to Dad's girlfriend Kiki's house. She lived in a little pink ranch on a little hill with a yellow Ford parked in the little drive-way. Her platinum blond hair in the shape of an upside-down bowl nearly matched her white jacket with the small white out-of-season rabbit fur collar. Her yellowish-white dress matched her shoes and pocketbook. It was a cheerful ensemble for a funeral. She looked like a middle-aged woman getting married for the third time on a cold day instead. But compared to the four of us in dark blue, black, gray, and Frank in brown, it was fresh and light and happy, and I had an idea that Marisa would have probably liked it. Marisa loved rabbit fur, and she liked Kiki, even though she didn't see her that much and didn't know her very well. It was a nice outfit. It was really nice, and it reminded me of something.

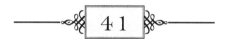

41

I couldn't remember when Marisa and I found out about the sudden death of Crescent Hills High School graduate of 1977, Laurie Schulman. She was a year older than Marisa, and for the entire time we lived in Crescent Hills, Laurie and her family lived all the way down the street in the cul-de-sac from the house where Marisa was murdered. Laurie's family, unlike ours, was very happy, solid, disciplined, religious, and about as perfect as a family could get. Her father was a well-known businessman in the area, and her mother taught first grade at the Rothschild Jewish Academy in Crescent Hills for early education. They kept strictly kosher and had a dishwasher in their dining room.

The year before she died, Marisa said to me, "Hey, did you hear about Laurie Schulman? She died in a car accident."

"What?" I couldn't believe it.

"No, I'm just kidding. She knocked herself unconscious during a softball game when she ran into a softball thrown directly at her head. She had to be rushed to the hospital. Serves her right, the little self-righteous snob."

"Marisa, how can you kid around about something like that?" I was stunned. "That's not funny at all! You shouldn't joke around about people dying. And you shouldn't joke about people getting injured. What is wrong with you?"

She plopped her butt down on the bed and looked at me as if I had the problem. "Oh, Alice, you are so damned serious all the time! You gotta cut it out, or else you are *never* gonna get a boyfriend."

"I don't think it's funny," I said as I continued to fold T-shirts.

"Just listen." She sat up and tucked her thin legs under her. "The third base coach told her to stay exactly where she was and not try to score, but what does she do? Try to score for her team, and she gets lobbed right in the noggin. Might have knocked a little sense into her."

"Is she going to be okay?" I stopped what I was doing and turned around.

"Who cares," she mumbled. "But no, really, I heard the doctor told her she was lucky she didn't have a fracture in her skull."

"Are you fibbing, Marisa?"

"No!" She shook her head, and it went on that way: Laurie's hard head and her perfect figure.

The Schulmans. They were very smart people. They valued a good higher education. It was very important to them. Getting good grades was a definite goal in their household. Laurie's parents were strict, but their family unit was good and tight and cohesive and structured and loving. Everyone around here was that way except for us. We, the Ionescu-Buchner-Withers, Catholic-Jewish-Catholic all mixed up clan? We were loose.

It was a year later after the softball incident when it happened. Laurie Ann Schulman graduated from Crescent Hills High School, summa cum laude. It was typical for someone like Laurie to graduate with highest honors; it was expected of her. Laurie was like a rock made of pink cashmere. No matter how many people where behind her rolling her up a hill, she really didn't need the help, but she was grateful for the support, and that showed in her radiant smile. Laurie had a beautiful smile. If I were to graduate from high school with honors as I had hoped and expected that I would, the experience would most likely be far less celebratory. But with Laurie, it was ceremonious.

She decided to take one year before college and spend it in France. Apparently, her parents weren't too happy with that. They wanted her to go directly to college. She hadn't even been in Paris a month when she and some friends planned a picnic. As they drove down a busy street, Laurie apparently spotted the park where she wanted to stop. Her friend parked the car, and Laurie quickly exited her friend's parked car and, without noticing, crossed behind the car and directly into the path of an oncoming tour bus. She was thrown in the air over thirty feet and run over by another car, which the driver was trying to stop. She was killed instantly.

The shock of Laurie Schulman's death was numbing from my throat all the way into my stomach. I didn't even feel as though I had a core left. I knew that people died—just not like this. A brilliant eighteen-year-old girl with so much promise, full of endless hope, and with the most beautiful smile that one of her friends labeled it five hundred watt. She was loved so deeply by so many people, and now she was just dead? Hit by a car in France? How do these things happen? But she was so bright. Didn't she look before she crossed the street? Why didn't she *look?* Her friends yelled for her to stop, but it was too late.

My mother told us that Laurie Schulman's body would be delivered back to the United States in a pine box for "pronto burial" and that I should know this since I was smart and "half-Jew." Laurie was "d-e-a-d," so there was no point in crying over spilled milk. I remember whispering to Marisa that this had been some sort of prophecy that she had predicted.

"Did you know that?" I reminded her one night in a darkened room. My lips did not feel the words as they formed Laurie Schulman on them. Suddenly I had become very spooked by her name.

"I could never do something like that!" she hissed back. "No! No, I don't remember doing that. Alice, you are as whirly as a bird. Just shut up and leave me alone!"

She didn't remember or she was pretending not to remember, but I did. Marisa's memory was spotty and tentative; she was creative and flighty. She never concentrated well, and in many ways, that's why I found her so magnificent.

While Mom was upstairs dressing Helena and explaining to the child what a memorial service was and what would be happening at the synagogue, Marisa was sitting all the way downstairs on a love seat in front of the massive fireplace in the family room. She was absolutely distraught over the death of a neighbor and an acquaintance from school. I noticed her outfit right away. She wore a white frilly blouse, something that a man might wear during the sixteenth century. Around her neck lay large white plastic beads separated by a couple of gold plastic ones in no particular order. I remember when she found them at a thrift store. She wore light purple wide wale corduroys and bright white ankle boots that she bought on a school trip to New York City. My mother's old white rabbit fur jacket was slung over the back of the love seat, and her thick long auburn hair cascaded over her shoulders in rich natural waves. I always envied my sister's flare. I couldn't put a stylish outfit together if my life depended on it, regardless of her constant nagging and input. I always looked like a cow.

I was so shocked over Laurie's sudden death that I couldn't even find tears to shed at that moment. The only thing I could do was try to remember everything I could about her. I thought so hard that I became frightened, and I actually thought for a minute that she could be haunting me. I doubted she even knew much more than my first name. But Marisa was different and I was worried about her. She cried so hard that all her blue mascara was gone. I wasn't sure what troubled her so much. She really didn't know Laurie that well, but because she was so clearly upset, you would have thought they were the best of friends.

"All right, Marisa, that's enough!" My mother whisked by on her way to the kitchen, her butt jiggling under her silky mustard-colored dress. Suddenly, that same feeling I had when we went on that ski trip to Northrington crept over me like a slow all-consuming fire. I wanted to reach out and slap that jiggly ass so hard, it would send a jolt to her heart. If there was even a heart in there on that day.

"Why do these things happen?" Marisa asked quietly, her elbows resting on her thighs, head down between her legs.

"Because they just do!" my mother shouted from another room. "That's life, my dear! When your number's up, your number's up. There's no point crying over it. You can beg and pray and cry all you want, and it's not going to bring her back. She's gone. That's it."

* * * * *

We saw the Schulman family in a room off to the right of the temple's sanctuary. Mrs. Schulman seemed to be holding up much better than Marisa was, and when she saw my sister, she immediately went to her and began stroking her anguished face. She said a few inaudible words to which Marisa nodded to and gave her some tissue to tuck away and wipe her tears.

The service was so shocking—such a horrid intrusion into regular life we seemed to all take for granted. Laurie's sisters sat directly in front of the rabbi, their arms over each other's shoulders. Two girls in front of us sobbed and sporadically embraced. A little cousin read some of the stories that Laurie had written about France and the French. I had no idea of her fondness for France. Why would I? She wrote in French about its history, its beauty, its life, its fight. And it was all in beautiful prose. She wrote so beautifully, just like Marisa wrote. The Schulmans had two daughters now. They had lost their youngest daughter, who was an obvious beam of light to them and to so many others. Marisa was right. How could God be so cruel? Then I had a thought—maybe he needed a special angel to help him in heaven, and if anyone was up to the task, it was Laurie Ann Schulman.

Marisa was inconsolable, much like everyone else at the service. My mother kept nudging her and whispering for her to go to the restroom and clean her face, but those pews were so packed full of mourners that even if someone had screamed fire, it would have been difficult to escape. Marisa just sat and cried and cried, like most friends, neighbors, and family who were tormented by this sudden tragedy—the sudden death of a young girl who should have still been alive.

When the service ended, people slowly flooded out of the synagogue and onto the sidewalks with little energy into the overcast afternoon and to the reality of men working construction across the street. Marisa looked as though she had cried every tear she had; her ashen face blended with the sky as she gazed off into nothing.

I tried to feebly lift her spirits. "You look so pretty, Marisa."

As she turned to me, my mother said, "Those boys back there. They were laughing. At you. One of them looked at your outfit, shook his head, and rolled his eyes. You're very dolled up. It's a bit much."

Marisa scanned the crowd as if she were looking for the culprits, but only briefly. It was like she had been distracted by something else. Her green eyes darkened, and I remembered that familiar look. It was the look of shock and withdrawal. It was as if she heard my mother, had listened to her comments, but remained silent, like it washed her many times over again. Time after time like a familiar old dance.

I felt my sister's sadness, and there were times I pondered how much of this sadness a person could carry. But then I looked at Marisa, and what I usually saw was immeasurable beauty in a tiny package and a strength that no one else could possibly possess.

42

As I thought about Marisa and her beautiful and flamboyant outfit the day of Laurie Schulman's memorial service, I tried not to stare at Kiki's white rabbit fur collar she wore in early summer. I noticed that it did have streaks of light reddish brown in it that made it look so alive. Marisa would have loved this jacket, and it made my mind whirl faster and faster.

The five of us walked toward the church on the tree-lined boulevard. As we made our way down a slight incline, I began to notice that the church seemed to be moving farther and farther away, and I wanted to be there less than I had thought. Kiki reached over and put an arm around my shoulder, and I breathed in the warmth of her scent. We were silent. I noticed my father, Frank, and Scotty, who looked so handsome in his gray suit. For a tiny window of time, I felt the comfortable cushion of family.

Dad and I had no idea of what would be happening at Marisa's service, and Bunica had been left out of the planning too. She was devastated. We didn't know who was speaking. The obituary didn't even contain any of our names as her survivors. All we knew was where it would be and what time, and so we just showed up. But it wasn't about any of us; it was about Marisa, and Marisa deserved so much more than she was given. So many had been devastated by the sudden and tragic death of Laurie Schulman, yet there would be such a celebration of her life. Had Laurie lived, I believe she would have been content and accomplished, but Marisa would have ultimately had that legendary strength. She had been through so much.

My mother and little Helena sat in the front row of the church. When Helena spotted me, her eyes became wide, and she bounced, her smile beaming. She pointed at me. "Ah! Sissy!"

I was amazed she even knew who I was. I avoided her because I didn't want to become attached. The little girl was like a cherub—that little kid Marisa loved so dearly. She always wanted to spend as much time with her as possible, but the killer did everything he could to keep the two of them apart. He took Helena to the Schuesters' home in Northrington, to the beach in the Bahamas, Morocco, Spain, on and on, away and away. Helena probably would never have memories of the older sister who doted on her, sang to her, rocked her to sleep, and strapped her into her stroller and took her on mile-long walks in the spring. She looked so much like Marisa, I had to turn away. I fought to not get any more attached to her than I already was, and yet I really wasn't. Her father had put his hands on my sister's neck. Helena was a Withers and the spawn of a killer. It didn't matter to me that it wasn't her choice, that she was an innocent little girl caught in the middle of this nightmare, and the only thing she wanted to do was love me. I didn't want any more sisters. I had no love to give back to her.

My mother looked over at us briefly as we were seated. Her glance was quick and threw huge darts poisoned with helplessness and fright. For a moment in time, I felt sorry for her. She looked lonely and small as she sat between her friend, roommate, and real estate agent and some man I didn't recognize.

I shook people's hands, so many hands because I felt like I was supposed to, but I wouldn't look at anyone's eyes, and I had no interest in conversing with anyone, not even the people I came with. I would just say "thank you" a couple of times, and that would have to be enough. My grandmother set a beautiful large framed photograph of Marisa's most recent school portrait near the ornate altar. She sat between Frank and me and reached over and took my hands in hers. Something made me feel the need to turn around and look toward the back of the church. There were so many of Marisa's friends, teachers, and neighbors in attendance. Mark was there with his family, and then I saw him—my grandfather.

I was amazed yet furious with the fresh new tears that sprung upon my cheeks. I wished it would all stop spinning, that it would all end. But there he was, my grandfather, standing in the back of the church in a doorway for easy escape. He had not been in a church for thirty years until today. He wouldn't do it for his daughter, but he would for his granddaughter.

Detectives Holloway and Archer were to Bunic's left, and then there stood DDA Giles looking down at his folded hands. I was shocked they were there.

The priest said some lovely words about my sister along with the usual scripture. But what I remembered most was when he remarked on the heinousness of the crime and how he could only pray that justice would be served on earth before it would be served for all eternity by the Lord, our Maker, which, of course, was in his hands and that we must believe and have faith. It was the first time since Marisa's murder that I heard another person express my own inner convictions. Sort of.

As people slowly made their way toward the exits of the church, each trying to avoid each other as if they were passengers on a train, I found myself knelt in front of Marisa's photograph. I saw a glimpse of my grandmother's shoes, and I heard Scotty speaking low. I caught a whiff of my mother's perfume somewhere off in the distance and wondered why she wore perfume to her daughter's memorial service. I let my fingertips touch the glass that held the image of my sister's face. "Oh!" I jerked back and felt myself smile back at her for an instant. Then I whispered back to the image, "I'm so sorry that I left you behind. I'm so sorry that I ran. I'm sorry, Marisa. I'm so sorry." I didn't think anyone heard me.

"Come on, doll." Kiki helped me up as if I were an old lady and ushered me out a side door. We walked down an incline and then on the gravel path that led to the day school. "There has got to be a ladies' room around here somewhere." She pulled the handle on the glass door, and it opened with one smooth whoosh. "Thank you, Jesus!"

"I'm sure there was one in the church," I said.

"Yes, dear, but we didn't want to linger in there, did we?" She put her hands on my shoulders.

It didn't look like there was anyone in the building. Then I noticed a custodian at the end of the hallway mopping the large tiled terrazzo floor. He nodded at us and continued to work. The place smelled like an empty hot elementary school—paints, crayons, sticky paste.

"I don't have to go to the bathroom, Kiki, do you?" I looked back at the door.

"Oh, Lord, you are a man of miracles. Sorry, Alice, but here," she whispered as she saw a water fountain with a dispenser of cone-shaped white cups. She opened her pocketbook and pulled out a prescription bottle, then took out a tiny pill and gave one to me. "Here, baby." She shoved the pill in my mouth and filled the cone cup with water. "This will help you relax. They are wonderful. I'll have one with you."

I swallowed the pill with the water. "What is it?"

"It's just a little sedative-like thing. Perfectly harmless, don't worry. But it will help you feel much better, I promise, and you won't cry so much."

"That's good," I answered quietly. "I'm tired of crying."

"I'm sure you are. But listen closely now." She pointed a perfect red nail at me. "Don't say *anything* to your dad about this, and for god sakes, whatever you do, don't tell your mother."

I shrugged. "I won't."

We headed back toward the door, and then Kiki stopped again and turned around. "Oh! And after you have taken this, do *not* sneak into the booze. Rudy would be so pissed off at me if you OD'd. Got it?"

Sneak? She caught me. I felt my face burning, and I'm sure she could see it.

"Yes, baby, the gin is mine. Your dad prefers vodka. I'm the gin girl."

"I'm sorry."

"It's okay." She smoothed out the empty space in front of her with one long gesture. She was also shaking her head from side to side, so I knew that it was anything *but* okay. "Just remember what I said, capisce?"

I nodded, and she looked at me like I was a pitiful dog and threw her arms around me. We stood in the hallway for a little while, letting the pill take its effect, which didn't take long.

"That poor child. That poor little Marisa. Oh god. We better get back."

We both started walking back up toward the church, and then I noticed her.

"Who is that woman walking toward us?" Kiki murmured. "I just heard her say your name."

I stopped dead. The clouds had parted and scattered, and the sun poked its head down into the sky. Danny had grown so much since the last time I had seen him—since my mother had married that monster. That fateful wedding day.

"Hi, Alice! Hi!" He grinned broadly and waved as if there had never been a terrible thing in the world. It was easy to smile back at him, but as soon as I did, my face snapped back.

Kiki turned and looked at me and then at Mary Jo Withers McLaughlin.

"Alice!" Mary Jo said. "You have grown so. You look—Alice, oh my dear, I am so sorry. I am so, so sorry. Honey, are you all right?"

"Alice? Is everything okay?" Kiki asked, looking first at Mary Jo's extended hand.

Danny ran back up the hill.

"Danny, don't go too far."

He stopped and turned around.

It felt like we stood there for hours, but it was only seconds. The three of us were completely still. Paralyzed in our own space. I could feel the commotion of people still leaving and gathering around the front of the church. There were faint sounds of voices traveling toward us with the light breeze, piercing the eternity that surrounded us.

I noticed Detective Holloway watching from the top of the incline while Mary Jo said, "I've been trying to get in touch with you. I've been—I would like to see you."

"Alice, please tell me what's going on? Who is this woman?" Kiki put her arm around me, but I wiggled away.

I walked closer to Mary Jo. I must have been closer than I thought because she actually stepped back. "Did you know that your big brother will be spending the rest of his life in prison because he is a cold-blooded murderer?"

"Oh god," Kiki said.

Mary Jo's eyebrows collapsed inward, and she bit her lower lip. Tears filled her eyes like little pools. I had never made an adult cry before. "I—I'm so sorry. Danny—"

"Your brother broke my sister's neck. That's what the cops say. I saw the whole thing—the whole fucking thing. She suffered and died. Aren't you proud of your brother?"

I didn't wait for her response as Kiki pulled me away from Mary Jo and practically dragged me up the gravel hill nearly as quickly as we descended it. She was strong as I tried to get away, but I couldn't.

"Goddamned dope. Went right to your head."

"What?"

"Don't look back there, Alice."

I loved that hate-filled thrill that warmly tingled through me. I would squash each Withers one by one until there was nothing left. At some point, we passed Danny. My head was down. He called out to me.

"Bye, Alice! Bye-bye! I love you!"

43

In August 1978, the monster pleaded guilty to voluntary manslaughter that carried a sentence of eight to twenty-five years in prison. DDA Giles told us that with "good behavior," he could be out in twelve years. Giles also informed us that there was an overcrowding problem in the Department of Corrections, and since Barton Withers had not been convicted of actual murder, he could possibly be granted an early release after eight to twelve years.

The mitigating circumstances the district attorney's office wanted to nail him with all tumbled by the wayside. My testimony could not be used. It didn't even come in that I was an eyewitness to Marisa's murder. Supposedly, I had seen things that never happened. Never happened—blood and water spewing from the wall where Barton Withers had thrown my sister's entire body up against; Pinkie, Mrs. Goldstein's cat, walking into my room and under the bed, offering me solace and comfort as I lay terrified, knowing what this monster had done and wondering when he would strike next. I would go to my grave knowing what I saw, but that didn't help the case against Barton Withers. Denying all this made me feel like I was lying—and I wasn't. I know what I saw, but it looked as if none of that mattered.

Big Barton and Sunny hired a team of defense attorneys that made the DA's office look like confused ants scurrying up and down a sidewalk. She was murdered, and he murdered her. It was so obvious. Marisa could not rest because Barton Withers told the most fantastic stories and lies about her. He said she was a "terribly unruly teenager who had pushed him to the point of insanity." He claimed he "just snapped" and that he never meant to kill her and that it was a "terrible, tragic, accident." He was not only a murderer, he was a

238

liar. I remember the malice on his face that day. It was *he* who pushed Marisa, figuratively, literally, and it was no accident. He had also been drinking that morning, I smelled the alcohol on his breath, but no one ever bothered to run a blood test or made him pee in a cup or whatever the police were supposed to do.

That was one of the things that ended up getting Detective Holloway thrown off the case. He was angry, he was upset, and I'm sure he cried about it. Giles had a very expressive face, and I could hear the emotion in his voice when he explained it to my father. I was eavesdropping. Dad knew he screwed something up. Investigators Holloway and Archer never conducted blood, alcohol, and drug tests on Barton Withers, among other things.

I didn't take a lot of time to think about Detective Holloway, his mistakes, or his career. I was just a kid who was home sick from school with a possible fever, which was another thing they attributed to the bullshit *hallucinations*.

"She watched her sister die and started to hallucinate."

They made damn sure they did a toxicology screen on me. Just not on the killer. My testimony was worth nothing.

Barton Withers's plea arrangement was all over the local news media and in the morning paper. Newspapers mysteriously disappeared from the house, the counter at the store next to the lobster tank, from Bunica's kitchen, but my father was busy, and he didn't have time to babysit me. Kiki had her own life too, putting a new roof on her house. And she was getting ready to be promoted to manager of the makeup counter at Sterns Department Store at the new boulevard mall not far from the church where we attended Marisa's memorial service.

I didn't like to read newspapers anyway. They always left that black print on my fingers that felt dirty and transferred on to everything else, so I usually waited until everyone else was asleep, and I switched on the eleven o'clock news. I knew every detail of Mario Santaro's ugly face. He was the lead attorney who defended my sister's murderer and the obvious spokesperson for Barton Withers and his broken parents. They stood behind Santaro like the pathetic characters that they were. The performance Big Barton and Sunny attempted to entertain Maidenhead county with was worthy of an award. Words and phrases like *accident, passionate crimes, teenagers these days,* and *drug culture* were thrown around like garbage on city streets. Santaro appeared supremely confident in his supportive sources, one of which I believed was probably my mother. He also conceded that he felt the sentence was "unfortunate but entirely fair." Marisa was made to look like a spoiled, privileged teenage girl who used drugs and drank alcohol, had sex with boys, and mouthed off one last time to a pressured, vulnerable man who did absolutely everything he possibly could to provide "his children" with "the best of everything in life" and that it was a "horrible, tragic, unfortunate accident." Lies, lies, lies.

Even so, Barton Withers would be spending twenty-three hours a day in a cell at Bellmorrow Correctional Center. He also divorced my mother.

I kissed the velvet pouch that contained the plastic bag of Marisa's ashes each night before I curled up with Shelly and stared into the darkness for hours. I took out the card that Detective Holloway gave my father with the psychiatrist Dr. Kilburn's name on it and twirled it around in my fingers before carefully placing it back in my top dresser drawer.

Time. Time was a staple of life that I didn't have that much experience with. I had always been good with numbers, but numbers had little to do with time.

When I first heard that Barton Withers could possibly be in prison for eight to twenty-five years, I was instantly elated. I thought about the minimum eight years. Eight years before, I had been six years old and in the first grade. Marisa was alive and just a little girl as well. My parents were still married. Eight years was so very long ago, and so very much had happened in that eight years. This was all very new for me, and at first, I enjoyed exploring this new thing called time, but that was only at first. Fifteen years. That would be a little over the time that Barton Withers could possibly be paroled if he didn't qualify for any type of early release that DDA Giles had been concerned about after those first eight years. Fifteen years? Fifteen years was one more year than I had lived, and my life had already felt like an eternity. Twenty-five years. I could not even picture that in my mind's eye. Ten years was a decade, and now we were talking about decades.

And my father? "Are you fucking kidding me?"

Frank: "Eight t' twenny-figh? *Eight t' twenny-figh?*"

Kiki: "That son of a bitch."

Bunic to Bunica: Silence.

Bunica to Bunic: "Radu, Bellmorrow is a maximum-security prison. One of the worst."

In a conversation my father and I had when I was a little kid, a time that seemed so long ago, my father reminded me that I should seize this very moment and be grateful that I was young. He told me, finger in face, that when I got to be an adult, it was all downhill and that the time would fly by so fast, I wouldn't realize where it went. He said that the older a person gets, the quicker time passes, and he felt like he was pulling the trash down to the curb every day.

At the age of fourteen, my life had *apparently* not begun yet. Life was supposedly too short. Lately, I didn't think that life was short enough until I thought of Marisa. In twenty-five years, Barton Withers would have been about Bunic's age. Bunic was healthy, ran his stand on Bean Street, and was free. If I looked at my grandfather, I really didn't see an old man, except for the grayish black naturally curly hair that showed he'd never be bald. Barton Withers would most likely not die in prison. He would not spend *the rest of his life* behind prison walls for murder, as was the original plan and my hope. Barton Withers could be out walking the streets again, a free man, spending his parents' money, after murdering my sister.

As I sat on my bed in the dark, I thought maybe, just maybe, I understood this dilemma, and I would have to figure out a way to not let that happen. I had time. I had to go back to school. I didn't want to go back to school, but I needed a distraction, even if it was mundane. But if what Dad said is true, wouldn't the monster's life just fly by?

"No, Allie. Because he'll be living a rotten existence every day. So rotten that I'm not even going to get into that with you."

That's right. I'm a minor.

241

"Maybe I'll have to repeat the ninth grade," I mentioned to Dad as we were going over the matriculation papers for South Wellton, the institution of fine education where I started and I would be finishing.

His shoulders bounced as he chuckled. "No way, Allie. I talked to your new guidance counselor. You have been a straight-A student all along. You probably could have even skipped a grade somewhere along the line."

"Not so much in my art and creative writing classes. That's where Marisa had always excelled." I began to get that nostalgic depressed feeling again. "I had a terrible time with short stories—couldn't string two sentences together."

"Well," he paused as he read something in silence for a few seconds, "it's a good thing they don't give a shit about any of that. You're in good shape. All set to go the day after Labor Day." He shuffled some papers around, put a paper clip on them, shoved them in an envelope in the desk drawer in the library, and went off to the store.

I stood on the back patio smoking a menthol cigarette. I wished I could find a job and quickly so that I could buy my own smokes, liquor, and pills. That wasn't going to happen. I knew I would have to draft someone of age to do my shopping for me. The trouble was that I had no friends. I preferred it that way, but when it came time to depend on others to get what I needed, it became a problem. I quickly tallied the people in my head, my supposed friends and contacts. It was pitiful.

Aubrey Meslier: Not of age either, useless, clingy, would probably tattle on me like two elementary schoolgirls on a playground.

Dad: I was already stealing his cigarettes and his booze; that was most likely the extent of his usefulness.

Kiki: Same. Her usefulness ended with my stealing her pills and her gin. She was good for something.

Frank: Dad's employee and best friend, nothing there.

Scotty? Way too loyal to my father, took classes at night, didn't drink.

Bunic and Bunica: What was I thinking? Although Bunic liked beer and vodka. Might be a secret prospect.

Then I felt a slight jar that caused me to look to the sky. I missed my sister so much. I found myself pacing back and forth on the patio slowly, back and forth. Things came into my mind that I hadn't thought about in what felt like years, like my old friend Bruce, who, with his parents and two cats, disappeared into the night, never looking back. I never saw him again. I wondered if he had heard about Marisa. Probably not—not if he was far away from Wellton.

The morning sun continued to climb higher and higher into the sky, the bright blazing yellow ball burning its way through the hot and helpless Wellton air, stretching over the rooftops with authority, owning the earth. A sharp shadow was cast over the purple-and-gray slate patio lined with old pressure-treated wood.

I stubbed out my cigarette in my father's overflowing outdoor ashtray, then, shaking my head, fetched a cardboard box to empty out the cigarette butts and disposed of everything in the metal trash container.

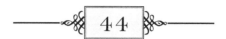

44

Marisa had a name for Mark the boyfriend's penis. I was so shocked that the first time she told me this, I was numb. I could not stop staring into space. *She did do it with him.* I could not believe that my sister had actually seen a man's thing. Our babysitter Nina at the Stanhope had a magazine filled with naked men, but that was the extent of our debauchery, or so I had thought. Marisa had denied it vehemently, but something told me she wasn't being completely truthful with my mother when she came home from school acting tense and angry. Vengeful, it seemed.

Marisa was friends with a girl named Marlene Cavendish, who was a very smart girl from a good family. I never understood why Marisa and Marlene were friends in the first place. They had nothing in common. They always seemed to be bickering over something or arguing with each other over the phone, gossiping about each other, and giving each other the silent treatment. Although they liked to go to the movies and the mall together and hang around the hall-ways in school before the morning bell, they were very different girls. Marlene was a tall girl who was involved in after-school programs and clubs and was very book smart. Marisa was a tiny porcelain doll who loved to draw and chase boys. Their friendship was deteriorating long before Marlene's twin sister, Elaine, came onto the picture.

Elaine tried very hard with the mounds of blond permed hair, lots of colorful makeup, and what looked like socks skillfully stuffed into her bra. Elaine never liked Marisa for two possible reasons: One, Marlene was probably complaining at home about Marisa equally as much as Marisa was complaining about Marlene. The Cavendishes were yet another tightly knit, incomprehensibly close family unit, and Elaine and Marlene were very protective of one another. And two, Elaine was jealous of Marisa's natural beauty. They were in the same fine art programs, and Elaine played clarinet very well. Elaine also seemed to spend large amounts of time in the girls' restroom fixing her hair and face in the mirror. Marisa never had to bother with any of that, and it was a very well-known fact that Elaine had an unrequited crush on Mark the boyfriend. Marisa would soon be at war with the Cavendish women, and it would be bloody.

Marisa claimed that Elaine accused Marisa of naming this male body part and blabbed it to everyone and anyone who would listen. She also wrote it on the ladies' room stall in her signature calligraphy that she was known for being so good at: Marisa loves Herbie. Herbie was the name. It was *the* name that Mark the boyfriend and Marisa supposedly named his penis. Why would anyone name a body part? Especially a private and disgusting one for all the world to know about? And how did Elaine know about it?

"That slutty little bitch!" Marisa said quietly as she slammed her schoolbooks down on the kitchen table.

I instantly cringed and shoved a finger in each ear. My mother was about twenty feet away, and she heard Marisa's language and the tone that accompanied it. A fury of anger would have imploded within her. "What is the matter?" She approached us carrying a white linen tablecloth.

"Elaine Cavendish. *That's* what's the matter."

Oh god.

My mother put the tablecloth down, burped, and picked up a glass of water. "Marlene's twin? That strange girl? What did she do?"

Marisa was spun into a frenzy. I wished she hadn't talked to my mother about this whole *Herb* or Herbie thing. The two of us could have gone somewhere else to talk about this. We could have worked it out without my mother's involvement, but it was too late for any of that now. The whole problem was out in the open. "It's just something he says the guys go on and on about in the locker room after baseball."

I knew she was lying. I didn't know if my mother picked up on it, but I suspected she had. And if she did, she didn't seem to care because she appeared to have other things on her mind. I could see just by watching that she was thinking through something far beyond Marisa's explanation.

"They were laughing, Mom! Everyone!" I heard Marisa say as I looked away from my mother before she caught my eye. Marisa was vehement, but she could get that way even when she was lying. "He told me this in confidence. One of the other boys must have said something about it, and she found out."

Marisa didn't look at me.

My mother stood in front of her. It was so quiet, surprisingly quiet for several seconds, an eternity. I looked through the giant picture window. Two birds tweeted and flew past the huge maple tree and off into the afternoon sun. I wanted to be among them, fluttering through the breeze. It must have been so much easier being among the wild, with nature.

Marisa popped into my thoughts, and I came crashing down out of the sky. She had this ugly sideways smile on her face. Her deep green eyes lost their shine as she gazed off in the distance.

"I know *exactly* what I would tell everyone about Elaine Cavendish if I was the gossiping type. We should all buy her more penicillin for her venereal disease," Marisa said.

At first I thought my eyes would fall out. I watched my mother carefully. My head stayed slightly down toward the table. "I don't know if—"

"Shut up, Alice!" My mother's eyes were so wide. A smile slowly crept across her face like a bright red snake. "Elaine Cavendish has a *venereal disease?*"

Marisa cocked her head to one side. It was like two people losing themselves to some sinister and invisible being that stalked the earth, stealing people's last drop of goodness and replacing it with something else. Something very bad. They looked normal on the outside, but really, they were dark and horrible. I didn't want to hear it. I didn't want to watch, but I found that I too was one of them, and I couldn't help myself.

"That was the rumor," my sister said, "a couple of years ago. Her boyfriend at the time, Jeffrey Salazar, Salisario, something like that gave it to her. Everybody's heard the rumor. She's always by herself in the hallway. She's really weird, and no one wants to be around her." She let out a wicked laugh. There was this incredible rumor out there.

My mother walked over to the olive-green phone that hung on the kitchen wall and picked it up. "Come over here, Marisa. You are going to call Ms. Elaine Cavendish, and you are going to tell her exactly that. You are going to tell her that you are going to tell everyone that she has a venereal disease."

Marisa's face broke into a wide grin. "Really? I can call her and tell her that?"

My mother's jaw was firm and square as she nodded deeply. "If Elaine Cavendish can embarrass you, *you* can embarrass her. Twice as much."

Marisa leapt from her chair toward the phone. Helena was in her little seat looking at some talk show on the little color TV. She didn't understand the ruins that were accumulating in the kitchen, but I still tried to make sure she was distracted as much as possible. No matter how young she was, I still didn't think it was a great idea for her to be hearing about penises and teenage venereal diseases. Thanks to her parents, she had already heard some really rotten words. Barton Withers seemed to have a problem with Jewish people and used two words thrown together an awful lot: "fucking Jew." I guess no one reminded him that I was half Jewish. I didn't, and so I supposed I was equally to blame. The problem was if I said anything to my mother or Marisa about their bad language or behavior, my mother would have lost control, and all of us would have paid for it. I didn't want that for Helena either.

And there I was, nursing this large part of me that wanted to watch this whole thing unfold. What was it that people call that? Watching a train wreck? I was a bad person too. And Elaine Cavendish messed with the wrong people. I could exhale for just a moment though because when Marisa made the call, Elaine wasn't home. She was at her part-time job at the mall. When Marisa tried to reach her at Parfait, a handbag store, Elaine promptly hung up on her.

"She hung up on you? Fine, let's go down there. Alice, bring Helena, we're going to Parfait," my mother ordered.

"Mom, why don't I just stay here with Helena? I've got home-work, and I can watch her." I knew halfway through my feeble excuse that my mother would shoot that down.

"Absolutely not. No one is staying here. You have plenty of time for homework, Alice. Besides, it might do you some good to get you out of your goddamned routine. Let's go."

Parfait happened to be owned by one of our neighbors, Mrs. Martie Adler, who also owned two other luxury handbag stores and a women's clothing store. She had a very nice retired husband, three very nice grown children, and a bunch of grandchildren. They were smart, peaceful, and content, a close family, and I always went out of my way to say hello and chat with them briefly whenever I saw them. I worried that one of them would see me now.

My mother made me sit with Helena on the side of the large fountain in the mall while she stood vigil in between us and the mid-dle of the entrance to Parfait. She looked like a small ragged statue, her back to me and the baby, not moving an inch as Marisa went into the store to confront Elaine Cavendish. My mother did not look like the typical suburban housewife that she so much wanted to embrace. Her freshly washed auburn hair hadn't been styled; instead, she had brushed it out, and it hung like a heavy cloud. She wore a plain beige trench coat, and she had tied the belt in the front. It was tight and made her look as if she had gained weight. She had on tartan track bottoms and blue and brown rubber shoes. She stood as still as a cat, patient and waiting to pounce on an unsuspecting mouse. People noticed the ominous fixture in the middle of the floor and steered as clear away as they could.

I took a penny out of my pocket, closed my eyes, and threw it into the shallow water as I made a wish. My wish was that Elaine Cavendish had left the store for a break and that I could somehow be redeemed, but when I noticed mounds of blond permed hair by the register, I knew that my penny had been wasted. I looked at Helena and then at Marisa. My mother was still stationed like a military policeman at a border crossing. As hard as I tried, I could not stop watching and waiting for the impending shoot-out, hoping that my sister would make it out of there alive and unharmed. There was some older woman in her thirties standing behind the desk where the cash register was. Marisa passed her and appeared to have said hello when suddenly, she was on Elaine Cavendish like a surprise attack. From where I sat behind my mother, over the sound of the fountain, I could hear Elaine shout, "Marisa?" For an instant, as she looked at Marisa, her face shook with a mixture of fear and embarrassment, then suddenly she laughed. Marisa said something to her and then walked away. The woman at the register walked closely beside Marisa, pointing a finger at her neck, her face twisted in fury as she said something to her. I heard three words: *ever, out, again.*

I took two more pennies, and I tried as hard as I could to focus all my attention on baby Helena and the rushing monotonous sound of the fountain as my mother and the woman stood nearly nose to nose, my mother throwing her pointed finger at the store's entrance and hissing a diatribe about "that girl" who I presumed was none other than Elaine Cavendish.

Now Helena heard my mother's voice, and she looked over. She wanted my mother.

Yes, everyone, this is her baby. Not mine. Can you believe it? Well, believe it.

I wasn't going to be able to keep this child fascinated with the fountain forever. She watched her mother silently rip another woman to pieces. I could do nothing more but bounce her and talk to her in my singsong voice. "Oh, they're not mad, honeybunch. They're just talking about the store and the paint."

The paint?

"Go ahead! Call Martie, she's my neighbor," my mother chided.

The woman walked over to the clothing store that Mrs. Adler also owned and which happened to be next to Parfait. She waited in front as she scanned the shop for her. She wasn't there, and so my mother motioned for us to follow her, leaving the woman standing there and Elaine Cavendish back inside Parfait with God knows what kind of thoughts running through her head. I got close enough to the woman where I could pick up a weak scent of shampoo or perfume, but I kept my head down until I was safely buried in the back seat of my mother's Chrysler.

The Adlers were such nice people, such decent people. Like our other neighbors who lost their daughter, the Schulmans, the Adlers similarly were very conservative Jews who performed kiddush every Friday night with their family and went to their synagogue every Saturday morning in recognition of the Sabbath. There were quite a few Jewish people in our neighborhood. If Barton Withers didn't like us, why did he buy a house in Crescent Hills where there was a strong Jewish community? The Adler family kept a kosher diet as well, which I was fascinated with, and Mrs. Adler and I talked a lot about this in her driveway. I wasn't exactly sure what it was about the Adlers. I knew Mrs. Adler thought that I was smart, she admired that, but there was something else. I wanted a relationship with this family that was fresh and started out on the right path. We always talked for a while, usually Mrs. Adler and me, and I normally didn't do that with people I wasn't related to or hadn't known my whole life. I wasn't good at that. I wanted her to see my family as nice, friendly, quiet, good neighbors. I wanted her family to see my family as stable and happy. I wanted them to look across the street and know that there was the right family living there. Now it appeared as if the jig was up. Now the Adlers would know the truth about us. About me.

"Marisa"—my mother started the car—"you know—"

"I told her, Mom. I said I was gonna buy her more penicillin for her venereal disease."

The car was running, and the front seat *seemed* far enough away. Helena was preoccupied with a road map sticking out of the back pocket of the driver's seat, so I gave it to her. "Well now, wait a minute," my mother continued. "I'm confused about something. When you told her *venereal disease*, is she—she doesn't have a second venereal disease, does she? And didn't you say this was just a rumor?"

"What?" Marisa quickly looked at my mother.

"Elaine Cavendish. You know, she looked very pretty in a blouse and skirt. You look a little rough with what you're wearing, all that denim. People are probably going to feel sorry for her. They're probably going to think that you bullied her."

I looked at the back of my mother's puffy brushed-out hair. She looked so alive at that moment.

"She was working! She had to wear those clothes! She wears stuff like mine all the time in school! Worse than this!" Marisa said.

I heard that familiar sound again. The sound of defense. The fear and protest was rising in my sister's throat as I watched my mother's bobbing head. The words spilled silently from her mouth as I clenched a fist.

"Mom, you argued with that lady! This was your idea!" Marisa pleaded helplessly.

"Oh no, it was not, dearie. I drove you here, that's all."

Frustrated tears that I had seen too often sprang from Marisa's eyes. We were powerless.

Marisa protested further. "No, I said what I wished I could say to her! You told me to do it!"

My mother jabbed her finger at my sister. Helena was now shying away and pulled the road map up closer to her face, frowning. "Don't you raise your voice to me!"

Marisa tried to reason with her. "I'm not trying to raise my voice, Mom, but when Alice and I were sitting at the table, I—"

"I'm not arguing with you anymore!" my mother shouted as Marisa finally burst into more tears. "Stop crying, you're acting like a baby."

I continued to watch the back of my mother's head. It wouldn't stop moving. If I had something strong and heavy enough, I could hit that head with all my might, the car would flip, and this would all be over. Helena was wearing little white socks and tiny white shoes that were beginning to wear. They had bows on them. I couldn't do it. I couldn't hurt that innocent baby girl. I felt so sorry for her. I would wait until we got home, and I would go sit with Marisa.

* * * * *

I gingerly followed her into the bedroom. "I like what you're wearing."

She huffed quietly and rubbed her eyes.

"You put those studs on your jeans yourself, didn't you?"

She nodded.

I was going to sit down, but I was too afraid. "What do you think is going to happen with you and Marlene?"

She sat down at her desk and looked out the window next to her. It had been a still, quiet twilight. She pulled out one of her many scrapbooks. My mother didn't like her to do her sketching and writing on her bed, so she sat at her desk, looking crowded and uncomfortable. She just shook her head. I could hear her breathing for a few seconds. It was so despondent.

"Marlene hasn't spoken to me in about three weeks now," she said. "She's done."

"Done?" I asked. I should have known what *done* meant, but I asked anyway. She wasn't even annoyed with me.

She turned to look at me, draping one arm over her chair. She was still wearing Mark the boyfriend's faded jean jacket with a big red lips patch sewn on the front pocket. "Marlene has totally given up on me. She doesn't want to be friends anymore. I mean, we had our differences before, but we always seemed to work things out and make up. It's different now. I've tried to talk to her a couple of times, but she just ignores me. She's moved on with her schoolwork and her other friends who are not exactly my friends. She seems happier now to be away from me."

"Marisa, that can't possibly be true."

"No, it is, it's true. I know it is, I can tell. And now with Elaine? It's over, Alice." She turned back to her sketches and resumed her work.

I watched her for a while and finally left her alone. As I closed her door behind me, I walked over to the top of the stairs and waited. I wasn't really waiting for anything. I just stood and listened. Helena was babbling something, the TV was blaring, and then Marisa's light went out. Then I heard my mother on the phone with Mrs. Cavendish, saying that she wanted to "forget about everything." A few minutes later, she came charging toward the stairs. I quickly backed into my bedroom, closed the door, and turned off the light.

"She never acknowledged anything about a venereal disease, Marisa, but then again, I never said anything about it either." My mother's voice had a tinge of glee running through it. "Her daughters don't like you. They say you use terrible language—you swear too much." Then she was gone to another part of her oversized house.

I opened my door a crack. Marisa never responded. She was still in her bedroom with the lights off.

I avoided the Adlers. It was just a matter of time before they figured out that I was a mean and crazy girl and that we were a mean and crazy family. Within the year, Mr. Cavendish's company promoted him to a new job, and he and his family relocated to Belgium. Marlene never spoke to Marisa again. I wondered after Marisa's murder if Marlene had ever heard about the killing of her old friend. I guessed not.

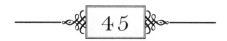

45

I watched my shadow on the slate tiles. Tiny strands of my hair separated in the wind. I thought I heard the phone ring when suddenly it stopped. I opened the back door to the kitchen, and I heard it again. "Hello?"

"Alice?" For heaven's sake, why do you not answer the telephone?"

"Hi, Bunica."

"What's wrong in that house?"

"Nothing, Bunica. I was just out back."

"Oh? Is something wrong with you, Alice? I can hear in your voice."

What could possibly be wrong?

"No, no, no, Bunica, I'm fine. Everything is okay."

"Good, good. Why not come for a visit soon, Alice? I miss seeing you. Maybe you can come for the weekend or next weekend?"

"Sure."

"We haven't seen you in such a very long time, your grandfather and I. Come and visit before you have to go back to school. Spend the night. I will make all of your favorites."

"Sounds good."

"Remember, your grandfather. He would like to see you as well. You can go up to the market with him."

"What on earth—?"

"What's the matter?"

I said nothing.

"Alice. What's happening now?"

It was Scotty. He burst into the kitchen like he was being chased by a dog. His eyes were wild, frightened. "I'm sorry, I—I see you're on the phone."

"What?"

"You hafta come quick. Your dad fell."

I made a loud sound as I sucked in air. I held the telephone several inches away from my ear, but I could still hear my grandmother. "Alice? Alice!"

"I have to go, I'm sorry. Dad fell. I'll call you back, Bunica, promise." And I put the phone down on my grandmother in a way that would have torn me apart at another time.

46

"Don't worry, Allie, I think I broke my arm."

"Don't worry?" My father was lying on his back, legs bent, face contorted into a splattered mess with the fluorescent light beaming above us.

Frank was kneeling next to him. He looked like he was in a lot of pain, but at first, I thought he seemed okay. It wasn't as if he was dying, but still, I felt as if something was pinging through my heart. Then someone mentioned an ambulance, and my father refused.

"Just get me to the hospital! Quicker in the car." It looked like it was hard for him to talk. Then he let out a shriek that horrified me. Frank and Scotty helped him up off the floor. I thought he was going to pass out from pain. I saw Scotty's breathless face just moments ago, and it was something that I had never seen from him and never imagined I would experience. It felt like nighttime in one of those flash rainstorms. The room was so cold and dark even with those artificial bright fluorescent bars above.

I put my hands over my ears. I was afraid I was about to scream. I don't know why Scotty even came to the house to alert me about my father. I was no help to any of them, no help at all.

4 7

I had three dimes in my pocket. As my father was heading into surgery, I decided to call back my grandmother.

"He fell from where?" she asked.

I didn't realize how much worse it could have been until she asked that question. I squeezed my eyes shut and put my finger in my ear. "Oh, Bunica, no. He tripped over a mat he didn't notice. His arm is broken, and they have to operate on it. It was a bad break, but one of the doctors said that he's young and strong, and he'll be fine."

I never thought of my father as young.

My grandmother rattled a few words in Romanian that I wished I could understand then said, "All right, my darling, please tell your father that we are praying for him night and day, and call me very, very soon to let me know how he's faring. You come to visit us, Alice."

"I promise I will, Bunica. I will. Goodbye." Now I had two dimes left. I had no idea where Kiki and Aunt Nancy were, but Scotty said he would find them. I found two business cards in my blue jeans pocket as I was returning my change. I walked away from the payphone and toward the rows of orange plastic chairs all attached to each other. One card was for Dr. Gwynneth Kilburn, the psychiatrist. Why did I take her card out of my drawer and put it in my pocket? I wondered. The other was for Detective Kenneth Holloway. I wasn't going to be using my dimes on either of those numbers.

I circled around the mostly empty waiting room and sat on a semi-detached chair near the window. I hadn't been in a hospital since Marisa died. Apparently, I had spent three days in this very one when I was being treated for severely low blood pressure, shock, and catatonia. I'm surprised they didn't throw in "cat hallucinations" and "seeing nonexistent blood" while they were diagnosing me. I barely remember a thing about it possibly because I was taking medications to sleep.

"How's my favorite girl?" It was Frank, still wearing his apron, carrying two ice-cold cans of soda, one of which he handed to me.

"Thanks." We sat across from each other in the orange plastic chairs. I was relieved when he moved farther away. I didn't want anyone sitting close to me, even Frank. I felt like I smelled bad.

"He gonna be perfectly fine. He gotta bad break, you know. A broken arm? Lor'. But everything gonna be okay."

I wondered for a moment if God was punishing me by hurting my father. I was very rude to Mary Jo McLaughlin and Danny at the memorial service because her brother killed my sister. I put my finger in my ear. "Is there anyone else I should call?"

Frank took a sip of his soda and shook his head. His arms rested on his lap as he leaned toward me. "Naw, I don't think so. Scotty got Kiki comin' down from Stern, and Tommy goin' over to sit wit' Nancy. She in the cellar cleanin' at the time. Didn't hear a thing."

It would have taken a lot more than Dad's broken arm to get Aunt Nancy into this hospital. I wondered what she could be possibly cleaning in that creepy clean cellar this time with her rock music blaring so loud.

"Maybe you shoult call your mom." He looked serious.

"I don't think she would come if Dad broke every bone in his body."

Frank's face broke into a wide grin. He laughed heartily and nodded at me. "Now, there my girl again. See? You gettin' your spirit up again! Ah-ha!"

I manufactured a smile for him as he continued to laugh. My spirit was anything but up, but I didn't want to hurt his feelings by telling him how wrong he was. I was glad that he asked me to hand him the newspaper that lay splattered on the little white table area between the seats. Now I didn't have to talk.

My thoughts turned to Barton Withers rotting away in prison. My mother told me once that the man who shot a politician was living a comfortable life in a cell all by himself with his own television set. That couldn't possibly be true. I thought about asking Frank as he leaned into the sports pages, but then I quickly decided not to. Seeing Frank still in his work clothes made me think of the store and its vast collection of knives. The fat thirteen-inch ones were my favorites—that is, if I was willing to do some real damage to someone like Barton Withers. I would stab him until there was nothing left of him but bones and blood on the ground.

I looked over at Frank again and then caught a glimpse of my reflection in the window. Bunic sold street maps. When I went to visit, I would find out how far Bellmorrow was from Boochie's. It was so stupid. I was so stupid. I knew exactly where it was—all the way up in the mountains. Marisa hated it there. She also hated Northrington. She hated skiing. Marisa was going to the city, New York, Paris, not the great outdoors! She would paint and write poems and be beautiful. But she was dead because of that monster.

How would I get there in the new ten-speed my father bought me for my birthday? My mother always drove it into our skulls the dangers of young girls hitchhiking. Didn't she think about the dangers of holding young girls up by the throat against her freshly papered wall until they died? Blood or no blood. Pulling the skin off Barton Withers like he was a chicken felt easier now than it was when I had the perfect chance. I was too frozen to move for the kitchen that was only about ten feet away and grab something, anything, to kill him with. Those knives.

Bunica once said that God paves a path to opportunity for us, but he only holds the door open for so long. It is up to us to walk through that opening, and it is our responsibility if we decide not to. Guilt and consequences were my concrete tomb. Pain is bad enough, but for some people, all they have to do is take an aspirin, and it subsides for a little while anyway before it comes back, possibly not as bad, but different. Carrying a concrete slab on your shoulders, having to drag it around wherever you go in addition to existing pain makes regular pain seem easy. I would get to him. I had time.

"You must be Alice."

Frank and I both looked up at the tall slim nurse standing in front of us. Under her white and blue cap, her silvery blond hair was pulled back into a shiny bun. She had kind brown eyes, and her teeth were large and white as she smiled down at me.

"My name is Paula. You can visit your dad now if you would like."

I was confused. "I didn't think I was old enough to go into his room."

Nurse Paula bent down a little and gave me a reassuring frown. "If you're under the age of twelve, you've got to stay in the waiting room with an adult." She said *adult* with the emphasis on the *a*. *I* said adult with the emphasis on the *dult*. "But you look like a pretty teenage girl to me."

"Thank you." Another manufactured smile. I followed her to my father's room. Pretty teenage girl. Why did she have to lie?

Paula turned around before we entered the room and lowered her voice. "He's very sleepy, so just a few minutes, okay? I'll leave the two of you alone."

I nodded and saw my father. It was dark outside, and the curtains were already drawn in the small greenish blue room. He was lying on his back, and there was another thin artificial fluorescent light over his head. I wished I could turn it off, but I thought about those artificial lights. There may have been something important about them. I didn't dare turn it off. He was snoring lightly, and his arm was in a heavy plaster cast almost all the way up to his shoulder and elevated in a sling.

Trying not to make too much noise, I dragged a chair over to his side of the bed where his good arm was and sat very close to him. I wanted to stroke his forehead and move a couple of black strands of hair with the smallest trace of gray away from his eyes. I wanted to tell him that I was there and I loved him, and I wanted to touch his good arm and kiss his cheek. I couldn't bring myself to do any of these things though, and so I put my head down next to his sleeping body, and I sobbed.

48

It took my father no time at all to bounce back to good health. Frank was right. As soon as he was awake, he wanted to leave the hospital and immediately get back to work. The doctor told him that he could find any chair he wanted, sit down, and supervise, but under no circumstances was he to do any physical labor for at least two weeks until he had his next examination. I knew the doctor would stretch that out even further and that he was taking baby steps with Dad's mind; otherwise, Dad would have lost that mind. My father wasn't going to be doing one physical thing for months. Not with that arm. He also told Dad not to drink alcohol, and cutting down, maybe even *quitting* cigarettes altogether, would be the best thing for him. He had bottles upon vials of prescription medication, and after seeing how he reacted after taking them, I found it incredible that he wanted to do anything other than stare into the fireplace or out the window. This gave me the idea to skim a couple of them here and there for myself. He wouldn't miss them. He had so many of them.

We began reading a book together on Hasidic Judaism at night, and during the day, he made sure he was at the store open until close to at least "fulfill my supervising duties," he said.

Aunt Nancy scrubbed every inch of the floors in the store and in the house and moved absolutely anything that my father, or anyone, could trip over. She was scared to death that he was no longer capable of watching where he was going and could not put one foot in front of the other.

"What about Scaly, or, um, what's his name, Shelly, Shelly?" she asked me one day.

"What about Shelly?" I looked up from my book, Shelly on my lap.

"Do you think Rudy will trip over the cat?"

"No!" I hollered, moving forward, and Shelly jumped off. "No, Aunt Nancy! Dad will *not* trip over the cat! Shelly is mine, and he stays!" I looked her directly in the eye, and my top lip quivered. She looked frightened and turned away. That was exactly the response I wanted from her. Then I added darkly, "Do you understand me?"

She nodded fast and looked down at Shelly, who was looking directly up at her with his peaceful face and perfectly round green eyes, and she turned and left the room. She never brought it up again.

By looking at my father's plaster cast, it looked like there had been hundreds of customers and friends who signed it. By the time he was ready for his first checkup to have his cast changed, his arm was a mirage of signatures, well-wishes, little proverbs, and drawings, all in colorful magic marker. Kiki bought some fruity-smelling ones so that people could choose from strawberry to blueberry to peach, all to match their color choices. My grandparents continued to insist that they see me on a regular basis, and so my father, against everyone's advice, drove me over there on Friday afternoon for a weekend visit. I promised my grandmother that I would spend the weekend with her and Bunic, and she could cook all my favorites for me, as if I needed to get any fatter than I already was. It was the last thing I wanted to do.

I did not want to leave my father. Although I would never tell him my thoughts, I had this nagging fear that if I left him this time, even for one night, I would never see him again. At first, I refused to go, but he wouldn't listen to my objections and made me pack enough clothing for two nights. He told me I needed to get out more, see my grandparents, my mother, and Helena. I hadn't seen much of any of them since Marisa was murdered, and the only bedroom I wanted to sleep in was my own. I had no desire to be anywhere else.

It felt like it did when my mother moved us out the first time. My father claimed that he didn't need me to take care of him, and he was insistent if not excited about my spending the weekend with my grandparents. He would be back on Sunday, and he and Shelly would be perfectly fine. He gave me his word. I was stuck. I had no choice, the minor child that I was. I wanted to be an old lady, someone who had already been through the whole life thing, was independent, and didn't care anymore. It was depressing and confusing.

The store got a little bit too lively for me on the Friday morning I was about to leave for my mandatory scheduled visit. Everyone wanted to sign my father's cast. Was there even room on that thing? Customers wanted to talk about the fall, the break, the hospital, the doctor, this, that as he sat on the stool in front of the lobster tank by the telephone and unraveled the story. The fruity-smelling magic markers were a big hit.

I slipped out the back door, up to the house, and up to my bedroom. People were so happy, talking normal, telling stories, smiling, laughing too much. It wasn't right. Marisa was still dead, and a lot of these people knew her. Not all of them were even at the service for her. I didn't see what was so funny and wonderful about life. This wasn't a time for celebration; this was a time to get back at those who harmed people. This was a time to corner evil and destroy it, and then maybe we could celebrate our victory, but not until that time. Why was I the only one in this fight?

I took the blue velvet bag that contained the portion of Marisa's ashes out of my desk drawer and held them close to my heart as I tried to breathe. *I'm really sorry*, I said in my mind. I didn't need anyone sneaking up behind me eavesdropping. Then I whispered, "I don't understand. Why did you want me to go? I could have—" I stopped and shook my head. It was pounding.

There was something there, something in the room. Shelly rubbed up against my leg. I saw something behind me, her chunky wooden bracelet, handmade, the import from Africa that Kay gave her. I turned around and looked at my bed. There was nothing there. I carefully placed the blue velvet bag back in my drawer.

There was a noise outside. I went to the window and peeked out through my white lace drapes. I saw Detective Holloway's police car, the one my father referred to as the undercover green wrapper. I breathed out frustration through my nose. He was always coming around. He usually bought at least two pounds of something from my father, shrimp most of the time, and I was getting tired of him following us around like a damned shadow. Why would anyone want to hang around someone who hallucinates? I always kept my door ajar so Shelly could come and go as he pleased, but today I lifted him up and put him on the bed. He circled and purred, looking for the perfect soft place to curl up. I shut the door and went back to the window, where I closed it tight, then knelt down on the bed behind the cat for protection. "I'm not talking to him today, Shelly. I really don't want to see him, and I don't have to see him. He's not even on the case—there *is* no case anymore. I just wish he would just—I'll open the door again. Why don't we wait a little while, and maybe he'll go home."

Later that day and against his doctor's advice, my father drove me over to my grandparents' house for my mandatory scheduled visit. My mother's car was in their driveway. I was *not* expecting to see her. Bunica's kitchen smelled of potatoes, cabbage, and tomatoes, but I just wanted to go home with my father. Yet it was made clear to me that I *would* be spending the rest of the weekend there in that house.

"Rudy, are you sure you're able to drive under these conditions?" My grandmother was worried as usual as she looked wide-eyed at my father's cast.

"Yes, Ana." My father nodded deeply. "I'm perfectly fine, perfectly fine. Really."

That's when we both spotted my mother and little Helena.

"Are you moving in here now, Lavinia?" Dad's words were biting, and when I looked at my mother, I could see the venom boil.

"No, no, Rudy. She's dropping off the little one and picking up some things. She's driving back to Ponopoly's—"

"Penelope, Mother. Penelope. You have met her several times now," my mother said with frustration.

My grandmother retorted, "It's the best place for her."

My grandfather took Helena out of the kitchen, probably knowing that at any moment, a pressure cooker in the form of his only daughter was about to skyrocket. The four of us stood there for the briefest of moments before I saw my father. He looked like he was pretending to cry, but he wasn't. It was real. I had never seen my father's tears before, and the shock made me feel totally removed, even though I was still standing there, my feet frozen to the floor.

"Dad?" I wanted to touch his good arm, but I couldn't move.

He turned to my mother. "How could you do this?"

"Rudy, you cannot blame—"

"Be quiet, Mother, please!" my mother hissed as she pointed a finger in my father's face. "Don't you even *think* about blaming me for anything, Rudy. I have done nothing wrong!"

"Nothing wrong, Lavinia? Nothing? How many years were you planning—Did, did she even kn—"

"Rudy! My god!" My grandmother screamed so loud, I jerked backward and made a strange sound.

My father instantly stopped. I have heard Bunica holler, but never like that. I was stunned. My mother's hands covered her mouth, and for once, she said nothing.

A facetious smirk twisted my father's lips, and a shiny fresh tear rolled down his cheek. "You married the guy," he said quietly. "What the hell is the matter with you? Your daughter is dead, Lavinia. *Your daughter*. And this one here? Alice? Do you even know who she is? Do you give a shit? She too is your daughter."

"Oh, come on now, please!" my grandmother begged in a wretched snappy voice that always sounded like a stern warning and would frighten Marisa and me into silence.

My mother swiped my grandmother's hand off her shoulder and continued her advance on my father, but Dad was not backing down. He stood firm in front of her. "Your flesh and blood, Lavinia. What were you thinking? You need help. You know what you need? You need psychological help."

My breathing stopped dead. My mother had her back to me. She screamed, "I have never hurt anyone! I didn't lay a hand on her—"

What a lie.

"Her?" His good arm was outstretched as he leaned forward slightly. "You mean Marisa, right? That's who we're talking about. Marisa. Can't you even say your dead kid's name?"

"I can!" she yelled and sobbed more.

He turned his sad face to the floor, and his shoulders slumped.

My grandmother glanced at me, but I stared motionless at my father's pathetic sling. He rubbed it, and he looked as broken as his arm. He started to turn to the door, but he stopped and turned back to my mother. "You know, I can't argue with you. I never could win the war of words, and I never really wanted to. But he's a murderer now. He killed your kid, and nothing is gonna fix this. Money doesn't fix things. Do you see that now? Nothing is ever going to bring that child back."

My mother started to yell again, and my grandmother begged and complained. I wondered about little Helena, off with my grand-father somewhere in this house, learning at a very young age what constant strife and grief are and how you must learn to bury it. I didn't hear them any longer. I did manage to catch a few words, in English this time, words that seemed to keep repeating themselves over and over again like *accident* and *death* and *brainwash*, even *Alice*, and all of a sudden, I heard something else, something much quieter in my vacuum of silence. It was the little patter of Helena's tiny feet running upstairs and the sounds of my grandfather's slower, larger creaking following. They were both singing, humming.

"I'll pick you up Sunday morning at eleven, Allie." My father threw his good arm around my shoulder and kissed my hair into the side of my head, then he disappeared. My mother and grandmother continued to argue as the door closed behind him.

"Alice?" my mother called after me as I ran to the large picture window in the front. "Where are you going?"

I had a couple of my father's pills shoved in my front pocket. I also found a forgotten bottle of something the other doctor had given me when I was in the hospital, and they still worked perfectly fine. They were tucked away safely in my blue overnight bag. I had taken one of those before we left home that morning.

"Dad?" I uttered the one word as I watched him pull out of the driveway. "Dad. Wait?" I was tired.

"Alice." It was Bunic at the top of the staircase. "Come up. Come upstairs."

I remained exactly where I was, listening to my mother and grandmother cry but not hearing any of their words.

"Do you want to play checkers with Helena and me?" he asked despite the shrill, yet his quiet voice was so clear.

"No, thanks." I thought of Big Boobs, the waitress at the saloon in the mountains who brought Marisa that huge cheeseburger. She was too afraid to eat it because she had thoughts about bears mauling her to death, so I finished her lunch for her. Those were the biggest boobs I had ever seen in my life. Had she touched me with those things? I think she brushed my cheek with one. Fat boob on a fat cheek.

I wiped my face with my hand, but the images remained. I kept wiping and rubbing. Oh my god, I could smell her perfume—sweet, sweaty, greasy, old womanish. It was all still there, and I kept wiping and rubbing my face and eyes over and over.

Bunic and Helena silently descended upon me. "We're going for a walk around the block, Alice. We might go around twice. Come with us?"

"No thanks."

Helena said something inaudible, and I ignored her. I continued to look out the big window as I watched my grandfather hold Helena's hand, both of them walking away from me toward the sidewalk. I watched until they disappeared around the corner. Why would he ask me to go with him? I didn't want him thinking about me; I wanted to be invisible, and I didn't want to be there in the first place.

"I feel like I'm going to vomit." From the other room, I heard my grandmother wretch. It was a frightening and wicked sound.

"Well, Mother, maybe if you stayed off the sauce every once in a while, you wouldn't find yourself in this situation, would you?" my mother said.

"Sauce? Sauce? What is sauce? What are you talking about now, Lavinia?"

"Oh please, Mother, don't play poor immigrant 'my English is terrible' routine! You have been here for decades, and you know exactly what I'm talking about. All that cheap goddamned white wine! Who do you think you're kidding? And please stop all that pleading. Nobody knows anything."

"How can you speak to me this way, Lavinia? I'm your mother. I raised you."

There was heavy movement in the air, and I felt it. I tasted it. A storm was coming; dark thunderous clouds were hovering like someone would be struck down.

"I can speak to anyone any way I want, Mother. I am no longer a child that you can spit on. I have had you and Dad to my home, I have treated you both, I have my—"

"Your what? What do you have? You don't have a home anymore. It was never your home anyway, and you cannot get anywhere from where you are right now, my dear. You could not pay for a house if you had one, eh? But you don't see these things that are right in front of you. It is like you're still a child. I am—"

"Barton's family will take care of all of it." My mother sounded like a bumbling fool looking for those perfect words. She shouted again, and I turned around from the window. "All you need to do is mind your own business, keep your mouths shut. For once in your rotten lives."

"Ahh, no, no, no. No one will be taking care of you anymore, my Lavinia. You will now have to take care of yourself, if, *if* this is even possible. He has taken one child away, and he has left you, and now he is locked away. The only thing that family will be doing is making sure that their only son achieves freedom. They can. They will move the stars and the skies above and fight God, pay Satan himself the dearest fee to free him. They will want everything appealed and you—"

No, no there's no way. Sure there is. Big Barton is beneath an insect, but the best part of it? He had bales of cash to simply throw away. He had connections, he knew politicians. He's even met the president. Satan is very powerful on earth.

"Bunica. Bunica?" I raced into the kitchen. "No! Can they really do that?"

"Mind your own business, Alice!" my mother roared into my face. I could smell her rotting cigarette-laced breath.

My grandmother ignored me as she continued to taunt her daughter. My palms went watery, and cold sharp blood slammed into my heart and trickled with ease up through my chest over my shoulders. "You're stuck with nothing."

My mother threw a wineglass. I heard the shatter and then the loud rumbling. While the screeching hiss of my grandmother made me want to hide again, I was uncommonly cheerful as I listened to her demolish my mother. "Get out of this house!"

My mother continued to holler wildly. I was sure the neighbors could hear, and I wondered if they would call the police. The more I listened to her not make any sense, the more I wanted to shove the nearest thing in her mouth to shut her up. Then she pushed my grandmother, not hard, but just enough. Surely my grandmother had known that she had done this to me and that it was a way of life for Marisa. She had done it to my father. But I had never seen her do it to my grandmother. My grandmother advanced on my mother and then quickly ducked as my mother's palm came crashing down between my grandmother's shoulder blades.

"Peasant!"

"I will have you arrested for assaulting your mother, Lavinia." My grandmother was calm. "You will not like jail."

"You would know."

Bunica was in jail?

My grandmother shook her head and smoothed down the front of her dark brown skirt. I still had Detective Holloway's number. I was hoping I wouldn't have to call him. "Go now, Lavinia. Leave my house."

My mother turned around and left. There was no "I'm sorry," no goodbyes, nothing. That was not out of the ordinary for my mother. And all I thought about was my father and how I had never seen him cry, how I had never seen him talk to her like that. I doubted I would ever see it again.

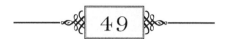

49

South Wellton High should have been a place where I remembered a lot of people from my and Marisa's early childhood. I took pride in my long-term memory. But not only did I not remember, I didn't care to even try. But what was funny was that I would all of a sudden see a face I would recognize from elementary school, and that face would look at me as if I had three heads.

Some people remembered Marisa. Everyone must have known about her murder by one of the richest monsters in town. After all, it was all over the newspapers. You would have to be one of those creatures that lived underground with no eyes not to have known, but not many said anything about it. At first. The principal, teachers, and a few of the students offered me condolences. I didn't want to talk about Marisa and her death to people whom I barely knew and didn't care about, and I was sure most of them only had a morbid curiosity about her murder anyway. They didn't care about her.

It didn't take long to get back into the regular routine—lockers slamming, endless chatter of people filling the hallways, the smell of a dusty layer of invisible grime atop a hard tile floor. I did not belong there. I was angry and sad about my life being torn apart. I didn't need school. I knew which one of these people were the drunks. I could almost smell it, and I knew which ones had the dope, which brought me to another dilemma.

In order to be supplied with booze and drugs at South Wellton, you had to have money, know someone, or slut around, which seemed to be pretty easy for most dirt balls except for me. The only friend I had since Bruce left town was Aubrey Meslier, and not only did she go to another school, she liked me more than I liked her. And Aubrey's idea of a mind-altering substance was the caffeine in a strong cup of black coffee. She was as clean as the cellar floor after my aunt finished mopping. Dad and Kiki appeared to be clean at the moment too, with those nice pills anyway. Pills were making me sleep long hours at a time. I wondered if anyone suspected.

One alternative when it came to finding what I needed was to get involved sexually with one of the boys who had drugs. There were plenty of pretty girls here. I hadn't even kissed a boy, let alone had sexual intercourse with one, and unless a girl is going to put it around, no one from the opposite sex is going to supply her unless she has that magic of all magic—cash. And even if I was ready and willing to, I didn't get the feeling that anyone would be interested in a tall, unattractive, flat chested girl with a big nose and frizzy hair. My only option would be to find a job, which presented a myriad of problems in and of themselves, beginning with Dad. He would never understand my working a part-time job on the weekends or after school, unless it was at the store, even though he knew exactly how I felt about that. He said that when he died, Boochie's was mine regardless of whether or not I was capable of decapitating a curious-eyed flounder or boiling one of those poor lobsters to death after I had named the entire tankful.

Yet once again, like her ashes, intervention in the form of Marisa swung a door open for me. I was asked by my guidance counselor, Mr. Milklader, whom everyone referred to as Mr. Milk, if I would like to tutor students a couple of days a week in business math for $3.10 per hour. Problem solved.

When I started tutoring, life became a combination of business math preparation and watching other young people fumble their way through their lives with their own sets of problems that were so foreign to me. Marisa probably would have been able to understand the dynamics of interpersonal relationships in high school society so much better than I ever could.

How terrible of a girl she must have been, how mean, how selfish. Someone in those cramped and endless hallways would have wanted to ask her a question, another girl perhaps, just of a "lower rank." Maybe she wanted to get her attention, and she would turn around, torn up and frustrated that the person calling her name wasn't the person she wanted to be calling her name. There were two prevalent adjectives to describe certain girls and boys for that matter in high school, and I have moved clear out of my own way not to mention them, but I feel that they are so important that I must. They are "popular" and "stuck-up." It would be impossible to bury or ignore these words.

Marisa Ana Ionescu

On Saturday morning at the store, Dad had on Pick Hudson's *All Soul All the Time* show on the radio. There was this new advertisement featuring some psychologist-type guy who quickly said that after high school, people will no longer have any use for the word *popular*, that "it will not be thrown around in the same way in which it was in terms of the ranking, if you will, of people." I wondered how he felt about the other term *stuck-up*? Would that not be thrown around in the same relentless and careless manner?

I wished that Marisa had been around to hear that advertisement. She would probably just say the guy was an idiot and leave it at that. Crescent Hills, where Marisa was held prisoner, was a horror show of teenage snobbery. South Wellton couldn't have been *that* awful. It was impossible. South Wellton itself was a peculiar place. It wasn't the best part of town, that was for sure, but the district encompassed the trashy south side and a good area of the countryside, including some farms and lots of land.

It was ultimately important for the lower-ranked girl to get that one stuck-up boy to come down off his snotty little shit-stained perch and grace her with a hello that would maintain her beaming glow for the rest of the day. The euphoria may even last well into the evening until quite possibly, she wouldn't be able to stand herself. How pathetic she was. The insecurity must have blazed above her head like a neon sign, and she didn't even understand the misery of her mind and the grief of her heart. Why not her? What was wrong with her? Why was she failing? Her assigned locker was all the way at the other end of the school, yet she chose an empty one next to "those girls." A couple of them she had pretty much known her entire life, even their parents knew each other, especially that "one very special girl." Although the two were friends (or a much looser association of the word), she really wasn't privy to "her interior." She couldn't understand what the problem was, and it killed her inside. That little cluster of about four or five of them would collect in that same corner like horny daisies, and one by one, sometimes in threes and fives, the bees would swarm around and pollinate. Sometimes there would be a new bee or a strange but somehow beautiful hornet. How had a homely and strange hornet become beautiful? And there she stood, flies eating away at her core, not even a wallflower but a dead flower. They weren't even all that lovely. One of them had expensive clothes; one of them was fat. One of them flew onto the scene like a witch on a tattered broom, only to be welcomed home like a long-lost soldier.

What was wrong? Why not her? Was she a little weird? Was it because she was a virgin? Was it because she didn't have a car? Didn't do the same things they did and couldn't keep a secret? What did they truly know about her? She wanted to be laid-back like the artsy types, respected because they didn't care. The problem was that she did care very much, but she wished that she didn't. She watched people smiling, laughing, chitter-chattering all around her, but no matter how much she wanted

their eyes to meet hers, she was never really invited,
not regularly anyway and not the way she wanted.
Her eyes would turn into two polluted dark lakes,
and when I think about that poor invisible girl, it
is I who weep.

—*Marisa*

50

There were a couple of things I had to prepare for before my day started, and one of them was to make sure that Aunt Nancy wasn't going to do something dangerous. Tommy, the superintendent of the apartment buildings she lived in and Dad's lifelong friend, had more patience than anyone I knew. But even he couldn't tolerate her chasing neighbors up and down the street with a broomstick like some wacko. Tommy was very familiar with mental illness not only because of my aunt, but because he had worked in the state system and the VA ever since he had come home from Vietnam. He regularly rented apartments to what he called higher-functioning people with psychiatric illness like Aunt Nancy. I suppose that would depend on the day. But Tommy, being that teeny, tiny cog in that enormous wheel of bureaucracy, could not exactly hold on to her abode until her doctor said it was fine for her to be living alone.

So here we were together. It was different now that I wasn't a kid anymore. It wasn't as if living with my aunt was a bad thing, it was just that *I* had changed, and I very much believed that Nancy *had* to change one thing: her curling iron. She had put on some very much-needed weight and claimed that her medications were helping. She was also growing her pretty blond locks, and Dad bought her one of those new hotshot curling irons that she had to have been using three times a day. Her hair was already naturally curly. How many more curls did she need? This curling iron was exactly what it was, an iron, and when she plugged it into the wall, it heated up all red and steamy. What if she forgot to unplug it? I spent countless times checking and double-checking, making sure that the thing was unplugged before I left the house in the morning after she finished styling herself and before I went to bed, over and over. It wasn't fair. It was scaring me, and I wanted to take it and throw it in the dumpster behind the warehouse. What if Shelly jumped up on the counter and burned his little paw? I couldn't even think about that possibility. I knew one thing: her curling iron would be in about thirty-three billion little pieces if anything ever happened to that cat.

I decided one morning to sit in the bathroom and watch while she was primping in front of the mirror. I was astonished at how well she had the curling iron technique mastered. What was my father thinking when he gave her that stupid thing? He wasn't thinking at all. "Aunt Nancy, you—"

"Hey, honey!" She nearly knocked me backward into the tub as she held her curling iron in one hand and a menthol in the other. "Did I tell you I'm volunteering a couple of hours a week at the hospital? Can you believe it? The hospital! I'm mostly doing some work with old people, but today, they said I was going to stuff a box full of envelopes."

I didn't care about her job. I cared about her getting her curling iron as far away from the house as possible.

She continued. "So, you know, I *have* to look good, being around all those very important people at the hospital like the doctors and the nurses and the secretaries. It's not so much like the store, you know, because no matter what you do, you still end up smelling like a trout! A rainbow trout! Bloop! Bloop! Bloop!" She laughed hard at herself.

I wasn't smiling.

She put her cigarette down in the ashtray, probably another problem I needed to worry about, turned around, puffed her cheeks out, and used her fingers to crawl through the air toward me. "Bloop, bloop!"

"Aunt Nancy, you don't need that curling iron to look pretty, you know. You are very pretty anyway."

"Well. Alice. You said I didn't need a curling iron to look pretty, but I do because when I grow my hair longer, I've got to style it."

I learned a long time ago that in order to communicate with my aunt, I needed to make my point clearly and concretely. Subtlety and abstraction were never going to get me anywhere. It never had in the past, and there was no reason why I should have been putting forth the effort. I was having a hard time doing a lot of things that I should have been able to do. "Okay, what if it gets wet?"

"The directions say your hair has to be completely, completely dry, or you won't get a curl."

"Nancy," I said firmly.

She turned from the mirror and looked at me. She held that curling iron on the top of her head with a big roll of hair in it that looked like a calzone "See? It's really easy, Alice. I can style you sometime."

As she spoke, I felt guilt over my small outburst, but something had to be done about this problem in the house. I stood up quietly. "Aunt Nancy, can you just put that thing down for a second please? And just listen to me very carefully."

"Sure, I'm finished. Are you okay, Alice?' She half chuckled and unplugged the curling iron.

I exhaled. "Can you just promise me, *promise* me that you will always, always, *always* unplug your curling iron when you are finished using it?" I pointed to the outlet, and she followed my finger. "You understand? Just do what you just did, all right?"

She looked confused but nodded sincerely.

I didn't like the confusion. There was nothing to be confused about. Not even for her. "Just...just leave the curling iron in the middle of the counter, like that, like where it is now, until it cools off. Leave it there until it is completely cold. Okay?"

She nodded again. "Of course I will, Alice. I have to, or it will overheat and break, and I won't be able to use it anymore."

I looked at her for several seconds. "Do you promise?"

She nodded again and smiled.

"Just tell me."

"Tell you."

"Say, 'I promise I will always unplug the curling iron when I am finished using it.'"

"I promise I will always unplug the curling iron. Oh. When I'm finished with my hair."

And she always did—or I think she did. I checked, but I couldn't remember if she did it, even though I knew she really did it. I went back again and again at different times of the day until I was nervous.

My brain was always playing tricks on me. I could believe one thing, but then my brain would make me check just to make sure I was absolutely correct, and it didn't stop at Aunt Nancy's curling iron. I was constantly worried that the oven wasn't turned off; the stovetop burner dials all had to be at Off with the Off word right up perfectly straight at the top of the dial. The doors and windows all had to be locked; the refrigerator door never felt shut. I couldn't breathe.

School helped a lot. There weren't too many things I had to check, except maybe the back of a chair when I stood up, and sometimes I would have to push it back under a desk or a table in the library. It was very important to me that none of my secret notes had fallen on the floor in case someone picked them up and read them out loud, even though I hadn't written any secret notes, nor had anyone written any secret notes to me. I knew this, but I could never be that sure, and that's when I knew that my brain was playing tricks on me. It didn't matter what I did either—I could fight it all I wanted. Once that brain decided to play tricks on me, there was no stopping it.

I tutored five pupils in business math, and my goal was to make sure that each one of them not only passed, but received an A. I drilled them like they were preparing for battle. I made them read, write, and explain. I'm sure they hated me, and I didn't care. Four out of five of them received an A, and then they loved me. I would receive extra money from their parents, movie tickets, dinner invitations, and a small plaque on the wall in which Mr. Milk insisted on hanging in his office above a small filing cabinet. Then he placed a small plant next to a chair where all the parents and other students sat and, if they wanted to, could look up at it.

The only pupil I felt unable to truly help, who was unable to rise to my expectations, was a boy named Walter Tifton, whom everyone called Tift for short. Except for me. I called him Walter. There were too many nicknames. It was tiresome, and sometimes I had to stop myself from thinking about *that* too, which was another difficulty. He was only able to achieve a C. He was a nice boy. I couldn't help but notice that he was a gentleman, if there was such a thing in that day and age. He was very friendly, gentle, but as dumb as a doorknob. I felt sorry for him. I liked him. He and Marisa probably would have gotten along very well.

Then there was Louis Dagher. Louis Dagher slowly and methodically appeared in my life like a poisonous crawling insect. This boy had his eye on me, and I had no idea what he wanted. It could not have been what I thought it might be when our eyes met for the first time, not with his sinister provocations as he tried to make me as miserable as possible. I kept a low profile. Having a quiet life and remaining anonymous were two very important things to me, so I didn't know what prompted him to be so intentionally cruel. Louis Dagher came from a working-class family in Wellton, and somewhere along the path of his boyhood journey, he became acquainted with Mark the boyfriend. That was the only way in which we were connected, and it was pretty distant. I hadn't seen Mark since my sister's memorial service. Dagher was a year ahead of me and very much a part of that "in crowd"—not the athletes, the raging rah-rahs in crowd, but the in crowd that knew where to buy drugs, get fake identifications, and where the best parties were on the weekends. He dated a girl in my class whom I remembered used to play the violin in elementary school named Nellie Manziel. The only thing that girl probably played now was his yucky bony naked body and whatever bong was set in front of her. She was so disgusting, I found it difficult to look at the needy pathetic excuse for a person she turned out to be. I think she was worse than I was.

The two of them shuffled around together like a couple of hobos. They wore beat-up moccasins and beads intertwined with peace signs, which was hypocrisy since Louis Dagher was far from peaceful. Their hair looked heavy and dirty, and they carried themselves as if they were stereotypical hippies from the previous decade. Both of them attempted to be who they were not. Nellie insulted my sense of smell with that smoky oil she rubbed all over her body in the locker room. I felt like I was the only one with the insight to recognize that Dagher too was *not* a loving person, a nonconformist, that laid-back flower child he wanted everyone to think he was. He was mean, loud, and domineering, and Nellie would just stand there with his skinny arm draped around her shoulder. She gazed up at him with blue doped-out doe eyes. Then I came into their line of fire.

"Here come da bomb!" he shouted one afternoon in the hallway. There were only a few people around. It was late.

I looked behind me to see who he was hollering at. I kept walking.

"Nope, that's right! She don't even know she's a bomb." Dagher laughed as Nellie looked over at me with nothing but distance and indifference in her big eyes.

I stopped. The two of them were now standing against the wall, she twisting around like a toddler trying to free herself from her parent's arms. Then she buried her little face in his underarm. I pointed to my chest. "What are you talking about?"

His smile was rotten, but he didn't answer; he just raised his voice again. "She's the bomb! Oh, hey there, bomb."

The few people who remained in the hallway stopped for a moment and looked at him, then at me, before they continued on their way. Nellie smiled and snorted. I was equally as annoyed as I was baffled. I didn't know him. I had hardly spoken to his girlfriend. I had my own way of getting wasted when I needed, and I sure as hell didn't need him for anything, yet he was singling me out for some reason.

Could that have been the problem? I was taking my business elsewhere? And what was with the whole bomb thing? I looked at myself in my bedroom mirror that night. What was he talking about? I certainly was no sex bomb. He must have meant something else.

I can't remember Louis Dagher or his girlfriend or anyone at school seeing me cry or losing my temper. I kept my feelings very private. I only cried when I was on my own. Maybe I cried once or twice around my family, Kiki, Detective Holloway, I don't know, when Marisa died and at her service. Was that what he meant by bomb? That I was explosive? I checked Marisa's ashes, and then I double-checked them. As I looked at her ashes as intently as my eyes would allow, I said "Marisa's ashes" over and over again. *Here. They. Are.* And in different variations, showing myself, reminding myself, convincing myself that I was indeed looking at my sister's ashes.

Do not take them out of the plastic. Do not take them out of the plastic. Have I taken them out of the plastic? No, I have not taken them out of the plastic.

It would go on and on. I kissed the velvet bag and placed it carefully back in the dresser drawer. I opened the drawer, and I opened the velvet bag again and again. I lived this way in a constant state of worry and perfection that was never quite perfect, but what this invariable agony and torment did manage to do was wipe me out mentally and eventually physically until I would hunker down with Shelly. I would crawl under my quilt with darkness as my other companion, and Shelly would curl up beside me, the door ajar for him. I would have a small measure of peace and solace.

Bomb, bomb, bomb.

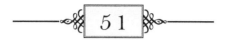

51

I could feel the wind drive into the fish-scale shingles outside my window, signaling that winter was closing in soon. Despite my exhaustion, one night would be unbearable. I couldn't doze off for a long time as the big bright colorful words continued to blast away within the confines of my mind: *Bomb! Bomb! Louis! Bomb! Ashes! Bomb!* They wouldn't go away. Neither would Louis Dagher or the stoned doe-eyed girlfriend he had draped over him like a sloth. I didn't know anything about stalking or harassment, but it felt like he was doing just that. It killed me to not understand why, since I didn't even know him or Nellie, and I hadn't had any type of conversation with her since we were about eight years old.

Then there it was again. The nasty hippie shouting as a field of people made up of confused, now-curious students parted an uncertain path leading to me. "Oh *no*! There she is again. There's the bomb!"

I looked around. Was I mistaken? Maybe he really wasn't talking to me? Given the way everyone was staring and smirking, I knew he was talking to me. "Why are you calling me a bomb, Louis?" I asked and then tried to walk across the crowded hallway, only to be blocked by what appeared to be bodyguards for the anointed free spirit and his scraggly princess.

There was a booming adult voice behind me, a social studies teacher I didn't know very well. "Come on, people, the bell has rung. Let's move along please."

I kept walking, grateful for the intervention, and then I remembered that I was wearing a bright orange T-shirt under an off-white cardigan, blue jeans, and blue sneakers. Did I clash with my loud shirt? Too many colors? I wondered if it was too much. Too bombish? That sounded ridiculous, even to me.

I looked back, but Louis Dagher had disappeared into the masses with that drippy girl of his.

"What's the matter with him?"

I turned around and saw Walter Tifton standing there, shaking his head slowly.

"Oh, hello, Walter. I'm sorry, I didn't see you standing there. I—I don't know what's wrong with him. I have been racking my brains trying to figure that out."

"Call me Tift. No one calls me Walter except my mother and my sister."

I smiled and nodded. *And now me.* He looked like a Walter, which was a very nice name. I was breathless, and my heart thumped hard. I was angry, embarrassed, frustrated, and distracted. He continued to walk with me, and I felt guilty about thinking he was dumb. He wasn't, and it was obvious that I had been way too hard on him. I had already known how kind and witty he was, and he was a lot more caring than most people I knew.

"I'll tell you what I think," he said. "I think Dagher's problem is this—way too much boozing. He's got whiskey brain, and he's always hungover. My grandfather was a big drinker, and he was mean as hell. And Dagher, he tries to chase away that shitty feeling with some weed and a few uppers here and there."

We both looked behind.

"The damned fool. He's just fried himself and, in the meantime, turned into an obnoxious bully," he said.

We stood for a minute outside my math class, which was about to begin. I tried not to smile as I looked at the big off-white comb stuck in his huge blown-out Afro.

He turned around and tapped my shoulder. "Let's have a cigarette sometime, Alice, if it's no problem for a teacher to fraternize with the students."

I nodded. "I don't think it's a problem."

I didn't even finish my sentence before he disappeared down the hallway into the audiovisual room where he helped out. It had never occurred to me that chatting with another person so briefly could give me a small measure of peace and perspective. I instantly felt better than I had in days, and I didn't have that knotty butterfly feeling in my chest. I wished that it would last. The problem was my mind—I couldn't distract it. I couldn't be happy ever since my sister was murdered. I was aimless and lost.

* * * * *

The next afternoon, I found Louis Dagher sitting on a bench in front of the auditorium. Nellie the orangutan waif was nowhere to be seen, and his throng that surrounded him were also absent. And so there was Louis Dagher, alone.

I smiled to myself, and I tried not to catch his eye, even though ignoring him completely was becoming more and more difficult. After all, I couldn't shake the curiosity as to why he was so keen on tormenting me. And so I *did* catch his eye, and he looked over, cheeks puffed, skinny mouth closed for a change as he peered at me like a rattlesnake about to strike. He said nothing. He only sat there, nodding his ugly face at me. What I found amusing and what Louis Dagher did not realize was that I had plenty of experience and years of practice not letting people know what I may or may not have been thinking at any time, and I could put on an award-winning performance if I needed.

On this occasion, I figured that he could nod and peer with his puffy face all that he wanted. I could deal with him if he engaged me. He was alone. One grab to his groin, a slug to the nose, my finger in his eye, he would go down like the bag of shit that he was. One of us would end up dead, and Louis Dagher probably didn't realize that I didn't care which one of us it was. He may not have felt quite the same.

I always hated school lunches, so I usually brought my own. I had an old gray lunchbox that looked like it belonged to a construction worker, and Aunt Nancy, when she wasn't preening herself in front of that mirror, liked to fill it up for me. My mother never bought mayonnaise because I liked it so much, and it made me fat. Aunt Nancy slathered it all over my sandwiches.

I headed for the cafeteria because for dessert, one of the ladies prepared giant peanut butter squares with the luscious dark chocolate ganache on top. I never missed a giant peanut butter square. I was regularly putting on weight again, which was something everyone except my mother was happy to see.

Louis Dagher was backed up against the wall by the trophy cases holding court with his posse and his Nellie. Once again, I tried to avoid him, but before I knew what was happening, his large pale face was in front of me. His round protuberant eyes in mean, careless brown peered down a long skinny nose. I could tell right away he was stoned; his breath stank of nonfiltered cigarettes and his clothes of yesterday's beer. I had never been that close to him before. He was a deeply cruel, vicious person—that was the reality. He had the look on his face like "I'm going to speak to you now, and you're not going to move until I'm finished with you." I knew Marisa was there. She was with me like she was the time I checked her ashes in my bedroom. I just didn't know how. I couldn't see her, hear her, or touch her. I sensed a presence all the way down in my bones, and I knew exactly what she thought.

His head looks like an upside down hardboiled egg, doesn't it?

I let out a laugh.

"What's so funny?" Louis Dagher demanded, blowing his girlfriend's floppy hair out of his mouth.

"Louis, I don't know why you keep bothering me. I have no business with you. I don't even know you. I want you to please leave me alone. Quit calling me names. I mean it."

The hallway was dark and felt more crowded than normal. The overcast sky at the noon hour filtered through the wall of doors, opening and closing, letting in the cold autumn. The smell of a bologna-like substance and thick industrial American cheese wafted from the cafeteria and took over the space, which was getting smaller and smaller.

Nellie Manziel's emaciated little body barely fit between us. "What did he say?"

"What?" My eyes shot daggers at her. "What did who say? Who's he?"

"Your little nigger friend, what's his name? Tippy?" Dagher said.

"Oh my god, *Louis*!" Nellie Manziel lifted her dainty fingers to her mouth. She blushed and tried to hide a smile.

"You know, Louis, for someone who wants everyone to think he's this open-minded hippie guy, you're anything but. That was a racial slur. Both of you should be ashamed of yourselves with that language," I said.

His mouth turned into a thin white line, and his eyes were charged with anger. I should have just walked away. There was no point trying to reason with a sick mind, but something was keeping me there, and everyone was watching us.

"What did he say? Nellie's been upset about him talking behind her back, and I want to know what he said."

In the meantime, Nellie was chatting with some girl standing practically on my feet as she continually stroked and snuggled Louis's ribs. I was nauseated. I looked at Nellie as I gently pushed her unaware friend out of my line of sight. "She doesn't look upset."

"Tell me what your little pussy-bitch friend said about my girlfriend!"

Girlfriend. Boyfriend. Those words sounded so silly when said aloud. "Walter hasn't spoken a word to me about you or Nellie. Do you know why, Louis? Because he has better things to do with his time than worry about either of you—"

"Your sister's got my tapes."

I stopped breathing. Everything stopped for that one second, and Louis Dagher knew it because he saw it too.

"My sister's four years old." I knew he wasn't talking about Helena.

Everything started up again.

I said, "I don't know anything about that. You know Mark. You should be talking to him."

"How do you know what I know about Mark?" he spat. He looked angry and scared. Not a lot made sense, and I thought Walter was right. His head was really messed up with drugs; he obviously didn't know how to control it. I wondered for a second what he would be like when he was my father's age.

"I don't know how you know him." I shrugged. "I just knew that you did. What's your problem? You really need to just leave me alone." I wanted my peanut butter and chocolate square.

Louis Dagher started to use his fingers to count the various tapes he said my sister had. "Oh, and you know I'm not talking about whatever sister you're talking about. I'm talking about Marisa. The dead one."

"Oh my god, *Louis*!" Nellie chimed in once again. "You can't say that to her."

I had already walked away, but I looked back at Nellie.

To hell with him, Alice. Come on. You know I don't give two shits about what that idiot says or thinks about me. Anyone who talks about a dead person that way is a real asshole. Come on, ding-a-ling, stand up to him. You're doing great. Don't be a chicken. Don't be a chicken.

He pointed a finger at me, and more people were slowing down to look at the escalating interchange between Louis Dagher and me. "She owes me money too."

I stood there and looked at this ridiculous boy. I didn't want to know why Marisa owed Louis Dagher money. It didn't matter anymore. "You have just acknowledged that my sister is dead." My voice was raised just a little, and I could now feel a collection of eyeballs burning through my back.

He shrugged as if he didn't care to respond, but he did. "I'm glad she's dead. She got what she deserved."

"Louis, stop," Nellie half whispered, half whined.

"Whatever, Louis," I said, fuming inside, "but this means you won't be getting your money or your tapes back. The dead don't return borrowed items, or didn't you know that? Louis?"

"And she accused me of raping her."

"Did you?" I didn't move a muscle.

"*Louis.*"

"Shut the fuck up, Nellie!" he warned.

Nellie slowly recoiled.

"No, I did not!"

I felt my top teeth tuck behind my bottom teeth. "I knew my sister pretty well. If she said you forced—"

"*No!*" He screamed like a little boy. The monster entered my mind. I remembered him, his screaming. I steadily trembled. "But I will tell you one thing, bomber. Your slut sister was screwing her rich stepdaddy Barton Withers *thee third*, and when she started accusing *him* of rape and started stealing his shit, he just crushed her scrawny throat like a fucking chicken!"

Louis Dagher laughed. He was howling, and a few of his male followers joined in. He pushed Nellie hard into the darkening crowd as he turned around and attempted to shake a hand. A group of boys rallied around him.

I continued to stand there and watch for several minutes, but it really wasn't that long. I was beyond angry—It was a madness, and I was filled with hatred. I was in disbelief. The frustration was unbearable, and I was so sad. I was simultaneously so harried yet so numb.

He lost his footing and fell backward ever so slightly. A wisp of his hair brushed against my nose in utter disrespect, and I could smell the faintness of his shampoo. He actually washed his hair.

I wrapped my arms around his neck, my right arm positioned in a perfect choke hold, and I pulled as hard as I could. I squeezed his throat with the total amount of strength I could attain as my teeth continued to grind. It was a wonder they didn't break, crush, and I didn't swallow them and choke myself. I looked off straight ahead and then to the left, but my sight became a pitch-black room. Thick, heavy curtains were drawn tightly closed where I could only see bits of streaming light. It was just me and Louis, and one of us was going to die that day right in front of the South Wellton cafeteria.

Dagher's hands and arms flailed furiously as he tried to grab my face. He tried to bang my nose with his head, but it was futile as I buried it in the back of his neck and shoulder blade and simply kept dodging him. Poor thing, he was having such a terrible time, and no one was helping him. Why?

He was finally able to pull my forearm off his soft pale throat long enough to let out an excruciating and comical gasp, and then the gasping and choking and sputtering went on and on to the point of silliness. I thought Louis Dagher was crying. Then I realized he was really crying—crying hard like a little boy who had just spilled his milk or who had fallen out of a tree. He was lucky to be a strong-enough boy to be crying, to have been able to pull my arm off his face and neck and fling me away like lint.

I sat up, my back against the shiny yellow tiled wall next to the janitor's closet.

"Teacher, that was something! You just blown my mind. You oughta go out for the wrestling team—you just beat up a guy! Ha! And he got what he deserved too. Look at him over there bawling like a baby."

It was Walter Tifton.

"What? Are you there?"

"What, am I here? Course I'm here. You're okay now, Alice."

I nodded and reached out to touch his hand.

He knelt down beside me. "Yeah, of course I'm here, Alice. That's what friends are for, right?"

"Yes," I said. My voice was hoarse, and I was scared. Everything around me began to move very quickly, including my conversation with Walter Tifton. There were far too many people in the hallway—teachers, students—and there was an air of madness and a sudden need for control and someone to be in charge. I tried not to listen to anything but Walter's voice and the sounds of Louis Dagher's fearful sniffling and weeping.

I pondered for a moment if he would come after me, and so I quickly sprang to my feet and waited for his advance. Walter gave me a surprised look. It was immediate, and Dagher was ushered like a celebrity into the kitchen of the cafeteria where my peanut butter squares were sitting on an aluminum cookie sheet. I was dragged into the vice principal's office where I got to sit and wait for first, my father, and second, Detective Holloway.

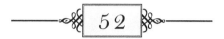

52

"Someone calls the police, and instead of sending a patrol car with a uniformed officer, in walks Detective Holloway. That's strange. Or am I hallucinating again, and you're not *really* here?"

"So now you're a tough guy?" he said without looking at me.

I was in trouble, and I didn't care.

"I called Detective Holloway, Allie, and you're damned lucky he *is* here." My father sat across the room from me. He was eerily calm.

"Why, Dad? Why would you call the cops on your own daughter? That sounds like something Mom would do."

He winced at that remark. He was obviously taken back, but he was mad as hell.

"No one's called the police, Alice. Not yet, anyway." Holloway's strangely gentle voice seeped into the space between the five people sitting in the drab yellow office.

I looked at the vastness of diplomas and certificates on the wall, and I wondered how they were fastened to cement.

"Your dad's concerned about you. We all are."

"There's nothing to be concerned about," I muttered.

"Nothing?" Mr. Milk, my guidance counselor and the one responsible for getting me a job as a paid tutor, said. He looked uncomfortable as he sat in someone else's office. "You could have killed that boy."

"Killed him?" I sat on the end of my chair, my palms soaking its wooden arms.

I watched as Detective Holloway looked at Mr. Milk. "Mr. Milklader, that *boy* has been stalking me for days, calling me names, saying I'm a bomb, and then today he started mouthing off about my murdered sister. He said she owed him money, she stole tapes from him, that she accused him of rape, she—not to mention he called Walter the n-word."

"But, Alice, your friends say you were doing a swell job of ignoring him."

"When?" When did anyone say this? He was lying. I didn't tell anyone what Louis Dagher said that angered me so much. I also didn't admit that if I had happened to squeeze every last breath of life out of him, then fine, he would have deserved that too, and I still wouldn't have cared what happened to me. I smiled inside at the thought. "None of these people are my friends, and if I happened to squeeze the wind out of him a little bit, he deserved it."

The vice principal dropped his pen on the desk. It hit with a hard click.

"Maybe it seemed like he did deserve it," Milk said unsteadily. "Mr. Dagher is a troubled boy. That is no secret around here. He will be duly punished for his part in all of this. We have enough witnesses to his taunting and bullying, but we just *don't* expect this behavior from you. You cannot put your hands on another person. He is injured. This is no joke. You are a straight A student, your standardized test scores throughout your life have been nearly perfect. I understand you have undergone tremendous loss and tragedy, but I…I don't know what to say. I'm still disappointed. I'm very, very disappointed."

My father said nothing.

Detective Holloway held up his giant hand. "If I may."

Milk nodded with relief, and Holloway turned and leaned toward me. "No matter what anyone, *anyone, ever* says to you, you cannot put your hands on them first. I say 'first' because you know this was no self-defense. You have committed a violent assault. If his parents decide to press charges against you, you could end up in juvenile hall, and if you think high school is bad, you ain't seen nothing, young lady. Nothing."

"I thought you people cared about Marisa—"

Holloway furrowed his brow.

"He said Marisa stole things from that monster that killed her!" I couldn't stop the tears, and my voice was rising. "He said she had sex with him and then called it rape!"

"It doesn't matter what anyone *says.*" His voice was sharp but steady. "You can't do this. You will go to jail the next time, Alice. You might go this time," Holloway said.

"But my sister—"

"There are judges in this town who may not be sympathetic to your ordeal. You will have to deal with bad people in this world for the rest of your life. Turn your head and continue to walk away. Every single time. Then see your guidance counselor or the vice principal, a teacher, your dad. That's what they're here for. You have a problem with your anger. You've got to get control of it."

"It isn't always that easy." I was openly weeping. I couldn't control the tears any longer. "That…that asshole just slaughtered my dead sister's character in front of a corridor filled with people that don't even know Marisa or the fact that she died for no reason. I already told you what he said. He accused her of having sex with… with Withers and that he killed her because she turned around and accused him of rape! He accused her of being a whore and a thief."

"Did he really say all that?" My father stared at me.

"Yes, Dad. Please don't tell me you think I'm making this all up."

He briefly turned to Milk and then to Holloway. "I mean, come on, guys, this jerk had it coming. I would have done the same thing if someone had talked to me about my mentally ill sister that way, and believe me, it's nearly happened a time or two—"

"Really, Mr. Buchner?" Finally, the aging voice of Vice Principal Richard Vorhees made the four of us look at him. "Would you really go as far as your daughter did this afternoon? No, I don't think so, and I think you are doing Alice a disservice by encouraging this."

"Hey, wait a minute, I'm not encouraging anything—"

I caught Mr. Milk's eyes as they sparkled quickly in agreement with Dad, although his face was twisted in disgust, probably to satisfy Vorhees.

Holloway put his hand up again, as if trying to both silence and ignore my father. He noticed Milk too. "Again," he warned even more sternly, "this is not going to be the last time you're going to come across mean, coldhearted people in this world. This Dagher person is exceptionally cruel. I know he's got some problems with drugs, and he's apparently already got one strike against his record before expulsion. But you, young lady, need help, and you need to get it fast. You need to get in touch with Dr. Kilburn. I have already discussed it with your father."

Jesus Christ. What was Louis Dagher's first strike, I wonder?

"If, for some reason, this young man wasn't able to break free of your grip, if there weren't other kids around to pull you off him, he would have passed out and eventually died if you continued to hold that choke. And with the amount of anger you've had brewing up in you, that's exactly what would have happened. You would be arrested and tried for murder. If found guilty, you would be on your way to juvenile hall, if not to a women's penitentiary."

"No truer words have been spoken, Ms. Buchner," Vorhees said. "Mr. Buchner, I suggest you see to it that your daughter gets the psychological help she needs."

My father gazed at the floor. Did any of them actually think I cared about penitentiaries or death? There was no justice to begin with. Barton Withers should die in prison, but according to everyone within two miles, he probably wouldn't. Louis Dagher can go around saying whatever he wants about anything or anyone at any time, and the minute I step in to try to shut him up—

And nobody pulled me off him. He just got lucky. Holloway was wrong.

"Question for you," Holloway said.

"What?"

"How much different from Barton Withers are you going to be then?"

"What? When?"

"When you're locked up because you have allowed some asinine little joker get the better of you?"

"My sister was no asinine little joker, and I guess I'm going home today."

"Violence never solves the problem, Alice," Holloway said. "You of all people should know that. It only makes things worse, no matter who you think deserves what and how gratifying it felt at that one half second of time that you can never get back. Look what it's done to your family. Look what it's done to *you*. You are the smartest, most intelligent youngster any of us have ever had the pleasure of knowing. Don't destroy your life."

Milk said nothing.

"He's right, Allie."

"Consider yourself warned, Ms. Buchner. Two weeks. Suspended. Now, get out of my sight." Vorhees stood up, and with that, at least I was dismissed, but the door shut behind me, and I wasn't allowed past his secretary.

Well, just like one of those little sayings, "All's well that ends well." Oh yeah, and what's the other one? "No harm, no foul." He's still alive. He didn't pass out. I'm not this robot. I knew when to let go. I mean, if there's any justice that's come out of this today, it's that I defended Marisa's honor. She would have done the same for me.

I didn't know if I even made sense in there, if they understood me or even believed me. I was so distressed. I heard myself talking, but it was as if words were dripping and sliding out of my numb mouth.

The omnipresent Detective Holloway got kicked off the case a long time before the monster even made his plea deal. Why does he even care anymore? He fucked the whole thing up. At least I didn't have to sit in a hot kitchen and wait to be escorted to another vacant yellow cinder block office and have to sit and wait for my turn with Vorhees like Louis Dagher. He was also suspended for two weeks, and so was justice served in this case? I suppose.

Then the ultimate in punishment came when, according to Walter, Louis Dagher's drunken slob of a father took the buckle of a belt to the back of Louis's scrawny legs and marked them all up for getting the shit kicked out of him by a girl. Then Mr. Dagher found out that Louis cried about it in public. That revelation got his ass beat even more. I'm sure Nellie Manziel thought that was really sexy.

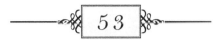

5 3

I sat in my room for a long time, looking out my window at the darkening winter sky. I could hear the brakes of a semi far off in the distance somewhere. The cold air sat still with hopelessness as the blue industrial landscape wore heavy on me. My heart and stomach tightened and ached. All I wanted to do was cry, but I couldn't find any tears. They needed some time to rest and dry up again. It was ironic how sometimes I wanted to cry but couldn't, and other times I grew so weary with grief that I couldn't stop myself from sobbing. I was tired having that feeling of not knowing what to do with myself next, of not knowing how to remove myself from my skin, and yet at the same time feeling like I was about to jump out of it. Taking a couple of hits of a joint helped, and so did a few pills here and there, especially sedatives, a drink or two, smoking a few cigarettes, hanging around with Shelly, checking Marisa's ashes, and so I decided to partake in these activities as often as I could. If it made me feel better and knocked me out, I should do it. I had also attempted to write the monster in prison, but I could never get the words down on paper the same way they were lined up in my mind. I must have made three attempts, but each time I couldn't get what I wanted to say to connect with my pen. It was a bad feeling, but I decided to try again anyway.

> *Dear Barton Withers, former stepfather, present-day monster,*
>
> > *I would like to remind you that you are currently incarcerated for murder. I don't care what you "pleaded" to, I also don't care how many lawyers you*

have or if they are good ones because everyone knows that you are a killer. What is it like in prison? I heard that Bellmorrow is one of the worst places.

That was it. I threw my pen against the wall. All I wanted to do was get revenge on him, but I couldn't even do that. It was hopeless, and I was frustrated, and I felt as if I was failing at the one thing I was supposed to be doing. It was almost as if it was a job.

Dad knocked on my door. "Allie? Come on down. I need to talk to you."

Shelly ran through the cracked door, and I followed down the long hardwood staircase. I smelled a familiar scent, that sweet dark oily smell of the cosmetics department at Sterns, but it wasn't Kiki. She had left earlier for work. This was deeper, more expensive. No, this was my mother sitting at our kitchen table with a steaming mug. My father appeared nervous as he ambled around the table, combing his fingers through his falling wisps of hair.

"Hello, Alice." She addressed me as if we were in a movie.

"What are you doing here?"

My father motioned for me to sit down. "We're having a family discussion. Go ahead and sit."

"Who's having a family discussion?" I gazed at my mother, who didn't seem right. She was clearly not her normal miserable self. She seemed fraught, beaten, and defeated. She didn't return my gaze.

"We are," my father said. "The three of us."

I smiled. I tried not to laugh out loud. I was doing a lot of things like that lately, being sarcastic, acting mean, showing obvious anger, getting in trouble. Why not give poor Mom a break? Why not make an effort not to laugh in her pretty face? Family discussions? We never had a family discussion before. We weren't a family, and besides, wasn't it a little late for that?

I sat down at the kitchen table anyway with my mother, who looked brutally out of place, but I was so relieved to feel Shelly strolling back and forth, rubbing his little scent glands on my pajama bottoms.

My father put his face down. He was exhausted and overworked. That's all he ever did was work. He was still wearing a heavy bandage on his arm, and I could tell when it hurt by the way he rubbed it and the how his face contorted in pain. His good arm was spread out in front of him as if he was about to crawl across the table in an attempt to escape his daughter and ex-wife. He raised his palm to his forehead and looked at me hard.

"What's going on, Dad? Why are you looking at me that way?"

"Alice, do you think you might need to go and stay with your mom for a little while?"

"Huh? What? No!" I yelled. Shelly ran out of the room. I was panicking, and I knew I would be thinking about this forever, wondering when my bedroom door would fly open in the middle of the night with such astonishing force.

"Okay, all right, all right, Allie. You don't have to do anything you don't want to do," he said.

I wiped my nose with the back of my hand as I felt more hot leakage from my eyes. More tears. More and more. Crying was my friend. Where were all these tears coming from? This couldn't be possible, could it? But it was.

"Don't you want me, Dad?" I didn't know what else to ask. "Why are you doing this? It doesn't make any sense." I jabbed a finger in her direction. "The last time you and she were in the same room, you were blaming her for Marisa's murder. In my grandmother's house!"

He couldn't answer that. He hated it when I caught him out on stuff. It made him so mad. He rubbed his temples with his thumb and forefinger. He said quietly, "That wasn't what I was trying to say."

I agreed with my mother on one thing. My father was weak a lot of the time. That's where I got my chicken shit from. I still hadn't looked at her. I was expecting the pain of her green flaring daggers in the side of my neck. Instead, I felt her tired eyes getting very large, then tightening up again, as if they expelled some kind of poisonous gas. My father's wrinkled brow rested in defeat.

"Alice," she began, "I bought this adorable little house in the old Pennington neighborhood. It's got a little round door with a stone front. You know, like the fairy tales. You loved those books."

"Marisa loved those books."

"And…and Helena? Helena misses you so much. You're all she ever blabbers about."

I missed that poor little kid too, but I couldn't afford to waste any more of my love. "I'm not going to live with my mother, Dad, and as long as you won't make me, I would be appreciative. Very appreciative."

I almost told him I would work in the store. Thank God I stopped myself.

"I won't make you go anywhere, Allie, I promise. Besides, you're going to be eighteen before you know it. I remember what it's like being your age and getting fed up with the adults telling you what to do."

No, I don't think you really have any idea.

"It's just that your mother and I are concerned about you. Come on, Alice, you're suspended from school for two weeks for assaulting another kid."

I was surprised it took so long for that to come up in our family discussion.

"Getting violent with boys? That…that's not you. That's not the little girl I raised."

I said nothing. I wanted to laugh.

"I think you need to get some counseling. Ken Holloway is right—"

Oh, so it's Ken now? "God, Dad, is that guy ever going to get out of our lives? Doesn't he have anything better to do with himself? I know, why doesn't he catch a murderer and see if he and DDA Giles can actually get a real conviction without being beaten with a plea bargain?"

My mother's head flopped forward.

"Alice, I know you're unhappy. I know you're angry—"

"I *am* angry, Dad. We already went over this Louis Dagher thing. He had no right to say those things. You *know* he had no right. You even said so! Why are you crumbling like this? Is it because she's sitting here? And what is it with that fucking Holloway?"

My father reached over and half tapped, half shook my face with his fingertips. "All right, Alice, that's enough. That fucking Holloway kept *your* butt out of jail! And don't you forget it. I don't know what ever gave you the idea that you were a badass."

I sat quietly. I waited for my mother's uncontrollable backhand. I was in the mood to grab hold of that arm. But nothing happened. I started to panic. It was always my mother whom I had to appease in order to live an anonymous peaceful existence, but now it was my father who was in charge.

"Dad, I'm sorry, really I am. I'm sorry about all the bad things I did. I'm sorry about what I said about Detective Holloway. I'm sorry about choking Louis." But I really wasn't. "Please, please don't make me go." Living with my mother only made bad things happen. I was the only one who came back alive, and it was this that I regretted and hated myself for.

He shook his head, "I won't make you live anywhere you don't want to live. You have my word." Then he turned to my mother as I finally glanced over at her. She looked disinterested. "I don't want to make things any more difficult than they already are, Lavinia. She wants to stay here with us. I think we should just have her stay. This is her home."

"Fine." She raised her eyebrows. "I'm too tired to force anyone to do anything they don't want to do."

No one spoke.

"But just know, Alice, I have a lovely little bedroom decorated and all set up for you when you want to visit."

"Where are your new slacks? You know, the gray ones that flare out at the bottom?"

"Hmm. Yeah, they're called bellbottoms, Alice."

"Where are they?"

"Mom has them."

"Why?"

"She got mad at me and took them back. She also took that hooped stripe sweater, and she broke that sterling silver L I bought her for Christmas. She threw it, and I didn't see where it landed."

"Those were your Christmas presents."

"I know, but I can't have them unless I buy them back from her. Where am I ever going to get the money to do that? I'll have to get a job."

"Do you want money?" I asked my mother.

"What?"

"For the decor, the time you put into the room."

"No, no, no." Her voice trailed off into a smoky croak.

My father looked over at me with a strange and questioning look on his face.

No one spoke again. The round glowing light from my mother's cigarette was kind, friendly, waiting for us, pleading for someone to say something. I could hear my father breathe in and out.

"Alice, I was thinking. Your dad and I were both in agreement on this." She sounded awkward, not her brazen, shameless self. "That boy in school. Anyone for that matter. You have to do your best to ignore them when they bully you, when they say mean things. You have to turn your head and walk the other way."

"Mom said the weirdest thing to me once about going to the movies, about going to the ladies' room at the movies."

"What could she have possibly said about that?"

"She said that sometimes men will go into the ladies' room to sit and wait for girls to come in so that they can rape and kidnap them. Sometimes kill them!"

"No way! She told you that?"

"Yep. She said always look under the stall for men's feet, and if someone comes out and surprises you with a gun? Just tell him this: 'Shoot me.' Then turn around and walk away."

"Turn and walk the other way. You don't say, Mother."

"It's true, Allie," my father said. "I know…I know we've gone over this…what do want to call it? An exception, okay. But you can't put your hands on anyone. You…you can't strike them first."

The urge to laugh welled up inside me again as I watched my mother inspect her perfect long red fingernails as my father lectured me on the near strangulation of Louis Dagher. She was still wearing the big ugly emerald and those shit diamonds the monster gave her. I ran my short fingernail down the crack between the two leaves of the shiny wooden plastic table and then slid it back up again, zigzagging my way back down.

"I tried to ignore him, Dad. I really did. But it didn't work, and when he said those things about Marisa, I just got so upset, so, so pissed off. I couldn't help it."

My father looked at me as if he didn't know what to say next. But finally he spoke. "I know. But you just keep walking away. Walk away from bad people like that. Let someone else punch his lights out, just don't let it be you. Eventually, he'll get tired of it. Even *he* will. Everyone knows what that kid is like. Believe me, he's in some trouble right now. And you know, these are things you can talk to someone about. There's nothing wrong with needing a little guidance when things get a little overwhelming."

I agreed with the guidance part, but I also thought that a little overwhelmed had nothing to do with how I felt. I didn't think either of them handled Marisa's murder properly. They didn't care like I did. No one did.

My mother suddenly threw her hands together. "Oh, Alice, I meant to tell you. Lil Schuester and her husband John are divorcing. She asks about you all the time. You remember Aunt Lil, of course."

I remembered Lil Schuester, but she wasn't my aunt. Instead, she was the older sister of the prisoner, the murderer, the monster.

I felt my nostrils flare and wondered why people continually forgot how things were so interconnected. It was like a house on fire. My mother poured gasoline around the perimeter of the house, then lit a match. When the house burned to the ground, she stood in the rubble, in the ashes, surrounded by smoke, and asked what happened to the house.

"Lil," she said slowly, "has two daughters." She paused as a flash of something I couldn't tell, guilt or pain, struck her face. "Kay and the other one? Robin, I think that's her name."

Oh yes, Mom. Do you remember those old days? You know, when you too had two daughters, close in age. "Yeah, I remember Kay. She was supposed to go to medical school. She didn't seem like the doctor type though."

I was jealous of Kay. Her life was good. Normal. She had parents who adored her, believed in her. Her mother gave her everything just to make sure she became this happy, well-rounded productive person where only good things came to her. Her older sister was still alive, and because she lived out of town and had a different last name, it would be hard to identify her as the niece of a killer. Reporters occasionally came around here, but not as much anymore, and I think that's one of the reasons Dad was beginning to like Detective Holloway so much. He kept those rats away for the most part. They seemed to gravitate to the Withers family much more, and the Withers family, for some pathological reason, appeared to welcome them.

My mother waved a hand at me and shook her head in resignation. "Good god, no! She's a hairdresser in Brooklyn."

"Really? Is she really?" The news perked me up.

"Yes, really. Why are you smiling?"

"Because that's what she really wanted to do all along."

The look on my mother's face was a combination of confusion and revulsion. "All that opportunity just thrown away," she said under her breath.

My father just shrugged. "Someone's gotta do the hair, Lavinia. Just like someone's gotta sell the fish, and someone's gotta pick up the trash."

Family discussion. Not sure what we accomplished. At least no one screamed.

Way to go, Kay.

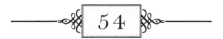

54

Dad decided to pull me out of South Wellton High and send me to the old convent. He thought it would give me the education I needed, the opportunity to stretch and excel, and put the fear of fire and brimstone the nuns would instill in me if I ever stepped out of line again or even thought about choking another student. I didn't mind. A change in scenery might have been a good thing. I could wear my blue wool knee socks and plaid mini skirt and go around pretending to be a good girl. Perhaps that would keep people far away from me. It would be like digging my own hole and crawling into it or putting a sheet over my head and cutting out the eyes like a ghost. I could walk around and see you, but you couldn't see me.

Aunt Nancy went to the convent. She was on the archery team, and that's where she met Mary Jo Withers McLaughlin. Then I reminded my father that the convent no longer provided bus service for the girls in the city due to funding, and so I would have to take the slow-poke Wellton public transportation, which was peppered with crime and would take about two hours to get to school. Dad was too busy to give me a lift, so that left hitchhiking.

"Oh shit, that's right! They made a big stink about that on the news maybe six weeks ago. You got one hell of a memory, don't you?" This had really been my mother's idea, I'm sure. Dad was secretly relieved because now he didn't have to dole out thousands of dollars for my Catholic education. I couldn't blame him.

And so that was that. I would not be attending St. Mary's, the Academy of the Immaculate Conception for Girls, or more commonly known as the old convent or just the convent because back in the early nineteen hundreds, that was exactly what it was: a convent. What was so ironic was how they renamed it so poorly because there was nothing immaculate about that place at all. Those Catholic girls were bigger sluts than the ones at South Wellton, if that was possible, and they smoked just as much pot, and so I suppose everything worked out exactly the way God and Dad wanted it after all. I would be continuing my education at South Wellton for the rest of my high school life.

Milk was hesitant to give me back my part-time job as a tutor, but apparently, some of the parents complained. They were on my side. They thought I was the wronged party, and Walter's mother and sister waged a campaign against Louis Dagher, telling Mr. Milk that if I was not allowed to tutor anymore, my "little incident" with Dagher would look like a "roll in a field of flowers" when they got through with him. It didn't take long for him to crumble. I was pleased.

As for Louis Dagher, he was not the same Louis Dagher anymore. As I continued to secretly observe him from afar, I think he may have gone a little crazy. Gone were the beads, the suede hat, old untucked flannel shirts over T-shirts sporting the names of bands, the ripped jeans, and the sandals with socks. Instead, Louis Dagher now looked like the perfect preppie boy with his pastel-colored sweaters, perfectly pressed shirts, cream-colored chinos, and penny loafers with the pennies in them. The odd thing was that no one said a word about it, and I never mentioned it to anyone either. Not once. I thought I was the only one who even noticed the complete transformation of this monster. Transformation or not, I knew underneath it all, he would always be a monster. Most people didn't understand that one could be wearing a suit, a creepy pair of sandals, or a prison jumpsuit. A monster was a monster, and I found it very difficult if not impossible to believe that a monster was capable of finding its heart and changing whatever soul it had because really, there was nothing there.

Monsters could not be forgiven nor forgotten, not ever. They needed to be destroyed the way evil should be destroyed. Barton Withers was a monster. Louis Dagher was a monster. I wondered how many monsters I would encounter in my life and how many I would be tasked to destroy before my death, when I might finally see my sister again. Every so often, I would position myself in a corner somewhere and try to catch Louis Dagher's eye so I could throw him a nasty grin or hiss at him as silently as I could like a trapped cat. But he ignored me and avoided me as Nellie Manziel was hanging off someone else these days. Poor Louis Dagher spent his time alone, hopefully stewing in his own hell as the former posse of devil worshipers dispersed in a frantic disappearing act like the giant cockroaches they were.

Hatred was a beautiful thing. It was delicious and motivating, and it fed me. You just had to know what to do with it that was all. Louis Dagher was destroyed.

Dear Barton Withers, former stepfather and current murderer,

I hope this letter finds you facedown in your prison cell with your cellmate's knee in the small of your back. Hopefully, he is deciding whether to beat the shit out of you or put his "you know what" into your "you know where!" You know what? I didn't even realize that this kind of stuff even went on until a friend of mine told me all about it! What a delightful thought for me, fantasizing about your suffering, because there isn't any love lost between you and me, even though I'm sure you already know that. You are a beast, Barton Withers. You aren't even good enough to be an animal. I pray night and day that you are traumatized and tortured, just like you traumatized and tortured Marisa. I hope you are forced to think every single day about what you did to her. I have to, and so should you. You have caused so much hurt and pain. It will never ever go away. I have heard people say that you have no feelings about what you did, but I know better. Everyone has feelings about something, and I remember what you used to be like long before you were a murderer. You liked Marisa. The two of you used to be friends. You got along really, really well. Maybe you killed the wrong stepdaughter, did you ever think of that? Marisa helped you do that sewing machine charity thing and that hospital stuff with those sick little kids. How can you ever be trusted again outside your dirty little cage? Well, I am here to tell you that you can't ever be trusted again. Not ever. I will find your feelings, and I will exploit them, press them, hurt them, and beat them until you are feeling just the way I am right now. Do you know how I will do that? I will write letters to you every chance I have a pen and piece of paper within my reach. I will save all the money I make and spend every nickel on stamps. Every time I pass the post office in my neighborhood, I will send you one more letter. Make that two more letters. You will never stop hearing from me, Barton Withers. I will chase you and chase you until my last breath on earth, and my life's work will be to make yours a living hell. You had better pray that you stay right where you are, you murderer, right there in that dark mudhole because what awaits you in the free world is far worse than anything you can imagine in there. You will pray for your death.

Have a nice day,
Alice

Of course, I couldn't get myself to send it. I was way too, what my sister used to call me, *chicken shit.* I read my letter to Barton Withers over and over again. I couldn't stop looking at it. It made me panic, and I had that chilly stabbing feeling in the middle of my chest again. What would happen to me for having these thoughts? I worried now that I had finished the letter and put the contents of my mind into words that somehow, the world already knew about them. I kept going back again, changing words around, checking and rechecking my spelling until the sides of my head pounded, and I became angrier and more frustrated than I was when I first sat down at my desk with a blank sheet of paper.

Finally finishing one of my hundreds of letters to the monster did not bring me the relief I was hoping for. I thought of Detective Holloway bulldozing his way into my room uninvited. He would hold up the envelope with his big hand right up near his chubby face, the address of Bellmorrow State Prison staring back at me, and with a wink say, "Alice, honey. You can't do this."

And Marisa. Ironically, she would have been the one who could have helped me put the right words together and turned my pitiful attempt at expression into a masterpiece.

I quickly ripped up the letter into teeny, tiny little pieces before any further damage could be done.

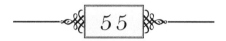

5 5

"Dad? Don't you have to be a Catholic girl to be enrolled at the convent?"

"Ah, oh, I don't know. Well, yeah, I guess. I don't think they care about any of that these days, Allie, as long as they got your money. Why?"

"Aunt Nancy went."

"I know that."

"Hmm. I just thought you had to be from an observant Catholic family or…you know what I mean. Don't you have to at least be baptized by a priest or something like that? Was Nancy?"

"Jesus, I don't know. That was a long time ago. You're not hitchhiking, Alice."

"No, Dad, it's not that. I was just thinking. I don't think I was even baptized a Catholic, was I? Surely, Bunica would have mentioned something over the years, but she never did. Once she gave Marisa a gold crucifix with a tiny diamond in the middle for her birthday. I never got anything like that. Was I baptized?"

My father was silent. We were both in different rooms as we were talking, so I couldn't read his face. Then he walked into the library where I was sitting. His face was twisted with worry. "No," he said very clearly, "you were not baptized Catholic. I have to go pick up Kiki. See you in a little while."

I sat there and gazed into the air. It came to me.

I could not see Marisa's face, but I knew how terrified she must have been. The overhead light was on in the bedroom, and everything lit up like a hot white bulb. I shivered underneath the gray quilted bedspread as I struggled with one eye to see my mother. She was hunched over Marisa, and I could tell she was poking my sister between the eyes.

"You made your First Communion, young lady!" my mother jeered in a frightening low voice. "What you did with that girl was a sin! I am so ashamed of you. You make me sick. Sick to my stomach!"

First Communion. The Holy Eucharist. I didn't know anything about it except for the books that were piled high in the cases behind me. But I remembered bits and pieces of that harsh scolding. Did Marisa make her First Holy Communion? I don't remember being there for any of the festivities. But I would have only been just under five years old. I didn't make mine, and I would have been baptized had I gone through this rite. I would have remembered all this had I been there.

I knew I would have to ask someone, like Bunica. The truth of the matter was that I was scared to ask, and I didn't want to think about it, but I couldn't help that. My head swam and my brain bounced around the inside of my head. I was frightened again. I was afraid of the strange inconsistencies of my life. Something was not right, but I was too frightened to find out what it was. I just wanted to be normal. It was so hard being so scared all the time like this, especially when I was alone with my thoughts. My mind hated me.

Dear Mary Jo,

I hope this letter finds you, your husband, and your two sons in the best of health. How is Danny? I think about him a lot. He has always been such a nice boy, and he said very nice things to me the last time I saw him at Marisa's memorial service. Nothing is his fault, and it was mean of me to just walk past him like he didn't even exist. I know he doesn't understand me. Maybe you can tell him more about me, and that might help him understand a little bit more. I'm sure I don't need to tell you any of this because you know how to do all these things. I'm also very sorry about making you cry on that day. I really am. I hope you will believe me and accept my apology. I don't like to be mean to anyone,

I really don't, it's just that you are his sister, and I know it's not your fault and you didn't do anything wrong, but I know you're like on his side, whether you want to be or not. Your parents have really stood behind him and seem to believe his lies. I'm not saying that you have done the same or anything like that. I mean, after all, you did come to Marisa's memorial service, and you were the only one. You and Danny were the only two from your entire family to even show up and pay respects. When I truly think about that, I know how much I owe you this apology. I saw the small wreath of flowers your parents sent and that bouquet that was propped up by that weird marble thing that Lil and her husband sent over, but the fact that you made the effort to come all the way from Denver with Danny only to hear me hurl insults at you was really quite admirable. I guess it was probably best that no one else in your family came. I probably would have been a lot meaner to them than I was to you. I just remember seeing your parents on the news saying that their son "would never intentionally hurt that girl" and that it was an accident and all of that. It was no accident, Mary Jo. I saw the whole thing with my own eyes, so please understand why I was so upset when I saw you. I really hope that you and Danny can forgive me.

I heard that Lil and her husband are getting a divorce. I know what it feels like, you know, divorce and all. Everything gets all turned around and confusing. I don't know what else to say about that stuff. I know I'll never get married, that's for sure. I thought it was so neat that Kay moved to the big city to become a hairdresser. She wanted to do that more than anything in the whole world. She wasn't interested in becoming a doctor, that's for sure. I remem-

ber the three of us had so much fun when she used to style our hair, and sometimes we would put on a ton of makeup. That was one of the other reasons I wanted to get in touch with you. Something about Kay deciding to do what she loves, what she's really good at, made me miss you more, and I wanted to finally send a letter to you.

Well, I'll stop here. I'm not very good at writing letters, so I hope this doesn't sound too weird. Anyway, take care.

From,
Alice Buchner

I sent this letter, but I knew it would be a laborious process. I sat at the desk forever, looking down at the letter but not really reading it. I kept asking myself, *What if this?* or *What happens when?* and the ruminating over it caused me so much frustration, I cried dry tears. But if I was going to send this letter, I would have to just send it. It was important to me that Mary Jo understood that I wasn't angry with her. I also felt awful about being rude to Danny.

I wondered how she would feel about the letter, if she would accept my apology. I know what it was like when Marisa used to apologize and ask for forgiveness when my mother made her believe that she had done something wrong. I remembered those constant silent treatments. I worried so much, it just wore me down.

* * * * *

We didn't do much praying. We never went to church—only when my grandmother took us did we ever participate in anything remotely religious, but when I saw my sister praying that day, I knew something was very wrong.

It was a Tuesday in the dead of winter. School was closed. The roads were very bad due to the heavy snow. The basement in the house in Crescent Hills was always cold. The plush yellow carpet felt as if it were laid directly over a frozen slab of concrete by the way the soles of my feet chilled. Once my mother pushed the side of my head down hard on that carpet. I corrected her about something, and she was less than pleased. When I looked up, I saw spots and light. It sure felt like concrete.

Marisa knelt in front of a little table by the cold inactive fireplace. I knelt down beside her.

"What are you doing?" As soon as I asked, I knew she would do something like roll her eyes and ask me something like "What does it look like I'm doing, donkey face?"

Instead, she put her hands down on the table and shook her head slowly as if in disbelief. "I don't know what I'm going to do now. I really, really did some bad things, and now I'm scared. I'm really scared, and it's all my fault."

I knew this had something to do with my mother and most likely Barton Withers, and so I made it a point to keep my voice down. "What do you mean? What happened?"

She turned to me. Fear and resignation were in her eyes and all over her face. "Barton left this morning. He moved out, and it's my fault."

That couldn't have been true. I didn't hear or see anything. "Where did he go?"

She raised her hands. "I don't know. Sun Chance, I guess. And I'm so worried about it. I mean, what if he doesn't come back? Mom said this was all my fault."

"Well now, of course he's going to come back." I looked around the vast room, the comfortable leather furniture, the television, the cable box, newspapers strewn about the large coffee table, the stereo, the fully stocked bar. "I mean, look—all his stuff is still here. And…and why is Mom saying this is your fault?"

I sort of already had an answer to that.

Tears formed in her eyes. "She said I drove him away from here. She said that I have a big mouth, and I'm an emotionally dist-distribute-disturbed girl. She said I was babyish and it's me that is breaking apart her relationship with her husband."

"She said those things to you?" Of course she did.

She nodded. "And if he doesn't come back or if he does come back, gets all his things, and then leaves again, it's gonna be all my fault. I'm scared. I don't know what to do. What should I do?"

I thought hard for a minute, and then I shifted myself off my knees and onto the floor where I sat, shaking my head, looking beyond my sister. "Marisa, this doesn't make sense at all. How does a kid like you or me break apart a grown-up's marriage or relationship or whatever you want to call it? He's moved out because of her, Marisa, not you. It can't be you. I…I don't understand. I mean, we don't have any say in what the adults do. This isn't your fault. It's hers. I just think she's blaming this on you because she blames everything bad that happens on you."

She didn't answer me. She was convinced that this was her doing. "I've been praying a lot, you know." She fell back on her butt and lightly scratched the surface of the table.

"You have? I didn't know that. I guess it's good to pray."

"Remember that one night I was at Suzanne's, and I wasn't supposed to leave the house?"

"No." I shook my head.

"Well, Mom was so mad, you wouldn't have believed it."

I would have believed it.

"I could hear her screaming just about three houses over. I was so embarrassed. Suzanne was already frightened of Mom as it was. I ran up the side of the yard as fast as I could, and there was Mom screaming louder than I think I had ever heard her. She was pregnant with Helena. I even remember what she was wearing, if you can believe that."

"And that's when you started to pray?"

"Yes!" she exclaimed in a near whisper. "When I got up to my room, she was already standing there at the window, looking out over the garden. She wouldn't even look at me, you know? She was just standing there with tears running down her cheeks, you know? She was crying and just slowly shaking her head back and forth, back and forth. I tried telling her I was sorry, but she just said that if anything happens to this baby, she will never forgive me. I never prayed so hard in my life. I had three months to go, maybe? I was so scared."

She brightened up immediately.

313

"But look at Helena! You couldn't ask for a more perfect little chubby cheek."

I sat speechless. Stunned.

All of a sudden she asked, "Why does she hate me so much? You don't hate me, do you?"

"Oh, no, Marisa, no." That question snapped me right out of my trance. "You're my sister, I love you. I could never hate you. I would love you even if you weren't my sister."

When she looked at me, I saw a warm appreciation as she tried to hide her sadness. It was a loss that seeped out of every angle of her face.

"And with Mom, I...I..." I didn't know the right words to say. I wasn't sure what I believed. I didn't know what to believe. I was numb. "I mean, Marisa. A...a parent, a mother, can't hate her own child. That's impossible, don't you think?" Unconditional love. I heard some character talk about it on a soap opera. The man said to his character son that although adults fall out of love, they can never stop loving their children. That was unconditional love.

"I don't know," she said and just shrugged. "I think it can be that way."

"What way?"

The basement door flew open, and our mother's irate voice came crashing down the steps. "I'm making soup. I don't know what the two of you are doing down there, but it's time for you to come upstairs."

I opened my drawer and looked at the secret contents inside, the ones that only I knew about, and stared at them for a long time. I needed to make sure they were still there and hadn't disappeared into a puff of smoke. I didn't dare take them out of that velvet bag because the tediousness in my mind combined with my letter to Mary Jo was far more than I could handle. Although I was tempted. I was very tempted.

"I'll get him, Marisa," I said as I looked down into my dresser drawer. "I'll get him. I know I will. I promise."

I carefully and quietly closed the dresser drawer and turned back to the bed where the letter to Mary Jo lay next to Shelly. He was sprawled sideways so that the little white fluff on the very bottom of his belly was exposed. I was so tired of going over and over things in my head, and I briefly thought of my old friend Bruce. Aside from my sister, he was the only real friend I ever had. Sometimes I could put my aunt in that category, but it could be hard having any type of meaningful conversation with her when either of us was in one of our states.

I read the letter over again. I changed a few lines, checked my lousy spelling and grammar, and after eleven times and almost four hours, I had my best penmanship inked on lavender paper from an old stationery package that Marisa won in a raffle at the school carnival in junior high. I read it over one last time and ran my finger along the inside of the envelope for anything evil that may have inadvertently fallen inside. I may have put something in there by mistake. The stress was unimaginable. It wasn't until the next day that I was finally able to drop it at the post office. It was brutal, but it was my way of life, and I figured that I would get used to it, which, in many ways, I did.

I remember when I was little, I used to enjoy the rain, especially when I used to stand on the front porch of our house and watch a storm roll in. I loved thunder. Dad would tell us that God was either bowling or moving furniture. He said that was the way he was able to keep Aunt Nancy calm when they were children. I was fascinated with the crackle of lightning, but the dull steely sloppiness of rain toward the end of March where the melting black snowbanks were peppered with dog shit only depressed me. I never knew what to do with myself. If it weren't for Shelly, I would seriously have to contemplate what I was doing and why I even bothered to fool with life.

* * * * *

"Aunt Nancy?" The house was dark when I walked in—darker than usual. It was six in the evening, so I figured she would either be messing with her hair and makeup or cleaning something.

I threw my knapsack down next to the telephone table and walked the long dark hallway ahead of me to the kitchen. I noticed the small lamp next to my father's chair was barely illuminating the room in a bitter orange glow. I stood in the doorway. "Kiki?"

"I need to talk to you, Alice. Come sit down." She sat in the dark, smoking a cigarette. She was not smiling. The pack sat sideways on the tiny round table beside her. I was dying for one.

"What's wrong?" Where's Dad?" I stood motionless in the doorway.

"Where do you think he is?" Beyond the large windows and the French doors, hidden by an assortment of hanging ferns and Dad's favorite African violets, the glow of the original Boochie's sign blinked and faded with its distinctive rhythm: Boochie's, B-O-O-C-H-I-E-S, Boochie's.

"Ask a stupid question, get a stupid answer?" I smiled, instantly regretting my cuteness. I didn't move from the doorway. "Where's Aunt Nancy?"

"Alice," she said firmly, her mouth full of smoke as she stubbed out her cigarette, "I don't know where she is, I don't really give a shit where she is, and I'm not in the mood for any more goddamned roll call. I should have never given you that—"

"What is your problem, Kiki?"

"Are you stealing from me?"

"Huh? No!"

"You wanna sit down?" It was more like a demand as she pointed to the chair adjacent to her.

"No, I'm fine here. I don't want to sit down next to you. I don't need your stupid money, Kiki."

"I'm not talking about money, Alice, and you know it!" Her voice rose to a level I'd never heard from her. "I'm talking about pills, my sedatives. Are you going into my pocketbook and taking my pills?"

I started to move a little back and forth.

"Answer me!"

"Don't you yell at me, Kiki." I backed away. "You're not my mother. This isn't even your house! It's Dad's."

She let out a deep breath and relaxed a little. "No, I am not your mother, and this is not my house, but I have a right to know if you have been taking my prescription medication without asking me first—without even the decency of getting my permission, not that

I would have given you any. You were very sick at that funeral those years back, and I made a big mistake, one that I regret to this day."

"It was just a couple—" My plan was to blame all of it on my aunt, but I just couldn't. I wouldn't have gotten away with that either.

"A couple. A couple? Half the goddamned bottle is gone, Alice. Did you not think I was going to figure this out? No wonder you have been walking around here like some kind of wacky, sped-up zombie. You are depressed. My god, Alice, these could kill you."

Good. Oh, gee. Now why would I be depressed? Hmm. Let me think. It's not because of your fucking sedatives. "I'm sorry. I'm sorry, okay? I mean, what am I supposed to do now? It's not like I can just regurgitate them back up. They're gone."

She sighed and leaned back in her chair.

I remained in the doorway. I knew I was wrong, but I didn't care.

"You know, a lot of this is my fault."

"Don't try to pull a guilt trip on me."

"Hey, why don't you just shut your mouth for a minute, huh?" She shot up from her chair. "For once, stop feeling sorry for yourself and open up your ears."

I just stared at her. "I am *not* feeling sorry for myself," I said finally.

She ignored me. "I knew when you started sneaking into the gin when you were barely out of diapers that there were gonna be problems. I was wrong not to put a stop to it there and then. Jesus Christ. A child sneaking into a bottle of gin. Then I come along and give you one of these to calm you down. I should have never *ever* done such a ridiculous thing. Your sister's funeral." Her tone became accusatory again. "Unless of course, you were lying to me and had already been doing pills."

"I wasn't."

She shook her head slowly in defeat. "You're right. I'm not your mother. I'm not even your stepmother. There's not a damned thing I can do but tell you this: keep your hands off my drugs, and keep your hands off my booze. You want something? *You ask me.* Then *I* will decide whether it's a yes or a no."

"You're talking to me like I'm a kid."

She smiled at me as if she were the one who felt sorry for me. She leaned forward and looked at me straight in the eyes. I could see her pupils, feel them even from the distance where I stood. I shuddered.

"I have been around drug addicts my whole life, little girl. I'll tell you what, you are heading down that same tragic road. Do you even realize that stealing certain kinds of prescription medications is a crime? If you continue with this kind of behavior, you are going to end up in jail, or you're going to end up dead with a needle in your arm. You will eventually overdose. You need to get help. You *are* a kid, and you know you are, and you're frying your brains. I've seen you sleep for days. You've gone through some horrible shit already in your young life. Your parents can and should force you to get help, and yet Rudy won't, and I cannot, for the fucking life of me, understand why he won't. You're his daughter, for Christ's sake."

"Are you going to tell him about this?"

"I knew that would be your next question. No, not this time because no one has discussed any of this drug shit with you. But next time? Count on it. And if Rudy melts? I'll call the police. And he *will* melt."

"Look, I'm sorry. It won't happen again. I don't know what else you want me to say." I was getting tired of this bitch lecturing and threatening me with the cops. My great-grandfather built this house she was sitting in so comfortably. Who the hell did she think she was?

I decided that right then, I was going to hate her forever. She, like everyone else, had no idea of what I was going through. I was sick of everyone around me thinking that Marisa's murder was no big deal. How they could go through life not caring about something like this was an absolute mystery to me. I'm the one in pain. Kiki had no right to—

"So," she stated, "are we clear? You do not take from me what does not belong to you."

"Yes. I got it." I turned to walk out.

"Alice, stop."

"What? I said I understood you."

"You're a good girl. You're much smarter than this, and please don't start sighing and rolling your eyes and breathing, breathing heavy. Get help. You need to talk to someone about Marisa."

"Can I go now? I'm tired of talking, Kiki. I'm sorry I stole from you. It will never happen again."

She didn't seem angry anymore, even though I was sure that she still was. She looked more sad than anything else, and I was glad. I hated her as she nodded her head and dismissed me from my own library with a wave of a bony hand. Everything was gone—my appetite, my craving for cigarettes. God forbid I take one of hers. She might call the cops and have me thrown in the slammer. She says she doesn't want to hurt my father? Well, what the hell does she think *that* would do? I despised her. Monster.

I still didn't know where Aunt Nancy was. I looked in the bathroom across from my room. At least that damned curling iron was turned off.

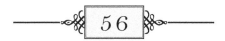

56

I sat in in the library in front of the fireplace looking through an old book. I had probably thumbed through that book at least a hundred times. Then I heard them talking. They were both fed up with me. I couldn't hear what they were talking about because the TV was too loud and I was paying attention to what was in the book, but I knew it was about me. Did they ever have a lot of nerve.

It was sinister—their low talking, the sound of Kiki flicking her lighter and then dropping it on the kitchen table with that plastic-sounding click. She acted like she owned this place. Everything was fine between me and Dad before she came along and turned him against me.

God, did they ever hate me.

I turned down the volume of the TV and quietly put the book on the rug in front of me. They knew I was listening because they stopped talking, and then when they resumed, it was only soft whispers. I heard them from very far away. I padded quietly out of the room down the endless darkness toward the kitchen, ever so slow. That's when I heard Dad say, "I look at her and I say to myself, 'Why couldn't that have been my daughter?'"

"How could you?" I shrieked.

"Hey! Go to bed!" my father shouted back.

"No! I'm not going to bed! I'm leaving! I'm going out!" I headed toward my room, but then I saw Kiki creeping up behind me. She was wearing this awful, ugly dress. It was a rose-colored contraption with big poofy sleeves like something a prostitute from the Elizabethan era would wear. It was monstrous. Like her. She had a cigarette dangling from her mouth, and my father ran and disappeared behind a corner somewhere as she did his dirty work for him.

320

"You go to your room right now! You do not tell us what you're going to do!" Her eyes blazed with the most vicious revelation of evil I had seen from her yet. They shot pin-sized bullets at me. She grabbed my arms, her burning cigarette centered in her lips.

"You bitch, you bitch!" was all I could say. It was pathetic.

"You're a lunatic, Alice!" She tried to holler as her cigarette stayed firmly in place. "You're a drug addict lunatic!"

"She's trying to burn me, Dad!"

But Dad made his way back to the kitchen. He was shouting and throwing things around the room, but I couldn't hear what he was yelling, even though I stood right next to him. I was ready for a fight. I was petrified. I felt a numbness come over me, and I couldn't move quickly, but I knew I had to defend myself against the monster.

She gripped my forearms as slowly, my knee came up in an effort to jab her in the stomach, but she moved back. It was futile. The lit cigarette remained stoutly in place.

She lost grip of one of my arms, and I was able to break free. I turned and ran up to my room as fast as I could and locked the door. I could hear them laughing, and Kiki was imitating my mother. "I called Lavinia the other day to tell her to get her rotten daughter out of my house, she's stealing from us, and she said, 'If Alice misbehaves, send her to her room without dinner!'" She laughed again in a rancid, hysterical cackle.

I pulled on a pair of purple three-quarter-length jeans, a white top, a knit vest, and slipped on a pair of old black flats, no socks. I was at the front door within seconds. It was pitch-black outside, late, probably well after midnight, but I wasn't frightened. I was ready to leave, to run, run far.

"Where do you think you're going?" my father shouted. There they were, both of them hovering over me like moths.

"You want me to go, I'm going. I'm leaving now." I was very calm. I didn't have any direction, but at least the second I walked out the door, I would be free.

Then my father started to punch me. Once on the left side of the head. Then twice, three times.

"Rudy, come on, that's enough."

The monster changed. She defended me. She must have been feeling some guilt deep down in that ice-cold vat of hers. But monsters don't change.

I never did leave that night. My father wouldn't let me, not without punching and punching and punching me until I was nearly blind. My father. A monster. Monsters are evil, and evil must be destroyed.

I woke up in my room. I didn't know how I got there, but a jolt of breathlessness catapulted me upward. The window was open, and the air was warm. A slight breeze rippled the soft petals of the petunias laid out perfectly manicured in the flower box beneath. That was Dad's project. He loved his flowers and his plants.

I lay back down.

I must have screamed loud enough to wake myself up for a second time. I heard the trailing end of my voice. Shelly leapt from the bed and into the hallway like a startled patch of gray flying through the night. I was soaked in what I thought was my own urine, but then I realized it was sweat. It was salty and cold, and it hurt to pull my knees up to my chest and huddle in the freezing room.

I walked out into the hallway feeling sticky and drenched. Very slowly, I opened my father's bedroom door. He lay sprawled out on his back, mouth wide-open, and snoring loudly. Kiki wasn't there. I thought she could be at work, but it was the middle of the night. Aunt Nancy's bedroom door was half-open. She lay on her stomach in her pink two-piece pajama set and thick white socks. She had green and pink curlers in her hair. Curlers and a curling iron. I didn't ask myself why. She snored too, only a little softer, and had a long pillow that looked like a rolling pin over the back of her neck.

I went back to the doorway of the room where my father slept. He looked like a little boy.

"I'm sorry about that dream, Dad, those terrible thoughts," I whispered into the darkness. "I hope you didn't hear anything."

I walked back to my bedroom to the loud harsh sound of my father gasping at the night with Shelly just a step behind. I stripped down completely and put on fresh pajamas. I ran my hand over the raspberry-colored fitted sheet. It wasn't as wet, so I lay back down, and Shelly began to knead my flannel chest in an effort to get himself comfortable enough to fall asleep in a warm ball. I gently stroked behind his ear. He purred loudly. It was a beautiful sound, and I felt protected. I guess all was forgiven.

"Sorry I startled you awake, fella. I hope it doesn't happen again, but I'm afraid I can't promise. I've been having a lot of strange dreams since Marisa was murdered. Maybe I'm smoking too many drugs. Why do you like me so much?"

I looked up at the ceiling. The hint of light from the warehouse out front showed a spot of a shadow I never noticed before.

"I wonder if Mary Jo's gotten my letter?"

57

Wellton in the spring had always been an illustrious time. There was a strong stirring in the morning air, as if a tiny clean bubble had popped out of a dusty cave full of cobwebs. It was as if a white rose had quickly opened and emitted the first ever scent of dew. Maple and wisteria bloomed again in places that I had forgotten even existed. Off to the northeast beyond the tree line, a deep indigo sky collided with the morning mist and broke off into little patches and sprinkles. I knew that if I was going to have any type of conversation with my father, meaningful or otherwise, I would have to take my place at the 1950s yellow telephone chair smooshed up against the old telephone books in front of the lobster tank.

"Hey, let's talk about you starting at State," he said as he ruffled through a cardboard box filled with oysters that said *Pensacola* on the side in big black letters.

"Before we do that, have you noticed Shelly? He looks like he's lost weight."

"Well, you'd never know that by the way he eats. Oh, and to answer your question, I don't notice him much unless he's scrounging for food. You're the one he loves, Allie."

"You love him too. Admit it." I was worried about my cat. I shifted in my seat so my voice was facing my father, even though none of my father was facing me. "He's eating, that's not the problem. He's still losing weight, and he's drinking more than he ever did before. I think I should take him to Dr. Campbell. He's got all his shots and everything. I don't think he's sick or anything like that."

"How much is this damned cat gonna cost me?"

"Nothing, Dad. I have money from my tutoring."

"Not enough to cover that rip-off veterinarian." He handed a clipboard to Frank and waved his other hand at me. "Don't worry about it. Find out what's going on with him. Little shit bag needs a job—I've been feeding him for years."

"Thanks, Dad."

"Now." He looked up at me as if he had just come up for air. "State, Allie! Damn, am I proud of you. You're gonna be the first person in this family who has ever gone to college. Can you believe that? You're grandfather's watching over you. Aww, he's so happy."

"Marisa probably would have gone if she wasn't murdered." I felt that twinge of anger again, and I was ready to lash out at someone who didn't deserve it.

"Oh, Alice." I deflated him, and I felt bad for a second. "Life is gonna go on whether we want it to or not."

Like it or not. Life moved on perfectly fine around here. I said nothing. My father gave me an ultimatum. He told me that turning eighteen meant that I was an adult, and if I was going to continue to "live under his roof," I was either going to join the military, go to college, or work at the store.

"I remember a long time ago my mother told me that I would go to Bertrand and become an astronaut," I said.

He sounded like a Chihuahua as he let out a yelp that nearly tossed him into one of the display cases. I thought he was laughing at me. "No, it's not that you aren't Bertrand material, Allie, because you are, really. In my estimation? You are. But your mother? Your mother. She hears the word *Bertrand*, and she's off like a torpedo. It's not about the grades. It's about the money, the connections, the lineage, all that horseshit that she finds so impor—" He stopped and waved a hand.

All those things I despised. All those things that destroyed my life from the top down. I watched from the outside as I measured my and even Marisa's values against those who ended up having none. My life was ruined even if I was the only one who would ever notice, and my sister would be dead forever.

"And besides, Allie, you go to a place like Bertrand, you won't be able to take your cat or your bedroom. See? This is the best way all around. You got the cat, you got the room, and you don't have to boil lobster. What else could you ask for?"

What else.

"And no matter what"—he threw a damp towel over his shoulder and backed away—"this is all gonna be yours someday. Don't wanna deal with the crustaceans? Get Scotty to do it."

"What if I just get rid of the lobster tank?"

"You'll regret it. You won't make nearly as much money, and Boochie's will no longer be Boochie's. Bad move, girl. And if you're gonna be stupid in business, please, wait 'til I'm dead."

"Do you and Kiki have plans tonight?" I wondered if she had ever said anything about the pills.

"Kiki? Kiki's gone. Where have you been over the past ten days?"

"Gone?" I sat up straight in the old yellow telephone stool. "Gone? What do you mean gone?"

"Gone. Moved out. Moved on. Got a transfer with Sterns to their flagship store in New York. Doing cosmetics or something, I don't know." He was always so damned nonchalant about the most important things.

"You broke up."

He nodded, not appearing in any way upset, which was exactly the way he was when my mother dragged Marisa and me away from him and out of our warm beds so many years ago. "She dumped me, yep. Now she's gone like a big fancy bird. Do you remember how that old song went?"

"Is it my fault?" I didn't even think. It just fell out.

"Whose fault?" he said, halfway turning to me. "Your fault? What? Of course not, what kind of a question is that? Jesus, Allie."

I faced down. My chest tightened. I said nothing.

"It's *my* fault," he said. "I work too much, I read too much, I snore too much, that is when I finally come home. Same old crap." With that, he disappeared into the back. I heard him say something to Frank. They laughed, and he picked up a distant telephone.

I hopped off the chair and out the front door and started walking back up to the house. Dad never seemed to know anything about the pills. Or the booze. Good. She was the one who got me hooked in the first place. Another monster gone.

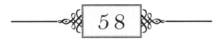

58

The South Wellton Animal Clinic had an excellent reputation. People from all over the small metropolitan area brought their pets to South Wellton to see the veterinarian from Scotland, who, like Dad, kept long hours and weekends to accommodate his business. I tried to explain to Dad that Dr. Campbell was a proud Scotsman and was not interested at all in applauding specific historical victories of the English. That just made my father want to provoke him even more by referring to him as the traitorous rip-off merchant whose head should belong to the king. I could never tell if Dr. Campbell's laugh was real or not.

The clinic had been in business since 1965, and it still had the same flooring—chips of irregular-sized terra-cotta tile set in thick grout that was now black from its years of wear and tear. Dark wooden paneling adorned the walls, and there was a little black-and-white TV set in the corner of the front desk that was always turned on to a daily game show, soap opera, or matinee movie. The volume was always turned down. Gentle music stirred the air. It quieted my head and relaxed whatever twined my stomach and bound the inside of my chest.

I peeked into Shelly's little crate carrier and watched him as he slept soundly. He purred as if all was right with the world.

"Shelly Buchner?" A robust redheaded man with wire-rim glasses and a golf shirt burst through the receiving door. I was expecting to see the elder Dr. Campbell with the loud brogue, soft complexion, and thick glasses.

I looked up at the redheaded man standing in front of me. He made me smile instantly. I didn't know if it was his fiery red hair, the small explosion of freckles on his ivory skin, his lopsided smile, or his eyes that were so acute and caring. I had never seen eyes like that before.

"I guess I wasn't sure if you were talking to us at first," I said as I picked up Shelly's carrier and followed Dr. Redhead. "No one has ever addressed him as Shelly Buchner."

His laugh was really nice.

We walked down a long bright hallway that showcased lots of funny photographs of dogs and cats, crayon drawings from children with their pets, sunshine and balloons, posters, and an assortment of pamphlets on how to take care of a pet.

Dr. Redhead led me to the usual cheery examination room with the giant scale and the plastic models of a dog's heart and cat's ear. I noticed they had another plastic heart infested with plastic worms. The large composite of every dog imaginable was included, broken down by breeds. One wall had the same exact composite, but it was cats.

"I refer to my patients with their parents' last name just because… Well, there are so many Sams and Shelly… Short for Sheldon?" Dr. Redhead expelled a childlike laugh. It was contagious, and although I had been so worried about Shelly, for that one moment, I was happy and I laughed too.

"No, no. My dad owns a fish market, and Shelly likes shellfish. Well, he eats all fish of course."

"I'll bet he does! Lucky you, Shelly. Dr. Paul Keating." Dr. Redhead stuck a freckled hand out to me.

"I'm Alice." I shook his hand. "Shelly Buchner's mom."

I was surprised at my spry humor and how relaxed I felt without a cigarette, a highball filled with gin, something quick to pop, anything.

He laughed again. "Shelly Buchner's mom. I like that." He carefully lifted Shelly onto the examination table. Shelly looked up at me and meowed and then looked at the new veterinarian with wonder.

"Where is Dr. Campbell?" I asked.

"Would you believe the south of France?" He continued to examine Shelly.

"Oh."

"A very much-needed vacation." He turned to find a thermometer. "Can you hold him? Will he scratch?"

Shelly wasn't happy, but he was cooperative. We both stroked and tickled him at the same time, and his head went back as he showed off his neck and closed his big eyes.

"Oh now." Dr. Keating's voice was low and gentle. He once again rubbed and pressed both sides of his stomach and looked into his ears. Then he stepped back and let out a breath, never taking his fingers off Shelly.

"What's wrong with my cat, Dr. Keating?"

"Did you get him as a kitten? I see he's been neutered."

"Yeah, my dad brings in him. No, he was a stray tomcat hanging around the fish store."

"Right, right."

"He came to us when I was about ten. My sister spotted him first. My father took him in, and we started to feed him regular cat food so he would get the right nutrition and not just something like shrimp all the time."

"Someone is getting a good deal, aren't you, old boy?" Dr. Keating smiled and continued to scratch Shelly behind the ears. "And when he, let's say, adopted you and your family as so many cats do, he was already a full-grown cat."

I thought for a second. "Well, yeah. I don't know how old he was. He wasn't a kitten, I know that."

"Ms. Buchner," he said, quickly removing his stethoscope, "your cat is probably suffering from kidney failure because he's old. You must know from seeing Dr. Campbell that Shelly is a very old cat."

"We never talked about his age." I never wanted to admit it.

Keating's face was slightly sorrowful. He began to thumb through Shelly's little yellow chart. "I'm going to go ahead and conservatively guess that after examining him, this cat is about twenty to twenty-two years old. This is extraordinary. A healthy indoor cat, one that is well taken care of, will usually live to maybe fifteen or sixteen."

"What about—"

He knew exactly what I was thinking. "Yes, there is the rare case of the twenty-seven-year-old cat, but…no. This is a first for me.

Shelly is the oldest cat I have ever examined, that I have ever seen. We have to be honest here. He's had a very long, very happy life with you. And he was a stray? Remarkable."

"Do I have more time?"

"Not much."

I bit my lip. I stroked the only living soul on this earth who knew and understood me—who could communicate with me. He looked up at me with perfect green eyes and closed them softly as he continued to purr. It was the only sound in the room.

"Lately he's been drinking more water."

"And he will continue to drink water. His organs are failing. I wouldn't do anything different than what you are doing. Look at him, he obviously loves you very much. You have given him excellent care, and he is stronger than most. He's holding on. He's holding on for you."

"We can't hold on forever."

"No, we can't."

Neither of us spoke, then Shelly suddenly found some energy and rolled over on his back, exposing his deep bluish-gray belly with the little white fluff.

"I think that death is one part, just like life is one part," Dr. Keating said.

"Part."

"Maybe there are more parts of this remarkable journey of ours, I don't know."

We both stood over Shelly, scratching and stroking different areas of his body to the joyous roar of his purring.

"The fact is that the time is now, he is here, and that's what matters. Enjoy every moment that you're alive together. There's got to be a reward for that."

I took Shelly home and fed him his favorite meal of liver and special salmon pâté that Dad prepared for him once a week. He ate heartily and drank lots of fresh cold water out of his metal bowl as I sat on the kitchen counter watching him. I thought about Dr. Paul Keating, his kindness and his insight. I hoped I wouldn't see him

again. Seeing Dr. Keating meant that poor Shelly was very unwell…
or worse.

There was a brief and unusual peacefulness that surrounded me,
the sound of Shelly lapping and swallowing his food. It was something that he had done for so many years, every day right under my
feet. But this time I really listened. We would enjoy every moment
that we were alive together.

Shelly left the room to go lick his little paws. He would stay
with me in this part—life. He was holding on for now.

I thought about Mary Jo. I wondered if I would ever hear back
from her.

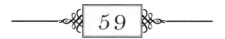

59

My mother thought it would be in my best interest to lecture me on the consequences of becoming involved with the "wrong crowd." I ate lunch with her a couple of times at the new and up-and-coming myriad of what Dad referred to as fern bars. A couple of them dotted the boulevard. Some of the old buildings were torn down in favor of them, and old beer joints that served legendary ethnic food sold out to them. They changed the landscape of the Wellton metropolitan area, all in the interest of money and the new trend. It was the era of the commercialization of chain restaurants where dolled-up cheeseburgers cost six dollars, and the feathered hat–wearing waitresses were mandated to wear heavy makeup. Everything from tubas to rusty gas station signs to antique carpet beaters covered every inch of wall space. And the ferns? There were so many plants in these places, I wondered if anything might crawl out of one.

Now that I was no longer a minor, I didn't have to do anything with my mother if I didn't want. But it was my father who was always pushing me in her direction, saying "It would be nice to" or "Why not have some girl time?" It was always some sort of passive little shove. What went through his mind? How did he spring out of bed every morning and face life as if the train just kept chugging along? Why couldn't I just ask him? Asking was impossible, and it always scared me to unimaginable scenarios. My chest would feel constricted, especially on the inside of my right breast and way deep down in my sides. I was so fearful of what I might face, although I could never articulate the exact consequences.

When my father pushed a normal mother-daughter relationship upon me, what I originally felt was guilt, but I realized that wasn't it. It was something else, although I didn't know what. I had to spend

332

time with her and play make-believe daughter regularly. It wasn't as if it was something new—I had done this my entire life. Pretend. I pretended countless times when Marisa was alive. Marisa did not pretend. She was only herself and revealed herself in her light-filled glory. Maybe she would still be alive if she pretended just a little.

I supposed my mother knew a few things about getting involved with the wrong crowd. After all, she did marry the person who murdered her oldest daughter. It would have sounded so biblical if it hadn't been so vulgar, and yet the two could sometimes go hand in hand. She still talked about Big Barton and Sunny as if they were closer to her heart than her own parents, which should not have been a surprise to me. She had no use for Lil Schuester anymore since the two of them got into an altercation over a fine china tea service, but it didn't stop my mother from discussing her or others she now loathed but once overvalued with exceeding energy.

I told my mother the year one of my professors earned his PhD, and all of a sudden, her beloved Sunny would appear. All I could visualize were the people who were feverishly and without success trying to get the monster released from prison by hoping they could convince the little people of the Wellton area that this had all been a terrible accident. While Barton Withers was flawed in only the most human of ways, he was a good, gentle boy and a wonderful son. He did charity work, he loved animals, he helped the poor. I didn't have to ponder over whether my mother ever countered their claim. The couple insinuated that her daughter, my sister, was "a troubled girl." She didn't deserve to die, but she was, they claimed, "a disturbed teenage girl" nonetheless.

My top row of teeth remained firmly planted behind the bottom row, and my lips were twisted shut. My head screamed. She never spoke of Mary Jo, and I never asked, but I would continue to do my best to heed her warnings about that despicable, questionable crowd at State University at Wellton. After all, this was not Bertrand, and so there were probably no aspiring astronauts there. Instead, one might find older students, kids on financial aid, some from poorer backgrounds.

But for now, at the naïve age of eighteen, I could ask my mother these questions. Would the wrong crowd come along and force-feed me pills? No, Alice. All these hippie types and their filthy friends had to do was convince me of how good these drugs would make me feel, and then before I knew it, I was hooked. The wrong crowd. How amusing it was to me that nothing, even the sweet feeling of drugs, was going to drag me in the direction of the wrong crowd, probably because I didn't even like any crowds. I didn't like people. I enjoyed my drugs alone, without the wrong crowds.

My mother had no idea. People were in my life when I needed them—the mailman took my mail, the professor graded my work, the pupil's mother paid me for tutoring her son in algebra, the man at the shop sold me the pump to put air in my bike tire, that guy had good pot, that girl had good uppers. The wrong crowd.

Walter and Aubrey were around. Maybe I could put them in my mother's wrong-crowd box. I'm sure they would fit, especially Walter, the poor black boy who was awarded a technical scholarship from the drama department. I wondered where monsters fit into the wrong crowd. What about murderers? How about men who killed young women? What about women who marry monsters? Monsters, Mom. Let's have another powwow about monsters, Mom. Should we stay at this fern bar, or should we choose another? Monsters never change. The wrong crowd.

Walter and I met for coffee and cigarettes, and I mostly drank beer regardless of the time. Walter was paranoid of losing his scholarship money if he even looked at a bottle of booze. Aubrey liked to bring her little colorful toothpick umbrellas along with all her ingredients to make her piña coladas. Virgin or not, Walter still didn't want to partake. Aubrey was the farthest thing from my mother's wrong crowd as the mind could encompass. Or not. She *was* from a middle-class immigrant family after all.

I used my studies as an excuse to get out of visiting my mother in her peculiar little old house. It wasn't exactly a lie. I was keeping straight As even though I was working a few hours a week at one of the campus libraries, and I continued to tutor high school students in an empty office at Dad's warehouse. My mother made it clear that she was exactly point seven miles closer to campus than my father was, and so moving in with her would be the optimal choice. That choice was the following: *No. Way. Ever.*

What I could never understand was why I continued to have these feelings of sorrow and guilt when I thought of my mother or when I forced myself to go and visit Helena. It irked me that I actually allowed myself to suffer this way because there was no reason for it, and my mother didn't deserve it.

Dad picked me up one Sunday afternoon, and I found myself looking out the back window, watching my mother's little stone house disappear as we drove away. Where was this melodrama coming from? I felt so sorry for her rattling around all alone in that house as Helena spent so much time at her grandparents' compound, most likely hearing all kinds of wonderful things about her father. I felt sorry for the little kid too. But my mother didn't deserve my sympathy.

I was tired of listening to my father complain about my not visiting her. Why her? Why not Bunic and Bunica? He knew what she was, and I pondered the question as to whether he was developing some sort of dementia—dementia that excluded anything to do with the store. A deficiency, an enmeshment that he possessed his entire life, and the older I became, the more I noticed it.

I would spend a night in my lovely perfect little room with little Helena right next door. I would force myself to play with the pretty little brat. Once I was smoking marijuana, and I thought I was going to die from laughter. Then the kid was laughing too. It was so weird, but it was a great trip, and Helena and I hung out and played around until she fell asleep. I played with her toys for another three hours straight. We never saw my mother. I decided I would never take a drug around the kid anymore or in my mother's perfect little stone house.

I would listen to my mother pay reverence to monsters like Big Barton and Sunny Withers. She would cackle during her card games with Penelope, the spider-eyed witch, as if she was having a great time and never missed Marisa.

There were many times when I avoided Helena because I didn't want to worry about another sister. My mother customarily lost tolerance with most people and would eventually implode. Sunny and Big Barton lost tolerance with her first. I could evaluate because I was an anonymous shadow from learned behavior. I had to survive and stay alive—the one thing Marisa could not do. No matter how much I tried to avoid Helena, I found it increasingly difficult to do. She looked so much like Marisa did when we were kids, except she was much taller. Where Marisa had the fine bone structure of my mother and appeared small and fragile like a porcelain figurine, Helena was growing into a healthy, athletic kid—robust. She wasn't exactly a linebacker like me; she was built more like her monster father. I could see him in her, and that was another reason I felt sorry for her. I never knew how much detail she knew about her father, about the fact that he was in prison for killing her sister. What I did know was that she had been indoctrinated by her family, and this was the time to do it, while she was fresh and tender.

She spent countless hours at Sun Chance. She loved to ride those stinky unintelligent horses, just like Marisa used to, but Helena was a seasoned rider and had all the gear and the frippery and all the other shit that went along with being an equestrian. She played four square and liked to be in school plays. She sang in the kiddie chorus, had her little friends, and always seemed to be around when I didn't want her to be. She shocked me once when she told me she remembered Marisa. I asserted to her that this would be impossible—she was an infant. In addition, I told her I did not want to discuss Marisa with her ever and to please not broach the subject with me again. She never did. And she never spoke of her father either, not to me anyway. She either had superior insight for a kid, or somehow I had put the fear of God into that cute little red head of hers. I didn't know which, and I didn't care. All I wanted was for her to shut up about these things and stay out of my way when I wanted her to. I could admire her from a distance if I chose, and if my mother became hostile and dangerous, I was waiting for her in the corner.

I was able to comfort the little girl, and that both surprised and disgusted me. I did not want another sister. We couldn't have long talks like Marisa and I once did. Helena and I would look at each other and smile and then look away, as if we didn't speak the same language. She would show me what she learned in school that day, we would color, and the most ironic and boldest move that left me so awestruck that I drank a bottle of white wine at a gazebo on campus and had to go over it again and again in my head was when she stole one of my mother's mascaras and a lipstick. She also had the nerve to swipe makeup remover and tissue so that my mother would never know what we were doing. Not only was this girl a prodigy, but she was growing up to be as emotionally abused as Marisa.

One evening before I was about to leave, Helena showed me her new violin Big Barton bought for her. She would take private lessons, but listening to her practice was like Shelly's claws on a blackboard. Of course my mother had to remind her of that from downstairs as she *screamed* about how shitty she sounded. One tear fell from the outside of her left eye as she continued to play despite my mother's hollering. I pulled her head close to me and kissed the tear. She embraced me, but she didn't cry after that.

I relished the times she was over at Sun Chance gathering information for me. I was tempted to ask her about her aunt Mary Jo, but I never did.

I just didn't want another sister.

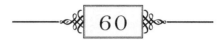

60

Oftentimes, I liked to lie on my back on the perfect green grass in front of the giant bronze statue of Arthur Drake Wellton sitting stoically on a smelly horse. Captain Wellton was rumored to be an ancestor of the Withers family, or so insisted Big Barton, but that was a lie.

I thought he looked familiar from a distance, but the evening sun meted into my eyes, and I couldn't be sure. I squinted and used my hands as a visor, but I knew that walk and those long legs. He was with a woman, tall like he was with long dark straight hair.

I rolled over on my knees and pushed myself up off the crushed lawn. I brushed down the backs of my legs and butt where the grass continued to cling. It was definitely him—Mark the boyfriend.

He approached me first with a heartfelt hug. "Alice! Wow! What's up? Are you in school here?"

I nodded and looked at the woman standing beside him. She looked as if she had just fallen out of a fashion magazine. She was too thin and had perfect white teeth when she smiled, which was only once. The majority of the time she was standing there with that fish-lipped model look. She too looked Asian, and by the way she was standing so close to Mark, for one moment, I remembered Louis Dagher and his pathetic girlfriend Nellie Manziel.

"Tosh, this is an old friend of mine from Crescent Hills. This is Alice Buchner."

Tosh flashed her light bulb smile and thrust a long tanned arm at me. Her hand was so soft, it seemed like she had never shaken anyone else's before. I always thought that was for businessmen, but it was the mideighties, and people were changing.

All of a sudden, a voice called out for Tosh. She turned around, beamed her toothpaste-ad smile, and waved. "You guys, I am like so sorry. I *really* have to take care of this. Alice, it was like *so* nice to meet you." She turned to Mark and, with a peck on the cheek, said, "Baby I'll see you later, 'kay?" Off she strutted to a pack of pretty people, but not before crying out, "Oh my *god!*"

The look on Mark's face was one of partial embarrassment as I stood in front of him. We stood there for a while and said nothing. Then I caught his eye, and he appeared more relaxed.

"You know, Mark, do you think it would have killed you to introduce me as your girlfriend's sister? It's not like the two of you broke up or anything like that. You stopped seeing each other because her stepfather murdered her."

"Wha—"

"Who *is* that Tosh?"

"Hey." His face immediately brightened. "I heard about that whole thing with Louis Dagher when you were at South Wellton. You know, his mother called him at a friend's house while he was tripping on LSD, and she threw him into an inpatient rehab. I wouldn't be surprised if that dude was dead by now. Or totally done a one-eighty."

"I guess he surrendered his penny loafers," I muttered.

"What's that?"

"Mark, I don't give a fuck about Louis Dagher, his drug habit, or his long-lost cassette tapes that you and Marisa stashed away somewhere. I don't care about any of this. Who is this girl?"

"Tosh!" he answered gleefully.

"I got the name," I snapped. "I thought you loved my sister."

It just spilled out before I had the chance to stop it. I knew it sounded strange, unrealistic maybe, but I wanted to hear his answer. Everyone was an impersonator, including me, but this was different. How could he do this?

He looked at me in a peculiar way, as if he finally saw what was running around on the track of my mind.

"Marisa is dead."

"You don't have to *remind me of that today.*"

"It's been…" He looked up at the sky and shook his head. He ran his hand through his thick straight black hair. Was he trying to find her? I doubted it. "What? Five years?"

"Six. How soon we forget."

He opened his mouth. Then he closed it. "Alice, come on." He stepped closer to me.

I stepped backward.

"Do you think you're being fair? Are you even being serious?"

"I can see that you have *thoroughly* moved on with *your* life. Congratulations, Mark."

"Hey, Alice, hold on a second. What the hell?" His tone changed. "What am I supposed to do?"

"You cried for days!" I plugged my nose in anticipation of the tears I did not want him to see. "Weeks. I thought we were in this together. I thought we were going to get him."

I knew we weren't in on anything together. I knew I was provoking him, and I was angry that he had moved on. He was just one more ass who had this ridiculous vision of moving on with his life.

"Get who?" He held his hands out as if he were giving up on me, that familiar pathetic look of confusion on his face. "The district attorney?"

"The monster, you idiot! Withers! Mark, god."

His head snapped backward as if I had thrown something at him.

"Get him. What do you mean get him? He's in prison. He got man one, and he's still in a maximum-security prison. They got him. What else can anybody do to him? Man one at Bellmorrow? I wouldn't have thought that would be common, Marisa."

And so he did still think of her.

"I'm Alice."

Neither of us looked at each other or said anything until I broke the silence. "I can think of a lot of things I would like to do to him."

"I know, I know." He quickly scanned the landscape, spotted the glamorous Tosh still chatting with her posse, and turned his attention back to me. "But Jesus Christ, don't you think he's putting up with all kinds of horrible shit in a place like that? That's what we wanted, wasn't it? He's going to suffer in that hell hole for the rest of his life, Alice, you know that. That's what we wanted all along."

"No. Oh no, no, no." I shook my head. Mark the boyfriend clearly hadn't kept up as well as he thought he had. "He made a deal, Mark, because he was caught, and that was all they could get." I closed my eyes hard and remembered all the endless and futile pleadings to Detective Holloway. "Eight to twenty-five goddamned years. And he could be out in twelve for good behavior and overcrowding. He could even be out by the time I graduate from this place."

He shook his head and kicked the grass. "That is very unlikely."

"Why? And what if it's not? Worst case? And I use that term very loosely. Twenty-five years. By the time he has finally done every second of his time, he'll be my grandfather's age. And my grandfather is doing just fine—he drives, he runs his stand, he reads the paper, he watches baseball, he eats good food, he's got a garden."

He watched me carefully. I think he was actually becoming frightened. He should have been. He didn't speak for a while. He just stood there looking at me. I stared right back. Then he got a little loud, and people started to notice. Not Tosh though. "What are you gonna do to stop any of this? You gonna, you gonna what? You gonna lie in wait in a tree with an automatic rifle until you just happen to see him decades later? Hmm, I know, bake him a poisonous cake and take it up to Bellmorrow on visitor's day? You're probably separated by three inches of iron with a tiny hole. You've lost control, can't you see that?"

"There's a hearing coming up," I went on. "His parents are trying to get him moved. He's appealing the sentence on some sort of duress grounds—"

"Stop!" He held up his hand. His voice was loud enough for more people to turn around and probably realize we were arguing.

I felt like I was standing alone atop a lighthouse in a black raging storm. Tosh was nowhere to be seen.

"I know Marisa was your sister, but let me tell you, I knew her. I knew her very well. I understand we were very young, but I still loved her, and she loved you. She would not want this for you. She would not want you to live like this."

He didn't know what anyone else wanted.

"I'm not living any other way than what I was put on this earth to do, and that is to fight for the memory of my sister. At least that. That family destroyed her dignity. That monster murdered her in front of me, and my job is to rid the world of these monsters."

When he looked at me, he made me feel like such an idiot. But he was wrong.

"No. You got it wrong. No one could destroy her dignity. No one." He pointed a finger at me. "But they're coming for you. You need to get help. You need to talk to someone who knows about grief, who knows how to guide you through this awful shit you're going through."

"You sound like Holloway. Leaving some psychiatrist's card on our table." And that bitch Kiki. I was so glad she moved to New York.

"Well, whoever that is, they're right," he said.

Guess Mark the boyfriend never picked up the papers either. State was a good place for his sorry ass.

"Here." He scribbled something on a small piece of paper. "Take my number. I'm working on my master's in philosophy."

I saw Tosh again out of the corner of my eye.

Then without either of us saying a word, he kissed my cheek, turned around, and walked off toward his new girlfriend and his new life.

Just like that.

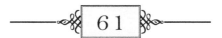

6 1

It had been a year since I first took Shelly in to see Dr. Paul Keating and years longer since I sent my apology letter to Mary Jo Withers McLaughlin. I never heard from her again. But Shelly was still chugging along. He ate, he drank lots of cold water, but he was very slow and very thin. He didn't go outside anymore. All he wanted to do was sit on my bed and listen to me praise him for being such a good friend and a good listener. I made him another litter box and stuck it in one corner of my bedroom, and I made sure he had plenty of food and water in the other corner.

One night I was helping a pupil from South Wellton High School read a practice math test when I overhead my father talking to a customer whose voice I didn't recognize. He said words like *morose* and *dour* and *poker face*. He even told this stranger that his daughter was "way too serious" and "way too introverted" for a girl her age. He either didn't realize I was in the back office tutoring, or he couldn't have cared less because the two of them discussed how tiresome their children's presence and our problems were. And this was no dream.

I was hoping my pupil wasn't also eavesdropping, but this poor soul had a hard-enough time focusing on the task at hand, so he probably wasn't. I had to remind my father that talking about what a pain in the ass I am was probably not the most appropriate discussion around my pupil, and if he would prefer, I would take these strange high school students into his beloved library, and we could do our work there.

It was time for me to move out. Being angry with my mother was not exactly breaking news, but what had transpired between the two of us a couple of days prior was what probably motivated him to spill his guts to some jerk buying french fries and haddock.

* * * * *

"Mom, why are you calling so late? The cat's not well, Nancy's asleep, and the ringer startled me. What?"

"Oh, shut up," she said proudly. "Your aunt will be perfectly fine. She is well taken care of living off the taxpayers' dime in her warm bed. I wanted to remind you that it's supposed to be cold this weekend, so if you decide to come by, make sure you bring a sweater because you won't be able to fit into one of mine."

"Is that why you called at eleven thirty at night? To remind me to pack a *sweater?* I'm an adult. I can dress myself."

"Alice, why do you have to be so fresh?"

"I won't be coming by this weekend anyway. I have work to do."

"Well, that's fine," she quipped. "Whatever you want to do. You're the adult. Oh, guess what? Finally. I finally scattered Marisa's ashes. It was just Helena and me, and it was a beautiful ceremony."

"What do you mean scattered them?" Fear began to brew and bubble up inside me.

"*Scattered.*" She enunciated the *T.* "Don't you know what *scattered* means?"

"What did you do?"

"Keep your voice down!" she shouted through the phone as if she were standing right in front of me. "Helena and I drove up to the mountains to watch a tennis match at Chiswell, and we found a beautiful waterfall, and the wind was perfect, the sun was out—"

"Marisa hated it there!"

"Oh, she did not, Alice, that's not true."

I tried to gather myself as much as I could, but I was seething.

"It *is* true because she told me she hated it there! Because I knew my sister. You didn't. You just hated her. She didn't *like* the outdoors. She was cold all the time. She *hated* the snow, she *hated* skiing. She was afraid of bears and bridges that folded up and swallowed up cars—"

"What the hell are you talking about? You are nuts!"

"I'm nuts."

"Your sister is dead. She's gone. All that there was left of her was her ashes…"

But not all of them, Mom, not all of them.

"Found a lovely place to scatter her—"

"You and Helena—"

"You're just jealous of that beautiful little girl, my precious baby."

"I'm not jealous of a goddamned thing."

"I don't have anything else to say to you."

"Well, before you go, listen to this one more thing, Mom. Marisa is dead because you married a murderer. That's why all you *had* left were ashes. You married a killer, and now, *now* you don't even have her ashes."

Her reply was inaudible hollering. She heard my entire sentence, which surprised me. I smiled a little as I held the phone away from my ear, but I thought I heard the excuses again: "It wasn't my fault, I didn't kill anyone. If your sister wasn't so unruly, Sunny and Barton are good whatevers—"

"Go to hell!" I slammed the phone down so hard, it popped out of the wall and came crashing down on the red brick–colored linoleum floor. For a second, I was reminded of Dr. Paul Keating, his hands, and that old terra-cotta floor at the animal clinic.

I picked up the phone and hung it back up on the wall, grateful for not damaging it. It wouldn't be the first time I threw something, and it probably wouldn't be the last. I walked down the hallway all the way into the living room where I noticed a distant light on. I was so full of anger, I would have pulled my own guts out if I could.

"Alice, what the hell is going on down there?"

I barely saw my father standing there in a T-shirt and boxer shorts, hair all over the place, smelling of a combination of fish, cigarettes, and that blue-and-white deodorant soap.

Aunt Nancy yawned as she made her way to the bottom step wrapped up like an indigenous person ready to harpoon dinner in bright orange footie pajamas, brown slippers, and a dark blue bathrobe.

I began to sob, and Dad ran his fingers through his black and slightly graying hair, exactly like Mark the boyfriend did recently when he too was annoyed with me.

"What's the matter with you?" He just stood there, barefoot, nothing in his hands, no drink, no cigarette.

"Dad, do you love me?"

He reached around for a cigarette.

"Never mind. If you can't even answer a simple goddamned question without having to smoke, I'm going upstairs."

"Allie—"

I whipped around like a sailfish. "Don't call me that. Anymore."

My father's face softened into a childlike sadness. I looked away immediately. Aunt Nancy burst into laughter. It sounded louder because of the stillness of the hour.

"Hey! You listen to me. I'll call you Allie until you're eighty-seven years old."

"You won't be here when I'm eighty-seven years old."

"That's exactly my point, you little smart-ass. You're the genius in the family, good for figuring that one out. Now. What's the problem this time?"

"She scattered Marisa's ashes." *Just not all of them.*

He looked up at the ceiling and then back at me. "Isn't that what you're supposed to do with ashes?"

"No. You're not supposed to scatter someone's ashes when the person is not supposed to be ashes in the first place."

"Alice." He put a palm on his head.

"Sorry I woke you two up, but you're the one who had a fleeting moment with that bitch—"

"Enough with the mouth!"

I ignored him. "That in turn produced me, and that's why I'm here, and now I'm going upstairs. Move, Nancy."

My aunt turned around and followed me up the steps. "Alice, you are wanting to know if Rudy loves you."

"Jesus Christ," I heard him mutter at the bottom of the stairs.

"Aunt Nancy, I really don't want to talk about this right now, okay? Really, I apologize for waking you up. I didn't mean to wake you up."

She ignored me like she always did when she needed to explain something. "Rudy *does* love you because Rudy is your father."

"That's nice."

"It is nice to have a father who loves you. My father has been dead for a long time. But Rudy is strange." She giggled. "That's funny, don't you think? But he is. He is sometimes strange. Maybe when he was born, maybe when he was a little baby, he was strange back then too."

I turned to face her.

She took a deep breath as if she were about to say something explosive. "You know. You are a loving person, and you are a lovable person. I know the difference. There's a difference. And *I* love you very, very much. I am your aunt, after all."

I put my arms around her. "I'm so sorry I woke you." I could smell the soft warm scent of her strawberry lotion.

"Hmm." She giggled again. "It's Rudy who wakes me with his snoring."

I closed my eyes and nodded deeply. If I didn't borrow some of her unused minor tranquilizers, I wouldn't sleep, and I would be up all night too. I wondered why she never used those lovelies. She never noticed.

"I love you too, Aunt Nancy. You are always such a big help."

She nodded slowly as if that had been something she had been waiting to hear for a long time. She continued to search my eyes as if she had something else she wanted to tell me. Hope it had nothing to do with those sedatives. "No. *You* are always such a big help."

She kissed me hard on the cheek and turned around and walked toward the stairs. I was so tempted to ask her about her old friendship with Mary Jo, but I didn't dare.

Shelly was sprawled out sideways on the bed. There was a small lamp light on the tiny table where my clock sat. I listened to the gusty draft rippling through the thick walls as I thought of Marisa's ashes flying away, fizzling off any which way that dreaded mountain wind decided to take them. It swallowed my sister up and spit her out over that cold, desolate landscape that has sat, lurking in its own noiselessness for over a thousand years, wanting to blow those ashes far from the lovely little waterfall. Off she fluttered to some toxic waste dumpsite the next state over where bears go rummaging around garbage looking for bits of food and end up devouring my sister.

I didn't care how many people traveled miles to see the beautiful foliage in October. Marisa hated it there, and she made it pretty clear several times. My mother saw it; she knew it. She was always looking for some other direction purely to be oppositional. And Helena was now clinging to her like barnacles on a whale. Was my mother so far gone into her own self that she couldn't pick up on the most obvious circumstance right in front of her? This is what she did—torched your house and burned it to the ground. Then she stood over the smoking and stinking debris and asked, "Where's your house?" Time and time again.

God forbid I showed any emotion—negative emotion. They were all culpable—my mother, Dad, Mary Jo, Bunica, Mark.

I heard Aunt Nancy in the hallway.

"She is *mad*. She's mad, and she's mad at you, Rudy. I can tell."

My father said nothing. At least I didn't hear anything spew from his mouth. He was just going to stare off into nowhere, no response, only deafening silence. I could light a stick of dynamite, roll it under his bed, and even *that* wouldn't make much of a difference. Not until he arrived at the store in the middle of the night with his Rudy Boochie's head on did he give a fuck about anything. He was lucky because he did not face the daily pain. So many people were lucky. I coveted. One of the big ten.

Shelly wouldn't be there forever, and I was so close to being alone. Sometimes I thought I would slit my wrists and just bleed until I was dry. But I wasn't ready to give up.

I looked in my special drawer and stroked the purple blue velvet jewelry bag that contained what was left of my sister's ashes. I stroked and stroked, but I didn't dare take them out of the bag. I knew what would happen. I would worry. These ashes were mine. My mother would never know. No one, *no one* would ever know.

My soul—I marveled. It was that one part. Parts of our journey like Dr. Paul Keating revealed to me on that day I brought Shelly in.

A part. A part of me that no one could ever touch, ever reach, ever know. It was like a disk of sorts, a little ball that sat behind my heart and expanded so immensely into a big sunlike ball ablaze with energy that was all mine, although I would never understand it completely.

Marisa's ashes. A part now. A true part.

My part.

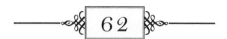

62

Shelly was slowing down day by day. He had to be close to twenty-two or twenty-three years old if Dr. Paul Keating had been correct in the age assessment, which I'm sure he was. I picked him up and placed him on my chest as we lay together on my bed. The door didn't have to be ajar anymore because he didn't need to leave the room. Everything he needed was right there with me, and soon, he would be leaving me too.

Death. I didn't care if it was part of a journey. I didn't care if it was a part of life. The only thing death accomplished was ruin the lives of people who loved whoever died and still had to live. It didn't matter to me that death was supposed to be natural and that eventually, every living thing dies—people who are not monsters will be transported to heaven or paradise or wherever and be with God. That was people. Trees, birds, Shelly all go to be with God. They are the innocent, even though they were animals and nature and cannot reason. Perhaps that's what makes them so innocent. And nature will not speak, but it will come back to earth and be eternal.

What worried me most about death was that I was even intrigued by something I hated so much. I could leave with Shelly. Shelly had no idea how much he touched me, how much just one tiny behavior brought me the miracle of love. He didn't know how much I loved his big green eyes and his loud purr, how I saw his tail and nothing else when I opened his food container, his following me everywhere and curling up with me and me alone—it all added so much to my otherwise shit life. He would never know how much I would miss stroking him for hours while he was on my lap as I read microeconomics out loud. Or calling his name and hearing him run and meow at the same time, only to come to me and rub his scent all over my calves and roll all over my feet.

As I stroked him, he purred softly, but it wasn't the same hearty roar. It was so faint and distant. He was moving farther and farther away from me, my poor little old man. I hummed to him as he purred ever so softly until we both eventually fell asleep.

A thin yellow ray of light woke me up. Shelly was no longer on my chest. In a panic, I bolted upright, and then I saw him. He looked as if he were trying to get somewhere. He lay sideways on the warm hardwood, still—very still. I knew right away he wasn't sleeping. I knelt down beside him and gently picked up his thin lifeless body and rocked him in my arms. "Shelly," I whispered as clearly as I could. "Oh, Shelly, no, no. I love you, baby. I will love you forever."

I was in shock. Then I noticed her perfect new white sneakers and her bright pink socks under her blue jeans. Her always rough hands from constant cleaning lovingly massaged my neck.

Aunt Nancy knelt over me. "Come on, honey," she said. "Let him go now. Let him go, sweetheart. He's gone."

63

My father thought it would be a good idea to bury Shelly in the backyard by the wall where he sunned and watched the birds sing. There was a cement company behind us up the hill that made noise with their big red trucks. Shelly's ears and his entire body would perk up when he heard the people and their beeps and swishes. He would readjust himself, get comfortable again, and fall back to sleep on the old stone wall behind the patio.

I had never known anyone die of old age. It had been so long since Shelly had been outside, scrounging around the warehouse for scraps of food, watching blue jays dive and squawk while he tried to catch them. He was a terrible hunter, entertaining himself instead with the song of the cardinal, being woken by cement trucks, lounging on his wall. I didn't want his precious frail little old body to be buried in the dark cold ground outside, especially in the wintertime and away from me. I told Dad that we could create a memorial plot, but that I would prefer to have Dr. Keating arrange for a cremation. Dad bitched about how much that would cost him, and once again, I had to remind him that I was making money tutoring, and he wouldn't have to pay a dime toward it. I would gladly dip into my drug money for Shelly. This way, I could have Shelly and Marisa with me. I didn't mention this to my father. Still no one knew. Only God and I knew, Marisa and now Shelly.

Dad built a wooden cross, which was supposed to replicate a crucifix, but in the space where Jesus's ebbing was supposed to be, he actually built a Star of David and placed it at that exact spot. "Well"— he shrugged with an earnest need to explain—"we're Ashkenazi Jews and Roman Catholic. I'm sure we got some kind of something else sprinkled in there like everyone else does. I-I don't know what to do, so let's just do the whole damned thing."

"Dad, are you serious?" I was so stoned and thirsty. Just looking at that monstrosity was making me a little paranoid. "No. No way. That's…that's…" It was just downright horrific and offensive. "It's iconoclastic."

"The hell it is."

"Just, just—Buchner, okay? Shelly Buchner. Either a Star of David *or* a cross would be beautiful. Please, Dad. Can you do that? Please?"

"Sure," he said without complaining, although his voice was resigned. It didn't even look like he took an hour out of his life at the empire to put that thing together.

"Do you think we can grow some edelweiss around the memorial?" I asked, coming back with two glasses of water.

"Look who's talking about iconoclastic."

"What?"

"You wanna put a Hitler flower next to a Star of David?"

"It's not a Hitler flower. What on earth?"

"Can't do it anyway." He pulled the "star crucifix" out of the ground.

"Why not?"

"Edelweiss are only found in the Austrian Alps at high altitudes, and besides, it's not the right season to plant any type of flower in Wellton."

I knew nothing about flowers. My father was trying to remind me that he knew a lot about many things.

Aunt Nancy gave me these beautiful crystal-type colored stones. She had no idea where they came from, but we took them out of the drawstring bag and placed them around the little cross. Dad said a little prayer. I cried at the beauty and sadness. My father prayed because of me for Shelly. I couldn't believe what I was hearing. I stood and looked at the memorial cross at the little wall for a long time, even after my father went back in the house. I was splintered with God. I was not even sure if he wanted me.

I didn't cry again. Shelly was an old cat, and I knew it was his time, whatever that really meant. His death was anticipated, unlike Marisa's, whose death was violent and unforeseen. Neither was easier, just different. I knew one thing—Shelly's death didn't anger me, but it reminded me of so many horrific sequences in my mind that I tried to push away over the years. And I knew another thing—it was time to leave.

I understood why Aunt Nancy had been trying with no luck for years to get back to her little efficiency after her last psychotic break right around the time Marisa was murdered. I think she was waiting for some old lady to die so she could move back into that shithole she preferred over the home she grew up in. When Shelly died, there was nothing left for me at home.

I increased my hours at the library. My tutoring business was slow. I guess high school kids weren't as dumb as they used to be, and besides, I had always detested tutoring, even though I had been doing it for years beginning way back when my friend Bruce Collins and I were eleven years old. That worked out well at first.

Walter worked diligently on his degree. I laughed to myself. I remembered when I tutored him in business math. He had come a long way since then. Maybe I was too hard on him. He told me as long as he had a roof over his head, he would find a way to squeeze me in too. I was grateful, but there were too many people coming in and out of that new four-story house everyone called the silo. It was noisy, and there was always a television on somewhere. I didn't know how you could think in that place.

Aubrey begged me to come and live with her and her mother in her childhood home up the street from the Stanhope Ridge Apartments where my mother, Marisa, and I led an uncertain existence. The last thing I needed was a view of that rotten place. She said that moving into their spare bedroom would keep me away from "the marijuana." The offer was very kind, but I was on my own, and I wished to be completely alone.

Dad gave me the old blue Plymouth because he had just bought himself a new red Honda Accord. It was such a nice car. I was surprised that the Plymouth was still working, but Dad always kept excellent care of it, and I always had affection for the Plymouth because it had the long "way back," and I kept a blanket back there. Why would I need to move in anywhere? I spent many nights in my

Plymouth. I read, I slept, watched the stars as I sat on the hood with my back against the windshield. I parked up and hunkered down at the local truck stop where a full tank of gas got me a free breakfast with a shower. Why did I need anything else?

At times, there would be something about sleeping in the "way back" that would frighten me. I was sunk into the deepest despair as I tried to rest with my sister's and cat's ashes, thinking about both of them. I was so depressed. I was weakened into a deep despondency, and sometimes, I couldn't leave the car unless I had to pee. I hated death, yet I wanted it.

I tried to finally slit my wrists while sitting in Dad's bathtub. Marisa used to call me a dumb chicken, and that was exactly what I was. I looked at what I had done, and I realized that my gash was about two millimeters away from the main artery. Oh, I bled. It just wasn't the right blood. Something was holding me back, keeping me away from my sister, grounding me to this life. I guess I just wasn't ready to surrender.

I remembered trying not to think about taking Shelly in to be cremated. I also couldn't get the reel of Marisa out of my mind that day.

* * * * *

I wrapped Shelly's little body in a clean fluffy towel. I took him to the vet, and as we sat in the parking lot of the South Wellton Animal Clinic, poor Shelly in the passenger seat, I looked in the rearview mirror about three thousand times, making sure my lip gloss was perfect. I went to the drugstore the day before and bought one of those fruity roll-on things that were supposed to make your lips look sexy. It was the only makeup I had ever worn, except for the time my mother married a murderer. That was the day I met Mary Jo. I was sort of hoping I would run into Dr. Paul Keating.

I noticed the front door of the animal clinic. Someone had stenciled a cartoon puppy, kitten, and bunny rabbit on the glass. I suddenly cried so hard, my nose drained on Shelly's lifeless head as I held him and rocked him like a baby. "Dammit, Shelly, why you too? I know, I know. Why did you have to die? Why does everyone have to leave?"

I cried for a long time. I hadn't cried that hard since the day he died or since I sat alone in my room at times with Shelly, thinking of my sister for years without her. I wiped my face down with a napkin and blew my ugly nose hard. Then I wiped what was left of the gloss shit off my lips and looked at Shelly. "How could I have been so disrespectful?"

Dr. Keating wasn't even there. It was Dr. Campbell behind the desk with a harem of receptionists. A pretty girl with dark brown hair and the dark eyes of a vampire took my best friend from me as I cried loud like a child in front of everyone in the room.

"Ms. Buchner," Vampire Eyes said, handing me a box of tissues, "he was very, very old."

"I was good to him, you know?" I wailed.

"*Of course* you were. He wouldn't have lived so long!" She smiled as a tech slipped in and took him away.

I stepped back in horror.

Shelly was gone forever.

* * * * *

I curled up with his little purple tin box and a photograph of him under the bright lights at the local truck stop in the way back of the Plymouth, wishing that someone out there in the parking lot would miraculously come by and set fire to my car so that I, a dumb chicken, could turn to ash as well. But no one was feeling like a criminal that night.

I had terrible dreams. Dreams of bears. Though they weren't really dreams like the one I had about Dad beating the side of my head while Kiki stood by in her ugly rose-colored dress with a cigarette dangling from her mouth. They were daydreams almost as I lay awake under a blanket in the way back of the Plymouth deep in the middle of the night. I was so frightened sometimes that I shook. I had to focus on the handle of the back door to steady myself. Thoughts would enter my brain without preparation. They would come from nowhere. Once I thought I was at a zoo. I stood in front of an enclosure of this new habitat where the animal wasn't in a cage anymore. It was a bear. A big brown bear sitting at the top of a huge pile of rocks staring back at me with eyes full of hunger and anticipation. His huge head bobbed up and down as he continued to glare at me. The sun beat relentlessly, but it was nowhere in the sky. There was only an overcast bluish-gray hue as all around me were the sounds of some sort of unusual language, an old Celtic language—Gaelic or Welsh? All of a sudden, a man whom I didn't recognize shot out of my peripheral. A skinny wispy man with faded blue jeans and a gray shirt threw me over the fence and into the bear enclosure.

The terror that split my insides in half was an experience like no other. I was a baby again, and I was going to die as the bear would rip me apart. All I wanted to do was go home and find my father. I wanted to crawl into his lap and stay there, never having my feet touch the ground again. That way, nothing could ever hurt me again. When we died together, I would make sure we were holding hands so that we would never be separated. But my father would never understand any of my wide-awake dreams, and so I lay under the bright cold light, wondering what would happen to me next, night after night.

64

I couldn't fail one of my advanced accounting courses. I would purposely cut a class, go in the next day, and everything would all be there in my head, as if there was a quill stabbed all the way through some tube and ready to drip directly into my brain. I would lie in the way back of the Plymouth clutching what was left of my sister and think of numbers, small, insignificant vile numbers and little painless and undemanding words. They were all shiny, and they burst out in a blaze of millions like teeny, tiny light bulbs. Then the sequence would repeat over and over again. I decided I would find a new place to sleep, eat, and shower first thing in the morning.

My luck was a lot better than usual. I hit the jackpot. I couldn't believe it. I found this nice inexpensive place not far from the schools of business and education. It had some interesting history and stories like the home I grew up in. I would keep this discovery from my father as long as I could. On the outset, it looked like a four-square house with two front porches on the top and bottom and a dormer attic window. There was a modern addition in the back. The inside was clean and in good shape. I thought I would have my own efficiency on the downstairs level, but it really wasn't an efficiency because it had been refurbished to include three rooms: one bedroom, one bathroom, and an uncommonly large kitchen with a perfect round oak table and chairs right in the middle of everything. There were about two or three guys who lived in the new addition. I didn't see them much because they used a separate entrance. There were two friendly young women around my age who lived upstairs, Candace and Amanda or Miranda, something like that.

Candace, whom I found out later was a graduate student, had an enormous cinnamon-colored Doberman pinscher named Arturo.

I was reminded of that brown bear on top of that rock pile that inserted himself into my head at will. But the thing that was strange about this dog was that he didn't have his ears clipped. They hung floppy like a hound dog, and he looked silly. When I saw the way he jiggled his rear end from side to side in a desperate childish dance and whined like a spoiled puppy, I realized that he wasn't a trained killer. Candace walked him all the time, and because she was a strict vegetarian, poor Arturo had to follow the same regiment. It was a small wonder at night he would hear me come in the main door, bound down the stairs in a fast and clumsy flop, and sniff and scratch the kitchen door until I let him in.

"Look at you, Arturo," I said to him one night as I sat in my huge bright aquamarine kitchen reading some textbook on statistics. He sat next to me on the blanket I used to use when I slept in the way back of the Plymouth at the local truck stop. I laid it out for him in a big folded square and watched him lick under his leg as I spoke to him. "It seems like your mother takes good care of you, I guess. You have a very shiny coat, but you are a little trim. Don't *ever* let her find out I've been feeding you hot dogs."

He looked up at me as if he knew the word *hot dogs*. I scratched underneath his chin, and he stretched his strong neck. He was still just a puppy.

"No wonder you want to hang around here. Look at those long sharp eye teeth. Look at how white they are too. They're for ripping flesh, meat. Vegetarian," I scoffed. "You're a dog. You're not supposed to be a vegetarian, are you? You know who would know the answer to that, Arturo? Do you? Dr. Paul Keating, that's who."

I pondered what sort of excuse I could make to get Candace to allow me to take her dog to the vet. Then I heard Marisa's voice very, very faintly, distantly. She was so far away. I spent the next three hours scratching, reading, and talking to a dog.

The next afternoon, I came in the front door, and Arturo bolted down the stairs like an ungainly horse to greet me. I wondered if Candace was annoyed with me because her beloved companion enjoyed spending his time with me. We settled into what was becoming our favorite spot, with my working at the round oak table and

Arturo lying on the folded blanket at my feet. Once we were sharing a blueberry muffin when Scotty appeared, presumably on my father's instructions, with a bag of salmon and a twenty-five-pound frozen turkey. What was I going to do with a twenty-five-pound frozen turkey? He also packed a small paper bag of tiny sample bottles of cologne and red nail polish from Aunt Nancy. Care packages for my new pad. I could oil up a pan and throw some seasoning on that salmon, but I would have to think hard about cooking a huge turkey. I would be able to feed the entire household with that bird, even the boys in the back, except for Candace, and I would have to sneak Arturo his share. Of all things, a turkey. From a fish market.

After about twenty minutes to a half hour after Scotty left, my kitchen light flickered. "Damn it." I got up and dug around the kitchen drawers looking for a light bulb when the phone startled me. I decided to let the answering machine pick up the call. Wise decision. It was my mother.

"Alice. Alice? Are you there? Listen, I need to talk to you immediately. Do not talk to your father or anyone else before you talk to me because…because I know what you're like. I need you to call me as soon as you get this message, please. Please call me as soon as possible. I need to talk to you. Alice, are you there?" Then the call ended with a beep, and I smiled as I turned on my flashlight. The power had gone out.

Could it be a blown fuse? I asked myself. "Great. You stay on your bed, Arturo. I have to go down the cellar."

I twisted the tarnished brass handle to the cellar door and crept down the small glossy gray wooden staircase to the musty cement-and-dirt cellar. It was an old and awful place, and had I not grown up with an octopus furnace in our basement, there would have been no way I could have gone down there. I had to hoist myself up a few feet through a large square entryway and walk about another ten feet to the end just underneath the kitchen. I looked around for rats, but there weren't any that I could see. I twisted in another glass fuse. The house needed to be completely rewired, just like ours.

I wanted to get the hell out of there as quickly as I could and smacked a cobweb out of my way. I jumped down from the large square opening and heard Arturo's footsteps coming to the rescue.

"I told you to stay upstairs, you dingbat dog," I said, rubbing his head and neck and giving him a big hug. I grinned. I sounded just like my sister.

I could see at the top of the steps that the kitchen light was back on. Slowly making my way toward it, I turned off my flashlight, Arturo marching behind me. I was taken aback when I saw Candace, her roommate Amanda-Miranda, and Aubrey Meslier standing in my kitchen. I closed the cellar door behind me as I continued to gaze at the three of them and wondered what they wanted.

"Alice, what are you doing?"

"I'm sorry, Candace. He followed me down the stairs. I wouldn't have kept the door open, but it's kind of creepy down there   "

"Oh, no, no. All I was going to mention was that if you ever need to have a fuse changed, just go around back and ask one of the guys to do it for you. I'm *way* too scared to go down into that cellar all by myself. And Chick is always around." Amanda-Miranda rolled her eyes and shuddered in disgust at the mention of the landlord's name. "If the guys aren't home, you can always call him."

I shook my head and wiped my dusty hands on my jeans. "It's no problem, really."

"She's always been so gosh-darn stubborn, you two. I have known her pretty much my whole life," Aubrey said.

"Aubrey, what are you doing here?"

She knew the girls from upstairs. That was how I found out about this place. The two of them just stood there awkwardly looking at me, smiling nervously, glancing at each other. Amanda-Miranda twirled her long hair, then her wristwatch. She couldn't even look at me.

"Would everyone like to sit down? You're making me nervous, and I'm getting worried." I was becoming frustrated and suddenly very alarmed as I anticipated some sort of confrontation. Candace was probably pissed with me because I was feeding Arturo animals and muffins. He was sitting on the blanket.

"Do you want to sit down, Alice?" Aubrey asked, looking at me with sorrowful eyes.

"What the hell is going on?"

The phone rang.

"It's probably my mother."

"Don't get that!" Aubrey yelled and leapt to the other side of the table where the answering machine sat on the small counter. She hastily unplugged the entire system.

At this time, I was about to fall over. I was having a hard time breathing, and my chest was clenched in a vise again. The anxiety was unbearable. I pointed to the three of them. They were wrong for doing this to me. They didn't have it together. They didn't have it planned out. They were torturing me. "You three better tell me what's going on right now."

Arturo put his head on my shin for just a moment, then he lay back down. Candace didn't even seem to care one iota about that. Then a pang of terror sped through me like a pin. "My father? No, Scotty was just here!"

"No, no, no," Candace cooed. Her hairstyle was so perfect. "Your dad? No, no. This is about Miranda."

That was her name. Miranda. Miranda. Miranda Something.

"This guy I had a few beers with the other night, Jack is his name. Jack Strait. His father is a producer over at WELLocal, and you know the TV station is owned by Barton Withers's parents, right?"

I said nothing. I just looked at her.

"Well, Jack and I were just talking about that new high-rise glass building downtown, and that's where his dad's office is moving. That's the new Wither-Chambliss Building, and the TV and radio stations are both moving if they haven't already. It's supposed to be this thirteen-million-dollar project."

"I hadn't noticed," I said. "And why are you telling me this? I mean, who cares, Amanda?"

"Miranda."

"Sorry."

"Miranda, just get to the point," Candace scolded.

Aubrey continued to guard the telephone and answering machine.

Miranda walked around the table, her hands near her face as if she were going to bite her nails. She pulled out a chair. "Lisa Jupiter," she said, referring to the buxom blonde who read the evening news. "Lisa Jupiter is doing a piece on Barton Withers and your older sister's murder. She's interviewing him at the new prison—"

"What new prison? What on earth are you talking about?" I stared at her.

"You didn't know he was out of Bellmorrow?" She had the eyes of a hound dog.

"No," I said quietly. I put my head in my hands.

Aubrey gingerly rubbed my shoulder. I couldn't speak, I couldn't cry. I was done fighting. I was incredulous. Every bone in my body felt as if it were about to snap. It hurt to breathe.

"He's been transferred to a medium, no, minimum-security prison. One or the other." She continued. "For what reason, I don't know. Good behavior, I guess? Overcrowding?"

Good behavior?

"He was transferred so that he could be closer to Maidenhead County."

Mommy and Daddy.

"Jack got to see the preliminary footage, and the trailers went out this afternoon."

"That's probably why your mom's trying to get in touch with you," Candace said gently.

"We know you don't have a TV. You've always got your nose in a book. That's good, you know?" Aubrey said, still standing guard.

"There's another thing, Alice."

"There can't be another thing." I brought my head up.

"Yes, yes, there's another thing, and you should know, Alice. It's not sympathetic to your sister. The Withers family is putting their own spin on the whole thing. We just wanted to make sure you heard it from us, you know?" Miranda said.

My nose and the sides of my neck ached with anger. My chest closed in on me again. I was so embarrassed because I kept forgetting this girl's name. I stared at the toxic space between Candace and the door.

Aubrey squeezed my knee, but I only saw it. I couldn't feel. The dog licked the back of my hand as it dangled in front of his nose.

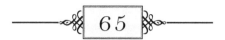

65

Late-afternoon television exploded into this phenomenon that Dad referred to as media-driven tabloid sensationalism. Reporters from New York, Los Angeles, Sydney, and even small suburban cities like Wellton were interviewing, and their producers were creating ostensible splashy and intense documentaries on everyone, from some Colombian drug lord smuggling cocaine into the United States to serial killers to a woman with eighteen personalities and just about every killer and bank robber in and among them.

I hadn't sat in front of a television set in years, and since I had been at State and living in the way back of the Plymouth, reading into the wee hours of the morning, I never had the need or the desire. I didn't even own a television set. I already knew that we lived in a fucked-up world, probably always did and probably always would, and so what difference would it make?

I also hadn't picked up a newspaper since Marisa's killing either. It's not like there was ever anything positive in the newspaper. After Marisa was murdered, Dad and Kiki did their best to hide all newspapers from me anyway, and so I took that as a sign. In addition, I never liked the way my fingers felt after I handled a newspaper. All that black ink made my hands feel filthy. I always hated that.

Marisa and I used to watch television all the time, especially when we were little. Bunica even claimed we were addicted to it. It was fun back then. Nothing was fun now, especially when I had to go into battle. The monster was transferred to a medium-security prison thanks to his rich parents and his purported good behavior. His behavior at Bellmorrow was supposed to be good. He was in that hole for a very good reason. I suppose I have to admit that it wasn't exactly as if anyone intentionally lied to me. Both Detective

Holloway and Deputy District Attorney Giles informed my father long ago that this could happen. Here we were at eight years, and the monster, along with his poor concerned parents, would grant Lisa Jupiter an interview that would launch her career into a trajectory of unlimited possibilities of opportunity and prestige. That is exactly why I needed to discuss my reservations with her. I had seen her huge blond head advertised on various billboards and along the lengths of city buses. If she wanted to become involved with Satan just to make enormous amounts of money and top ratings, no one could stop her. That I was sure of, but she would not be doing it at the expense of my sister.

Walter and Aubrey cautiously followed me around for hours, even after midnight, explaining to me all about freedom of the press, freedom of the media, freedom to do whatever the fuck you wanted to do. I found that to be complete bullshit. My sister had no free-doms anymore because she was dead—murdered before she even fin-ished high school. Instead of her young beautiful body buried, she was burned to a crisp and her ashes scattered by a mother who never wanted her. Scattered near a damned lovely waterfall in a part of the world she despised. Marisa never had any freedom.

Since I was the only one who had any feelings for her and felt anything at all about any of this, I would be the one who would continue to fight for her and her memory. I would fight until my last breath because I owed it to her. I didn't care about Lisa Jupiter or her freedom. I didn't care if it was too late either; it was going to take place. Marisa would have done it for me.

I decided I would take my bike. I had not slept the night before, but that wasn't unusual for me. I rarely captured sleep my whole life, unless I took a sedative. Then sometimes I would really sleep.

The humidity immediately clung to my arms and back like a magnet. The smell of lilac and damp earth hung in the air. Riding was a good way for me to get somewhere, especially if I was angry and had a purpose. It took longer, but I could spend time thinking while pedaling. Sometimes I felt a bit calmer at the end of my jour-ney, but this time, I had the feeling that nothing would calm me, unless they did what they were told.

I wasn't sure exactly what to think about Lisa Jupiter and the TV station. It was the monster and his parents that I tried to push out of my mind, even though the task had been impossible for nearly half of my life.

I had never been to a TV station before. No wonder they were moving. It was so far below the Withers family. Adams Street was in a scrubby industrialized area on the south side. I would have to go up a hill before I reached the building. It was a shithole, but that's where they had been located my entire life. Dad was wrong; it was Big Barton who owned his favorite DJ, Pick Hudson. What a shame. I never boycotted Pick. After all, it wasn't his fault. He probably never even met the man who raised the monster that killed my sister. I should have taken the Plymouth.

I popped off my bike and locked it to a pole. There was a small anteroom area right inside the front door that was old and empty, most likely because the station was relocating. It smelled dusty, like the inside of our piano when you opened the top.

I was shocked at how dark and narrow the hallway was that led to Lisa Jupiter's set. It was spring and warm, but even in the summer months, there wasn't much need for air-conditioning, unless you're rich and idle like Big Barton, or if you happened to be a bank or a restaurant or a fish store. Out of nowhere, an unexpected blast of freezing-cold air from a noisy old vent sticking out of the wall almost knocked me backward. It disturbed my thinking as I found myself walking toward voices and then into a large room.

I blinked quickly as my eyes adjusted to the lights. I had no idea a television station could be so chaotic, so disorganized to such an extent that it caused me disappointment. I felt an urgent need to start moving things around, placing them somewhere else, anywhere but where they were. It was riotous, as if a bomb had exploded in the middle of the floor, and no one seemed to care. No one even noticed that I was standing there, a stranger. No one recognized Marisa Ionescu's younger half sister. How funny. What if *I* had that bomb? Oh, wouldn't that be lovely. We could have all gone out together in one big pink plume. No more Lisa Jupiter, no more me. Why hadn't

I thought of that? Because I had no idea I could just walk into these places unannounced. That was one reason.

I continued to stand there in silence, watching, absorbing. Several people entered the room behind me with an "Excuse me" and joined the bustle to prevail upon whatever it was these mindless folks were trying to accomplish. They were so mindless, they didn't even notice me and my prospective bomb. I briefly thought of Louis Dagher and how he had called me a bomb.

I looked at the wall to my left. It was covered with this faded yellow and brown vertical pinstripe wallpaper. It was ugly, but my sister would have loved it because it would have reminded her of her childhood art classes in school and the old decorating magazines she used to thumb through. My eyes watered slightly, and I smiled. It had to have been hanging there for at least twenty years, and it was peeling. There was also a collection of diplomas or certificates on a wall behind a tiny wooden desk and what looked like a broken secretarial chair. They were too far away from me to see who they belonged to, although I'm sure that one of them had to belong to Lisa Jupiter. They were in dire need of cleaning, and it appeared as if someone had thrown them up against the wall to purposely let them fall into a lopsided fashion. No one straightened them out. My top teeth dropped behind my bottom teeth. Someone threw those diplomas up against the wall. I had to stop thinking of things being thrown up against a wall.

I was dying to walk over to that wall and straighten out those diplomas, but I didn't dare. As people continued to scurry around, in and out of different rooms, over floors lined with wires and cords in every color, length, and thickness, I always believed as much as I knew to believe that there was something greater about the way people on television were supposed to look and act. They were supposed to be beautiful, in perfect proportion, dressed to a precision, no threads out of place, no creases, every color should alternate and match, their shoes should never be scuffed. According the billboards and the sides of the city buses, Lisa Jupiter was a majestic creature of the screen. Her smile was warm but explosive, her blond hair was shiny and silky, her clothes were expensive and of the latest fashion.

Lisa Jupiter certainly had Wellton fooled. She was buxom but was unfortunate to have the rest of her figure like mine. She was tall and chunky with those oversized boobs that I would think the average man would not find attractive. What did *I* know about men? I think I knew that anyway. I pictured an enormous white lacy bra with huge straps. Her calves were encased like pork sausages in dark pantyhose. She was wearing thick older white sneakers that looked out of place with her blue dress. I figured in Lisa Jupiter's case, it was all for comfort since no one was supposed to see her feet when she was interviewing the monster and its parents. That long blond silky hair, like the kind you would see in a shampoo commercial, was more like a giant yellow wavy overstyled, overdressed wig. The more I eyed this despicable woman, the more I realized that it *was* a wig! What a liar and a phony. In the short time frame I had been standing about twenty-five feet from Lisa Jupiter, I thought about what I was looking at, and I began to question what I was actually seeing. It was true that people could appear so differently than what they actually were. I remembered Marisa's death, and as much as I wanted to pull the thought back out and away from my mind, I knew that I would never be able to as long as Lisa Jupiter was around.

I had seen so many things, and from what I had seen about Lisa Jupiter, she wasn't so beautiful; not on the inside, not on the outside. I would have believed her to be educated and smart, perhaps she graduated near the top of her class, but when I barely had to rouse the courage to merely stroll into this dumpy studio, I realized that the monster with the sausage legs, yellow head, and caked-on makeup was exactly that—a monster. A monster that would interview three other monsters.

I was so nervous as I paved my way through a couple of what might have been crew people, watching carefully not to trip over the mine field of cable and wires. "Ms. Jupiter?" I didn't think she heard me. "Ms. Lisa Jupiter? My name is Alice Buchner."

The woman standing closest to her turned to face me. She tilted her head and was somehow able to tuck it under her chin so that rolls of chin fat held it up. She opened her mouth slightly. Her large brown eyes were filled with terror and confusion. It looked as if she had an idea who she was glaring at, although it wasn't quite a glare, it was a look with just the tiniest hint of regret, and then it was gone. I don't know how they accomplished it, but both my father and Detective Holloway were able to keep the press away from me and my story; however, it was obvious that Triple Chin recognized my name immediately. The regret, the sorrow, the guilt, whatever it was that I saw, died almost as soon as it was birthed.

"What are you doing here, Ms. Buchner?" Triple Chin asked and turned back to her boss. "I'll call security, Lisa."

Security? What security? Who? Where?

"No, no, Amy, let's not do that. I'll talk to her," Lisa Jupiter said in a syrupy voice to Triple Chin and loud enough for me to hear as she dismissed her and walked over to me with a big fake white smile. Those teeth didn't even look real. She offered me her outstretched hand. I took it.

"What can I do for you today, Alice?" She looked right into my eyes. I looked into hers. Brown entangled with blue; she knew exactly what the answer to that was.

"I don't think you should do the interview with Barton Withers, Ms. Jupiter."

"Well, my dear," she scoffed, "I have already interviewed him and some of his family members."

Mary Jo?

"It just hasn't *aired* yet." That bogus smile remained pasted on that plastered face as she tilted her head and blinked a few times. She probably thought I was pathetic.

I became more and more irritated with her as she gazed at me with that mouth.

"Why don't you *please not* air it? This man, if that's what you people want to call him, murdered my sister. Why would you want to talk to him?"

She stood up a little straighter. "It's quite simple, Ms. Buchner. The people want to know the entire story, and Barton Withers wants to tell his side of it. He was not charged with murder either. He was charged with manslaughter in the first degree and given a very harsh sentence, having to spend several years in a maximum-security prison. I am a journal—"

"You are incredulous, Ms. Jupiter. Don't you have any soul? Where are your scruples?" My voice was shaking, and I was getting louder.

She smiled. I knew that was what she wanted—to infuriate me.

"What about Marisa's side of the story?"

People were looking at us.

"What about my side of the story?"

"Your side of the story, Ms. Buchner." She crossed her arms in front of her and pinched her lips together, all the while nodding. "*Your* side of the story? You mean the one you *couldn't* testify to in court, the one they couldn't use? The story that was nothing more than one big fat hallucination?"

The room emptied. There was only Lisa Jupiter and Alice Buchner left in the world.

"And as for Marisa Ionescu? She has no story. Oh, maybe she does to the medical examiner, dear, but her story is told from the perspective of Mr. and Mrs. Withers and their son, who has never wavered from this being purely an accident, no more and no less. Marisa was a very, very burdensome teenager who was difficult and heading down the wrong path. Your stepfather was only trying to discipline her. You're a good young woman with your whole life ahead of you, Alice. All I can say is that it's time to put the past in the past and move on. She wasn't even your real sister."

I was stunned into silence. How naïve could I be, thinking that this vile woman might help me? She had no standards. I knew she was a monster, but I was astonished to the degree. My stomach roiled with hollowness, defeat, and rage. How did she think she knew about Marisa? How could she—she had no idea. She too was fooled by Barton Withers.

Lisa Jupiter placed her hand on my arm in an attempt to lead me out, but I brushed her off me. "What is wrong with you people?" I looked around the room and back at her. "There is no *his* side of the story! Aren't you supposed to be objective, Lisa?"

Her voice lowered, and her smile disappeared. "It was a terrible accident. I am so sorry for your loss, Alice, but Barton is doing his time."

"It was no accident!" I shouted. "I was there! Were you? No! I don't care about hallucinations or whatever else you heard or think you heard. It's all wrong! *This* is about you and your damned ratings! Your career! I saw him. I saw the entire fight. I saw lots of fights. He tormented *my sister* for years. I saw his face that day. He was drunk at nine in the morning, lady. He was always drunk! I'll bet he forgot to mention *that* in his interview! He's glad she's dead—he hated her. He tried to strangle her but ended up breaking her tiny neck instead. How, *how* can that be an accident?"

I barely noticed someone taking photos of me. I knew Lisa Jupiter wouldn't be a part of her own slanted story. There was so much fury running up the sides of my neck and into my head.

Lisa Jupiter snapped her fingers and motioned for someone to come immediately. "I will not discuss this with you any further, Ms. Buchner, this is absolutely ridiculous. I will not have you barge onto my set and treat my colleagues and me in this fashion. Security has been notified, so I suggest you leave this instant. The next call will be to the police."

"Barton Withers is a murderer," I said as calmly as I could, my voice shaking as my body became hot. "He is a cold-blooded killer, and his diabolical family thinks there is nothing wrong with that. He already had a criminal record, or did you forget to research *that* as well?"

"Get out!"

"You need to have that big blond head of yours examined, you liar! You fool. Don't you turn your back on me!" I hissed like a rattler and went after her in slow motion. I ripped at the top of her head, but her wig was sewed and glued on somehow. She shrieked in pain. When I looked at my hands, there was only a chunky tuft of yellow hair between my fingers. A clump of Lisa Jupiter was in my right hand.

"Assault!" she cried.

That's nothing. Ever had your neck broken?

371

"Sh-she assaulted me!" Lisa Jupiter shrieked and sobbed. She was a fake. Then she collapsed into her group of people as I was led out by a man with big arms and a black shirt.

"I barely even touched her," I protested as he half led, half dragged me down the same filthy dark corridor I had easily entered and into the piercing afternoon sunlight. "Her hair just came out."

The man reached over and took the ball of blond hair out of my hand. "She's an important figure," he said at last. "You shouldn't have touched her. How did you get in here in the first place?"

"I walked through the front door."

"We're going to have to take care of that problem." Big Arms walked me out front to greet three policemen and two patrol cars. A small group of people gathered across the street to watch the entertainment as a short policeman who was about as tall as he was wide asked me some basic questions and directed me to sit quietly on the curb as Big Arms showed a tall and extremely well-built cop Lisa Jupiter's hair ball.

The third cop, another chubby one, appeared. He had strawberry blond hair and a solid dark blue uniform unlike the other two. He went back inside the building with Big Arms, presumably to get a statement from the pitiful Lisa Jupiter, whom I had just so brutally attacked. She probably wouldn't even allow herself to realize that the insect she interviewed caused far more permanent damage than I could ever do yanking at her head. This was how shallow, vain, and unintelligent this woman was. She wasn't capable of seeing the evil in Barton Withers, yet she most likely could see evil in me because I, in a split second, could have possibly caused her not to be attractive anymore.

Whatever gave this woman the idea she was attractive in the first place? Inside or out? An accident—she was his *mouthpiece to the world*. I would preach to whoever would listen that what happened that day was no accident. It was a premeditation that no one believed but God and me.

How cruel life could be. Thinking about it angered me more and more.

"What happened here today, Ms. Buchner?" Short Fat Cop asked.

It wasn't difficult for me to answer quickly. "I heard from some friends that Lisa Jupiter would be airing an interview with my sister's murderer and his parents who are defending him."

"And?"

"And I came down to the studio to ask her to please pull the interview." *Pull.* Probably not the best choice of words.

"She said she wouldn't do that."

"Yes, that's right. I was trying to reason with her, but she wouldn't listen." I stood up, threw my hands on my hips, and shifted my weight to one leg. Maybe I could make this one cop understand. These people were the ones who found my sister. "She was being cruel, bringing up things from the court case, the files, how did she even—never mind. She said my sister's death was an accident. I am so *tired* of hearing that!"

"All right."

"This is the lie that the Withers family is trying to put out there. It wasn't an accident, sir, Officer. I was there. Why do I have to keep repeating myself? It was no accident! And I don't care what she or any of these people say—"

He put his hands up in front of my face. "Ms. Buchner. You need to calm down. Now. You don't have any right to trespass on this property."

"Trespass? I just walked in." I quickly scanned the immediate area. "There's no sign. No one was even at the front door to stop me."

He looked at me as if I were no more than merely argumentative. "I said calm. Down. Do you understand? If you can't, I'm going to cuff you and throw you in the back of the car right now."

I stopped as tears of grief and frustration began to form in the corners of my eyes once again. What was the point of his asking me questions if he wasn't even remotely interested in what I had to say? What was it about police that made them decide what to believe and what they wanted to hear, even though it was so grossly wrong? When it came to Marisa, it always appeared as if my family, what few friends I had, the law, and now the media had their own ideas, which were clearly stacked against her and me.

"Why did you pull her hair?"

Why do you think?

"Go ahead." He waited.

"I didn't mean to pull her hair out." That wasn't his question. "I really didn't. I don't know why, I mean, it's not like I yanked it hard or anything. I just reached over and tugged at it."

I was lying, and there were witnesses.

"A big chunk just came out. It wasn't even her hair. It was a wig. I doubt it even hurt her, Officer. What about me? Look what's she's doing—"

"You never know what hurts other people, Ms. Buchner. That's why you're not supposed to put your hands on anyone. And you? You were pretty angry. This could have escalated into something bad."

I briefly thought of Louis Dagher. He and Lisa Jupiter *both* deserved it, even if I would take the punishment for it. I looked at him as carefully as I could in the afternoon light. There it was again, rearing itself. That irony, that little twisting, nagging incongruity. Was he serious?

Poor Lisa Jupiter. I yanked a tuft of her yellow wig off her ugly head. Louis Dagher, I choked him hard enough to make the poor, pitiful young boy cry. They didn't like it at all, did they? But they were alive, and they started the fight. Lisa Jupiter was so offended by what she started. Listening to that beast scream assault? After I saw what that monster did to Marisa? Did she really think this was appropriate? Really? Was she capable of feeling? Was this policeman standing in front of me capable of feeling? Did these people truly have empathy for a giant monster who puts his hands on another human being, throwing and pounding her little body up against a wall, strangling, twisting her neck like a jar until it ripped to shreds?

I could hear Aubrey saying something very faint and droll: *Two wrongs don't make a right. I know, I know, this is so much different. I understand that this is not exactly like two children in a playground squabble, but, Alice—*

My thinking was far beyond where it was only an hour ago.

"The good news is that Ms. Jupiter won't be pressing any charges against you, Ms. Buchner."

"That's good. That's great news. Can I leave now? Any more questions for me?" Now that it was all smoothed over, I figured Lisa Jupiter and the station would now decide not to air the interview with the monster and his diabolical parents and whatever other Withers decided to partake in this atrocity.

"No, I'm afraid you can't leave now." He moved in on me. "I'm going to place you under arrest, Ms. Buchner."

"But why? She's not pressing charges." I didn't care if she did.

"No, but the state takes trespassing and simple battery seriously."

Simple battery? Her hair would have fallen out on her next trip down in the elevator.

"Please turn around and bend your elbows. It will be more comfortable for you when I put the handcuffs on."

"What about my bike? Will it also be arrested for trespassing?"

"You need to watch your tone, Ms. Buchner. We are going to have to impound your bike."

"You're going to impound my bike?" *What?*

"Yes, Ms. Buchner," he snapped. "We're going to impound your bike. Now I don't want to hear another word out of you. Do you understand me? Not one more word."

I nodded slightly, and he was gone, off somewhere in a different direction, probably to find my bike. I didn't know. I looked down at the sidewalk. It was old and cracked. Parts of it were buckling furiously with the impatient earth. My top row of teeth were firmly tucked behind my lower row and I stood, hands cuffed behind my back in powerlessness, as the fat strawberry blond cop in the different colored uniform ushered me into the back of his car. I was expecting him to be just as rude and authoritarian as his friend, but he was surprisingly easier to talk to. I hoped they didn't make me pee in a cup because they would see a whole bunch of weed, and I could have possibly been penalized for that.

"Where are you taking me?" I already knew I was heading for a holding cell.

"Maidenhead County Public Safety Building. Women's Unit. That's the only place I know of." A comedian. He pulled away from the curb, and I watched out the back window as my bike, still locked to a pole, got smaller and smaller, and we drove farther and farther.

"How come you didn't read me my rights?"

"We don't normally do that for something this minor."

Hmm. Minor. That didn't sound right.

"I've never been arrested before."

"I figured as much."

"You did? How?"

"I'm pretty good at these types of things."

I hoped that while I was in jail, he would come and visit me. I was becoming fearful of one of those women making me do things to them or a bunch of them holding me down and forcing a shampoo bottle up me. "They're going to rape me in there."

"No, they won't."

"Yes, they will." I was scared. I had all kinds of ideas running through my head. Anything could happen to a person in jail. I didn't want to ask, but the question fell out of my mouth. "Do you know Detective Holloway?"

"Oh, sure," he said. "But don't think he can get you out of this one."

"I didn't mean to pull—"

"That's a lie."

I said nothing.

"I've known Holloway for about twenty-two years now—fine, solid, good cop."

"I had a right to be angry that she interviewed the animal that killed my sister. If you could even call him an animal. He's no animal, he's a mon—They're going to air it. He's a liar, his parents have no idea what they're talking about. Lisa Jupiter is supposed to be a journalist. Did she once get my side of the story? No. She's on his side, I mean—and it makes it even worse that he's been transferred to a medium-security prison." I didn't care if I cried now. I was going to jail.

"I can't say I disagree with you. If it had been my sister and I didn't know what I know now, I probably would have done the same thing. Not to a woman, but if it was a guy and I was a young man around your age, not a policeman, obviously, I probably would have kicked the shit out of him—for pullin' a stunt like that."

"Really?" We were now on parallel planes. I wasn't sure if he was even being completely truthful with me. Maybe he was trying to keep me as calm as he could before the guillotine finally got its taste of my blood. And it was unlikely that as understanding as he wanted me to think he was, he would take these cuffs off and let me out of the car.

He peered at his driver's mirror and then straight ahead again. He was smiling. I wasn't.

"You won't be in there long. I'm sure if you just give someone a call, say, your parents maybe? They'll come get you out."

"No."

"Sorry?"

"I don't want either one of my parents to know anything."

He nodded. "That's perfectly fine. You're an adult. You don't have to call anyone."

Finally, Dad. I'm no longer a minor. Remember how long it took to get here? I thought it would be a big party when I became an adult. Instead, I'm as depressed now as when Marisa died.

I felt guilty about calling fat strawberry blond cop in the different colored uniform fat strawberry blond cop in the different colored uniform. His real name was Sergeant Gregg Hayman. He was an okay guy. It could have been a lot worse, and so in my mind, I made a note to myself to refer to him as Sergeant Gregg Hayman from then on.

We pulled into a large garage-type structure that could have doubled as a small airplane hangar. Sergeant Gregg Hayman led me through a gray steel door and then a windowless room where he filled out one sheet of paper. He led me out of the room and immediately took off the handcuffs as he turned me over to a short hearty-looking middle-aged woman named Dee.

"Don't let your grief ruin what's left," he said. Those were his last words to me.

I looked at Dee. "They're going to beat the shit out of me in here and rape me, aren't they? These women?" I pointed beyond her. I was suddenly frightened and felt very alone. "They're going to shove some object in my vagina, aren't they?"

377

She looked up at me with a furrowed brow. Her head bobbed so very slightly from side to side. It felt as though her gaze lasted forever. Then a smile slowly crept across her face. I thought she was about to spit at me, but she startled me with her soft voice. "You watch way too much TV, kid."

I stared back at her. I didn't watch any TV.

I learned two things after Dee accompanied me down a long corridor and into another room where a pretty blond guard dressed me out. I learned that I had to leave my underpants behind because they were blue, and only white undergarments were allowed. Thank God my bra was white. I learned that my bail was set at $750, and for seventy-five bucks, all I had to do was go home, come back, and enter my plea on Monday in front of a judge. I knew that I could make a phone call, even though with all the questions asked and all the forms filled out, it appeared to me that the elderly man who discussed my bond with me was also going to make a phone call or two. To whom, I did not know, but it could not be to anyone I did not wish for him to call. I repeated this to him so many times that finally he looked at me and said, "Young lady, I realize that I am older than dirt, but I am not senile, nor am I deaf. You have my word. I will not call your parents. I am obligated by penal code not to infringe upon your rights as an American citizen. May we move on?"

And so I did not use the one and only jailhouse phone call I was allowed. Who was I going to call? I didn't know anyone who had seventy-five bucks in their back pocket—well, maybe Chick—but then he would expect something in return, and the thought of that made me want to vomit. I would have to swallow the indignant lump in my throat and sit in that cell until Monday afternoon and hope and pray that some four-hundred-pound monster and her buddies wouldn't hurt me…or worse.

A spark flickered in my mind, and I briefly laughed as I thought about Lisa Jupiter's wig. My thoughts turned to the seriousness of Louis Dagher, and I realized this: I too was an angry prisoner. It all subsided. I was not about to let the bear see the fear in my eyes.

* * * * *

I was making my way up the rear stairwell when I turned around and saw her, the back of my sister's deep wavy blue-red hair pulled up in a long ponytail at the nape of her neck, fastened in little areas around her ears with bobby pins. One of them glistened when it caught the evening light. She may have been coming up behind me, casually scuffling along our mother's shiny cherry floors in thin white socks as she was about to make that right turn when he caught her, his voice buried in yet another thoroughly decorated space in this maze.

"I know you called my mother a cunt." The voice out of nowhere pierced through the twilight.

She turned around in shock as his shadow was now visible on the ruffled curtains that matched the wallpaper. She opened her mouth and then closed it again. Her hand was on the stair rail. "I never said— Barton, what?"

The shadow came bounding over the wall like a rabid dog. "Let me tell you something, little shit. You are not going to call my mother a cunt!"

I looked around, worrying if his little daughter could hear him; the language, his yelling on a peaceful evening in July. Where was my mother? The last I saw her, she was loading china into a storage closet, so she couldn't be far.

"I did not say that, Barton! Never!" Marisa protested, backing up. She looked scared as his monstrous physique hovered and loomed like some sort of mythological giant creature.

"You don't call my mother a cunt!" He was stiff, and it looked like he was using his whole body to point to her, not gesture with his fingers. Something was wrong with him. "I don't care if you don't like her. You don't get to call her a cunt!"

"I said I—"

"I know what you said because your mother told me!"

Marisa was crying openly now. She had protested long enough for me to believe that she was telling the truth, although I did nothing to defend her, and I said nothing to stop him. She was backed up onto the stairs; her face was a shade lighter than newspaper white.

He clamped a massive hand between her shoulder blades and twisted her around, causing her to stumble down two steps. She remained upright on her small feet. I cringed and slid down to a sitting position at the top of the landing behind the banister. He had to have seen me.

"You see that?" He pointed into the next room. When my sister didn't respond, he grabbed her by the face and pulled her into the giant doorway and made her look in the exact direction he wanted her to look. "Do. You. See. That?" With each word, he yanked her face. She would be bruised for sure.

She nodded, his gargantuan hand never leaving her face. He was pointing to a very old restored upright piano that belonged to Sunny Withers when she was a little girl.

"You stay the hell away from that, do you hear me? Don't you ever let me see you within one foot of that piano, do you understand, you vicious little witch?"

She nodded again as much as she could with his strength combatting her.

He threw her face aside and walked away.

Marisa loved to play that piano. She was a remarkable musician. My sister played music by ear. She wanted to take piano lessons, but my mother said she couldn't afford to spend that kind of money. I couldn't understand what my mother was talking about. How much could piano lessons cost? I knew some kids at school who took piano lessons, and they didn't live in mansions like ours. How could anyone say they couldn't afford piano lessons when they lived in a big fancy house and had a really talented kid who could actually play *the piano before their very first lesson? My mother ordered sheets and a bedspread for herself and Barton Withers that had to be shipped all the way from Egypt, for god's sake.*

What was wrong with me? Why was I such a coward? Was I ever a chicken. Marisa was right about that.

* * * * *

I was terrified when Dee led me into a tiny anteroom behind a steel door that slammed shut behind us. In the anteroom were two doors on either side of us, and I was led through the one on the left. I looked behind, and that door too slammed shut with such a heavy and final ferocity as I held my cup and my sandwich bag filled with travel-type toiletries in one hand while positioning my green cot mattress under my arm. Six women stared at me and smiled, and after rapidly scanning the room, I felt a sudden surge of relief. They did not give the impression of eagerness to rape me, particularly the elderly one who had been arrested and charged with armed robbery. I was still on guard.

I heard a collective "Hey," and a tall thin girl with long dirty blond hair, blue eyes, and freckles bounded over first. I didn't. I was cautious.

"You can put your mat down there next to the wall, down on the floor. Sorry, all the bunks are taken. What are you in here for?"

I couldn't remember where I heard the conversation from, probably at the store, but it was a long time ago, when Marisa was alive, and we were really young. I was probably hiding behind some wall or door somewhere, listening to something I shouldn't have been listening to about the politics and behavior of those condemned to the inside. It could have been one of Kiki's trampy loser friends, a customer of Dad's, a combination of both, I didn't remember, which would drive me insane and start the launching sequence for my poor tired mind again. When you're in jail or prison, you never discuss your crimes. You never ask anyone for anything. You always keep your area tidy. You'll be expected to fight, so make sure you don't completely kick the shit out of the other, otherwise everyone else will want to fight you. No one is your friend, you come in alone and you leave alone, if you leave at all.

I doubted that the monster was paying attention to any of these little house rules as he had no regard for anyone in authority. He was the authority, or so he believed. He was the omnipresent. He was the axe that killed the most beautiful flourishing tree. A new prison. Good behavior. Such bull.

"What did you say your name was again? I'm Sharon. What did you do, girl?"

"I assaulted Lisa Jupiter." Fuck it.

"Wa' dat *you?* Hahaha, *ha, gurl!*" Even my mother wasn't that loud.

An obese black woman lifted her huge round head and looked at me as if I were the Messiah. She had cheeks on top of cheeks on top of chins. Her smile was vast and white except for the one gold tooth in the front. I was worried she would collapse that top bunk onto the woman below her. How the hell did she get up there? And I'm glad I wasn't the only one who thought it was funny.

"You *heard* about that?" I was stunned. How could she have?

"*Honey?* News travel fas' 'round here!" she shouted and laughed heartily again. "You a celebrity."

"No, she isn't, JR. Don't scare her on her first day in."

"I ain't!" She shrugged, pointing her fingers to her chest in protest. Then her face softened when she looked back at me, and she smiled again. "Dat bitch deserve it."

"I agree." That was the other thing. You always act tough. I noticed a television set hanging in the corner of the cell. Maybe JR saw me on the news? No, impossible.

"You ain't gonna be seein' none a dat shit in here, baby. Dat TV way up? All Jesus network. It be good."

I was relieved. It would have been cruel and unusual punishment for me to have to sit in this cell all weekend, forced to have to listen to Lisa Jupiter and the highlights of the upcoming interview with Barton Withers. The girls back at the house got the day wrong, but it was happening. It was real now, and there was no stopping it. I was going to be locked up for three nights before I went before the judge on Monday afternoon. I was no longer frightened for my safety, but suddenly, I felt very constricted, as if I were being squeezed by the four walls all approaching me at once. I would move but then realize that I couldn't. I kept patting myself down as I sat on my lumpy green mat up against the wall, looking for a cigarette, which I didn't have. Sharon gave me two of hers and shared one with me. Some of the other women sat at a shiny metal table with attached matching stools and played cards.

"Who is this Lisa bitch?" Sharon asked as she blew out smoke and flicked an ash.

"Lisa Jupiter. She's been a reporter at WELLocal for a few years. Now she's started to do what's called these 'sensationalized human interest stories.'" I hoped I wasn't insulting her, but I felt like I needed to give Sharon a bit of an education. "It's all bullshit."

"How did you know her?"

"I didn't know her personally, but I went to find her at the TV station." A trickle of anger crept its way up from my stomach into my mouth where I could taste it. I wish I had done more damage to Lisa Jupiter's wig.

Don't talk about your crimes, Alice. Watch out for rats.

"She interviewed the man who murdered my sister after he was transferred from a maximum-security prison to medium. Practically nothing for a monster like him. They're supposed to air it the beginning of next month."

"Fuck," Sharon replied softly and took another drag off her cigarette.

I didn't want to talk about Marisa. It was enough feeling helpless and closed up in a jail cell built for six, and it made the pain that much more insurmountable. I tried futilely not to cry, but I couldn't control the tears. Sharon gave me the cigarette and put her arm on my shoulders. I wondered for a second if she thought she was going to have sex with me. I hadn't even done it with a guy yet, and going to bed with a woman didn't sound appealing. But I guess if I was forced to, I would have to make the best of it since no one outside this cluttered cell would give a damn. I thrust my fear and anticipation aside.

"I tried to reason with her, Lisa Jupiter. She didn't care though, she wouldn't listen."

"Man, I'm really sorry about your sister though. She was murdered? Shit, when did that happen?"

"I was thirteen."

"How old…" She paused. "And how…" She was grappling for the obvious words, the right words. I noticed the same confused eyes, the twisted features that clouded the face of a person when I told them about Marisa. "Murder. Man, that sucks."

"It was a long time ago."

"Yeah," she countered, "but you never get over something like that."

I had never thought about it in those very simple terms. Once again, I was frightened. That was routine. How was I going to live the rest of my life with this? I wouldn't if I died tomorrow. What if I didn't die in the near future, and I lived to be an old woman? It was an impossible feat to think that far ahead. Everyone else who was affected, or at least I thought was affected, seemed to be dealing with their emotions and grief just perfectly fine. I was never able to learn their secret, and I didn't want any of them to teach me that secret.

"No wonder you're so pissed off," she said.

I looked around the cold beige room and said nothing.

"I went to this doctor a couple of years ago," she said. "He told me I was manic-depressive because I got really mad really easily, you know? So he put me on this medicine that didn't do a damned thing, but I don't think he knew what he was talking about. I knew about manic depression 'cause my mother had it. She drank all the time, she was sick, man. She would stay up all night for days, you know? One time she tried to take me and my brother horseback riding like at three in the morning." She shook her head. "When my little brother reminded her that we didn't have no horses anywhere near our apartment in Scranton, she went fucking berserk, man! She slapped that poor kid's face so hard, it sounded like a firecracker goin' off—like one of those cherry bomb things."

Her mother sounded eerily like Aunt Nancy in her bad years, but I was not going to immerse myself in discussion about that. I preferred to listen. And cry.

Sharon put her arm around my shoulder again. "Don't worry, you'll be outta here on Monday." She pulled her knees up to her chest, and my eyes caught sight of her feet. She wore white crunchy socks and thick comical-looking brown earth shoes. The pretty girl with the big grayish-blue eyes and the bit of freckles on and around her nose resembled more of a college student than a prostitute looking at a possible ten-year sentence for selling marijuana and cocaine.

"Is your mom still alive?" I asked.

"Don't know, don't care. Last time I saw her, she was walking out the door, saying she had to go because her brain was rotting. Come on, man, what the hell is *that* supposed to mean? That's why I knew that doc was full of shit. I never been anywhere that crazy.

I know I got real bad days, you know. I mean, you push me hard enough, I get so pissed. I can't help it."

When she gazed at me, I noticed the dark circles and tiny blood vessels under her distant eyes. She couldn't have been much older than me, if at all, but she was going to age quickly if she continued her life of turning tricks, booze, and drugs.

At least I didn't turn tricks.

"This is your first time in jail, isn't it?"

I nodded.

"I thought so."

"How can you tell?"

"Ah. You just look worried. You shouldn't be. And your hands. They're soft."

I wondered if she was trying to get me to touch her private areas. I looked at my hands.

"You're a big girl though. I bet you could do some damage if you really wanted to." She made that sound like a good thing. I was relieved.

"Hell yeah," one of the women said as she walked by us. "You'll be out on Monday."

Suddenly, it got very loud. I had an instant and frantic urge to escape the airless room when I realized that this was exactly what jail was for—a place to escape. I now wished I had called my father or grandfather for bail money.

Jackie, a robust and stocky dark-haired girl, started seizing. She was what my mother called a street walker who had been involved with drugs. I was also involved with drugs, and so I really didn't know what the big deal was unless you couldn't handle your drugs and alcohol, *or* you were an idiot and tried to sell large quantities for huge amounts of money. I never sold drugs. But Jackie had also violated a former probation by shoplifting a mascara *and* a thirteen-inch color TV from a Shoppers Paradise. She had to spend the next twenty-seven days in that cell.

The girls were able to get her over to Jackie's bottom bunk and hold her down while she thrashed and stiffened like a washing machine about to break down.

"What about her tongue?" I asked, frenzied. I had never seen anyone have a seizure before. "Do you think she'll bite it?"

One of the girls looked up at me with tiny helpless eyes.

"She's never done it before," another one said.

"Do you think we should get help?" I asked, looking over at the bolted steel window with the little crack at the bottom. The other side was the corridor, and guards walked by frequently.

"Honey, they ain't gonna come and help nobody!" JR shouted facedown from her top bunk. She kicked her feet as if she were swimming; her Peds bore her last name in black marker for the laundry. "Ain't nobody cares about us in this damned place."

Suddenly it stopped. Jackie let out an enormous burp and then looked as if she had fallen asleep. I knew people with epilepsy had seizures, but Jackie was not epileptic. She had a head injury from being attacked by a monster who, unlike Barton Withers, was spending the rest of his life in prison without the possibility of parole. This guy picked her up off the streets in Wellton in a stolen van and raped her. I had come to the conclusion that in many ways, if not in all probability, I had been so immature, so coddled and sheltered compared to these women that in the deepest ends of my mind, I struggled with the idea that a prostitute could even *be* raped. After all, she was getting into the van to inevitably have sex with him, and he would be paying her to do this. But I was wrong.

When he was finished with her, he tried to throw her out of the speeding van, but she was somehow able to hang on, albeit not before her entire body slammed into the windshield, breaking nearly every one of her bones and crushing a part of her skull. The stolen van belonged to woman he had robbed and stabbed to death.

I sat next to her when she woke up.

"You look like you seen a ghost, Alice," Jackie said.

"Are you okay?"

"Oh, yeah, yeah. I'm fine," she said from the darkened end of the bunk. A dark green blanket covered her up to her chin, and the remainder of her stiff body resembled the outline of a mummy. "Oh, Jesus," she complained, stretching and cracking, "would you mind givin' my legs a rub? I'm sore as hell."

I looked at her.

"Don't worry, girl. I don't have the energy for no fun stuff no more."

"Two cigarettes. One for each leg."

"Ahh, fuck."

"You got a whole pack, unless you crushed it when you were flailing around before."

She reached under her pillow and found her cigarettes. "It's a box. Thank God. We got a deal?"

"Yep," I agreed. "Give them to me first."

"Ah, come—"

"Come on." I motioned for my cigarettes.

"How about one now, one when you're done."

"As long as I get two." I glared at her, and she smiled.

"It's a deal, bitch."

I would get my two cigarettes. She was in no condition to go on the offense with her broken and deteriorating body.

"Here," she said, "what you're doing is putting me right to sleep. Damn, girl, you're good at this."

"Never even done it before."

"Oof. You better take your other one now." She reached under her pillow again, pulled out the box, and retrieved another cigarette. Within minutes of my beginning her leg massage, she was snoring.

I sat alone on my cot with my back against the cold cinder-block, realizing that there was no way out of there. Everyone was asleep, except for this one temperamental woman in her late twenties named Sarah Jane.

Sarah Jane sat at the permanent metal table directly next to the little crack at the bottom of the steel window that looked out upon the corridor. I stayed away from her because she hadn't been in an agreeable mood since the day I was locked up. However, she was fastidious about looking after the elderly inmate Beth, whom the girls called Miss Beth. Sarah Jane also liked to keep herself busy with little projects like mopping the floor, making sure the cell was fully stocked with tampons, the cups were neatly arranged on the shelves, and she liked to draw. This skinny girl with the long nose and ponytail that touched the small of her back had a large assortment of finely sharpened colored pencils she kept at the end of her top bunk. I was shocked that those pencils were allowed within a mile of this place; they could so easily be used as weapons, and considering she was so bitchy, I wouldn't trust her with a dull pencil, let alone a sharp one.

I noticed Sarah Jane's pencils a few times—the vibrant reds, yellows, orange, blues mainly—and thought that if my life got any worse than it already was, I would grab a couple and plunge their needlelike ends into my abdomen. They were sharp, but probably not sharp enough, and therefore wouldn't have caused my desired damage. In addition, Sarah Jane would have most likely unleashed unrelenting fury on me.

I smiled to myself as I imagined my mother's reaction to my being in jail. It really wasn't supposed to be funny, but her clamoring for words and excuses painted an entertaining picture in my mind. Here I sat surrounded by hookers, drug dealers, and an old lady accused of holding up a local bank branch with a thirty-eight-caliber revolver. Not bad for an overweight girl about to graduate from college eighth in her class with an accounting degree she hated but could do nothing else with her life.

"I'm not bailing you out of jail!" my mother would have hollered in my ear and down the poor telephone line. It would be like she waited her entire life to communicate that very quote. She would be so proud of herself. For once, a comical thought about her embraced my mind. The woman was so pathetic. Who cared anymore?

I couldn't sleep much at night. The central air-conditioning blew so hard that I froze, and no matter how many lights were turned off in the cell, it always seemed like there was another one on somewhere. They did that to us on purpose just to drive us crazy, remind us that we were criminals, and punish us even further. I still preferred complete solitude and darkness, unless it was Arturo who bounded in and nudged me awake or let me know with a few sniffs of a wet nose that he would be spending the night next to me and my queen-sized mattress on the floor. Or old Shelly curled up in a gray soft-purring ball at my feet, or Marisa's ashes resting comfortably in my closed palm under my chin for the night. It wasn't about what I preferred now. I was locked up tight.

Eventually I dozed off and fell into a very deep but short sleep. I dreamt of terrible images of snakes that woke me up immediately. I saw giant pythons quietly slithering around the permanent metal table. They were looking me directly in the eye, but they didn't come close. They were ugly and thick and brown, and I was horrified and suddenly very lonely. I cried hard and silently as I thought about Marisa.

I got up and went behind a green shower curtain into a tiny room that had a metal toilet with an attached sink and drinking fountain, ingeniously put together into one unit. I was so ashamed of myself, I couldn't even look in the mirror above the toilet. I was not regretful, nor did I feel any guilt about the whole incident with Lisa Jupiter. I thought she deserved everything I gave her. I was ashamed of myself and everything that comprised my life. I was so sad and lonely and worn out from being left behind to fight the wars of the living.

The next morning was a Sunday, and Protestant Church services were available to most of the women who wanted to attend. Most everyone in my cell went, I believed just to get the hell out of there, except for JR. She stated that she didn't want to have to deal with those two "bitches fra' nex door."

"You can just ignore them if you want, JR. Why don't you just sit with us?"

She looked at me as if I had an eye in the middle of my forehead. Jackie also decided to stay behind because she was tired and sore.

Sarah Jane plastered on at least an inch of foundation that was way too dark for her fair complexion, topping it off with gobs of dark blue eyeliner and shiny brown lipstick. I had no idea who this girl was trying to impress, but it was pretty clear that she thoroughly enjoyed being locked up. Sharon told me that Sarah Jane had three small children back in New Hampshire and that maybe she was purposely trying to get away from them. She dutifully took Miss Beth by the arm before the guard made us snap to attention like good little criminals and walk in an elementary school–style single file.

The last time I had heard any type of religious service was at my sister's memorial. I still believed in God, but I sure as hell had no personal relationship with him, certainly nothing compared to my grandmother's reverence to Jesus Christ and Holy Mother Mary. But it was a way to get out of that cramped cell.

The female guard who led us out looked at me, and I smiled. She quickly looked away. I didn't know what I was supposed to do; I just behaved in a way I normally did. It seemed like everything I did lately was the opposite of what was expected of me.

Dee, the guard who processed me the first day I was arrested and hauled into this place, met us at an open door and asked me how I was holding up.

"I'm all right."

"Nobody's beaten you up or anything like that, have they?" She made the joke and winked at me.

I cracked a half smile just for her. "No, I'll just be glad to be out of here tomorrow."

"You'll be going before the judge, so there's always a fifty-fifty chance."

"Fifty-fifty?" I felt that familiar burn of panic again in my weary chest. Does that mean I would have to stay here another night? Would he sentence me? For how long? What would they want from me? Aren't they locking up the wrong person? What about Lisa Jupiter? All right, maybe I was wrong to touch her big yellow head, but it's not my fault that a mass of blond came out in one big clump. It just happened.

I surveyed my surroundings, and I realized that no matter what I was thinking and how frustrated and desperate I was, there was no way I was going to relieve my boxed-in worries and anger in there. I was not in control. These people could keep me in here for as long as they wanted, and there was nowhere to hide nor get away.

My whole body stiffened like a corpse, and I knew I had to do everything in my power to keep my lips from spewing the poison that would only infect me time after time. It would be a daunting task, but at least I had a brush of clarity. I had control, yet I had no control.

We filed into a small conference-classroom type windowless room of white cinderblock with completely bare walls and powder blue linoleum. It was a newly built wing, and it was a fresh and clean-looking room. Ultimately, if we were going to be praising the Lord, we should be celebrating in the newer, cleaner, freshly painted part of this shithole. There were about four rows of long tables and powder blue plastic chairs, none of which were attached to the floor. A guard with hair so short she looked like a marine and with bright red lipstick sat at the end of the next table from me. A woman with a thick Hispanic accent sat at the end of my table and complained about how expensive collect calls were from this place. I bowed my head and looked at my broken and half-bitten nails as my hands lay indecisively in my bright orange lap. Once again, I tried not to cry as the tears stung my eyes. My freedom had been taken, and I couldn't stand being closed in and locked away with inmates who wore too much rouge.

A woman possibly in her early sixties stood before us. Her name was Marianne, and she was from the Beckwith United Methodist Church in the suburb of Beckwith, a small upper middle-class town due east of Wellton. As I studied Marianne, she looked so vanilla, so plain, so pure. I wondered what Bunica would think. Proud would be my guess, to some extent. I might be wearing an orange jump-suit, but I took the initiative and went to a Sunday Church–type service without anyone, specifically her, having to drag me like dead weight—even if we weren't going to focus on the Blessed Mother. Then again, the only reason why I was in this brand-new room was because I was so desperate to flee the other one.

Marianne was a short hearty woman with big square-rimmed glasses and short sandy-colored hair. It had that puffy full-bodied look that was the usual result of one of those home perms my aunt liked to experiment with. She wore a short-sleeved off-white blouse and a beige cotton skirt with copper snaps down the front. Her ankles were swollen as they spilled out over her tanned shoes with rubber soles. She talked about her grown sons and her husband Tom, who got together for a barbeque at their church the previous Sunday. It all sounded like the normalcy I had always longed for in my life, even if it was a long and boring story. I would be glad to have it any day.

"We find solace in our families *some* of the time, but not always," she said. "Because we do not choose our families. We choose our friends, our jobs, but our families are not chosen, and with many of us, herein lies the problem that we are sometimes unable to recognize. We cannot give thanks to the Lord when we are unhappy with what we are given. We do not see God."

"Praise the Lord, ain't that the truth," Sharon muttered next to me, and I coughed, trying not to laugh.

"So we are stuck, not such a reassuring word, I might add, stuck with what we have, not feeling grateful for it, and all the while Jesus is right there in all his presence, in all his glory, in all his grace, and he is telling us and showing us every single step of the way how to love and accept others exactly the way they are, including ourselves. No one is perfect. No family is perfect, regardless of what we see on the television set. It's a creation of Hollywood, a creation of a commercial developed in New York. It is not a reality, and this is where we lose our way, many of us. There are problems, big and small, some not so bad, some terrible, criminal. We will speak honestly here. Only Christ our Lord is perfect, and there is nothing he cannot fix in his way and in his time. But it is up to us to learn, to have faith, give thanks, and to believe. You do not have to second-guess God."

I have no idea of what she's talking about. Being grateful for what we have. Accepting others. Families. She didn't know the monster.

After she finished with her spiel on families, she asked us to open up our soft-cover Bibles as the women volunteered to read from the Scriptures. It was painful. Some of the girls sounded as if they had never gone to school for one day, let alone twelve years. They had a terrible time getting through a sentence, and it wasn't just the seasoned tutor in me critiquing them. It was obvious that some of the women in there were so challenged, so uneducated. To speed things up, I could have volunteered to read, but I decided not to; I didn't dare.

I never liked reading from the Bible. I found it boring, nonsensical, and wide-open to all types of interpretation. But that's exactly what these women did—interpret the scriptures.

Once when Marisa and I were very young, Aunt Nancy had to be hospitalized after spending part of the week with blue bungee cords wrapped around her head as if they were the crown of thorns. Then one morning, she carried around a cross on her back, which was only visible to her. By the way she was struggling to walk, "the cross" must have weighed over twenty pounds. I remember how terrified we were when we thought she would throw a tea kettle of boiling water at my father when he told her that the crown of thorns was not blue bungee cords, and she was not Jesus Christ. It took him, Tommy, and Frank—three grown men—to wrestle her to the floor. Dad was somehow able to shove something into her mouth without her biting his finger off. Her strength was astronomical that day. My mother had left the house the minute she saw Nancy walk into the kitchen pulling "the cross" behind her. Marisa, at the age of nine, waited on the porch for the police to come.

After listening some more to Marianne and reading more from the New Testament, the Puerto Rican girl at the end of the table who was previously complaining about collect phone calls was nodding, her dull puffy bangs bouncing between her forehead and the rubber band that held back the rest of her hair.

A thin black girl with fine bone structure sitting at the table directly across from me placed her hand on her chest as she commented on the all-loving Lord who never moves. "It doesn't make a difference what I am feeling, I know that," the woman said with a toothy beige grin and oversized dark brown eyes. Her name was Marisol. She looked around the room and specifically at me and two other people at our table. "God is *always* there, ladies, and he's gonna make sure everythin' works out jus' fine. No matter what. It's his will. Not ours. We have to follow him, not ourselves. Once we understand that?"

She shook her head slowly and looked down with a smile.

"I have to consciously bring myself back to God each time, each time I stray. I can be hateful and angry. I can be deceitful even to myself. I can be stubborn and completely turn my back on him. But when *I* finally decide to come back to the Lord, you know what I see? I see he is there with open arms. He is ready to receive me every single time. God don't hold no grudge. And he is *in love* with you! It's almost like he is runnin' in place with you. His arms stretched out around me, protectin' me. He won't chase me though because you know why? He has given me and all you ladies free will. And that's why we here!"

I could see the progressively excited Marisol had one cigarette left sticking out of a smashed pack of cigarettes in her orange breast pocket. She seemed to know an awful lot about God. I wondered what she did to get herself locked up. For somebody so comfortable knowing the elusive coordinates of where God hid and waited for her with his arms outstretched, she did something pretty bad at one point. It couldn't have been a traffic ticket. I suppose she wasn't so sure then. Maybe she didn't pay a fine. Maybe she was a hooker who shoplifted makeup and electronics, like Jackie. She appeared way too nice for the rest of us. Sharon was looking more bored than she did back in the cell as she alternately examined and bit her fingernails. Sarah Jane was sitting on the far side of the room with this weird smirk on her face as she held the hand of her surrogate grandmother Beth.

Toward the end of the service or whatever that provocative last hour had been, Marianne pointedly asked each one of us what we wanted the rest of us to pray for. I was petrified when she looked at me first and asked my name. I didn't realize my mouth had opened when I said my sister and my cat. Right after *cat* left my lips, I noticed Marianne wince just a little bit in surprise, as if there was a tinge of confusion. Maybe she wasn't confused. She may have loved people more than animals, more than cats. But given who she appeared to be, she was most likely accepting and empathetic. And after all, this was about praying to God, *not* to Marianne. I worried that I would have a hard time shoving Marianne's quick and confused look out of my mind. At least I had removed myself from that cell. That was good. That was very good. I stuck my finger in my ear and hoped that no one would notice.

And like good and obedient little hourly criminals, we bowed our heads in prayer anyway. All I could do was think about Marianne's wince until she let us back up for air. She told us to keep our little bibles and also doled out a paperback book to each of us titled *How Jesus Frees When We Are Shackled and Chained.*

The ladies in orange filed out of the freshly painted room like soldiers. I stopped in front of the podium and observed some flyers.

"Come on, dear, come on." Marianne stood at the doorway, urging me to catch up with the rest of the ants. I had forgotten protocol, I guess. We were in jail after all, not high school.

It happened so quickly. Marisol stood directly in front of me and began to walk backward. I noticed the guard up in front was talking to some of the girls and didn't really seem to care what we were doing at the end of the queue.

"I hope you're doin' okay, you look so deeply sad. I'm Marisol. What is your name?"

"Alice. Alice," I said, nodding and feeling like I was speaking to a nun.

She took my hands in hers and squeezed them, smiling wide. I could see she was missing some back teeth. "Oh, Alice. I will pray for you. And your sister and your cat."

As I thanked her, she nodded and gently slipped away to the front of the line, leaving Sharon and me at the tail end. We walked.

"She seems like a real nice lady," I said to Sharon, who was nonplussed.

"Yeah, she's nice."

"What on earth is she in here for?" It was no big deal. We were all talking about our crimes in there. Some were even laughing about them.

Sharon looked down at her nails again. "Waiting for trial. Murder. Two people, I think. No, wait. Three."

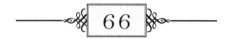

66

"Alice? Ready to go home?"

I looked up from the cot on the floor. Every light in the cell was on, and the Christian network was blaring from the overhead television.

Dee stood at the open steel window to the corridor that was otherwise bolted shut.

"How can she sleep at a time like this?" one of the women asked. "God, if I was getting outta here, I'd be dancing like a cheap stripper."

"You is a cheap stripper, bitch."

"Fuck you, JR."

"She tired!" JR hollered from her top bunk, referring to me. "She ain't slept since she been here."

I stood before a tired and exasperated judge and, on the advice of Sharon and Jackie, pled guilty. I was warned, "If you plead not guilty, there'll be a trial date set for God knows when, and you'll be sitting in this joint until you can get your seventy-five bucks together. It ain't worth it."

And so I threw myself on the mercy of the court and pleaded guilty, like I already knew I would. After all, I was guilty. I yanked Lisa Jupiter's hair on her head in a threatening-like manner, and by doing so, I pulled out a clump of her closeted wig. I would not argue the case to the contrary. I came away with a sixty-five-dollar fine and an order to enroll in psychological counseling for no less than twelve sessions. Both the fine and the first appointment with the shrink had to be satisfied within sixty-one days of my release from the Maidenhead County Department of Public Safety. I also received my green signed copy of the agreement outlining the stipulations ordered by the burned-out judge. I was convicted of simple battery, which was classified as a level 3 misdemeanor. Unless I wanted to be back there again, I had to do exactly what was ordered within the time frame it was ordered; otherwise, I would end up like Jackie—thirty days to one year for a probation violation.

To celebrate, Beth, the gun-toting grandma, bought me a grape soda. She pulled me aside, sat me down on her cot, and put her arm around my shoulder. "All that matters is that little green paper, honey. Now, don't come back here. If you feel like you're getting angry, think hard first about the consequences of your behavior. Take some deep breaths, in and out, in and out, and just walk away."

Everyone had such stellar advice shortly before my departure, yet look where we all were. Some found their wisdom. Some found their Lord. Was it too late for others? I would spend much time pondering that question again and again as I thought of Mary Jo all those years ago. I knelt down beside Jackie's bunk to say goodbye, and just as I did, I realized she was fast asleep.

"Don't go waking up the girls who are staying behind!" Sarah Jane yelled from across the cell as she folded and refolded towels.

The only thing that's going to wake anyone is your big mouth, I thought, but I ignored her. She was a nasty woman, and I knew if I stayed in there one more day, we might turn on each other like a couple of mad dogs. I took Beth's advice and walked away.

Just before the steel door slammed behind me, I turned around and looked back at Sharon, who smiled and flitted her fingers in a wave. I knew I would never see her again. I knew I would have to avoid every television set, whatever newspaper that was scattered throughout my path, and most people for at least the next ten days.

I followed Dee down the long corridor. I was joined with another released inmate. The two of us were led into the large gray windowless room where we could be dressed in and processed out. The released inmate standing next to me didn't look any older than about seventeen and wore a flat affect that announced, "I'll be back here in a couple of months. Count on it." As soon as she had the nod from Dee, she was out of that room like a road runner until another guard threatened to shackle her, and she was calmly escorted down the exit hallway to the bus stop outside.

Dee walked me halfway down the exit corridor and pointed to the glass doors at the very end where I could see the bright afternoon light bursting its way into the foyer beyond. "You just go through those doors down there and out to the left. And I don't want to see you back here, Alice. A girl like you doesn't belong in here."

She turned and walked away.

I stood motionless, standing sideways, looking at her walking away back up the corridor. "Okay, I'll try."

"Don't try," she warned, her back to me. "Just stay away." She turned around. "You know what?" She walked back toward me.

"Hmm?"

"If I ever write a book? It's gonna be about you."

"*Me?*"

"Yeah, you."

"Why?"

She shrugged and raised her hands. "I don't know why. You're one of a kind. I've never met anyone like you before. Now go on. Get out of here." She turned around again. I could hear her chuckling softly as she shook her head.

One of a kind? I thought. She obviously didn't know anything about me. I found myself to be boring and quite ordinary. The only thing I could do well was crunch numbers. Wow. Big deal. I'm a hero. Oh, and I could tutor idiots. All pioneer attributes. What was she talking about?

I made my way outside. It was as if the day had never changed from Friday, when I had been arrested. I looked down at the faded gray pavement, and I thought about kneeling down and kissing it until I saw a wad of smooshed beige chewing gum splattered like a dead bug and quickly changed my mind. There was a small cement stairway at the crest of a little slope down into a parking lot near the garage-like structure where Sergeant Gregg Hayman originally unloaded me. I sat on the top step, thinking about my impounded bike and how I was going to get it back and get home to my apartment when I spotted him. I quickly looked around for an escape route, but the doors I had just walked through only opened in one direction. I couldn't believe the luck I was having. I was trying to figure out how I could *escape into* this jail. But it was too late as I cursed in despair as he was already strolling over in my direction at a faster pace than I thought he was capable of.

"You hungry?" he asked, staring down at me, hands in his pockets.

"Detective Holloway," I said. "What are you doing here?"

"I work here." His answer was matter-of-fact. "Some of the time, anyway."

I put my head in my hands. I knew where this was going. First stop, Dad. Then my mother. Eventually Bunic and Bunica. Why couldn't people just leave me alone? Louis Dagher was a long time ago.

"Where's your partner? Where's Archer? Doesn't he ever need you for anything? Don't you have any friends?"

He turned around to look as a patrol car pulled up behind, then he glanced at his watch. "To answer your questions, my partner is at the hospital right now waiting for his wife to give birth if she hasn't already done so. So I would say no, he doesn't need me for anything right at this moment." His face brightened as he inhaled sharply. "As far as friends go, I got about maybe three to four really close ones. They say you lucky if you got one *good, true, real* friend in this life. Speaking of which, I know you got some friends who care about you and are concerned about you, one of them bein' Walter Tifton."

I was exasperated with the full intent of walking back to my apartment. "How do you know Walter?"

"He gotcher bike outta impound."

"Imagine that!" I snapped, my back to him. "An impounded bike. Never thought that would happen."

"Where you goin'? You walkin' home?"

"Yes, I'm walking home." What was he going to do? Arrest me for walking? Then I stopped and thought. I could not stop my mind from whirling. He could very easily arrest me if he wanted to. He could have made something up. The girls told me the cops pull that stuff all the time, planting drugs, lying—I wasn't sure if I believed it. I couldn't go back in there. I turned around, defeated and worried.

"I thought you're walkin'?"

"It's too far, really," I said.

His giant hand came down gently on my shoulder. "I'll give you a ride back to campus, and if you want, we can stop off for something to eat. Jodie's got some chicken nuggety things now."

"They do?" I looked at him.

He nodded. "Good too. Real hot."

I was famished. I probably couldn't make that walk after all. All I had to eat over the last two days were undercooked pancakes and cold lima beans. I had to force food into my stomach. I had no appetite, but the girls warned that if an inmate doesn't eat or won't at least try to eat to keep up her strength, one of the nastier guards like Holmes or the one who escorted us to church service would throw her in the hole and force-feed her. I believed they would throw her in the hole and take away her cigarettes, shower, Christian TV, and probably any chance of getting out in a timely fashion. And so I made the effort to eat freezing-cold gruel after it passed through the slot under the locked steel opening to the cell three times a day.

We got into a brand-new car. "So Walter knows I was arrested."

"Of course. Everyone knows. He's the one who picked up your bike from impound."

"How does *everyone* know?" Then I remembered the cameras at WELLocal. I should have known the answer to this ridiculous question, but I was actually afraid of the answer I was about to get. JR knew. She informed me that news travels fast in there. How did she know, and how fast did news travel? JR hardly ever removed her rear end from that top bunk.

"Anyone who reads *The Wellton Morning News* is gonna find out too." There was an underlying exasperation in his voice, yet at the same time, I thought he might start laughing at me. "Anyone who watched the five o'clock news on Friday would have seen it."

My mother popped into my head. I didn't know why it mattered, but I had just received a slug of reality right to the mouth.

"Honey. You're lucky this town's the size that it is, otherwise, you girls would have an entire tabloid paper dedicated to you. Wellton City Police Department? County Sherriff's Office? We got police blotters. Some people read 'em for fun, see if they know anyone."

"Oh no."

"Anytime anyone is arrested and charged with a crime in this city or the county, their name, the date of the charge, all the details is goin' right in the blotter." Was he really enjoying himself as much as it sounded? "And you walking into a television station and attacking one of the most recognizable faces in town is gonna get your mug shot on the five o'clock news. Not even five seconds, I would say. Now. You ain't a celebrity, but I would say most people who watch the news probably know you. And there was a few seconds of you arguing with security as you were being escorted out of WELLocal. That came before the mug shot, of course."

I had a mug shot.

"'Member the days when you had a few reporters comin' around? There were two this past weekend out front your dad's place. He's okay. He thinks it's helped his business." His voice lowered. "Like he needs any more help with his business."

Typical of my father to think of that store first. What about Aunt Nancy? I'll bet she was really confused and scared. "I did not attack her!"

"You pulled her hair out."

"It was a wig! It wasn't even her real hair. It just came out. I barely even touched her."

"Alice, that is a lie, and you know it. There was a roomful of witnesses. Don't you think it's time to start taking responsibility for your anger? How about taking responsibility for your behavior?"

It started to rain fast. Holloway pumped the wiper blades.

"This was the same thing that nearly took out Louis Dagher back when you were in high school." His voice was even, stern, almost pleading. "This is your anger, and it's not going to go away by itself. You see a pattern here? You are damned lucky Ms. Jupiter didn't press charges against you as well. You keep getting off! One day you won't. You could have been locked up for *at least* another year. You like it in there?"

I should have just called my father or grandfather to come and bail me out. It wouldn't have made a difference though. I was dying for something to boost my mood. Anything.

"It wasn't nice." I was tired and jonesing. The hunger and rain were making it worse. I could have curbed the hunger if I had a beauty.

"That pretty little jail back there? The one that's had a brand-new addition built on and a fresh coat of paint? That's a hell of lot nicer than the women's prisons in this state. And you got lucky again, didn't you?"

I didn't answer his question. I thought about Marisol, and I was sure Holloway knew all about her case. I studied his head, his flattop hair with the perfect sides, his triple chin, and the silly thick light brown glasses. I wished I could have gotten inside that head and learned all about her. The thought of just asking him about her made my stomach flip-flop.

"Next time you might not be so lucky. People go to prison all the time, and I've seen it time and time again—that anger that festers like a poison. It changes and evolves. It mutates like a virus. People in this country have been executed because their anger has gotten so out of control that they commit heinous crimes—awful, terrible crimes."

Like the monster. Right? But unfortunately, there's no death penalty anymore in this screwed-up state, so he's still alive and breathing. Tell me, Ken, what point exactly are you trying to make?

"And you, honey? You *this* close." He showed me how close I was with his thumb and forefinger.

We both said nothing for a minute. I stared straight ahead.

"At least you're gonna get to talk to someone. Thank God for that."

"How do you know that?" I asked when I realized that he seemed to know everything about me even before I did.

"Because I know Judge Kaufman would not have let you outta there without some kind of treatment. Good for you he's a very deep-feelin' generous type who will catch a problem early and try and fix it fast—that's *before* it goes too far, and he's got a repeat offender in front of him, which happens more often than not."

Again, I said nothing. That judge looked at me like he was about to fall off his bench from boredom.

"Do you have any kids?" I surprised myself by asking suddenly.

"I did. A boy. Ken Jr."

"You did."

"He died of the cancer, leukemia."

"Oh no." I wished I hadn't asked. "I'm sorry."

A gentle smile swept lightly across his face, and his furry eyebrows perked up as if someone from above was pulling them with a string. "His twenty-fifth birthday is coming up in December. He had been sick for a very long time. His whole life, as a matter of fact." His face turned ashen, and heavy gray clouds crowded over us as the rain began to pelt harder. Traffic slowed down to nearly a halt because of the heavy rain. Despite the loud distraction of the skies, Holloway talked about his dead son.

"But that boy, lemme tell you what, he never let out a complaint. He was always smilin'. He loved to play that tetherball, and he was good at it—and four square, you know, where you gotta keep the ball within the lines."

"Sure."

"Oh, you would have liked Ken Jr., Alice," he said but grimaced slightly and immediately, as if he regretted telling me that. He scratched his nose and said evenly, "He was a smart and tough kid. And he was good at math too. He could solve his times tables backward and forward faster than you could blink."

I nodded and stared straight ahead again. Traffic came to a standstill. I cleared my throat and again speculated on what Detective Holloway knew about Marisol's case. I was positive he knew everything about it. I wouldn't dare ask him about it since we were talking about his dead kid.

Traffic started to pick up.

"I know we were prepared, but—"

"You're never prepared."

"But in little Ken's case, it was a lot more sudden than my wife and I expected. My wife? Wanda? She was so mad at me that morning." He surprised me with a chuckle. "Oh lord, it started as a good day. He got up and had a good breakfast. I found an early birthday present for him the weekend before, and I just couldn't wait. I wanted him to have it so bad. It was a gold-color transistor radio in the shape of a balloon that was twisted together in the middle so there was a bubble on the top and a bubble on the bottom. It was the neatest thing I ever seen. So I wrapped it up and gave it to him that morning before I left for work, and I am so damned glad I did."

"Why was she mad at you? Because you gave him his birthday present early?"

"Because I wrapped it in tin foil!"

"Tin foil?"

His eyes got wide, and he laughed heartily. "I thought we had wrappin' paper in the house somewhere, but I guess we didn't! That was the last time I saw him. He was eleven years old."

I was silent.

"Alive, anyway. I went off to work, and within an hour, he was dead from respiratory failure."

I was silent.

"Respiratory failure killed him."

I looked out the passenger window at the violent and thunderous sky. The rain had stopped, but the heavens breathed fire. A young child dying. What a sad story.

"Do you know if he liked his radio?"

He nodded slowly, and his face cracked into a big grin. "He was over the moon with that radio."

The rain was back, and we were in the parking lot at Jodie's. Detective Holloway dropped me off at the front door while he parked. I counted the green concrete tables outside as I waited for him to make the short run. I ordered the smallest cheeseburger and the largest onion rings and strawberry milkshake. He ordered a small box of chicken nuggets and a black coffee.

"You're not eating much," I said, looking at his chicken nuggets.

"It's time that I start losing a little weight. I'm fifty-one now. Time to start getting serious. I've been puttin' on a little bit lately, and your old man's french fries don't help."

"No, they certainly don't."

"Jail food ain't so good, is it?" He nodded at my pile of onion rings.

I shook my head, my mouth full. "Why are you wearing those big glasses?"

"You think they suit me?"

"No, not really."

"I lost a contact somewhere at the station. Until I get a new one, I'm gonna' have to wear these. They're actually a lot easier. Just put 'em on. Hey, can you do me a favor?" He didn't wait for a response. "Can you stay out of jail now? Girls like you don't belong in there."

"So I've been told."

67

Detective Holloway dropped me off at the front door of my apartment as the twilight worked its way through an angry sky. Now that my stomach was full, I was annoyed with him. Then I felt guilty for feeling annoyed. He did, after all, give me a ride home in a thunderstorm and buy me lunch, and I felt bad for him because his little boy died. Detective Holloway saw a lot of death.

The blue Plymouth was still parked in the exact same spot where I left it Friday, except the tires were about an inch and a half buried in what looked like quicksand. My bike was locked up in its usual place, on the large cement porch, dry and safe from the elements. I had to remember to scrape together the thirty-five bucks Walter paid to get it out of impound.

Bike out of impound. That had to be the silliest thing I had ever heard. I suppose I *should* have found some way or another to be grateful. They could have tossed it directly into a dumpster. But they wouldn't. Because it was my property. And then I could have sued them. I should have told Holloway all about that. Never mind. The less he knew about my fights with life, the better.

I opened the old walnut front door as slowly and as quietly as could, but that was no easy task since it was heavy and squeaked. I could never sneak in the front door. It was impossible, especially to the keenly sensitive ears of Arturo, who came flopping, wiggling, and dancing down the stairs and into the large foyer as if he hadn't seen me in years. Other than the dog, I did not want to see or speak to anyone. I just wanted to crawl all the way to the back of my cave and remain there until I felt like coming out. Isolation was where I found the most happiness and the most peace.

But before I could take another step, I heard the muffled creaking of footsteps, and there was Candace about halfway down the stairs, gazing at me with her mouth half-open as I could feel the sky rolling in on itself again. The room darkened.

"Oh my god. Are you okay?" She stood frozen, one leg in her dark blue jeans behind her, looking as if she was walking but suddenly stopped. Her hair was perfectly curled and tied with a small pink ribbon on the top that matched her pink sweater. Her white socks looked new.

I said nothing. I didn't want to speak. I just nodded.

She slowly descended the staircase, and Arturo happily wove himself between the two of us. "Good boy." She scratched his head. "Can I do anything for you? What was it like in there? Oh! Walter brought your bike back. I mean, what happened?"

I slowly shook my head. It felt as if a weight was on top of it, pushing me down to the floor as I looked at her. "I'm really tired. Maybe we can talk about this later?"

She closed her eyes and put both her hands on my arms. "Of course we can. I'm sorry about him, but he's so happy to see you."

"Can he come in with me while I just hang out?"

She nodded quickly, closing those eyes again. "Sure, sure. Just let me know later if he gets fidgety."

"Thanks. That's great. I will." I started to walk toward my door, the dog following.

"Alice, I'm so glad you're back. We, we were all so worried about you."

I turned around. She looked pensive.

I forced a smile. "Thanks. Don't worry, Candace. I'm fine." I turned around again and gently closed the door behind me.

The first thing I had to do was find the thirty-five dollars to pay back Walter. I also had to pay the court fine, and I wasn't sure if I had a job to go back to at the library. Tutoring had long since dried up. Although Walter's mother had always been my most staunch supporter, even she was having a hard time finding pupils to throw in my direction. Now that she knew I was a jailbird, she probably didn't want to believe in me anymore. I was most likely gaining the reputation of a girl with little self-control, a lot of anger, and a scumbag who had now completed three days in the county lockup.

It made me continue to have the sleepless nights I sometimes had throughout my life. I would get up out of bed in the middle of the night, take the dog out, and the two of us would walk the streets and parts of the campus for an hour or so. We were alone, and it was perfect.

Sometimes I wanted to find a map and navigate my way right into a real cave where I could be completely alone and happy in a dark people-less quiet place. I would move everything I needed all the way to the way back of that cave where I could be in total solitude and leave a note letting people know not to bother to try and find me because I had no intention of wanting to be found.

I pet Arturo's head.

But what I really needed to do was call and make an appointment with Dr. Gwynneth Kilburn, Detective Holloway's trusted psychiatrist friend. I'm sure he would be supervising every aspect of my progress. Dr. Gwynneth Kilburn would in all likelihood blab my story to Detective Holloway—that is, the pieces he *didn't* know about. If I violated my court order, I would be right back in that boring and claustrophobic concrete hovel with Sarah Jane and her nasty attitude. I could have found myself another counselor, but I already had Dr. Kilburn's phone number, and so I decided to do the easiest thing.

There were five messages on my answering machine.

Beep! "Alice, are you home yet? Bunic and I are very worried about all of this. We would like you to please call as soon as you hear my voice!" Then she mumbled something to my grandfather. From what little I could hear and understand, he said, "no" and "adult."

Beep! "Allie, it's Dad. Jesus Christ, what the hell is goin' on over there? Jail? Why didn't you call me? Don't they give you a phone call? What's going on? I want to know. Okay, call me."

Beep! "Ms. Buchner, this is Catherine Mays, Dean Vann's secretary at the School of Business. Please call our office at your earliest convenience so that we can arrange a time for you to come in and speak with the dean."

That didn't sound good. What did they want? No need to wonder, and I wouldn't be returning Ms. Mays's call either. It was a twelve-minute walk up the hill and to the left. If she wanted to, she could tell the jailbird what she wanted to say directly to the jailbird.

Beep! "Alice, this is your grandmother again. I do not like these machines."

Bunica became easily frustrated, but her lividity was quiet, and she stewed for a long while. There would still be no reasoning with her, and so I decided not to even make the attempt to do so. At that moment, I didn't want to discuss the past three days with her either.

The last *beep!* was followed by a lecture from my mother: "Alice? Alice. Had you answered your telephone the first time I called you, you would have realized what was about to happen. So. Don't you *dare* say I didn't warn you. Your sister is crying. You are an embarrassment. I am so ashamed of you and your behavior, and I am so glad, *so relieved,* that you never called me to bail you out of jail. Jail, Alice. You were in jail! Let your father take care of this. It wouldn't kill him to do something for you. You know, Alice? I don't think I want to bother with you anymore. This is not the—"

And because my mother couldn't shut her mouth, the answering machine shut it for her by running out of tape.

I was thrilled my mother wanted to disown me. This meant I didn't have to force myself to see her or talk to her when I didn't want to do either. It was regrettable that I wasn't watching Helena grow up, but that was the fault of Big Barton and Sunny. They deliberately kept her away from Bunic and Bunica, from her mother, which was ironically for the best, and particularly from me. She was always accompanying them on trips when she was out of school or at their compound riding one of those awful horses. The kid was an innocent by-product of a murderer, and I thought and worried about her often—too often, and it hurt me. I felt so sorry for that little girl. We used to have so much fun when I was over at my mother's playing with her and stoned out of my head. We used to click perfectly into place.

It felt good to be home, and it felt even better to be alone. I poured myself a glass of white wine and lit a cigarette. I opened the drawer of my dresser in the bedroom to look at the ashes of my sister and of my cat, repeatedly checking and double-checking them, making sure they were still there until my head hurt. I never took those ashes out of the drawer because I would check them over and over again until I wouldn't be able to move. I knew I wouldn't be able to put them back in that drawer without panicking for air. Just thinking about it made my insides twist up and around like a wet sponge.

I was finally able to walk back into the kitchen, Arturo at my feet the entire time. I glanced over at my freezer and remembered that inside was a twenty-five-pound turkey Scotty brought over the week before. I knew my father wouldn't be in the house at this time of day, and so I thought I would just walk in the front door of the store and take my place on the banana-colored chair in front of the payphone, next to the stack of worn telephone books encased in the plastic cover with the metal string attached.

This day was different. I was too tired and happy to be home to name the new lobsters and plead for their lives. It never worked with Dad, and it never would. They were doomed. And I was in no mood to walk through the front door lest a lone reporter or photographer was hanging around. It might have been the case since the monster's stepdaughter spent a weekend in jail for roughing up Lisa Jupiter. It was more than that. I was in no mood to walk through the front door.

I walked around back and lingered around the small dock area as I waited for my father to eventually see me. I heard a love song as it blared loudly from a transistor radio in a parked truck. I looked over at our old dark green house painted against the bluish-gray sky, overcast and cluttered, looking as if it would rain again. Muddy dust from the dry edge of the road kicked up by the wind became lost in my eyes, and I had to flinch and rub out the tiny particles. A couple of people were talking, but I couldn't see their faces. Suddenly, a gust of cool wind rippled through the pine trees behind the house, and the sky darkened further with a chill.

"Alice! Allie, hey! What's going on?"

I turned around to see my father standing above me in an empty dock. The wind was picking up like the sky would reopen and pelt rain again, but then a stream of light shone through the clouds and gave me energy.

He had his hands in the air as his eyes briefly darted from side to side. His face was confused as he looked at me with incredulity. Someone in my periphery, either Frank or Scotty was behind him in the warehouse, way in the background.

"What the hell are you standing out here for? How long have you been back here?"

"You called me, Dad."

"I know I called you. Why haven't you called me back?"

"I didn't feel like talking. I just got your message a while ago." It wasn't a lie.

He hopped down off the loading dock with the energy and flexibility of a much younger man. "Oh, is that right? You didn't feel like talking?"

"Dad." I didn't like the sound of his voice. "I didn't come here to argue with you." I felt like I was on a stage somewhere, delivering the lines of an actor, not my own.

"Hey, come on, girl. Don't you think you owe me a little bit of an explanation here? You spent the last weekend in jail. What the hell happened?" He knew what happened.

"Detective Holloway said the charges were in the pap—"

"I don't give a shit about the newspaper, Alice!" He looked me squarely in the eye as I pretended to proudly stand tall. "I want to hear this from you. Why were you arrested? You hit that Jupiter lady? What were you thinking? Were you on something again?"

"What was I thinking?" I ignored the last question. I was on something then. A driver looked at us. "What do you mean 'what was I thinking'? Are you kidding me, Dad? I mean, do you not know what's going on? Are you so wrapped up in the store that you don't even see what's going on outside of those walls?"

"I don't like your tone," he said as he lit a cigarette.

"Lisa Jupiter," I said, lowering my voice and trying to remain calm despite the fuel that ran through me, "got paid by that damned family who employed her to do a hit piece on Marisa—a special, sympathetic, 'oh no, the poor parents of this traumatized, brutalized,

411

and misunderstood man,' who, by the way, has been transferred to a minimum-security prison, Dad. A *minimum-security prison!* A pretty little puffy interview of a kil—"

"I think it's medium," he stated casually, blowing out smoke. "Everyone knows. Actually. Now listen, you can't breathe a word of this to anyone, but I've got a bootleg of the real show before it even airs. You know Stern, the guy I thought owned WELL? Origin—"

I looked at him. Disbelief took control of me, and my mouth flopped open.

"You can't tell anyone about this, Allie."

"You have a video?"

"*Sshh!*"

"Why would you even want to be in *possession* of this? Have you lost your mind for good this time, Dad?"

"I was gonna tape it anyway." His voice was low and cunning. "I don't have time to watch the boob tube even when I get out of here at a decent hour, which is next to never."

"You, a smart man, have completely missed the entire point. You aren't so smart after all, are you? I can't believe you! *What* is *wrong* with you?" It was right then at that moment I had felt the loneliest and most unloved in my entire life. I realized there was never a team, a family. I was completely alone. I was by myself. Totally without anyone beside me.

I wanted to vaporize. The tears fell again, stung my eyes, and I wiped them away. I backed away from him.

"What do you mean 'what is wrong with me'?" He gazed at me with bright questioning eyes.

I pounded the tip of my finger into my palm. Some realizations now swarmed around me like hornets, and they sickened me. "This is a betrayal of Marisa, my sister, your daugh—no, never mind, not your daughter. Mom drove that point home, and you were only too proud to acknowledge it!"

"Lower. Your. Voice."

"Am I the only one who ever loved her?" I felt completely powerless and exhausted, but I persisted. "I am the only person who really cared about Marisa, and I'm probably the only one who will continue to remember her in the way that she should be remembered, as much as she should be remembered. We should never forget her, and yet everyone has. Everyone has. Everyone has just simply moved the fuck on with their rotten, insignificant lives—"

"That is not exactly true." He pointed a finger at me.

"Yes, it is!" I hollered.

He grabbed my face lightly and positioned it so that I was looking directly at him. I wanted to bite him. "You have allowed that girl, the death of that girl, to *ruin your life.*"

He quickly looked around, most likely to make sure no one was listening to the great, adorable, funny, laid-back Rudy talking seriously and shouting about his dead stepdaughter.

"It's been almost a decade, Alice. Grief like this—grief that you can't let go, grief that stops you from moving on—is going to put you in a grave before you're forty! Your life *has* to move forward. Life *itself* moves forward. It never stops until you're dead, and, little girl, you are looking at an early death if you keep this up! You have no choice. You *have* to move on someway. Somehow. You are committing a slow suicide, goddammit, Alice. *What is wrong with you?*"

"That girl, Dad? That girl."

"Oh, Jesus Christ, Alice."

"Marisa was treated like garbage, and now she was be—"

"She didn't deserve you. She does not deserve this. Any of this."

I looked down at the ground.

He put his hand on my shoulders. He stank of raw fish, and his breath smelled of cigarettes. "You are so good. You've taken all of this so hard. You need to get help. You need to talk to someone. This has gone on for far too long—"

"I've made an appointment."

"Good," he answered quickly. "Good."

"What do you mean she didn't deserve me?" I wiggled out of his grasp.

He backed away and lit another cigarette. I was dying to smoke and wanted to get one out of the car, but I didn't want to smoke with him. I had a feeling I knew what he was talking about, but I wanted clarification. I wanted to hear it from him.

"You would follow her around like a puppy when you were kids—hang on her every word," he said quietly. "She laughed at you, teased you. She called you names. You were good to your sister, but she wasn't always nice back, even when you girls were teenagers. She blew me off like a dead weed, and Nancy missed her—she rarely came around. Look, I don't want to speak ill of the dead, but Marisa looked out for Marisa first. I know you girls loved each other, but, Allie, your heart was a hundred times the size of hers—"

"There were so many things you didn't know about our relationship—"

"I'm sure—"

"She did not deserve—"

"No, not really, if you want to know the truth—"

"She deserved me. I didn't deserve—" I stopped midsentence.

"She wouldn't have done this for you—she wouldn't have *grieved for you like this*, okay? She wouldn't have destroyed herself for you." He used his fingers to count each of my offenses as a cigarette dangled from his mouth. "Look how this has affected you, you're… you're isolating yourself from the world, your family, your friends—"

"I don't have any friends."

"Bullshit. And not only that, you're assaulting people and getting arrested, you nearly killed a classmate, confronting people who are just doing their jobs. You're not well, Allie."

"You did the same thing, Dad, the same exact thing just before Holloway got kicked off the case." He chose to blame me and my sister for everything.

"Drinking too much, smoking weed, popping pills, *stealing* fucking pills. It's a miracle you can get through your classes."

She told him. Kiki told him I was stealing from them.

"You're gonna end up in prison or worse if you don't start getting control of that anger. I know this isn't you. You can't let this wound stay open for the rest of your life, don't you see that?" He stood back and smoked. He moved around as if he had to go to the bathroom. I had seen that dance before. He shuffled like that when he was nervous. "I should have thought good and hard before I gave you that car—"

"You want the Plymouth back."

"No, no, no. Your sister. Like I said before, I don't want to speak ill of the dead, but—"

"Then don't."

"Because you need to hear this. You can bet your ass right now she'd be married to some schmuck, having kids, living in the suburbs, shelling peas, and watching soap operas all day. Moving on with life! She was a self-centered girl—everything was all about her. I'm not trying to say bad things about her, I'm really not. I loved her too, I did, I really did, but she was an instigator. She knew how to manipulate to get what she wanted, she knew how to push people's buttons. She treated you like dirt most of the time, and don't tell me otherwise. I watched you kids grow up, both of you."

I shrugged. "Up to a point you did, Dad."

"What?" He couldn't have forgotten.

"You didn't do anything to stop my mother from dragging us off with her when she decided to leave you!" I snapped.

"And what the hell was I supposed to do about that, huh?" He threw his hands up in the air and backed away. "She didn't *want* to be here! She wasn't even my kid."

"Instigate," I continued, ignoring his excuses. "On the day she died, she stayed home from school because I was sick, and she brought me orange juice. She didn't instigate anything."

We were both yelling now, and I didn't care who heard or was listening.

"And for no reason whatsoever, no reason other than he hated her guts, he threw her up against the wall by the neck, Dad. By the neck! And he killed her. I watched him do it, and I did nothing to stop him. I didn't save her. I saw him kill her, so please don't tell me she was—"

"You don't know what you saw."

He might as well have punched me in the throat. The bomb of butterflies finally exploded in my stomach with a crash of thunder and a loathsome streak of lightning. After all these years, I knew exactly what he thought, where he stood, and at that moment, I hated him.

I opened my mouth to speak, but for that one second, I couldn't as rage clouded my vision. Had he not been my father, I would have ran toward him, but then I briefly remembered Marisol. I couldn't breathe as my chest closed in on itself. I forced myself to remain calm, to relax, to inhale and exhale. It was only for a few seconds, but it felt like a lifetime. I could hear the sound of my mouth grabbing the air around me.

Finally, I cupped my ears. My father looked at me curiously.

"Don't you ever speak to me again," I said with extraordinary cool, my hands still over my ears.

My father stepped toward me, but I turned and walked through the old dust turned mud by heavy sloughs of rain. The wind swished through the pine, pushing and pushing me off and away from his voice trailing behind, trying in futile desperation to keep up. I glanced at the newspaper stand in front of the store: "Maidenhead County Sheriff's Investigator Killed in the Line of Duty: Arthur Frosh."

No, no, no. It's not him. It's not him.

I got into the Plymouth and drove off into the new storm.

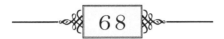

68

Mrs. Margaret Ferguson, the front desk librarian, looked at me sideways when she informed me that they wanted an employee who was more dependable. It was her boss, Ms. Lampell, who didn't like the way I turned off the lights in the building at the end of the night, claiming that I usually missed many of them. I would have liked to have seen them try it. There were so many light switches in that building: behind doors, next to partitions, on one side of the wall, at nose level, at naval level, over here, over there. Ms. Lorelei Lampell, according to Mrs. Sideways Ferguson, did not like the fact that when I closed the building and turned off whatever lights I could find, I did so in my socks while carrying my shoes. This was *after* the library closed and so no one *saw* my stocking feet, and I'm sure no would care if they had. What Ms. Lorelei Lampell didn't understand was that I could run faster without my shoes if I had been chased around a dark building by a rapist, a murderer, or a combination of both. Chances were that I *might* have been able to outrun the monster and eventually escape.

She had a tremendous amount of audacity, that Ms. Lorelei Lampell. She never said anything about the lights or my socks before. She and I ran into each other late one evening, and she was very kind and said she was "so appreciative" of my services. Horseshit. Who did she think she was lying to? Why not just come out with it? She had the authority and could delegate the task to Mrs. Sideways Ferguson:

"Alice, you were arrested and charged with assaulting a member of the local news media. We do not condone violence of any sort and do not wish to have you on our team at the Eastside Campus Library. We thank you for your services and wish you the best of luck in your future endeavors."

I was fired from the library.

Dean Vann and his secretary, Catherine Mays, were more sympathetic. The dean made sure that he let me know he went to bat for me with certain members of the administration. Because I wasn't charged with a felony, no one really thought it was anything more than what it was. I tried to stop Lisa Jupiter, a yellow journalist and opportunist, from airing her prejudicial TV hit piece on my murdered teenage sister, and I yanked out a clump of her wig.

"In my hometown of Kansas City, way back when, I found myself in the county jail, so I know exactly where you're coming from." He smiled, displaying a row of gnarly yellow front teeth. "This was a long, long time ago, before you were even born. One night I had too much to drink and kicked the shit out of this guy in a bar because he said something about my future wife being fat. And she *is* a little chubby, but I didn't exactly want to hear it from him. The only thing violence does is get us into trouble. I haven't kept this little story a secret because it's a good teaching point for emotionally troubled young people like you, Ms. Buchner."

"Emotionally troubled."

He nodded. "I suggest you see someone. Someone you can talk to."

"I have it all set up."

"Great. That's exactly what I want to hear. You *have* been a first-rate student."

It was possible, even though I liked to drink and use drugs. People were so uninformed, so misguided about alcohol and drugs. You just had to know your limit.

He bent over the side of his disorganized desk and slapped another stack of papers in front of him. He thumbed through them. He was eerily understanding. I couldn't imagine the dean punching someone out, even in his younger years. No way. I think he made that up.

"I see you are graduating eighth in your class. Out of forty-two hundred students. That's astounding, Ms. Buchner. I assume you'll be applying for graduate school."

I hadn't thought about it, but since I had nothing else to do with myself… "Probably," I said.

He said nothing but looked at me as if he understood.

I studied Dean Vann's face as he studied my files. There was something about him that reminded me of Deputy District Attorney Martin Giles, way back all those years ago when he interviewed me in that break room at the police station. As Vann continued to pour over files presumably containing snippets of my academic life, I stuck my finger in my ear, hoping he wouldn't notice. I didn't want to think about DDA Giles, although what I thought about and what I wanted to think about had nothing to do with each other.

"And it's going to be an honor to have you stand with your class." He continued to talk to me as I paid little attention. I then tried to refocus my attention on him.

"Do I have to stand with my class?"

He looked at me with no attempt to hide his horror, and his mouth fell wide-open. "Are you kidding me, Alice? Are you really asking me if you have to participate in commencement ceremonies? Well, you know what? The answer is yes, young lady, you do. You owe it to your family, your friends, to this school, to me, and most of all, to yourself. I won't have it any other way. You damn well will!"

He calmed down again, but he was still irritated that I even dared to ask.

"And next week, come find me. I'll still be here. I want to talk to you more about graduate school. You have a great mind. Let's not waste any more time in jail. Next time, it may not be so pleasant."

"I don't remember it being pleasant this time."

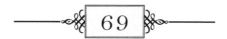

69

My landlord Chick told me I could stay in my apartment as long as I wanted. With a toothpick in his mouth and exposed hideous tattoos on his arms and legs, he informed me that if I wanted to continue to live in an undergraduate dump, he was more than happy to take my money.

"It's not so bad, Charles."

"Oh darlin', my birth name. What a turn-on. You know I keep this place in tip-top shape just for you now."

I scoffed. He could be so incredibly vulgar.

Sensing my disgust, he laughed out loud and ruffled my hair at the crown.

"Go away!"

He was gone, laughing all the way to his pickup.

I had nowhere else to go, and I could be alone. I preferred to be alone. But things would change soon. Candace, who always said she wanted to live in the wilderness and eat bark and berries, had been offered a teaching job in Portland, Oregon. Clear across the country, it wasn't exactly the wilderness, but I suppose it was a lot closer to it than Wellton was. As much as I didn't want to think about it, this meant that the dog would be gone forever.

"I'm a great letter writer," she insisted in her most compassionate voice. Candace would make a great elementary school teacher and an even better mother someday. Her father came to help her pack up her belongings and furniture in a little trailer as Arturo sat on the front porch, swishing his tail. I rubbed his head and kissed one of his ears. I didn't want him to see my tears. I didn't want to upset him. He already knew something was wrong. And I knew I would never hear from her or see either one of them again.

70

I changed as much as I could in my apartment so that I wouldn't have to live in the past. My first task was to throw out Arturo's little towel bed. Being reminded of the past had always been depressing. I found it remarkable that people like my father could reminisce and then forget so easily. I couldn't. I wanted to move the round oak kitchen table, but there was no other place for it to go, so it just sat there, exactly where it was, the refrigerator to the left. The only thing I could do was choose another chair to sit in and not feel the need to look down at a dogless towel anymore. Now, when I sat in a different chair, I would force myself not to look down at the old linoleum tile. I wouldn't see that empty space where Arturo used to sit and keep me company.

One day, I found myself looking in my mailbox for a letter from Mary Jo McLaughlin. Nothing. It had been years. Whatever gave me the idea that she would write to me? She didn't even know where I was. No response ever came from her, and I don't know why I had a hunch that on this particular day, I would somehow receive one. I was sure she hated me.

I spent a lot of time avoiding Aubrey, the phone, Miranda upstairs, the new people in the back, and any other stimuli that I felt should remain outside my cave. I argued with Walter over paying him back the thirty-five dollars I owed him for getting my bike out of impound, but he refused to take any money from me. While he was in the bathroom one day, I stuck two twenties in a zipper-folder thing in one of his three-ring binders. Then when I wasn't looking, I found the two twenties in my refrigerator. I gave up after that and baked him some pretty good chocolate chip cookies.

Then my great-uncle Nick from Florida died from a stroke, and my grandmother gave me $23,700 in a cashier's check and made me promise in front of the bank not to tell anyone. Great-Uncle Nick, whom I met once when I was eight and Marisa was eleven, was a very successful businessman, although I had no idea what he did for a living. He had been widowed for decades and never had children, and when he died, he left his entire estate to his only surviving sibling—Bunica. She knew somewhere in the back of that head of hers that she didn't have to worry about *my* loose lips. I was frugal to a fault. I knew exactly how to save money and multiply it if I needed to, *and* $23,700 would keep me going for a while until I could figure out which direction I would take next.

I knew one thing—I would not be attending graduate school just to please Vann. And I knew something else—it was time to sober up a little bit if I could. Wine? Fine. No more downers to sleep or uppers to wake. Coke was a hundred dollars a gram. A joint here and there? Okay. Now what? There was no leaving Wellton. Not until I completed my sentence with Dr. Kilburn.

I looked at it from every angle, and there was no way around it. If I didn't complete my twelve sessions with Dr. Kilburn or *someone* certified to deal with a crazed, criminally insane, and violent maniac like me, I would be heading directly back to the stockade.

I was amazed that someone like Detective Holloway was actually acquainted with someone like Dr. Kilburn.

Her life most likely happened like this: Dr. Kilburn went to medical school because her father was a doctor. She wanted to model but was too short. Daddy was a doctor, and he had no sons, and so it was expected of her, as it was expected of me to run a fish store. Decent grades probably helped, but money was what clinched it for this old woman. Well, she wasn't that old. She was perfectly groomed, from her exquisitely planned gray bob to her squared red toenails that adorned soft white crushed leather sandals.

"Do you have a boyfriend?" she half asked, half sneered. I didn't think this woman was capable of sneering, but her top lip looked as if it was being pulled by a string on one side. I was astonished at how rude she was. I was stunned and embarrassed, but of course, I couldn't respond in the way I wanted to respond. What does this have to do with anything? Was I the only adult woman on the planet who didn't have a boyfriend and was still a virgin? I'll bet I was. "No."

"No?"

"No."

"No boyfriend."

"No."

She actually looked surprised.

Maybe I should have taken that look as a compliment. I shook my head as she scribbled my lack of love life in her notes, keeping in mind that I was court-ordered to sit across a teakwood coffee table from her. I decided to give her some juicy information for her yellow legal pad.

"I haven't met anyone special in my life yet." I gazed out a large window across the room as the words tumbled out of my mouth. It felt like a strange thing for me to say, and I thought of Dr. Paul Keating, the redheaded veterinarian who took such good care of Shelly. I decided it was time to get it off my chest.

"Dr. Kilburn, I understand this may be a silly question, but when you take those notes, I mean, in my circumstance, will you be turning them over to the court or—"

"No, no, Alice." She scratched her powdery pale cheek with her red pinkie fingernail. I noticed the beautiful diamond tennis brace-let that lay delicately at her wrist, which slipped down slightly. The clouds were puffy, and the sun streamed hard across the Oriental rug. "Everything we discuss in these anger management sessions is confidential. I just have to sign off at the end of our twelve sessions that you completed your court order for your probation within your allotted time. So you must show up or at least call if there is an emergency, and you can't make your appointment. What you say to me goes nowhere, and I want you to know that you can say anything you want within these four walls. Now, if I feel that you are a danger to yourself or others, *these* would be situations I must report to authorities."

It was a little reassuring, but I still didn't trust her. I didn't trust anyone, and no other human being was ever privy to my mind.

"Am I making sense? Is all of this understood, Alice?" She gently tilted her attractive made-up face to one side, as if she could obviously see my discomfort.

"Yes," I said, looking over at the clock.

"Very good," she said quietly. "Tell me what happened at the TV station."

She had to ask even though she already knew. Ironically, I had been a "danger to others." And that's why we were there.

"Well…" I shifted a little on the bright peach floral love seat. "I heard from some friends that…" The word *that* was drawn out as long as possible. I had gone over and over this again in my mind, and I didn't want to talk about it, but I had no choice. I had to do it. She was making me. "That the big blond newswoman who's really famous in town, you know, Lisa Jupiter, was about to air an interview with Barton Withers, the man who murdered my sister right in front of me. She would also be interviewing his parents, Sunny and Big Barton."

I thought for sure that Dr. Kilburn knew them personally. If she did, she was going to hear every last drop of my vitriol toward them.

"Okay. And?"

I wasn't talking fast enough for her.

She looked up and stretched her neck a little. "So your friends told you about a—"

"Friends and upstairs housemates, I guess you could call them," I interrupted.

She nodded and wrote something down as if on cue and then continued, "All right, that this interview would be airing. Did you see a trailer or read about it in the paper?"

I wasn't getting help. I was being interrogated. I knew all about interrogations.

I shook my head. "No, I don't own a television, and I don't like to read the newspaper."

"So how did they tell you? Did you go out for lunch, or did you overhear something at first? Did they warn you or 'Hey, by the way'?"

She gave me a few options here, and it was really rather ridiculous since I knew she already knew the answer to all these questions.

Formality, I suppose, in addition to the ream of paperwork I had to fill out when I walked into this office. Or it could have been my original thought—interrogation.

"I guess you could say they warned me." I pushed the hair out of my eyes and looked up at the white tiled ceiling while trying to gather my thoughts. "The girls from upstairs, Candace and ah, ah, Miranda, came down to my apartment with Aubrey, this girl I've known most of my life. I was just hanging out with Candace's dog. He liked to come downstairs and visit me all the time."

I felt a flash of sadness as I thought of Arturo, which led me to think of Shelly and then Dr. Paul Keating. Then I thought about the fact that I had never had a boyfriend and that I was still a virgin.

"All three girls?" I waited for her face to react, but it didn't since the sneer about my boyfriend-less existence.

I nodded.

"What did they do, sit you down and tell you?"

"Yes, that's exactly what they did. I mean, at the time I knew it was something very important because they looked worried, and they just kept beating around the bush. And they just stood there. Aubrey even turned off my answering machine and wouldn't let me answer my own phone. Then she stood over it, guarding it. Finally, I just made them come out with it. I was so worried, and I was getting pretty pissed with them. The anxiety was killing me. I thought something had happened to my dad or something like that."

"From the way you describe their behavior, I can understand your anger and anxiety." She smiled, I suppose to put me at ease. Naturally, her teeth were perfectly white and straight. "Alice, do you think their dramatization, perhaps their fear of hurting you with this information, fueled your anger? Sadness?"

I said nothing at first. "Hmm. I never really thought of it."

"Let's just sit with that for a moment."

We sat until I felt like we were wasting time. But then I figured that it didn't really matter, and so I used the rest of the wasted time to really think about her interesting question.

"I don't really know how to answer your question."

"That's all right. You don't have answer it. But I would like for you to think about it. Write down how you feel about it when you leave here if you have to do so."

I never wrote things down. I didn't have to write things down. My mind was a steel trap. Detrimental.

"They knew about Barton Withers." *The monster.* "They knew about Marisa. I'm sure they knew it would piss me off, this interview."

"Are all three women local? How would they know about your sister's death—"

"Murder."

"With the exception of Aubrey, whom you have known since you were a child. Do you ever talk to your friends about your feelings?"

"No."

"Aubrey?"

"No."

"All right." She wrote something down again on her yellow legal pad. "You decided to go to the television station. How did you get in?"

I looked around her perfectly decorated office. "I don't know how I—what do you mean? I parked up my bike and went in the front door, walked through the offices for a little while until I found her."

She looked at her notepad and said with a friendly smile, "I am assuming the security will be better at the new building?"

I half smiled. Oh yes, let's not forget about the shiny new building. The Withers Tower. I wanted to throw that vase of lemons directly at the window, but I manufactured everything in my capability not to do that. I had to pull my mind away from my own thoughts. I had to be there. I did not want to go back to jail. My viscera burned. The arteries on the sides of my neck burned. Dr. Gwynneth Kilburn held my whole life in her tiny perfectly manicured hand. I was still in jail. There were no walls or steel doors that slammed shut, no guards or cots or seizures. But none of that made any difference because I was still not free.

"The assault," she said, not noticing a thing. Shitty psychiatrist. "Tell me about that."

Like you haven't already read every detail about it backward and forward. Did you also know I nearly killed a kid in high school too? He also deserved it.

"The assault? You see, it wasn't actually what I would call an assault. I've seen an assault, but then—"

"Yes, the assault. Ms. Jupiter didn't press any charges against you, but the county took you into custody. What happened?" She looked directly into my eyes, and so I had to try really hard not to show her what I was thinking.

"I. Just. Had. She wouldn't cancel the show." I felt tears again, and I quickly wiped them away.

She gently pushed plush pink tissues in a gold forever box toward me.

"Suddenly my fingers were in her hair, and I tugged at it, and this ball of blond just came out." I was laughing and crying at the same time. She knew I yanked the hell out of Lisa Jupiter's head. "I'm sorry, Dr. Kilburn, I know this isn't funny," I lied. "But I was really, really upset with her for what she was doing to Marisa. It was just a wig. I was so angry. I wanted her to feel as humiliated. She was humiliating my sister."

"Marisa is dead, Alice. She can't be humiliated. People are smart. They will make up their own minds."

That was something I *sat* with.

"You don't have to remind me that she's dead." I tried to remain calm. "But it has been my experience that people are not as smart as you may think they are. You may be smart. I may be smart. Most people are not smart."

She continued to write and talk, write and write, flipping that pad of hers over the top as if she were taking notes in class where the minute her attention was deviated from the topic was when she lost everything. She made me talk about the murder, my thoughts, my mother, my family, my grades, my drinking and drugging, which I implied was normal for a college student, even though I knew I was way out of control. I just didn't tell her that. She forced me to talk about the house where I grew up in, the store, my three days in jail,

427

and the subject I wanted to avoid even more than my virginity—my paranoid schizophrenic aunt.

"Please tell me I don't have what she has." I regretted my vulnerability. Dr. Gwynneth Kilburn had me right where she wanted me.

"Maybe not."

The terror was back.

"You may have some sort of atypical mood disorder or obsessive compulsive disorder." She threw me that sneering look again as if to say, "So what? What's the big deal? There are a lot of crazy people out there. What makes you think you're immune?"

That ball of panic burst in my throat, but I didn't cry.

"I had a patient once." She balanced the air with her palms, her bracelets delicately sparkling and clinking together. "Brilliant man. Very educated. Very cultured man who continually had to wash his hands because he couldn't stop smelling horse manure. He *knew* that there wasn't any horse manure on his hands, but he couldn't stop smelling it, and he couldn't stop washing. He suffered tremendously."

"I don't do weird shit like that."

"No, you don't, but this man was a very angry person. His anger was turned inward, and he became very depressed. He was depressed for many years and never got help for his depression, and *that* is what depression turns into when you let it go and let it fester. It consumes your life, and you hit rock bottom. Rock. Bottom. He thought he was schizophrenic too. He wasn't. You both came for help at the right time."

At least she didn't mention that I had to be there.

"I've seen Aunt Nancy do similar things, even when she's taking her medication or at least we all think she is. Even at her best, she still goes down into that creepy cellar and scrubs the floors and the walls. The huge steel octopus heater used to scare the hell out of Marisa and me. It still does kind of scare me. She says she has to clean away bad memories, that she was chosen by God to do so, and is the only one on earth who can accomplish the task. She plays loud music just so she can drown out voices and yells *back* at them, she says, as she washes them away. That's when she's off her medication. My aunt isn't like your patient. She doesn't think she has a problem. She's doing God's work. She thinks I have a problem a lot of the time, and of course, that thing with my dad where she acts like she can't stand him. But it's not real. It's some sort of delusion."

Dr. Kilburn flipped through her yellow legal pad. "Right. Alice, look. I am going to clearly state after seeing you for one hour, you don't have paranoid schizophrenia. When you leave here today, at least you can take that one piece of information with you."

I visited the powder-puff-pink ladies' room and splashed some water on my numb face, then made my way back to the small reception area where a woman sat on another fluffy beige love seat. Nonmedicated staff with normal lives and nonmurdered sisters giggled.

Dr. Gwynneth Kilburn appeared through a back door with my file, presumably, and joined her little team. I picked up my papers from one of the ladies and left the office. I climbed into the blue Plymouth and sat outside the medical building for a while. I lit a cigarette and put my sunglasses on, and naturally, everything darkened, for which I was grateful.

Off in the distance was a new building I had never noticed before. The tile roof tiered and became smaller as it got higher. It reminded me of a church steeple. It was probably just one more building owned by the Withers family. They didn't deserve to own a town and the people in it. They didn't deserve to own the radio stations and develop tall buildings that twinkled at night. They deserved nothing, every single one of them—even Mary Jo, Kay, and Helena. The only good thing about that family was that their monster murderer was still in prison, if you could even call where he was a prison. He had passed right through those years and never did receive that early release I was so worried about. To my surprise, he didn't get paroled either. I was so happy for one minute, I couldn't believe my luck. I thought for sure that he would be released into the sunshine and directly into his mother's adoring arms. Nope. He was no longer locked away at Bellmorrow, but at least he was locked away somewhere.

I thought about Marianne giving us that sermon at the Maidenhead County lockup. I suppose that God was watching over me when it came to the monster. He could always change his mind like he often had over the years. The thought of taking medication regressed and terrified me. The last time I was prescribed medication was right after my sister was murdered and my father took me back right away. Since then, I had experimented with all kinds of drugs, sedatives, and speed being my most valued, although I would settle for whatever I could get my hands on, whatever I could afford. Maybe being zonked out of my mind after seeing Marisa plastered all over my mother's fancy wall was what precipitated this whole thing—blood and water pasted on there like some kind of spackle.

I'll kill him if I ever see him. I don't care what happens to me then.

This was a prescription that was written out to *me* in my name, not because I broke my arm like Dad or because I couldn't sleep like Kiki, but because I attacked the poor blond monster Lisa Jupiter. I wasn't a sick kid like Holloway Junior or an old lady with joint trouble like Mrs. Sideways Ferguson. I was a crazy person like my aunt Nancy. Just different. And I didn't smell shit on my hands. At least my aunt had Tommy. I had no one, and I guess that was the way it was intended to be. It wasn't bad.

I walked up to the pharmacy counter, and I was embarrassed. Why would I suddenly care if the pharmacist and his assistant would now know that I was a crazy person? I thought for several seconds until the thinking tired me out.

"Good afternoon. Can I help you?" a weird-looking woman behind the counter asked. She had huge grayish-blue eyes that were set very far apart and low on her face. Her ears were enormous. Marisa would have said she looked like a Martian. I was ashamed of my thoughts. Marisa could think this way.

I noticed the woman had thick sandy-colored hair though, shiny and pretty as if it could be in another shampoo commercial. I hoped she couldn't tell what I was thinking as she looked me straight in the eye, and the light behind her in one of the medication aisles flickered. I looked passed her at the light, then back into her eyes. I handed Martian woman with the pretty sandy-colored hair my prescriptions, and within ten minutes, she brought back a little white paper bag containing a bottle of white and yellow capsules and a bottle of yellow pills. I had to control my thoughts.

I had to control my thoughts.

Why was I spiraling off into nowhere? *I* was out of control, out of sway. I was terrified—exactly the way I was when I was a child. I could not keep looking at this woman and keep thinking what I was thinking. Eventually, I would be punished. Maybe she and her boss didn't think I was crazy after all. She didn't seem to even know what the pills were, and when she grinned like a vampire and said goodbye to me, I didn't get the feeling from her that she cared, even though I didn't stick around long enough to find out.

I sped out of the store. She saw me. Other people saw me. I hurried home so I could open up my packages and inspect their contents. It suddenly went dark and rainy again. Fall was here, and the days would be getting shorter and shorter.

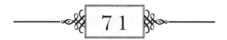

71

The breezy blue perfect Saturday afternoon where students in their turtlenecks and sweatshirts walked arm in arm to State football games when legendary yellow, red, and orange leaves fluttered to the ground meant little to me. But it seemed to waken and bring joy to those ordinary and normal people with good families and perfect lives. I would instead have to listen to Miranda's way-too-loud TV set playing and replaying that same commercial about back-to-school supplies that made me feel like retching as I remembered having to go back to school when Marisa and I were little kids.

It was starting to feel so long ago since Marisa was murdered. No one probably even knew who she was anymore, like those early presidents whose faces hung on the bulletin board in elementary school. No one cared. I couldn't remember the last time I felt so alone. I normally liked the dark, but when the rain decided to fall again that afternoon, it hurt me far more than it helped.

I walked down the long driveway to the mailbox in the drizzle. Maybe there was a letter back from Mary Jo.

Don't be ridiculous, you're a grown woman now. She doesn't even know who you are anymore. And she doesn't care.

I was supposed to take my pills at bedtime, but I was bored, so I decided I would go to sleep early. The house was dark and quiet. Not even Miranda's TV was giving me the irritation I needed. I thought I would call Aubrey, then I quickly decided not to do that. I knew she would only chat for the next hour or worse, and then insist on coming over.

I sat on the end of my bed on top of my blue and gray comforter, the one I had for as long as I could remember, and stared at a red pocketbook that used to be my grandmother's. I always admired the fake alligator dyed to a bright red in the shape of an upside-down half moon with long gold chains. After commenting on it once, she dumped out all of its contents and handed it to me. "You take it, Alice," she said in her heavily accented English. "You like it. I want you to have it."

I knew nothing about style or fashion, and my idea of a pocketbook was either an old green knapsack I found in the front closet at my father's or an attempt to shove as many things as I could into the pockets of my blue jeans. But I liked this pocketbook. I liked to just look at it and touch the shiny patent leather, smell my grandmother's musky warm scent.

I swallowed the little yellow-and-white pill, and suddenly, my mouth opened wide. I had this type of feeling before, but this was different. It was a thousand times worse, the fear, the inability to breathe, knowing that within twenty seconds, I would be dead on the floor in front of Bunica's pocketbook. I gasped. My god, I was dying, I was really dying. In my mind, I saw an eight-millimeter film, a fast film of a woman, blue and black, dark colors, a heavyset older woman sitting at a table. I think she was me. She suddenly stood up with such a look of terror and excruciation on her face, I had to close my eyes. But the image wouldn't go away. Someone didn't want her to live because they poisoned her. She, like me, knew she was dying.

I stood up and jumped in place, waving my hands. I wasn't dead. It had been at least twenty seconds, and I was still alive. I was breathing, and blood was beating through my body, back to my heart, and out again. I was still there. I wanted to be dead for a long time, and in many ways, I was, even though I was still breathing and walking. Death was now the new enemy.

I felt a little calmer as each moment passed, exhilarated that there I was in my bedroom in front of my grandmother's old pocketbook, still alive. My lungs swelled and collapsed, swelled and collapsed, and even though I was still very traumatized, I no longer was all consumed by that fear of terror.

I picked up the phone and dialed Walter. When he answered, I was still staring at the red pocketbook, and then I wondered if I should quickly hang up. "I had that appointment with that doctor today, you know, Dr. Kilburn?"

"Oh, yeah, yeah. That's right. What did she have to say? How did that go?"

"She said a bunch of stuff." I looked down at my fingernails, thinking about some of the nonsense that spewed from Dr. Kilburn's perfect mouth. "She put me on some medication. Crazy pills." I reached for one of the bottles.

"I think I've heard of those. My mom takes a bunch of stuff, I'm pretty sure I've seen them."

I knew immediately by the sound of his voice he was lying just to placate me. There was no way his very grounded and organized mother was taking crazy pills.

"Look, can you promise me—"

"Easy, girl, I'm not gonna tell a single soul anything about your business, but look, you know you've got friends who want to help—"

"No!" I was panicking. "Not a fucking word. Like you said, it's my business. I'm goddamned trusting you with this. Can I trust you?"

"Yes, you can. You can trust me."

"Good."

"So how often do you have to take this stuff? Is this an everyday thing?"

"Oh yes," I answered facetiously. "I'm supposed to. I have to, but I don't think I can do that."

"What do you mean you don't think you can do that?"

"I'm scared. I'm too scared. I can't swallow them."

"Why can't you swallow them?"

"What if I die?" This was all very new to me. Dying didn't seem to matter once. Now it did. Now after experiencing whatever had happened in my bedroom, I realized that like most everyone else, I was terrified of dying.

"You are not going to die, Alice."

"How do you know that? You don't know that! What if the drugstore tampered with these capsules? All you have to do is open them up. It's easy, Walter. The pharmacist seemed normal, but you never know. His assistant looked at me funny. I think she was an alien."

"That didn't happen, baby."

"No, but—"

"Listen, Alice. Listen to me. The pharmacist isn't going to tamper with your prescription. He's a medical professional. He could lose his license, could go to prison. Why would he risk that? He doesn't even know you!"

"Oh, Walter, he might not even be a real person! You have so much to learn about monsters." I knew a lot about monsters. "Do you remember a year ago or whenever when that guy tampered with those over-the-counter capsules? He spiked them with poison! People died. A little boy died."

"I'm coming over, Alice."

"No, don't—"

But he had already hung up the phone. Fuck! I didn't want any visitors. But it was too late. He would be over in about ten minutes, maybe sooner if he was quick.

I threw my pill bottle across the room, making sure I carefully watched where it landed, knowing I would have to go through the whole thing again later.

Before I could even light a cigarette and find the coffeepot, I could hear Walter's footsteps clomping on the large cement front porch.

"Want some?" I shook the coffee bag at him without turning to face him.

"No, I don't. Thank you."

"What the fuck is your problem?" I turned to look at him. "Walter, you're the one who insisted on coming over here. I never asked you to."

Then I heard what sounded like the evening news bellowing from Miranda's TV upstairs. Was she goddamned deaf? I sat down in my new chair at my kitchen table.

Walter looked at the ceiling, and his face relaxed, as if he was pleased that there was someone else breathing in the house besides me.

"What's going on with you, Alice? You're not okay."

I folded my hands in front of me in the sanest way I could fold them. "Listen. I need you to listen to me, Walter. This is important. I got out of jail. I've got this court-ordered probationary period, and I can't have any trouble, Walter, you know? Do you understand me?"

The look on his face was full of sorrow as he pulled out a chair and sat down next to me.

"There is nothing wrong," I continued, frightened of what he could do to me. "I am sorry that I even called you in the first place—"

"Well, I'm not." He shook his head. "I'm glad you called me. I'm glad we're best friends."

Tears welled up in my eyes.

He put his hand on my arm. "You're slipping away somewhere, girl, and I don't know what's going on. I don't know how to help you. But I can tell you, you won't die if you take your medication. It will help you. I know times have been tough for you, but it's just getting worse. You have to take your medication even if you're scared. You have to do it, baby. You won't die. It will help you."

He got up and poured black coffee into my mug. I lifted it to my lips. It smelled so fresh, and it was so perfectly steamy and hot, but when I tried to take a sip, I became panicked. I couldn't do it. I quickly put it down on the table.

"I know, I know." I felt a tightness in my chest that I had never felt before, and the room looked different. Things were different. There was an awkwardness to the environment. "But you have to be scared. *I* have to be scared. You don't know. What if there's something in that medication that's going to kill me?"

He shook his head. "Baby, there's nothing in there. Besides, you already took some. That's how you know."

"But in a bottle of thirty, there *could* be that one pill, that *one little pill*—"

The look on his face was of sadness and fear. "Why aren't you drinking your coffee? Aren't you gonna drink your coffee?"

"No," I said quietly.

"You know what?"

I said nothing.

"I remember when I first met you, when Milk assigned you as my tutor in business math. I remember the look on your face half the time. I think *you* thought I was a shithead." He smiled. "I remember sayin' to myself, 'That girl's eyes are half-closed. She's got a lot of thoughts.'"

I said nothing.

"What do you want? You...you wanna be an accountant or something? I'll bet your old man would love to set you up with an office in that warehouse of his, the way you crunch those numbers, ace those exams—"

I shook my head. "I wouldn't work for my father if his was the last job on this earth. Ever. *Ever.* We aren't even speaking."

His look of surprise annoyed me. "Why aren't you talkin' to Rudy?"

"Walter, you don't know him. You don't know what you're talking about."

"Okay, no, I know. You're right."

Suddenly, I felt like I was talking to a male version of Dr. Gwynneth Kilburn. I glanced over at him. His black hair was trimmed so short, he almost looked like he was bald, but the cut was about a half centimeter above his scalp, so perfectly planned out. Gone were the days of the bushy Afro with the white pick.

"So what do you want out of life?"

What exactly was this line of questioning?

I looked him right in the eye. "I would have thought you would have known what I would have wanted by now. All along. I want revenge."

He raised his eyebrows as if he had no idea of what I was taking about, but I knew he did. "Revenge?"

"Revenge. Yes, revenge. Revenge on that monster that broke my sister's neck. And you know what else? I want people to care. I actually want people to give a shit, which they never did about her and her death."

"Oh, baby, that is so not true."

"I want the people who were in her life to care, her family, her boyfriend Mark who these days acts like she never even existed. I am

437

the only one who holds her light in my soul, Walter. The only one. How many photographs of Marisa has my little sister Helena ever seen? Not many, I can assure you. And the reason why? They *hide* her from the very truth. That kid spends all of her time, practically every waking moment when she's not in her private school, with those horrible parents of the man who murdered our sister."

"Bastard," he whispered.

"So you tell me? When is he really, *really* going to pay for what he's done?" I didn't want to cry again, but Walter made it so hard as he grabbed a roll of paper towels and pulled off too many of them. He made me wipe my face and blow my nose. Then he once again put his hand on my arm in a similar way Detective Holloway did all those years ago in that break room at the police station.

"Listen to me, and I know you know this." He pulled his chair closer to me. "People are funny creatures. They grieve in different ways, Alice. It's different and it's harder and it's full of horror that will never go away because she was your sister, and the two of you were really close—"

"That's bullshit! She was brutally attacked! I saw him kill her. I was thirteen years old, and she was only seventeen! And I'm so tired of hearing everyone tell me the same thing over and over again."

I looked quickly at the paper towel I just wiped my face with and felt a pang of sorrow. I looked at Walter, whose face was full of questions.

"Marisa was strangled, and her neck was snapped. She was murdered in cold blood. I was the only other person in the room, not even six feet away. I saw everything. Everything, Walter, and I did nothing to stop it. I couldn't save her life. This was *not a fucking accident.*"

I wasn't even crying now. It was as if everything was gone, and terror had taken over my mind, my viscera.

"And for some reason, I am the only one who truly grieves, who really understands, who knows the truth. The damned doctor barely wanted to touch it at our first visit. Probably because the police never believed my account—things didn't add up right, so they accused me of hallucinating." My voice trailed off into nothing.

"I don't know what I would have done if I saw my sister—if I saw that." He didn't doubt me. He looked around the room. It was as if he was trying to get me to understand him, had he been in my situation. "Alice, if I had gone through what you had gone through, I would have found the tallest building downtown, gone up to the rooftop, and I would have jumped off headfirst. But you? There could be a line of tanks coming through this kitchen about to run you over, and when they did? You would still get up and dust yourself off because *that* is how strong you are."

"Walt—"

"Because you haven't had a choice. You *had* to be."

But I wasn't strong. This was the worst I had ever been, and still, I was slipping farther away. I was deteriorating, and I knew it when I looked at my friend's round sad eyes and the sun as it began to set and pierce through the kitchen window in its finale.

"Do you know what revenge does to a person?"

"Which person? Me or Withers?"

"You know what I'm talking about. You're not well, Alice. We've got to get you better. For now, Withers is in prison. I know for a while you were worried about him getting paroled, but he hasn't yet. I know he's been transferred out of Bellmorrow. Do you know when his next hearing is?"

"That's a tightly guarded secret," I said quietly, my chest closing in on itself. Again. It was bad enough they let him sleaze his way out of Bellmorrow. Giving him his freedom was too much for me to visualize.

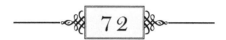

7 2

I was aware that my functioning was worsening, as were my social skills, which weren't very good to begin with. I reveled in social isolation and whatever I needed to keep what was left of my rabid mind occupied. While I lay on my bed in the perfect black stillness, looking up at the ceiling, for some reason, I remembered one of my father's little sayings: "Small cog in the big wheel, Allie. Small cog in the big wheel."

Then I thought about Walter telling me the same thing that others had said to me so many times in so many distinctive ways: "Marisa wouldn't want this. Marisa wouldn't like to see you doing this to yourself. Marisa wants you to move on. Marisa needs you to carry on."

People had no idea what they were talking about. I was sick. She would be laughing at me right now because that's what she always did. I was so sick. I had hardly eaten all day. I had half a pear for breakfast, a few bites of pasta for lunch, and not a thing for dinner. I wasn't the least bit hungry. I became sicker as the day wore on.

I took a blanket and pillow along with Marisa's and Shelly's ashes and drove to the truck stop where I could fall asleep in the way back of the blue Plymouth with the seats down under the big fluorescent light of safety. In the morning, if I could, I would sip some coffee and take a shower.

73

I put on an award-winning performance for Dr. Kilburn and showed up for my appointments wearing a tentative smile that said, "Oh gosh, I'm not at my zenith of mental health, but I am getting better every day, and I'm learning a little with each anger management session with you, Dr. Kilburn."

I did everything that was required of me, including completing my anger tabulation. I was assigned to write down each time I was angry, what made me angry, how I handled my anger, and what I would do the next time I became angry. I perfected a tailored diary for Dr. Kilburn. If I had written down each time I was angry, I would have had a whole encyclopedia-sized novel. I wondered if she knew how much bullshit I was throwing at her wall. I was too sick to care about it at the time. I just wanted to get out from under her watchful eye in the sky, get all of this legality out of the way, and move forward with my life. It wasn't so much of a life though. I was barely functioning.

I could not eat. One night I picked up a vegetable pizza, and I just sat there and stared at it. I worried that it was poisoned, and if I ate any of it, like my overweight elderly self, who didn't really exist but continued to pop into my head, I would end up cold and dead. I knew the pizza wasn't poisoned, but my mind wouldn't let me touch it. My brain played tricks with me as it had in the past. But this time, it was far worse.

I could not keep a job. After being fired from the library, I went to work as a bookkeeper for a local company that distributed hot water heaters. It started out fine; the money was okay. It was in an old building downtown in the basement where they decided to shove my desk in a windowless corner room with the boss's nephew, Will.

I didn't trust him. Once I lit up a cigarette, but I couldn't smoke it because naturally, I thought it was poisoned. He simultaneously blew up at me and made me take it outside because of his asthma and allergies. I didn't dare remind him that *he* didn't mind stinking up the place. He was filthy. He changed his clothes every two days. He was about six feet seven inches tall and terribly thin. He had long greasy brown hair that wasn't styled and thick brown glasses. He obviously rarely bathed because he smelled like a combination of body odor and chili con carne.

I went upstairs one afternoon and explained the situation to the owner. I asked for a new work station. He promptly fired me. I should have done what I normally did   not dare say a word and suffer. But I was suffering in other areas of my life, and I was getting sicker. I was panicking. I was losing my functioning as a person.

I went to work in a steel-coating factory. A lot of people who worked on the floor had been there for decades and were part of a union. Although new people like me who came through a light industrial temporary employment agency were made fun of or ignored, some of the workers seemed pleasant and gave me my space. It felt good to be able to wear sweatpants and sneakers to work. I treasured the mornings where the line boss, Bonnie, would stick me all the way down on the end where I could be quiet and anonymous. I attached my little plastic whatevers onto the little spikes that hung from the ever-turning ceiling about twenty-five feet above me.

Then my slow solace was shattered when Bonnie began pairing me on the line with other people from the agency. Donavan, with three kids under the age of four, was a black guy about my age with a fresh mouth. He was rude, obnoxious, constantly telling dirty jokes, and bantering with the other men. Some of them engaged him and others ignored him, but not many. Then one day, Donovan turned his attention to me as if he had hung a magnifying glass directly in front of my face. Each morning, I dreaded the possibility of being paired up with him. On a Tuesday morning, he yelled over to me, informing me that diapers were very expensive. After the first fifteen-minute cigarette break bell, he asked me if I had ever worn a diaper. Then he laughed uncontrollably.

"When I was a baby, I guess. Sure. Everyone did." I was trying to remain calm, uninterested, and slow.

Just before the lunch bell screamed, Donovan told me I was the most gorgeous girl in the entire plant. He said it loud enough for people to take notice, and some of the men looked over at me while a few of the women made faces. One of these women was an eighteen-year-old girl who had a child with one of the men. Her eyes went directly to my breasts shortly after Donovan made the comment. The younger girl glared at me like she wanted to rip my throat out with her teeth.

I wasn't the most gorgeous woman in there. None of us were gorgeous. The eighteen-year-old with the kid sure as hell was not gorgeous, and I sure as hell was no threat to her. I didn't want her man. I didn't want any man. I only wanted to be left alone so I could do my job in peace. But there was one thing I learned about this life and that was there were people out in the world who had no intention of leaving me alone.

Later on that afternoon, Donavan told me that I had a nice stomach, and it looked like I worked out a lot. How could he have seen my stomach? It was covered up with an old extra-large navy-blue T-shirt. Donavan was quickly gnawing away at my nerves, but I was too frightened to say anything. No one had ever talked to me that way—in a sexual way. Maybe Chick, but that wasn't real. He did that with every single woman he walked past, young or old. And I had known and had been used to Chick for years.

But there was something tingly about being told I was gorgeous when clearly I was not. I liked it even though I wasn't supposed to, and that secret lie so far buried in my mind that it may have somehow dictated my behavior without my even realizing it. Maybe the whole thing was my fault.

The next day, I asked Bonnie if I could move to another line. Maybe I should have told her that Donavan was pestering me, and I wanted to get away from him. But Bonnie always had this hurried look on her face, and I didn't want to frustrate her any more than she appeared to be. Throwing Donavan into her new mix of problems would end up giving her bigger problems than I think she was willing to deal with.

"No, baby," short, intense, gray-headed Bonnie said, looking up at me with crinkled eyes and a loud voice. "You're not fast enough, honey. I'm sorry. I need you to stay right where you are. You see Sidney over there? He's been with the union for over twenty-eight years now. You can't keep up with him." She patted my arm and waddled off.

She was right. What did I know about throwing plastic cologne bottle tops on a vertical rack and filling it up enough so that when it moves down the line to the big acid vat, there would be enough tops on the rack that no one would notice there was an incompetent slowpoke stuck in the line somewhere from the temp agency? And so I had no choice but to endure Donovan, his remarks, and that no one within earshot ever told him to shut his fat mouth.

The next morning was more of the same. Had I not been so sick, nervous, and depressed, I might have laughed or at least been outwardly flattered; it was so ridiculous. The women glared at me like I was some sort of exotic creature with lovely boobs strutting down a Paris runway. I couldn't believe it. They were pathetic. Eighteen-year-old with the kid watched me like she couldn't decide whether she should cry or run me over with her car. Bonnie was on vacation, and so we were assigned a replacement supervisor named Carmine.

Donovan continued to annoy me. By ten o'clock in the morning, I couldn't stand it anymore. I got permission from Carmine to go to the ladies' room, and I walked off the slow end of the line. Just as I was about to climb the steps, Donovan and two of the other men passed me from behind. Donovan reached down and pinched my right butt cheek. I whirled around in a circle. I knew it was him who touched me just by the way his legs slipped by—skinny brown legs in blue sweat shorts and white socks with blue stripes up to his knees. I opened my mouth, but before anything could come out, he was gone. I tried to scream, but I couldn't. I began to sob loudly. One of the male supervisors casually looked over but simply went about chomping on his gum. It seemed as if I was suddenly the only female in a sea of males, and none of them seemed to care or did anything to help me.

I climbed the wooden steps, bolted through the door, and ran down the hallway to the ladies' room. I was mad, I was repulsed, and my face was soaked with tears. No one had ever touched me like that before. No one. I cried loudly.

"Wassa matta, honey?" A thin black girl, tall like me, cornered me by the sink. "Wha' happen?"

"You know Donovan?" I choked the words out. "The black guy, the temp that works on the line with me?"

It didn't look as though she knew either of us, but she nodded quickly, a look of worry seared from her eyes.

"He grabbed me!"

"Wha'? He ain't spoda' do dat!" She surprised me by grabbing my arm and hauling me out of the bathroom and down the brown-paneled corridor.

Another woman came toward us. "Wass' goin' on?"

Still holding my arm, the woman who found me crying in the bathroom said, "One of those temps she paired up wit. Grabbin' at her."

"Grabbed your bee-hind?" she asked, looking straight at me. "He gonna find hisself in some big trouble. That a sexual harassment thing."

"You got that right. Come on, you gotta talk to Mr. Kichens. He the boss of the whole plant. Wass your name, honey."

"Alice," I whispered.

"Alice, you say? Thas' my mama's name. Alice. Come on."

The three of us walked down another wood-paneled corridor and toward a small wooden door with a square window that looked like it belonged on the side of a camper.

The second woman looked through the window. "He ain't there. Figures."

I should have asked them their names, but I hadn't been thinking clearly for weeks, and this incident made things even more impossible. I was concentrating on myself and what Donovan had done to me. In front of people.

"Who the supervisa' down there, Alice? Bonnie?"

I nodded and sniffed like a baby.

"She on vacation, Lola. Carmine down there now."

"Aw, great. Another man."

The three of us walked back to the break room. I had stopped crying, and just as we sat at one of the white tables, the buzzer cried its warning.

"We gonna have to go back to the floor, honey," the first woman, Lola, explained as the other nodded. "You sit here for a few minutes, then you go back there, and you keep checkin' that window for the boss man Mr. Kichens. That grabbin' binn-iss against the rules, and Kichens need to know."

Kichens was a medium-sized, medium-built union man with greasy skin and a reddish-purple nose. He was hardened from years of working in factories. He chain-smoked unfiltered cigarettes, and his fingertips were stained brown. He looked worn and ready to find a new life, possibly on a beach somewhere with a pretty young blond. And he wanted corroboration. He wanted to see Carmine and the one guy walking alongside Donovan when he touched me. But Carmine was no help to me. Not only did he whine about "not wanting to get involved," but once in Kichens's office, he said very little, answering Kichens's questions like a tired puppy hiding behind big eyes. Why was this so hard for him? He was a supervisor, for god's sake. This was his job, to supervise and stand by his workers. He was a man. Why were they so weak sometimes?

Kichens dismissed Jimmy, the chubby little creep who wore pointed-toe snakeskin cowboy boots and the same filthy baseball cap every day. He sheepishly denied seeing Donovan putting his hands on me.

"I didn't see nothin', Mr. Kichens, honest to God" was all the little liar could say.

Kichens furrowed his wrinkled brow as he continued to smoke one cigarette after another. He didn't give me the impression that he didn't have the time for what he was doing, but he wanted to get to the bottom of it quickly. I could see that he wasn't feeling like he was accomplishing much. He had a huge amber glass ashtray that was a final resting place for a couple hundred cigarette butts. His marcelled golden hair needed trimming as he held court behind a large wooden desk in a paneled disposable office with a dirty white vinyl floor. He wore a solid blue tie with a white short-sleeved shirt and gold-rimmed glasses plopped on his spongy purple nose. He wore a wedding band on his big craggy hand. He looked and sounded like a mean person. And he never even talked to Donovan. He talked to Carmine though, right in front of me, about me.

"I don't know how long this assignment is going to last," I heard Carmine say as I surveyed the cheap smoky den of Percy Kichens.

"Wait a minute! These people are temps?" Kichens leaned forward, clenching a fist.

He was just finding this out?

Carmine nodded.

"Oh, Jesus Christ, Carmine. I don't need this horseshit. She's from that Greenway agency? Her and this who? Donald What? No, no. That's it. Go home. Carmine, I want you to go down there and get rid of all those Greenway people right away. We're not gonna use any more of those temps."

There was no negotiating, no protesting, no begging. I felt like a little speck of dust on Kichens's veneer wall. The old man picked up the phone, and Carmine ushered me out of the wooden room and through the camper door with a look of finality on his face.

"When is Bonnie coming back?" I asked when we were out in the hallway. I thought maybe another female could help me.

"Not for another ten days. You'll be gone by then."

"Carmine," I said, pointing to the camper door, "you can't let him do this! I need this job. I'm not the one who did anything wrong. That Donovan touched—" I was so mad. "Come on, you know what he's like. You know how he is, what he is."

He shook his head slowly. "It don't matter. You don't have no witnesses. Jimmy's like—"

"Jimmy is lying, Carmine!" I was so desperate for justice and my pittance, and neither was coming easily. "He's lying. He was standing right next to him, and he looked at him and laughed. I saw him."

I saw him. I saw him. I saw him. You don't know what you saw. I know exactly what I saw.

"Why would he lie?"

"This is sexual harassment—"

The words made him wince. He raised his long thin hands. He stood close. I noticed his salt-and-pepper chest hair popping out of his white undershirt. "Look, there's nothing I can do. I can't do anything. Mr. Kichens is the boss. He makes all the decisions. I'm just a floor supervisor."

Suddenly, a door swung open, and a voice called out to Carmine. He looked relieved as he slithered down the hallway away from me. I watched his white sneakers slip over the white vinyl. Everything from behind matched—his white shirt, white pants, white shoes, white floor, white lights. I could have mistaken him for an angel making his way back to heaven, but I knew much better than that.

I didn't know what to do as I stood in the middle of the hallway. This was another job that I had lost, another job I had been fired from. There was always turmoil wherever I went, and trouble liked to creep up behind and around me like a curse. Not only was I fired, but everyone from Greenway Light Industrial was fired, including that nice guy Sam, who was working his way through music school, and for what? Because I happened to be the object of affection for some piece of trash that I didn't want putting his hands on my body?

I wanted to scream and let tears of frustration stain my cheeks. Though a disillusioned haze filled me with guilt, especially when I thought of Sam, I went back downstairs to retrieve my sweater. I was glad Sam wasn't there, but Carmine was, hovering around a back door leading out to where the trucks offloaded. He tried to avoid my gaze as he shuffled around, slumped over like the weakling that he was. For a second, watching him worm around reminded me of my father, whom I still was avoiding.

I headed toward the front doors to the outside forever, and a familiar voice crept up behind me. "I got my woman at home! I neva' touched you! I got my woman's ass! I don't need yo' stank ass!"

"You can't even face me, can you?" I heckled. "You're nothing but a goddamned low-life liar!" I grabbed the end of a metal table and squeezed. My insides were ablaze again. My reasoning was completely shut off as I watched the back of Donovan sneak away. I wanted his blood to run down the front of me. I wanted to run fast and catch up with him. I wanted to plunge something, anything, into the back of his head. But I wouldn't, and I stopped. I squeezed my eyes shut as again, hot tears of rage screamed to be released. I didn't want to go back to jail. I remembered the suffering Marisa endured. My anger was a poison, just like food and water were a necessity. I would write all of this down on a new list. Dr. Kilburn put me on a new pill. She said I had to "help" the medicine work. No more capsules so no one could tamper with them, unless…

"Don't give it a second thought, Alice. You're an educated woman."

I felt a small hand on my shoulder. How did she know who I was?

"I'm Rochelle."

I looked down at an older redheaded woman with a smooth and fair complexion. Her smile made me cry.

"Go, get out of here and live your life. A lovely young girl doesn't belong here. You're too good for this place."

She sounded exactly like Beth. Dee. Why was I too good for anything? I wasn't too good for anything. I was a crazy person, and I was getting worse by the day. I was afraid of my food, my drink, cigarettes, medicine—I thought someone was poisoning anything that went into my mouth. I knew they weren't, but my brain was playing tricks on me, and I couldn't stop it. I would turn into my aunt. Dr. Kilburn was wrong, I just knew she was wrong. And as I looked out into the bright gray of the afternoon, I caught the side of Donovan's face in the passenger seat of an old rusted-out sedan pulling away from the parking lot. He looked as though he had supreme confidence. He was gone. I couldn't pretend to kill him anymore.

* * * * *

The clouds balled up, scattered about, and bulldozed through the sky as the rain pummeled my lonely roof. I sat on my mattress on the floor with my back against the wall like I had done so many times before. I looked at the ugly black metal tray with the painting of Granny Smith apples that was fastened against the opposite wall. It was there when I moved in, and I never removed it. I don't know to whom it ever belonged. Maybe they thought it was ugly too and left it on purpose. I felt sorry for it. It should have been on some kitchen wall somewhere, or maybe once this room had been a dining room. I wanted to smoke a joint, but I was afraid to put one to my lips. I could have used a cigarette, but I couldn't even smoke one of those. I supposed that was a good thing, but in the grand scheme of things, nothing was good. I couldn't even drink a glass of water without thinking it would kill me.

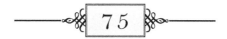

75

"You look so thin." Bunica put her hands up to her mouth.

"I needed to lose some weight."

She was going to make me eat, especially if she thought I looked thin. The smell of the bread was so beautiful, but actually having to put it to my lips terrified me at a level that I had never known, even as a child when I was scared of everything. My brain would play tricks with me again. I squeezed my eyes shut.

"You come sit down." She pushed me at the small of my back to the kitchen table. "I will make us some tea."

Thank God that tea would be coming out of the same teapot. We would drink together, and we would die together. I was so desperate to live. Please just let me live. No one could understand this. How could I tell anyone? Walter knew, sort of. My grandmother, who was angered and intimidated by any strife, any negativity whatsoever, could never help me.

I turned around and watched every single motion when she made that tea. My own grandmother poisoning my tea? Her home-baked bread that I had eaten with her my entire life? But would she put something in one side of the loaf or in just my piece? It wasn't real, I knew this wasn't real, but my brain was fooling me. Again.

I remembered the brilliant man who kept washing his hands. I didn't think I was too thin, but I guess I might start to be too thin if I continued to avoid eating or drinking.

I did a lot of dancing. I chopped up a tomato and swallowed a piece of it. I panicked so badly, I started to dance. I thought if I could keep dancing, I could stay alive. One time I ran. I sprinted. I ate some green salsa out of a jar. I must have forgotten that I couldn't eat. I spit out what was left in my mouth and bolted out the front door of my apartment and ran like a world-class sprinter up the street, then up the hill. I left my front door wide-open, with Marisa and Shelly's ashes in my top drawer. That was very bad. Dancing, running, not eating or drinking might eventually make a person too thin.

"Alice, you have barely touched that bread," Bunica admonished as she put her cup of tea down on her saucer with a clank. I watched her take a bite of her bread. Then I took a smaller bite. "Why are you breathing like that? Are you coming down with something?"

My grandmother equaled food. What the hell was I doing there?

"I just thought I would spend some time with Bunic."

"Sure. You can go to the stand with him." She scoffed. "I do not know why you would want. He is not much company, you know. Don't expect any kind of talk."

I didn't, and I was perfectly fine with that. Maybe that's why I went there.

"So you are not working now?"

"No."

"It is just as well. As an honor student with a degree, you should not be sweeping the streets."

"It wasn't exactly sweeping the streets." I tried to sound as cheerful as possible, even though I was teeming with snotty sarcasm. "I put these little plastic things on this rack, and it moved along to the next person."

"You are an educated girl. You don't need to be working in a factory. It was your grandfather who was most unhappy about that. The men in those places."

She was right about that. I thought about that filth Donovan and how he touched my ass. I never told Bunica. My front teeth tucked behind my lower teeth.

The lady at Greenway told me it would be quiet. Right. The whole idea was for them to stick me in a room somewhere and have me stuff envelopes all day for $3.90 an hour. Undisturbed. With my thoughts. That was fine. It was exactly what I was after, and working on that slow rack would have been perfect, had that monster who ruined everything kept his hands to himself and had not lied about it afterward. No one gave a shit about the fact that I was an honor student or a college graduate. Who cared? Whoop-de-do. I had nothing else to do. It was all I had going for me—numbers. I wasn't creative like Marisa; I wasn't king of the world like Dad. I could tutor more pupils if I wanted, but I was too lazy and sick to market myself, and my quasi agent, Mrs. Tifton, moved to Florida to be closer to Walter's ailing grandmother. Besides, I was tired of all that nonsense anyway. What did it all get me? Not a thing. I was just a grunt. A poor grunt. To hell with it. Fine. Although I did visualize the expression on my mother's face when my grandmother told her I was working in a metal-coating factory over on Beaverton.

"You're grinning from ear to ear. Not listening to a thing I say," my grandmother observed. "At least you like the bread. Good girl."

I was so glad to be eating a little.

76

Bunic declared the following: "You can come to work with me anytime you want."

We marched up the hill like two soldiers heading toward East Mosh. It was really Marsh, but because I pronounced it "mosh" when I was little, it was a habitual pronunciation that stuck. Bunic carried an oversized nylon sack full of food, and I was in charge of these two green thermos-like things filled with coffee. Bunic wore this strange bluish-gray shirt. It was a workman's shirt that had the guy's name stitched into the white oval over the breast pocket, except there was no name stitched into the white oval.

Bean Street wasn't that bustling scene I once remembered as a child. But it was very early in the morning on a weekday, and most normal people were probably still at home getting ready for their jobs in an office somewhere in town. There were still a few people roaming around—a few elderly immigrants, shop owners, delivery drivers, stand owners, some young man who looked like he worked in one of the banks, and the smells of something baking filled the waking skies. At a different time, I would have been starved, fighting my watering taste buds and then losing, succumbing to a slab of breakfast meat, egg yolks, and flour. But nothing could make me hungry anymore. I would be lucky if I could get down a piece of fruit. It was different when I was little and scared all the time. I couldn't swallow my food because I had this lump in my throat. Now, my brain kept playing those nonstop tricks on me, and I was terrified all the time again, but it was different. I didn't want anyone to hurt me, and I didn't want to die anymore.

The best thing was that my grandfather didn't notice and didn't nag, and for that, I was so thankful that I looked up at God and smiled. I could hang around Bunic, hide in his shadow, and immerse myself in his world while trying to forget mine. I may not have been safe, but I felt a little more protected.

It also helped to have Bunic's cronies in and around, particularly Mr. Petran, who must have been close to ninety. He chattered on and on like a gossipy high school girl, waving his arms up in the air above his broken body. But as the street came to life, a few people recognized me as Radu's little granddaughter Alice. I was hugged, poked, squeezed, and kissed so many times, I thought I would catch something. One woman started to cry as she shouted something in Romanian, which I thought were probably glorious embellishments of lovely Alice, but when I heard the names *Lavinia* and *Marisa,* reality caught itself and hid away deep in my mind and in my heart. I soon kept my back turned when people would approach. Lots of them were too observant, had so much sentiment, and seemed to want at the time, more than anything, to shower me with more affection than I was able to receive and give back. My skin reeked of food and cologne, and my lips tasted of someone else's breath. If these people knew me, really knew *me*, knew *us,* there would be no love, no affection, no reminiscing about the past, no empathy. There would be anger, despair, and disbelief. None of this. Everything would be dark and dirty.

I sat on an old barstool with my eyes closed tight. The beating sun finally found its way through the afternoon sky and pounced on me, acting as if it were feeding me something healthy. For a few minutes, I felt like I could relax. I read newspapers in Romanian, understanding a few words here and there, but not as much as I wanted. I always wished I had known more. My grandparents wouldn't communicate with me in English; I don't know why I would ever assume they would communicate with me in Romanian. It was their fighting tongue that captured me, even though it was such a beautiful sound—rolling and romantic, gorgeous and picturesque.

I watched Bunic stack fruit, smoke his nonfilter cigarettes, trade booze, count boxes of stereo equipment in the back of a long white trailer. It looked like it had been backed in by a twelve-year-old. I examined the immigrant boy. He was so young. I wondered if he knew my father. I wondered if he had any pot. Never mind. What would be the point of asking the kid anything of the kind? My lips were so dried, I was afraid to lick them, let alone ingest all my old favorites.

I used to see certain things in this world that gave me such a longing for the love of family and the realness of a unit where there weren't any conditions applied. I had a difficult time defining the feeling to myself, and I was glad I never had to explain it to anyone else. I tried on several occasions to explain it to Dr. Kilburn. I think she probably knew what I was talking about, but I didn't know for sure. Maybe I explained it to Marisa, and she understood me. I'm sure she did in her own way. I certainly saw what was lacking even back then, but those days were over.

The Adlers across the street, the Schulmans, the two men in the mountains. I cringed when I thought of the Withers family. Even Big Barton and Sunny moved the earth to make sure their monster son didn't get convicted of first-degree murder of a minor child, made sure that he didn't have to spend the rest of his pointless existence behind prison walls without the possibility of parole. Had that been me or Marisa? My mother would have told them to throw away the key.

When I looked at people, there were so many other things I longed for, and maybe I had taken my conditional life for granted. Maybe I hadn't appreciated life. I knew I couldn't make the best of what I had, and I briefly thought of Marianne, the lady who conducted church services in jail. Did I move away from God? Did he want me? Was he punishing me? Was he even there? Was there even a God? I didn't know what to believe, but I prayed and prayed a lot since I had gotten sick. When I did, the clock always said 7:00 a.m. I wonder what that meant, if anything at all.

A skinny very attractive woman about in her fifties stopped near Bunic's stand. She had that short stylish wedge-style hair that a lot of women started to wear in the seventies. She had very high cheekbones and a very strong jawline. She was dressed in such a classy fashion, with a tan silk blouse, matching pencil skirt, a string of large fake bauble pearls, and lots of bracelets. Her shoes matched her leather handbag, in which she fished around for what looked like a mint or a cough drop. When she found it, she plunked it into her mouth and carried on walking. As I watched the back of her disappear up the street, I surprised myself with my envy. I would have done anything to be that woman; older, sophisticated, probably been through everything she had been dealt with, but most of all, she could swallow a cough drop. The simple task of being able to swallow a mint, a cough drop. I couldn't do that anymore. Not without the panicking feeling, impending doom, oncoming death.

It never occurred to me that my sister would die right in front of me, murdered in front of my eyes. Maybe if I had been a better sister and a stronger girl, I could have saved her life. Maybe if I hadn't been such a fat glutton, always on the hunt for food, I could eat. Maybe I would be able to laugh more, pretend to complain about ridiculous things like the weather or a bus schedule. Maybe if I had been a better daughter, I would have had better parents—a mother who wasn't so mean and angry and looked at Marisa and me as her enemies. Maybe my father would work less than his hundred hour weeks and care more about his family and what happened to us. Maybe Bunica would cry, and Bunic and I could actually have a conversation. Maybe Aunt Nancy would show up to a funeral for her murdered niece instead of acting like a spoiled and crazy woman while everyone made excuses for her. Maybe Detective Holloway could have made his case against the monster stick like superglue so that we could have gotten that life sentence without parole, and I didn't have to see his parents on TV making a mockery out of my sister's death. If only I had just been someone other than me.

An old lady with a tiny round face shuffled by. I couldn't fathom what she had experienced in her life. What bothered her now, and what did she do about it? I wouldn't suppose it would be so great to be that old, but to have that kind of wisdom might make it all worthwhile. I wondered if I would make it to that age. Would I be an old happy lady who would laugh? Would I ever eat again? I decided to return to my apartment in the morning. I could take about twenty-four hours of Bunica, and then it was time to leave. She was thrilled for the visit but constantly moaned about my weight and "new eating habits." Of course, she made me take two grocery bags full of food back to the house, which would go right upstairs. Maybe I could eat a little—not much, just a little.

The medication had strange side effects, and one of them was wild but vivid dreams. I dreamt one night that I went over to my mother's charming little stone house with the round wooden front door, and before I could knock, she opened it.

"Bunic died," she said with a sadness that I had never heard from her before.

"What? Why? How?" I asked, still standing outside in the frozen winter.

"Heart attack. He had two. He gave Bunica a kiss and then had a second one." Then she handed me a beach bag and said, "Don't forget you have swim class today. Do you want to come in, or shall I just close the door now?"

I woke up with a jump. I knew I had been dreaming even while I was dreaming. I worried that I screamed out loud, so loud that the people in the back of the house could hear me. I walked out toward the hallway and saw the familiar light of the streetlamp outside the front window. I felt myself breathe again as I watched a cat walk with determination in the middle of the sidewalk toward the hill. I shivered in my nightgown as my sweat clung to me and froze.

I shuffled back to my room. Dr. Kilburn would have to give me more of that minor tranquilizer stuff if I could swallow it. I walked like an old man on this purple junk, and it made me hunched over. I couldn't stand up straight as I dragged my feet along. It was another rotten side effect. I dreamt like a crazy person in living color, and I was a psychotic who was afraid to eat when there was nothing to be afraid of. Nothing was helping. But I was happy to know that my grandfather was still alive.

"You're gonna need a whole new engine, miss," the mechanic with the light brown eyes and black hair informed me. "I mean, you can get a second opinion if you want." He wiped his hands on a terry cloth towel. "But my advice is that this is just an old car that's coming to the end of its life."

He was even more handsome than Dr. Paul Keating.

"I know, I know," I said, trying not to blush when I looked at him, but still feeling frustrated and annoyed. "It's over twenty years old. My dad bought it when I was a kid." When my parents were actually married. When my sister was alive.

"And it's gonna cost you plenty. You're probably better off just getting yourself a new car, even a used one. This old Plymouth ain't worth much. It's a gas guzzler, for sure."

"They don't make station wagons like this anymore," I said, feeling nostalgic, my voice barely audible.

He gave me a funny look as if to say, "No, and why would you want one?" He shook his head. "Nope, these are long gone, but if you need room, you know, for dogs and kids and stuff like that, you can get yourself one of those minivans or an aerodynamic wagon."

Oh. So do you think one of those would work when I needed to go sleep at the truck stop after a bad day?

He looked at me and smiled. His teeth were crooked, but they were very white. He had a very nice smile. "You'll get okay gas mileage, not great. But a heck of a lot better than what you got with the Plymouth."

We settled on $208 for my faithful old car and occasional bed. We didn't exactly settle; he told me he couldn't give me any more than that, and the old thing was dead anyway. I virtually coasted into the repair shop.

"What are you going to do with it?" I asked, removing what little of my belongings were still inside the car and placing my hand on the driver's side window as if I were betraying it.

He shrugged. "We might be able to use some of the parts, but not much. It's mostly scrap metal."

"I see."

"Can I give you a lift somewhere?" he asked.

"No thanks, I only live a few blocks away."

He nodded and thanked me, then the handsome mechanic disappeared into the garage.

I turned to leave before I started to cry. It was more than mere frustration, anger, and inconvenience. Why was I crying over this? I knew the reasons. It was greater than just a car. The car was my solace, and there were memories of my murdered sister. I missed her so much.

Quit crying over the car, you crazy wacko.

I sniffed and wiped my nose with the back of my hand like a child. I still had my bike to get around. As I walked to the cross street, I thought I smelled something cooking, possibly burning. I didn't know if it was coming from somebody's kitchen, chimney, or backyard, and then I realized I hadn't eaten anything other than half an apple that morning. I had no appetite.

It was the end of April in Wellton, and it was unusually warm. It almost felt like the beginning of summer with the sun way up high, beating a path right to my shoulders. I always remembered the new spring and how everything was a shade brighter, how my heart was renewed and lifted. But the seasons melted into each other a long time ago, and time either scurried past or paddled by slowly like a rainy and gray weekend where the day had no texture.

A figure of a woman wound its way into my peripheral. It was my aunt walking fast and with determination, as if something was on her mind. She stopped the second time I called out her name and looked around. I noticed how trim she looked. When she recognized me, her face exploded into a huge smile, and she trekked over, the air fluttering through her long streaked blond hair. She hugged me hard.

"Alice, I knew you lived around here. I knew it!"

"What on earth are you doing all the way over here?"

"I'm taking a walk," she said, giggling and moving a strand of hair away from her face.

"Taking a walk? You walked all the way over here from your place? Isn't that like six miles? That's an awfully long way to walk, don't you think?"

"No," she admonished. "It's *not* six miles. It's four-and-a-half miles." Her eyes darted right to my stomach. "Alice! You're skinny. How do you get so thin?"

"I always needed to lose weight." I wanted to change the subject. "Look at how thin *you* are."

She wore faded denim shorts, a bright yellow blouse, matching ankle socks, and white walking sneakers. She looked like a teenager. She hugged me hard again. "Sometimes you can be the nicest person. You're a good niece. Thank you so much."

"How's Dad?" *Sometimes* I can be the nicest person?

She laughed and shook her head. "He's the same. You know Rudy, he's always the same. At the store all the time. You're going to stop by soon? You don't want to, I know. I know. Oh! Mary Jo stopped by to see you! Oh! I forgot to tell you. I forget a lot of things, Alice."

"Mary Jo? When? She's here?" I was shocked.

"I don't know when—"

"Is she still here?"

"I don't know."

"She's probably at the castle."

"I don't know any castle."

"No, no, I'm sorry. She's probably staying at her family home. Is she staying at her family home? Is she staying with her parents? Her mother and father?"

"No, no!" she said, smiling. "No, she's staying at a round building. I don't know where it is. She said she was staying at a round building."

The Wellton Inn downtown.

"I wrote it down on a piece of paper, but I don't know where—"

"No, no, don't worry about it. It's okay. I'll find her. You have done a great job."

If my aunt remembered this, it had to be very recent. Maybe that's why she walked over here. I prayed that Mary Jo was still in town. A part of me doubted it, but it was worth trying to find her.

I took my aunt's hand in mine. It was dry and coarse. She gave me a huge smile again. She almost looked embarrassed. Then her face turned dark and angry.

"What's wrong?"

"She told me her brother is sick." Her eyes darted from side to side, as if she were telling me a secret. "You know, the bad brother, the one who hurt poor Melissa—no, Marisa I mean. She died."

I nodded in resignation. I was about to ask her what she meant by "sick" when she looked down at her feet and shook her head.

Then she said clearly, "Killing his own daughter. He murdered his own daughter. How could a father do that?"

"Stepfather," I said. "He was our stepfather. It doesn't make it any better though."

"No, not stepfather," Nancy said slowly, as if she were explaining something to a child. "Father, father. He was *your* stepfather. *Rudy* was Marisa's stepfather. Oh, it's confusing!"

She put her hands together as if to pray.

"Okay. I can remember now." She looked up at the sky, hands still together. "Your stepfather is Mary Jo's brother. Rudy is Marisa's stepfather. Okay? Rudy is your father. Mary Jo's brother is Barton, right? Barton is Marisa's father. But Marisa died, so she doesn't have a father or a stepfather now."

I didn't notice the car slowing down to pass us as we stood in the middle of the road.

My aunt took my arm and waved to the driver. "Alice, he wants to go by, let's go stand on the sidewalk."

She was mistaken. She had to have been. My aunt didn't know anything.

"You're not making any sense."

She looked hurt by the comment.

"No one except maybe my mother knows who Marisa's father was. My mother married Dad after Marisa was born, then they had me." I was confused and becoming irritated with my aunt. "Marisa had two stepfathers—first Dad, and then there was Barton Withers, Mary Jo's brother. Barton Withers was Marisa's stepfather. He killed her. Why are you saying these things, Nancy?"

She put her head down and began to cry like a little girl. She looked at me as if I had just struck her. I looked around to see if anyone was watching us. Something was wrong.

"Well, me and Mary Jo were friends, and you know, we went to the convent. We were just talking this morning. I didn't know. I didn't know what I was supposed to say—no one tells me things that much. I don't remember things that much."

I could see it now. I was shocked. I felt like getting sick, but there was nothing in my stomach. I turned away from my aunt and retched over a patch of grass between the sidewalk and the street.

"I hope you're not coming down with something."

"Who else knows about this?"

She just stared at me with tears still in her eyes.

"About Marisa's stepfather and her father?"

"I don't know." She shrugged and glanced over at someone getting their mail.

I was losing her attention. She had been delusional like this in the past, and I was hoping this was just one more thing.

"Did you tell Dad about this?"

"No! Rudy works all the time," she said, giggling again. "Rudy doesn't know anything unless it's fish."

The visit from Mary Jo was what brought everything to the surface. My mother and all her scheming. This was obviously part of her grand plan. Did she know she would get a dead daughter out of it?

"Nancy," I begged, "next time you know something important like this, you have to tell me."

The words sounded so absurd. I didn't know what else to say to her.

"Please don't be mad at me."

"I'm not mad at you. I should be apologizing to you for making you cry like that. I'm so sorry."

"Do you promise me you're not—"

"I promise. I promise I am not mad at you." I put my arms around her and held her close. She was doing so well with her job at the hospital, her apartment, and a good combination of medication. I didn't want this latest fiasco to set her back. I was so grateful that she had stopped crying. I was so tired and worn out. "You have done a great job. I am never mad at you."

She reached up and smooshed what was left of my thinning face. Then she kissed me on the nose. "You are always my favorite," she said. "I love you."

"I love you."

She looked at her watch. "I gotta go."

"Now? How are you going to get home?"

She looked at me strangely. "Walk." She turned and powered away. Then she looked back, never breaking her stride. "Tommy's taking me and Scotty to the Lobster House. Then we're going to the movies."

"The Lobster House? Very nice. Don't tell Rudy."

"What do you think, I'm stupid?" she called back and then finally turned around for good.

I watched her fade out of sight.

There were a few times in my life that I was ready for war. The problem was that I was a very weak fighter, and I never won in battle. And I was a coward. The last time I embarked on a bike ride through lush green maples under blue-bird skies was when I went to ask Lisa Jupiter kindly to hold off on her piece about the monster. Poor Lisa. She and her so-called investigative team were so smart, so fresh, so brand-new—everything Wellton commanded for a different style of news—and they couldn't even dig up enough dirt to figure out that the tall handsome guy from the prominent local family who contributed *so much* to our community had murdered his own child.

Couldn't Lisa Jupiter and her staff find Mary Jo? Did they not even remotely have a lead that would find them in the vicinity of my paranoid schizophrenic aunt? I presumed that even if they had everything at their disposal, they probably didn't want it. After all, Lisa Jupiter wanted to spin that story into the most sugary web possible for the Withers family. She was a liar, not a real journalist. A yellow journalist. I wondered how much she really knew. I wondered who else knew. I'm sure if this disco ball ever dropped, her career would be over or at least severely hampered. Her show had already been cancelled, and the Withers interview apparently received very low ratings. She certainly deserved everything that landed on her. People knew who she was and what she did. It was worth getting arrested for pulling out that tuft of hair that was eventually going to fall out anyway.

I was surprised that Mary Jo was staying at the Wellton Inn Plaza Hotel downtown. It was a beautiful hotel, but it wasn't nearly as luxurious as her family estate. The hotel was built in the sixties. When we were little, we would sometimes drive past it with Dad. Marisa always commented on the fact that the building was circular, and the beige drapes in every window were always closed. I argued with her that not every single curtain could be closed, but when we looked at the building as a whole, it looked like they were. Every once in a while, I would pick out a window where the curtains were open, and Marisa would pretend not to see it. Then we would start to argue, and Dad would get irritated.

There was a bar and restaurant on the lobby floor. A man quietly played a black concert grand piano. Much of the ground floor was trimmed in brass, teakwood, and frosted glass. The beige-colored marble floor was so smooth and shiny, I could almost see my reflection. There were small teakwood half doors that partitioned off different areas. It was quite impressive, and I was dying for a drink. The problem was that I was far too frightened to put the glass to my lips and even more terrified to drink. I hadn't had a cigarette in ages, and I needed one. I didn't have time to sit and talk all that fear out to myself. I walked over to the desk, assuming she was still at the hotel.

"Alice?"

I turned around quickly.

Mary Jo Withers McLaughlin stood before me with a tentative look on her face. She smoothed down the front of her skirt even though it didn't need it. She walked toward me slowly, her arms slightly outward, as if she were going to touch me.

"I…I recognized you by your height. Your hair too, it's so long and beautiful." Then she looked at my legs. "You're so thin, Alice."

I shrugged. I wanted and needed to ask right away about my sister's paternity. That was the only thing that was on my mind. My head was burning with questions for this woman, but I couldn't ask. I couldn't because I might have lost her again. This time forever. I had to hold in my hysteria. I had never been this sick. Never had I reached this point. I had to keep my head and pretend as much as I possibly could.

"I needed to lose weight."

"So…so how have you been? I came by the store this morning to see you." She sounded both hopeful and embarrassed.

"Why did it take you so long?" I was accusatory. "I wrote to you a long time ago. Years ago. I apologized to you and Danny, and I meant it."

She nodded quickly. "I know, I know you did."

"Maybe I should have written more than once. But that one time—that was really hard for me. I'm not a very good letter writer. It was hard enough—"

"Alice, I'm sorry, I'm really sorry. Could we go sit down?" She motioned to some tan chairs over by the floor-to-ceiling windows. "Would you like some coffee or tea? Something to eat?"

"No thanks." I followed her through the lobby, and we found a place to sit together. She ordered some kind of French coffee with a lot of whipped cream. It looked delicious, but I didn't dare.

"I was rude to you and Danny at Marisa's memorial service." I didn't tell her it was my first experience with Kiki's tranquilizers, and I was tired, angry, and a little high. "I was still angry at the time, and I blamed your brother's actions on you. It wasn't your fault, Mary Jo."

She smiled when I mentioned Danny's name. Then she put her cup down and held up her other hand. I couldn't wait much longer. "I'm the one who should be apologizing. Please. You mentioned all of this in your letter. Do you think for a second that I don't blame you?

I know exactly what my brother is. I know exactly what this family is. Why do you think I live almost three thousand miles away?"

I said nothing at first. I was shocked. And then I blurted out, "Your brother was my sister's biological father, wasn't he?"

She lifted her square rimless glasses with her thumb and forefinger and massaged the sides of her nose. "Nancy," she said.

"I'm glad you reminded her. I'm glad I just happened to bump into her taking a walk five miles from her home."

"I didn't remind her of anything. We never discussed a word of this. Seeing me after all this time obviously triggered those memories. I could tell by the way she was acting that something like this would happen. It was so long ago. Barton was having one of his parties. I don't remember any one of our friends having wild parties in 1959, but then again, your aunt and I went to the convent. My brother? He was obscene. You already knew that.

"We had just come back from India, all of us, the whole family. It wasn't even ten days later, and my parents were jetting off again to some other part of the world. I can't even remember where now. They were always gone when we were young. Lil was at college where she met her ex-husband. Nancy and I were very good friends who were on the archery team together.

"It was a weekend night. Barton was supposed to be supervising us, what a joke, but instead he relegated me to my room and made me stay there for the entire night. Nancy had come over earlier, and we had a slumber party, you know, trying on clothes and makeup, doing each other's hair, that sort of thing. Meantime, Barton was downstairs throwing a wild bash, and when I say wild, I mean he was smart enough to have as many people in the house as possible without drawing negative attention. Barton was cunning, and he felt the need to constantly impress those around him."

"Your brother is a narcissist," I said, nodding and looking down at my feet. Then I looked up at her straight in the eye. "No, really, I meant to say he's a sociopath."

"I agree. And he was always so arrogant and insecure," she added slowly. "I blame my parents for nurturing this egomania." She looked down and shook her head. "Like I said, we had just returned from India."

She kept saying *India*. Sorrow filled me. I knew something new and truthful was coming. I was so sad for my sister.

"It was an awful trip. My father was in constant business meetings with a supposed member of nobility, an 'Indian prince,' he told us. Of course, Barton had to throw a party and tell everyone about the supposed 'Indian prince' he had just become great friends with, which was complete bull—a total lie. The gentleman was born of some sort of lineage, but he was not the prince of anything. He was an elderly man who treated us like the young people that we were, but was particularly fond of Barton because he was a young man.

"We spent two days at this gentleman's estate. In the end, he and my father decided not to do business together. But Barton embellished his stories and bragged and lied because he is only a shell. Barton is a caricature of himself. He never had a soul. None of them do. Even my sister Lil. The only thing that woman cares about are appearances. She has nearly disowned her own beloved daughter for moving to Brooklyn to go to school and become what she has always wanted to be—a hairstylist. Not a doctor, a hairstylist. And when Danny was born with Down syndrome? That…that lovely young man is nothing but an embarrassment to the Withers family, my family." She took a deep breath and took another sip of her coffee as a single tear fell from her eye.

I suddenly felt guilty for coming.

"Anyway, Nancy and I did everything we could that night to watch the events of this party unfold. We wanted to be a part of the fun too. We listened through the vents, behind closed doors, we spied from the staircases. Then Nancy saw her, your mother. It was all quiet at about five in the morning. We stayed up all night. Then later, we watched the sun come up through the large window in my room. I remember the sky was dark still, but pink and blue at the same time, and we could hear the birds singing loudly. Nancy pointed at the woman who was walking, well, jogging really, away from the house. I will never forget her hair or her long tan jacket. The hair, medium length, just to the back of her neck, very thick and full and auburn, like a bluish red, unusually beautiful. Nancy knew it was Lavinia right away."

"How?" I was shocked as I listened to Mary Jo talk about the Indian prince who would eventually murder my sister. "Nancy didn't know my mother, did she?"

She nodded. "She did because she spotted her and said, 'That's Lavinia Ionescu.' Apparently, your dad was smitten with her."

"My father was a part of this too." I was sure of it. The morning of Marisa's memorial service. We sat on the porch. He lied to me—he almost slipped up. He'd actually slipped up a few times. I remembered the time they were all arguing at my grandparents' house. That was what they were arguing about. That was why my grandfather wanted me to go for a walk with him and Helena. My grandmother was so worried.

"I don't know your father. I know I never breathed a word of this to anyone. Maybe Nancy said something, but I—"

"She didn't. Nancy really doesn't have a memory. Her way of letting me know that you stopped by this morning was to take a walk over to my apartment. But she never went to my apartment. I just happened to see her on the street. She said she was 'taking a walk.' This is what Nancy does. Nancy didn't say a word about this. She mentioned it in passing, and I confronted the poor woman and upset her."

Mary Jo looked upset as she sighed. "Nancy became very ill in her early twenties." She looked down at her hands. "I've only seen her a couple of times over the past two decades."

"You're not exactly very good at keeping in touch."

"I know. I'm sorry. My mother is an incredibly self-centered woman. They all are. I've tried to distance myself from this place. And in a way, I've taken it out on you too. I'm sorry. But I was so glad to see Nancy. She looks wonderful. But I…I couldn't take it. I just had to flee, Alice, for the safety of my marriage and my sons."

"I understand that." My mother. How could she be so cruel? How could she do something like this and then lie about it for all these years? "Let me ask you this: does your brother know he murdered his own flesh and blood?"

"Yes"—she nodded—"he does now. I told him after he made his deal with Martin Giles. I could barely get near him. He was surrounded by his lawyers and my parents. Even the press seemed to be able to get closer to him than his own sister. It didn't look like he even believed me, but shortly after our visit, he had divorce papers drawn up. And when I watched that horrible interview with Lisa Jupiter—"

"You watched that?"

"Yes, but for different reasons…" Her voice trailed off, and I stopped listening. I didn't want to know what her reasons were.

I watched other people in the lobby and tried to listen to their conversations.

"The ratings for that show were supposedly deplorable," she carried on. I didn't care whether they were or not. "I think that was the end of her sensational documentary career. I don't even think she's in Wellton anymore."

"Your brother is sick? With what?"

"He has intestinal cancer. He is suffering greatly, and I have a feeling that his illness has been exacerbated by guilt."

"Guilt? You're kidding, right? He doesn't feel any guilt! He just doesn't like being locked up. He's probably just pissed off because he killed a Withers. He's evil, and I don't have an iota of sympathy for him."

"I don't expect you to have any sympathy for him. He's exactly where he belongs." She thought for a time. "I failed you too, Alice. Typical of a Withers, I guess."

"Just because you didn't write back, that's not failing—"

"No, that's not what I mean. You came to me. You needed help, and you were so young. I don't even know how much you realized that you needed help. And there I sat. With all the cards. I knew about your mother, I knew about Marisa, I knew she was hurting you and that Marisa was being brutalized, and I was too much of a coward to do anything to try and stop it. I let you down, and if it weren't for me… I'm sorry. I'm so, so sorry about Marisa. I could have saved her from my brother. I should have saved her from my brother. Oh god."

I should have saved her from your brother.

471

I bit my lower lip as Mary Jo's eyes filled with tears. She grabbed a cocktail napkin and quickly looked away, then our eyes met.

"I don't want you to blame yourself. You didn't kill anyone," I said.

"I know, I know, but—"

"Just listen for a minute," I said, and she quieted down quickly. "I've tried my whole life to get people to come around to my way of thinking. It doesn't work. It never works. I shouldn't have burdened you with my thoughts. I was so worried and scared after I confided in you. It frightened me for the longest time and made me crazy. I mean, come on, what were you going to do? Stop the wedding?"

I felt as though I couldn't say one more thing about it. I was so exhausted. But then something occurred to me, and I was able to push out one more thought.

"Now I have another answer."

"For?"

"My sister made her Holy Communion. She was 100 percent Roman Catholic like you. I'm not. She was baptized in the Roman Catholic Church. I wasn't. No need for anything further. By that time, my mother was working toward getting everything she ever wanted."

We sat in silence. A tall thin black man was changing a tablecloth. A blond woman in a gray pantsuit said something to him, and they both laughed. I would have done anything to exchange lives with either one of them. Just to be normal.

"How long are you staying?"

"I'll be leaving next Monday. I wanted to see you and Helena. And you know, I haven't been very good at keeping in touch. So do you see her often? Helena, I mean?"

"No. Not anymore."

"Why?" she asked cautiously. By the way she looked at me, she had to have understood why.

"I don't want any more sisters." I stood up. "I have to go."

She stood up, and we hugged.

"Alice." She looked at me sadly. "I am so glad you came."

"Thank you. I am too." I turned and walked off. I wasn't as angry with her as I thought I would be. But I didn't have anything more to say, and I didn't want to listen anymore. To anyone. It was my mother that I wanted to spit on, but I didn't have that kind of energy. I was so tired, but I couldn't sleep. I couldn't eat, and I was past hunger. I used to be thirsty, but I was past that too now.

Thanks to my little purple pill, I shuffled through the lobby and toward the main front door. I slumped over, and my back hurt. It was difficult to stand up straight, and when I tried, I felt as though people were watching and evaluating me as if I were on display. All I wanted to do was get out of the building, but I couldn't move fast enough. It was like a dream. My hair was getting too long, and I thought about getting it whacked off. Maybe I would go and see a movie.

Then I noticed there was a man walking behind me. He was a little taller than I was with a wiry build. He had thick sandy blond hair that fell to his jawline. His facial features were fine and structured. He wore a white dress shirt, gray pants, and a black belt matching his black shoes. He would have been very handsome had he not been up to something. What the hell did he think he was doing, and why was he right behind me? When I looked back toward the other end of the large lobby, I could no longer see Mary Jo past all the ornamental woodwork. Maybe she went up to her room, or maybe she was still sitting in her plush tan club chair, but it was too far away and out of my line of vision. I was panicking. I was so afraid that I forgot where I was going. I knew what that man behind me was about to do as I stopped in front of a mural by the front door on a curved part of the wall. It was a painting of the Battle of Oriskany in New York State during the Revolutionary War. It was supposedly the bloodiest battle of all.

I whipped around quickly in hopes of catching the man before he injected me with a syringe full of cyanide. I glared at his hands and studied them quickly to see just how fast he could put his murder weapon back in his pocket without my catching him. Rotten, sly killer.

But the tall handsome man with the invisible syringe only nodded and smiled, then gestured like a gentleman for me to walk ahead of him so he could hold open the door for me. I knew he wasn't going to try to kill me, and I knew that he had no intentions of hurting me. He was just a man. The two struggling ideas were becoming harder and harder to distinguish as my brain continued to ruin me. No amount of medication could help. No combination of medication was helping, and changing to different medications wasn't helping either. I was decompensating, and I was far over my probationary period. I was still seeing Dr. Kilburn because I was a crazy sick person who was in desperate need of help that I could not find. I was dying. Eventually, I would starve myself to death because I had no other choice.

It took an inordinate amount of strength to run toward my bike, and after fumbling in frustration, I was finally able to unlock it and whisk away. I could feel cool air on my wet snotty face. I was surprised I had any fluids left in my body since I couldn't even take a sip of water, soda, or orange juice unless I was choking down a psychotropic pill that I had to spend several minutes talking myself into swallowing. Then I would do my ritual dance around the room just to let myself know that I was still alive, still taking in air and letting it back out again.

I should have been thrilled to learn about the monster's impending death from a painful and terminal illness, but the fact that even that couldn't give me a wisp of joy was a clue that I knew I was losing my functioning in a way that was beyond reality. There were few things more frightening than coming to the realization that you're breaking away from the real world. Seeing my sister die was one of them, and knowing that a monster was milling around downstairs while I was upstairs hiding like a coward was another. Spending a perfectly good weekend in jail was harrowing, but I most likely learned my lesson from that.

Remembering the days when my aunt had to turn all the clocks off was dreadful for Marisa and me particularly because we would be alone with her and didn't know how to help her. Such pieces were the essence of my life, but there was a particular horror that went hand in hand with breaking from reality and actually knowing that I was losing functioning as a human being. Regardless of any of the so-called accomplishments I made in my young life, nothing mattered if I was crazy. Nothing. Nothing meant anything after a psychiatric break.

I was able to find my way home. The sun was lower in the sky. I pushed the front door open and shuffled across the old black-and-white linoleum floor. It was so quiet, I wasn't sure if anyone was even home. Normally, I would hear Miranda's television or some other movement, but it was deadly quiet except for the humming of the refrigerator. I was glad.

I turned the key into my lock and walked as best as I could into my kitchen, the twilight streaming from the window above the sink. I closed the blinds. The room was tidy and dark. I doddered into the bedroom, which was already dark, exactly the way I always liked it. Everything was picked up, put away, and in order. I went over to the dresser and opened the top drawer. I didn't want to have to do it, but I found I had no other option. I had to look, check, and make sure that everything was safe. I picked up the little square box with the flowers and carefully opened the top. I kissed the bindle of Shelly's pale yellow ashes. I picked up what remained of my sister and did the same. I looked at the alarm clock next to the bed and realized that it was nearly forty-five minutes later when I was able to finally convince myself that the ashes were back in their cases and sacks, the covers were on, and the strings were pulled closed. Everything was safe and tucked away neatly in the right-hand corner of the top drawer in my dresser, and all was covered up and perfectly silent. I was very sick. I knew this with the last drop of rationality I had lurking around my mind.

After packing a small bag, I had to force myself out of my bedroom. My brain told me in a clear bold thought, *If you go back into that bedroom and check those ashes one more time, you will suddenly die. That will be certain. You will lie on your kitchen floor gasping for air, and your death will be slow, heinous, and filled with terror. You will suffer in pain. You will be alone, and no one will hear you or be able to save you.*

My brain informed me of this fate over and over again with each suggestion more and more gruesome until finally, I was lying on top of a sea of dead birds with huge heads, and all my ashes had been blown away forever. I stuck my finger in my ear, but that no longer calmed me down. I slapped the side of my head several times, and that seemed to make the thoughts subside for a little while, but they just found their way back into my mind again.

I went outside, unlocked my bike, and brought it inside, and I stood it next to the kitchen counter. I already had the surprising forethought to pay Chick eight weeks of rent in advance, and all my utility bills were paid through the next month. I was the most organized psycho in the history of psychopathology, but I would need a job as soon as I was well. And I knew that one day I would be well again. I had to be. Or I would die.

Maybe again this was the God that Preacher Marianne was talking about. I had moved away from him. But somewhere there was a little perfect beam of light that lifted me up just enough for me to think clearly, even if it was for a few minutes one day and maybe a minute the day before.

You're not your aunt Nancy. You're not paranoid. You're irrational. You know *you're not losing your mind. Aunt Nancy didn't know when she stopped functioning. You need rest and intense medication to make you well again. When Nancy was your age, she truly believed there was someone on the roof trying to get into her bedroom window and that he had already drilled a hole in her head so that he could place his thoughts into her brain. You are irrational. You are not paranoid. There's a difference. There's a difference. There's a difference.*

I sat at the kitchen table and dialed the number. He picked up on the first ring.

"Can you help me?"

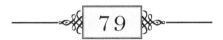

79

It was a tiny windowless peach-colored room, more like a closet.

"Are you going to give me electric shock therapy?" In that very second I believed that someone would be doing that to me soon. I may have not realized it at the moment, but I was no longer irrational, I was paranoid.

The intake coordinator gave me a look and then went on to discuss a problem she was having with her word processor with some equally disinterested coworker.

I sobbed when I walked down the hallway to Adult Ward B. The male nurse was pleasant as he tried to offer me trite words of encouragement, but it was Detective Holloway who put his huge arm around my shoulder and promised me that everything would turn out better than before. He promised me that I didn't have to be scared and that I was finally on the road to recovery. He also told me how proud he was of me for getting myself organized, deciding that I needed help, and realizing that I couldn't do it anymore on my own. We walked slowly toward the ward, and I cried so hard that all I could see in front of me were dark colors and unusual shapes.

I reminded Detective Holloway that I was nothing but organized as the thought sprouted in the back of my mind as to how I was going to pay for this place. I knew something about an insurance plan that my father had for the store, but I never paid any attention to it. And this place was far more upscale than the state shithole my aunt had been in and out of over the years. Detective Holloway simply said that the medical director, Dr. Herbert Ling, was a good friend of his, and he wouldn't let anyone who genuinely needed help bankrupt themselves.

I thought of my father. He knew everyone, and everyone knew him, probably even Dr. Ling. I never acquired that type of social skill and probably never would. I was isolated and needed to be taken care of. Detective Holloway gave me his word that he would be back the next day to see me, and just before I entered the locked ward with the nurse, I turned to see him walking back up the corridor. I was just about to ask him to please feed Shelly, and in that very instant, I remembered. Shelly had been dead for years.

I felt a warm gush of peace and relief run through me. The door clicked shut behind us. There was no turning back. There were several minutes of chaos and unstructured time before I was led to my room. I sat in a chair next to the nurses' station and adjacent to a huge area with the setup of a living room that included a television, stereo, and grand piano on the other side by the windows. All the furniture and the carpet were mauve, gray and peach, the popular colors of the eighties.

A few of the patients descended upon me at once. A young-ish-looking man with an orange T-shirt and jeans and shoulder-length brown hair approached. He had a bad speech impediment, and I found it very hard to understand him at first. He handed me a plastic carton.

"Wan thom zoos?" he asked, and I looked up at him for a moment, then I registered that he was offering me some apple juice.

I lost it. The floodgates not only opened, they exploded. My sobbing was so intense, I felt as though I was roaring in despair. Suddenly, I felt such incredible regret for allowing Detective Holloway to lock me up in this swanky nuthouse. What had I done? The man-child who had offered me the apple juice looked at me like I had just slapped him hard across the face.

"Oh, oh, oh, I'm thorry. I'm…I'm thorry."

I wasn't able to respond to him, but another female patient appeared to come to my rescue. "It's okay, Jimmy, she's not angry with you. It's just her first night here. She's scared. You can't always go up to people like that, you know."

He nodded like a boy, and the masses backed off.

"I'm Robyn." The woman sat down next to me and shook my hand.

"Alice."

"Why don't I show you around? Everyone is really nice here. Maybe if you take a little walk, it might take your mind off things."

I watched this pretty woman who was about my age with the olive complexion, dark brown eyes, and long chocolate brown hair. A mental patient. I was one of them now. Robyn decided this was the best time to give me a tour. I had not been "officially processed" by the intake nurse, and so she thought it would be great to take advantage of this opportunity. The girl was very nice, very caring and nurturing, but I didn't feel like making any friends. I never remembered a time when I was keen on making friends, and one thing was for sure—I didn't feel like making any on Adult Ward B. But this Robyn person had a way of forcing her kindness on me, and I was too tired and vulnerable to resist.

She took my arm, and we walked. She introduced me to a short pudgy woman with a round soft face. I immediately noticed her beautiful skin and naturally rosy cheeks. Her blond hair was perfectly feathered and fluffy all over. She held out her hand, shook mine, and promptly showed me a ping-pong table. I lost it again.

"God, she's in bad shape." Puffy blond looked disappointed. "Looks like I upset her more. I don't think she wants to take your tour, Robyn."

"Or maybe she doesn't want to be introduced to a ping-pong table, Susan. Can't everyone just go easy on her?"

I was systematically offending people one by one, but I felt so out of control by the utter despair and regret that rocked my body.

Finally, I was led down a long corridor to my room while a passing nurse haphazardly told me she would be in just a minute to do my intake. I was surprised to see how relaxed and laid-back everyone appeared to be. Could have been drugs. Robyn walked by my side every inch of the way as we walked into the room where I would be living in until whenever. This was not what I remembered as a kid in the waiting area when my father went to see Aunt Nancy. That awful place had bright linoleum floors, brown plastic chairs, and glass with the hole in the middle for some nasty staff member to sit behind. The exterior looked like a huge ugly block of concrete, like a prison.

My room had two beds, hospital beds, deep dark orange wall-to-wall carpet, two desks with lamps, a couple of average wooden chairs, and a private bathroom with a stand-up shower. The fact that it appeared to be comfortable provided little comfort to me. I knew that it could have been much worse, but my mind had not been functioning rationally for a long time, and I was too terrified and exhausted to be working out "grass is greener" assessments.

My roommate Bernadette appeared. She was fifty-seven years old and weighed at least three hundred pounds at about the height of five feet three inches. She carried around an oxygen tank with her. The look on her face was a mixture of surprise and happiness when she saw me. There was a softness to her, and she was gentle and calm. She was hospitalized for major depression. She had not been able to get out of bed for over a year. Robyn attempted suicide by taking an overdose of sleeping pills and had to have her stomach pumped at the hospital.

"I can't eat," I said finally.

"You're anorexic?"

I shook my head. "No, it's not that. I'm—I just have this really bad fear that someone is trying to poison me. I know, it sounds crazy."

Neither of the two women flinched. It was as if they had heard everything.

"Who do you think is poisoning you?" Bernadette asked as she sat on her bed.

I shrugged. "Well, no one really, I guess. It's just that I feel like everything I'm about to put in my mouth, like food or drink, medicine, a cigarette—all of it is contaminated with something that could kill me quickly and aggressively. And there would be nothing I could do. No antidote."

I could hear my voice trailing off. I felt ridiculous.

"Yeah, that's just your mind," Robyn said in such a tone that something inside me shifted. "Did you eat anything today?"

"I had half a pear."

"You're going to have to eat more than that," she said, "because before you go to sleep tonight, you're probably going to get meds, and if you have an empty stomach, they're going to tear it right up.

There's a big basket of cheese and peanut butter crackers up there. You should really eat some first."

"Can you help me?" As soon as I asked the question, I thought for sure I would need to follow up with an explanation as to what I needed help with.

"Yeah, sure! We'll go up there with you."

"Of course. That's not a problem."

A skinny woman with very short silvery hair, a red polo shirt, and blue jeans stood in the doorway. Robyn stood up as I remained sitting on my bed. The woman looked at Bernadette. "Bernadette, I hate to have to kick you out of your own room, but we have to do an intake."

Bernadette laboriously rose from her bed and dragged her tank behind her. We waited almost a minute for her to leave the room. Then she finally closed the large hospital door behind her.

"I'm sorry," I said as she left.

"You don't have to apologize to her," skinny woman quipped. I could tell right away that she was going to be difficult. This was not the time for me to be surrounded by difficult hospital staff. But did I have a choice? I felt desperation and fear rise up in my stomach. I knew this was one ass I was going to have to kiss.

She clanked her clipboard down and sat at the desk. She sighed and sprung upward. "We don't *need* the door closed, Bernadette. I just need *you* to go somewhere else." Skinny woman sat back down at the desk and looked me over. She slapped the fabric on the seat of the chair next to her three times. "Come sit down, Ms. Buchner. This shouldn't take very long."

I doggedly walked the few feet to skinny woman with the clipboard and sat down, exactly as I was told to do. She asked me to confirm my birthdate, asked a series of general health questions and questions about my background, when she paused at something and then glared up at me. She had small tired black eyes. "How tall are you?"

"Five eleven."

"You're way too skinny. Do you know how much you weigh?"

I shook my head.

She kept writing. "We'll get your weight in a minute."

"Are you a nurse?"

"Ah—yeah." She looked at me like I was an idiot.

"What's your name?" She never did formally introduce herself to me.

She never took her beady black eyes off me. "Reardon."

I lifted my hands up to the side of my face. I wasn't used to asking for help. "Okay. Hmm. Reardon." I took a deep breath.

"What?"

"Can you help—can you stay with me while I take my medication?" I felt so foolish. Detective Holloway said something about the staff being supportive. After meeting Reardon, I wasn't so sure.

Her nose crinkled up like a weasel's. I knew it was a mistake to ask. Maybe Robyn and Bernadette would keep their word. I doubted it.

"I don't know what you're talking about. I don't have anything to do with medications. That's Billie's job. Any allergies to any medications while we're on the subject?"

"Codeine." I thought of all the drugs I had ingested over the years. I never could tolerate that one.

"Does it upset your stomach?" How did she know? "You're not allergic. That's a common side effect." She smiled for the first time, even if it was for a half a second. Pretty good answer for someone who had nothing to do with medications. "You don't really want to be here, do you?" she sat back and asked with a sadistic glint in her eye.

"I don't know." I hadn't realized I had given her that impression. I was so tired. Detective Holloway told me that this wasn't a jail. I wanted to go home. "I thought it was a good idea, but now, I'm not so sure."

"So you don't think you need to be here."

"No, I don't think so." But I must have known, otherwise, I wouldn't have called Detective Holloway. "But I also know that I can leave if I want. I can leave tomorrow if I want."

She leaned forward. Those tiny soulless eyes bore holes into my face. "Oh, you can leave anytime you want, but it would be against medical advice. And if your doctor thinks you're a danger to yourself or anyone else, he can turn around and commit you. Then you won't be going anywhere until the doctor discharges you."

I didn't know what game Nurse Reardon was trying to play, but she was clearly in the wrong line of work. I looked at her and did everything in my power to keep that tiny smile from perching on my face. She glared back at me. It was a good thing for both of us that I refused to go back to jail and had enough self-control left in me, or I probably would have had my hands around her throat. Thank God I was spent from starvation and thirst.

Like me, she was angry and burned out with life, most likely from her job. Her tactics reminded me of my mother's. She was a habitual tormentor who liked to scare people into thinking a certain way. I lowered my eyes and didn't meet her gaze again. I couldn't win, but I knew how to survive a person like her. I would let her think she was in charge and that I was awestruck by her, when all along in my mind, she was just one more in a long queue of monsters.

Nurse Reardon continued to write about a minute's worth of more nonsense before she threw her pen down on the desk. "All right, skinny Minnie. Let's go get your weight."

She moved swiftly down the corridor as I tried to keep up. I followed her into a little examination room behind the main desk, and she ushered me onto a scale. "Five foot eleven. One hundred and two pounds. And that's *with* your clothes and shoes on. Very, very thin for a tall girl like you. I'm sure your doctor will put you on some form of liquid nutrition because, baby, you need it."

She abruptly opened the door and motioned for me to leave.

"Very good. We're done here, Ms. Buchner. Thank you."

"Thanks," I said and left the room as Nurse Reardon held the door for me.

I sat on my hospital bed. What the hell was I thinking? What have I done? I regretted my decision to check myself into this place almost as much as I regretted some other things in my life. Like not stabbing the monster when he had hold of my sister when there was a whole set of knives within my view. Thoughts raced through my head, whipped through my mind, round and round. There was no end point. I was terrified again and very lonely.

My sadness escalated when I saw a middle-aged man struggling to make his way down the corridor. "I'm goin' home in the morning, I'm goin' home in the morning," he sang gleefully. He sounded infantile and droll.

Upon my arrival, he was one of the patients who descended upon me at once and was happy and eager to shake my hand, which was something I was trying to avoid. I could see that he was thrilled about something, and then I knew what that something was: he was going home in the morning. His dark eyes were suspicious, wild, and in them they told me that he would be back. Hopefully, that would be long after I left.

Bernadette eventually waddled back into our shared room, dragging her oxygen tank alongside her. "Usually I just turn this thing on at night, but it's been a rough day for me," the well-spoken morbidly overweight woman said. She placed a heavy hand over her mouth and coughed.

"Do you want to come and sit down?" I asked in the friendliest voice I could summon. I felt threatened in this place, and I knew I needed to make friends. It felt worse than jail because of the degree to which my mental illness had deteriorated.

She finally plopped herself down in the chair next to me and took hold of my hand. She had long fingernails that she filed but didn't polish. I sat and stared at her hand for a long time. I had no idea why I began to talk, but once I started, I couldn't stop myself. My voice had its own mind. I hoped that my voice's mind was working better than the mind in my head, but I doubted that to be true.

"I made a terrible mistake," I said. "I should not have signed myself into this place. Fuck. I'm running out of money, and I need to find a job. I just wish I could make some phone calls."

"There's a phone out in the hall down by the nurses' desk. I saw a couple of people waiting for it though. I don't get on it much. Everyone seems to want to eavesdrop on what you're saying."

"That's just great."

"Do you have any family? That big black chubby man. He's not your dad or anything? Adoptive maybe? He's a cop."

I continued to watch her hand clutch mine. Our fingers were intertwined as if we were lovers. I caught my breath. "Ah, hmm, no. He's not my father. That's Detective Holloway. How did you know he was a cop?"

She raised her eyebrows. "He looks like one."

"Really? What does a cop look like?"

"Official. And he had on those black shoes with the rubber soles in case he has to run fast."

I couldn't imagine.

"Do you have his phone number?"

"Whose?"

"The cop's."

"Detective Holloway's? Yeah, I have his phone number."

"Maybe you can call him, and he can come back here and get you out. If you want to go home, that is."

I looked at the clock on the wall. It was ten past eleven at night.

Oh my god.

I looked at Bernadette's fingernails. They were very strong for fingernails. Thoughts and faces were speeding through my head. I remembered a girl named Tammy from elementary school. She wore her hair in a shag—bowl on top and the fringe hanging down only in the back. Quite ahead of herself for an elementary schoolgirl. She had a little brother. It was the first time in over a decade I had thought about her. There was no reason to think about her. We were not friends, yet her image in my mind was astonishingly clear.

"Are you okay?"

"I'm afraid if I call him, I'll wake him up." Why did I call him in the first place?

Now he knows. What have I done? I looked back at Bernadette's hand. I wanted to pull mine back. I watched hers intently. Bernadette was planning to rape me. Here I was sitting next to this strange woman, and I was holding her hand. How many minutes have passed since I managed to allow some of my deepest fears to take a strangle hold of me? And I was there, holding her hand. I could have choked on my foolishness and dependency. How did I let this happen? There was so much silent terror brewing inside me, I wondered if I would simply fall over and die right on the plush carpet in front of me. Death not from poison, not from murder or starvation or thirst, but from hot, bubbling fear that my body could no longer hold.

I didn't die though. I never died. I was alive, and I had to stick around, and I had to think. I had to strategize and kiss as many asses as I had to survive in this place—Nurse Reardon, that wild-eyed guy who was going home in the morning, Jimmy, and now Bernadette, my roommate with the oxygen tank. I would watch her. She was going to rape me, stick her fat fingers with those long finger-nails in my vagina where *nothing*, not even a tampon, had ever been. She would force me to suck those enormous flabby breasts. I would watch her all night if I had to. She was four times my size in weight, but I was four times taller and far wirier. I just didn't have much strength to fight her off.

Go for the nose. She's planning on raping you.

Another nurse appeared in the doorway. She wore a white hip-length lab coat, matching white pants, and ugly white old lady shoes. She was elderly, her hair was bleached blond, and she wore big brown glasses. I noticed her long very thin legs.

She glanced down at a clipboard. "Alice Buchner, it's time for your medication."

Bernadette looked at me with big eyes. "I'm going to have to take my hand back now, Alice."

I didn't look back at her at first. I didn't want her to get the upper hand when she noticed my acid stare.

"Come on, Alice." Robyn trotted into the room, nearly shoving Old Nurse Blondie out of the way. "Meds. We're gonna sit with you, remember?"

Old Nurse Blondie put her hand up in protest and snapped, "I'm only interested in Alice Buchner, ladies."

"We know, Billie. We're just going to give her support while she swallows her pills. She's having a hard time eating, you know. And drinking." Robyn asserted herself graciously.

Billie shook her head. "Whatever." She lightly touched my shoulder as she ushered me to the dispensary. I had no idea what I was taking. I counted four pills in a tiny paper cup. I swallowed them easily with water.

"Here." Robyn handed me a pack of cheese crackers. "If all you had this morning was half a pear, then you should really eat these, otherwise, those pills are going to rip your stomach apart."

Robyn, Bernadette, and I sat down on a plush sofa in the middle of the giant room. There weren't a lot of people around, probably since it was close to midnight. I ripped open the plastic package of crackers and examined Bernadette's new white sneakers under the fluorescent lights. She smiled at me, and I noticed a little sweaty sheen on her face. She was breathing heavily. Suddenly, I felt terrible for thinking she would rape me later and the revenge I would perpetrate on her had she succeeded. She could barely make it down the hallway, yet she trekked along after me so that she could sit with me as I contemplated swallowing medicine, water, and crackers. Both had kept their word.

Dr. Kilburn told me once that hospitals would include a lot of round-the-clock support from caregivers. So far, I met two caregivers who appeared to be overworked, hostile, and just plain burned out.

I thought briefly about that prison-like bedlam that Aunt Nancy frequented before her medication was managed in a more efficient way. Two strange women who knew nothing about me—suicidal, depressed, fellow mentally unstable women—took the time at midnight to sit with me because I was too terrified to even swallow. I ate the crackers without a problem. I doubted the medication worked that quickly. I even took the medication itself and drank all the water with ease. It was the first time in months I didn't have to choke down something for fear that I would drop dead within the minute.

"You did a great job," Robyn said, her voice full of encouragement. "You just ate the entire pack of crackers."

"And you took your pills," Bernadette said.

A feeling of contentment and exhaustion washed over me.

"If you do that every day, you'll be fine in no time," Bernadette continued. "Someone like you won't be here for long. You're just going through a really hard time. It probably won't last."

But it's lasted for years, this "really hard time." Someone like me. Somehow I gave off some sort of impression that I was special each time I landed in an unfavorable situation, and I was vastly unaware of where that vibe was coming from. She knew nothing about my life, and I wanted to keep it that way. We sat for a while and didn't say a whole lot.

I believe it was the first night of total uninterrupted sleep I had gotten in a very long time. A cocktail of psychotropics, antidepressants, and minor tranquilizers made it impossible to be my normal crazed self. I had always considered myself to be a fairly experienced drug addict, and I was happy to be receiving the tranquilizers. They fed right into my needs. I had bought, used, and stolen plenty of pills, but these were a whole new category. I drank myself into an oblivion most weekends, smoked marijuana most days, and used cocaine as often as I could afford to. I had seen people lose control, *really* lose control. Once I saw some guy outside a party hanging on to a streetlamp, stretching his body way out behind him and screaming to God so loud, it made me think of the monster, and I had to stick both fingers in my ears and run back to my apartment. I didn't like to go to college parties much after that, and I didn't want to lose control of myself any more than I had already had.

These drugs were a whole new experience. I wasn't exactly blacked out, but I was floating around in some unknown gray area where I knew where I was but most likely didn't want to be where I was. I just couldn't do anything about it but enjoy the ride. And eventually, I found myself not even caring. I was merely going along, doing what I was told and not really remembering the details.

Bernadette had not raped me during my first night in the hospital. If she had, I might have not known it with all the sedation, but I felt strongly that she had not. When I peered at the triple vision of her in the morning, she was covered head to toe in pink sleepwear like an over-the-top Easter egg flanked with her oxygen equipment, yet still snoring loudly.

I was comfortable in my mind that I had not been raped, and just because of that, I was able to relax. To my surprise, I was also able to eat breakfast without a single problem exactly like the night before when I ate the cheese crackers and took my new medication for the first time. I was an A patient. I didn't know what the *A* stood for, but I had to have direct supervision anytime I left the locked ward.

I don't know how I got to the dining hall; presumably I walked. Robyn was with me. There was also a staff member present, but I didn't know who was who. What I did know was that I amazed myself by eating. *Amazed* wasn't the right word because I couldn't think of the right word. I couldn't understand how twenty-four hours ago, I had been terrified of my poisoned sliced pear, and the next day, I was eating large portions of scrambled eggs, bacon, sausage links, home fries, and bagels slathered with butter. I also drank what seemed to amount to a gallon of orange juice. Despite the amount of food I was consuming, Nurse Billie at the dispensary had orders to give me a canned milkshake that was a type of food supplement for anorexics. I drank it. I did what I was told, and I didn't argue. I wanted to get well, and I wanted to go home.

That morning, I briefly talked to the staff social worker. I wished at first that I could remember her name because she was so gentle and compassionate and very kind to me, unlike that awful Nurse Reardon. Jennifer or Jessica. I was so unfocused, and as hard as I tried to come across as my intellectual self, I knew it was the drugs talking, and the more of an attempt I made, the more I came across sounding like a babbling fool. I only hoped that Jennifer or Jessica or whatever her name was understood. And so I rattled off anyway, as loose and as tangential as any crazy person could be. "I wasn't eating. I was scared to eat so I. I stopped. But today. Today, I did eat. I ate breakfast."

"But you weren't too happy about it, were you?" Jennifer or Jessica asked.

I shook my head, but that was a lie. I *was* happy about eating all that food. It was the greatest accomplishment of my life as of late, but I was too unsure about how to discuss any of that with her. She was so sweet, and I didn't know how to disagree. I was too tired to explain. I also didn't know how to begin. I didn't know where that terror came from and why it all happened. All I knew was that it all started when I picked up my first prescription at the pharmacy.

As she spoke, I watched her carefully. I attributed that to the medication. She was chubby, like I used to be, but much shorter. She had straight brown hair that fell to her shoulders, and part of it was perfectly pulled back with a barrette. Her skin was a creamy white smattered with tiny freckles everywhere. She wore funny lavender harem pants and high-tops. I could tell she was smart, empathetic, and I wondered what she thought of Reardon.

As it turned out, her name was Gemma, and she could teach Reardon a thing or two. That was for sure. *And* I found out Reardon was her last name. Her first name was Colleen, but she went by her last name. What a bitch.

Meeting Gemma that first morning helped me to relax even more, if that was possible, and I understood that I could easily smile at and brush off Reardon and the snotty dispensary nurses with little effort. I also knew for certainty that Bernadette would not be raping me in our room. Although I think I already knew that earlier after I saw her sleeping with her can. When you go to jail, you get thrown into a concrete cell and left there. When you are hospitalized, for the first day or two, people are tripping over you and each other as you remain dazed and listless in their effort to organize you into groups, sessions, classes, and whatever they have planned for your daily life. I still had no idea how I was going to pay for all of it.

I suddenly and without warning found myself in the same room Reardon dragged me into on the first night and told me that at five feet eleven inches tall, I weighed 102 pounds with my clothes on. A man in his mid to late fifties with thick silver wavy hair held court before me. His face was silken, and he was impeccably dressed. He wore a dark suit, pink shirt, dark tie, and dark shoes. Everything matched, and it was perfection. He even smelled perfect. He looked like he had tumbled out of a men's fashion magazine. His voice was loud. I may have been imagining that there was another door to the room and that people were coming in and out.

He introduced himself as a clinical psychologist, and I wasn't sure if he kept turning around and talking to and giggling with the people who kept coming in and out of the room. There were lots of them, presumably staff members, but I didn't recognize any of them, and I wasn't clear what was real and what wasn't real with these people and this second door. What kind of drugs had they put me on that day? I thought I knew what it was like to fly, but this was out of this world. I never did get the man's name. I'm sure that I *did* get his name, I just didn't remember it. What I did know was that he methodically asked me lots of questions about my life, beginning as far back as childhood.

Samuel. That was it. Dr. Timothy Samuel.

He began with questions about my parents and their divorce. I didn't have much to tell him about that except for the fact that my mother was always yelling at my father. She was never happy. She never smiled unless she was having one of her lunches with Penelope the black widow spider, who had long since moved to Florida with her boyfriend. He asked me about my relationship with my mother. That was a tough one—a question that could probably be answered several different ways, and although I didn't want to discuss it, I knew I had to. I liked Dr. Samuel a lot more than Dr. Kilburn.

I shrugged. "I never had a relationship with my mother. I was invisible to her. Most of the time I was." I thought of Mary Jo. "It was probably better that way. Marisa wasn't invisible. She always had to argue with our mother. I was a sheep. Marisa told me that a lot, but she also knew she should have been one too. She couldn't help herself. I stayed alive. Didn't get me very far, did it?" I started to laugh.

He frowned and started looking through his notes. "I see you have a bachelor of science degree in accounting, and you have minors in business and education. You also say that you graduated eighth in your class at State. That's quite impressive, to say the least. I'm glad you added that, Alice. It shows me that you take pride in this accomplishment."

"I've always done well in school." A small wonder considering the fact that my brain was fried.

"But you've never been happy. Not since your sister died."

"Well, no. No, I guess I haven't been. No. I haven't been happy."

"You said your mother slugged the two of you around, but Marisa got the worst of it."

I nodded. "She did. She just couldn't leave things alone. Sometimes she could, but not very often. But my mother really hated Marisa. She really hated her, and she hit her all the time, even with the two-pound wooden spoon. I got that too, a few times on the side of the head. That really hurt. I saw bright spots when she banged my head into the floor once. She smashed Marisa with a tennis racket, she hit her with a cutting board. One time I saw her try to shove an umbrella up her ass. It was a good thing Marisa was wearing shorts because it didn't go in very far. But sometimes, sometimes I think it was the humiliation that was even worse. My mother was always making fun of Marisa, laughing at her in front of people, calling her names, belittling her. No one did anything about the bruises. No one helped her. I remember Mrs. Cranston, an old math teacher. People. They just looked the other way. I'm just as culpable."

"You were a child, Alice."

"No, no." I shook my head. "That doesn't matter."

"A child's mind doesn't have the capability to reason under those circumstances. If you were to ask my opinion, I don't believe a person's brain is even developed fully until they are about twenty-three, and even that is debatable," he said.

"Somebody should have helped. Everyone knew. My grandparents, my father, Frank, her teachers. Okay? They were all adults, so their minds were *supposed* to work better than mine, right? Right?"

He nodded. "Yes, you are absolutely right. They had the moral authority to do something for her."

"She didn't just die. She was murdered. I saw it. I saw him."

He began to frantically whisk through a pile of loose paper.

"You're not going to find anything in there," I said.

"What do you mean?"

"Our stepfather killed her."

For the first time in my life, I felt nothing when I said it. It had to be the medication and the fog. I knew my detail. But I wasn't sure if it was the accurate detail.

"But he was only my stepfather, not hers. I found out from his sister, the one who has been avoiding me since I sent her a letter apologizing for my behavior at my sister's funeral. My behavior. Toward her. She also avoided my aunt for years. They were friends in high school until my aunt went—she got sick too."

"Sick how?"

"She's paranoid schizophrenic."

"You say your stepfather murdered your sister?"

"My aunt. I love her very much." My words drooled, and I couldn't stop myself from talking about nonsense. "She is the closest thing I have to a best friend—I…I guess. Not really. I don't want to talk about Nancy."

"We don't have to talk about her."

"Barton Withers killed my sister. No one believed me. I found out from—he is Marisa's real father, not her stepfather. He met my mother at a party when they were young, and she found him several years later, and they married, but he didn't know that he had a daughter at the time."

He was furiously taking notes as people continued to walk in and out of the office. "You're telling me he didn't know he was Marisa's father?"

"Nope."

"Barton Withers is incarcerated for voluntary manslaughter," he said, reading some notes.

"Yes, and he's dying of some sort of intestinal cancer. I hope it kills him before he ever gets out, and I don't care how that sounds."

He leaned forward. "I don't blame you. If someone murdered one of my family members, I would feel the same way. You said you witnessed a murder and *no one believed you?*"

"Yes. No one. Not even my father. I haven't spoken to him that much in such a long time."

"What did you see? Can you remember?"

"I remember everything. But this medicine makes me groggy."

"Do you want to tell me? As best as you can?"

"I stayed home from school that day. Marisa stayed home to take care of me, but knowing her, it was just an excuse to play hooky."

He smiled.

"I wish she hadn't done it. She would have been alive today if she hadn't stayed home to take care of me, but he probably would have killed her at some other time. He's a monster. She gave me some orange juice, and he was outside the kitchen window looking in, and then he disappeared, and then he was in the house. He taunted her, like he always did. He made fun of her, but this time, it was worse. He called her names. He said she had to have all of her shit moved out of the house by noon. He was drunk. I know he was because I could smell it. And he looked different that morning. He was dirty looking, and he hadn't shaved. He was wearing a ball cap and an old shirt and corduroys. He never looked like that.

"They walked out into the hallway, and they were fighting. She had a hard time ignoring things, but this time I didn't blame her. She did nothing wrong, and he was being so mean to her for no reason at all. He was yelling at her, calling her a good for nothing, one of my mother's favorites, telling her that he was going to throw everything she owned down to the end of the driveway. A coward like me runs and hides under the bed, but not Marisa. She wasn't going to take any more of his mean remarks. She pissed him off by calling him a drunk, and they kept arguing. I followed them into the hallway. She ended up spitting in his face. Do I have to keep going?"

"No. Not if it's going to make you uncomfortable. But you know, we will eventually have to confront this."

"He picked up my sister by the throat and threw her up against the wall in the hallway. She kicked and struggled, and finally, it was awful. It was just awful. The problem was that her spitting in his face and her struggling was like gasoline on a fire, and it made it worse. I have to stop. I can't tell you what happened next. It was…it was horrible—"

"It's okay, you don't have to."

"He screamed." I had no tears. "He screamed at me to get out of there, but I only ran when I saw her eyes at the end. They were dying, and then they were dead for sure. I know that's what she wanted because I could tell when she was dying. Marisa and I knew each other very well. Even though I believed she wanted me to run, I never forgave myself for not staying and helping her. I was wrong for leaving her. I was wrong for just thinking about myself. I shouldn't have run away."

"You had to run away," he said simply. "You said yourself you saw it in her eyes."

I was surprised by his response.

"You had to run and hide or, for heaven's sake, get the hell out of that house. You may not have survived. There would have probably been a chain of events that would have occurred very differently. He could have turned on you, and he would have. The passerby may not have heard the commotion at the time or your screams and cries for help as you ran through the house."

How did he know that? The police report, I guess. Is that what happened? I thought I remembered everything. "But I don't have anything left."

"Of course you do," he said. "I'm looking right at her."

I let out a laugh. "So are you going to tell me that latest thing? That I come from an abusive family? An *abusive background?*"

He looked me in the eye. "Yes. Very much so. And I am so, so sorry for your loss."

"It happened a long time ago," I said. "But thank you. I miss her so much. Every day."

"And you will continue to miss her every day. A tremendous amount of physical and psychological abuse led up to Marisa's murder, and the aftermath has caused you astronomical suffering throughout your life. This is what finally led you here. And you made that decision. You checked yourself into this hospital, which was an incredibly brave thing to do. Now, what we need to do together is to get you well. Do you want to get well?"

I nodded. "Yes, I've hit the bottom. I really want to get well and live a good, productive life."

"Then let's start now."

He continued to ask more questions about me, and we talked for what felt like a long time.

80

I found myself in the dining hall again, this time without the company of one of the male nurses or Gemma. Apparently, the weekend doctor thought I was taking too much sedative and cut down my dosage. I don't know what the reasons behind it were, but when I talked to this doctor, to me, I sounded perfectly intelligent. But then I completely forgot what I said to him, as if I had too much to drink. It wasn't a pleasant experience, and I felt as if I was dreaming and knew I was dreaming at the same time.

As he was about to leave, Robyn insisted that I ask him for a B pass, which I suppose stood for "big girl." I couldn't have cared less, but she thought it was so important I could eat lunch with her without staff eavesdropping on our conversations.

Robyn tried to convince Bernadette to join us and celebrate my newfound freedom, but Bernadette preferred to sleep through lunch and then stuff herself until she was sick at dinner. Instead, Robyn dragged the angry girl at the end of the hallway with us—the one with the thick black glasses and the perpetual pout on her face. She introduced herself to me as Squizzy.

"Squizzy?" I asked.

"Yes," she answered with a tone of annoyance. "My real name is Suzanne, but I couldn't say Susie when I was little. I said 'Squizzy,' and it just stuck. I get really tired of telling that story over and over again."

"I understand what you mean," I said. What on earth was wrong with Suzanne? It was a perfectly nice name.

"We all do," Robyn said. "They ask you the same questions over and over again in here. That's my doctor over there." She pointed to a woman who, to me, didn't look like a doctor. I remembered

Bernadette commenting on Holloway looking like a cop. She had an enormous butt, and her beige skirt was way too tight. Dr. Kilburn looked like a doctor.

"That big blond woman?" I asked.

"Hmm." She nodded with a mouthful of food. "Dr. George. She's discharging me on Tuesday."

I put my fork down and wiped my mouth. "What? What are you talking about, Tuesday? Are you sure? That's in two days."

"You are so lucky," Squizzy said.

I looked at her. Her glasses reminded me of Holloway's. They were so awful.

"I wish I was getting out of here on Tuesday, but my asshole husband's thrown me out. I don't have anywhere to go anyway."

Robyn perked up. "That's no problem at all. You can come live with us. My boyfriend and I have a guest room, and I'm sure like whatever—"

"Wait a minute," I said.

They both looked at me.

"Why is she discharging you? You tried to commit suicide with sleeping pills. You said you had vomit all down the front of you. They had to pump your stomach. You're lucky to be alive."

"Could we please change the subject?" Squizzy put down her tuna sandwich. "That is really disgusting. Alice. If you don't mind."

I ignored her.

"Dr. George thinks I'm ready to go home," Robyn said with supreme confidence. "If she thinks I'm ready to go home, then I'm ready to go home. But don't worry, if you're still here, I'm gonna call you. You'll be here on Wednesday for sure."

"For sure." She didn't hear the sarcasm in my voice.

"Dr. George is great. She's really wonderful. Fantastic…" Robyn yammered on and on about Dr. George. I was jealous and resentful. Here I sat, the result of a person suddenly scared out of her mind at the prospect of sudden death, and there's Robyn ready to embrace it. Yet she's the one who gets turned loose on the world. She was a danger to herself. I knew she still was, and I knew I was missing something. Maybe it was because I didn't know this woman at all. She had been kind to me when I actually needed and wanted the comfort of another human being, but I didn't know her or her situation. She seemed to be the kind of person who could do anything she wanted to do in life, but there was something.

I looked over at Dr. George, who was eating her salad with a table full of patients. Unusual, but I wished at that moment I could have traded Dr. Kilburn for Dr. George. I decided to leave Robyn alone about her discharge. I had stirred up enough. I knew nothing, and I wasn't going to be able to trade in Dr. Kilburn.

I had already seen Dr. Kilburn twice since I admitted myself. I remembered sitting down with her once, but I was so drugged up that our meeting seemed senseless. She probably enjoyed it because I could merely sit there and stare off into nowhere, agreeing with anything she said as the spittle dried in the corners of my mouth. But there was something interesting I captured the next time we met. Dr. Kilburn was being so nice to me. Her face softened, she smiled a lot, and she talked to me in a pleasant tone, as if she were talking to one of her neighbors. I thought about it, and then I thought about it a little more when I felt my mind was a little less bogged down, and I concluded that all along, Dr. Kilburn *wanted* me to be hospitalized. I supposed the problem was that she couldn't quite bring herself to commit me because at the time, she really didn't see me to be a danger to myself or anyone else. It was like she told me once, my sanity was right on the edge, but it hadn't quite crossed over that line yet. And so I did it myself, and she was apparently proud. Maybe she was happy that I fulfilled the task for her. Robyn said that the professionals called this *transference.*

Or had I imagined the whole thing? That could also have been a possibility. After all, when I saw the weekend doctor, I was so high, I most likely could have walked in front of a train and never have known it. I supposed I would find out later when I had my next meeting with Dr. Kilburn. I had to be as charming as possible in case I had to undo whatever I had done.

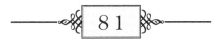

81

"Robyn, are you sure about this? I mean, I have never worn makeup before in my life. No, wait—that's not true. I have once." How could I have forgotten? My mother's wedding day to the monster who murdered Marisa. His own daughter. A little secret that my mother decided to keep from everyone until she was absolutely sure she could sink her talons into the Withers fortune. What a stupid plot that would never work.

"See? I knew you must have worn makeup *at least* once in your life, a tall skinny girl like you," she drawled, her head tilted back, fingers under my chin as she slapped powder on my face. "Bernadette, hand me that brush, will you please?"

"I wasn't always so skinny," I said, keeping my head in place.

"Well, you are now, and you're learning how to eat again. You're not afraid anymore. Hell, I saw you put away that chocolate iced doughnut the other day. It's okay. For right now. But you, Bernadette—"

"I know," Bernadette answered slowly. "I already have a mother, Robyn. She lives far away in Idaho, thank God."

"I'm only looking out for the health of my favorite friends. Now."

Bernadette rolled her eyes and shook her head while Robyn tapped both sides of my face. I was reminded of my aunt who still had a habit of touching my cheeks even though they had lost all their flab in recent months.

"You're smiling! You like it!"

I looked over at both of them as they beamed with excitement. "I've have never seen myself look this way before, Robyn."

499

"That's *you*, Alice. That's you in the mirror. You look beyond beautiful." She powdered my fair skin with a similar color and evened out the tone so that it was close to perfect. My eyelids were a velvety combination of purple, pink, and white, blended together as the color got darker closer to my eyes. She lined the bottoms of my eyes with a bright lapis liner and finished off with a deep black mascara. I was surprised they let her have all this makeup in there. My cheeks were a deep soft fuchsia, as were my lips. My face glowed with warmth and a surprising vision. "You look beautiful, Alice."

"You do," Bernadette said softly and nodded. "You are stunning."

Robyn put her fingers in my hair and frowned. "Bernadette, hand me that bag of rollers and that comb. We have to do something with this hair." She began to run frustrated hands through my unruly hair. "What to do. This is a tough one. You have a lot of hair."

I looked back at her and shrugged. "I've never been able to figure it out."

She settled on a french braid tucked at the nape of my neck with what felt like a million bobby pins and half a can of soft-touch hair spray. I felt like a princess. "If you even think about crying and ruining that eye makeup, Alice, I swear to God—"

Bernadette held up her hands. "Whatever you do, don't cry."

"I promise I won't." It was ironic. They were both so teary-eyed, and I wasn't. I had spent years sobbing my way through life. At that moment, I felt so much peace. "But can you show me how to do this french braid thing? I get tired of the ponytail, and the bun is so old ladyish." Kay showed me once, but I never got the hang of it.

"Oh, definitely. It isn't hard at all. I'll show you right after your appointment if you want."

Dr. Kilburn received me in the ping-pong table room. I cried so hard the first evening because seeing that ping-pong table made me realize what a state I was in. With Detective Holloway's help, I admitted myself to a locked ward of a mental hospital. Apparently, it could have been worse right here in this building. Directly on the opposite side was the Intensive Treatment or IT unit where, according to Bernadette, "folks who had holes in their brains" were housed. There were people coming off drugs and alcohol, people refusing to take their medication, people in need of electroconvulsive therapy, people whose behavior required them to be in restraints, people like Aunt Nancy at her worst.

Our ward recently acquired one such transplant, a tall handsome nineteen-year-old. He actually bragged about being so manic that he was pretty much constantly in restraints. I stayed away from that kid as much as I could. I didn't even make eye contact with him. He was wild and scary like a cheetah. He was fast, wiry, and he talked too loud and too much. I was afraid he would snap in half. Someone in this place needed to give him something to take him down a notch or two. Maybe they already had, and it wasn't working.

I passed Reardon as she was walking out of the ping-pong hall, crazy cheetah following and then skittering past us and off to wherever. She was wearing a bright blue blazer, and it fit her very well.

"You look really nice today, Nurse Reardon," I said, and I meant it.

"Well, thank you, honey."

"You're welcome." I was shocked. She was being very pleasant. She must have had a date later.

"Why, Alice." Dr. Kilburn stood up as I approached the chair across from her. "You look lovely." We both sat down. "You're wearing makeup, and your hair is just gorgeous. May I see the back?"

I turned to show her the tucked braid. "My friend Robyn is really good at this kind of stuff. A couple of us sat around and had some tea while she gave me a much-needed makeover. Girl stuff, I know."

Dr. Kilburn smiled broadly while I remembered that one night in Northrington when Kay Schuester dressed my and Marisa's hair.

"I hear you've been eating well. You're taking a supplement, and you're taking all your medications as prescribed."

I nodded. "I'm surprised that the medication worked so fast. Maybe it was the combination?" But I was skeptical.

"How do you mean?"

I thought about that for a moment as I pulled my knees up to my chin. "After I admitted myself, I ate that night. Robyn and Bernadette helped a lot. But it seemed a little implausible."

"You're right. Medication doesn't work that fast. It takes time to even find the *right* medication, as you know, and once we do, the right medication has to work itself through your bloodstream. Then get to your brain. That's why we have to prescribe minor tranquilizers to help you to relax and cope while the process is taking place. Now I know you've had some trouble with these before, but we were out of options. You were clearly, consciously or not, starving yourself to death." Her voice was so clear and precise.

"I'm sure that helped it along." I still felt a little dopey, just not quite as much.

"It did, of course, but what I really believe is that somewhere in your mind, you hit your bottom. Thankfully, you decided on your own to get help, and by doing so, you found that there was nowhere further to fall." She paused, and we looked at each other. "Now. You may not have been aware of that. You have found strength in others. More strength. You are already a very strong woman. You may not be aware of that either. You have found support in people who have also suffered through tremendous crises and are not apt to judge you, and in just a few *hours* of your being here, you have garnered further strength and wellness. If you can continue to work hard and take this combination of medication, I believe you will continue to improve. However, and this is very important, you already know that medication can be a bandage. *You* have to *help* the medication. There is a total here. It's a combination of people, therapy, anger management, and medication that will help you heal. You will never be cured, but you can live a long, healthy, and happy life."

I didn't want to sound like I wasn't taking in her every word, but I was so anxious to start my new life. "Can I go home soon?" I asked quietly, my chin resting on my knees.

"How does Thursday sound?"

I smiled. "Thursday is fine."

"I have a condition," she warned.

I waited, feeling the tension crawl through my stomach.

"I want to see you get into a group."

"Like the one—"

"Yes." She seemed to read my thoughts. "A therapy group. And I'm going to tell you why."

"Okay." I listened but was very against the idea. I put my feet back down on the floor and sat straight up.

"This is something that I strongly recommend, and in this instance, I am prescribing it to you. You are a loner, Alice."

"But I like it that way, Dr. Kilburn," I quietly protested.

"And some people do. Generally, there is nothing wrong with that," she said, casually throwing her hands in the air. "But in crisis, you withdraw into yourself and turn your anger inward, which can be very dangerous to you. And to those around you."

I sat and listened to her continue to explain, actually not minding the sound of her shrill. She seemed so convinced that she knew what she was talking about, and in many ways, she was right. But there was the soul that she could never know, the one who had to navigate canyons, the one who had seen cats that supposedly weren't really there. It was the person that *I* didn't even know, yet I knew existed like a large dark shape that lived in the center of my body. Sometimes the shape was there, and sometimes it was gone. Dr. Kilburn would never know me as well as she thought she did, but I was at her mercy, and at that very moment, I had to give her the illusion that she had me all figured out. That I had myself all figured out. Figured out enough to go home.

"I would like for you to try it for ninety days." She handed me a card. "You remember Dr. Tim Samuel?" She sat up a little in her chair. "I know things were probably a bit daunting."

I nodded. "I remember."

"Dr. Samuel will be conducting the sessions. They'll be in the building right across the street and down the hill." She pointed over my shoulder, and that forced me to turn around and see nothing but large closed double doors.

Logistically, it would be all right. I had my bike, and at least the weather was fine and spring was in bloom. When it rained, I could take the bus from College Avenue right to the medical buildings. Of course, the bus would take me around hell and back, but I didn't see any way out of this no matter how many angles from which I examined my situation.

And examined I did, with Robyn, Bernadette, and even Squizzy. I was, in a sense, committed to Dr. Samuel's group therapy sessions for ninety days if I wanted to go home. Dr. Kilburn knew exactly what she was doing. She pushed me right into the deep end of the pool when she knew I didn't know how to swim. People were not my strength, even though she thought I had been progressing in that area. I never loved that woman. Why did Detective Holloway think she was God's gift to the world? I should have asked him that when he came to visit and brought me these new chicken wings from Jodie's.

"Aren't you going to have any?" I asked, unrolling the wings from the paper.

"Got me a salad," he said with pride.

"A salad? You're boring."

"They got some great chicken soup now too. Remember the days when it was just burgers and fries? You knew it was a cheeseburger if it came in the little yellow packet. You only got a strawberry milkshake? I didn't even *know* what cholesterol was back in them days."

"These chicken wings are so good," I said, feeling as if I was eating too fast. "You're missing out."

Groups. I didn't like them much, and I usually hung back like a forgotten dusty drapery in an old house. No one really noticed. I didn't mind that movement thing I had to do on one of my first days. I was sitting in the huge front room. A patient named Vince who always looked ready for the golf course was playing a song on the grand piano. He had musical talent and he could sing, but the words meant little to me. I did find the melody very sad, and so I started to get up and leave the room.

"Alice? Alice Buchner? Is that you, dear?"

I looked down and saw a tiny little hippie woman with blondish-gray hair and blue eyes. She was wearing a flowing white combination cape dress with white tights and gold sandals. I wasn't sure if I was hallucinating or if I was actually seeing a good witch. We left the locked ward with one other guy and an older glum black woman with big thick gray glasses named Amy who went out for a walk one day and never came back.

The good witch named Sally led us to a beige room with a large thin mat on the floor, and for about twenty minutes, we engaged in something she referred to as movement therapy. She played music that reminded me of that Chinese restaurant Bunica sometimes took me to after church where she would order a double gin martini that tasted like rubbing alcohol. It may have only been the four of us, but I found it to be a group. Not by Dr. Kilburn's standard, I'm sure.

I liked movement therapy. I felt guilty because I was having fun. We created a dance. We each invented a step. Sally asked us to dance out how we felt when we were admitted. I jumped in a circle with my arms squeezed across my chest.

"And, my dears, how will you dance when you get to go home?"

Amy wiggled her rear end like she definitely had some funky moves. Sally was so excited, you would have thought we had just created a masterpiece. Then somehow Amy wiggled her ass right out of there.

So what was the big deal? This sense of urgency? These huge groups of people sitting around talking about their feelings, complaining, whining, all pushing for their turn, the tired nurses trying to do the impossible—troubleshoot with each person among a pack of unstable people. It was all bullshit to me. I always felt left out, and that didn't hurt me. I *liked it* that way.

But Dr. Kilburn knew that, and that was the sticking point. And so I would be grouping for the next ninety days after my discharge, and there was no escaping it. People were going to know about me and Marisa, and they were going to walk me through something I really didn't want to walk through again, even though deep down inside, I knew I needed it.

Ninety days.

More group therapy. It would be the last one before Robyn was discharged early the following morning. I still worried about her, and I hoped she would be all right. I gave her my home number, and she promised to call. I was glad to see Gemma facilitating because it always seemed as if she wanted to be there.

A tall attractive woman in her fifties with short curly hair, a black blouse, and a long maroon skirt entered the room with a large satchel that she laid against the wall. She nodded and smiled and asked to sit directly across from Gemma. She called herself Sandy and introduced herself to us as a clinical nurse specialist who would be Gemma's co-therapist. She appeared to be cheerful and pleasant, exactly like Gemma always was. And like Gemma, she seemed grounded, very smart and kind.

Gemma had requested that we write in our journals, a task that I always found difficult and tedious. Marisa always loved these mind-numbing hobbies. I would do a little journaling just to make sure I got the most important facts right, but generally, journaling put me to sleep. It was a hard day to concentrate too because Robyn wouldn't shut up about leaving, and when she found out I was leaving the following day, I swear she wanted to throw a ticker-tape parade for the two of us.

The group was unusually large that day. Normally, a few people were in some individual session or talking with their doctors, but there were exactly twenty-two people who were free and clear and ready to have something interesting to discuss or cry over.

I sighed and tried to be positive and feel present as I looked over my shoulder out the giant windows into the sunny parking lot. I needed to get used to it since it would be my life for ninety days, beginning as soon as Dr. Samuel captured me like a trapped animal. Bernadette and her oxygen tank sat on a recliner at the end of the mauve couch, then Robyn to my left. I noticed one more person whose name I couldn't remember, sober or not. Since I graduated from high school, I had a terrible time putting a name with a face, but I was told I was not alone. Dad always remembered names and faces, even from decades past. That's one of the things that made him so unique. That was wonderful for him. He did have some strengths after all. I still hadn't talked much to him in months, and I wondered if he was going to get a gigantic bill for my hospital stay.

Pam was her name. No, Patty. No. Pam. That was it. She had a friendly husband. I met him twice when he came to visit her. He smiled and nodded a lot, as if he understood he would forever be married to a troubled woman. That is, if he stayed with her forever, but that was hardly the norm. Even though he displayed perfectly straight white teeth, Pam never smiled. He wore the same ball cap and T-shirt on both days. I surprised myself by noticing that, considering how drugged up I was, although greatly less so as time went by.

Once as we were standing in line for our medication, I overheard her telling someone that she had been a fashion model. I found that to be odd and refrained from making a smirk or just bursting out with laughter. It had to be one of those delusions of grandeur that Dr. Kilburn, some of the staff, and even Dad would go on about with Aunt Nancy. Poor Pam was more unattractive than me, Bernadette, *and* Squizzy, and that was no small feat. She was a very light-skinned black girl with a million pimples and greasy curls that looked as if they were pinned to her head. Her face was very large and round, and her body was so tiny, she could have been mistaken for a nine-year-old boy—*if* you had removed the huge head. And all she ever did was eat sweets. She seemed to like the sugary, wrapped, manufactured type that dispensed from the vending machines, especially if they had icing on top or were cream filled so that she could stick her tiny fingers into them.

My lips curled as I watched her eat, but Gemma caught her. "Pam, honey, you know there is no eating in here. You'll have to get rid of that Danish." Gemma was always so agreeable, so patient. How did she do that?

Pam rolled her eyes, got up, maneuvered herself through a row of chairs, threw out her dessert, and sat back down, alternately licking her fingers and wiping her hands on her blue jeans. It became hushed and quiet in the room as one of the nurses from the hallway outside pulled closed the double doors.

Gemma crossed her heavy legs. She was wearing some kind of art smock, a purple skirt, black tights, and shoes that kind of looked like regular leather Mary Janes. With her freckles, her ponytail, and her broad smile, she looked very lovable and approachable, and she made me feel exactly the same way I felt when I met her on my first morning. I was immediately calmed by her presence.

Sandy had a very professional and different approach to doing things, and I suddenly felt a ping of anxiety in my chest. Without hesitation, she sat up straight in her chair and raised her hands. "Group? Who would like to begin?"

Oh, come on, I thought. *Since when does this motley crew need an invitation?* This was just an opportunity for Jimmy to start panting and falling all over the arms of his chair and Caroline to put on a silent open-mouth show for about fifteen seconds before we hear a "Waaaa! Why do I have to go through this!" Here we go.

Then to my surprise, Robyn raised her hand like a schoolgirl. "I will begin." She cleared her throat. "Just so you all know, I will be leaving tomorrow morning, *and* Alice will be discharged on Thursday."

The room exploded in loud applause, and Robyn lifted my arm with hers, as if we just won a sporting event. I was so embarrassed, and I looked across the room at Pam, who was smiling and clapping as she looked directly back at me. It was the first time I had ever had any eye contact with the woman, and at that very moment, I wanted to vaporize. I hated Robyn for embarrassing me like this.

Gemma glanced over at Sandy. "Thank you, Robyn. We were going to get to those discharges in due time, but you beat me to it."

"No problem, Gemma." Gemma's cheeky answer went right past Robyn as she was leveraging for more. "In case any of you haven't noticed yet, Alice looks pretty damned gorgeous, if I do say so myself—"

"Robyn," I said quietly and calmly as I looked downward to my left. There was a lot of chatter in the room. She looked directly at me.

"Don't you even think about 'Robyning' me," she said. "You're beautiful, and I made you even more so."

"Now just a moment, everyone, if we could all pipe down." Sandy threw her hands up again. "This is my first session with this group, and I haven't met Alice or anyone else for that matter. Would someone mind filling me in?"

How about putting a piece of tape over Robyn's mouth?

"Robyn gave Alice a makeover today," Pam said in a louder-than-usual voice, "before she went to see the doctor. So now, Robyn thinks it's all her doing that Alice gets to go home, not that Alice earned it herself—"

"Don't tell me what I think, Pam," Robyn shot back.

"You look great, Alice." Tall skinny boy from the IT ward opined. He gave the impression of having found his balance since he joined us. That was a good thing since I wondered which one of his limbs would catch me or run into something or someone. "But just a word of caution. Too much makeup on chicks is a turnoff."

"What do you know, Ben?" Robyn asked.

"I know all about these things."

"This is the most incredibly stupid conversation we have ever had in this room," a woman named Sarah blurted out.

"Why, because it's not about you?" Robyn slumped in her chair and crossed her arms. She was angry and put out, but she was right. Sarah didn't participate in any group discussion unless the topic was solely hers, and she had been called out on it a few times. But no amount of coaxing could get her to become active in someone else's life problems. Until that day.

Sarah was a great beauty as a woman in her early fifties. She had very thick shiny chocolate brown short bobbed hair that fell to her ears in deep waves. Her skin, although a little saggy and wrinkled around the eyes, was very smooth, and her eyes were the most beautiful shade of a light indigo blue. I had never seen anyone with eyes that color. They were almost purple, and I knew they weren't contacts because sometimes I saw her wear huge glasses. She wore very comfortable-looking clothing, expensive cashmere tank tops and pants and slipper shoes, and she was very thin. She smoked a lot in the one room patients were allowed to go, but she didn't talk much to anyone. Robyn claimed she was married to a very wealthy stockbroker who was mean to her and cheated on her all the time. That was not her first hospitalization. Apparently, she suffered from deep and chronic depression.

"Here we are rejoicing about makeup and people *going home?*" Sarah used her slender fingers as air quotes around *going* and *home*. "Lovely. So we can go back to our wonderful healthy lives. How many of us have been right back in these very seats? How about you, Jimmy?"

Jimmy purposefully dropped his head down hard. I wished I could have reached over and tapped him under his chin.

"Doesn't anyone know who this girl is?" Sarah's words sounded like a harsh one-woman choir.

My eyes darted around the room. I glanced over at Robyn, who was glaring back at Sarah, but I knew Sarah wasn't asking about Robyn. My insides froze.

"Something is troubling you, Sarah," Sandy stated. "Who are you referring to?"

Sarah scoffed and waved her hand.

"What is your problem, Sarah?" Robyn leaned forward and past me so that she could eye Sarah further.

"I don't *have* a problem, Robyn."

"Is it just me, or does it sound a little hostile in here?" one of the men asked.

"I am not—look. That is Alice Buchner." Sarah pointed her finger at me as if I were a defendant in court. "She is leaving the day after tomorrow. She's been here for what, five days? A week? We've been sitting around this room for days talking about whatever, and she's been hiding in a corner. That young woman should not be going anywhere. Not one of us, including me, has even mentioned the big elephant sitting right here in the middle of this room."

"The what elephant?"

"It's an expression."

"Her daddy owns that fish market down on the south side," Robyn said proudly.

"I'm not talking about that," Sarah stated.

"Maybe she doesn't want to talk about her father. He's kind of insensitive," Robyn sneered, sounding like a child. She examined her freshly polished fingernails.

"I said this isn't about him." Sarah's voice was becoming louder as she was becoming more impatient. "Well, not *all* about him. I mean, come on, you people are unbelievable. Art, Vince, Dean, you three have lived here longer than I have. Sandy, you too for that matter." She shot an incredulous look in the direction of the nurse therapist. "You all have had to have read at least *one* newspaper. This poor child was witness to a murder."

As she finally said it, she was looking in Vince's direction, but she was pointing at me. An eerie silence fell upon the room. Sarah peeked at me, and an instant pang of fear and regret washed through her striking blue eyes. Her face went pale. "I'm sorry, but—"

"The papers never said murder." The only sound in the room was my voice. "Nowhere that I could see. I snuck them from my father who used to try and hide them from me for a while." I looked down at my hands. I saw myself rubbing imaginary ink off the tips of my fingers. Then it came crashing through—activity, movement, and noise.

Robyn rubbed my arm. "Sarah, you are the nastiest person—"

"Robyn, what did I tell you about being everyone's mother?" Bernadette asked. "Most people already have one."

"Just be glad you don't have Alice's mother," Sarah announced.

I stared at her blankly.

"I watch the news, I read the news. When I'm not in here," she said. "I can also read between the lines."

What was that supposed to mean?

"Alice, there's a lot of focus on you right now." Gemma turned to me with empathy in her voice. "It must be pretty intimidating after everything you've been through these last few days."

"What has she been through?" Ben, the teenager from the IT ward, asked. "Did you really see someone get murdered? Really? No way." He was a kid with a silly hairdo, short in the front and long in the back. He wore short white tennis shorts, and he waved his skinny long legs like two flags in and out.

"Hmm." Pam nodded. "She did. Her sister. Her older sister. I can't remember the name. Sorry."

"You don't have to apologize," I said quietly.

"I remember it," Vince said. "It isn't a nice thing to remember, but I'm sure Alice can't forget."

"I can't believe it."

"You really didn't have to out her though, Sarah."

"No wonder she's in this place."

"I thought she was anorexic. They were making her drink that milky shit."

"Isn't he in jail still?"

"You know, I'm sitting right here," I interrupted. "I don't know why you feel the need to discuss my life while I'm here having to listen to you babble on and speculate. If you have a question or a comment? I'm right here." I couldn't believe myself. What was I doing?

I noticed Sandy raised her eyebrows and nodded to no one in particular.

They weren't going to let me out of here now. Sarah would see to that. I had to say something useful. Otherwise, I thought I would be locked up in here for God knows how long.

"I have to get revenge," I blurted out without thinking.

"He's in prison," Vince said. "How are you supposed to get revenge?"

"The police just screwed up," Sarah said slowly and deliberately. "The. Whole. Thing. I think so anyway. Someone high up in that department must have been on the fat slob's payroll, and those two cops that led the investigation?" She once again looked over at the older men, Vince, Art, and Dean in the wheelchair, who looked like he had slept in a ditch for a week. He kept glancing at me with one eye. "Holloway," she said, remembering his name. "Detective Holloway? He's the one who came in with you. He's the only one who's been to visit."

"Sarah, we're getting a little off track here. Vince *did* make a very important point." Nurse Therapist Sandy swooped down like a giant hawk. I didn't want to talk about myself, but I had to now, especially if Sarah was throwing it out there that I *shouldn't* be discharged.

"What did I say?" Vince said.

Ben's face exploded into a huge smile, and he burst out with laughter. He halfway covered his mouth with his hand and looked to his left at Vince. "Vince, man, you're always forgetting stuff. You did way too many drugs. Look at you now, you look like you're about to play two rounds of tennis. Look at me! You asked her how she's going to get revenge on that bad dude if he's already locked up, man!"

"Oh, right." The room darkened to a normal calm. Vince swallowed and seemed to be organizing his thoughts. I allowed him to take his time. The longer he took, the sooner someone would change the subject again, or we would be out of this quiet room. "Withers," he said. I cringed at the sound of someone else saying his name. "The man who killed your sister. He's in prison. It's been about twelve years?"

"Almost eleven."

"Trying to get revenge on him. How? How can you get revenge on him when he's in prison? I don't understand."

I shook my head slowly. I didn't understand either. It was hard. It was an impossible task. I hadn't gotten anywhere. Look where my thoughts got me: the county lockup, a psychiatric hospital. What was next?

"Revenge. Hmm," he said. His face was sad. I didn't want to continue with this, but there was no turning back. "And his being behind bars isn't enough?"

"No," I said. "He's been moved to a medium-security prison for good behavior, I guess, which shouldn't have happened. I understand the fact that I at least know where he is, but I don't exactly like the way he got there. Process versus content."

Gemma furrowed her freckled brow. "Explain that to us."

"I think it's pretty simple, even though I've had a hard time getting anyone else to understand it. He wasn't charged with murder. He pleaded to a lesser charge of voluntary manslaughter. I wasn't even a court witness. My father wouldn't allow it, even though I begged and screamed. He didn't care. My mother didn't care, of course. But it didn't matter because no one believed me. The police and the DDA didn't believe me. They said I was seeing things that weren't really there, and maybe I was. But I know for sure that he picked her up by the neck, and he slammed her against the wall. That I saw."

"Like you were hallucinating? At ten?"

"Almost fourteen."

"Were you taking drugs?"

"Not at that age."

513

Ben leaned back in his chair. "Early onset schizophrenia. That's what a doctor told me once. I was sixteen and already a drunk. But thirteen is kinda young. And your sister did just die right in front of you. No wonder you were seein' shit." He giggled to himself.

"I've been saying those words, 'I know what I saw,' for what seems like forever. I've actually read about people who have been through severe trauma, and they say they can't remember certain things because it hurts too much or they have suppressed it or whatever, and I envy them. I really do because I *can't* forget. I wish I could. And I've spent so much time trying to figure out what to do about all of it. It was a murder, not manslaughter. That's exactly what it was, a murder. He was drunk, he was angry, he hated her, and he killed her. And the people in her life that were supposed to love and take care of her didn't."

Including me.

Pam shook her head. Her black eyes were watery, but she wasn't crying. She seemed to look right through me when she spoke. "What did you see?"

"I saw him kill her. Deliberately."

"What else did you see?"

Jimmy sat up straight in his chair, paying attention and waiting for my response.

"Yeah, I want to hear this," Ben said.

"I'm not here to entertain you with gory details. I've told the cops, the doctor, the psychologist—" And then I remembered that group Dr. Kilburn was making me go to. I remembered that I was going home that Thursday on that condition.

Fine. Do it quickly. You want a real life? A better life? They've trapped you, and no one is coming to your rescue.

"He was a monster. He is a monster. Marisa was a tiny little thing. He picked her up by the neck, higher than he stood, and smashed her into the wall. I was scared, and I lost my balance and fell backward into a chair. He screamed at me to get the hell out of there. I saw blood spring from the back of her head, and it poured down the wall and flooded the floor. The police told me later that there *was* no blood. They said she had bruising on her neck and that she died from a broken neck. There was no blood. He also threw her so hard against the wall that I thought a pipe behind it burst because water then came pouring out of the wall. According to the police, there was no pipe behind the wall, and there was no water anywhere. I insisted that I saw blood and water rolling down the wall.

"My sister had the most beautiful green eyes. They looked like the inside of two avocados or emeralds even. But when she was dying, they darkened to a grayish green. A sad, sad gray, and they didn't speak, but I could read them. They begged me to run. I couldn't help her. I didn't help her. I did nothing to help her. I didn't even run into the kitchen and grab the knife that was right there and plunge it into his back. No, like an idiot, I obeyed those eyes, and I ran and ran and ran through that giant house, and it felt like it took forever. I thought he was coming after me."

I amazed myself that I didn't cry. I felt as though I had complete control over my behavior. It felt strange. I had to talk. I had to go home.

"Finally, I got myself to my room, and I hid under my bed. I was so fat when I was a kid. I could barely fit under the bed. I still thought the monster was coming after me, but I never heard a sound. It was so quiet. It was as if there was no one home. Just perfect silence. Total silence. I can't even explain how terrified I was. I wanted to die because I knew my sister was dead. I…I saw her. I knew she was dead, but I was so afraid because even though I wanted to be with her, I didn't want him to kill me too. Then somehow the neighbor's cat got into the house, maybe through an open door or window. He was an enormous Persian cat named Pinkie. He stayed under the bed with me and comforted me until I couldn't stay awake anymore. When I awoke, Pinkie was gone. According to the police, Pinkie, who was very old at the time, was an indoor cat who never left his owner's sewing room that day. It was a police officer who rescued me. Detective Holloway's the one who brought me here and has been coming to visit me."

No one spoke for several seconds. I wondered if I had betrayed my conscience and exposed my heart. At least I could go home without any second thoughts from the staff or Dr. Kilburn. Now the sharks could swim away. I was going home, starting a new group, and starting a new life. I wasn't the same Alice anymore. I was too strong to stay sick forever.

I spoke first. "Please don't think I'm crazy. I'm not, I'm really not. Well, no more than anyone else."

Dean shifted in his wheelchair as much as he could, smoothed his long gray hair on the back of his head, and flashed an eye. "Oh, you're not crazy. I knew guys who came back from Vietnam. Great guys. I couldn't go 'cause I got one hip. Good guys seen things we can't even imagine. And it sits with them forever. You been traumatized."

A rumbling of agreement weaved its way through the group.

"If anyone is going to empathize with you, it will be people in here," Sarah said. "I'm sorry that it took so long and that you're leaving so soon. I know you must be happy about it. Those first couple of days, you were pretty out of it."

It doesn't exactly help when you announce that I shouldn't be going anywhere. What if the right person heard you and thought, "Maybe she doesn't need to be going anywhere after all?" That was my head again. No one was going to listen to—

"After listening to your story and observing those of you who are participating today, it's very obvious to me that you have a remarkable history, one that interests others," Gemma said. "People will always be very curious about this tragic part of your life, and that must be very difficult for you to cope with. I can only speak for myself, but to me, it is very understandable why you would want to seek vengeance on the perpetrator who put your family through this."

Well said. My family doesn't give a shit.

"Revenge is a powerful motivator," one of the women pointed out.

Jimmy popped up in his chair. "Do you go to school?"

I shook my head. "I graduated from State. Still in my same place. I know it's time to move on, but I really like it there. It's quiet and—"

"At least you did that!"

"I bet you don't have many friends."

"Yeah, she's way too quiet."

I shrugged. "Anger and wanting to, you know, lashing out makes you want to get drunk and be alone. I have enough friends." What the hell did I do? That secret slipped out of me without my even realizing it. Again. Another one. I could feel my face burning. How much was getting drunk a danger to myself or another human being?

"Do a lot of drugs?"

"No," I lied.

"Had a little scrape with the law." Suddenly, Dean was becoming more involved in this conversation than I thought he was capable of.

I glared at him.

"That's right! I forgot all about that." Sarah slapped her skinny thigh.

"Hey, don't get mad at me, kiddo. It's public." Dean smiled, revealing crooked brownish-gray teeth.

Sarah admonished the group for not knowing the details of my "felonious" assault on Lisa Jupiter.

"That's not exactly what happened, Sarah," I asserted in a way that was unusual and new for me. "I did not strike her. I pulled out a tuft of her wig. It was fluffed up on top, and I just…I just pulled it out." I lied again. Sort of. "And I wasn't charged with a felony. I was charged with a misdemeanor."

Ben laughed hard and rocked backward in his chair. "You what?"

"You ran her out of town anyway. Her little tabloid TV thing didn't last."

I was tempted to ask Sarah if she watched the Witherses' interview, but I suppressed the urge to foolishly open my mouth again. She answered my question for me.

"Her interview wasn't thorough, and people didn't want to see it without both sides of the story. She made the Withers family out to be victims, and everyone in Wellton with half a brain knows that they certainly are not." Sarah's voice trailed off, and although she was the only one talking, she wasn't making any impact on the rest of the group. For that very moment, I felt sorry for her, even if she was talking about my life.

"I was just sitting here, thinking once again about revenge." Gemma redirected the conversation. "And I really wonder if you have been seeking revenge on yourself."

Immediately, my top teeth tucked behind my bottom teeth. I didn't understand what she meant, and I wasn't sure if I wanted to hear more of what she had to say.

"Okay, he's in prison," she said. "That's a good thing. But it doesn't answer your questions, it doesn't stop your pain, you don't get the justice for your sister that you believe she deserves, and it doesn't bring her back. But revenge is like taking a sledgehammer and clobbering your own head with it. You are punishing yourself. Exacting revenge on this person is useless because first of all, he has been physically removed from society. You can't have access to him unless you were to visit him, and of course, I don't think that would be something that you would do. Have you? Have you gotten any response from him?"

"No." I lowered my head.

Robyn played with the bits of my hair that were coming loose.

Sandy turned to the group. "What I believe Gemma is saying is that you, Alice, have been angry and depressed for a very, very long time. No one could *ever* fault you for that." She studied me. "But the revenge that you feel you must seek on Withers is falling squarely on your shoulders."

Gemma and many of the group members nodded in agreement.

"I could have stopped him," I said out loud. I did everything I could to avoid my tears. But they fell freely. "I was behind him. I was steps from the kitchen. My mother kept a sterling silver knife block next to the sink. I could *see* them. But I was too scared, I froze. If I had plunged a thirteen-inch butcher's knife into his back, my sister might still be alive today."

"Oh no, no, young lady." Dean waved a hand at me in disgrace. "By the time you got back fumbling with your knives, your sister mighta still been dead. You know how hard it is to stick a knife into a man's back? It ain't like TV, and you were just a little girl. He woulda taken that knife away from you in a second and killed you with it. You weren't thinking straight then, and you're not thinking straight now. You did nothing wrong. You go home and get well and live a good life. Stepfather. Shoulda been taking care of his young family."

Actually, he was her father.

But we never went into that. It was someone else's turn.

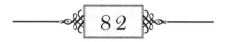

82

"Why are you isolating?"

I opened an eye and squinted. Reardon stood before me. The overhead light was on, and I noticed Bernadette wasn't in the room. "I'm not isolating. I'm taking a nap. It's been a very long day. This medicine's making me sleepy."

I had to explain myself to her since *isolating* was a curse word around there. I was to be discharged the following day, and I wasn't about to allow Reardon to ruin it for me too.

She looked down at her clipboard. I tried not to laugh at her silly hairstyle, which looked like she had gone through great pains to make sure every piece was curled under. She would have really done me in for that.

"Well, you gotta phone call. Sounds like Madame Makeup."

"Who?"

"Get up."

I threw on a pair of shoes, shuffled down the hallway, and plunked myself down. Someone had shoved an old desk up against the wall directly across from me. It was one of those desks that we used to have in elementary school that was square on four legs with a big square hole in the middle to jam all your stuff into. I stared at it while Robyn talked.

"Oh my god. You have no idea. It feels so good to be out of there. Dan and I are going to the civic center tonight to see a concert. It's some group I've never even heard of before, but Danny says they're so great! Are you okay?"

"Who, me?"

"Yes, you! Who else am I talking to?"

"No, I'm…I'm fine," I answered as I yawned.

"Because you don't sound fine. You sound depressed. What's going on?"

I suddenly snapped to attention.

First isolating *and then* depressed. *What was next? Witchy Reardon and suicidal Robyn running hand in hand to the perfectly coifed Dr. Kilburn, all the while sneaking back glances and spilling their tales about Alice, the unstable young woman who thought she saw a murder, but it was really an accident? Alice, the girl who was afraid to eat because she thought someone was poisoning her food and cigarettes and hallucinated blood and cats? Detective Holloway would be my ride home, but he would be no help. He couldn't even close an obvious murder case. What was he going to do about a psychiatric patient who wanted to leave the hospital against medical advice? Against his "friend" Dr. Kilburn's advice? Robyn, I would slam the phone down in your ear if I didn't think that one teeny, tiny part of my brain actually knew it would make it worse.*

"I'm very sleepy right now. I don't know why. I think I was dreaming when you called. Haven't you ever been in a deep dream when the phone or the doorbell rang? I'm not depressed, I was sleeping. Really, I'm happy! I'm really happy to hear from you." I sounded desperate, but I knew I was being irrational.

"Well, all right!" I could see that smug look on her face right through the telephone line. "I've got your number at your apartment, and I promise I'll call you. I promise, I promise, I promise. Here, let me give you Dan's. Do you have a pen?"

"Yep," I lied.

"Call me tomorrow when you get out, okay? Go back to sleep. Got to go. Bye. Love you!"

"Bye, talk to you soo—"

She was gone. She was so hyper, more so than usual, and there was no way I would call her at her boyfriend's. I met him when he came to visit once, and he reminded me of another boyfriend—Mark the boyfriend. The difference was that this guy was older, slicker, and more experienced, and I had a feeling Robyn wasn't his last conquest. She seemed a lot more smitten with him than he was with her. He would end up breaking her heart, and that would be a disaster.

I looked down at my fingers and noticed I was twirling one of her hair bands. It wasn't mine because I had never had one of the thick gray ones. And she didn't have that boring bland hair like mine; hers was more of a chestnut or mahogany with red glints. I decided it was time to color my hair—like Robyn's. Hers was so pretty. The hair messily clung to the band. I put it up to my nose and smiled. He perfume was so unique. A little square purplish bottle she liked to use like water. I went back to my room.

Providing no one messed with me, I needed to pack the one knapsack I brought with me. A receptionist gave me my discharge papers even though I was still waiting for my ride. It was strange how endings happened. I pleaded guilty to pulling out a tuft of Lisa Jupiter's yellow wig. I got the green paper from the court, but I still had to sit in the cell until Guard Dee processed whatever she processed. The thin girl with the long white nails that clicked on her countertop desk area slid me my yellow copy while she kept at least one white and one pink for Dr. Kilburn and God knows who else. I'm sure Reardon's slithery little fingers would weave their way into those big beige filing cabinets just for some fun reading.

Obsessive compulsive disorder. Generalized anxiety disorder. Major depression with acute psychotic episode. At least it didn't say what it said on Aunt Nancy's paperwork.

"I don't have that."

The minute the words dribbled out of my mouth, I knew how much of an idiot mental patient I sounded like. I crossed my arms. I didn't have psychotic anything. I was not psychotic. I was fully aware of what was not real, and I objected to that word. I did not have psychotic depression. I *did not* have psychotic depression.

She looked at me with that "sure you don't" face, and I decided immediately that I wasn't going to argue with her. I didn't need to get into a disagreement with someone who was more interested in her fingernails than she was in the meaning of psychosis.

I walked back to my room to say my last goodbye to Bernadette. She was already standing in the middle of the room talking to Detective Holloway. He obviously snuck in without my noticing.

"I see you've met Detective Holloway," I said.

Bernadette turned and slowly made her way toward me. "It's awfully kind of the detective to come and pick you up."

"It really is."

"Taking time out of his busy schedule catching murderers and bank robbers, I would think—"

I could see Detective Holloway all puffed up and proud of himself like some kind of fancy bird.

"You come over here, Miss Alice." Bernadette reached up and threw her chubby arms around my shoulders and squeezed harder than I thought she was capable of.

"Goodbye, Bernadette."

She pulled me in so that she could look right at me. Detective Holloway left the room. Her bulbous eyes were a blazing watery gray. Her breath was sweet. "Now you listen. Nothing is going to hurt you. Do you understand me? Nothing."

I nodded quickly. I knew that. I was going home.

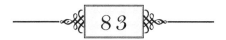

83

The sun smacked me in the face as if I had walked out into it for the first time. It was difficult not to love the springtime in Wellton. The shift of the sky and the sweetness of the air made my heart lighter. April was the time that Marisa was taken from me so suddenly, and for so many years, I fought this rare beauty of such a finite time. I didn't care about what sounded like a thousand birds chirping before dawn or the sight of the first robin on the leaf of a maple tree I didn't even know existed because it had been dead all winter. Spring in Wellton was hopelessly noticeable. But after Marisa was killed, it was more like the devil reaching into my intestines and twisting its grimy claws around my viscera. Similar to the way Aunt Nancy had felt. The whole idea of my hospital stay was to experience those feelings less frequently, then to the point of not at all.

I rubbed my eyes, remembering that I wasn't wearing a ton of mascara. Robyn would have been on me for that.

I noticed Detective Holloway right away. "Look at you. Seems like the last couple of times I've seen you this week alone—you're looking good."

"I appreciate that very much. Twenty-two pounds altogether. Still have a ways to go," he said.

"Twenty-two pounds?" We walked in the warm sun to the pea green GM. "That's a lot."

"Got myself a stationary bike. The handlebars move, you know, back and forth like this." He demonstrated how his handlebars worked, and I just smiled and rolled my eyes. He chuckled. "Still eating my chicken, nothing fried, no sweets. And look at you. You look a whole lot healthier than when I dropped you off a week ago."

"I put weight on," I said, patting my stomach as the car door locks clicked open loudly. "No one seems to want to gain weight, but I really needed to."

"Oh yes, yes, you did." Then his voice changed. "And you're still able to eat, and everything's all right?"

I nodded slowly. I was still in disbelief as to how it all happened the way it did. "I hadn't had one single problem since I walked in there. With the food." I remembered that first night when I ate crackers with Robyn and Bernadette sitting with me as I swallowed my medication with a tiny cup of water. I laughed to myself as I thought about it. That was right after Nurse Billie got all bitchy about the three of us coming up to the Dutch door at the same time. So ridiculous. I was glad to be away from her and Reardon.

"That's great, Alice," he said quietly. "That's real good. Are you hungry now?"

I looked down at the light blue men's oxford shirt I wore when I was hospitalized. I had the sleeves rolled to my forearms and a french knot tied at the bottom. It was my father's. "I actually have a craving for a Jodie's double hot fudge sundae with chopped peanuts."

"Not called Jodie's anymore."

"What?"

"Called Cosmic Burger now. Big company out of St. Louis bought out Jodie."

"*Jodie's?* Welcome to the eighties," I said.

"Hence the broadened menu," he said as he casually pulled onto the interstate. "Time marches on, kiddo. You can still get a really good sundae."

"Answer a question for me."

"Sure."

"What does everyone think about my being in a mental hospital for a week?"

A moment of confusion flashed across his face.

"Who did you tell about it?" I asked.

"Not a soul."

"Then no one has an opinion because no one knows? Dad? My mother doesn't know? Mary Jo? She was in—"

"Nobody. Unless you told them. Don't you remember what I talked to you about when you were admitted? The intake nurse gives you a set of numbers on a card. It's like a business card, and it's probably tucked away in your bag somewhere. Only the people you give that number to know where you are."

I sat back in my seat and stared straight ahead. "I vaguely remember the card, and I never called anyone with the number, and, well, it's not like it's the first time I've disappeared for days on end. I was pretty high in there for a while, and who knows if—"

"It's fine, Alice. You don't have to report to anyone unless it's your boss, and even then you don't have to say where you are."

That was one of my big tasks   finding a job.

"You're not required to tell your family or your friends about your hospital stay," he continued. "It's all confidential. But if you do, know that you have nothing to be ashamed of. If anything, I find you to be a very brave person to finally realize that you needed help. And you've got people out there who care about you very much. Walter, for instance. Now that boy is a friend. It doesn't get any better than that."

"Oh god, yeah," I whispered. "You've seen him? You've seen Walter?"

"Believe it or not, he called me. Thought you were in jail again."

Clouds moved up and over the dome of the sky. I stared out the window, watching vacant land whizz by. "Jail. What did you tell him?"

"I told him firstly you weren't in jail, you were safe, and you were fine and that you would get in touch with him when you could. I left it at that."

"It's funny. My friends don't know where I am, so the first thing they do is call the police."

Detective Holloway looked very philosophical.

"I guess he probably thinks I went into treatment for drugs or something like that."

"I don't know what he thinks, but I know it's impossible to try and keep up with what everybody else is thinking."

He was right. He had that annoying habit of being right a lot.

We decided to sit out on Cosmic Burger's, previously Jodie's, expanded river terrace since it was such a sunny day. I chose a table near a Chinese hydrangea with full lush leaves that wouldn't expect blossoms until the summer. My double hot fudge sundae with chopped peanuts was about the size of the child a few tables over from us. "What are you eating now, salad again?"

"This is called a 'go for it' salad. It's got chicken and almonds and these little snap green things and all this other good stuff."

"You still buying fish from Dad?"

"Oh, sure. Fish is good. Fish is real good. Supposed to be good for your brain."

"Right."

Holloway's eyes sort of darted around, and his face darkened suddenly. "All right, Alice, now look, I don't mean to change the subject, but there are some very important things we need to discuss, and we need to talk about them quickly." He looked at his watch and suddenly appeared frighteningly official. "What's today? Thursday. The story will be in tomorrow's paper. They've already had a press conference."

"Does this have anything to do with Withers being Marisa's biological father?"

"Well, partially, but that was never really proven beyond a doubt."

"When did you find out?"

"When he did. Shortly before he and your mother divorced."

"So you mean there's more?"

"I'm afraid so. There's much more. And you have to remain calm. Can you do that for me? This is very important."

"Okay," I said tentatively. He was scaring me. I was filled with the flutter of anxiety that ripped through my chest, but as I looked over at that toddler at the other table, I knew I could remain calm. I would remain calm for that little girl with the red-and-white Cosmic Burger balloon.

"Do you remember a girl by the name of Nina Averelle?"

I didn't have to think as I dug into my ice cream. "Of course I remember Nina. She used to babysit us when we lived at the Stanhope and my mother and Withers started dating."

Nina was small and skinny with dark brown hair and a dark tan in the summer. She always wore bone Dr. Scholl's sandals and played jacks and all kinds of different games with us. She loved her soft rock music and played her albums for us while we read the liner notes. Marisa and I would walk with her down by the creek behind one of the buildings and look for tadpoles and minnows. There were trillions of them. Our mother usually left us with boring TV dinners in the freezer, so her mother would sometimes bring us a box of chicken, mashed potatoes, and sodas for dinner instead. Mom would go ape shit. "This is a violation of my household!" She would say things like that. "I spend money on food. If she thinks she can feed you better, then go over to her house and eat as many deep-fried rats as she can stuff into you!" She wasn't the least bit grateful for Mrs. Averelle's generosity.

"How do you know her?"

"Nina Averelle disappeared in August 1974, just after your mother and Barton Withers married and the four of you moved to Crescent Hills." He shook his head. "A small portion of her remains were found seven weeks ago by a broker for a real estate firm looking at some vacant land near Seagramsville."

I gasped. The father of the toddler looked over at me and smiled. "Oh no." I put my spoon down. "Oh no, god, Nina."

"We couldn't determine at first how the person died, but we knew it was a teenage female, and dental records identified her as the missing Nina Averelle."

"There was nothing left of her but skeletal remains," I said quietly, stating what I assumed was most likely the obvious.

"Pretty much."

"Barton Withers murdered her, didn't he?"

"Yes. Yes, he did." He scratched the back of his neck and frowned.

My top teeth slipped behind my bottom teeth. I felt myself staring off into nowhere as fury began to creep through me.

"But this time it's different. The investigation brought forth evidence that at first was thought to be human bone, but it turned out to be ivory."

"Ivory? Like an elephant's tusk?"

"Exactly. Turns out, there was a part of a knife left at the scene, a hunting knife that had ivory on the handle. Somehow it broke or split. It was traced back to Withers's father."

I looked over at the little girl who was now grabbing at her hair and her balloon with her dad. He seemed to be the favorite parent. "Is he some kind of serial killer of teenage girls? Do you think he's done this before? Before Nina and Marisa? You know, he's traveled all over the world."

"I don't know. I don't know about anywhere else in the world. I certainly wouldn't put it past him, especially when he was a younger, stronger, wild little psychopath with no limitations on how much money and freedom was doled out to him. Drugs, alcohol—there's no telling what that animal was capable of in his day. So far, we know of two: Marisa and the homicide of Nina Averelle. And it *was* a homicide. That I know for sure."

I couldn't speak. I felt that old combination of anger and sorrow again, but at least I was eating. I sat back and looked at a half-empty cup.

"Alice," he said, "I'm so sorry. This could not have come at a worse time. I really wish this story wasn't going to be in the morning paper, but it is. Mr. and Mrs. Averelle are elderly now. Nina was their middle child."

"He hated my sister, but she hated him too. That was no secret." I was thinking out loud now. But Nina? Why her? I guess I was trying once again to think like a killer, and same as before, I didn't know how the mind of a killer worked. I should have been happy about that. "Nina was a sweet and caring person. I remember him being pleasant and cordial with her just like he was with me up until that last day. Not all the time, but mostly." I was in shock and so sad. But he was a monster.

"Do you think we should finish this conversation in the car?" He nodded toward my cup. "That hot fudge looks like it's about had it. You gonna eat the rest of it?"

"No, I'm fine. This is an awful lot to absorb," I said. "If you don't mind, I really wouldn't mind just sitting here for a few more minutes if we could."

"We can take all the time you need. And I wouldn't be telling you this if it weren't gonna be in the newspaper tomorrow morning," he said.

The irony of our meeting was that I didn't even read newspapers. I would have found out soon enough anyway, just like I did about Lisa Jupiter and her flopped sensationalized story about the wonderful Withers family.

"It's probably best that I know," I said.

"Okay," he said, as if he was waiting for me to speak but hoping that I wouldn't explode. "There's some more unpleasantness to this."

"There's *more*?"

Holloway was stern. "Remember what I said about remaining calm. I'm trusting you, Alice."

"I can remain calm," I said, quietly praying that I could. I looked over at the little girl again, who was now giggling and making faces with her mother. Daddy said something about ice cream, smiled, got up, and left the table.

"You may remember some of this, or you may not, I don't know, but Barton Withers had Nina Averelle on his radar."

"His radar?"

"Yes, his radar. She was in his way. Your mother was furious with her and her family, and Lavinia was a great big headache to him. Nina Averelle was allegedly sexually molesting your sister."

I opened my mouth to say something but closed it again.

"I'm sorry, Alice, but I have to ask you these questions. Do you remember anything about that time?"

I remembered everything. But it took Holloway's reminding me to once again bring it to light.

"Are you okay, Alice?"

"Yeah."

Daddy came back to the table with ice cream. Good, they're staying.

We used to walk down to the creek. Sometimes we would find frogs and salamanders. Nina would take her shirt off and lie in the shade, pretending to be under a spell. But a kiss from a handsome prince would not be what would wake her up. "Suck my boobs, Marisa," she cried in a sleepy voice. "Kiss my boobs."

"She told my mother," I said suddenly.

"Who told your mother?"

"Marisa did. I don't know why I can't remember if she asked me about it first, but I think she felt guilty. She knew it was wrong. I just can't remember. Marisa and I talked about a lot of things, but I just can't remember this time. I'm not sure about this time."

"But you remember the molestation." He lowered his head and looked directly at me.

I nodded.

"Did Nina ever touch you or make you touch her?"

"No. No, not that I can remember."

"That's good." He sat back slightly. "You understand that Marisa had no reason to feel guilty. She was a little girl who did nothing wrong."

"Yeah," I said, taking a sip of my water, "but my mother went nuts. I remember it now. That's it. That's it." It was as if the light broke through the clouding of my mind. Then I knew.

"What do you remember?" He was interrogating me, but more like the way Dr. Kilburn always did. He was gentler still, and so I didn't feel threatened at all.

"That's when I found out Marisa was a Catholic. Marisa was baptized in the Catholic Church. My mother let it slip when she was slapping my sister's face. It went something like this: 'You made your First Communion, you dirty little bitch! You better pray for forgiveness. You better get on your knees and say ten Hail Marys and pray that God lets you into heaven after committing a lesbian act! Such filthy heinous acts!' And there was Marisa kneeling in the doorway, saying Hail Mary, yeah, praying. Ten times. She baptized Marisa in the Roman Catholic Church because she believed her to be Withers's daughter. Now it all made sense. Were Bunic and Bunica in on this? How could they do this without the father? So many unanswered questions.

"She made us both walk over to the Averelles' house that night." I sat up and rested my chin on the top of my hands. Memories were flowing back to me easily.

"Lavinia."

I nodded, looking off in the distance at nothing. "Yeah. It was summertime, so it stayed light out until almost nine o'clock."

"Your mother took you and Marisa over to the Averelles' home to do what exactly? Confront Nina?"

"I guess. At first anyway."

"Did Withers go with you?"

"No."

"What happened?"

I stretched out my arms in front of me, placed my elbows on the table, and lowered my chin back down on my hands. "It wasn't far. They lived in those townhouses next to St. Dominic's. Mom made us wait on the steps. Marisa was crying her eyes out. I tried to comfort her by patting her shoulders, but she was so upset and inconsolable, I couldn't get her to stop crying. I could tell she was frightened out of her mind."

"Frightened of your mother?" He was attentive, but he looked sad and defeated. I knew he felt guilty about Marisa.

"Frightened of being beaten to a pulp. My mother was so pissed at her. She blamed Marisa for everything."

Detective Holloway's face didn't move.

"I could hear my mother from outside. Believe it or not, she wasn't yelling. Her voice was calm and so direct, but cold and threatening too. As I think back on it now, it almost feels as if it were yesterday." I scoffed and shook my head in amazement. "If you can imagine this, she even told Mr. Averelle, *in his own home*, that none of this had anything to do with him, and he needed to leave. No, really, can you believe that? Walking into someone's house and telling them to mind their own business? But this is my mother, and people were frightened of her. She did *nothing* to save my sister. Nothing—"

"Alice—"

"I know." I held back tears as I smiled. "I'm okay."

We both sat there for several seconds. I heard people chattering, cardinals singing, a loud car radio.

"Marisa and I just sat there on the front steps. And we could clearly hear our mother inside. And no one else."

"Did either of you ever see Nina that night? Did you talk to her?"

I shook my head slowly. I knew what became of Nina. "But we saw her brother. Sam? Thomas? Tim. Tim, that's right. Tim, yeah, that was him. I think he was in college at the time. I remember he was riding his bike up the sidewalk. I remember he was wearing ripped blue jeans, a maroon T-shirt, and he was smoking a cigarette. When he pulled up alongside us, he tossed the lit cigarette into the parking lot and asked us if we were okay. Marisa answered yes, but she was crying so uncontrollably, it was obvious that she wasn't. He locked his bike on the rack and walked over to us. I remember he put his hand on Marisa's shoulder, and he asked again, 'Are you sure you're okay?' Marisa said yes again through her tears. He was so nice. I remember wishing we could have lived with him at that very second. I mean, I was a child, but I had that feeling that he would have been kind to Marisa and me, you know? Then he said, 'Everything is gonna be all right.'"

"I could see why you would think that. It was unusual for people to demonstrate that kind of thoughtfulness to the two of you, wasn't it?"

I nodded and thought about that for a minute. "Yes, it was. Marisa never felt worthy of anything in her own home in the very short time she was on this earth."

"Unfortunately, you are probably right." I could have sworn I could hear him breathing. Then he said, "You seem to remember fairly vivid details about the events surrounding the time Nina Averelle babysat you and your sister."

Now he's going to tell me I need to testify at a murder trial for another one of Barton Withers's victims. This time the victim herself tricked a young girl into putting her little mouth on the victim's sixteen-year-old breasts. The victim also had a victim. Shouldn't I have been glad Nina's dead? Did he stab her with that hunting knife when a piece of it somehow got left behind? How did that happen?

But I was not happy about Nina. Maybe there would have been a time that an old obsessively angry Alice Buchner would have been, but I wasn't now. I was shocked and saddened by Nina Averelle's murder, and in a mind like mine, this would have once been celebrated.

"And you're absolutely sure she never touched you or forced you in anyway?"

Why did he keep asking me this? I wondered but didn't feel like continuing with that. "No. I mean yes, I'm sure. It was only Marisa."

He leaned back and finally looked a little more relaxed, as if he were done repeating himself. "Very good."

I turned to look over my left shoulder at the sky so blue, it looked almost purple. I had hardly been anywhere, but I learned that the sun never goes very high in the northeast, even in the summer months. Not like in the south anyway, but the sky looked so clear, clear like a cloudless indigo.

Two men waded into the Maidenhead with their rubber overalls and fishing poles. I should have known what they were fishing for, but I had no clue because I had never cared to take the time out to learn. I wondered if the occasional breeze that came out of nowhere scared the fish away. Probably not. I also had to wonder if their lives were normal, and I figured with a twinge of hopelessness and longing that they probably were. I always envied normal people. They didn't live among murderers, psychotics with depression, or little girls who coerced other little girls to perform sexual acts on them.

One more day and one more atrocity. Just one more atrocity I witnessed and did nothing about. I told myself to stop. What was I supposed to do about all this? I couldn't have been any older than ten at the time. Marisa was dead, and she's been dead for a long time. Nina Averelle was dead, and she's been dead even longer than Marisa has. I figured that if I continue to unravel everything I've accomplished, all the hard work I've done, I was going to end up spiraling down. The second break is always worse. I had to help the medicine. I had to help the medicine. I had to help this medicine because the medicine is only a bandage.

"Alice?"

"Yeah."

"What's on your mind? You've been staring out over that river."

I took a deep breath and shook my head. "My sister is never far from my thoughts."

"I know that."

"She was treated so unfairly as far back as I can remember. And for no other reason than for the fact that she was who she was, born at the wrong time and for the wrong reasons, resented. I don't know… I…I don't know what else to say. I think my mother was jealous of her potential, of her beauty."

"I don't think either one of you were brought up under the best of circumstances, to say the least."

I waved my hand at him. "Oh, no." I shook my head quickly and looked directly beyond him. "She always had it far worse than I did."

He looked at me curiously as if he didn't believe me. But I didn't need his opinion on this because he had no idea what I knew. I could ignore my mother a good portion of the time. He wasn't there. Not until the end. I was, and it was Marisa's body he found, not mine. That wasn't by chance.

"She was an incredibly special person. I think about all of the good now, more now. Marisa would just keep getting back up and leaping to her feet again. She fought back. She never gave up. She didn't cower to anyone, not even at the end. I know how scared she was all those times, especially when she was cornered. She would cry when she wasn't supposed to cry, and she would continue to tell the truth when she was accused of lying. She would hold her head up and pretend to be proud when she was purposefully humiliated and disparaged. I knew it all hurt her so much."

I smiled at the memories even though they weren't all happy ones.

"I would try to comfort her, and god, did she ever hate that, not always but sometimes, and I could never tell when she would lash out. A lot of times she would bark at me, call me a nasty name, or swear. She had a mouth on her. Of course she wacked me a few times, but it wasn't hard. It was just that our fighting would lead to worse things—like my mother's wrath—and Marisa always getting the worst of it, but it was like she never learned her lesson or she never wanted to."

Detective Holloway frowned.

"But I understood Marisa. And now after remembering all this horror with Nina, I…I… God, poor Marisa. I know she would probably start laughing if she heard me say that. That beautiful girl was in a lot of needless pain, and I was young and clingy and maybe a little too insecure. Insecure. What did that mean when you're talking about a young kid? I do know one thing. I loved her very much. I always will, and I'll never stop missing her and wanting justice for her. I don't know, the justice part? I guess that will never happen."

"I didn't know your sister, but if I had money to put on the bettin' table, I'm positive she thought you were just as special as you thought she was," he said, and I smiled.

I fought back tears again, but they were different tears. They were of happiness and contentment.

"And not only did she love you, but she still loves you because she never left your side. Her spirit will stay with you forever, until the day the two of you are reunited again. I believe that. I believe that our spirits are so much more capable than what our mere bodies are capable of in life."

I listened carefully as both of us sat over what was left of our food.

"When I was a boy, my brothers and my sister knew that every Sunday morning at 10:00 a.m. sharp, we were to be in Mass, and every Thursday afternoon, we were either at someone's house, including our own, or some basement or a room at the church studying the Bible and discussing Jesus or the Holy Mother Mary. It was all us Holloway kids knew. I was a regular black Catholic boy from southwest Wellton who married a regular black Catholic girl from southwest Wellton. But when it came to true faith, I don't know if I really ever had it, not at that age anyway. I don't know if I truly believed in anything divine, and I'm not sure if I even knew the definition of spirituality versus religion, if there even was a difference. We did what we were told to do. You had to in those days. When my son was alive, before dinner, he used to cross himself and say, 'In the name of the Father, and of the Son, and the Holy Asparagus, amen.'"

I laughed.

"Oh, I know, I know. I used to burst with laughter. I thought it was so funny. I mean, how did that kid get *spirit* mixed up with *asparagus*?"

We were both laughing now.

"Now my wife Wanda—giggling too, mind you, even though she was trying desperately not to—was a little less impressed. And when little Ken died, she threw herself into her faith. Mine was gone. You could say mine's been gone a long time, particularly since all the things I've seen over the course of my career, or maybe I never really had any in the first place. But there is one thing I've grown to learn over the years, and that is this—there is a god out there somewhere. Now I'm not so sure he coincides with everything I learned growing up or everything I learned as I've gotten older, I just don't know. Maybe that *is* faith. I don't think I'll ever know for sure, but I do know one thing *is* for sure. He chooses his angels wisely. They did not die in vain—Marisa, little Ken. We may not like the way they got there, but I know that both of them are in a much better place. Your sister is with God, and that feisty spirit of hers, her soul, will always be with you. She will not leave your side. You don't have to second-guess that."

Sounded like he didn't lose his faith at all. I knew he was right. It was a strange prospect, but I rarely felt her presence, probably because I wasn't looking for it or I was too busy pushing it away. But there were those times that I felt it in calming shadows and shifting breezes and when I knew I was able to eat again. We really don't know how much we take for granted. Swallowing food all the while thinking that it's going to kill you is terrorizing. When that stops, eating again is the most wonderful thing in the entire world. Marisa was still there…somewhere.

"But I'm worried about some, I don't know, I guess you could say loose ends."

"Which are?"

"I know he's sick, I know he's supposedly dying, but how's his family going to get him out of this one?"

"They're not."

"Oh, I'm sure they'll try."

"They won't. He confessed."

"Confessed? Why the hell did it take you so damned long to tell me?"

People looked over. I rubbed my palms together and placed them between my thighs and hunched over like I was a hundred years old. I noticed that the little girl with the red-and-white Cosmic Burger balloon was gone, and in her family's place were two middle-aged women. They were the ones who looked over when my voice was raised. Then the whole outdoor terrace seemed to clear out.

"That's incredible." I was absent-minded. "It's just amazing. It's finally over, isn't it? Will he be sent back to Bellmorrow? I guess they have to throw him into the infirmary."

Holloway shook his head. "No. He'll remain where he's at, and the taxpayers of this great state will foot the bill for his cancer treatment."

"Does Mary Jo know about this? The almighty family?"

"About his illness?"

"*No!*" I leaned forward. "*His confession. Killing Nina.*"

He turned to the side and waved his hand. "I presume his lawyers have corralled the—what did you call them? *The almighty family* well before the big news day."

"Which is tomorrow when the paper comes out."

"Hmm. Although like I said, we did conduct the press conference."

We drove in silence for most of the way back to my apartment. But then I became curious. "Why do you think he confessed to this? He never admitted what he had done to my sister. Is it because he's dying, and he doesn't think he has anything to lose?"

"Well, that's a very good question." He thought for a moment. "But I sure don't believe it. Underneath it all, Withers is a terribly weak and insecure excuse for a man. He's got an ego the size of the sky, and he's arrogant as hell, and that's how he pushes people around.

He's predictable in that way. But he's a narcissist and a sociopath. And he's dying and scared. Scared for himself, not out of any guilt or wanting to make amends. That I'm sure of. He's got nowhere else to hide, and really, I thought he liked getting a rise out of us if you wanted to know the truth. He was quite proud of himself."

"And he never admitted anything about Marisa."

"Not even when we pressed him as hard as we could. He'd rather go down giving me the finger than giving me what I want on your sister, honey. I'm sorry. I'm so very sorry. That—"

"It's in the past."

"Well, listen to you," he said. "I never thought I would hear you make a statement like that. You're makin' progress, young lady."

I shrugged and looked down. "Thanks."

We drove up the gray, lumpy potholed, and old tree-lined street to my flat in the old white house. It was one of those spring evenings that was perfect and went on forever. It felt like forever since I had been home, even though it had only been six days.

As soon as we pulled up to the front of the house, I could smell the familiar spring comfort of grilling food and marijuana. I was glad I stopped getting high. There were people all over the front porch. I crouched in the front seat like a third grader walking into a new classroom for the first time, and I was lost in the new school and late. God, the embarrassment. And to make the situation even worse, Holloway dropped me off. I knew what everyone thought of me. I was a classic nut job, and I often wondered if any of them were actually frightened by me. They knew what I had been through in my life, but still, why not *get* a life, screwball? Look at your aunt. At least not many of them knew about Nancy, so they had nothing to compare me to. But I worked hard to push those thoughts out of my head. I had no control over them.

I noticed Aubrey standing among a collection of paper plates, utensils, and wax paper under a ridiculous floral umbrella that she no doubt brought herself. Walter had a beer in one hand and was guiding Holloway into the driveway with the other. I recognized Miranda wearing a ball cap, sitting cross-legged under a tree. She looked stoned.

Aubrey came scurrying over. "I'm so glad you're here! We have so much food. The more the merrier!"

I'm glad you're glad because it's my apartment.

Walter assured Holloway that everyone was of drinking age, which was kind of funny because the entire front yard smelled like a dope den.

"Oh, I believe you, man, just promise me you won't drive if you had a little too many."

I walked over to Miranda and where a bunch of her friends were sitting. One of them was playing a guitar. "Alice, oh my god," she drawled. "Please don't tell me you were in jail again."

"No, no, no. Everything's fine, I just needed a few days away."

She was way too high to make much of a connection between Holloway's car and me.

"I'm good, really. Best I've been in a long time. Really."

"Really. Well, that's great, man." She squinted up at me in the setting sun. "You are thin, man, really, really thin. We have enough food for the whole street." Then she started to laugh uncontrollably. "No. Really." She took a sip of her beer. "Aubrey's made all this French shit, and there's burgers and ribs, and Walter's got—oh my god. We had no idea you were coming home with the cops." Her face was focused on the front door.

I looked behind me. Suddenly, the front screen door opened, and out walked a newer version of Miranda's old roommate Candace. Behind Candace, Arturo walked out and onto the porch.

"Arturo?" I was stunned. I could see the change in the dog's eyes as he recognized me right away. At first I thought he was angry. His head jutted upward, and his floppy ears perked up. He ran to me and jumped up, putting one paw on each of my shoulders, and furiously licked my face and my neck. Then he pressed the top of his head into my chin and the front of my neck. His tail wouldn't stop.

"Arturo, you're being rude," Candace called from the porch.

I melted into the cool grass with him and let him lick me. I scratched and petted him as he grunted and whined, and I let him continue to lick my face and my ears while trying to dodge that tongue at the same time. I spent so many years of my life crying, sobbing so uncontrollably that many times I would ask myself if I would actually run out of tears. But these tears felt different as the water filled my eyes and trickled down my face. They didn't sting with that constant and tiresome anguish and hatred. These *were* dissimilar tears, and they were a brand-new experience. I was happy. I might even say I was euphoric, and I was as sober as the dog was. It felt right to feel happy. I let myself cry. I was going to be okay. Really okay.

84

It was still dark when I sat on the front porch and waited for the paperboy to absentmindedly throw the Wellton morning newspaper at me. Arturo lay quietly. It was strange, even though I hated newspapers, I thought that opening this one first, I could somehow control the pain and damage it would inevitably emit. I knew I was engaging in what Dr. Kilburn referred to as magical thinking, yet it wasn't really magical thinking because I was aware that I was doing it. "I wish you could move back home here, Arturo. I suppose as long as you and I visit each other, we can most likely handle what comes our way—like awful stories from the newspaper that I'm about to read." I was still talking to animals. It helped me.

Candace decided that although Oregon was a beautiful place, she missed her friends and family, and "the wilderness" wasn't really for her after all. Lots of gorgeous and picturesque wonders, but also a lot of dangerous creatures that, if you weren't careful and, more importantly, inexperienced in the great outdoors, Arturo could have been a main dish. That was my opinion after seeing some of those wilderness photographs. And Portland was a city, a nice one, but Candace preferred good-old reliable Wellton. Her home. She got a job at the same school where Marisa and I attended while we were living at the Stanhope. It was the same school where my old math teacher, Mrs. Cranston, inspected a nonexistent stab wound on my sister's back but never thought to follow up with Marisa's unusual accusation and obvious bruises. I thought she should have been required to. I thought anyone in authority should have been required to report any suspicion of child abuse. But apparently, you're not required to do so. Someday there would be new laws. I never told Candace about our time at the school, nor did I ever ask about Mrs.

Cranston who was in all probability retired or dead. Candace moved into some new apartments up a hill behind Aubrey's mother's house. Up the street was the Stanhope Ridge, which was old, run-down, and in generally shitty condition. The whole thing was weird. I was just glad the dog was back.

"Miss?" The sound of the newspaper smashing into the concrete steps interrupted my thoughts and woke Arturo instantly. He didn't even bark at the boy, and the boy didn't even appear to be remotely frightened of the dog.

"Thanks," I told the kid who was halfway gone. "You're lazy, Arturo. You need a good long walk. We both do." I was putting off reading the article as long as possible by talking to the dog, but it was inevitable.

I knelt down and carefully pulled the atom bomb out of its cellophane wrap. Now I would have to dirty my hands and find the lifestyle section or the society pages or maybe even the gossip column. I didn't have to do any of that. The story was front and center and hit me right in the face.

Barton Withers III Confesses to Killing a Second Girl

So simple and to the point. He never confessed to killing the first one. There was Marisa's photograph. The one from her junior year. There was no talk about sexual molestation by the other murdered girl Nina Averelle, whose photograph was another school photo and was much larger. It was mentioned that Barton Withers committed manslaughter possibly on his own daughter. I wondered who leaked that little nugget? Could it have been my mother? I knew the rest. Barton Withers was finally going to hell. My head was aching, but at least I could eat.

It was time to do something with myself. The sun was peeking through the gray wispy clouds and purple vastness above. I rose from the chair and went inside, the dog at my heels. I needed to get to my group therapy session next Thursday afternoon, and the thought of taking the city bus made me feel even more like a mental patient.

The medical center was way too far away for a bike ride, especially in the dark. I needed a car. Badly.

I thought for a very long time as I sat in silence at my kitchen table. I knew the only person who could get me a smashing deal on a car would be Bunic. Without thinking, I dialed the number, and my grandmother picked up on the first ring. She was frantic and screeching in Romanian. I picked up the following: *God, the papers, my girl, your mother, spanking*—all of this.

"Bunica, I know all about it. I just read the entire article." I lied. All I could do was skim. "Everything is okay."

"Alice! Everything is not okay! That man is a serial killer, and he lived in your home!"

"I think you have to kill at least three times to qualify as a serial killer, Bunica, but he was certainly on his way," I said mildly.

"He is Helena's father! That poor little child! Her life is ruined. Ruined! Did anyone not ever stop and think about that precious little child?"

Didn't anyone ever stop and think about Marisa? Never mind.

"And your mother. She engineered this whole thing!"

Hmm. Engineered. Interesting word for my grandmother to use.

I took a deep breath and decided to handle this as calmly as I could. "Bunica, they *finally* got him. After all these years. He's still in prison, and he's going to die there. I know it took another death, but—look, I'm sorry to change the subject, but I actually called to speak to Bunic. Is he there?"

"No, dear." I was surprised she didn't fight me. "Of course he's not here. He is up at the stand."

"It's a little early, isn't it?"

She scoffed, and I imagined the look on her face and the way she waved her hand in the air. "He reads the newspaper. He leaves the house. Bunic doesn't show his feelings often, but he has them, I can promise you that."

"I have no doubt."

"You come over to visit today. Where have you been anyway? Come, I'll make you breakfast."

"It might take me a little while. My car finally died. That's why I need to see Bunic. I need to find a new, well, a used car fast. I'm riding my bike everywhere." A little stretch of the truth.

"Alice, it is not safe for you to ride your bike all the way over here. Why do you make my blood pressure go up like this especially on this morning?" She bristled.

I leaned my head back, shook it slowly, and closed my eyes while I tried to think of a way to get off the phone. I was full of peace and relief. I just didn't feel like getting caught up in all the nagging with my grandmother on one of the happier days I've experienced in quite a long time. "Bunica, please have Bunic call me. If I can get a ride, I'll be over as soon as possible, you have my word."

"You can take the bus."

"The bus will take all afternoon."

"Bunic can pick you up."

"That sounds great. Just please have him call me."

"I love you, my darling girl."

I smiled. "I love you too, Bunica." That wasn't as I hard as I thought it was going to be.

My grandfather had a friend named Costel whom he had known since he'd been in the United States. I thought Costel was from Bucharest or maybe from somewhere not far outside that city, but the two did not know each other when they were young men growing up in Romania. I knew Costel most of my life, and I never understood why he and Bunic were friends. All the two of them ever did was bicker. They would rant on and on, fast, worse than the arguments between my grandparents, and I could barely pick up a word. Once in high school after Marisa died, I was staying at my grandparents for the weekend and had taken one of my father's pint bottles of vodka along with me. It was cheap and nasty, and I didn't think he would miss it. I was right. I lied to Bunica about my abominable hangover, and she bought my story about some forty-eight-hour stomach virus where I couldn't eat, my head felt as if someone had clobbered me with a claw hammer, and all I could do was throw up my stomach lining. Naturally, I refused to see her doctor. I received just punishment for getting drunk and lying to my grandmother because the first morning, Bunic and Costel were working on a plumbing problem in the bathroom, and they argued and complained over the project for hours. I thought my head would explode. I cried in pain, and their loud voices in a small tiled room made the vomiting all the more horrendous. I thought the whole experience would be enough to keep me away from vodka from that point forward, but it didn't. I made sure that I stayed away from Dad's cheap vodka, and when I turned eighteen, I only bought the better stuff.

Bunic was able to get me a super deal on a little brown Dodge Dart. I just needed to wait another day or two for Costel to find the plates, whatever that meant. Then I would have my car, and I could easily get myself to group therapy and work really hard to find a job. But before I did either of those things, I would spend the night at my grandparents' house and be sure to spend the day at the stand with Bunic so I could thank him and Costel for helping me.

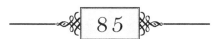

85

The sun sent shimmering shards of evening light over the rooftop of the bright white-and-black trim medical center Building A. I was pressed to find a parking spot. Finally, I saw someone pulling out, so I eased into her space and was glad that I left early. Leaving early had always been a habit I had to structure into my life so that I could check and recheck every aspect of both Marisa's and Shelly's ashes. That included their placement and safety and anything else that needed to be checked and done. It was part of the obsessive compulsive disorder. Since I had been taking my yellow-and-white capsules, I knew I needed to help the new medicine and try not to fall into what I called my double-checking trap. It was so much better since I had been on the right medication, and on this night, I picked up Marisa's little bindle of ashes and put them to my lips. I told her that I loved her and that the monster was going away forever. I told her I was sorry it took so long and that she had to endure so much. Then I put the ashes back into the velvet bag and closed the drawer. The old irrational thoughts did not plague me into irrational distraction or, even worse, starvation. It was a soothing and beautiful experience. Heart lifting relief.

I looked back at the hospital across the road and its huge windows. I wondered who was still behind them looking back upon me, knowing a few of my secrets: Sarah? Ben? Vincent? Pam? I turned back and hurried into Building A and the afterhours smells of a new purple carpeted corridor and air-conditioning that had been turned off about a few minutes prior to my walking in.

There were only about ten people in the group. It was different from the hospital. These people were more polished, clean-shaven, and less drugged. I noticed a bulletin board full of notices and felt eyes on my back. I turned around and noticed a strangely handsome man looking at me. He had mounds of thick wavy shiny black hair and a soft olive complexion. I noticed he had a large nose. His eyes were a large hazel, and it looked almost as if steam emitted from them. He smiled. I didn't smile. He was staring, and I thought that was kind of rude and creepy. I walked past him, threw down my straw bag, and took a seat.

"Hi, Alice, you look fantastic," an impeccably dressed Dr. Timothy Samuel declared from halfway across the room. I thought he was going to come over and hug me; he looked so happy to see me. He probably thought I wasn't going to show up. A few heads turned and glanced over at me, and I wondered if anyone had made the connection. "Doesn't anyone know who this girl is?" I could hear the shrill of Sarah's voice pounding my temples and feel her small indigo eyes drilling through me.

There had been a newspaper thrown around porches in Wellton, in driveways, on doorsteps. It ended up on coffee tables, in kitchens, in my father's little metal stand outside the store, in people's bathrooms, with my sister's face on it. The same face after so many years had passed.

I looked up, and Dr. Samuel was standing closer. "I am so glad you're here for group. You're going to like this group. Are you okay?"

"Do people—they don't know me, do they?" I was going to slip a little. I wasn't perfect.

"So what if they do? It's old news. There was a fire at an abandoned warehouse downtown last night. All over the news this morning."

I nodded as he led me to another chair. Apparently, the one I sat down in wasn't the one I was supposed to sit in.

"This is how our minds work. We are the all-powerful sun, and everything revolves around us today. When you're in the middle of chaos, it feels unusual to be *anything but* the sun. Think about that for today."

I said nothing. Dr. Samuel smiled and walked away. I was glad. Now that I had my wonderful new car, I thought about maybe sleeping under the lights at the truck stop again, but after more thought,

I decided against it. I didn't think I needed the truck stop parking lot or its lights anymore.

Dr. Samuel insisted that the members of the group introduce themselves before we got started. There were two new members, me and a thirty-eight-year-old lady named Kim who sat across from me. Kim was short and round and had shoulder-length brown hair with blunt bangs. She wore a beige and green dress and flat brown hippie sandals with a loop that went around the big toe. I knew she had to have struggled with drug problems—it was her eyes. They were the most peculiar things I think I had ever seen in my life. She looked like a cartoon or a comic strip. Her eyes were these little circles of green that actually matched the color of her dress. And her pupils were little pinpricks.

This night was different because every fifth week, someone in the group would volunteer to talk about their own personal experiences and what led them to that very room. They may talk about the progress they made and all the other bullshit that encompasses being in group therapy. I had this feeling that most of us were mandated to be there. I supposed my day to volunteer would come, even though I was already drafted into a performance across this street, which I resisted as much as I possibly could. I had to discuss my life story with a group of strange people again. I only did it so that I could be sure that I wouldn't have any problems in being discharged the following day. It actually turned out okay.

We were entertained by the man staring at me out in the hallway. He sat across from me but down a few chairs. He welcomed Kim and me to the group and introduced himself as Reza Khavari. I had a chance to examine him more closely. He was a very handsome man in an unusual and exotic way. It was obvious that he was Mediterranean or Middle Eastern. His skin was like milky creamy coffee, and I couldn't stop looking at his lush and wavy black hair. It was so thick and shiny. His large aggressive nose reminded me of my own. His broad smile displayed clean white teeth, and he had a little stubble on his square jawline, as if he was thinking of growing a beard but wasn't sure if it was really the right time of year. I wondered what brought him there.

Then he spoke. "Ten years ago, I had a sister named Estera." His accent was strange. He sounded British, but I could also tell that he had lived in the United States for a while. He had a sister. I had a sister too, and so I listened intently, hoping no one would interrupt with some ridiculous question.

His face darkened. "Let me go back just a little and preface this," he said. "I have never discussed this in a group setting. In fact, I have never discussed this at all, well, with anyone except the doctor who prescribed me the antidepressants that really don't work very well. And maybe that was a mistake, I don't know, but I maybe self-ishly need to get this out of my heart because it's killing me, and eventually, it will kill me.

"You're never supposed to speak ill of the dead. You're never supposed to think ill of the dead. My sister Estera was my parents' pride and joy. She received excellent grades in school, she was in mock trial because she wanted to be a lawyer someday, she was a cheerleader and homecoming queen. She had what seemed like hundreds of friends, and although I was already in veterinary school at the time, according to my mother, the phone never stopped ringing, and it was always a boy on the other end. We thought my father would lock her away somewhere. We were from Persia, and although we immigrated to London and eventually moved here, my father was still fairly protective of his girls.

"My parents had some very good friends who were also Persian, and they had a daughter about a year older than Estera. She went to a different school, and she was a nice girl. They were kind of thrown together and forced to be friends because our parents were so close. But apparently, one night, this girl, Yasmin, came over to spend the night with Estera while my parents were out at a dinner party. Estera started an argument over what to watch on TV and then decided to go upstairs to her room, leaving Yasmin downstairs alone. This wasn't the only time Estera took offense to something trivial and suddenly gave the silent treatment to Yasmin, or became mean and started to make fun of her, or even called to tell my mother to come get her out of the house. She even called Yasmin's mother once and demanded that she come pick up her 'loser daughter.' I remember some of these things when I was home and witnessed them.

"Once she threw an entire bowl of pasta and sauce at her. The next morning, they were supposed to go shopping, and they made up—for a while anyway. But Yasmin was the innocent. Estera was the instigator. Yasmin, who had taken plenty of my sister's abuse, had moved out west with her family, and my parents didn't really keep in touch with them much after that. But Estera remained the apple of my father's eye. He was particularly proud when she was on the winning debate team and made the honor society.

"Then a supposed 'accident' happened. On the way to a football game, Estera and her friend were in a large van. They let some of their friends in the van to ride along, but it got very crowded. When the van came to a stop, a girl outside opened the door and tried to get in. She said later that she thought alcohol was involved. In the packed van, *somehow* Estera's leg *accidentally* shoved her out of the van when it began to roll again. The girl had some scrapes, but otherwise, she was okay. Thank God. But I knew this was no accident. Estera did this on purpose probably because she didn't think this girl was good enough to ride in the van with her and her friends. It became perfectly clear to me that my sister was just not a nice person.

"One other time, Estera and a bunch of her friends were at the beach. Estera claimed that some of her money was stolen, some change. She blamed one of the girls and was somehow able to get the other girls to go along with her accusations. Then they just picked up and left. They took their towels, their bags, all of their belongings, and left this girl on the beach without a dime to put in a pay phone to call and get a ride home. An elderly couple she did not know finally gave her a ride home when they found her hitchhiking along a stretch of road. This could have very easily turned out to be a disaster, and it would have been my sister's fault had anything happened to that girl.

"My sister was given a full scholarship to attend a university out of state. She was a straight A student the first year, and of course, my parents were so pleased, they thought sun shined out her ass." He blushed. "Sorry for the expression."

The group mumbled their okays, and I smiled.

"The third year came, and my mother drove her to school with my younger brother and sister in the car. Estera had her own apartment junior year, and so they stayed the weekend to set up her new place. Nine days later, we got the phone call. Estera was out late studying at the library that was closest to her apartment. As she was walking home shortly after midnight, about half a block from her apartment, she ran into Robert Sweeney.

"Robert Sweeny was a senior at the same college and a star athlete. What happened next would change our lives forever. He stabbed my sister sixteen times with a pen and continued to relentlessly beat her. When he saw she wasn't dead, he strangled her to death with his bare hands."

The reaction in the room was a combination of gasps and pure silence.

Reza remained stoic and shed not one tear. He scratched his forehead. "Sweeney got life without parole. This is where my anger comes in. It's anger with myself. This piece of garbage never carried out a violent crime in his life, and he does *that* to my sister? He never raped her. He was a model student and a gifted athlete. You mean to tell me that out of nowhere, he just happens to take out his heinous violent rage on my sister? He won't talk. He hasn't said a word. Not in court, not in jail, I can't even remember what his voice sounds like. So this is what I want to know from Estera, and I'll never know because she's dead. What did you do, Estera? What did you say that set off this maniac?"

The group seemed angry with him.

One tear dropped from his right eye. "I knew you so well. And I'm not supposed to be angry with you. I should have taught you better because no one else did. I should have said what had been on my mind for years. 'If you don't start treating people better, be kinder and behave better, and keep your rotten thoughts and comments to yourself, someone's going to eventually come along and punch you right in the mouth.' I wasn't there, and I should have been. It was my responsibility because both my parents were incapable. I was the oldest brother in the family. I'm not supposed to feel this way. Please,

please do not get me wrong. I'm not excusing Sweeney. I'm glad he'll never come up for parole. I'm supposed to be 100 percent behind Estera. I just can't get there right now, and it's caused immeasurable anger and despair in my life."

The way Reza told his story sounded as if he were performing some sort of experiment that few people were ever going to understand. But he wasn't performing an experiment. He was real, and it was raw. I felt like although I didn't know him or his sister, I understood the fine line he walked.

"But that was your sister. And he stabbed and beat her. I know you know she didn't deserve that, but come on, no one deserves that, no matter what kind of person they are," Kim with the weird green eyes said.

Reza put his hands together as if her were about to pray. "And that I understand. No one deserves that. I'm glad he got life without parole, but if I *knew* there could have been that tiny percent of a chance that she could have prevented her death—I'm not saying that he wouldn't have killed her anyway, but the absolute rage. What was he so angry about? And… I don't know."

"And you feel guilty," Dr. Samuel said.

Reza nodded. "I feel guilty about a lot of things. And I feel guilty about thinking this way. I think that she said something, called him a loser or worse, or told him to fuck off in that condescending voice of hers. I knew Estera better than anyone. No one else would even admit it. Again, I'm sorry, I know you're not supposed to talk ill of the dead, but my beautiful sister was not a good person when she was alive. That doesn't mean she deserved to be brutally murdered, and it doesn't mean that Sweeney shouldn't be locked away for life. That's not what I'm saying. It's just the rage, the absolute rage. I don't know what I'm saying."

"I know what you're saying," I said and immediately got looks from the group. "He's being so brave and so brutally honest. I don't think I've ever heard anyone speak so honestly about their innermost thoughts and feelings. I mean, these are the kind of feelings that we are taught to be taboo. We don't think about them. In fact, we push them from our minds whenever possible. The idea that he's trusting a group of people with this is pretty remarkable. Whether you agree with him or not, we should at least give him *some* credit for his courage. This is amazing to me, and we *at least* owe him that. I'm sitting here, and I'm absolutely stunned by his candor. He's trusting us."

"You have very good insight, Alice," Dr. Samuel said in an embarrassing way. "Does the group have any insight into Reza's commentary?"

I doubted it. Most people were looking at him like he was a first-class asshole, and the women were the worst.

"She should have been able to walk anywhere she wanted to without someone doing this to her," one of them said. Well, yes, she should have been able to. Trouble is, you can't just walk anywhere you want at night. They just didn't get it. But that wasn't really the point. It was Reza's guilt and anger with himself for his feelings.

Dr. Samuel and the group continued to process Reza's story, but it seemed to me like they were getting nowhere. And it looked like Reza was getting a little burned out. They seemed to be upset with him for questioning his sister's murder.

When the session was over, I quickly got up and left through the back metal door to the outside. Down a hill to the left were some picnic tables and some old pots where people stubbed out their cigarettes. I realized I hadn't smoked since I became frightened of someone poisoning me, and I never started up again. I sat on top of the picnic table, elbows on my knees, chin cupped in my hands, and looked out over my favorite evening sky.

I thought about Reza. Now, we don't speak about the dead unless it's something wonderful—everyone knows that. His sister was a stuck-up nasty bitch. It didn't mean she deserved to be torn apart by an obvious animal. She was brought up to have no limits. Everyone knew what she was, but no one talked about it. Marisa spit in the monster's face before he killed her. It didn't help matters; he was still going to kill her. It just made him angrier. The same may have been true for Reza's sister.

I had my back to the small slope at the back of the building when I heard someone coming up behind me. It was Reza. "Hi, Alice."

"Hi."

"Do you mind if I sit down?"

"No," I said.

"Do you smoke?"

"Used to. Not anymore."

"Do you mind if I do?"

"No."

He took out a bag of tobacco and some rolling papers and started to roll his own cigarette. "Did I do something to offend you? I know the group thinks I'm some sort of insensitive—"

I cut him off. "You stare a lot."

He looked at me sideways as he lit his cigarette. "Do I? At what?"

"You know at what. At me."

He smiled and blew out smoke. "What can I say, you're a beautiful woman."

"Oh, come on," I scoffed. "I am not a beautiful woman. How can you even say something like that? I'm not even an attractive woman."

He sat there and looked at me, confusion all over his face. "What on earth ever made you think you weren't an attractive woman?"

"The mirror."

"I think you're very attractive. You're like a…" He stopped for a second and looked up as he thought. "Oh, I don't know. I think you're pretty attractive."

"Well. That's quite a compliment. I'm not very good at taking compliments."

"I've noticed," he said.

I took a deep breath and let it out. "Thanks."

"For what?"

"For the compliment. It was a kind thing to say."

"I mean it."

"And you are definitely not shy."

He shrugged. "I guess it just depends on the circumstances, but I got the feeling that we would hit it off."

"Confident."

"And thanks for saving my ass in there."

"I really wasn't," I said. "I knew exactly what you were talking about. I don't know how we got sidetracked by talking about how women should have the right to walk anywhere they want at night. I mean, they should, but let's be realistic. You were really brave. There is no way I'm going to be able to do what you did in there. It was almost like it was an experiment, you know?"

"Really? Explain to me how?"

"Well, you brought up what could be seen as taboo material."

"I couldn't function, and I knew it had everything to do with Estera. I was so pissed off all the time, I was hitting the bottle really hard. Depression was out of control. I couldn't get out of bed. Of course, Dr. Samuel knew some because I told him, so I decided to just throw shit on the wall and tell the group. Let the balloon go and see where it led. It flew exactly where I thought it would fly and landed right where I thought it would land."

"You were getting into some really heavy stuff in there. Has anyone else shared their stories yet?"

"I was the first. As far as I know."

"Well. This is something that's totally new to people. Once everyone starts hearing what's really going on in everyone's head, providing we're as honest as we can be—"

"Now I don't know if I really give a shit what anyone thinks."

"Did it help in there? Maybe a little?"

"Yeah, it kind of did. I, uh, should have brought her up better. You know how you feel like you're the only one who notices something?"

"Oh, sure I do. I felt like I was the only one who even knew what grief *was* when my sister died. That's one of the things I think drove me over the edge. But it wasn't your job to bring her up. You were her older brother, not her father."

"I felt like I was the only one who understood her. And she knew it. I knew she had a mean streak. Maybe she didn't do a damned thing. Maybe she just ran into this psychopath, and he just killed her. But I will never believe that. I can't even imagine what my family would think if they knew my thoughts."

"Your thoughts are your own, and they're real. Besides, you don't give a shit what anyone thinks."

He sighed and nodded somberly. "Tell me about your sister."

"I had a mouthy sister too," I said, and we both laughed. "She was also murdered, so we have some things in common."

"Really?" He seemed astonished.

I nodded. "Our stepfather." I didn't tell him he was most likely her father.

"You've got to be kidding me."

I shook my head. "He threw her up against the wall in a hallway in our house and broke her neck. I saw the whole thing."

Watching me carefully, he sat back and took the last drag of his cigarette. Then he flicked it away. "You were a witness?"

"Yes. But I was young, and no one believed my account. And he got eight to twenty-five years for manslaughter. He was moved from a maximum-security prison to a medium after eight, and now he's dying of cancer." That was all I told him.

"*Manslaughter.*"

I was suddenly spent. There wasn't much more I could say on the subject. There wasn't much more I wanted to say on the subject. "He'll die in prison now. He confessed to another killing. He'll die there."

"I should think so." He began to roll another cigarette.

I glimpsed at his hair, hoping he wouldn't notice. The evening sun still picked up shiny glints of blue. His face was chiseled.

"Are you from here? Wellton?"

"Born and raised. You said something about living in Britain?"

He nodded. "I was born in Iran. My parents brought me to England when my father got an engineering job with a firm in London, then we were transferred to the United States when I was just finishing high school. We lived in Atlanta. My family is still there."

We talked until stars flooded the sky. We remembered the lovely things we wanted to remember about our sisters. It was unusual for me. I had never had that conversation with anyone, certainly not a man. Possibly with Walter, but this was very different.

Suddenly, he looked up. "It's late. You should be getting home."

I didn't tell him I was a loner and sometimes an insomniac who could have sat on that table for hours. I didn't tell him a lot of things about myself. I had no other plans for the evening.

"Let me walk you to your car," he insisted.

We had already watched the custodian lock the door, so we walked along the darkened side and front of the building. I noticed the bright lights in the grand piano room in the hospital across the road, but I couldn't see anything beyond. I thought of Robyn and how ridiculously happy she would have been had she seen me walking along with a man.

We strolled over to my little life saving Dodge Dart. I unlocked the door.

"It was really nice talking to you, Alice." Then he stuck out his hand for me to shake, which I thought was kind of weird, but I took it.

"Same. And again, you were really, really brave in there. I only hope I can find some of your courage."

"Believe me, you have plenty of courage," he said.

I started up my car as I watched him get into a green Jeep. I had a feeling that he wanted to escort me out of the office park, and I didn't want that, so I backed out and drove away. I headed toward the interstate back toward the university. I had a strange feeling I couldn't identify. It was almost as if I was lighter, and it felt easier to breathe.

I turned on the radio and quickly turned it down. I scanned the dial, looking for Pick Hudson's new FM channel, but I knew he didn't have anything going on this late at night. There was another guy named Salvadore who played Cuban jazz on the university radio station the Rattler. This was what was probably playing at the store right as my father was at the warehouse loading dock, guiding some trucker as he backed up to the door. The rhythmic beat, the soft background voices in the romantic language I couldn't understand, the fast trumpet—I visualized the scene in my head as it could have unfolded in reality and turned off the radio so that I could have complete silence once again.

The house was dark and quiet except for the porch light. I was thrilled and relieved. This meant no questions, none of Miranda's new television and stereo blaring. I batted away a tiny mysterious flying creature and unlocked the door, immediately turning on the light in the front hallway. I checked the bolts on the ratty cellar door just to make sure they were secure. But I didn't check the main coat closet just to make sure that no one was hiding in there, and when I entered the door to my kitchen, I never checked the broom closet, nor the linen closet, nor the bathroom, under the couch, and in the refrigerator. When I entered my bedroom, I didn't enter like a TV cop, making sure everything was clear. What I did do was check Marisa's ashes then Shelly's by merely touching the velvet sack and the little tin. I knew the medication was helping me, and I was helping it work.

I turned on a small lamp that I believed to be an antique. It had once belonged to my mother, and I squinted up at the light and wondered how I became in possession of it. I thought of Reza and the first time I saw him. I marveled at his exotic good looks, the warmth of his smile, his aggressive nose, his smooth olive complexion, the way the sun played with his hair. He seemed to understand, and he said I wasn't alone, and then I felt as if I wasn't. He touched my shoulder once. I tried to remember everything about him, everything we talked about from the beginning, until I finally fell asleep, wondering about Reza Khavari without turning off the small lamp.

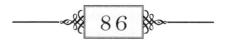

86

Jean Collins had been a certified public accountant and the chief executive officer of a small accounting firm since 1967. She worked hard to get where she was in life, and by the looks of her office, it appeared to be an interesting experience. She had memorabilia of women's liberation on just about every flat surface and an array of stickers pinned to corkboards. My first thought was that she had the same last name as my lost childhood best friend Bruce. I understood that the name *Collins* wasn't exactly an unusual surname, but Jeanne and Bruce were the only two that I knew of. I tried not to look at her as if I were pulling apart her features in an attempt to figure out whether or not there was any resemblance to the young boy who disappeared with his parents so many years ago. I wondered if Barton Withers tossed their bodies into a field somewhere when I forced myself to snap back to attention.

"It is very nice to meet you, Ms. Buchner. Please follow me."

Aunt Nancy once again walked to my apartment so that she could help me pick out a blue business suit, blue pumps and pantyhose for my interview. It took us nearly a full day to find something appropriate. To my surprise and shock, she showed up at my door at 6:00 a.m., ready for coffee. "Aunt Nancy, you can't walk in the middle of the night to get here. It's dark. It's dangerous."

"Well, who's going to give me a ride? Everyone's asleep."

I thought about her intriguing question for a moment and just decided to say nothing.

Not only did I need, but I wanted this job so badly. I was hoping that the small intense Jean Collins could look past my spotty résumé and see that I was a true professional. I could work with general ledgers, read financial statements, prepare and file taxes. I didn't exactly love accounting, but I was very good at it, and if she decided to continue to grow her company, I had years of experience in teaching and training. It had never occurred to me how exhausting a job interview could be, particularly when I wanted the job so much, until I had shaken Jean Collins's tiny hand for the last time that day and walked out of the little brick building, the formal wooden door slowly closing behind me.

I was dying to remove the uncomfortable navy-blue pumps and scuttle to my car, but I knew that would be most unprofessional. Jean Collins could have been sitting back in her cozy and snug desk chair watching me from her window as I made a complete fool of myself, thus defeating my entire purpose for the morning. But as soon as I was far enough away and behind a row of cars, I released my poor feet from the treacherous navy-blue pumps and walked the short remainder of the way in my pantyhose through the old potholed parking lot to my car. My sneakers were waiting on the floor of the passenger's seat. I lovingly put them on, threw the pumps in the back seat, pulled out of the parking lot, and wondered. I wondered about the interview, and I wondered about Reza.

I found him even more attractive the next time I saw him at evening group therapy, so much so that I couldn't bring myself to look at him. Being in his presence all of a sudden made me become warm and flush. I hoped no one else noticed because it could have been embarrassing. Marilyn brought homemade banana bread and told us her story about how both she and her older sister and brother were repeatedly raped over the years by a friend of her parents.

Reza and I spent hours talking out back at the picnic table, dodging bats and mosquitoes. We didn't discuss Marilyn, her baked goods, and her tragic upbringing, but we talked about everything else. It was only a matter of time until I had to share the story of Marisa and the monster and the police officer finding me under the bed. I was tired of thinking about it and tired of reliving it. It would never go away, but I had no other option. Everyone else had to do it, so it was only fair that I had to do it too.

One afternoon, the phone rang. It was Jean Collins. She didn't offer me a job, but she wanted me to come back and talk to her business partner, Leah McGillis. I saw that as a positive sign, even though I had forgotten she had a business partner; I had been so nervous. I should have remembered since the company was called Collins & McGillis Certified Public Accountants, Inc. Leah McGillis was the type of woman I could imagine being a wonderful aunt. I could see little children crawling all over her in her spare time. She was overweight and had a soft gentleness to her. Her brown hair with the blond highlights was wavy and fell almost to her shoulders. She wore huge purple glasses with her initials pasted in one corner, and when she smiled, her eyes disappeared. Originally from a small town in New Zealand, she and her son Andrew came to the United States in 1969. She had a picture of Andrew nearly front and center on her credenza. He was a giant man with bushy hair, a fat face, and a beard. Oddly, Leah McGillis never asked me much about my work as an accountant or a bookkeeper or any of the sort of work I did in my past. She was more interested that I had spent so many years tutoring and had always found myself doing it once again when I needed extra money. I made notes in my head about what she found so fascinating about me and decided to just leave them there for future reference. I was learning more and more about people and how much I didn't know. I was learning more about everything.

Then Leah McGillis dropped a bomb. "Alice, I certainly don't want to embarrass you, and I hope I'm not being too unprofessional," she said in her heavy accent, "but I must mention that you and I have met before, a very long time ago."

"We have?"

"I doubt you would remember—"

"When did we meet?"

"It was at Boochie's. We were picking up fish and a bag of chips, I'm sorry, fries. You would think after twenty years in America, I would stop calling french fries chips. You were there. I recognize you, your hair and your eyes. You were tall then too. There were some other children. You couldn't have been any older than about seven or eight. There was a massive crowd in that store. Well, there always is."

I worked quickly to unfreeze my smile. "Oh. Well. No kidding!"

"I don't get over there as often as I would like. I don't like crowds very much, but here's the funny thing."

I wondered for a second what could be funny.

"I *was* in there, oh, about a year or so ago, and I was talking to your father for a bit. And then I heard him talking to another customer about you, Alice. He spoke very highly of you. You are the apple of his eye." She smiled, and her eyes disappeared.

My chin rested on my thumbs. Not the most professional posture. "Ms. McGillis."

"Leah."

"I'm sorry, Leah. I'm not embarrassed." Embarrassed wouldn't cover the way I felt at that very moment. "I don't want you to think that you have to hire me because you know my dad's store, or he's proud of me, or—"

"All fathers should be proud of their daughters," she said resolutely. "Jean and I are both very impressed by you, and we would like you to join our team. That is, if you want to."

"Of course, yes. Thank you! Thank you very much."

She took my hand and enclosed the other one around it. Her grasp was firm.

We walked down a short corridor to Jean Collins's office and picked up paperwork that I started to fill out in what looked like the boardroom.

When I finally got to my car, my eyes stung with tears, but they were different again. I was elated that I landed a decent-paying job. I wanted to share my good news with Reza, but I had no way of getting in touch with him. And I would never want to call him. He would have to call me, that is, if he had my phone number, which he didn't.

As I drove home, I thought about the only men in my life who called me: Dad, Walter, Scotty to deliver a turkey, Bunic to deliver a car, a connection when I needed drugs, my landlord Chick. Maybe there were others. No, I think that was about it.

But it wasn't like this, not with Reza. When I thought of him, I felt a stirring, and I would sweat. I was happy with peace of mind, but it was also a silly and euphoric happy that only I knew. Then we would sit on the picnic table behind the medical building and talk for hours about everything—his father's dementia, his mother's sad death because of the stress over losing Estera, his sister's cucumber farm in North Carolina, Farsi, food, America. I found it was difficult to talk to him now because I sweat and found it hard to breathe. He didn't seem to find it difficult at all, and he didn't seem to notice my struggle. He was a handsome, accomplished, intelligent, very sensitive man. Why would he want someone like me? Did he want me? I had to stop that way of thinking. He told me I was beautiful, and I believe he meant it. And it was not just that. I was intelligent and accomplished. I had a job to do, and it was an important one. I was Alice Buchner, staff accountant for Collins & McGillis, Certified Public Accountants, Inc., and I would soon have cream-colored business cards with the raised brown print to prove it.

I flitted around my kitchen with pride, and it wasn't more than two minutes after I stood over the sink drinking a cold glass of water that the phone rang. I jumped and caught my breath.

"I'm so glad you gave me your number. Finally."

It was Reza.

"When did I give you my number?" My chest started to feel hot.

"Yesterday evening. Don't you remember? I asked you for it."

"Of course, of course, yes, I remember." I couldn't believe I didn't remember.

"You know," he said hurriedly, "I think it's time to celebrate getting this new job. Let me take you out to dinner Saturday night. Are you free? There's this great Persian restaurant in Harbins, right on the water. It's as good as my mother's cooking. Really. I want to see you. Should I pick you up at seven?"

I didn't know if he raced through that whole spiel out of fear of rejection.

"Okay, sure, yes. That would be wonderful." As soon as I put the phone down, I wanted to scream out of fear, anxiety, and that euphoria that my life was actually changing. I took three hard breaths and exhaled with my eyes closed, then I ran into my bedroom and looked for Robyn's phone number, thinking she could come by and give me a makeover in the morning. I stopped digging and sat still for a minute and tried to let my stomach decompress. Reza didn't know me by all that goop on my eyes and paint and hairspray. He liked the way I looked exactly the way I was.

I closed my eyes and smiled. Then I realized I didn't have a dressy thing to wear, and I knew that if I was going on a dinner date in Harbins, I needed a nice dress and a great pair of shoes. I leapt out into the front hallway. The first time I needed something.

"Miranda? Are you up there?" Miranda's father bought her a new TV and stereo system for her birthday, and she had been blaring them both ever since. "Miranda?"

With one whomp, her loud music ended into complete silence. I heard the door fly open. "Hey, are you okay? What's going on? Are you laughing?"

"No. I have a date Saturday night, and I don't know what to wear. Can you go shopping tomorrow morning?" They were words that surprised both of us.

She ran down the stairs wearing a caftan and nothing else. Her eyes danced with glee. "You have a date Saturday night? Who is he?"

"You don't know him."

She looked me up and down. "If I'm going to help you find something to wear, you're going to have to give me details. Is he taller than you?"

"Maybe an inch," I said with disbelief.

"What's his name?"

"Reza. Reza Khavari." I liked saying his name. I tried not to smile. I didn't want to give her any more than what I she felt she needed.

"What kind of name is that?"

"Persian."

"Persian?"

"Yes."

She leaned back against the refrigerator. "You like him, don't you? I can tell."

"Well." I crossed my arms. "So far, I think we mix very well. Are you going to help me buy a dress or not?"

She looked skeptical. "Where did you meet?"

"At a group for people who have experienced violence," I said. "Can we please talk about dresses now?"

We both looked at each other and said nothing. Then she pushed herself off the refrigerator. "I always thought Sterns had the best quality for the best prices. Let's go to the one on the boulevard."

"I'll drive," I said.

I couldn't remember the last time I had been to Sterns. It had been years. I went once to the downtown store with Kiki to pick up her paycheck. I had been such a recluse over the years, and I was beginning to realize how sad that really was. But it wasn't easy. I was like a prisoner coming out of a hole after years and years without ever seeing the sun. The good thing was that I didn't have to pretend about any of this with Reza because he knew. We talked about avoiding people and not trusting anyone. I didn't have to hide anything from him.

The updated Sterns hit me like something falling from the sky. The smell of the sweeping cosmetics counters when we entered the store—new, powdery, colorful, buttery, loaded with perfuming opium in the air. Although the peach carpets and twelve-by-twelve shiny marble floors were replaced by vast smooth gray and mauve carpet and beige limestone, I remember Marisa taking her shoes off and pretending to be an ice skater on that marble. My grandmother would give both of us a dirty look, but that wasn't enough to stop my sister. She would hide behind the yellow lattice décor where the handbags used to be displayed and pretend to be a bird in a cage, sticking her tongue out at customers who came too close. When one customer stuck *her* tongue out at Marisa, I sprinted toward my grandmother, leaving Marisa to fend for herself.

I finally settled on a beautiful black sleeveless dress with tiny white polka dots on the flowing skirt. Simple, pretty, kind of retro. I bought a pair of black sling-back low-wedge heels, not exactly killer, but I didn't want to be taller than my date either. I also bought some fake pearl button earrings. I had a matching bracelet already, a tiny silver chain at home, and a clip for my hair, which I had recently cut to my shoulders and dyed with the red glints, like Robyn's. So much better. Tame.

"You are going to look perfect, Alice. That dress fits you so well. It's like it was made for you. I didn't even realize how tiny your waist has become."

I really, really had to watch it with some of this medication.

"Thank you." I felt shy. I thought it actually looked good. I smiled to myself.

"Where is he taking you?"

"Some Persian place in Harbins. He says the food is as good as his mother's."

"Oh." She tossed her head back. "Ramin. It's right on the river, the nicest part of the river, of course. I've never been there, but I've read some of their reviews. Food is supposed to be fabulous, really authentic. Apparently at night, it has an incredibly romantic atmosphere. Alice, are you up for this?"

"Yes, I believe I am," I said, smiling.

"Oh god, you will look perfect. They have a hookah bar to the side for all the rich Harbins boys to try to show off and pretend. You know, those big bong-looking things with all the tubes for smoking fine tobacco?"

"I don't even smoke anymore. We won't be doing that, I can assure you."

"No hookahs for you?" she said playfully.

I looked over at her. "No. We have far more important things to discuss than bongs and fine tobacco."

"Listen to you. No, he'll just be whisking you to a quiet and dark candle-lit corner table."

"That's the whole idea."

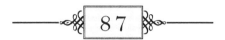

87

I was so nervous on Saturday. My anxiety couldn't be controlled. But why? It was Reza. We knew so much about each other. We had spent hours talking about the tragedies that comprised our lives. I cried in front of him. He cried in front of me. We were a comfort and solace to each other. We almost kissed one time, but I became frightened and retreated by looking down. Instead, he brushed a strand of hair from my face. I had never experienced these feelings before. I kept forgetting things, misplacing things, walking into things, laughing to myself. I tried to take a nap, but I couldn't sleep. I went out for a walk, but I was so distracted by noise, I had to turn around and come home. Then I got into the bathtub, but that didn't help. I painted my fingernails and toenails pink, then burgundy, and then I finally settled on a classic bright red. I showered, washed my hair, shaved my legs and underarms. I brushed and flossed, I used plenty of mouthwash, and I especially dressed carefully. With a vintage black clutch that used to belong to my grandmother, I was almost complete. I applied three strokes of black mascara to each eye and a tiny bit of red lipstick.

At 6:45 p.m., Miranda, Candace, and Aubrey insisted on seeing the finished product.

"Alice, I am in awe. You are beautiful. I could cry. Look at her," Aubrey said at the height of her dramatism.

I looked at each of them pointedly. "Thank you, I really appreciate your compliments and your support, but promise me you're not going to stand at the top of that staircase and listen through a cracked door like a bunch of silly sorority girls. I'm an adult woman, and I feel pathetic enough that this is my very first date with a man *ever*."

They looked at me liked they knew what to say but didn't know how to say it. Even Aubrey was at a loss for words. And then she wasn't. "Alice, you have been through more than most people could even fathom. You had a right to want to be alone for a long time. I'm not even sure if I'm saying this the right way, probably not, but lately, you have really seemed so much happier."

I nodded. "I believe I am."

"You're here now, and you look and feel great," Candace said. "Right now. Be in *this* now. Then maybe you can look to the future when you feel you have the strength."

Miranda nodded.

I knew they would still be one flight up eavesdropping on everything while they had the very best view they possibly could of Reza. And when he parked his Jeep and showed up at the front door, I could actually *feel* the three of them breathing off some distance somewhere.

My face was flushed, and I could feel the heat radiate off it. There was a tiny tickle in the center of my chest. My smile was wide and felt so warm. I felt such calm, peace, and contentment on this night, as if he was all mine.

He came to the door wearing a gauzy antique white shirt, a casual sport jacket, black chinos, and loafers. His regular work watch was gone and was replaced by a stainless steel one with a black face, and in his elegant hands were a bouquet of yellow roses. I took them from him and kissed his cheek. He seemed surprised but happy. Then I felt absolutely ridiculous because I knew I didn't have one single vase for them. Why would I? No one had ever brought me a bouquet of flowers before.

"Reza. They are exquisite. Did I tell you I love yellow roses too?" I could smell the deep richness of his soap.

He smiled. "Once. You look so beautiful." He ran his finger down my cheek.

I closed my eyes and quickly opened them again, realizing I was still holding the roses.

Then Miranda, knowing I had nothing suitable to put them in, quietly padded down the staircase. "I'm so sorry to interrupt the two of you, but I have a perfect crystal vase for you to put those gorgeous roses in." She lied and said she forgot to get the mail, and when she came back in, she would trim the stems and arrange them in the vase for me. After brief introductions, she told us to have a great time and took the roses from me.

We headed toward the Jeep. I could have been annoyed and embarrassed, but I wasn't, and neither was Reza. She stepped in there and saved me.

He opened the passenger door to the Jeep for me and helped me in. "Upstairs roommate trying to get as much information as possible?"

I laughed. "How did you know?"

"I grew up with five sisters." Then he silenced me with a kiss. It was delicate and lovely as our tongues brushed against one another. "I've been wanting to do that for the longest time."

"Me too," I agreed quietly.

"There will be plenty of flowers, Alice, and I will make sure you have a vase to put them all in." He leaned over and kissed me again. I looked back at him, nodded, and smiled. Then he touched my nose, and we drove off.

It was a warm August evening in Harbins. The days were long, and the quaint village center was still bustling. People were on the docks, in the cafés, and browsing the boutiques. I hadn't been there since I was a child with Marisa, my mother, Sunny, and Lil Schuester, tirelessly poking around musty antique shops while the older women gossiped about who had what and who married who. It was a different crowd this evening, and being with Reza made me feel like a strong woman, not a frightened kid. I wouldn't have to think about the next expression on my face for fear it might offend someone. I wouldn't have to cringe when Marisa made a comment or challenged my mother. All I needed to do was enjoy the stroll as Reza put his arm around me, and we crossed the main street.

Miranda was right about the hookah bar on a side alley as we walked down a flight of stairs into the restaurant. Like she said, it was crowded with obvious wealth and entitlement, all young men on that one weekend they may have been home from summering somewhere else and getting ready to go back to college. Had this establishment been there thirty years prior, the monster would have been in this very spot holding court, commanding attention, and acting like every inch the drunken thug that he was. But I had no time to think about him. He was gone.

A woman in her late fifties wearing more makeup than I had ever seen met us inside and introduced herself to me as Nadine. Reza seemed to be acquainted with her and kissed her quickly on both cheeks. She in turn did the same to me. There was so much warmth and a soothing calm of the unfamiliar fragrance of spice. There was soft music playing, foreign but recognizable, with a tinge of the west. There was handcrafted art on glass walls. The stone and hardwoods were shiny, and candles flickered on every table among the chatter and clinking of glasses. The aura sizzled with evening celebration and romance. It was as if daytime didn't exist.

Nadine led us through the back door and onto a stone deck overlooking the harbor where we were the only table set.

"Reza, this is lovely," I said as I looked out over the iron rail.

He stood very close to me, and his deep hazel eyes looked directly into mine. "Congratulations on your new job," he said.

I smiled and wanted so much to kiss him again. We locked lips, but when the kissing became intense, we both reluctantly pulled away, and I turned back to look at the harbor. "I've come here a few times for lunch, you know, for a smoke and to speak as much Farsi as I can. There aren't a lot of us in Wellton."

I smiled broadly and laughed.

As if reading my thoughts, he gave me a cheeky grin and scratched the back of my neck. "I promise I'll never ask you to join me for a smoke."

"I don't think I'll ever take it again."

"Good for you. I *should* follow suit, but as long as you don't mind, I don't think that's going to happen any time soon." He laughed and then said quietly, "I had never been back here before until the last time I was here. I happened to walk out on this deck, and I said to myself that if you got the job, I would take you right here to this beautiful spot. And if not, even though I knew you would, I would still take you here to this beautiful spot."

I smiled and wanted to throw my arms around him, but out of the corner of my eye, I saw a man with a white shirt walking around beyond us. "Shall we sit?"

"Yes, let's."

The man in the white shirt was of stocky build and was somewhere in his thirties. He and Reza chuckled and greeted each other warmly. "Alice, meet Nadine's son, Zack."

Zack humbly reached for my hand and held it in both of his. "Congratulations on your new employ," he said in a thick accent.

"Thank you," I replied. "Thank you very much."

Reza and Zack spoke quickly as he ordered for us. I briefly thought of my father and how fascinated he would have been with this place and the people. I drank a strong glass of wine or maybe what felt like one since I hadn't had a drink in a long time. But it was good wine, and I felt comfortable. I was in good hands, mainly my own.

We dined on rolled grape leaves with currants and plain yogurt, hot flat bread, kebabs with rice lentils, vegetables, and orange zest. We drank tea and had homemade vanilla ice cream with fresh spearmint.

We talked until the last light flickered on the table. We laughed so hard that at one point, I could see a waiter through a window chuckle as he bent down to pick up glasses. We walked along the harbor arm in arm, but when it started to rain, we ran for the car, and we drove home slowly. It would give me time to tell Reza the one thing he knew nothing about and might find difficult to believe.

As we pulled up in front of the house, I became suddenly panicked. I looked out onto the lit street. My mouth opened, my brow furrowed, and I could feel my breath heaving irregularly.

"Alice, are you all right?" His elegant fingers were in my hair again, and his touch stirred me and made me warm.

"I would really love for you to come inside."

He sat back in his seat and looked at me thoughtfully. "Are you sure?"

"I am sure, but I must tell you, I'm a virgin."

He didn't move. There wasn't even a flicker of his pupils. "A virgin?"

"Yes, I'm a virgin. Hard to believe at my age, but true."

"A virgin." Now he sat up a little. "A virgin."

"A virgin. I know. It's the eighties."

"A virgin."

"Reza, don't you know what a virgin is?"

"No, oh, no, no. Of course I do." He looked out the windshield with a pained expression. "The last thing I want to do is cause you any pain. Are you absolutely sure?"

"I was the one who asked you in."

"I'm falling in love with you. No, that's not right. I *am* in love with you." He put his hand on my cheek. "I want you to be sure this is what you want."

I put his face in my hands and drew him close to me. "I'm in love with you. And what I want is for you to park this Jeep in that makeshift parking lot over there, come inside, have another glass of wine, and make love to me."

We kissed for a long time. I felt those same stirrings in my body that I never felt before, that I never knew existed because I had never felt like this. Once his mouth was on my neck and shoulders, I could have positioned myself to do it right then and there on the dashboard, but I felt it was probably best that we go inside. I had an old bottle of white wine that had been in my refrigerator forever. I knew it was going to be cheap and bitter, but at least it was ice-cold.

I laughed as I tried to remove the cork, which refused to budge. Reza stood against the counter watching me silently, then he gently took the wine bottle from my hand and led me into the bedroom and closed the door. I went to turn on the one low light that I had, the antique lamp, but he gently took my arm away, turned off the lamp, and instead opened the blinds just a crack so the light from the streetlamp at the corner of the block could seep through just a little and from afar. He unzipped my dress as I worked on removing his linen shirt and his belt. Within seconds, we were naked and on my bed, exploring each other's bodies. We melded together as if were made for each other, our bodies entwined, our damp hair brushing against each other's skin. Silently I was frightened of all the pain I would endure when he rolled on top of me. I wrapped my arms and legs around his back, and he plunged himself inside me. I let out a little sound of anguish.

"Are you all right?" he spoke gently.

"Yes," I gasped softly. I buried my face in his neck and took solace in his chest and in his hair. Our bodies came closer and closer together as we rocked as one. He was all mine, and I could let go and give everything to him. Then he shook and groaned loudly, sweeping me up in his pleasure.

When he finally rolled over, I noticed blood on my thighs. He looked over at me and put his head on my stomach. "Are you hurt, Alice?"

I stroked his hair. "I'm perfectly fine."

"You are beautiful."

We fell asleep to the joy of each other's breathing and Miranda's blues and rock selections. I smiled to myself, thinking of the women in my life who were so hell-bent on blaring music at the most inopportune times. Were they also trying to drown me out?

I woke in the middle of the night to the rumbling of thunder and clash of lightning. Reza leaned over me and cupped my cheek. Instinctively, I went down and took him in my mouth until he was ready. The room was very dark, and neither of us spoke a word. I mounted him, and he pulled his knees up and outward until he was deeply inside of me. There was some pain again, but not like before. I began to experience the most unbelievable ecstasy. I shivered and sweated at the same time as Reza tickled my nipples, and I glided hard back and forth, back and forth.

"Reza," I gasped, "I can't. What is—"

He smiled up at me. "Just wait."

I screamed as I exploded in pleasure. "My god." I fell back on his thighs in exhaustion.

He rolled me over and lifted my legs onto his shoulders and ground himself into me. We made love until we were both spent, until Sunday morning's light was desperate to make its way through the slits of the partially open blinds.

"I have dark bold coffee beans and my very own grinder." I lay on my belly and rested my chin on my arms.

"Hmm. That sounds great."

"I also have two-day-old blueberry muffins—homemade. I haven't tried one yet, but I hear they're very good. I wasn't expecting an overnight guest." I smiled.

"Two days old is just the perfect time." He rolled me toward him, and we made love again. Finally, we made our way out of bed. I threw on his shirt and a pair of panties. It was soft and worn and smelled of him. He put on his red and blue boxers and an undershirt, and together, we padded into the kitchen. There was a lightning bolt as I poured the two of us fresh brewed coffee. We both took it black. I heard the unmistakable sound of a door slamming and female voices followed by scratching sounds at my front kitchen door.

"Sounds like a large dog is trying to get in," Reza remarked as he stood, back to the sink, shoving blueberry muffin into his mouth.

"Oh, damn! I forgot to lock the door last night."

Just as the words plummeted from my mouth, in bounded a smiling cinnamon floppy-eared Doberman heading straight toward me at full speed.

"Oh, Arturo! You sweet boy. Here, have some muffin."

He had a friendly look of confusion on his face when he spotted Reza, who patted and talked to him immediately.

"Arturo, you can't just walk into Auntie Alice's kitchen uninvited on a Sun—oh my god, Alice." Candace stopped dead and looked at Reza and me standing half-naked in front of the sink. Arturo kept trying to put his nose on my thighs, and I gently pushed his head away as I tried not to laugh.

"So how was it last night?" In walked Miranda next. She had a knowing smirk on her face as if, despite blasting her music all night, she had her ear to the floor the whole time. "I see it didn't take long for that dress to come off."

"Arturo, get over here now!" Candace commanded.

"Man, is it comin' down out there."

Arturo barked at Scotty, who walked in with a cardboard box full of presumable offerings in the form of food from my father. He was wearing a ridiculous navy-blue raincoat with a hood that had this huge visor attached to it.

He looked at me with eyes the size of silver dollars. "I got a box," He said in a trancelike state.

"I can see that," I said, feeling sorry for him. "Just put it on the table. Thanks, Scotty."

"Now. Arturo, go with your mom, and the rest of you, as you can see, I have company." I backed into Reza, who put his arms around my waist and his face in my hair.

It was the dog that led the way, then Scotty, then Candace, and finally Miranda.

I immediately went to lock the door.

"I'm so sorry about that." I shook my head and smiled. It was actually funny, and I felt relaxed.

He walked toward me, put his arms around me, and kissed me. "We could always go over to my place," he said, looking around my kitchen. "But with the books and the socks, I think I have far more clutter than you."

"Or I could learn to lock the door."

"I'm sorry I distracted you." His mouth made its way down to my breasts again, and within seconds, we were back in bed. His hands went to the small of my back, and he lifted me into his mouth. As much as I tried not to make any noise, I moaned with the pounding relentless rain. We spent more time exploring each other, took a long hot shower together, ordered Chinese food, napped, read, and talked.

Eventually, it was late when the rain let up again. Both of us were exhausted and had busy mornings. Although I wanted him to stay, I reluctantly let him slip off into the finality of the Sunday evening.

I frowned at the sound of his Jeep speeding away as I longed to hold him again. I could hear Arturo's toenails on the hardwoods upstairs right after a door closing, the sound of a low female voice, and the sound of loud folk music. I smiled as I listened to the dog. Sometimes the silence in the house was so welcoming, but I was grateful to not be alone right then.

I lay on my stomach. The only light in the room was from the small antique lamp. I was amazed how much I loved the light it gave off. With one eye, I looked at the amber warmth it gave back to me. I never asked Reza if he noticed it, but I'm sure he did. Reza knew warmth and passion.

A deep roar of thunder returned through the winds, and the light flickered. My thoughts turned nearly as dark as the sky.

I was no longer a virgin. I really took a gamble. I supposed every woman did her first time. I had been attracted to Reza for a long time. I had been attracted to other men in the past, yet it always felt like some sort of ridiculous game we were playing. I would always end up tongue-tied. He would always end up with a prettier girl on his arm, so to hell with the whole thing.

Reza and I were in love. At least, that's what it felt like. I had an aching, longing feeling for him that, although it frightened me, would not be satisfied until my clothes were on the floor. I gave him my mind; he had all of my soul, and now I would give him every inch of my body. Yes, we were in love. He said it first. We told each other. I knew we were. Or were we? Next would be the test.

I turned off the lamp and lay back down in the pitch-black. We had not met what was left of each other's families; we were not engaged to be married. We had one date, and we had made love on and off for nearly twenty-four hours. Maybe he was longing for me as much as I was longing for him, or maybe he had gotten exactly what he wanted—to get into my pants. My mother would have thought so. The thought of her mocking me right now made me want to curl up like a ball of gray yarn and roll away. Bunica would have thought so. I could only imagine what raced through her mind when my mother came home in 1959, unmarried and pregnant with Marisa. Marisa would have thought so. She seemed to think she was the guru on guys and their one and only motivation.

But my thoughts returned to Reza. The man was a genius, a man of science, an animal lover who also knew unimaginable horror and grief. He knew doubt. He was a person who suffered tremendous loss. No one cared to understand him, not like I could. And now I loved him so much, there was no turning back. My god, help me.

Were there degrees of love? Can it be measured? It was all happening so fast. Other women my age already had careers and husbands and families. And there I was. I didn't think Reza would have told me he loved me if he didn't really love me.

I understood the pattern my mind could get caught up in, and I wanted to be cautious. I decided the next weekend, I would spend time with my grandmother replenishing flowers at my sister's would-be grave, but which turned out to be a memorial place instead. I would allow Reza to be the one to make the phone call. I would not play games with Reza, not like the heady stuff that Candace and Miranda were always complaining about over bottles of wine while Aubrey would stand on the sidelines, lecturing them because she had the key to a man's linear mind. I wouldn't even try to understand Robyn's obsession with being in love with the idea of a relationship with a man. She would deliberately put up with asshole after asshole just to have a guy around.

I thought my new life as a possible whore may have been just that, but Reza called that evening to say good night, to tell me that he had a wonderful weekend with me and hoped to see me again and have many, many more. He did not tell me he loved me again. I knew better than to push. I went to sleep warm and happy. It had been the happiest time in my life.

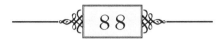

88

I didn't know if it was fate or pure coincidence, but I would be working directly with Reza's employer, the New Wellton Zoo and Conservation Center.

Formerly the Wellton Zoo, the New Wellton Zoo and Conservation Center was supposed to be a super educational state-of-the-art nonprofit project that would be relocating to its new grounds in October. But with construction behind schedule and tens of thousands of dollars over budget, it didn't appear as though that was going to happen. The zoo had acquired an outside agency that created the mess, and that's when Collins & McGillis stepped in to advise. Keeping full disclosure in mind, I reported to Jean immediately that I was dating one of the veterinarians. She didn't find that to be a problem since we were not dealing directly with them on this project. She stated to me that all confidentiality policies and laws remain the same regardless. I was surprised but grateful that I didn't have to either dump Reza or dump my job.

There were stacks of paper, ledgers, and unopened mail on what would be my desk. I thought to myself that it would take a forensics team to sift through this chaos. I didn't tell Reza how unconfident I felt in my abilities, but then I didn't see Reza much. Both of us were so busy those first couple of days that we were only able to say good night over the phone before we each crashed at about twelve o'clock.

On Thursday morning, I was given a slight respite when Jean Collins accompanied me into the conference room and sat me in front of what looked to be more personnel material and asked me to read and sign the majority of it. She sat down with two steaming mugs of coffee.

"Thank you." I said.

"I know you take yours black," she said.

"You do?"

"Yes. I've been watching you all week."

Little antennae perked up all over my body. I looked at her as I sipped. Her eyes were down.

"Look," she said, putting her cup down, "I know it's been tremendously hectic around here, but eventually, *eventually*, things will settle down, and it will begin to feel as if you're moving forward." She didn't sound sure of anything. "I see that you are very self-motivated and focused. But please, don't feel like you are a prisoner to that desk. You're getting to know the girls in the office, aren't you?"

"Oh yes. Everyone's been great." It would have been impossible *not* to get to know the receptionist Kathleen. She was as tall as I was and just as heavy before I became ill and lost all the weight. She was impeccably dressed in fine business suits that made her look more like a lady district attorney than a receptionist. When I remarked on her lovely summer plaid suit, she stated that real estate was her business. She was a licensed agent, and she never knew if she would have to show a property after work.

"Always have to look my best," she said with a beaming smile. "Never know when you have to chop-chop!" Her bubblegum personality went with her perfectly styled and sprayed light brown coif. Not a single strand was out of place, and she had a different style almost every day. Her makeup was thick and perfect. Her teeth were straight and white, and her nails were long and always the same color as her lipstick. Her shoes always matched her handbags. She must have gotten up in the middle of the night to put the whole ensemble together.

Shirl was Jean and Leah's secretary or administrative assistant. Her real name was Shirley, but everyone called her Shirl, and she liked it that way. She was a thin intense woman of medium height, in her midsixties, who, according to Kathleen, was always moaning about old age and retirement. I had only been here a few days, and I already heard her say something about her sixty-sixth birthday. It was funny, I thought she looked a lot older than that with that gaunt, pale skin and her far from fashionable dishwater to gray hair. She was, however, devoted to the partners and made it clear to me that as far as clerical needs went, I was on my own.

At about three in the afternoon, I saw a little blue note on top of my cluttered desk.

> Came in to introduce myself. Will call first the next time.
>
> —Kinsey

I frowned, got up, and strolled over to the reception area where Kathleen was talking to a man who was dropping off a giant white metal wall-mounted first aid kit. "Who is Kinsey?"

Kathleen slapped her purple metallic pen down as the delivery man walked away and turned the corner. "Oh my god, Kinsey. She stopped by when you were filling out all that paperwork. Kinsey is the executive director of the New Wellton Zoo and Conservation Center."

The Zoo as a description would have been adequate.

"She is the sweetest! And a herpetologist. Can you imagine? A master snake wrangler. I have seen her stroke an eastern diamondback like it was a puppy."

"Lovely. When did you see that?"

"Well, you see, my boyfriend, Denny, is a keeper at the zoo." She continued to tell me about what her boyfriend's job responsibilities were. "This is her extension," she continued. "Here, I'll write it down for you, fifteen, oh, six."

I stood for a moment, wondering what to do.

"Alice, don't worry, she's not going to carry a snake with her to lunch."

I smiled, but my thoughts were somewhere else. I wasn't worried about snakes. What I was wondering about was doing something out of the ordinary again and taking the initiative. I was learning to do things that were uncomfortable, like loving people other than Marisa, meeting new people, exposing myself in ways that may have been so easy for others but were more difficult for me. "Maybe I'll go find her."

"Oh, that's a great idea." Kathleen cheerfully approved and grabbed a small piece of paper. "Here, I'll draw you a map. She's in the A building today. Don't know why they call it that, but that's what it is. If you go through the main entrance, take a left and go all the way down the hill. Take your second left, and it's the second building on the right. It's a dark green stucco building with a maroon metal door. No *A* in sight, and I don't know why. It's just called the A building." She smiled broadly and tapped my wrist. Her bracelets jangled, and I could smell her perfume even more. "She will be so glad to see you."

I took the diagram and pretended to study it. "Thank you, Kathleen."

"You betcha." Her phones rang as I walked away, but I could feel her smile and her eyes on me the whole time.

It felt good to get out, stretch my legs, and take the five-minute drive to the old zoo that had been there my entire life. But when I arrived, there was that feeling in my stomach, and my heart filled with the flutter of anxiety. I walked up the concrete steps to building A and stepped inside to a beautiful sight. I stood directly in front of a large barred room with a baby giraffe inside. I threw my hand over my mouth. The man on a stepladder to the left of the baby feeding the animal greens was apparently Denny, Kathleen's boyfriend. Behind the baby lay Reza, who was on his back with a red bandana wrapped around his head, concentrating deeply as he appeared to be changing a bandage. The other person hovered closely and quietly as he fiddled with a toolbox-type medical case. I didn't want to be a distraction as I looked around for this Kinsey person.

Suddenly, the baby stopped eating the greens and lowered its head. It looked directly at me.

"Oh no," I said quietly. "I should go."

"No, don't go anywhere. Look, she likes you."

"She?" I moved in a little closer.

"Holly, this is Alice. Alice, this is Holly." Reza introduced me to the baby giraffe as he continued to work on a sore leg.

I spoke softly as Holly seemed to forget about her greens and continued to examine my face. I was surprised that this magnificent animal found a human being so intriguing. "You have the face of an angel, Holly. You're just a baby girl, aren't you?"

"'Cept when she starts kicking. Then she's a beast."

"Don't listen to Denny. He's negative today."

"He's always negative."

"Cut me some slack, man."

"Keep her occupied."

"You got it?"

"Got it."

"You want some more green stuff, baby girl? You all done?" Denny said.

Reza rolled away from Holly and got to his feet. Both he and the other man looked at the leg, and then he and Denny led Holly out a back door. It was the first time I had seen Reza since Sunday. His smile was broad and his teeth so white. He looked so pleased to see me, and I hadn't realized how much I had missed him.

"Hi," I said.

"What a nice surprise. What are you doing here?"

"I came down here to meet Kinsey Forman. She put a note on my desk."

He turned around. "She was here a while ago."

I put my hand on my chest. "I had never seen anything like that before in my life. She looked right into my eyes. She's so beautiful."

His smile was joyous. Our long noses were almost touching.

Denny walked back into the barred room with another man.

"But what happened to her poor leg?"

"An infection," he explained. "I've been treating it with antibiotics. She'll be fine. She's been doing much better. You obviously brightened up her afternoon." He smiled again, and I could feel myself turn bright pink.

"Was Holly born here?"

"Hmm. It was all over the news and in the paper…" His voice trailed off. Reza knew that I wasn't exactly out of my own head eight months ago. He looked down at my hands.

"I know," I said.

"So we must live in the now."

583

Our eyes held for a moment, and I turned that bright pink again. I was sure he noticed.

"Alice?" A fast-talking woman with long thick wavy brown hair and round tortoiseshell glasses came up behind me. "I'm Kinsey."

Reza touched my pinkie finger. "See you later."

I nodded. I wanted to go back to my office. This was hard and tiresome. I had a mile-long dot matrix printout of problems with potential solutions that I had to come up with, and after looking at the first ten, I knew I would probably be sitting there until ten in the evening. As I looked at her, I immediately noticed the faint scent of mint balm at her temples, her purple crochet choker, and her peaceful smile.

"I see you got my note."

"Yes."

"Hey, great. Why don't we take a walk across the street?" She said it so quickly, it almost sounded like one long word. But she seemed nice. She had this enchanting, earthy demeanor about her. "I'll put some herbal tea on. Can you stay for a few?"

Not really, but it wasn't like I could say no. I followed the lady with the long and thick brown hair, pristine white starched lab coat, tan baggie pants, and work boots into a room full of aquarium-type vessels. It looked like all of them were occupied by snakes.

"I also make a freshly ground vanilla hazelnut coffee. Please say you have ten minutes?"

Remembering Jean's suggestion about not chaining myself to my desk and at least getting to know my colleagues, I obliged. "It smells delicious," I said as I sat down in a comfortable green chair across from a long fat twisted sleeping monster whose head and presumably poisonous fangs were resting tranquilly.

Kinsey handed me a hand-thrown clay mug full of vanilla hazelnut coffee. "Puff adder. Just arrived a day ago. One of the most venomous vipers in the world."

I saw her catch the look of uneasiness on my face. I think she actually liked it.

"They're fat, short, and lazy, and that's how they trick their prey. They make a puffing sound, thus the name."

"Do I want to be sitting here right now?"

"We're perfectly safe." She watched every move on my face. She knew I was frightened out of my mind. I liked animals, but I could have done without certain reptiles…like venomous snakes. She told me how *he* would have to be "milked" before being handled. She was so passionate about *him* that I was tempted to ask her if she had a name for the sleepy killer, but I decided not to.

"What made you decide to get into this line of work?" I asked, sitting back in my overstuffed chair, sipping my coffee, staring at the horrifying thing in its little aquarium-type enclosure, praying to God it wouldn't find its way out. Kinsey Forman liked this room, and she wanted to meet me in here. She didn't mind my fear one bit.

She put her cup of coffee down on the mosaic table directly in front of us. "Well," she said, "I'm originally from Phoenix, Arizona."

"I heard it was really nice out there. Hot."

"Hmm. Indeed. And I was eight years old when one night, my father and I were coming home from buying a Christmas present for my mom. The front porch light was out, and as we went up to the walkway toward the front door, this giant rattler came out of nowhere and struck my father in the leg."

"Oh my god."

"Yes, but"—she nodded—"the snake never bit my dad, it just banged my dad's leg. Hard. We never understood what happened. It was a mystery and a miracle at the same time because it could have killed my father, who wasn't in the best of health at that time. My father ended up with a bruise on his leg that nearly covered his entire thigh. That's when I decided that I would never be beaten by a snake again, if you will. I made it my life's goal to understand the reptile."

Understand the reptile. I never heard such a strange story.

"So." She picked up her coffee again and sat back in her chair. She had a dreamy smile on her face. "What's going on with you and Reza?"

"I don't know what you're referring to, but I thought we were here to talk about numbers." I surprised myself at my assertiveness with a stranger.

"Oh, I can talk about numbers anytime with Jean," she said in a condescending tone. "He can't take his eyes off you."

I felt my neck become warm. "I would prefer to not talk about my personal life."

"So there *is* something going on." She put her cup down and put her hands out. "Look, just forget I even asked." I noticed her blouse was a pink silk. "Everyone is really laid-back around here, and no one really cares about anyone's dating habits. It's just that last year, he took one of the keepers home after the Christmas party. She was quite drunk."

"I'm not interested in what anyone did last Christmas."

"Well, you know what? This keeper, who shall remain nameless, might have some unresolved feelings. I just wanted to tell you that Reza might like to make the rounds, and I'm not just talking about with the animals."

"Kinsey"—I rose from my seat—"it was really nice to meet you, but I have mounds of work to do, and I really should be getting back."

"Don't rush off because of the Reza stuff."

"Thanks again for the coffee."

"Uh-huh." She looked at me for just a second and then turned away.

I hoped I didn't have to have contact with Dr. Kinsey Forman again. She was unseemly, gossipy, and generally not a very nice person. I needed to stay away from people like that.

"You're back!" Kathleen announced loudly as soon as I walked through the front door.

"Did I miss anything?" I prayed nosy Kathleen wouldn't ask me how my meeting went with Kinsey Forman.

"Not a thing," Kathleen said as Jean leaned on the reception counter. "Jean, I sent Alice over to the zoo to meet Dr. Forman because she stopped by first to meet Alice, who was busy with paperwork. I'm so glad she was able to finally get up and get out."

Jean looked tired.

"I understand you're busy, Alice," Kathleen continued without taking a breath, "and you're the new gal, and you want to make a good impression and everything, but everyone here knows you'll do a great job. There's nothing wrong with stretching those long legs of yours every once in a while. Right, Jean? Jean knows."

Jean exchanged a smile with me and nodded.

"I haven't been here very long, Kathleen. Try not to run me off too much," I said.

Jean chuckled, and Kathleen's face broke into a horrified look. She tapped the desk. "You are so bad. Here." She placed a little blue glass bottle down. "This is for you. A little welcoming gift from me. Nothing much."

"Nail strengthener?" I asked. I looked at my fingernails.

"It works great." Jean nodded in the direction of the bottle

"Hmm, thank you, Kathleen. I wonder if I'll ever get mine to look as good as yours. I doubt it."

She waved a hand at me. "Honey, these aren't even real."

"Really?" I looked at her perfect mango-colored nails as Jean said good night.

It was seven thirty in the evening when I felt I was at a stopping point and could safely leave my desk and prepare for a return in the morning. Pushing thoughts out of my mind still wasn't easy for me, and I had to work really hard to help the medication as best as I could. I didn't want to think about Reza taking some drunken keeper home from a Christmas party, but I couldn't help it. The thought continued like an endless loop, and it tortured me for a while. I understood Reza was a man, but I certainly didn't need the Executive Director of the New Zoo to be reminding me of it. And why was she? Why did she want to see me? It obviously had nothing to do with work. I had never had my heart broken by a man, and this relationship was still early enough for me to back out if I needed to. But this was my first relationship, and I was a weird adult who should have been through all this a long time ago.

I was still planning to visit the memorial site my grandmother meticulously put together for Marisa on Saturday. I thought I could bring up the subject of men and premarital sex and get her to convince me out of something.

The evening was blissful. It reminded me of the long nights when we played capture the flag and kick the can when we were kids. Even later at night, it was still so light in the summertime. My mother would stand along that side door and scream for us to get in the house "right now." Why did she even want us to come home?

Reza asked me to meet him by the lion's exhibit. I sat behind a section of secured glass where the zoo's mascot and oldest resident lived, a lion named Chacha. He seemed to like to sleep in the same place, a cave or den type of area, but from where I was perched, he would come up close and look right at me. His head backed up, he tucked his chin under, and his golden eyes met mine. I remembered the big cat from when Marisa and I were little girls, and my father took us to this zoo. He looked ferocious and majestic then, but now he was old. Marisa used to refer to him as Eric, not Chacha. Regardless of how big and fearless he was to two little girls, she said he had a sad face that reminded her of a little skinny boy in her class that the other children picked on and laughed at, Eric.

"Eric," I said aloud.

"Alice?" I looked up at Reza.

"Hi."

"I saw you come in."

"Did you?"

"Yes. Who is Eric?"

"Oh. Hmm. My sister named that lion Eric when we were kids."

"Interesting." He crossed his arms.

"She said he reminded her of a kid in school who got laughed at a lot."

"Really," he said. "How sad."

"It was something in his eyes, his face."

Both of us looked silently through the glass at Chacha as he ignored us. His back toward us, he slapped his tail.

"I don't know what she saw back then, but now that he's so old, there's a little bit of weariness in his eyes, like he's had enough. He never did have much of a mane, and those folds under his skin— is there a chance he could be Gir?" I was tired and felt like I was rambling.

Reza shook his head. "No, he's African."

We said nothing for a moment, then he looked down at me.

"You know the Gir?"

"No, not really. I don't think I was paying a whole lot of attention. The only thing I know is that they were the lions of the Bible, and there are about four to six hundred left in India. My dad's got a book about them in his library. You know, we used to read a lot together. A long time ago."

Reza knew everything about me, emotionally, physically. Maybe more than I knew about him, and I couldn't look at him. My face was hot. Then our eyes met.

"You're making me blush."

"You amaze me."

"Why, because I know a little trivia?" I looked at Eric, who ambled to the other side of the exhibit.

"I don't want to wait until this weekend to be with you again. See me tonight," he said.

"Okay."

"I really want to kiss you right now."

"Go ahead and kiss her, Doc."

I instantly stood up and looked around.

"No one's watchin' but that old cat who's been livin' on borrowed time for the past three years." It was Kathleen's boyfriend Denny, trotting by with two full garbage bags.

"How long have you been eavesdropping?" Reza pretended to be annoyed.

"Eavesdropping? *Eavesdropping?* You two are on Denny's turf now." He opened a nearby metal bin and dropped in the bags. "You don't think everyone noticed the two of you makin' googly eyes at each other earlier?"

"What?" I said.

"Body language, my dear. I'm an expert." He mumbled something else and walked off.

Reza must have taken that as permission. He took my face in his hands and kissed me passionately. "Let's go," he whispered.

Eric came back and sat at the glass with his back to us.

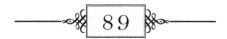

89

My grandmother's plain flannel button-down blouse matched the color of her hair. I didn't understand why she wore so much clothing when the weather was so warm.

"I'm glad you're out here so much, Bunica," I said, "taking care of Marisa's memorial."

She shrugged. "You do the things you have to do."

"Sometimes I hate coming out here."

"Hate is a very strong word, Alice. You know that. I have told you," she said as she clipped away at an overgrown pine. She never looked at me as she spoke. "I know what it is that you, my dear, are most likely thinking. Now, although God is everywhere, he does not force power over our will. *That* he has given to us. And so"—she paused—"if we want to sin, we will sin."

"Bunica."

She looked at me. "Alice, that man will receive proper judgment. Now what you need to do is stop this. Stop all of it."

"Stop what?" I touched a flower petal.

"Blaming yourself."

"I'm trying. I'm really trying so hard."

"Don't try. Do."

We placed some purple and red geraniums in front and to the side of the stone, and Bunica removed an old palm from Easter. "I didn't see this," she mumbled.

"Did you know there was a very strong possibility that he was her father?" I should have thought before I asked, but her reaction surprised me.

"Oh, yes." She was resigned.

"Oh, Bunica," I said, sitting back on my legs. "What did you and Bunic do?"

She lifted her hands to the sky. "What could we do? Your mother was eighteen years old. Unmarried. She worked as a typist for his father's company. One in a million girls. She was an adult, just barely, but I couldn't send her to a convent. She wouldn't go. She threatened us. And if I threw her out of the house, where would she go? Who would take care of her and her child? This is America, Alice, yes, but in 1959, things are not as they are now. She stayed hidden in the house until little Marisa was born. Your grandfather and I tried to protect them as best as we could."

"It sounds like you love my mother a lot."

Her face pleaded with sincerity. "Of course I love Lavinia. She is my daughter. You have to understand these things, Alice, and one day, you will."

I was confused. "What things?"

"My own sister beat our mother with a hairbrush for decades," she said. "My mother. A saint. She prayed for all those decades. Your own father's sister Nancy. I remember that young lady when she was becoming ill."

"No, no. That's different. You must know that's different. Aunt Nancy would have never *purposely* hurt someone."

My grandmother looked at me with tired eyes as her shoulders slumped. She nodded her head. "You're right," she said quietly. "It is different. My daughter has problems, and most of them she has brought on entirely by herself. Marisa went through her own hell."

I had never heard my grandmother use that word.

"And that beautiful child never complained. Not once."

"Bunica." I felt that sting in my eyes and the swell in my nose.

She took hold of my hands. "My dear Alice, your grandfather and I were the adults, and where were we? Where was Rudy? I knew she didn't get along with that Withers man. You two were teenage girls. Even an old lady from an old country should have known better. I knew my daughter, but I didn't realize how far she could stoop. She chose that man over her own child. I have thought so hard about it. I have been up at night, night after night, wondering what I could have done to save her. Alice. Please. Maybe when she was older, they would tell her that he was her father?"

"He didn't even know he was her father. If he even was. When he found out, he divorced my mother. That's when the divorce went through, while that monster was at Bellmorrow."

My grandmother's face fell weakly onto my shoulder.

We clung to each other for a long time.

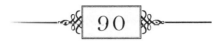

90

I took my place in front of the lobster tank. I knew the best time to drop by—Sunday around noon when most normal people were having lunch with their families after church. My father was in the store, but I was surprised to see Frank, Scotty, and Nancy all working diligently. My aunt was wearing a powder blue camouflage army jacket. I don't think I had ever seen one that color before. I ran my fingers across the bottom front of the tank that looked less populated than the last time I visited. I also avoided making eye contact with Scotty.

My father was finishing some heady conversation with a customer about the arms race between the United States and the Soviet Union when the customer finally turned to me and said, "Well, goodbye, Alice. My, you're all grown up now. What a beautiful young woman you turned out to be."

I smiled, wishing I knew who the person was. "Thank you. Thank you very much. Take care."

The glass door swished closed behind him.

I turned to my father. "Dad, you talk too much about politics. What happens if someone decides to disagree with you?"

"No one has in over thirty years, and if they do?"

"We throw 'em out!" Frank finished his sentence from behind a wall.

They laughed. I smiled. I shook my head and was glad my aunt wasn't around to give her opinion. He was in his world. My father. He had his own world, and that would never change. I noticed his clothing under his black rubber apron—red chef pants, red like the stripes in the American flag, which he hoisted up the pole each morning outside and took down each night and properly folded. His shirt perfectly matched his pants. He looked like he was wearing bright red emergency room scrubs. He put his hands together as if he were about to pray.

"Allie, this is big. Big. Big!"

I said nothing and looked toward the doomed lobsters.

"This is out of this world," he continued. "You got some Brit who drives a Jeep? Why are you hiding this guy from us? Come on!"

I looked at my father, whose arms were open as wide as his grin. Loud soul was blasting over the airwaves. Finally, Scotty and I looked at each other. "Gee, I wonder why. Could any of this be the sweet, innocent, hardworking Scotty and his big fat mouth?" I said.

"Ah, my dear daughter. The great Rudolph Buchner knows all," my father said as Scotty pulled a disappearing act.

"Bullshit," I said.

I was an adult and shouldn't have felt like a complete fool at this stage my life. Dr. Kilburn *did* happen to mention that being around your parents had a tendency to regress a person.

"That's what I've heard, and that's what I know to be true," my father chimed in with that exact same singsong voice that Marisa used to taunt me with.

I looked down at my new tan flats.

"Rudy!" Suddenly Aunt Nancy was back. "Alice has a new job and new friends and a new car. Why can't you just be nice?" She was drooling her words again. She was probably dieting and taking medication on an empty stomach.

But it was a fine question, Dad. Why *didn't* I bring Reza around to meet the family? Oh, I don't know, why not? My father. He really is so sensitive. So kind. If I didn't know better, I would have mistaken him for a fourteen-year-old boy in a fifty-something-year-old man's body.

He and my aunt were still bickering, Frank was running water, Scotty was still nowhere to be seen, and I was looking at my new shoes. What family? This one? I knew I should have been grateful for everything my father has done for me. My new shoes. I loved their smooth oily smell of leather and how much they felt like slippers.

My father walked around to my side of the tank. He put his arm around my shoulder. "Alice, honey, I'm sorry. It was wrong of me to humiliate you like that. You wanted to talk to me?"

"Do you have a few minutes?" My father and I hadn't had a solid relationship in quite a while.

"I didn't mean to sound sarcastic, but it could have been construed that way," he said.

"I'll show you the way to the back, Alice," my aunt volunteered loudly with a chastising glare at my father. "I'll get you a chair and a drink."

"Nancy, she knows where the back of the store is, for Christ's sake!"

"It's all right, Dad," I said quietly. "She's doing a great job helping. Thank you, Nance."

Like a child eager to please, my aunt practically pushed me into the old blue recliner next to my father's desk, brought me a plastic cup full of water, and quickly left the room.

My father whipped around the corner with his bright red scrubs and landed in his swivel chair. He smoothed back his thinning hair on top, and I observed the gray around his temples. He still didn't have much. "So what's on your mind, kid?" But as quickly as he asked, he changed the subject. "No, really, I want you to bring your new friend by. *I* don't care about anyone else around here. Why are you making that face?"

I breathed in, ready for whatever was coming at me. "Dad, I'm not here to talk about that." I chose my words as carefully as I could. "Did you know who Marisa's father probably was?"

I saw the electricity flicker in his pupils. He knew he was cornered. His shoulders relaxed in defeated exasperation, and he finally rubbed those burned-out eyes. His elbows tiredly found the mat on his desk, and his head went from side to side. I quickly looked over my shoulder to make sure that no one was coming. It was as if the hand of God held back any and all who could have disturbed us. "Alice, why are you rehashing all this bullshit again? Why?"

I squeezed in my stomach as I held my breath. I bit my tongue until I could almost taste the blood. I thought of everything I was grateful for in this life. I did everything I could not to lose my temper with him, not to throw his stapler across the room. I breathed in and out. In and out. I counted to ten, then twenty, as he sat there looking at me.

"I mean, come on."

"Dad," I said. "I am asking you a simple question."

"You know the answer!" he shouted and reached for his cigarettes.

"I thought you were cutting back," I observed quietly.

"I am," he said as he blew out smoke. "But now you're here giving me crap." He threw the pack down and looked over my shoulder. He waved his hand, smoke rising from his nose. "They can't hear. They could if they really wanted to badly enough. What the hell difference does it make now? Everyone knows. Nancy knows. My father knew."

I nodded. "But no one ever did a blood test. I mean, we can never be sure. It's just speculation," I said. "And perfect timing."

"Your mother is a sick woman, Alice. I know she's your mother—"

"You don't have to apologize, Dad."

"She knew this whole train wreck was going to happen by the time it left the station. Big Bucks knocks her up. Wouldn't it have made sense to tell him?"

"I don't think we'll ever know the answer to that," I said. "But you *raised* her. You were the only father she ever had."

"I've been racking my brains for years trying to figure out how a man could kill his own little girl. She was supposed to be his pride and joy, just like you are to me."

I looked at my father with helplessness, and he returned my gaze with sorrow-filled eyes. "She never did tell him, Dad. I guess everything came out after the arrest."

He shook his head slowly. He looked so sad. "Stepdaughter, niece, neighbor's daughter, *my* stepdaughter. What difference does it make now? Who cares?" He lowered his head. His face was full of regret. Then in anger, he lit another cigarette. "Want one?"

"No thanks."

"Does your guy smoke?"

"Roll-ups."

"Good."

I smiled.

"Alice, I don't know. Your sister. She was, you know, only seventeen years old. Beautiful child. Would grow to be a stunner, that's for sure. She didn't deserve that. Believe me, if I had the chance to do it all over again, I would have kept you both here. But that's all in the past. God, I had no idea this would happen! You can't turn back the clock. But I would have. Then both of you would have been safe. I wouldn't have been the best father, but at least she would have been alive."

I closed my eyes and prayed I wouldn't cry.

"So what? She wasn't my kid? I should have fought Lavinia tooth and nail. She would have backed down. Eventually. She would have gotten tired of it, you see. She would have tossed the two of you out on your little asses if I had just done what I should have done. You know how many goddamned lawyers come through that front door out there? How many you think?" His voice raised as his eyes turned wet.

"Dad." For the first time, I reached over and held my father's hand.

We sat in silence for a minute without moving, until quietly and finally, he said, "It's all right, Alice."

Slowly I rose from my chair. I decided to go out the back door by the loading dock. I turned around to look at my father. He sat hunched over and broken in his brown swivel chair in front of his desk. I knew he wanted to be left alone.

Then God lifted the hand, and the afternoon sun shone brightly. I heard the sounds of people, laughter, chatter, and the distant voices of the radio. Somewhere was the sound of Boochie's front entrance bell and a car door slamming off in the distance.

When I turned back to look at my father, he was gone.

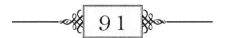

9 1

Autumn was unusually warm and long. It was as if every day, the sun was high in the sky, and each leaf was ablaze in a brilliant vermillion, yellow, or orange. The maple trees were always my favorite and brought back memories of how Aunt Nancy would find the perfect ones with Marisa and me and iron them between two pieces of wax paper. This had to be done under my father's supervision, of course. My mother didn't like us participating in any activities with Aunt Nancy, particularly if they involved a dangerous appliance.

I was happy. Not happy in that ongoing yet temporary euphoric way that a drug would make me feel. I was content. Reza and I were spending lovely times together. We had attended two operas, both at the Wellton Civic Center downtown. The first one took place during the French Revolution and then a more contemporarily written one, which featured in one of the beginning scenes a prince in chains being sent off to his gruesome death. I cried a little and clutched Reza's hand, but they were both so beautiful, and the music took such command of my soul.

It felt right to be myself around someone, even though I wasn't sure what being myself actually meant. Maybe it meant to feel perfectly comfortable around someone else so that I didn't have to worry or think over and over about what I might have done or said. That's what it was like with Reza. I tried to be a little more social than I normally was because I knew it was good for me. I was a natural recluse, and being out in the world was difficult for me, but I forced myself. I had good friends, and the people whom I worked for were very nice. I also had a good family who loved me. I was beginning to understand that more and more, regardless of their flaws. I had them too.

One afternoon, I decided it was time to discuss the meeting with Dr. Kinsey Forman with Reza. We were walking Arturo around campus. "She's reading a standardized exam to a special education child," I said, referring to Candace's Saturday afternoon.

"How many questions are there on one of those things? Eight hundred?"

"More like two," I said.

"Two," he said quietly.

"Hundred. You're avoiding my question, Reza. Why?"

"I don't even remember it." He shrugged and smiled.

"Don't bullshit me," I said, laughing.

"You're laughing now?" he said. "Okay. The Christmas party last year."

"I know. I know it was last year, but can't I get just a little bit jealous?" I tried to make the conversation light so that my obsessive worry didn't show. I guess I wasn't really being myself.

He turned to me, and a slow smile broke through his face. He put his hands on my shoulders and rubbed down my arms. Arturo sat at our feet. "Nothing happened between me and that keeper. I drove her home. She was drunk, very drunk. I helped her to the toilet where she got sick more times than I care to remember. Then once she cleaned herself up, she flung herself down onto her couch. I helped her get into her bed and turned her on her side, just in case she vomited again. When I left, she was snoring."

We continued to walk.

"I should have known. Kinsey. That wretched woman. Don't pay any attention to her. She's not working directly with you, and she had no business bothering you."

"She's your boss," I said with apprehension.

"I'm keenly aware of that. She shouldn't be anyone's boss. She's immature and unprofessional, and we're all constantly feeling like we have to just put our heads down and do our jobs to the best of our ability, which is obviously the right thing to do. But some people feel the need to kiss her ass. She's a spoiled troublemaker, and everyone knows it."

"So she *doesn't* soothe eastern diamondbacks to sleep?" I couldn't help laughing. Something told me that Kathleen got the name of the snake wrong, or from everything I know about the great Dr. Kinsey Forman, poor Kathleen was fed a load of shit.

Reza stopped quickly and looked at me. "Lord Jesus, no."

"And milking puff adders wouldn't be a part of her job description either."

He smirked, and we kept walking. "Not in a very long time."

"She had me sitting right in front of one in some kind of aquarium enclosure. We drank coffee, and she asked me these personal questions, of which, to her dismay, she got nothing in return. And not a thing had anything to do with the job or the project, and then she threw me a condescending curveball by telling me that if she needed any information about the project, she could just talk to one of my bosses." I was repeating myself, and I didn't care.

"Dan Renquist used to be the executive director about eight months ago, before he retired. He was a herpetologist too, and he had this habit of picking up strays: stray dogs, stray cats, stray rabbits, stray people. And Kinsey was one of them. She comes from a very wealthy family in Phoenix, she graduated at the top of her class, and all of that impressed Dan, even though she was so obviously after his job, it was sickeningly obnoxious. And when her father gave an enormous endowment to the new conservation center, Dan became just as obsessed with her as she was with him. The new reptile exhibit is going to be named after her father, James B. Forman. In the meantime, we're stuck with her. No one even got to interview for the job. Dan just *appointed* her. Money and politics. Such bullshit."

"Having the reptile house named after her family seems very fitting."

He nodded and smiled with an unlit cigarette in his mouth. "One day I'll introduce you to some sweet, harmless reptiles."

We dropped Arturo off at Candace's new apartment in the newly built beautifully manicured complex with the terraces and the grand brick landscaped entrance. I looked behind me all the way down the hill at Aubrey's house where her mother still lived, the little blue ranch with the oversized glass enclosure in the back where

Aubrey had that one birthday party that Marisa and I both attended. I smiled at the memory.

The sky was a lovely blue. There were so many memories, it was as if I could reach out and touch them. Beyond the now-busy four-lane road was the bus stop where we all used to wait and the long grassy field where my friend Bruce and I used to talk about our inventions. The Stanhope Ridge was so run-down now, and if they kept building apartment complexes like Candace's, it was just a matter of time before they tore the whole place down altogether.

As if sensing my longing and the nostalgia, Reza gave me Arturo's leash, and we walked toward Candace's door. It all happened so fast, my descent into sadness over the past. But the medication was helping, and I was able to smile so much more when I thought of the good times with my sister.

We drove out to Seagramsville to the new site where the New Wellton Zoo and Conservation Center was being constructed. It was about two thirty in the afternoon, and the sky was almost as perfectly blue as I had ever seen it. I couldn't stop noticing the beauty of the leaves and their radiant colors as barely a breeze interrupted them. People came from all over the country just to see the foliage in our little part of the world. I felt so fortunate to be born of it.

We rode past several pumpkin patches, large apple orchards where hundreds of people were out picking, several homes displaying their scarecrows, witches, and dancing skeletons, and then finally we drove to what looked like a giant crater in the earth and parked in an area that would eventually be a parking lot. There were a few construction workers milling around but, from what I could see, not many, probably because it was a Saturday.

I stayed in the car for a minute as Reza went to talk to someone in a trailer. "Are we allowed to be here?" I asked as I climbed out of the Jeep.

"Oh sure, but we have to wear one of these." Reza handed me a yellow hard hat he received from a man he seemed to know on the steps of the trailer.

I looked around in awe at the vastness of what would be the new zoo. "Reza, this is going to be incredible, so far, I mean, from what I can see from where we're standing," I said, observing the impressive view. "I was beginning to think that this was never going to happen. Thank God we have such incredible donors."

The Withers family was not one of them. I was surprised and suspicious as to the reason because there obviously had to be a big one. I was just glad.

"This could have been a hell of a lot worse than what it turned out to be financially," he said as we continued to walk past the trailer.

"I'm almost afraid to ask how," I said.

"Well, for one thing, the local news could have turned it into some kind of 'way over budget' scandal. I mean an actual scandal—not just because the old accounting firm really mismanaged the allocation of funds."

I nodded, my mind elsewhere. I briefly thought of Lisa Jupiter, who was apparently now living in Los Angeles.

As if reading my thoughts, Reza asked, "Can you imagine if that hack Lisa Jupiter was still around? I could see it right now: 'Girl who pulled out my fake hair is connected to the poorly planned New Wellton Zoo. Way over budgeted and taking far more time to build than originally planned. Could this scandal possibly be criminally related?'"

I chuckled. "Believe me, she would *never* admit to 'fake' anything. That woman was so vain—good lord!"

I stopped dead.

"What's the matter?" He put his arm around me. "Are you okay?"

I had seen that bright red color so many times, I wanted to get sick. But the bright white writing on the signs and banners was different. "Chambliss? Chambliss Enterprises?"

Reza looked over at the huge red banner covering one of the temporary chain-link fences like an oversized shawl. "Yes. Chambliss started to swallow up Withers about eight months ago. Apparently, it's been a good thing lately, although I don't know that much about the acquisition as I probably should. Withers sold out to Chambliss, the market took a tumble for about a minute, but then things went back to normal pretty quickly."

"I should know this, Reza," I said, horrified with my irresponsibility and childishness. "I'm amazed that Leah McGillis even hired me in the first place. And to think I've been getting almost hundreds of pieces of mail from Chambliss—my god, Reza, what is wrong with me? I am fastidious to a fault. This is my job—"

"And you are doing your job." He stopped me and put his hands on my shoulders. "And by the looks of things, I'd say you're doing a fine job. What, you didn't do a tap dance and give everyone a balloon when Withers Chambliss dissolved? I don't even think they're totally dissolved yet, if that makes you feel any better. But they *do* have that banner up, and I know Withers has nothing to do with this project. Right now would be a perfect time to trust yourself. Have some faith." He let his fingers quickly explore my face. "Alice, I think this is progress."

We continued to walk around an area that was going to be for a certain species of tiny blond monkeys. *"Progress?* Tell me. I'm dying to know how you think this is anything *close* to progress."

He stomped his cigarette out. "Well," he said quietly while standing and surveying the surroundings and the view in the perfect afternoon. I watched his hair blow slightly under the hard hat. "There would have been a time when seeing the name Chambliss Enterprises in huge bold letters would have completely knocked you sideways, and it almost did. But for different reasons. One time in your life? That banner would have instantly made you think of Withers and what he did to your sister, the justice that he never received, justice that *Marisa* never received. Inside that head of yours? It would have gone on like a loop. A nonstop loop until the one person who was really hurt and in terrible pain? Was you. You—while everyone else was moving forward, getting on with their lives, *never* understanding anything about you and your grief."

Like an old memory, Nina Averelle appeared. Her remains were probably found very close to this property. She sexually molested Marisa while I was doing what I was best at—nothing. And Marisa seemed to enjoy it too. Another young girl whose life was taken by the monster—Nina Averelle. A monster too?

"How do you handle this so well with Estera?"

"You know, I have my dark days. Sometimes I don't." He rapped on my hard hat, and we continued to walk. "But Estera and I had a far different relationship than you and Marisa did."

I pictured the attractions that would be heading our way, breathed in the smells of cement, sand, and autumn. There were so many things that I wanted to enjoy at that very moment that I decided to make every attempt to do what Reza tried to do each day—live in the now.

"I have a little surprise for you," he said all of a sudden. "Ahh, look at this."

"Is this my surprise?"

"No," He smiled and winked. "This entire acreage will be the lion sanctuary. This is where Eric will live."

"Oh, you remembered his name."

"Of course," he said, turning around with a huge grin. "How could anyone forget a lion named Eric? I hope the old guy adapts well to the move. That old place has been his home for decades."

I nodded.

Quietly we made our way back to the parking lot. It was about a twenty-minute drive over red and green farmland and up and over rolling hills until we finally stopped. There wasn't a soul around. It was so peaceful, so quiet, and the panoramic views from the top of the small hill were like nothing I had ever experienced. They were breathtaking, and I was filled with exhilaration. I had grown up only about forty minutes east of this exquisite area and had never known it had even existed.

We rode slowly up a gravel driveway to a large white house with a huge wraparound porch and gazebo area in the corner, a white barn and stone detached garage outbuilding, and another garage beyond. I saw a little girl in pink pants and a pink jacket running around near the barn.

We parked the Jeep.

"Reza, who lives here?"

"Some single guy."

I pointed to the little pink spot in the sun. "Is that his little girl?"

"No," he said, chuckling. "The little blond one? She belongs to the caretaker."

"The caretaker?"

He was already walking up the stone walkway leading to the front door.

"Where are you going?"

"Let's go ask the caretaker if we can go in and check the place out. I know the guy." He didn't even turn to look at me.

"We can't just go inside," I said, standing next to the Jeep. "That's trespassing. I've been in jail before, and not too long ago, I was on a year's probation for third-degree battery, in case you forgot."

He said nothing as he looked up at the house and then made his way up the stairs to the front porch.

"Reza, you need to come back here. Come on, let's go."

"Don't you know that Detective Holiday?"

"It's Holloway."

"Holloway. Can't he get us out of trouble? I'm a very reputable vet."

"Who cares?"

"Alice, come here now!"

"No. You're crazy. I'm not trespassing. It's bad enough we're in the guy's driveway."

He grinned and shook his head slowly. Then he walked back down the steps and toward me.

I said, "I don't know what you think is so funny, but you are not making me a part of this—"

"You are the most stubborn woman. You make me insane, you know that? Or are you just being smart?"

"I'm an idiot."

"Oh yes, you are. I told you I had a surprise for you."

"You bought this house."

"Yes." There was so much joy in his face. "I can't believe it took you that look to figure it out."

"So this is my surprise!" I put my hands over my mouth. "Reza, it's beautiful. But it's so big."

"I like big houses. But this is only half of the surprise. You have to come inside."

"*Half?*" I looked at him with skepticism. "It's so old."

"Built in 1883. So what are we waiting for?"

"I don't know. I'm now dying to see the inside." I was so happy just to see how excited he was. I took his arm, and we walked up the front walkway together and onto the huge wraparound porch. "This is more than beautiful. How did you find this place?"

There was a breeze that swished among the leaves and rippled through the freshly cut blades of grass that we probably wouldn't even feel had we not been on top of the hill.

"Look over there." Reza pointed off to the right as both of us languished in the unusual wind against the bright white wooden railings. "Can you see Wellton?"

There it was. The modest skyline of downtown Wellton.

"It's actually quite beautiful when it's all lit up at night. Let's go inside."

The heavy wooden front door had a square lead stained-glass window with one yellow tulip. The walls were all painted an antique white, and the hardwood floors in the entranceway were stained and glossed a shiny deep cherry. There was a huge rustic kitchen with a large island in the middle. This would suit Reza since he enjoyed cooking, especially Persian food, and he had gotten me interested too. The basement boasted a real wine cellar, which I had never seen before, and there was a large wood-paneled library similar to my father's for all of Reza's books. It was smaller though and cozier, and since it was an inside room, it had no windows, unlike Dad's, which had several.

There was a huge master bedroom on the main level, which he had restructured with a separate bathroom and a custom-made modernized bear-claw bathtub and a separate stand-up shower. There was also a powder room on the main floor, four more bedrooms upstairs, and two more bathrooms. All of the original moldings were intact, including the rare picture hangers from one hundred years prior.

Reza had all the plumbing, heating, and electrical ripped out and completely replaced and even had central air installed. I thought the house was ready to move in, but he insisted there was far more work to be completed on the old place.

It hadn't been the first time I had seen the inside of an impressive house. I lived in one, and the memories from that place in Crescent Hills nearly destroyed my life. A portion of my life was destroyed for many years, and those were years that were in the past and I would never get back. The Withers monstrosity was supposedly one of the grandest mansions within a ten-mile radius of Wellton. The only thing about that rotten castle I could say is that it was no home. It produced nothing but sorrow. And all these things really turn out to be are mortar, stone, wood, heating elements, garages, doors, and the rest of it. Happy people became happier, and unhappy people became unhappier.

And it wasn't the first time I stopped and wondered, not worried, but wondered about Reza. He was too good to be true. I knew he did well, but he was no millionaire, not that I was aware of anyway. I didn't know how he afforded this place. He did, after all, keep much of the original house intact, unlike the other two owned by the Withers family, which were ripped to shreds and turned into ostentatious eyesores. There were a lot of the same floors, same doors, same walls, and same moldings. He worked with what he had. But there was still something gnawing at me, which wasn't unusual. There was always something gnawing at me. It was just different this time.

I stood at a back window, looking out at an old yellow house and the land beyond. "I wonder what it's like up here in the winter. How many acres are you sitting on?"

"Bob's got a snowplow, snow blower, everything you can possibly imagine." His voice was trembling a little. "And to answer your question, thirteen."

"Oh, that's incredible." I whipped around to face him.

In his hand he held an open ring box. He was visibly trembling.

I threw my fingers up to my lips. Nothing would come out of my mouth.

He knelt down on one knee in the old-fashioned tradition. How did he know I would love that so much?

"Alice Buchner, will you become Alice Khavari and fill this house with children?"

There was never a time in my life where I cried out because of pure joy. The feeling was so euphoric, stupendous, and perfect. I ignored the tiny worm in my mind that reminded me that we hadn't been dating for a very long time.

"Yes, yes!"

We wrapped our arms around each other as my tears spilled onto his neck. I never dreamed I could find such happiness. The house had not one piece of furniture, and I was itching to get back to my place for a full evening of lovemaking as an engaged woman. Reza had thought ahead and brought a large flokati rug, which he placed in one of the upstairs bedrooms. We made love fiercely and didn't stop until we were both spent.

He pushed the damp hair off my face and held it in his hands as we kissed. I didn't want to stop, but he had something to say and reluctantly pulled his lips away from mine. "It is important that you know I went to your father first."

I sat up quickly. "You did?"

"I thought it would be inappropriate not to do so," he said, rubbing my back. "That was the first time I had ever met him, and there I was asking him for your hand. I prayed to God he would say yes."

"And did he?"

"Yes. Yes he did, straight away."

"How traditional," I said quietly as I pushed him down and rolled closely next to him. Then my mind started to run. I thought of scenario after scenario where my father and Frank could have really messed with him. I became embarrassed just thinking about what the two of them could have concocted without my knowledge and supervision. "When?"

"What?"

"When did you go over there? Well, I guess it doesn't matter. The hard part's over."

"Wanna climb back on?"

I just smiled and said nothing.

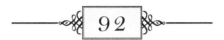

We finally headed for the stairway. "You know," I said, "I'm actually glad you went to see my dad. I know it was the first time, and it was probably a little awkward. I should have introduced the two of you first. But it was so nice, so traditional that you asked him for my hand. I'm sure he really appreciated that. Soon I'll have to meet the millions of people in your family."

"It turned out a lot better than I thought it would. I showed him the ring, which he loved. I told him that I loved you and wanted to spend the rest of my life with you, and then we went to Phil's Lounge at the end of the street, smoked a few cigarettes, talked a lot, and drank a couple of beers. Just the two of us."

"I can't believe he took you to that dump. No, I can, actually," I said.

"No, it was awesome. They have a huge beer selection, and they were selling bottles of English beer for a dollar seventy-five. Speaking of which, your dad went nuts over my accent. He could tell I spent a lot of time in England. I thought he was going to fall off his stool."

I nodded. "Oh yes, Dad is absolutely obsessed with Great Britain. Always was."

"Has he ever been?"

"Are you kidding me?" I scoffed. "No one could pull him away from that store even if there was a nuclear war."

"He adores you, Alice. You are everything to him."

I turned to him and pulled him in close. "I can't wait to be your wife."

"We have a lot to plan, don't we?"

I nodded. "Oh, yes. But we'll get through all that, and we have plenty of time to talk about what we want to do."

"Agreed," he said as if he really wanted to put the semantics and planning subject off for a while. "Would you like to go out back and meet little Diana?"

"Is that the little girl dressed in all pink?"

"That would be the one. That's Bob and Tina's daughter. Bob's the caretaker of the property, and they live in the yellow house back there."

"That would be nice." I was shocked and surprised as to how quickly my life had changed and the joy to which it could be measured. Maybe it was the combination of taking my medication and seeing Dr. Kilburn every eight weeks. It probably helped a lot that I had completely stopped smoking, drinking, and taking illicit drugs. I didn't think it was supposed to be this way for me, considering everything I had seen and experienced, considering everything I had done.

Reza joked about wanting to have one hundred children. I had never thought about marriage and children. I assumed as a young girl that one day I would grow up and marry because that's what you're supposed to do, whether I was interested or not. I knew that "he" was out there in the world somewhere; I just didn't know who "he" was. I understood that having children was an obvious result of marriage. It was not a choice. It was something that most married people did. People who got married had children, and I wasn't sure how ready I was for that.

But it turned out to be the one thing my mother did so beautifully. Although the circumstances were so wrong, what came from it was so lovely. I remembered Marisa and I played a game once with one of my grandmother's sewing needles and some white thread. I had to hold my palm out while Marisa dangled and rubbed the needle on the side on my hand. Then she dangled the needle directly over my palm. If the needle moved in a circle, I would someday have a girl. If the needle moved back and forth like a pendulum, I would someday have a boy. When the needle stopped, that would be the number of children we would have given birth to. I had three: a girl, then a boy, and then another girl. Marisa had two girls. We dangled that needle three times that one winter afternoon, and we came up with the same results each time. I thought about that day so many times over the years, that needle and white thread. It had to have been rigged somehow, but I didn't know how because I watched every move she made so closely. Marisa loved to pull one over on me in routine fashion.

It was Marisa who adored children. She would get so excited when were out somewhere like the bank or at the store, and there would be a baby with its mother. She particularly loved the bald infants with the really fat cheeks and the little fat square pillow feet. Naturally, my mother would become annoyed and embarrassed to the point of her usual anger. My sister didn't just make a comment about a beautiful child; she would run right over to that unassuming mother, look right in that little basket, and start touching the baby. It didn't even seem like the mothers cared. If anything, most of them seemed flattered. Marisa was just a young girl and wanted to see the baby. One time my mother twisted Marisa's ear so hard, I thought it would come peeling off. But as usual, no one ever seemed to notice, not the women with the big buns and the harlequin glasses, not the mothers with the babies, no one. I did, but I did nothing.

When Helena was born, Marisa was more overjoyed than my mother. Had we lived in a different place and time, she could have been mistaken for some ancient tribal mother, a mother far too young for the 1970s but a perfect princess from some other era. Marisa loved Helena, and then my mother and her monster took her away. Her little baby sister. Then the monster and his bride took everything away.

"Are you okay?"

I turned to Reza as I popped out of my trance. "Oh, yes. I'm fine. Just thinking about my sister. She would be so happy for me right now. She would probably be making some smart-ass remark too, like 'Try not to eat too much or you'll get fat and not fit into your wedding dress,' something like that. You had to know Marisa. She was really something."

"I'm sorry she won't be here," he said quietly and with sorrow in his voice.

"She is here. I believe that."

He grinned broadly. "You're right." He put his arm around my shoulder as we walked slowly into the breeze toward a split-rail fence. "I remember you told me once you didn't like horses."

"Oh. Yeah. It's really more of those uptight snobby types they have over at Sun Chance. But this old guy looks friendly."

A happy-looking brown horse with white markings clomped toward the fence as a tiny doll-like girl completely in pink, right down to her shoes, came running up to meet us. There was a man following her from behind.

"Hi!" she squeaked.

"Well, hello," I said. A smile grew on my face mostly because I had never experienced such happiness and peace, but also because the little child was so perfect. Everything was there—eyes, ears, nose, mouth, fingers, ponytail, but it was all tiny.

"Hello, Diana," Reza said in a gentle voice. Then he turned to Bob. "Bob, this is Alice. We're getting married."

"Well, congratulations. This poor boy's been a nervous wreck." The man extended his hand. "Bob McCarthy." Bob wasn't only the caretaker of the property, he was also an electrician and father to little Diana. He grew and sold vegetables and raised farm-fresh eggs. He and Diana also took care of one horse, a pig, two hens, a rooster, three cats, a rabbit, an old golden retriever, and a turkey that apparently liked to occasionally come up from the river. Bob's wife was Tina. She was the director of nursing at the large state hospital, Wellton General, about thirty minutes east.

"How old are you?" I asked the little girl.

Her little face snapped to a serious glare. "I'm four," she said and held up four fingers. There was something about her. She was a tough little kid.

"You're a very big girl," I said, looking at her little fingers and surprising myself. I remember when Helena was that young, and all I could remember about her was how loud and annoying she was. We once had a good relationship, a very close one. And I think I missed her. She was always gone.

While Reza and Bob talked about farm equipment, I continued to talk to Diana, who eventually noticed my ring. "You have a princess ring. Are you a princess?"

"No," I said, shaking my head. "I'm not a princess at all, but I feel like one today."

Diana knit her little strawberry blond eyebrows together. "That's probably because today you're wearing your ring, so you feel like a princess today."

I slowly looked down at the small child with awe. I loved what I was hearing and would have to mention it to Reza later. "My goodness, are you ever smart. Are you sure you're only four and not thirty-four?"

She started to laugh and jump in place with a mixture of self-consciousness and glee. It was as if I had embarrassed her, but she thought it was incredibly funny. "I'm four!"

"Can I give you a hug?" I surprised myself with my question.

She nodded deeply and held her arms up. I knelt down and took the child in my arms and held her for a few seconds. I gave her a little peck on the cheek.

"Now it's my turn to kiss you!"

We hugged again, and she kissed me softly on my right cheek. I was so overwhelmed with joy and contentment. I never believed I would find the warmth of happiness and love. And I found it with Reza.

I looked up at him as he talked to Bob. He looked back at me and quickly and effortlessly winked and then went on with his conversation. I was so blessed. I had everything.

The horse ambled over to the fence again. He seemed very social for a horse. I scratched his forehead. That was the first time I had ever scratched and patted a horse. Marisa loved them, and so did Helena from everything I knew about my younger sister, which was not very much anymore. I thought of those horses from Sun Chance. They were dark and mean and high-strung. Their eyes were always blazing as if they were prepared to jump their fences and trample me to death just because they knew I didn't like them. But this horse was nothing like the Sun Chance horses.

"Is this gentle sweetheart your horse, Diana?"

"Yes, but you can play with her too."

"Oh, thank you so much. She's a girl?"

Diana nodded quickly. "Hmm. Her name is Marisa."

"Name? *What?*"

"Little Melissa." Bob McCarthy and Reza joined us at the split-rail fence. "Melissa is Diana's middle name."

"Right, of course," I said, wondering how my shock came across. I looked at Reza but saw nothing in his face.

Bob patted the gentle creature's neck. "We just call her Little Melissa most of the time."

Reza put his arm around me while I put my head on his shoulder.

Bob McCarthy quietly hummed a tune. I wondered if I had scared little Diana, but I didn't think my surprise and misunderstanding was as bad as I thought it was. She just kept chatting with Melissa, Reza, and me. There were things I needed to be aware of.

The sky reluctantly took in the twilight.

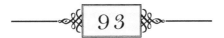

93

Our engagement announcement was very casual. But when I first received that ring, I knew I wouldn't be able to get past the reception area without Kathleen's eyes darting directly to it. What I wasn't prepared for was her screaming so loud when she saw it that poor Jean ran out of the office expecting a fire or a shooting.

Then Kathleen insisted on hosting a girls-only engagement announcement luncheon at this really posh French restaurant in Harbins. It was divine and very thoughtful of Kathleen to do something so special for me. It also was lovely to have Leah, Jean, Shirl, Bunica, Aunt Nancy, Miranda, Candace, Aubrey, and her mom there to help celebrate. We ate delicious French food, talked, laughed, and had a wonderful time. It was fun having Mrs. Meslier there to read the French side of the menu right down to the very last bean and explain in extensive detail what everything was. Aunt Nancy wore a little too much perfume, but she was balanced and lucid that day. Kathleen, obsessed with our biggest client, also invited Kinsey Forman, who politely declined due to meetings. My mother and Helena didn't even answer the invitations.

The first of December felt more like the end of September. Reza said Wellton reminded him of the English countryside in February: cold, rainy, dreary but no snow. I was secretly hoping it would stay this way for as long as possible. Kathleen and Candace would have burned me at the stake had I mentioned anything about a Christmas being other than starkly white.

As usual, my desk was piled high with seafoam green and white paper. The office was quiet at around two in the afternoon when Kathleen put a call through to my extension. It was my father.

"Dad?"

He sounded distraught and more hurried than normal. "It's not good, honey. Frank's had a heart attack."

"A heart attack?" I tried to keep my voice as low as possible. "What? When?"

"About an hour ago. Right here on the floor by the table." I heard tears and panic in his voice.

"Oh my god, Dad, is he okay?"

"The ambulance took him to Wellton General. Thank God I had a customer in here that knew CPR. Oh, honey, it was bad. He started clutching his arm, and I said, 'What the hell are you doing?' There musta been thirty people in here. I didn't know what to do."

"Dad, you have to say your prayers. Come on, everything's going to be fine. Take some deep breaths." I could hear him breathe for me. "In and out. In and out. Everything's going to be fine. Where is Scotty?"

"He went along in the ambulance." That surprised me, but I was glad they let him do that.

"What about Aunt Nancy? Is she there?"

"No, thank God. She's candy striping until six on the pediatric floor, then she and Tommy are going to get some dinner and cut down a Christmas tree for her apartment. I've talked to him, he'll keep her occupied. Thank God she didn't see this."

Sometimes I thought we coddled my aunt maybe a little bit too much and didn't give her credit for what she could handle.

"I'm on my way home now, Dad."

"Oh, Alice—"

"Dad, please don't argue with me."

"Okay," he said quietly, and his voice trailed off. I immediately called Reza, who didn't pick up his line, so I had to leave a message at his extension. I told him what happened and where I would be, and I had no idea what time I would be seeing him that night, if at all.

Leah was out of the office, and Jean was in a meeting, so I gave a note to Shirl to pass along. She heard the conversation and knew there was a problem. "Go and take care of your family, dear. Let us know if you need anything." She had definitely become a lot easier to get along with.

"Thanks so much, Shirl."

Kathleen wasn't in the reception area when I ran out the front door into the gray, cold, and wet afternoon. I knew I had to drive very carefully, not just because of the awful weather, but because my mind was so preoccupied with Frank. I turned on Pick Hudson's *All Soul All the Time.*

When I pulled into the driveway at my dad's house, I noticed Reza's Jeep was already parked in Boochie's front lot. He had gotten my message and beaten me there. The sign was turned off, and the store was eerily dark. I knew they were around the back. "Dad? Reza?"

"We're back here, Alice," Reza called out.

My father was pacing back and forth slowly, his head down as he shook it. A cigarette was between his thumb and first finger. Reza stood there, a cigarette between his lips, looking helpless and trying to console my father, whose face was streaked with tears. I didn't see this when my sister died, and for that one second, I was infuriated, but I pulled my mind away. I think Reza noticed something in my face. Our eyes met, and he nodded slightly.

"Dad."

"Allie," he said quietly. We embraced for a few seconds. "He's at the hospital. He's alive, and he's getting excellent care."

"Why are you wet? Have you been walking outside in this drizzle?" I asked my father.

"That's where I found him when I got here," Reza said.

I kissed Reza's cheek. "Thank you so much for coming. I'm so glad you got the message."

"Me too," he said quietly.

"Okay, Dad?"

"Huh?"

"We need to go to the hospital now, and you need to take your apron and this cardigan off. It's wet." I noticed his bright vermillion red chef pants were relatively dry, and so was his colorful fish shirt where the fish looked like they were drawn by children.

"Allie, I'm fine."

"Please don't fight me on this. You can't go to the hospital in wet clothing, *and* you can't sit on Reza's leather seats."

"I've got an anorak in the Jeep. Don't worry about the seats," Reza said.

"Yes, daughter. You sure you want to marry this one? She's awfully bossy."

Reza and Dad laughed nervously on our way out.

"Hey, man," my father said as he shut the door and reached over for Reza's arm. "Thanks a lot for coming. Means a lot to me."

"Of course, Mr. Buch—Rudy."

"That's it. Mr. Buchner. Mr. Buchner! Mr. Buchner was my ancestor from way back who had nothing to do with the store. It's Rudy or Dad, or whatever you're comfortable with." When my father gave Reza permission to call him Dad, the smile on Reza's face had a warmth to it that made me feel so full of joy, if only momentarily. We would be family soon.

Dad's spirits seemed a little bit more lifted. But when I turned around to look at him, he was a mess. Had I not known this was my father, I would have thought we had picked someone up off the streets, not the workaholic who was scared to death for his best friend's life.

"Hey, don't look at me. I stink like cod. I haven't changed, I haven't taken a shower. Sorry, man, I'm smelling up your raincoat thing you're letting me borrow here," he said.

"It's no problem at all, and you don't stink. That bad."

That got my father laughing, and I felt some relief. I looked over at Reza and smiled.

"Can we turn the heat up for you, Dad?" I asked.

"Oh no, honey, no. I'm perfectly comfortable, thank you. You guys are great for picking me up like this."

"It's not a problem at all."

"Oh, and by the way, I meant to congratulate the two of you, but we'll make sure we throw you a big party or, well, you know what I mean, as soon as we get poor old Frank back on his feet again, you know." His voice trailed off into a disorganized mishmash of promises to me and Reza and hopes for Frank.

I put my head down and rolled my bottom lip around under my teeth.

Reza looked at me curiously.

"Dad, listen. Don't worry about any of that right now, okay? Really, I'm serious. Reza and I are fine. Frank is our number one priority. Let's just take one thing at a time and get to the hospital. Just one thing at a time, okay?"

"You're right," he said. He took a deep breath and nodded, and for the next several minutes until we arrived at the hospital, the three of us rode in silence. The clearest sound was my father shifting nervously in the back seat.

It was a consistent and cold sharp drizzle when we reached the main entrance at Wellton General Hospital. I watched my father wearing Reza's anorak. It was almost comical being too big for him, but at least Dad was dry. There were about fifteen people—staff, visitors, and candy stripers—outside smoking and, of course, an endless stream of comings and goings. I wondered if we would run into my aunt on her candy striping shift, but I just couldn't worry about that. She was going to have to find out about Frank at some time.

We took the hallway in silence to the ICU. I remembered the last time we were at this hospital when Dad broke his arm by slipping and falling in the warehouse. And it was I, the wonderful daughter that I was, who stole his pain medicine. Frank and I sat in the same horrible attached plastic chairs waiting to go and visit with my father, whose arm had never been the same since that fall. I laughed to myself as I remembered Frank saying that those chairs reminded him of a police station in Mexico. How on earth would he know what the inside of a police station in Mexico looked like? I was afraid to ask then. I used to be afraid of a lot of things back then.

"What's funny?" Reza asked, looking at my smile.

My father went to find Scotty. The attached chairs in the ICU were navy-blue. Reza and I went to sit in the two closest to the floor-to-ceiling windows. We were the only people in the quietly buzzing waiting area who had happy faces.

"I was thinking about Frank, I don't know. Things he said, how he always made me laugh, his terrible singing voice. I've known him my whole life. And I took him for granted."

He took my hand. "Keep thinking good thoughts. Only good thoughts."

Scotty walked over to us with a wide-eyed look of bewilderment. He headed right toward me, threw his arms around me, and hugged me tight. I felt his shy sobbing face relieve itself into my shoulder, and we stayed like that until he could find a way to stand up. I was a little surprised. I never thought Scotty found that kind of attachment to me, but he was clinging to hope and full of desperation. He smelled warm and soft, almost floral, like he had just washed his navy-blue turtleneck.

He stood back and wiped his eyes and nose with his sleeve. There was a box of tissues sitting on the white free-floating table. I took out a couple and handed them to him. "Thanks, Alice," he whispered.

Reza stood up.

Scotty shook his hand. "Thanks for coming both of you."

"I'm so sorry about your father," Reza said gently. "Have you heard any news?"

Scotty shook his head. "Naw, they're not sayin' much. He's not even awake."

Unlike Frank, Scotty was what I would call a man of few words. Now, he was panicking and animated. His hands kept moving in and out of his pockets. He kept sitting down and standing up. He kept wiping his nose and scratching his head. He kept telling us that there wasn't really much news and that he came along in the ambulance with his father.

"Man, I know you're a doctor," he said, his eyes searching Reza's face.

"An animal doctor, I'm afraid, not human," Reza said apologetically, but Scotty surged forward.

"How did this happen? I mean…" He paused and looked around the room, probing for answers. "He's old, but he's not *that* old. He quit smoking about five years ago. He eats good. He loves his vegetables. He boils 'em 'til they mush, which I know isn't the best way to cook 'em. He's even been tryin' to get Rudy and Tom to go down to the Y and do the Nautilus weight stuff." He looked right into my eyes, and I had not a single word to say in return except "I'm sorry."

"Come sit down." Reza led him to one of several vacant plastic seats near ours. "Sometimes, *not always*, these days because of the way we eat, smoke, take care of ourselves, like I'm one to talk, but sometimes heart attacks can happen because of heredity. Does he have high blood pressure or cholesterol? Do you know your family's history when it comes to heart disease?"

I looked at Reza, and I think he already knew how Scotty was going to answer, but he seemed a little calmer as Reza asked him some simple questions.

But Scotty slowly shook his head. "One of the nurses asked me the same questions. Only thing is I really don't know. I don't remember my dad ever bein' sick. I don't remember him even goin' to the doctors."

Reza put a hand on his shoulder. Scotty looked dazed and tired. He opened his mouth to say something, but then closed it again.

"They'll probably run some tests and find out how this all originated," I said, not knowing what I was talking about but trying to add something useful.

Scotty put his head in his hands. The three of us sat there in long silence, as if there was nothing further to say. And then I glanced out the window, and my mind went to work. The monster. He was somewhere in this hospital. In the ICU perhaps? Was he on this floor? Or was he back in the prison infirmary? I wondered if I could just get up and walk around and inspect. Look through the windows. I could say I was a family member. I could do it, I could finally kill him. But there would be a policeman at his door who probably would say he wasn't allowed any visitors, and he would most likely be chained to the bed. Maybe not, he was hardly a flight risk.

No. Not anymore. I was different now. I took my medication. My thoughts were clearer. I wasn't sick anymore. I had Reza, and I was getting married. Marisa would have been so happy, and I was told time after time that she wouldn't want me to think this way. I didn't want to think this way. Barton Withers was dying, and he knew what he did. For that, he would get his just punishment. I could only hope.

I wondered as I looked around briefly where my father had disappeared to when Scotty's head popped up. His voice was horse. "I didn't think to congratulate you two on your engagement. Man, I'm sorry."

"Congratulations? Are you kidding me? You have so much going on right now." I was so empathetic to him.

"Really, don't apologize," Reza confirmed.

I saw my father with a cardboard carrier.

"I got some coffee here. Reza, I don't know if you drink coffee, but I got you some anyway."

"Thanks, Dad." I took the cup.

"Black is just fine, Rudy, thanks."

My father took a seat. Scotty poured two creams and a sugar into his coffee, and I took everyone's trash, put it in the cardboard holder, and placed it on the end table. My father reached for his cigarettes until he realized he was in a hospital and there was no smoking allowed.

"What do we do now?" I felt powerless.

"I wonder when we can see Dad." Scotty looked depressed, and my father looked helpless.

"As soon as he's stable and can have visitors," Reza said.

"When will that be?" I asked.

"It could be anytime. All we can do is wait. Have you talked to your father's doctor yet?"

Scotty shook his head.

We waited for about two more hours. The three men drank more coffee, went to the bathroom. We walked around. No one wanted food. We read old magazines, and we watched the rain. Not one person complained about the time.

Then a man in a white medical coat came waddling toward us. The four of us stood to attention at once.

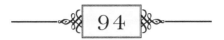

94

Dr. Andrew Stephenson introduced himself to Scotty first then to us as Frank's cardiologist. "Your dad is very touch and go right now, Mr. Watson."

Touch and go?

"Right now, Mr. Watson, we need to monitor him very closely. He's awake but very drowsy. A lot of that has to do with the medication we have him on. The most important thing is to get his blood pressure down to normal for a healthy man his age. It is unfortunately very, very high. He does have some blockage, but I don't think he needs surgery. Yet. I'm hoping we can manage him with medication. I just wished he had a checkup sooner, but that's in the past."

Dr. Stephenson had a thick strand of black hair at the back of his head that was longer than the rest. He was short and shaped like an egg. I had a feeling that *he* had a few blocked arteries, and I found it incredulous that at one point, he was so critical of the way Frank had been taking care of his health when it seemed like he really didn't even know what taking care of one's health meant. He had wide brown eyes rimmed with square silver-wired glasses and fluffy beige skin. His lips were the same color and shape as his fingers. His black shoes were scuffed and old-fashioned and looked like something you would buy at a thrift store. Worst of all, he looked as though he had slept in his clothing for at least a week. Maybe he had. I didn't like him and didn't want him within fifty feet of Frank. But that was not my call.

I wished I could have erased the last six hours, pulled Reza aside, and told him what I was thinking, but that would have scared Scotty even more. My father and Reza listened intently to Stephenson as I watched Scotty. He looked calmer and much more relaxed. At least that was good.

Stephenson shrugged and, with a helpless expression, continued, "Maybe tomorrow, you can see him. Look, there's no telling, but I am hopeful, okay?" He waved a fat finger and gave Scotty an admonishing look that worried me.

Reza reached for my hand because he knew I was exasperated. I looked at him, and he winked at me with his "we'll take care of it" face.

"Family may see him tomorrow or the next day. Family only," Stephenson said.

"Dr. Stephenson, we're all his family." Scotty motioned to all of us, even Reza.

My father pushed his hair back with his hands, "Doc, come on, Frank and I have known each other for over forty-five years. We're all he's got—"

"Fine." Stephenson raised two little hands. "I will call Mr. Watson in the morning first and immediately if there is any change. In the meantime, I suggest that all of you go home and get some rest. There is no point in hanging around here and fraying your nerves anymore." He ran out of breath. "It won't do you any good, and it won't do the patient any good. Now"—he turned to Scotty—"I'm actually on call tonight if you need me. Here is my card. Good night, everyone."

"Thank you, Doc," Scotty said.

As Stephenson waddled his way back to wherever he came from, I picked up the trash from the little end table and looked around for a receptacle.

"Are you okay?" Reza asked.

I looked over at Scotty and my father to make sure they were out of earshot and saw they were talking. "I didn't like that doctor, Reza."

"I know, I could tell."

"I hope Scotty didn't notice."

"I very much doubt it."

"There were so many negatives about him. He was a real turn-off. I could smell his breath from three feet away, for god's sake!"

"He was definitely rough around the edges. But it's right here that counts." He tapped on his head. "And he made sense on a lot of points. I think Frank is in good hands."

"You're too smart and too patient for me."

He said nothing.

"It's just that when the doctor tells you that you have to cut down on this and cut down on that, lift weights, jog, I mean, come on, does that guy look like he jogs to you?"

He laughed quietly. "Definitely not."

"If I'm going to have a heart doctor take care of me, I want him to look like he—"

"Like Mr. America?"

"You see, that's it."

"It doesn't work that way. It's all in the mind. Most of the time."

I was so exhausted and worried. "I don't think there's much else we can do around here right now."

"Are you two ready to hit the road?" my father called out.

Scotty answered instead. "I think so. Dr. Stephenson said he would call immediately if there's any change." He sounded so confident, and so I decided I would be too.

The four of us strolled slowly toward the corridor, not really wanting to leave Frank behind.

"I gotta coupla things I gotta do. I gotta call Aunt Shirley in Philadelphia and Aunt Pat in Detroit and let them know what happened. Maybe I can get some family history."

"Scotty, I didn't realize you had aunts," I said. There really was a lot I didn't know about Scotty and Frank, even though they were a part of this family my whole life. Marisa's murder and my subsequent depression and anxiety kept me so self-focused from knowing, wanting to know, or even caring. And now Frank was in the hospital.

"Oh, sure," my father said. "I remember Patricia and Shirley when we were kids. Frank was a little older, but—that was a long time ago." He looked down at his shoes.

"You know, Dad," I said, "it probably wouldn't be a bad idea if you kept up on some of that stuff. Blood pressure, triglycerides, cholesterol. That builds up in the arteries. When was the last time you saw a doctor about that?"

"Ah, probably the last time I was here when I broke my arm. I think my blood pressure is a little borderline high. Suppose I gotta give up these cigarettes one of these days. When we started smoking, no one told us they were bad for you. Before you knew it, you were hooked. You too, man. Those nonfiltered roll-ups?"

Reza nodded. "Easier said than done."

"Hell, don't I know it."

I chose not to talk about how I gave up smoking, but I never craved nor did I ever smoke anything again.

"I hope I can see him tomorrow. I'm prayin' I can see him tomorrow," Scotty said, shaking his head and looking around.

"I hope so too. We just have to think positive thoughts," I said.

"I don't think the doctor woulda said maybe tomorrow or maybe the next day if he wasn't hopeful. I really don't," Scotty said.

"All we can do is wait."

"And pray."

The sky was wintry and dark, and the temperature dropped from when we were last outside. The wind was whipping sideways, and sharp flecks of water stung my cheek. The four of us hustled toward the parking garage and Reza's Jeep.

"Whew!"

"Brr."

Another car door closed.

"Did it ever get cold or what?"

"I'll put the heat on, but we'll have to sit and shiver for a few minutes at least."

"It'll be over soon. I'll count to sixty."

"More like two hundred."

"Reza, you were sayin' something back there about praying?" Scotty said from the back seat.

"Yes." Reza looked in his rearview mirror.

"I'm not very good at that," Scotty said.

"No? Have you tried?" Reza asked.

"I have, you know? But I always think I'm angering God 'cause when I pray, I'm always askin' for somethin'. I had my head in my hands, and I was praying. I didn't have my hands put together, and I wasn't kneeling, nothin' like that. I was beggin' the Lord to please make my dad okay, please don't let my dad die. Please make my dad well again so I can take him home."

"There's nothing wrong with that at all," Reza said. "You may be asking for something, but look what you're asking for."

"But that's the *only* time I pray," Scotty said.

"You know, I've never been a very religious person," I said. "I certainly don't know what God thinks or what he will do, none of us does, but you are praying for your father's health, you're praying for him to get well. When I pray, I find that it can be very powerful."

I felt as though I was talking to a much younger person, even though he wasn't. Scotty was so confused and terrified.

"I can't imagine why God would be angry with you for praying for the well-being of your own father. That certainly isn't selfish, and if that's what you're worried about, you shouldn't be."

"Of course not, kid," my father said, trying to add some levity to the situation. "Of course if you prayed for one of those new Jaguars or a million bucks, *then* you would be *greedy*, and that would be a different story. But we all know you're worried about your dad. We're all praying for him."

"I might be going against God's will for my dad," Scotty said clearly.

No one said a word. I looked over at Reza, who looked at Scotty in his rearview mirror again. My father's head was down.

It was Scotty who changed the subject. "How we gonna break this to Nancy? I can't believe we got outta there without seeing her. It's a huge hospital, but—"

"You know," I said, "she's been doing well lately. I think she'll handle it okay, I really do."

Finally, Reza's Jeep was comfortable and warm. It was as if he had forgotten to drive out of the parking garage. And so off we drove through the dark and dreary maze of the hospital parking garage with each second moving farther and farther away from Frank.

"Look, guys, I've known my sister my whole life. The best way to deal with these things is to throw her as much normalcy as possible. There is no point in pouring sugar on it."

Right, this coming from a man who was so glad that Tommy was babysitting her again and had farmed her off on.

"Nancy, my dear little sister. Let me tell you a story when her illness really worked in our favor." He started to shimmy his way up to the front of his seat so we could all hear clearly.

"Oh god, Dad. Please don't make my cry." I turned around, pleading.

He patted me on the head. "You're not gonna cry, Allie. This one is funny as hell." His eyes got as wide as quarters. He reminded me of a little boy. Scotty looked at him with such interest. They were both so pitiful. "No, listen, Allie, this is a great one. It's so funny. You're gonna love it. You too, Reza.

"It was, oh, you girls, Marisa and Alice. You were little. You were just a kid too, Scotty. I'm thinkin' sixty-seven? Sixty-eight? Me and Frank. *And* Nancy. She liked to tag along. Tommy had already enlisted." He pushed his glasses up his nose with his forefinger. "It was really early in the morning. Frank and I hadn't opened the store yet. There was some diner across the street from the old W truck stop. They've spruced it up quite a bit from the old days. You know where I mean?"

Suddenly, we noticed a traffic jam up ahead of us.

"Oh shit, what's goin' on up there?" Dad asked to no one in particular.

Reza and I exchanged glances. I knew exactly the truck stop my father was referring to. It was the one I used to sleep at in the Plymouth in the way back of the car under the bright lights.

My father forgot about the traffic and continued with his story. "Okay. Now we were gonna meet with this old Italian guy, his name was, listen to this, Gazzer. Gaz. Short for Gasperino. But we were early, so we go and wait in this shitty little all-night diner called the Lunch Box. You shoulda seen your old man, Scott—he was wearing these brand-new maroon pants that were really stiff and way too long for him. He didn't want to cuff them, so they looked like these big bulging balloons around his ankles."

He described Frank's pants with his hands. I shook my head. I knew a lot of my father's stories, but this was a new one.

Scotty started to crack up in the back seat. It was hard not to laugh when my dad told a funny story from the past.

"And he was wearing these bright white loafers. Oh, he looked like a pimp, for god's sake. Anyway, we're all three standing right by the front door." My father's laughter was fresh, beautiful, and out of control now. "This fat black dude, and he says—he—he—pulls out a switchblade, but no one can really see how long it is because he's so fat, and it's in between the four of us."

"Dad!"

"No, wait, let me catch my breath, let me catch my breath. Oh dear Lord Almighty. So he says right then. He says, 'This is a stickup.' And *Nancy*"—my father points with exaggeration to the foggy window—"points down the aisle to the cash register where there was a waitress and about ten people standing in line, and she says, she says, 'Oh, okay, the cash register is right down over there.'"

The Jeep erupted into male laughter and seat and knee slapping as I looked around with confusion.

"Frank and I just looked at each other, trying not to laugh. But it was close to impossible. I think your dad did a little pee-pee in his pants. I knew if I let out a peep, this guy would have stuck me. And here's Nancy trying to find us a table! This guy was so, was so flummoxed. It was one of the only times I've seen a black man turn red. He reached into his pockets and pulled out a bunch of fake gold chains. He tried to sell us some hashish. He says, 'Here, some pretty jewelry for the pretty lady.' Jesus Christ! Nancy asks him if he played football in high school! Then before you can count to three, Gaz walks in, and this guy vanishes into thin air. My sister talked us out of being robbed and didn't even realize it."

"My ribs are hurting," Reza said.

"I hope I don't pee too!" Scotty answered.

"You better not!" Reza said.

"I'm cryin'," my father said, still laughing. "Those were some days. Unbelievable times. All we ever did was laugh. *And*, Scotty, we prayed for Tom's safe return. Yep, I remember it like it was yesterday."

"You and Dad got some good memories."

"Decades. *Decades.*"

I wondered why he was meeting this Gasperino person. I didn't dare ask because I didn't think I really wanted to know.

It was dark and cold and rainy. It was one of those awful week-nights that used to depress me to the point where I felt a waterfall of chemicals drop from the top of my brain to the bottom of my stomach. I was so despondent, I didn't know what to do with myself. I didn't want to live, and I was too afraid to die. But tonight, as Frank lay in a hospital bed fighting for his life, I laughed at the old stories because I had a strong feeling that everything was going to be okay.

We pulled up next to the loading dock.

"There's Bump," my father said, referring to the face in the cab window. "I'll go give him the news about Frank and tell him to get some sleep if he wants. We'll just have to get him unloaded in the morning."

The three of us stood awkwardly in front of the house, waiting for my father to come down off the side of Bump's cab. None of us seemed to want to break free. I wondered if anyone felt a twinge of guilt over the botched robbery story, the laughter, the smiles that hurt our faces. Most likely not. It was as if we were glued together by Frank's quest for survival, and it exhausted us and drained us of words, of voice.

And now Aunt Nancy would *have* to stop by the house and show Dad her Christmas tree even though it was tied to the top of Tommy's van. At least it was better than last year when she went out on her own and tried to take it on the city bus with her. This was a big accomplishment to manage a full day, and she wanted to show her brother she could do it. As I thought about her schedule, it would have been a huge day for *anyone*.

At first, I wasn't sure that telling my aunt about Frank's heart attack at this hour was such a great idea. She was probably very tired like the rest of us, but there were many times that she was very strong.

Her parents died when she was young, and my mother, who was terribly cruel to her, left my father, and she certainly handled Marisa's death far better than I did. But I'll never really know the truth to that. She was just coming out of a psychotic episode, but she adored Marisa. Kiki came, Kiki left.

The lives of this family had survived a myriad of changes. Over the years, I often wondered what the inner workings of her mind were really like. *Were* they similar to mine? Did I inherit some things from her? All I heard about time and time again over the years was that change was never good for Nancy—from my father, the doctors. Whether we liked it or not, change was a part of life.

The four of us walked the long walkway up to the front steps of the huge porch. My father looked around unsteadily as the sound of Bump's cab idled in the background. "I…I'm gonna' take a well-needed shower. Do you guys want to come in for some coffee or a drink or something? Ted did a party last week—the refrigerator is stocked if you're hungry. I've got shrimp, I've got crab dip and those nice pepper crackers." As he went on, I realized that he needed us there. I think it was the first time he needed me there for anything.

"It's fine, Dad, we'll stay for a while," I said.

"Sure, we would love to," Reza said. "Besides I've heard you've got an incredible library."

My father's eyes got big. "By all means, man, take a look at anything you want. You know where it is. You go show him, Allie."

"Great."

Scotty disappeared out to the garage to get some firewood. The house was a little chilly and smelled like my aunt had put some of that powdery-scented stuff on the throw rugs before she vacuumed them. I turned on the lamp just inside the door.

"Oh, Alice." Reza was stunned. "This is unbelievable."

I walked over to him, turned on more lamps, and then stood by his side. I could faintly hear the water running upstairs. "There was a time in my life when I actually believed he read each and every one of those books." I looked at the huge walls of hundreds of books on just about every topic you could think of.

"He may have," Reza said quietly. "You said he had a thirst for learning anything and everything."

I nodded slowly. "It's true. He thinks he knows everything, but he doesn't."

"Lately he works night and day?"

"Well…" I turned to walk away. "He's always done that, but something's changed over the years. He's become more of a workaholic. If that's even possible." I sat down on the sofa in front of the fireplace and rubbed the worn fabric. "We used to sit right here and read together, learn things together. But that was such a long time ago. Go ahead, pull one out."

He pulled out a book on Arctic wolves and sat down next to me.

"They're beautiful, aren't they? Have you ever seen one before?"

"No," he said, "not in the wild, no."

"I'm worried about Frank," I said.

As he sat in my father's place, he put his arm around me. "I see that you are."

"I keep saying it in my head over and over. And what about Scotty?" I put my head on his shoulder. "Do you want something to—"

"Rudy! I got my tree! Where is he? Oh god. Rudy! Bump's out there sleeping in the parking lot." My aunt stomped around the living room then up the stairs.

"Aunt Nancy?"

Reza looked at me as I stood in the doorway to the library. Tommy appeared wearing his army jacket. Then my aunt. Then Scotty with his arms full of wood. The hallway was crowded. I stood back while Reza stood up.

Nancy wore a powder blue winter jacket with a fake fur–lined hood that framed her pretty face. She removed the jacket. Underneath, she wore blue jeans, a beige sweater, and loafers. "Alice! What are you doing here?" She looked at Reza cautiously. "Who are you?"

"Tom McBride." Tommy thrust a hand at Reza.

"Scotty, how nice of you to start a fire," Nancy said. "Where's Rudy?"

Finally, my father walked into the library wearing blue jeans that were too big for him, a long-sleeved blue and white baseball T-shirt, and his moccasin slippers. "Nancy, where's your candy stripe uniform?"

My aunt slowly looked at my father and rolled her eyes. "Rudy, I went home and changed out of it before Tommy and I had dinner and went Christmas tree shopping."

"Right," my father said as Scotty carried the wood inside.

"Well, why don't we all sit down. Does anyone want something to eat or drink?" Dad said as Nancy examined Reza, her eyes darting around.

"Dad, um   "

Tommy took Nancy's coat.

"Can someone tell me why we're standing here? And who is that man with the black hair?"

With a gentleness of approaching a child, Reza held out a hand to my aunt. "I'm Reza. I'm a friend of Alice's."

Scotty looked up from the firewood for a second and turned his attention back to crumpling newspapers.

"Oh, hello," she said, sounding formal. "Your hands are very soft."

"Really?" Reza looked at his hands and then turned them over to look at his palms. "Thank you."

"You have an accent. Where are you from?"

"Well, I lived in Atlanta for a time, grew up mostly in England, and I was born and spent my young childhood in Iran."

From the corner of my eye, I saw Tommy wince when Reza said *Iran*. I thought it was obvious he was of some Middle Eastern origin.

"That's a long way from here, isn't it?"

"Yes." Reza smiled. "A very long way."

"How do you know Alice?"

I put my arm around Reza's waist. "Aunt Nancy, do you remember the luncheon Kathleen from work—"

"That's *right!* You're Reza. You're the boyfriend that I keep hearing everyone talk about. You're more than just friends. And you're getting married. Hey. You guys kind of look more like brother and sister than girlfriend and boyfriend. Alice never had a brother, but she did have a sister who died a long time ago. It was awfully sad."

I heard a muttered "Jesus Christ" slip out of my father.

"Brother and sister?" Reza said to Nancy. "I think Alice is far prettier than I am."

My aunt let out a loud laugh. Tommy rubbed his face as Scotty continued to build a fire that didn't need much more building. Nancy sometimes let out a loud guffaw when she was in a euphoric and manic type of state. She knew something was very wrong at this gathering, but she didn't know how to ask. That was what I was afraid of. And it felt like we were all making it worse.

She nervously turned toward the door and said, "Bump's outside, and my tree's getting wet." She turned to look at me with an annoyance in her eyes. "I taped my daytime soap opera," she said evenly. "I watch it at nine o'clock every night."

Reza remained standing while Scotty scurried to a corner of the room. I could hear the click of my father's lighter.

"That's the great thing about a VCR," I said. "You can watch your show anytime you want."

She sighed and rolled her eyes again. I knew she would fight me on this. Her daily soap opera was important. Standing there, she crossed her arms in front of her and bent one knee. She counted one by one what her regiment would be that evening.

I glanced over at my father, who was blowing smoke rings and not even looking at me.

"Alice," she said, "I *had* to buy my tree tonight, *and* it's raining."

"I know, I know."

"Wednesday nights I wash my hair, and I let it dry during my show. Then I smoke a cigarette and use my curling iron. Look at him with his little grin." She laughed loudly again and loped over to Reza and made him sit down next to her on the red couch in front of the fire. She tucked one leg under herself.

All of a sudden, I felt as if I had more control of the situation. Dad, Tommy, and Scotty had still not breathed a word of the situation.

Nancy was innocently flirtatious but childlike when she spoke with Reza. "Alice, your boyfriend is funny. Do you ever see the way he grins at things? You guys are so lucky to be guys. See? You don't have to worry about rollers and makeup, do you? Isn't that right, Alice?"

"It sure is," I said ruefully, scratching my head. Which one of us was going to tell her?

My father's head flopped back while Tommy and Scotty chuckled.

"Stay for just a moment, Nancy," I said.

"I *can't*." Her mood suddenly turned. The light was shining brightly in the hallway. The night was upon us. The time was now

I walked right in front of my aunt's path and made her stop. "Frank had a heart attack today, Aunt Nancy."

"Frank?"

I took her hands in mine. They were so dry. "Yes."

"Today."

"Yes, today."

"Did he die?"

"No. He's alive. He's in ICU at Wellton General."

Her face went flat, devoid of all color, affect, and spark.

"Scotty," she said.

"I'm here, Nance."

Then she looked at me as I tried with all my strength not to cry. I didn't.

"What are we going to do now?" she asked then turned her focus to her brother. "Rudy, we've been standing here for a long time."

There was a heavy silence in the room.

"And?" he said. He was tired and angry.

Her eyes got wide, and her top lip curled up. "Why didn't you just say something?"

"Nancy, what did you want me to say?"

"Well," I began.

She placed her hands on her hips. The look on her face was incredulous. "You're just going to sit there smoking your head off and let little Alice tell me about Frank?"

Tommy, who sat on the window seat clear across the room, was facing us but made no eye contact. He held his head up, and I got the feeling that he was annoyed with my father. Scotty sat in the small chair in the corner of the room with his head down, and Reza remained on the red couch and stared straight ahead.

"*Little* Alice?" He turned to her. "Alice is a grown woman, Nancy. Isn't it time we cut this shit out?" It was then that I recognized his fear and sadness. "*And* she was doing a fine job. Maybe she could have made her point a little sooner, but I couldn't have done a better job." A tear escaped his eye, and he brushed it away. "And who cares anyway? Frank is sick. Who cares who delivers the goddamned message?"

She ignored that. "Rudy, maybe you need to start taking care of things a little bit better around here." She put one arm around me and held my other hand. "Alice has been through enough. Give her a rest."

"Oh, Aunt Nancy," I protested gently. "Everything is fine, I promise you. I'm fine."

She pointed to Scotty. "When your dad is able to have visitors, please let me know. They won't tell me at the hospital because I'm not a blood relative."

"I don't think that's true, Nance," Scotty said. "They'll be glad to let you know. I'll tell 'em you're family too. You can tell 'em you been a great friend of his for a long time."

"You think so?" she said.

"I do."

She turned and left the room. I followed. Then she turned around and walked back toward me. She held my arms and looked directly into my eyes. "What are we going to do, Alice?" Her voice was just above a whisper. "What are we going to do about Frank?"

Scotty was directly behind me in the long hallway. "Nancy, Dad's gonna be okay. I talked about all that to the doctor."

He did?

He put his arm around her shoulder and led her back down the hallway.

I turned around and walked back into the library and sat down next to Reza. Dad took the Queen Anne chair. Tommy said goodbye and left the room. We both declined a scotch.

"You've always done such a great job with her, Allie. *A great job.* You *and* your sister." He stopped and looked at me. "Sorry about that."

"You don't have to apologize, Dad. We can always talk about Marisa. It keeps her spirit alive."

Reza said nothing.

"No, you're right. It does. It does." He paused to sit back down with his drink and what looked like his hundredth cigarette since we picked him up. He was exhausted, and he didn't want to talk about Frank anymore. "*My* sister? Doctors, nurses, therapists, hospitals. This one's a specialist, this one had a PhD. Everyone's got an opinion. Don't say this, don't say that. I should tell her, you should tell her, oh, for Christ's sake, just someone tell her. She's been on this earth for almost fifty years. She's made it over the bumps of this disease." He took a long swig from his highball.

"Dad, she came here specifically to show you her Christmas tree."

Tommy walked back into the library.

"I know you're exhausted. I know you're worried. But you have to show her some patience. She's actually been doing okay lately. Really."

"Oh shit, I'll bet that tree is soaked. What are you going to do, Tom?" my dad asked.

"I took the van. She said it was on it. It's not, it's in it. The weatherman got me all prepared the other day."

We filed through the long hallway to the front of the house to the olive-green living room. Scotty and Aunt Nancy talked quietly as they looked out a window at the black sky and the rain. Scotty had one arm around her shoulder, and I was sure they were talking about Frank.

"Nancy, is your tree out in that van?" Reza asked.

She slowly turned toward us and looked at Reza. "You never had a Christmas tree growing up, did you?"

"Yes, oh yes. I'm a Christian. We had a tree every year. I've always had Christmas trees."

It was the first time that night I had seen Tommy's face completely relaxed. "No kidding, man."

The conversation between Tommy and Reza appeared as if it bored my aunt, so she walked back over to the window to look at the blackness and the rain. "Your sister used to love to decorate the Christmas tree when she was little, Alice. She used to scare me with those lights. She loved the blue ones," she said.

"I remember," I said. "I remember those big blue lights."

"Do you think Frank will be all right, or do you think he's going to die?"

"I don't know, Aunt Nancy, I just don't know. I'm going to pray that he'll be okay."

"You pray?" she asked.

"Sometimes. Do you?"

"No," she said. "But tonight before I go to sleep, I will get on my knees and say a long prayer for Frank."

"I think that's a great idea."

Reza and I ran to our vehicles quickly in the dirty dark rain. It should have been snowing that time of year, but it wasn't cold enough. My arms still froze under my damp woolen jacket until the heat finally filled the car. I was glad that part of the night was over, Dad and Nancy bickering as usual, and I was glad someone other than me brought up my sister's memory. I was terrified about Frank, and I didn't want my mind to wander or maybe make an attempt to play a trick on me. Reza wouldn't want that either. That was something he hadn't experienced.

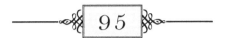

95

Bunica left a message on my answering machine. Reza was so tired, he took a shower and went straight to bed. I sat up at the kitchen table late that night thinking.

Bunica didn't mind leaving long-winded messages, and I was ready for something like the following: "Alice, please call me immediately. You are most likely driving a stolen car. You know your grandfather knew all about this, but of course, he does not include me in his dealings. I never trusted that Costel. Thank you for inviting me to your engagement luncheon. Although we could have had something much nicer here. The French think they know everything about food, but they don't."

Or "Alice, you are looking very thin, please come over and spend the weekend with us."

Or "Alice, please come spend the weekend with us, you are looking very thin."

But her actual message went like this: "Alice, thank you for the invitation to the lovely, lovely luncheon in Harbins. It was a kind gesture for your friend to arrange such a beautiful afternoon for you and the ladies. What a sweet girl. Is it Catherine? No, Kathleen. I am so sorry, I'm getting old, and I am very forgetful, as you know. I am so very sorry that your mother and Helena did not come. Your mother ought to be ashamed of herself. That's a discussion for another day.

"My dear, I have been thinking about you, and I would very much like for us to sit down and talk. I could come to you if you would like, or you know you are always welcome here. Maybe your fiancé wouldn't mind if you could spend the weekend with us, and I could make all your favorites. Just like we used to do. We could even go and tidy up Marisa's little plot. I know it's been cold, but it might be a nice time to do that.

"Please call me soon, my dear. I would very much like to talk to you. I love you, Alice."

In all the years I had lived in this apartment, my grandmother had *never* asked to come over. There was no reason. Miranda was still upstairs, a kindergarten teacher now with a graduate student roommate named Ellen, and there were a group of grad students living on the back side of us. The thought of my grandmother sitting at my round oak kitchen table seemed very strange, and I didn't want her to come by. I would go to her, and I felt as though I needed to soon because there was a peculiarity to her voice. I couldn't quite figure out what it was. I knew this had nothing to do with my mother. That she had pointed out, but the clarity of her words were like a flashing neon sign, and even her accent didn't sound as strong. She was very much in control, and I was a little confused, curious, and maybe a little worried. Maybe it had something to do with her and Bunic not meeting Reza.

Reza had to have some painting done on the interior of the house, and it would still be a while before we could move in. We were hoping by spring, and then the following May, we would get married. I didn't want to have a June wedding. Everyone had a June wedding, and I wanted to be different. May was a pretty month in Wellton.

I left Reza to take care of the house issues while I went to Bunica's one evening for dinner.

The three of us practically ate in silence, which was strange since Bunica normally chatted away while I listened and Bunic pretended to listen. After dinner, Bunica brought out the homemade blueberry cheesecake and the decaf. Bunic took his in the other room to watch a game.

She drew a deep breath, and I figured this was where we were going to begin our discussion. "Alice."

I put my head down and looked at my coffee. "What's on your mind, Bunica?"

"I know your temperament."

"My temperament?"

She took a sip of her coffee. "You have been through your own hell."

I was surprised again to hear her use that word.

"And you have come back so much better, so much stronger. Alice, my dear, you are the strongest, most admirable person I know."

I slumped a little in my chair. "Bunica, you're going to make me cry. Thank you."

She ignored me. "I don't want you to become angry with me. I know I did not tell you about Marisa's father. How can we be 100 percent… Anyway, please, let me say my piece. Will you? Please, if you become angry, don't lose your temper with me."

"I believe you're thinking about Mom. *Or* me a while back, right?" I said. "You're awfully worried about something."

"I think you are rushing into marriage." She looked directly at me.

I knew it. And I had thought about it. She was right. I closed my eyes and put my chin on top of my folded hands. My elbows sat on the table, my favorite cheesecake untouched. I looked down at my coffee again and then back at her.

"I'm a little scared, Bunica," I said.

"What are you scared of, dear?"

I sat up straight and took a sip of my coffee. "He wants to fill that farmhouse with children. Maybe I'll have children someday, but I don't want them anytime soon. And, and…"

"How well do you know this man, Alice? You have not even been seeing him a year. Have you met his family? Your grandfather and I have not met him yet. When is this all going to take place?" She rubbed my arm and leaned in closer to me. "I am not trying to scare you any more than you already are. And I am not trying to talk you out of *anything* at all. It's only that you must meet everyone in his family first, do you not agree? And he must meet us too."

"It does feel as if things are moving fast. We were planning to go to Atlanta, but then Frank got—he had a heart attack, and he's in the hospital, and, and everything just got all messed up." I turned to face her. "Bunica, he's a brilliant and wonderful man." Suddenly,

I was beginning to regret that I told her I had any reservations of my upcoming nuptials.

"I know all of this. I also know there's about a ten-year age difference between the two of you."

"You also know he was brought up in the Catholic Church."

She nodded and smiled.

"I love him, Bunica," I said. "You will meet Reza as soon as possible. I promise you. There are a few things that need to be smoothed out, but we will get through it and have a lovely wedding. We have a year and a half."

"Why such a long engagement?"

"Because we want to get married the following spring."

She sat back. "I understand." She took a bite of her cake. "Remember this, Alice. And I know we have never talked about this before, but you understand sex is only a small part of love. Many times, it's not love at all."

I smiled and nodded. "He makes me happy."

"Those were the words I was looking for. You must be able to talk to him, Alice. You must be able to discuss anything and everything with him. You must know him here." She placed her hand on her heart. "If you do not want children at this stage of your life, then you must tell him. You must be sure that you want this more than anything else in this world. Because if you do not, you will not be happy, and you may not see it right away, but you will. Later in your life. And by that time, it will be too late. You will resent him."

"Thank you, Bunica."

She took my hand and kissed it hard.

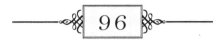

96

"Why are you still here? *Why are you still here?*" Kathleen was more than surprised that she wasn't the only one in the office. I think I might have scared her when I walked up behind her. "Just be grateful that *I am* and the phones are still on. I was just about to tell your dad you've gone home. He needs to talk to you right away."

I immediately scurried back to my desk. "Dad?"

"Hey, kid."

"How's Frank? Have you heard anything? Please tell me everything's okay?"

"He's awake. He's well."

Thank God.

"We can see him, but only one at a time. I'm here with Scotty. You're still working? I'm glad I caught up with you." He talked fast. "Can you come down?"

"Yes, yes, of course," I said. "It's after hours around here."

My father chuckled. "Someone's taking after her old man, I see. Now if I could get you to come down and crunch my numbers."

I ignored him. "I'll be down as soon as I can."

"The weather's not good. Drive safe."

"I will."

Kathleen and I locked up quickly and left the office together. Dad was right. It was dark, wet, windy, and cold, but still no snow.

Kathleen linked my arm. "This is what the Europeans do, Alice," she said cheerfully, despite the clattering of her teeth. "Have you ever been to Europe, Alice?"

"No, I can't say I have."

"Oh my!" she gushed. "It is something that you *must* do before you die."

I'm hoping I have a few years left.

"I spent the summer of '79 in the Stuttgart. What an amazing place. Wild. Unimaginable."

Just when I was going to ask her about Stuttgart, she ambushed me. "Where is Dr. Khavari tonight? I'm sure he'll want to hear all about this."

"He's working on a project. I don't want to disturb him." I hoped that she wouldn't ask me anything else. All I knew was that he was working on a project, and that was it. I knew nothing more of the details, so I changed the subject. "How are things with Denny?"

Kathleen giggled as she wobbled toward her car in her camel-hair coat. "Please tell me it's not that obvious."

"No, it really isn't. But he did turn a certain shade of red the two times I saw him waiting for you in the reception area. I'll be fine," I said as Kathleen arranged herself in the driver's seat and made room for me in the passenger's seat.

"No, Alice, I'm driving you to your car. It's dark."

I felt as though I had no choice but to get in.

She continued on about Denny. "He is as cute as a bug, Alice." She smiled sweetly. "Oh, I know, how many times have you heard that phrase before? Now. I am going to say a special prayer for your dear friend tonight. I'm so glad he's receiving visitors. That's a good sign. Be sure to let me know tomorrow how it all went, will you remember?"

"*Of course* I will. As soon as I get in. Thanks for the ride." I got into my little brown Dodge Dart and drove to the hospital. The monster suddenly entered my mind and shot like a pin through my body. I chose to ignore it and think only about Frank. I looked at the clock. It was twenty minutes to seven. Reza was probably eating a gas station sandwich over the kitchen sink for his dinner. Lately he was patting me on the ass and calling me Mama. I always laughed, but I wasn't sure how I felt about it, and he never said anything further. I never had maternal instincts. Ever. Even meeting four-year-old Diana didn't stir up anything. Maybe that would change in a few years. I did know one thing. I had mental illness that needed to be controlled with medication. The last thing I wanted to do was pass that along to a kid.

Frank was moved out of ICU and into a room upstairs. Apparently, he had made remarkable strides. His sister was scheduled to fly in from Michigan. The one from Pennsylvania was already there. Shirley was a tall regal-like woman who caught my eye right away. "Alice," she said as she touched my shoulder with her long fingers. "My goodness. What a lovely young woman you've become."

I've become? I don't remember ever meeting Frank's sister from Philadelphia. I thought for a moment, and then I realized where I met the slim elegant woman. It was at Marisa's memorial service all those years ago. "I'm sorry, Mrs.—"

"Shirley," she said.

"Shirley. I wasn't exactly at my best, you could say. I try not think about that day."

"Honey, of course you don't want to think about that day." Then she leaned in close. "So is that motherfucker dead yet? Withers?"

I was shocked, and I couldn't help but laugh hearing that come from such a high-class–looking woman. People looked over at us. I wasn't about to tell her he might have been in that very complex.

"I ain't jokin', girl," she said, shaking her head and furrowing her brow.

I looked down at her high-heeled boots. "No," I said. "He's still hanging on."

"Damned shame."

For a second, I worried that if I wished death upon the monster, then bad things could happen to Frank. I knew that was my obsessiveness, and I chose to let it go. "How's he doing? Have you seen him yet?"

"If you can believe it, he asked me to run out and get him a chocolate bar from the machine. I tol' him, 'Frank, from now on, you gonna be Mr. Healthy every day, not just when you feelin' like it.' You see, our mother died of heart failure at the age of fifty-two. Speakin' of mothers, how is yours?"

Shirley was among the vast outside. She, like just about everyone, knew that Marisa's death was no accident, but our mother was also a victim of a violent crime, not one of the principal perpetrators. But then how could a mother possibly allow this to happen to her own daughter? It was unthinkable. There was so much speculation, it cluttered my mind to the point of pain that I could barely return from. I could never really figure out a good answer to that.

"She's fine, thanks." I never thought I would be so happy to see my father. I could have kissed him for arriving when he did. I didn't want to talk any further about my mother. She stole my sister's opportunity at life by siding with and covering for that monster. I *could* have allowed her to ruin my life had I not sought help through Detective Holloway. I could have ended up a crispy dead leaf floating on top of a stream somewhere off to nowhere. Alive but very much dead.

"Kid, you wanna go in?" he asked. "Where's Scotty?"

"We sent him home," Shirley said as I looked around the waiting area. "That boy had pillow eyes."

My father and Shirley continued to talk as I walked with the nurse toward Frank's room. It felt like a walk to the gas chamber. I had known Frank my entire life. He was always there, like a father, sort of. I took him for granted, that much I knew. I never had a serious conversation with him. I never spoke privately with him, really, except for the time we sat in the waiting area of this very hospital after Dad broke his arm in the warehouse. Although that wasn't exactly *private* or being alone in the same room together. I didn't even know if he knew how much I cared for him.

Frank, I thought to myself as I exhaled.

The nurse stayed for a minute, checking on his tubes and wires. "Not too long, okay, honey?"

"Sure," I said.

As soon as the nurse closed the heavy door with her foot and her head bounced away from the square window, Frank was the one who spoke first. "She mean like a snake, that one." He showed me his big toothy grin.

"Really? She looked nice."

"What they say about looks?" He nodded his head, never taking his eyes off me. "They be deceiving. As they say."

"Few truer words were ever spoken," I said. I walked closer to him.

"Come on in and sit yourself down." He waved a hand at me.

He looked warm and soft, and he appeared to be comfortable as he lay in a bluish-green hospital gown all hooked up under pristine white sheets and a gold blanket. He had lost a tremendous amount of weight, and although his face was strikingly drawn, it looked calm.

There was a blue plastic chair near the wall. I pulled it closer to the bed and sat down. I noticed there was a spark of peacefulness in his eyes. He didn't look frightened like I thought he might, like probably anyone would. I put my hands together as if I were praying. "Frank, I'm so, so glad you're better," I sputtered. "I was so *afraid* for you. We just…just got down here as fast as we could, and when we spoke with your doctor, we all seemed to feel a little better." I hoped he couldn't tell I was lying about Stephenson.

He turned his head and, with a big grin, spoke to the ceiling. "Well now, honey, you ain't gonna get rid of me as fas' as you think you can."

"You'd better be right about that, Frank. I mean it, I'm serious. You know how much I don't want your job."

He smiled and nodded deeply, never losing eye contact with me. "You talkin' 'bout my singin' job."

"Yes, I almost forgot! Your singing too."

We smiled and sat in silence for a few moments. I found it easier to talk to him as the minutes flew by.

"Are you *feeling* better, Frank? You've lost quite a lot of weight, but I guess these things are all part of it. I'm sure you'll put it back on again."

"Doctor say I'll put some weight back on, probably not all of it, but I could stood to lose a little 'round the middle. But yeah. I guess so. Feel as good as I did before. Even better since all my friends and family come to visit. You family, Alice. I remember the day you and your sister were born, God rest that child's soul."

I nodded slowly and looked down at the floor.

"An' look at you now. All grown up, smart as can be, an' a real beauty."

"That's very kind, Frank, but—"

His eyes got big and white, and he pointed a craggy finger at me. "When Frank say you smart an' a beauty, you smart and a beauty. Jus' like that grandmother a yours."

"*Bunica?*" I was confused.

"Naw, the other one. Rosalie. She tall too."

I never knew much about my father's mother. She died before I was born. All we had were photographs.

"An' you could run over that old girl with a bulldozer, 'an she keep gettin' up, sweep off the dust, an' keep movin' on. One hell of a great lady."

I smiled and looked at my fingernails. "She sounded remarkable, like an inspiration."

"Aw, she wa'."

I wanted to cheer Frank up with an interesting little cactus I found at the plant store at the mall and maybe some small talk about the store, his health, maybe music, but he seemed to have so many things that he wanted to say. That's what appeared to really make him happy.

"An' you got a nice friend too," he said, referring to Reza. I saw that twinkle he always had in his eye when he was about to start the relentless teasing he patented with my father.

I covered my eyes and rubbed them with my palms. "I can't believe he actually went to the store and asked Dad for my hand. It was such a lovely gesture, but I thought the two of you? Poor, poor Reza."

"We decite' that day we gonna cut him some slack because we think you got a winner there," he said. "No," he corrected himself. "We *know* you got a winner. An' the most important thing? *He* got a winner."

"Thank you, Frank." It was all I could think to say.

"An' your dad? He so proud a you. Them customers comin' through that door, and he always braggin' 'bout you, accountant for that McGillis Company place, first one in the family graduate from college." He stopped with the accolades, and again we sat in silence.

I hoped the supposed "mean like a snake" nurse wouldn't come back to the room and separate us.

As if reading my thoughts, Frank looked over at me. "She hant' thrown out any visitors yet. She like to pretend she the boss. An' let me tell you somethin' else."

"Hmm?"

"You know, Alice. No one perfect. We all have our flaws, and we deal with 'em different. Some of us cry, and some of us gotta do a make-believe strong face. Your dat is the best man I know. The best. An' he loves you so much. That store is all he know. But *you* is all he got."

I could feel my nose burn as tears welled up in my eyes. I grabbed a tissue. I was happy. I stood up and bent down to kiss him on the forehead. A stray tear hit him, and I wiped it away. "Come home soon, Frank. This is no place for you." Those words rang in my ears.

"Now you better go on before Nurse Snake get back."

We both laughed. I put the chair back by the wall and stepped toward the door. I turned around and said goodbye again. His head was turned to the side toward me, and his eyes were starting to close.

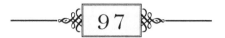

97

Frank Watson was one of the only people I could think of who never complained. Born and raised in Wellton like most everyone else I knew, I never heard him talk of the freezing-cold harshness of a Wellton winter, getting dark at four in the afternoon, the driving, the salt ruining your car unless you had it rustproofed properly, snow-plowing the driveways, dodging deadly icicles, snow tires, threatening moves to Florida, and my personal favorite, slipping and falling on your ass because you weren't wearing the right footwear. I heard Frank on a few occasions see a fresh snowfall at nighttime while the colors of the Boochie's sign threw a beautiful light on the huge slow and white puff balls. While the rest of us moaned about the "tip of the iceberg," Frank was able to see the allure of it all. His attitude was bright, and he spread happiness throughout like a thread easily working its way through cloth.

That was what was probably keeping him alive. He chuckled when he talked about Nurse Snake, and so I knew he wasn't serious, but when I finally did get to speak with her, she said that overall, Frank was in very good health for a man of his age. But this heart attack was bad. It was similar to the one that killed his mother, and he was very lucky to be alive, given his heredity. It wasn't the first time I noticed, but as I looked upon my darkened past, I knew I had taken things and people for granted. Frank was one of them. And I would make it up to him, without him ever knowing, without him ever figuring out what I was doing. Because I knew what he would do, and I knew what he would say.

The dreary light would eventually fight its way through the blinds, and with the wind chill, the temperature was supposed to *feel* like thirty-one degrees, but still, not a flake of snow. How could that be *possible?* Was there such a thing as being too cold to snow?

Reza lay on his stomach snoring peacefully from a late-night reading hangover. The huge ginger-colored cat Jacob lay on Reza's back with his head up, purring loudly. I scratched his head, put some coffee on, got into the shower, and made my way into work a half hour early. This was the second time in my life I had seen this. Dead grass for Christmas. No snow. Just a lot of cold, rainy, icy sleet. Sloppy rain. I thought about turning on the radio to get another weather report and then just decided it would snow when it snowed, so I turned on some pop station, listened to some music, and remembered the first Christmas it was like this when Marisa was alive.

We lived in the palace in Crescent Hills. It was where she was murdered. We were out on the driveway, all the way down at the end behind a pine tree where our mother couldn't see us. Julie Silver was there. We played hot potato with a tennis ball. I had a camera with a flashcube, and I wanted to take photographs of Christmas dusk without the snow. Julie's Hanukkah coincided with our Christmas. A lot of the neighborhood consisted of a bunch of rich drunk people celebrating, entertaining, and eating too much. Even though the Silvers were Jewish, Julie's older brother bought her ribbons and bows so that she could decorate the dog's water and food bowls for Christmas. The interesting thing was that her parents had no problem with it. That was a long time ago. Wherever Julie Silver was, I was sure she was married, had children, was doing well, and was smart enough not to live in Wellton anymore, at least during the winter months. I wondered if she knew about Marisa.

No snow. I was kind of glad in a way. I pulled on the freezing metal handle to the front door to the building and realized it was locked. I searched for my keys and shook off the cold air once inside. The fresh smell of coffee hit me head-on as Kathleen was preparing herself for the times when I was coming in earlier and earlier.

"This is *the* most incredible thing, Alice. This coffee maker has a digital clock and a timer on it. So. The night before you even *suspect* you'll be early, there will be a fresh pot for you."

"Kathleen, you *don't* have to do this," I said, suddenly realizing that I might hurt her feelings.

"Do what?"

I just hurt her feelings. "Come in early just because I do."

"Oh, no, no, no, no. I like to come in early sometimes, and when I don't have a client, I like to stay late. I go over my listings." She cupped her mouth and whispered as if someone else were there. "A little moonlighting, you know."

Kathleen juggled endless calls that morning, and then I received one from my father. It was weird because the connection was terrible. All I could hear were hissing and popping noises until I finally heard his voice. At first we tagged each other.

"Hello?" the familiar voice asked.

"Hello? Dad, is that you?"

"Allie?"

"Dad?" Then there was silence, but the connection was fine, and I knew he was still on the other end of the line. "What's the matter?"

"It's Frank. He's gone."

"Where did he go?"

"Gone, honey. He's dead. He had a massive heart attack at three fifteen this morning."

"Wait. What? Are you kidding me?" I lowered my voice. "Are you *kidding* me? No! Why? There's no way. I just *saw* him, Dad, he was fine. How could this happen?"

"I'm sorry, Allie." His voice was teeming with sorrow. "It can happen. It happened."

I was dying to catch my breath.

"His doctors said—"

"His doctor," I muttered. "I knew that Stephenson was a quack the moment I laid eyes on him."

"I know that guy gives you the creeps, but really, it's not his fault. Frank had—"

"Dad, I have to go now," I said, rubbing my temples. "I can't talk. I'm sorry."

"Do you want me to have someone come pick you up?" he asked. "You're in no state to drive, are you?"

I felt a twinge of guilt as I listened to the sheer despair in his voice, but I just had to get off the phone. "I'm fine, Dad," I said quietly. I put the receiver down and left yet another note for Jean. If I weren't bulldozing my way through this project, she probably would have fired me, but I didn't much care.

And once again, I walked out of the office into the cold air and made it to my car without anyone noticing. I stuck a note on Kathleen's desk as she was on the phone and was able to leave without any of her gushing interference. I was sad, angry, and focused on myself.

Frank and I didn't have a friendship. We didn't have a relationship. He loved me like a daughter. I knew that, and I loved him probably sometimes more than I loved my own father. *If* love was something that could be measured. I took him for granted as for years and years, I dug deep holes into myself. The desolation and loss I had for my sister ruined me. I was never able to get to know the people in my life who truly loved me, and I couldn't because I didn't know how.

I settled for the most comfortable thing I knew and drove to the truck stop where the lights would be turned off for the day. I sat and sobbed. Of course it didn't feel the same. There was no more way back to sleep in and no bright light to sleep under.

I wiped my face with a couple of tissues and drove back to Reza's, hoping that he was still home. I thanked God he was when I walked in and saw him feeding the cat. We embraced. "You know?" I asked.

"I know now. I can see it on your face. I'm so, so sorry."

"I was numb at first, shocked. And then I couldn't stop crying," I said as I stared at a door handle.

"Hmm. Come sit." He led me over to the overstuffed couch. Jacob followed us and jumped up behind me. He purred loudly and nuzzled my neck and chewed my hair. I turned around and gently put my hand between his face and my head.

"You just saw him the other day, and he was doing so well. Do you know what happened?"

I leaned forward and put my elbows on my thighs. "I couldn't stay on the phone long enough to find out the details from my dad. All I know is that he had a massive heart attack in the middle of the night, and this one killed him." I cried quickly. "And look at poor, poor Scotty now. I don't know what to do or what to say."

"You'll know when you see him. Maybe we should go over there."

"We have all experienced so much loss. All of us. The regrets. I have so many regrets, Reza."

"Alice, you can't go back in time. We can't change the past as much as we want to. It's over. We have each other right now."

I nodded and grabbed a tissue. "It's that one thing that keeps me from progressing, and I can't stop it. I long for it so badly."

"It's natural," he said. "Don't be so hard on yourself."

"Can we just stay here for a little while?"

"Of course we can. As long as you like." He wrapped his arms around me and pulled me close to him.

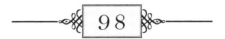

98

I don't think I had ever seen a darker day than that of Frank's funeral mass. The sky was filled with so much gray, and the rain was sharp and deliberate. I still didn't like umbrellas, but on this day, I was glad Reza and I were sharing one. The cars were parked all around the corner and all the way around the block. Frank was a very well-known and very much loved man. Had we not been experiencing so much gloominess along with the freezing rain and wind, I would have thought that on this day, even the earth was crying for him.

People were in shock by this death. The sanctuary was filled with sobs and exhales. My father wasn't doing well, and the look of distraught on his face was so sad. I looked around, extracting comfort from the familiar faces. I remembered all those years ago doing the same thing at Marisa's memorial. Every seat was filled. I noticed a much thinner Detective Holloway sitting in the back with my grandfather sitting next to him. I was so proud of Bunic for entering the church. Bunica sat on the other side. There were friends, relatives, customers from the store, and I was so touched to see Kathleen, Jean, and Shirl from the office. Walter, Aubrey, Candace, and Miranda sat behind us.

The priest read from the Scripture about life and grief. He confirmed that anguish was natural, but there was no greater gift than to rest in the palms of the Lord and that Frank had entered into an existence of everlasting joy and peace.

I glanced over at my father. His head was down. Aunt Nancy was sandwiched between us. She wept a little, but she was strong. I told her as she was putting on her makeup for her candy striping job that if she felt uncomfortable about Frank's service, she didn't have to go. Then I selfishly reminded her of Marisa's memorial service.

"I can go," she said. "I'm old now, and I have more negative symptoms. Young people have positive symptoms."

"What are you talking about?" I said. "You're not old, Nancy."

She sighed and clicked the roof of her mouth with her tongue like I was an idiot. "Stay there," she commanded. "I'll get the note he wrote it on." She came back with a piece of pink paper. "Here it is." She began reading. "Negative symptoms are complete withdrawal, flat affect, blunted affect, social isolation. *I just might* have some of these. Positive symptoms are auditory and visual hallucinations, paranoia, thought insertion, thought withdrawal, delusions of grandiosity. I have *none* of these, and you wouldn't want to experience them at a funeral."

"I see." I knew full well she had a bunch of that crap as Dad called it. "Well then, I guess you should go," I said.

As long as she remained on her medication, she did well. I guess both of us did.

"There's just one thing. I really want you to remember that this is going to be a very sad funeral. Can you keep that in mind?"

She looked at me strangely as she put her crinkled dry hands on my face. "Alice"—she tapped my cheeks with each word—"all funerals are sad." She continued to apply far too much perfume and left me with my somewhat ridiculous comment.

My attention turned back to the altar as I saw my father surrounded in the soft yellow lighting, hundreds of flowers, and the sea of candles. He wore an impeccable gray suit, and his medium-length black hair was only gray around the temples and in tiny streaks throughout, as was his mustache. He wore those silly perfectly round bright red glasses that sometimes he and Frank shared.

"The first thing I want everyone to know is that I'm not good at speaking in front of a roomful of silent people," he began. "But this is not about me. This is about Frank. The other thing I want everyone to know is that I'm not just saying kind words because Frank is gone. We always do that when someone dies. Because you only want to see the good in the person regardless of what kind of guy he was in life. No one wants to speak ill of the dead. If you do, you shouldn't say anything at all. We all know that. But everything I'm going to tell you about Frank is the absolute truth. *Everything.* I'll be 100 percent honest with you.

"Frank and I met in a stairwell in school when I was seven and he was almost eleven. He said his mother had some leftover ham, and he wanted to share. He said he felt sorry for me because I was only allowed to eat fish. Well, that wasn't exactly true, but I made him believe it because I wanted the ham."

There was muffled laughter.

"Frank was my first real friend. True friend. Best friend. I don't remember having a true friend, a brother, before Frank Watson. I wrote all this down on a piece of paper, you know, on this paper I have with me. This piece of paper right here. But I don't know whether I can read it or not. I don't know if this makes sense, but it feels strange to read notes about a person who knew so much of *your* life. Frank was an expert in kindness, in giving, in compassion. *His heart was open to everyone.* Father, I know your words. They are good words. They come from the Bible. I know Frank is here in spirit. I can *feel* him. But what I would give right now to reach over and punch him in the arm, what I would do to listen to his awful voice singing to that radio at the store."

More muffled laughter.

"Marisa, my oldest daughter. Beautiful girl just setting out in life. You all know what happened to that poor kid. *I did not know what to do next. Frank* had no idea what to do next. I selfishly somehow turned to my best friend, my brother, and he saved my life. Even though he too was *dying* of grief. I had my Alice to think of, to protect and watch over, but I didn't know how because I didn't do a good-enough job with the first one. Frank encouraged me to do the best I was capable of, just one day at a time. One hour at a time. One *minute* at a time, if that's what it took. *Frank Watson stood behind his friends no matter what was going on in his own life.* He stood behind me when I didn't want to wake up anymore and face the morning because I had a murdered child tattooed on my brain. I had a business to run. But more importantly, I had my daughter to raise. With Frank there, I knew I would eventually move out of this darkness, but I didn't know how or when, and I had to depend on *him.* Not once did I say to myself, 'Hey, maybe he's depressed too. He has a son to raise. Did you ever think about that? You need to be there for him too.' Oh no. Nope. Is this what we do when we grieve? I know what Frank Watson did. He helped out everyone else who needed him. He put *everyone else* first. He was selfless. And he loved his boy, Scott. Scotty was his whole world. You know that, man, don't you?"

My father looked at Scotty, who nodded quickly, tears on his face.

"We were all getting so tired, so fed up with the way things were going with Marisa's case. So tired. It was a humid, overcast Sunday afternoon when I decided I would get into the car and drive out to the Arizona desert, get out of the car, walk out into the desert, and just never come back. Die alone. Frank said, 'Let me come with you.' I said, 'No. I'm not getting into any suicide pacts. I'm gonna die alone. I can't take this anymore. Alice deserves better than me, and Scotty needs you.' Me and my mouth. Because after that, he got behind my car and lay down, actually lay down behind the back tires of my car, and he said, 'If you're going to Arizona, you're going to have to run over me first. You drive to that desert, you're driving over this one.'

"It's because of Frank that people could say, 'I have one true friend in this world.' It's because of Frank that people could always feel so very much cared for, could feel as if they had a brother. Oh Scotty, how proud he was of you and the man you have become. I love you, Frank, and I'm going to miss you forever. We all will. But I know you're still out there with my girl Marisa, so come around and visit us from time to time. Please. Ladies and gentlemen, friends and family of Frank Watson. That's all I can say right now."

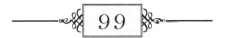

99

Kathleen said she was in Munich once in a cathedral that looked like it was lit up by God himself. At Frank's funeral, somehow I knew what she was talking about. It brought almost a joyous ending to such a morose wake the night before. I cried almost as much as at Marisa's memorial service all those years ago. I was devastated for Scotty.

My father had a lot of guilt over what he did and did not do about my sister. I was shocked and I felt numb, as if I had heard words spoken from another person in a different time. I was surprised and yet I was happy and grateful. I also reminded myself that this was not another day for me and my self-centeredness. Today was dedicated to Frank and his life, a life that had such a remarkable effect on others.

Reza took my hand as we slowly rolled along the city blocks in the long black limousine. Tears flowed from my eyes again. I glanced out the window and saw a young man standing on a corner. He made the sign of the cross as we crawled by. Although he had an umbrella, he was not weak.

My father talked about how Frank saved his life. Did any of us try to save each other? Did I ever think about Frank first? The answer was no, never. He was a background fixture whom I believed would be there forever. I wallowed in sorrow and guilt for so many years, and now I wondered what Frank was really thinking. What did he think about all of that? What did he really think about the girl who could never stop grieving? How could such a genuinely altru-istic man attach himself to such selfish people? Maybe Frank was so formidable that he didn't see the world the way I did. Then some-thing happened, and his heart gave in. The second time it killed him. Maybe Frank was an angel, and God wanted him back. I'll never know now, and I wondered at that point if I would allow another death to destroy my life. I didn't think so. I hoped not.

I sat thinking as I looked down at my skirt then up at the watery window. There was some quiet talk throughout the car. Scotty sat all the way up front with the driver, then Aunt Nancy, Frank's sisters Shirley from Philadelphia and Patricia from Detroit, then Dad, Tommy, and Shirley's husband Earl, then Patricia's husband Travis, Reza, and me. I never realized how large Frank's family was. There were two other limos that followed behind filled with relatives, and we all slowly followed Frank for the last time.

It was very rare that he talked about himself at all. His extended family came from Wellton's south side, just like my father, but then they all scattered throughout the northeast and the Midwest. Every one of them appeared to get along well and were relieved to see each other despite the circumstances and the wrenching heartache, but it was puzzling as to why everyone fled Wellton except for Frank and Scotty when everyone supposedly was so close. Wellton is terribly cold in the winter. You rarely see a person outside on a dreary overcast day when the wind blows snow sideways, but Detroit and Philadelphia aren't exactly balmy in February either. I hoped Frank hadn't stayed there to watch over my father. That would have been a wasted life.

My entire family was right there, and yet we were not close at all. It was becoming more and more clear. Frank had taken care of my father, and now he was gone. Most likely the stress on his heart was too much for him. He should have left, moved away with Scotty, and gotten the hell away from us. All of us. Anyone could have worked for my father.

"Alice?" Reza whispered.

"I'm fine," I said.

Frank would be buried in the family plot next to his wife Arlene, who died of brain cancer when Scotty was only nine. Scotty looked so strong when he touched the engraving of his mother's name. Suddenly I felt something cold touch my nose. Scotty and I both looked at each other as more and more of the procession somberly rolled in. He looked toward the sky.

"Alice," he said with a grin, "it's gotta be."
"Can you believe it?" I said.
"What is it?" Reza said.
"It's snowing."

100

My father had the reception at the house, and there were more silver trays piled high with more food than there were people in both the large dining room and the living room. Detective Holloway had gotten to know Frank well over the past several years since Marisa's death. He was sitting in the back of the church, and I wondered what he thought about my father's comments about Marisa's case. I imagined it still hurt him, but he probably didn't take it as personally as I would. It was so long ago now. It had been over ten years. Marisa would have been a nearly twenty-nine-year-old woman now.

I looked over, then approached Dad and Holloway. "What are you two doing?"

Detective Holloway had a photograph album open and was smoothing a page down with one hand.

"Looking at these old black-and-white photographs, Allie. Reminiscing," Dad said, peering at the photos and turning the pages slowly.

"Have you seen any of these, Alice?" Holloway asked.

"Oh, yeah. Lots of times. Dad's got plenty of photos too. It would take you days to get through every one of them."

"They certainly are beautiful. Such memories," Holloway said, and I was reminded of his own son Ken. The three of us were silent for a minute. I gazed at Reza, who was standing across the room. He was talking to a couple I didn't recognize. Holloway was about to say something else about the pictures, but he saw me watching Reza.

My father continued to study the old photos of Frank, Nancy, Tommy, and himself, either choosing to ignore us altogether or completely engrossed in his task. I think it was the first. He didn't want any more pain.

I surveyed the room. I watched everyone. It was so different this time because I was able to take a step back emotionally. I was a completely different person too. Friends and family mourned *so* deeply for Frank, and I watched the way they did it. It was all different. Emotions were a mosaic of unintelligence but a required foundation in each of us.

Grief. Which path was the best path? Which direction made a person the most stable of human kind? Was there actually a right way to grieve? I used to believe that there was, and I was resolute about it. If there was *anything* I was clear about, that was it, in my darkest, sickest moments. Now, I wasn't so sure.

And Dad. Celebrating Frank's life with food, booze, photographs, old stories, and laughter while others were so devastated, but still didn't seem to be nearly as devastated as I was when Marisa was murdered.

Bunica had seen me just outside the church. "Too young." She shook her head slowly and linked my arm. The rain had stopped. "Terrible tragedy. We can question God as much as we would like, but when he makes a decision, it is always for the best, no matter how much pain it causes us. Poor man. Terrible, terrible tragedy."

Scotty had a gray look of numbness and shock as he and the rest of his family had thanked everyone again for being with them and honoring Frank in such a special way. I heard the word *special*, and I wasn't exactly sure what they meant. I think they were just struggling for the right words. I didn't think Scotty should have been given the task to thank anyone at all. He should have been eating, drinking lots of water, and resting. He didn't look well.

"Ladies and gentlemen, friends and family of Frank Watson." Dad made an announcement in the living room, where most of the people were sitting. "You all know now how far back Frank and I go. We met over ham. Now, you also know that Frank wouldn't let you out the door without making a bigger dent in this food. It's not going to eat itself. Look, I know this was sudden and unexpected, but Frank wouldn't want everyone moping over a casserole."

The room percolated with laughter.

"Please try to relax, celebrate Frank's life, and I insist you make yourselves at home."

As if given permission, everyone did just that. Some people ended up in the kitchen, a lot of the ladies stayed in the living room, and the men went to the library. Kathleen and I were cleaning up some plates off the dining room table when the caterer took them from us immediately. I looked in the library and saw that there was some room around the fire for us to sit. Aunt Nancy nestled in a love seat, and Kathleen and I sat on a couch. The room smelled of the Christmas wreaths that hung on each of the windows in the library. The snow was falling in soft giant puffs. Some of the men sat across the room reminiscing about Frank, some looking at photographs, some old, some recent, and people asked questions. Walter, Detective Holloway, and Aubrey were chatting with Shirley.

Later, when most of the mourners departed, we went into the living room. Nancy was sprawled out on the front sofa in front of the television. She turned it off when the room began to fill up. She still had her dress on, but she was wearing her slippers.

"Aunt Nancy, you're going to wrinkle that dress." I heard my mother in my voice and closed my mouth fast. I instinctively picked up a cup and saucer as a caterer wagged her finger at me.

"I hope I never have to wear this dress again," she said somberly.

"Oh honey, I couldn't agree with you more," Kathleen said as she made a failed attempt to bus a napkin and a dessert plate with a large spoon. She turned to my father. "Mr. Buchner, I can't tell you enough, the service was beautiful. It would have been an honor to have met Frank Watson."

"Mr. Buchner was my great-grandfather," Dad said, sitting cross-legged, sipping his drink. "Call me Rudy, please."

"You are too kind." Kathleen remained standing.

"And if you're tired, had too much to drink, or don't feel like driving in the snow, we have plenty of room upstairs. My sister has scoured every room in this house."

"Someone has to do it, brother." Nancy replied in a singsong voice.

The phone rang suddenly. It sounded as if the ringer had been turned all the way up, and it startled me. I picked it up, and the room went quiet. "Hello?"

"Alice?"

"Mom?"

Every eyeball was on me. Everyone watched. Even Kathleen. Even Nancy. There must have been something in my voice, a packed-up defense. A fight. That look on my face and the way I stood there, armed.

"Alice, I'm moving as you know and—"

"No, I didn't know."

"Please let me finish." She spoke so loud that Kathleen looked up again. "You need to come over and get your things that you never bothered to get before. I packed up boxes of both yours and your sister's things and want you to get them tonight."

I stood staring at a painting on the wall. "Mom, Frank died. His funeral was today. It's late. And why would I have to pick up Helena's things?"

"Oh, for Christ's sake, Alice, not Helena. Marisa."

"Marisa?" I asked, feeling deflated.

"Alice?" Reza walked into the room.

"You can come over tonight, or it's all going in the trash tomorrow. Be here in thirty minutes. There will be a policeman to escort you."

"A what? Mom."

She was gone.

I helplessly looked over at my father. "We have to leave now, Reza."

"What did she say to you, Allie?" my dad said.

I tried to remain calm, even though I wanted to cry out in anger. "She wants me to drive over to her house in this snowfall within the next thirty minutes to pick up belongings that were apparently mine and Marisa's. She has a *police escort* meeting me there."

Detective Holloway reached for the phone. "Let me see if I can intervene on this one."

"She said that if I didn't pick up these boxes tonight, she was trashing everything tomorrow."

Reza put his arm around my shoulders. "Do you even know what's in these boxes? They may be things you have forgotten about."

"I'm sure they are, and I don't care about any of that, but Marisa's things? I don't want my mother throwing them away in some dirty trash can. It isn't like Marisa had a choice."

"Of course not, of course not," he said quietly.

"Why is your mother being so difficult? Especially on a night like this?" Dad asked.

"I don't know, Dad." The tiring and never-ending question. I didn't even wonder anymore. The whole situation was played out in public and was an embarrassing mess. It was as if she planned it like this.

He put his drink down. "Well, she did one good thing. She gave me you. Now. Should I call her?"

"I can handle this, Dad," I said and turned to Kathleen, once again embarrassed beyond belief that she had witnessed this. "I'm so sorry about this."

She shook her head and said loudly, "Don't even give it a second thought. If you ever want to swap family stories, just let me know. We'll play for money, and I'll win."

I scoffed. "Sounds good." Knowing Kathleen for the amount of time that I did, I realized that she was only trying to make me feel better. I looked around the room and realized that my aunt was gone.

The snow stopped falling, and the night was clear. Detective Holloway was right behind us in his car. But I felt self-conscious in front of Reza. "I'm really sorry about all of this."

"There's nothing to be sorry about," he said, then added, "Look at it this way, I'm finally going to meet your mother."

"I was hoping that you never got to meet my mother, Reza. Not like this, anyway." I realized my tone, and I closed my eyes. "I don't care about anything she's boxed up, anything that was *mine*. I didn't even live there. But…but *why* would she threaten to throw out the things that belonged to her dead daughter? A death she enabled? She egged Withers on when it came to Marisa. She hated Marisa. And I don't want her to see me cry."

"So what if she does see you cry? What the hell do you care anymore?" he asked matter-of-factly. "Any normal person *would* cry. And I have a feeling that meeting her will confirm my suspicions. She might be your mother, but you're nothing like her."

I laughed through thick tears that had not yet fallen. "God, I hope not. Neither was Marisa."

"Look what we're doing right now. Only a disturbed person would call you like this after a funeral. You don't have to struggle with her anymore. I love you, and I'm your family now. I'm here with you."

"How did I get so lucky?"

"I could ask the same question."

We drove down into my mother's dark driveway as if we were entering the serpent's lair. There were already two patrol cars parked out front, and Detective Holloway slid in behind us. The light in the garage was turned on, and the automatic door lifted up. There were about nine or ten boxes lying on the floor. Some had my name on them, some had Marisa's name on them, and some had neither.

The four uniformed police officers stood back with Detective Holloway. It was Helena standing at the door. I barely recognized her. "Mom wants you to get your stuff," she quipped.

I was taken aback, and for a moment, I stood still in time, remembering the little girl I once cared for. Then I decided I wanted to slap her over made-up face. She wore a purple sweater with a white turtleneck underneath. The sweater was so tight, it accentuated her breasts, which I'm sure she planned. Her acid wash blue jeans were so tight, it would have been hard for her to put her finger in her back pocket. She had long purple fingernails and lots of rings. I mused at what Sunny and Big Barton thought of their precious granddaughter looking like this. Although the patriarch had been ill for a while, and so he probably wasn't paying much attention anymore.

"I know that." I tried to remain calm. What had become of this child?

"She called earlier, you know. Who's he?" She pointed a finger at Reza.

"Helena, this is my fiancé, Dr. Reza Khavari. Reza, my younger sister Helena—"

"Oh my god, Alice," she said as she studied Reza. "He looks like one of those, like, terrorist guys that, like, hijack planes and—it's *half* sister. Mom! Are you on the phone?"

Detective Holloway raised his eyebrows and muttered something to one of the uniformed officers.

But Reza smiled. "I can assure you, what's your name again? Helen? That I'm, like, no terrorist, like, hijacker," he said in as close to a teenage American accent as he could muster.

I tried not to laugh, but when I looked at his facial expression, a ridiculous sound came out of my nose. We both quietly cracked up, even though I was so sorry for what had become of Helena.

Before we could regain our composure, my mother was at the door next to Helena, who was protesting our giggles and begging my mother for a cigarette. My mother did not look well. She wore a gold-colored bathrobe as she opened the door and stepped into her dimly lit garage with old tan leather slippers on her feet. Her hair was pulled back in a high ponytail, and the usual look of anger pounced from her face. The wonted cigarette dangled from her mouth, and she had put on a noticeable amount of weight.

It also appeared as if she destroyed her youngest daughter. Marisa adored that little girl. I was just as guilty too, really. I didn't fight for time with Helena. I didn't want to have anything to do with it. I was too busy figuring out my own problems, and really, I didn't want to have much to do with her. And between our mother and me, God knows *what* over at Sun Chance and her murderer father dying slowly, the poor kid turned out to be a rude, nasty excuse for a human being. It didn't take long for me to see that. And I knew a part of that was on me.

"Look at you, Alice." My mother talked through her smoke. "You've lost a lot of weight."

I looked down at the cement floor. It was uneven and broken up in a lot of places. I was surprised she let that floor get as bad as it did.

"Who is this?" She nodded her head at Reza, but before I could answer, her head snapped around like a turtle, and she shrieked at Helena, "Go back inside and close the door! This is none of your business."

"Marisa was my sister too, you know. I should be able to look through her stuff too."

"Go back inside!"

I winced at Helena's remark. But I knew exactly what she was thinking when she shut that screen door. She didn't dare slam it. My mother would have made her eat that cigarette. May have done her some good. I could have slapped the other side of her face regarding that comment about Marisa. She didn't even remember Marisa, and she had no clue as to how much Marisa revered her.

My mother was suddenly disinterested in Reza and waved her hand at Helena as she closed the door behind her.

"Mom, it's late, and it's cold out here. The most important thing is that we buried Frank today. Why are you doing this?"

She stomped out her cigarette and immediately lit another one. "Frank's funeral was today. How charming. Yes, I knew he died. I read his obituary. What I would like to know is why no one invited me?"

"Invited you? Mom, it was an open funeral. No one gets an invitation. You just show up. You were more than welcome to attend. Bunic and Bunica were both there."

She crossed her arms and then waved her hand again. "Your grandmother—"

I looked at one of the uniformed policemen who was answering a call.

"I can take it from here." I heard Detective Holloway say to one of them.

"Where are you going, officers? I said I wanted this woman escorted along with her belongings off my property."

"This *woman?*" Reza said.

My mother glared at him.

"This woman, as you say, happens to be your daughter."

"It's okay, Reza," I said.

"No, it's not. Look, we will very quickly load up the boxes, the ones Alice wants, and be off."

"Where are you from?" she said.

I had already gone through three boxes that contained nothing of any importance.

"I hear a British accent, but there's something else. By the looks of you, you're obviously foreign."

"I was born in Tehran."

"Tehran. Jesus Christ. Alice, are you out of your mind? These people are the enemy."

I turned around and looked directly into my mother's eyes. "Mother, I would rather marry a man from Tehran than one who would murder his own daughter. Now that's an enemy."

Her head tilted slightly, and for a moment, I thought that she would hit me. But Reza stood right next to me, and Detective Holloway was over by the garage door, so physically, I was safe. Even more than that, I was confident.

The silence was thick, and she appeared off track and confused, but once again she was causing pain, and I didn't care at that very minute if it was me who was causing *her* pain. Of course, it was a mind-blowing puzzle to know whether or not she even felt pain.

Finally, she turned to Detective Holloway. "You have fifteen minutes to get rid of this crap, or I'm turning out the light, and tomorrow, it goes into a landfill." She turned and walked back into her house and slammed the door behind her.

As I knelt down on the cold garage floor, I looked behind me at both of them. "I'm sorry you had to see that," I said, lowering my voice. "It's just so embarrassing. It's not the way things are supposed to be."

Reza walked over and knelt beside me. He put his hand on my shoulder blades and then rubbed my back. "You have to stop apologizing for other people's behavior. I'm so proud of how far you've come. You made it out alive, and that's not a slight against your sister. You made it out alive in so many other ways. *So* many other ways. She needs help. You got that, right?"

I nodded. Inside my mind, I was frustrated and angry, but I didn't let it show. What made her so angry with me on this night?

Now Helena was in trouble. But there wasn't a thing I could do to protect her. I couldn't protect Marisa. I couldn't protect Helena. There were a certain number of things that I had control over, and I learned those lessons over the years.

"Can I help you two put anything in the trunk of my car?" Detective Holloway asked. "I've got plenty of room."

"I think we have plenty of room, Detective Holloway," Reza said. "But thank you."

Holloway nodded, but I noticed a suspicious look flash across his face. I watched it, and I was curious what that was all about.

Altogether we had three boxes. Two had Marisa's name on them, and the third had Marisa's and my name on it. The other six boxes had nothing inside them that I found of any value, and they each had my name written on them. I remember after Marisa was murdered, I had taken some things that I thought were sentimental. I had no idea that any of these other boxes existed.

The Jeep had cooled down as we got in, but it heated up quickly as we headed out of the driveway. I could see Helena's face peering out one of the windows, but I decided not to wave.

"Are you all right, Alice?"

"Oh." I shivered. "It's been such a long day."

"And you handled it very well. With complete grace."

I had to laugh. "Now *that's* a first."

"What is?"

"The fact that anyone has ever told me I had grace."

"They don't know you like I do."

I looked over at him. "Oh, Reza, what has happened to my little sister? What have I done?"

"Nothing," he said. "You've done nothing. "What do you mean 'what have you done?'"

"She's mean, she's rude, loud. I won't fault her at her age for being overweight. I battled with my weight for years, but I sure as hell didn't emphasize it with blue jeans that looked like they were painted on. And not only that, she just had to make it clear that we were not sisters, we were half sisters. That's the kind of shit my mother used to pull when we were growing up. She had to drive that point home. Rudy was Marisa's stepfather, I was her half sister, and so on and so forth. She was a nuisance about it. We know how all that turned out, don't we?

"I ignored Helena. I mean, we kind of had a relationship when she was little for a while when I went over to visit, but for the most part? I didn't want any other sisters after what happened to the first one. Helena was his spawn, and I treated her poorly. She knew it, and this is her way of getting back at me."

"She seems like she's getting back at everybody. Don't forget the fact that she's right at that age where kids tend to do that," he said.

We stopped at a red light that stayed on for a long time. I studied it.

"It most likely wouldn't have made a difference. You told me that the Withers were always taking her away, traveling, spending days with them, off on weekends. You barely had any time to have any influence over her. From what I gathered from you, her grandparents did whatever they could except file for full custody to keep that young lady away from you and even your mother's parents. Even your mother, right?"

"Yes. I wonder why they never did try to file for full custody."

"Because I think somewhere deep down in Eloise Withers's conscience, she feels some guilt, I think she has to. She knows what her son is. And she knows how good you are. She never wanted to fully take Helena away. And the husband? He's no good, but he probably didn't want to be raising his grandchild either. I doubt he wanted that responsibility."

"Interesting. Never thought of it that way."

He smiled reassuringly. "You can't blame yourself for how other people are or the way they turn out."

He had a point. He usually did. I didn't think he was completely right because Reza didn't know Helena. When she was younger, she wanted to hang around all the time. She wanted to know all about Marisa, and I would tell her to shut her mouth. No wonder she hated me. But this? I had a habit of focusing on myself, I knew that. It didn't take a professional like Dr. Kilburn to remind me of that, although she did seem to bring it up in every other one of our sessions. Maybe none of this had anything to do with me. And there was another thing I knew—Eloise "Sunny" Withers couldn't have given a shit about me. Reza may have been way up on when their company stock rose and fell, when it was time to buy, and when it was time to sell, but he had little idea of the self-centeredness, the raw evil that ran through the veins of that old lady. Neither one of them ever apologized for what their son did to my sister.

I thought of the two people whom I probably would never see again: Helena and my mother.

101

It was warm in my apartment when we opened the door and shook off the snow. We carried the boxes to the kitchen and set them down on the floor.

"Don't you want to go through them?" Reza said. I already caught a glimpse of what was inside each of them. "Aren't you curious?"

"Well, yes, I am."

"Listen, I'm not trying to force you to do anything you don't want to do. It's been a long day. I know you're tired."

"We should put them in the bedroom," I said. I had the time to go through the boxes, and I knew I had the right ones. I got up on my knees on my freshly vacuumed carpet, but then I sat back again. "You're a really great guy, Reza."

He propped himself up on one elbow and laughed. "Thanks. What makes you say that now?"

I put my hands over my face, forgetting that I was wearing makeup to the service. "Because you put up with me and all of this." I waved at the boxes. "My family, these problems, the history. A lot of people would call it baggage. I like to be more specific like—"

"Alice, you don't have to say anything. Don't you remember how we met? We had so much in common that at one point, you actually thought I was making up a story."

"How could I forget?" I said, unfolding cardboard. "I was crazy that day."

"You weren't."

"I was."

"I don't think so, and you know you were never alone."

I said nothing more, and we just sat for a while as I breathed him in, and he kissed and stroked my hair. I got up and opened one box that had only my sister's name written on it. The first thing I pulled out were a pair of lavender pumps. "Oh my g..." My voice trailed off as I looked at the worn shoes that lay in the box for so many years. "I forgot about these. She used to love them. She actually wore them to school. They're four inches high!"

Farther down were burgundy-colored hiking boots with gold laces and the lustrous smell of clean leather oil. It was too much. I could hear her voice, I could see her slam a door as I breathed in the smell of the boots.

"It's like she's here. When I smell the leather on these boots. I...I wish you had known her."

He passed me a tissue. "Sometimes I feel like I do."

I wiped my nose and laughed. "It's amazing what smelling an old pair of boots can do."

We found a box of old cassettes. "Louis Dagher."

"Who?"

"Remember the guy I told you about in high school who I choked nearly to unconsciousness?" I tried not to laugh, but I couldn't help it. I knew it was serious, and I could have gotten into serious trouble, but it was so long ago.

"Ah, yes. The smart-ass, racist hippie."

We both went through what looked to be about fifteen or more cassettes.

"These are either his or Mark's. I didn't think Marisa liked this kind of stuff. Maybe she did. God knows my mother would never let her play them in the house." I wondered whatever happened to Mark the boyfriend after I saw him that day on campus. I heard Louis Dagher died years ago from a drug overdose. At least he went out doing what he loved.

"Why are you smiling?"

"Having evil thoughts about Louis Dagher."

"That's what I thought." Abruptly, he neatly stacked the cassettes back in the box. He was silent, and all of a sudden, I found him acting unusual. I wasn't sure really what to do because I had never seen him this way before. I wanted to say something, but I was torn between Reza and my dead sister. Marisa still had a way of getting me to do things, but Reza would be my husband. Then I thought with horror if that was similar to the silent oath my mother had given to the monster. Was it even silent?

Reza must have noticed something because his face broke into a smile again. "Are you all right?"

"Of course," I said.

"What else do we have?"

I opened another box still feeling like I was in the room with a different person. "Marisa's quilt, a bag full of her baubles, and costume jewelry. I remember asking my mother where this was, and she said she couldn't find any of it, yet here it is. Why would she lie to me about this?"

He looked at me carefully. "Why would she lie to you? You're joking, right? You saw the way she behaved in front of everyone, her own daughters. Your mother's pretty mean. I wouldn't trust her if I were you. Do I even have to remind you of that?"

I rose and sat back down next to him with my butt against the box spring. "No."

We sat for a while in silence. Both of us were very tired from the long and intense day. I crawled back over to the bag. I pulled out a pair of earrings that looked like they belonged to a belly dancer.

"Look at those." He reached for them and held one up. "Like an Egyptian queen."

"It's a little ironic that you say that." I marveled at the earrings I hadn't seen in so long. "I remember when she bought these."

"Were you with her?"

I nodded. "We took the bus downtown on a Saturday. We wanted to get something for Bunica for her birthday, and there was this little store owned by a man from India. She told the man at the register that her father was an Indian prince. I couldn't believe she did that after swearing me to secrecy."

I jangled the metal earrings, and they made the same exact sound they made all those years ago. I was brought back again.

"She just told him so casually and then flitted off somewhere. That man gave her the strangest look. I was so confused."

"Now you know why."

"Now I know why. When she picked out the earrings, she asked him if they were sterling silver or pewter, and he said to her, 'They are metal, miss. Metal!' Obviously." I jangled them again. "She bought incense and two huge tapestries for the wall, which was a waste of money because my mother was never going to let her burn incense or hang anything on the wall. We weren't allowed to decorate our rooms. They were already decorated for us."

Reza noticed the tapestries next. "Estera would have liked these," he said. He rarely talked about her.

We both gently smelled the tapestries at the same time.

"I have a feeling someone was burning incense behind your mother's back."

I grinned and nodded. This smell was different. It didn't take me back. It brought her to me. Although it was wonderful, there was still so much darkness. It was still difficult for me to think about her short life.

"Oh yes." I pulled out a heavy black jersey tank dress with a pleated waist. "I loved this dress and the pastel sash." Marisa could take any scarf and turn it into a belt. This one was a soft oversized crepe material with beautiful lilac and green colors. "She used to tie this around her tiny waist and let it cascade down the side."

"And I'll bet the purple shoes tied the whole look together."

"You never told me you knew so much about ladies' fashion," I teased, trying desperately to keep my nose as far away from that scarf as possible.

"I really don't."

We kissed, but when it became serious, I pulled away.

"I really want you right now," he whispered.

"Can I just put this away and move it across the room?"

"Yeah," he said, rubbing his face. "Want some help?"

"No, I got it." But I wasn't finished going through the box, and when I began to push it across the floor, I noticed a large book overflowing with papers, all different colored stickers, high school concert programs, and letters. This was nothing new. Marisa had a lot of these scrapbook-type things. She collected photographs, her sketches, she wrote poetry, although the last time she let me read anything was when my parents split up, and we moved to the Stanhope. I was far too young to understand and appreciate it. Besides, Bruce Collins and I were too busy building our first radio, which never came to fruition.

I opened the book, and out fell a little square cocktail napkin that had the old Sterns logo embellished on it. I remembered how Marisa loved old signs and took her instamatic camera with her everywhere. She loved the Boochie's sign, which were the same perfectly maintained bright lights since the early 1920s, and the huge loop at the bottom of the big *S* in Sterns was magical to her. Every year, birds would build a nest in that loop. I thought they were sparrows. Marisa said they were finches. No one seemed to know or care except for Dad, who agreed with me. The original building was still there with the old sign, but the store was gone, and the building had been empty for the past couple of years. I thought of something, but as quickly as the thought came to my head, it vanished.

I thumbed through the book some more, and the weight of pages caused me to drop it. When I picked it up, I saw one of her poems. Even now with her gone, I felt as though it would be a betrayal to read it. I also knew she would have hated my going through her things, but I ignored the inner warnings:

Street

You are confined in a mist
In a space, not my space
But a place that is thin, menacing
Yet new.
I cannot even speak.
For my love for you swirls in my stomach.
You are full of order
Task by task but no real
Task

Nothing binds together
I am not sure what to say;
For my love for you chokes me.
You are not able to move for
You are sick with the street.
Frightened by the man
Who is waiting for you.
I shall always listen closely.
For my love for you is a beggar.
Now your life remains empty
And your wrath screeches bloody disdain
Your back is now faded
As my thoughts are alone.
For my love for you is angered but waits.
And you are here and I am far
You will never be the one I knew.
The fury visits you once again,
I am a flower.
Now I am a weed.
For my love for you has turned to soot and blown away.

—Marisa Ana Ionescu

I sat back. I was stunned. Who on earth was she talking about? Mark the boyfriend?

"Reza." I was unable to hear my voice. My thoughts were interrupted by soft snoring. I turned around, and there he lay, half-on, half-off the mattress and box spring that so collegiately lay on the floor. He tried so hard to stay awake after that very long day.

I closed my eyes, then I looked to the ceiling. I looked at him.

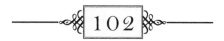

102

"You have to see it. I mean, why pass up a chance like this?"

How can her makeup last all day like that? It's even thicker than usual. And her hair, it was twisted up in a perfect bun almost at the top of her head. She didn't quite look like Kathleen today. She looked very strange, creepy even.

"Kathleen." I felt guilty, but why? I wasn't ever going to buy that house, even if I had the money. "There are a lot of bad memories there. My sister was killed there. How could you even expect me to step foot on that driveway? The same driveway where we used to sit all the way at the end just so we could talk about our day?"

"Why all the way at the end?"

"So our mother couldn't see us."

"That doesn't make any sense," she said, rolling her lips.

It had been years since I rode a city bus. I think the last time was when I was tutoring Walter in high school and had no other means of transportation. It took me an hour to get to his mother's little apartment when it should have only taken me about twelve minutes. Why did Helena own the house in Crescent Hills now? Why did she put it on the market? Whose idea was all of this? How old was she now? I tried to think of the year she was born, but the numbers kept winding up and unraveling, and I couldn't pinpoint a date.

The bus let me off at the street before the entrance to the old neighborhood. I remembered that the Crescent Hills Police Department was headquartered here, and I wondered if any of the village cops might be spying on me. I walked up to our old street and stopped. I had not been here since the day Barton Withers killed my sister. I wanted to turn around and run back to the bus. My heart was boxing my insides out, and I thought I would get sick. Why did Kathleen think this was such a *fine idea? Why did I let her talk me into this? Why was I always asking myself questions I could never answer? Because nothing changed. I lost any confidence I may have thought I had gained over the years. Just like I lost weight, I lost confidence. I gave up smoking, I gave up my self-esteem. I quit drugging, I quit me.*

I hated myself all over again. I wanted to pull my hair out, and then I found myself dragging my feet up that road. I was dragging myself to the gas chamber as if I were a condemned woman, but there were no guards on either side of me to push me or even hold me up.

It was different. It was older, more mature, sadder, and less glossy. The pines towered into the sky, and the maples filled in forgotten spaces. I saw the corner of Mrs. Goldstein's house, and I was curious to know if she was still alive. She would have to have been well into her nineties by now. It was so quiet, and the sun was beating down on me hard from a cloudless purple sky. The hot wind shifted through the trees. I passed the Adlers' house, the close family that seemed so solid, so normal. I would have been so proud and honored to have been born into that family. I remembered when no one was around, I would find a comfortable grassy place to sit in their yard and just stare with my little transistor radio playing pop music with a warm breeze coming from a purple sky. Just like today. I could almost see Mrs. Cruikshank up on her pseudo widow's walk wearing her blue terry cloth robe, and I could feel the shame and questions Marisa had as to why she was pulled out of class so that my mother could interrogate her over the phone and blame her for some adult neighbor's insecurities.

Then I saw Kathleen's tidy Corolla. I thought all real estate people drove nice cars, and somehow, a tan Corolla fit Kathleen. It was parked on the circular drive just past the main entrance. I stood on the street in the hot sun wearing my yellow and green T-shirt, blue jeans, and boat shoes, staring at the giant tan stucco façade that should have been a happy place and was anything but. This could have been a place that housed so many happy, smiling, playing children, well-adjusted and with good parents. They were parents who were there first, right from the very beginning. There was no hatred. There were no affairs, no divorce, no girlfriends, no remarriages, new kids from new people.

This house was sad. I could see it. Even the lawn wasn't as kept up as the other houses. There were tears here. This house cried. The walls cried. I cut across the lawn quickly to the main entrance that our mother forbade anyone to ever use, but it was chained and bolted shut.

What the hell is all this?

I dreaded going around to the side entrance because I knew where I would end up—right in the foyer where Barton Withers lifted my sister by her neck. "Kathleen. Kathleen? Why is there a chain on the front door?"

There was a familiar hiss of breeze through the huge hydrangeas, and I found my way up the steps to the same tan wooden screen door I couldn't move a step farther. Suddenly, I could smell what was inside the house. There was another hallway that led out to the garage that was lined in cedar. Marisa and I had to leave our shoes and winter items out there. I had almost forgotten about that little hallway until the open door forced the cedar smell into my face and into my memories.

I won't go in. But you have to go in.

I looked behind me. Way down across the street was a woman with a large muscular dog. She saw me. I walked straight into the house as if I belonged there, ready to see that wall. Instead, the first thing I saw was Kathleen's body crumpled up on the floor against it.

103

"Kathleen!" I cried and leapt over to her as quickly as I could. She was facedown, and her thick brownish-blond hair was covered with blood that was oozing from the back of her head. My hand was now covered in it. "Oh god, Kathleen, who did this to you?" I checked for a pulse and found that she was still breathing. I was terrified and could have run again, but this time I would not.

I looked behind me out the screen door at the magnificent purple sky. I wondered if that woman and her dog were still there. Then I looked into the darkened kitchen, too frightened to leave Kathleen as if her large injured body would protect me from harm. If there were phones in the house by any slim chance, I knew where they would be.

As I made my way through the kitchen, I realized my first mistake. I should have run to a neighbor's house as fast as I could for help. There was nothing in the kitchen but cheap drawn plastic shades on every window and a filthy shag carpet. None of this made any sense. This house was not for sale, and someone somehow had tried to kill Kathleen and subsequently lure me in to a lair that hadn't changed in decades.

Music was playing on our same old radio in the family room. But there was no phone anywhere in sight, and the 1970s soft rock did nothing to counter the sheer terror that smacked me in the face at my next turn. It was the old love seat. This is where he sat. His long huge body and a grimy faded green blanket lay haphazardly over him. My mouth went dry, and I couldn't move my jaw to speak. I could feel my heart stop, and a hollowness completely replaced my insides. I only stared at him. I couldn't move. The hideous smell of a sickly monster was now before me.

"Don't make one move," he said.

I stood frozen. I didn't even have enough air in my lungs to exhale. I didn't know much about guns, but from what I could surmise, this was a *sawed-off shotgun he pulled out from underneath the dingy blanket and pointed directly at me. I threw my hands in the air instinctively.*

"Didn't I just tell you not to move, bitch?"

"You're supposed to be in prison." I defied him. "You're supposed to be dying. You got an extra life sentence."

"I am dying, and I'm out. As you can see, Miss Smarty Pants."

"You confessed to murdering Nina—"

"Shut up!"

I thought I heard a cry from Kathleen, and I turned to look in that direction.

"And don't you goddamned move again! That skinny dyke deserved everything she got, and so did your sister. Excuse me, half sister." He knew that would burn me.

"Your daughter. Your own flesh and blood, Bart."

"Bart?"

"Did it ever occur to you that you killed your own child?"

"She wasn't mine. Besides, it was an accident. You were there."

"Yeah, so your Mommy and Daddy said—"

"You had better keep that trap of yours closed!" He began to shake.

"You really look sick. Shall I call an ambulance?"

"No!" He started to smile and then cough. Then he laughed. His mouth was hideous. There was spittle jetting out from the middle of his front teeth. The coughing became more violent, and he set the gun down on his ratty blanket. Blood was now spewing from his mouth. I wanted to look away but couldn't.

"You used to be so handsome," I said, eyeing the shotgun. "What was it that you caught again?"

All of a sudden, as if some burst of energy sprung from hell, he was up from under his ratty blanket and on his feet. "That's it, smart-ass, let's go for a walk."

"To where?" I knew. I was certain he was going to kill me now.

"Where?" He shoved the barrel of the gun into my right breast, and it hurt.

"Kathleen." I wanted to scream her name.

"Turn around. Now!" He held the gun up to the back of my neck, and his voice dropped to an evil and gravelly vibration. "Now, I'm going

to say this once and one time only. I do not want to hear you talk anymore. I do not want to hear your snotty, know-it-all voice. I don't want to fucking hear you. You walk where I tell you to walk, you do what I tell you to do, or I will blow your head off and wallpaper the room with your brain. Understood?"

I nodded and squeezed my eyes shut. I moved forward as a suddenly markedly strong Barton Withers shoved his gun into my back. I believed he could and would blow my head off. He forced me through the house. I tried not to think of Marisa as we passed through the main entranceway. There was a cheap white ceiling fan softly humming above where the chandelier once hung. For just a second, it was actually refreshing, even if there was a shotgun thrust in my back. The old slate floor was still there, but it wasn't shiny anymore. It was covered in about an inch of dust that swirled when I walked over it. The place was so dirty, I briefly thought about my mother and how she would have been more disgusted in that than in what was happening to me at this moment.

"Up the stairs," he commanded.

"Where are we going?" My short-term memory failed me, and I asked a question.

"What did I tell you about your mouth?" he hollered, but he still didn't blow my brains out.

I insisted to myself that I had to keep my mouth shut. The last time I had been on this staircase was when I was escaping from him. I had been an overweight thirteen-year-old girl trundling up these steps after just seeing my sister murdered. Running as fast as I could. I could still hear the radio from the other room, which was odd. As hard as I tried to keep quiet now, I felt sadness and pure terror that my life would soon end so violently and painfully, and I began to openly sob.

Once we were up the stairs, he used the gun to jam me in the back and push me into my old bedroom. There were strings of dust on the cherry hardwood floor and cobwebs everywhere. It looked like something out of a movie; it was that macabre and unreal. But the many windows didn't have any blinds, and the afternoon sun beat relentlessly through the naked glass. The room was heavenly bright, and a single piece of furniture sat staring back at me. My twin bed.

"Get under it," he said, seeming more infuriated.

I drew a breath and shook. I turned around, and the gun moved.

"And don't even think about arguing with me, you cunt. Get under that goddamned bed. I liked it the first time I saw you under there hiding and shaking. That was going to be the first place I looked. You knew that, didn't you?"

"You knew where I was?" Somehow I thought that whispering would keep his gun away, but instead, he only thrust it into my neck, which caused unbearable pain that made me cough. My coughing was contagious, however, because when I coughed, he coughed again too. The difference was he couldn't stop. It was like before, but worse. He coughed and gagged and choked, and the gagging turned to repulsive laughter. Blood and spittle dripped like venom from his hairy chin, and as he started to double over in front of me, he was no longer paying attention to the gun. I felt as though it took forever to pull my arm back, and when I punched him, I hit him once, and the punch seemed to travel all the way to the other side of the room.

The gun tumbled to the floor with a loud clunking noise that made me flinch just long enough for the two of us to lunge for it. We struggled. He was sick, but he was still stronger than I would have anticipated. I looked over and saw his knee, and I then I stomped hard on his right foot. He was only wearing those black slippers my mother bought him without any socks. I jabbed him with my elbow as hard as I could in the stomach. He screamed and coughed violently. At that point, I could smell his innards as he grabbed his stomach and toppled forward. But I kicked him hard in the face, and he flew backward. My elbow was scraped badly because it had somehow made contact with the gun, which had once again miraculously fallen to the floor. I jumped on it as if I were shielding a small child. I got to my feet, and I pointed it at him. But there was no trigger.

He looked at me and made a sound. "Oh no, clever little Alice. Where do you think the trigger is, you pain-in-the-ass piece of shit? Same place it's at on every gun. Point and aim, go on."

I had never seen nor had I ever heard anything like it in my entire life. It seemed as if thousands of bullets roared through the air at every angle and in every direction possible. I was amazed not one of them hit me. It was an absolute explosion. Windows were blown out from bullets, a huge mirror was broken, nearly split in half, and there were holes in the sheet rock, the bed, everywhere. I was covered in blood, and there was enough of it to repaint the walls. It was hot, and then it went eerily quiet.

From what I could tell, about a quarter of Barton Withers's bloodied face was mostly intact, but the rest was completely gone. Kathleen was up and standing in the doorway. She startled me, and I screamed. "Kathleen!"

She looked very stoic. There was dried blood in her hair and on her face and neck. "Honey, you did a wonderful job killing him. Just stellar. It's what you've been wanting to do for years. And now you've done it. How do you feel?" She clapped her hands. "You must want to celebrate."

I sat down on the floor, never taking my eyes off her. I rested the gun by my side and decided I would take it with me wherever I went. You never know when you might need one. Blood, blood, everywhere. I realized I was sitting in it. It was sticky and freezing cold like a reptile's, a serpent's. But that's what he was all along. He was a monster, and I just sent him back to hell.

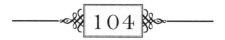

104

"Daddy!"

"Alice?" It was Reza standing in the doorway, not Kathleen.

My eyes tried to focus. I noticed my wet knees. I pulled the covers over me, but it didn't help. I was wet and freezing. At first I thought I peed the bed, but I felt huge relief when I realized it was only sweat.

Reza sat next to me and pulled me into his arms. "I think you had a nightmare."

"I dreamt that I wrestled a shotgun away from Barton Withers and finally killed him. Reza, it went on forever, Kathleen was there. It was terrible. Whose newspaper is that? I thought you didn't like that paper?"

"As a matter of fact, he *is* dead. See? Right there."

There it was. Front-page news with a big photograph of the monster with his five-thousand-watt smile and zero light emitting from his eyes: "Millionaire Businessman, Socialite and Confessed Murderer Barton Withers, III Dead from Intestinal Cancer at 53."

"Intestinal cancer," Reza said. "I wonder if all that consumption of top-rated scotch had anything to do with that?"

The article went on to say that Withers pleaded guilty to voluntary manslaughter of his alleged biological daughter, Marisa Ionescu, 17, of Crescent Hills in 1978 and confessed to murdering her former babysitter, Nina Elizabeth Averelle, 16, in 1974, whose remains were found in a field in Seagramsville last March. The article also went into the Witherses' long and extended boring history and the same old blather about their prominence and money.

"I don't want to hear any more of this," I said.

"Then I will go and place this paper back in its plastic bag and return it to the front porch. Do you want some coffee?"

I lay back and stretched, a huge grin across my face. "Well, I might, but I think I may want to celebrate first. In fact, I think we should celebrate all day. This is one of the happiest days of my life."

For the briefest of moments, I thought Reza threw me an unexplainable strange look, but I ignored it. After all these years, it was finally over. The monster was dead. He had cancer for years, and it finally killed him. And to his rotten parents who supported and stood behind him since Marisa's murder, I hoped it had killed them too. I wanted them to know my pain. But after all those years, Big Barton and Sunny were such sociopaths themselves, they most likely didn't know what pain was. Maybe the death of their son would give them a whole new perspective on what horror was all about.

I felt the cold wetness on the frosty window with my two fingers. "When we move into the new house, we'll have much better windows than these old wooden ones from when they put them in back in 1957, don't you think?" When I looked behind me, he was gone, but I could hear him out in the hallway. "Reza?"

He returned, closed the door, and slid into bed beside me. "You *are* sweaty. That must have been a bad dream."

"It was strange. It was one of those dreams where the more you think about it, the more it slips away. I remember the weather was beautiful, even though the sky had these unusual colors like purple and pink, yellow even. Beautiful colors for a beautiful outcome."

The feeling of euphoria was back. The monster was dead.

"This is such great news. I...I don't know what to say. I don't know what to do."

"I know what we can do."

I felt my face heat up, and the happiness throughout my body nearly burst through my skin. I wanted to feel more of it, but it was over too soon. I wanted to delve deep into the soulless hole of the monster and cheer on his pain and suffering, but that too was over and done. None of it was enough to satisfy me. "I hope he didn't go peacefully."

"All right, Alice. You're going to tear yourself apart." He put his finger to my lips.

I pulled back a little. "What do you mean?"

"Are you going to spend the next fifteen years doing this? Please tell me that you aren't."

"Doing what?"

He sat up and put a pillow behind his head. "He's dead. We don't know what the last minutes of life were like, but I am pretty sure that he didn't even know what was going on. Honestly? I doubt he was writhing in pain."

"That's too bad, but you're probably right."

"You don't need to do this. Not anymore. I don't want this for you."

"Reza," I said, feeling a little annoyed, "what if it was Sweeney? After what he did to Estera?"

He scoffed. "You of all people know I've gone the vengeance route so many times, especially when I'm angry or frustrated by anything. Even when I've had too much to drink, but being with you has changed so many things. I thought that being with me has done the same for you."

"Of course it has." I rubbed my eyes. I could feel a headache coming on. "You know that. We've talked about it so many times. I feel like a spoiled child most of the time."

"You're definitely not that." He ran his fingers through my hair, as if sensing my oncoming headache. "But first Frank, and now this. It's a lot to take in all at once, a lot to handle no matter how strong you are, and you know I believe you're a really strong person."

We sat in silence for a while as the wind cried and beat against the watery single-pane window.

"I know, I know. It's like it's the old me—angry, sick, and scared all the time. It just isn't worth taking the time out. He isn't worth our time. He isn't even worth being called a human being. I don't think I had ever had a happier yet stranger morning all at once. I've never known what it was like to be glad that a person is dead. We're used to grieving death, not rejoicing in it."

"Well," he said, "I don't want to see you get sucked back into those resentments all over again. I understand exactly what you're thinking and feeling, and I hope he suffered in prison as much as you, more than you if that's possible because I love you and want to protect you from evil and from the things that hurt."

I lay my head on his chest. "Right. It's just that we don't have to throw a street party or shoot off fireworks."

"The most important thing to know is that he's gone now. He's really gone. He'll never be able to hurt anyone ever again. And you already know that your sister is everywhere. That's a good way to celebrate by remembering that. I think so, anyway." He got up out of bed to go and lock the apartment door. When he came back, I was naked and waiting for him.

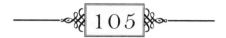

105

It would be a while before I would see Reza again. First he flew to Atlanta for meetings with Dr. Stephens, a zoologist. I wanted to accompany him so that I could finally meet his enormous family, but he preferred to wait until spring before our move to the new house. Then they left for East Africa for a three-week research safari. I was amazed at how much I missed him.

After the first snowfall at Frank's funeral, the typical subzero Wellton winter was up and running at full speed. I decided I needed to relinquish custody of Marisa's and Shelly's ashes. I never thought spring would arrive, and I had to hide my depression and anxiety that could have turned me into a shut-in. The medication helped, but pulling myself out of bed in the dark and cold mornings was a chore, especially with Reza gone.

Then one morning, the sun shone so bright through my new vinyl blinds, and the melting ice dribbled from their cones. It was a Saturday, and Miranda was awake and banging around upstairs. It couldn't have been a better time. I decided to take the bus. I didn't like parking downtown with all the one-way streets and being ripped off by the meters. The parking garages were all old and dark, and last summer, a woman was raped and murdered. The Wellton police still hadn't caught the monster who did it. There weren't a lot of Saturday shoppers down there like there used to be when Marisa and I were little.

Saturdays on the bus with Bunica would be special occasions— noisy and crowded. We would rise early at her house, and Bunic would already be gone up to the stand. She would fix us a huge breakfast, and then the three of us would lumber up the hill to catch the 9:30 a.m. The bus was never exactly on time, and Bunica and the ladies waiting with us complained loudly in Romanian. But I would pick up a few words. Marisa ignored them and popped the heads of dandelions. People dressed up. The shops felt alive with beautifully dressed mannequins in the windows with lights, perfume, and music. All of that was gone. That part of downtown became economically depressed.

Months before Marisa was murdered, she became more interested in her photography. The minute she turned sixteen, my mother told her that it was time to beat the streets and find a job, and if she had any plans to go to college, she would have to save her money, or she would be plumb out of luck.

※　※　※　※　※

"How am I going to save up that kind of money?" Marisa whispered to me one night while in her room. "College tuition is like seven grand a year, even more. If I don't go to college, where will I go? Barton and Mom don't even want me around now, and I haven't even graduated from high school yet." She was taking that instamatic camera with her everywhere, taking pictures of signs, especially the old ones.

Barton Withers was pressuring my mother to pressure my father to give back Marisa her old room. Marisa was trying to stay with friends as much as possible, pressuring them to see if their parents wanted to please take on another daughter. And if they were rich enough, maybe they could help send her off to college. She must have been so terrified; she had no idea how terrified she was. And to the outside? It must have looked like an utter mess. Complete devastation. But no one said a word.

Marisa found a part-time job at Weinstock Bros. or Weinstocks for short, a small elite department store that was shaped like an L. They called her a floater because she worked in all six departments but usually ended up in women's shoes. At three ten an hour, she never saved up enough money for college by herself. She would need grants, loans, financial aid, and someone's help, probably mine in filling out those hundred-foot-long application and loan forms. She really wasn't the college-bound type anyway, but she was very creative and artistic, and so there was that. Maybe she could go to art school. And what she didn't put aside for college, she put aside for a fancy camera with a long zoom lens. When she explained to me one day what she wanted, I sat there staring at her and her friend. It was fascinating. I was so impressed that my sister knew so much about cameras.

Marisa's friend Hope was a year older than her, and I had never seen her wear normal clothing. On the day the three of us went out on my first photo expedition, Hope was wearing a long shiny sandy-colored robe that billowed behind her when she walked. She wore silky harem pants and some strange tie-dyed blouse. Beads covered her neck, wrists, and feet. She wore what looked like worn-out ballet slippers with soles hard enough to survive the outdoors.

Wellton was full of those old signs Marisa loved. She shot the Sterns sign that lit up a pearl gray at night. She shot the original Jodie's, Reddy Dry Cleaners, Orbit's Drugstore, and Zee Bowling Alley and Billiards.

"I see your sister has plenty of money saved up for a fancy camera, doesn't she?" my mother crudely yelled past me one summer evening with a mouthful of food. "She's supposed to be saving for college. Although I don't think a girl like that will make college."

"That's not her camera, Mom," I offered. "She and Hope have been going out on these expeditions. She's really interested in photography right now."

"Is that so?" she said as she scraped her wooden salad bowl with her fork and washed the rest of her food down with red wine. "Hope's mother is worth millions. We don't have that kind of dough around here to—"

"Excuse me?" I knew Marisa was in no way going to take that lying down. She came flying down the stairs, screaming, face red with furor, mascara running everywhere from crying. "It's not my camera, Mom! It's not mine!"

"I already told her that, Marisa," I said. "It's okay." I actually tried to stand between the two of them, but it was too late.

My mother tugged at the leather strap around Marisa's neck, and the camera fell, crashing to the Oriental rug with a plunk.

"You broke it!" My sister shrieked so loud, her voice broke at the end.

I put my face in my hands, hoping not to see the fight that I knew was about to become hopelessly out of control when Barton Withers magically appeared.

"Don't hurt her, Barton," I begged when he came up behind Marisa, grabbed her arm, and did with it what he liked to do best—twist it behind her back.

"Get upstairs to your room!" he shouted.

She pulled away in defiance. "Get off me! Leave me alone!"

"I'll leave you alone, all right! Alone on the streets!" he said. He shoved her hard toward the staircase when she ran.

"Can I go upstairs to her room?" I asked.

"Get lost," he said dismissively.

I passed Marisa on the hallway phone quietly talking to Hope about the camera, but my mother was on her way up one of the back staircases and caught her. "Are you on the phone? Who are you taking to?" Then it would happen. The wild screaming and banging. The commotion was out of control, and I got so worried. I figured if I put my fingers in my ears, it would work itself out, and my sister would make it out alive and in one piece. It never occurred to me that there would be times I would be taken so far off guard. I had prepared for war before in so many ways and at so many different times, but this time, I wasn't as prepared. I should have been. I just wasn't ready that time.

Later that evening, Hope's mother, Roberta Weiss, appeared at the side door with her little gray poodle Trix. They lived on the next street over, and she had been out walking the dog. I wasn't surprised to see my mother, with a glass of red wine, loud and syrupy, welcome Mrs. Weiss into her home, but I was surprised that she let her bring in the dog. I supposed she had no choice. After all, she was in enough trouble after breaking the woman's daughter's camera. Barton Withers was off hiding somewhere with his bottle, no doubt. Marisa was ordered to her room, and I lingered in a private position on the balcony overlooking the dining room. My mother was drunk and in her stocking feet, dancing around on her one-of-a-kind Oriental rug, authoritatively reminding Mrs. Weiss that this was an accident, and we all need to get on with our lives.

Seeing Mrs. Weiss with her cute little dog allowed me to breathe. Her smile was wide and warm. She was a small woman with short and frizzy brown hair and brown glasses. She wore white pants, brown pumps, and a dark green blouse. Three long chains hung from her neck.

She had on lots of reddish-pink lipstick, and when she spoke, I detected a faint New York accent.

"Marisa seemed so upset, Mrs. Withers, I thought Trix and I should drop by. I'm worried about her. She was crying." She soothed and softened.

I felt my chin drop as I frowned in shame. I wanted to reach out to her, to bury myself in her, climb up on her lap, and be mothered by her.

"Oh, Marisa." My mother waved a hand. "Don't pay any attention to her, Roberta. She's nothing but a big baby."

Mrs. Weiss's smile froze, but I knew I was the only one who noticed. She changed the subject back to the camera that was sitting on the table. "Clearly, it's just a cracked lens cap. This is no trouble at all," she said in a quiet and kind voice. "Please, Lavinia, tell Marisa not to worry. We can replace something minor like this."

"For heaven's sake, Roberta. Now you're the one who's worrying, really. This discussion is over," my mother said.

I cringed and stuck my fingers in my ears, not that it would make my mother's rudeness go away, but it lessened my embarrassment. When I looked up, Mrs. Weiss was politely saying goodbye and thank you, smiling warmly, nodding her head, bowing almost. Then she disappeared with her poodle and her daughter's camera.

I wanted to fling myself over that railing and run to her, grab her tiny figure, and embrace her. I wanted to pull her warmth and beauty back to me, but it was too late. Not only was she gone, but she belonged to someone else.

* * * * *

I squeezed my hands together and rubbed my eyes. It became suddenly overcast as I sat on a bench across from the old Sterns building looking up at the old letters. There wasn't a bird's nest in the big loop of the *S* that year though, or not yet anyway. That would have to wait until spring if they even came back at all. I just sat not really knowing when to do it. It didn't feel right. Nothing was special, and so I decided to wait on the bench in the desolate loneliness of what had become blighted Wellton.

The old Sterns sign. They updated it in the sixties to give it that funky, groovy feel and then again a few years later. Then their ads looked space-aged and cheesy. But that one store never changed, and I couldn't stop looking at it, thinking of the birds' nests and my sister.

The clouds collided with each other, and the wind started to blow. We had recently had a warm front, and a lot of rain melted much of the snow. I looked down the street one city block, and I could see regular traffic: busses, cars, people. I opened up Shelly's little tin and Marisa's deep bluish-purple velvet bag. Tears of sorrow and joy streamed down my cheeks. I could feel the time.

I jogged toward the old building as the wind favored me. I held my arm up as high as I could toward the sign and held out my hand, and within an instant, Marisa's ashes were gone. "Go on, Shelly," I said as I let go of his ashes. "Go with her."

106

"Detective Holloway?"

"Alice."

"Is there something wrong?"

"No, no, nothing at all. I was just hoping that if you have some time this weekend, maybe Saturday morning, you could come down to Maidenhead. I apologize for the short notice. I have a friend in town for a couple of days that I think you might like to meet."

This sounded unusual. "A friend?"

"Listen, I hate to impose on your Saturday, but—"

"No, it's not an imposition." I had nothing else to do. "Is ten o'clock okay, or do you need to make it earlier?"

"Ten o'clock is perfect."

I put the phone down. A friend in town? What friend was he talking about? All I had to do was ask him. Why didn't I? It had been several years since I had been in the Maidenhead County Sheriff's Department. It was so long ago, and it seemed like so long ago. So many things were different now, most for the better.

The best part was Reza. We were going to move into the new house together at the first breath of spring if he ever returned from Africa. Then we had to really start working on the plans for our wedding, otherwise, it would be a Christmas one. I missed him so much.

The monster was dead—thank God. Hopefully he was burning in his own hell. Frank was gone, and Scotty was slowly learning to cope. A lot better than I ever did. Dad and I were getting along much better, and I noticed too that Bunica and I shared more of a special relationship. She admitted to me that she would have loved to have been a more demonstrative person, but she kept her feelings private. She was divulging a lot more. I told her it was an honor to be privy to those innermost thoughts and feelings. That was important for her to hear.

"Every time I see you, you're thinner and thinner." Detective Holloway stood next to a stocky woman in her forties with short wavy gray hair, large purple glasses, blue jeans, and a yellow shirt with palm trees on it.

"It's hard to believe Ken didn't always look this way." She spoke in a fond voice as she met my eyes and smiled.

"Almost a hundred pounds heavier than I am right now." He slapped his stomach with pride.

I grinned. *"Really?* That's unbelievable."

"Quit braggin', Holloway," someone said as soft laughter filled the halls.

"Alice, meet Rita Winkler. Rita, Alice Buchner."

After exchanging common niceties, Detective Holloway led Rita Winkler, her large tan handbag, her stack of folders, and me into a room with a one-way mirror. I was already beginning to feel a little creeped out by what was happening, but not enough to leave the room. I remembered the break room that my father and I sat in with Detective Holloway and DDA Martin Giles all those years ago. Martin Giles was now the district attorney of Maidenhead County.

The room was much smaller than the old break room with the huge microwave and the seventies-style refrigerator with the loud compressor that needed fixing. Rita Winkler seemed comfortable as she carefully laid out her file folders on the gray table. There was brand-new carpeting on the floor.

"I'm so glad you could make it this morning, Alice. If you would like to have a seat, we can tell you what this is all about," Rita Winkler said and in a professional tone and gestured for me to sit.

Trepidation shot through me. I knew how I sounded and I didn't care. "Wait a minute. Do you work for the Withers family? Please tell me there's no mistake—"

"Hell no." Rita Winkler waved her hand at me. "Withers is still six feet under, honey, and that's going to be forever."

At first I said nothing. "I still keep in touch with his younger sister Mary Jo and her son Danny. They know what he was."

She quickly reached out her hand and touched the tips of my fingers. "And there's nothing wrong with that." She seemed to stare at me for a long time. She took a deep breath. "I am a fairly young retired detective with a very small police department outside of Sacramento. Now I write true crime. Do you like to read?"

"Oh, I do," I said. "But true crime is not my genre. I've never read a true crime biography in my life for obvious reasons."

"Understood." She nodded deeply. "We had our fair share of murders, robberies, plenty of drugs, but nothing compared to what you and I went through as children. Detective Holloway has offered to help me with an initiative I have set up called Crime Impact USA. So far we have incorporated Crime Impact USA in three cities, smaller cities, but cities nonetheless. We concentrate on people who were afflicted by violent crime, victims of violent crime, survivors, and those who are willing to conquer. Someone like me would help someone write a letter to their parole board or *get* to a parole hearing *if they could in their state* and make sure that offender remains exactly where he or she belongs."

"I see," I said.

"Crime Impact USA is a nonprofit organization that has so far raised sixty thousand dollars in its one-year existence."

"If you're asking for money, I don't have any."

"I'm not, Alice, not at all. What I need is your brain." She smiled, not taking her eyes off me as she shuffled through her papers and folders. "Another fascinating thing I discovered on my journey is that there are quite a few people who are very much like me and you—people who have had a family member perpetrate a crime and have gone on to lead productive lives."

"Barton Withers was not a member of my family, if that's what you're trying to say." I sounded childish and disagreeable the moment I opened my mouth. I still wondered what this woman wanted from me. Why didn't I just come right out and ask her?

She was immediately apologetic. "No, you're absolutely right. I just meant that he was a stepfather, and he lived with you in your home." She continued before I had a chance to tell her how he always reminded us that it was *his* home. After all, he was *paying for it*. "Also, some children come from the same backgrounds, and one leads a terrible life of crime, and one is a respected member of society. One witnesses a violent crime like you and eventually finds good in the world and lives a violence-free, law-abiding life while their sibling does not and cannot—a witness to the same crime, same domestic violence."

I was more than a little confused and glanced over at the mirror. Then I addressed this friendly but unusual woman. "Ms. Winkler—"

"Rita. Please."

"Rita." I was silent for a minute. No one said a word. "I see that you know a little about me, either through public records or old newspaper clippings, Detective Holloway, I don't know, but you really don't know *that* much about me. I've had brushes with the law. I guess I'm a little confused as to why I'm here? I mean, why am I here? What do you want? To help you clean up the streets of Wellton? I grew up in one of the worst sections of Wellton supposedly, and I don't really care. The streets don't matter. I've learned that. Murder starts at home and—"

"Exactly."

"I don't understand. I'm confused. I'm flattered—"

"Are you? Let me ask you a few questions," Rita said. She leaned forward. "Do you remember a country singer by the name of Gretchen Connor?"

I lifted my head. I did know the name. "I do. I know that name, although I was never really a fan of country music." I instantly thought of Reza and his collection of country music albums. To me they were country and western, and I liked them. They were growing on me. I just didn't feel the need to tell that to Rita Winkler. And then I remembered. "Yes, yeah. Of course. That poor woman was murdered along with half her band. I was very young. It happened a couple of years before Marisa's death, maybe more. We were just moving into the Stanhope. It was in the news. Why, did you know her?"

I studied Rita Winkler's face. Her eyes were full of a strange far-off sorrow as she shook her head. "In 1973, Gretchen Connor was hosting a dinner party at her remote desert home outside Las Vegas for a couple of her friends and a few members of her band when an unknown intruder walked right in the front door and murdered five people in cold blood. His name was Edward Steven Winkler. Or as the press jumped on his childhood nickname, Eddie Winkles. Not only was he a prolific serial killer, but he is also my younger brother."

The air in the room grew hot and thick. I didn't move, nor did I say a word. There was an uncanny metallic taste in my mouth, and I tried not to make a face. I could almost hear the sound of my own heartbeat.

Rita Winkler's eyes became intense, and she stared as if she wanted to know how much I could take from her. I wanted to know the same myself. I knew I could have gotten up and walked away any time I wanted from this peculiar woman and her files, but there was something in Rita Winkler that I felt I could trust, and whatever it was, it compelled me to stay.

Next, as if casually dealing a deck of cards, she threw down black-and-white crime scene photos in front of me. I couldn't help but notice the first one, even though I looked away. It reminded me of the dream where I shot Barton Withers with what I thought was a sawed-off shotgun.

I turned to Detective Holloway.

"Easy does it, Rita" was all he said.

"Ken, this woman saw her stepfather break her sister's neck just a few feet away from her. She'll be fine. Right, Alice?"

I gingerly turned back to the photographs. "Are you out of your mind? Where did you *get* these?" I said matter-of-factly as I looked at her.

I got no answer. One of them showed what I thought was a large gunshot wound to an individual. What I could see initially were clumps of black sludge, a pool of dark blood, and legs in a fetal position. Another photo showed what was left of someone's face, a man. This was the one that reminded me of my dream. There was nothing there but a mass of black blood on the shirt except the very top of the forehead with just a few hairs sticking up. They looked like they were blond. Another photo was of a woman's head in a fireplace. The mouth was open, and the hair was swept off to the side as if it was flying. The eyes looked into the direction of the blowing wind.

I stuck my hand on my heart.

"Alice?" Detective Holloway said.

"I'm okay." I shook my head. Why was I still there? "What kind of monster lives and breathes on this earth? Was this the work of your brother?"

She nodded slowly, her mouth in a frown. "Took me many years to get my hands on those photos."

"Was he always a psychopath? My god, I've never seen anything like that in my life!"

"Most people haven't. But the close-up of the face is actually in your local library. And to answer your question, he wasn't *always* a psychopath, but there was definitely something wrong." She sat back in her chair. "You probably wouldn't believe it if I told you that he was the most adorable, chubby little baby boy you had ever seen in your life. I was seven when he was born. I felt like a little mother to him, and in many ways, I was and grew to be.

"My family's story, unfortunately, is one that I have to retell time and time again in order to keep Crime Impact USA moving forward. My father was a warehouse worker by day and a bartender at night where we lived in Torrance, California, near Los Angeles. He was also a complete and utter unadulterated drunk and dead by the time I was fourteen." She lifted her finger. "But. Fortunately for us, and everyone else for that matter, Dad was a fun drunk. He was the type who would get up on tables and start dancing like a fool, and a few times he got arrested for getting completely naked and directing traffic. He was never mean. Just an idiot. And when he died, both Eddie and I were crushed. Our father was our entire world, our moon, our stars."

She stopped and mused for a moment. Detective Holloway was called out of the room. I got a bit worried about what I was going to hear next.

"As you can imagine, he was *extremely* irresponsible as a father. Dad was our best buddy and nowhere *near* a proper guardian to two young kids, which drove our poor mother crazy. If on a Sunday afternoon she was making a ham or a roast, the two of us would be too full to eat because Dad had spoiled us rotten at the five-and-dime with a stomach full of candy, and then he would stop off for his gin. Dad was rarely hungry. Then he became sick and was hospitalized for internal bleeding of the stomach."

She took a breath.

"One of the last times I saw my father was when he was picked up in an ambulance and taken to the hospital. Eddie and I weren't allowed in because we were too young, which I thought was bullshit, but those were the rules in those days. I remember how upset Eddie was. He cried because he didn't understand, but I also remember how *angry* he was, and he was only seven years old. I guess it was just as well because our mother told us Dad looked like a pumpkin. His face was bloated and yellowish orange in color. She told me he had constant headaches because they wouldn't let him have his gin. Then he laughed that wonderful, joyful laugh of his until he'd make these awful hacking noises and spit up blood and mucus into a cup. Mother said it was horrible."

Her face twisted up in disgust.

"Finally, *someone* allowed us in the room to see our dad. Mom and I both knew how persuasive Dad could be, and we figured he charmed the nurse somehow even in the horrifying state he was in. Of course, the whole thing was ridiculous. The man was dying, and he wanted to see his kids. And the way Eddie was behaving, he needed to see him too."

She bit her lip.

"You know, it's amazing to see the psychopath that my brother turned into when all those years ago, I remember watching my father holding his son in his arms on the day he died." She shook her head. "The only thing my mother said to us was 'Be grateful your father was a good happy man who loved you to the moon and back.'

"Things got tough. We barely had enough money to bury my father. It was as if every single penny he was supposed to save was spent on booze and cigarettes. The electric bill hadn't been paid in three months. I was amazed we still had the lights on. My grand-mother insisted we come live with her, but nope—Mother was deter-mined. But determined or not, we had nowhere to go because Dad wasn't paying the rent either, and we got kicked out. So we went to

Granny's for a while, and Mother went out into the world and got a job answering a phone for a superintendent's office. It worked out perfectly because the job came with a free crummy apartment. Not at first, but right after someone got fired for stealing. Mother was ecstatic, and I was so happy for her. But Eddie? He didn't seem to care about anything. He just did what he was told. Then Mom got a boyfriend, and within a year and a half of Dad's death, I, like you, was blessed with a stepfather."

I scoffed at her sarcasm.

"His name was Neil Clifford. He was from Scotland and originally living in the United States illegally, so I found out much later. He was Mother's boss and, apparently, had *the best* apartment in the whole building, and of course, I hated his guts. He was an ugly, greasy, weedy little shit who chain-smoked and drank so much black coffee, it came out his pores. I told Mother she was too good for him, too nice, too sweet, too pretty. My mother always laughed when I told her she was pretty. She would say things like 'Rita, I am mousy, chubby, and ordinary at best, fat and unattractive at worst.' She had this way of putting herself down. Sometimes I just wanted to shake her!"

She sat back in her chair again, eyes downcast.

"And forget having any kind of ally in Eddie. You could put a plate of cold, canned, creamed spinach in front of him, and he wouldn't say a word. No 'I love this' or 'I hate this.' Just complete indifference. He would gobble up the spinach and just wait until he was excused from the table. I just chalked it up to an eight-year-old boy who lost his treasured father, and he simply wasn't the same anymore. For the most part, he had pretty much been a calm and quiet little boy, but after Dad's death? He was downright silent. And Mother didn't want to be bothered with it. She was too busy with Neil. But see, I didn't know it was what you would call *a problem.*" She put her hand on her chest. "I was just a kid too. It was all too confusing, and the worst was yet to come.

"Neil Clifford, in addition to all his disgusting habits, was what I called a nitpicker. He was vicious and controlling. He and my mother would go to one of my softball games with Eddie in tow and get talking with some of the other parents after the game. Then in the car on the way home, Neil would accuse my mother of giving Mrs. Whomever a dirty look. My mother was a saint. And she would have no idea what he was referring to. When she would protest, he would stick his finger in her face hard or slap her. I would scream and yell at the loser who simply ignored me or told me to shut up and mind my own business. Eddie would sit in silence and, at nine years old, shove his thumb in his mouth. I would say to him, 'Come on, Ed, you're too old for that,' and I would pull his thumb out of his mouth. And he'd keep it out if he knew I was watching or if I was still there. Then he'd wait and shove it back in his mouth again.

"It was Neil's little imaginary nitpicky things that frustrated my mother to the point of tears. But still, she stayed with him. One time he said something like 'When you said what you said to me last night, why did you say it in that tone of voice?' My mother would say, 'Neil, what the hell are you talking about?' And of course he would punch her on the back of the head. I would *beg* her. I would say, 'Mother, *leave* him.' And she would say, 'What about the apartment?' And I would say, 'Who cares? We'll get a new one!' And she would say, 'He's a good provider, Rita.' And I would get so mad, I would storm off mumbling a string of curse words under my breath. Of course, Eddie would be playing with a toy by himself in which he was far too old for. That's what I remembered back then. Eddie wasn't developing properly, and no one was doing anything to help him.

"One night, Mother blew up and took a swing at Neil's face. They had friends over for dinner, and when they left, Neil accused my mother of not smiling enough. Remember now, Mother had had it up to her eyeballs with Neil's constant torment. She had also been in the kitchen all afternoon cooking, baking, and preparing. She finally just hauled off and punched him in the nose. He bled a little—big deal. He deserved it."

Rita Winkler looked at the ceiling and took a deep breath.

"They didn't stop hollering at each other all night after that. I really believed she was finally, *finally* going to leave him. She sounded strong, like she was done with him. I could hear the independence in her voice. I kept my eye on Eddie for a minute, but then decided to go find a suitcase and start packing our clothing. Just as I was about to call my grandmother, I heard a tussle in the bathroom. Something was wrong. I went back into the living room and saw that Eddie wasn't sitting on the floor anymore. Suddenly I heard Eddie cry out, and I ran to the bathroom. It was the most surreal sensation, almost as if I was in a dream, you know, like when you're trying to run but you can't because your legs are so heavy? I couldn't move fast enough. It was as if the bathroom was ten miles away. But then I saw little Eddie."

She placed her hands together as if she were about to pray and chopped the air with each word.

"I. Will. Never. Forget. The. Look. On That. Child's. Face.

"He was chained to the radiator like a wild animal, and my mother was kneeling in front of the bathtub with a huge bloodied gash on the side of her face and her wrists handcuffed behind her. She didn't even look conscious. Handcuffed. I had no idea where those handcuffs came from. I had never seen real handcuffs before.

"Before I could open my mouth, Neil was right behind me, and suddenly, the room became so loud, I couldn't think. He used ripped pillowcases to bind my wrists behind me, and he tied me to the radiator next to my brother with some kind of cord. Eddie and I sat and watched him shoot our mother in the side of the head. Her death was brutal, violent, and cruel. He was wearing two pieces of a three-piece suit, a dirty old suit with scuffed-up brown shoes. He changed his clothes for the occasion. At dinner he was wearing his smoky, smelly, bright red shirt and those green suspenders. *He actually changed his clothes for the occasion.* Ed was screaming for her, and I kept screaming to him, 'Eddie, close your eyes! Don't look, baby!' All the while pulling ferociously on that damned radiator, trying to get that knot loose. My *hands* loose. Where did this animal suddenly get this superhuman strength from? Eddie was in hysterics now, and I kept screaming, 'Mother, I'm coming! Mother, I'm coming!'

"Neil Clifford just stood there and watched. I kept pulling and twisting as hard as I could, trying to free myself, but it was too late. Neil threw our dead mother's body on top of us, stepped over her, and simply walked out of the bathroom.

707

"Mother used to call herself a hearty gal. She was about five foot ten and weighed over two hundred pounds, and she was just perfect to us. Eddie suffered a broken nose, a broken collarbone, and a hurt leg. I guess you could call me *lucky*. Apparently, my head smashed backward against the radiator, and I suffered a really bad concussion and passed out, waking up with vomit all over me and my mother. I do remember the police charging into the apartment, but I wasn't glad to see them. It didn't matter anymore. I thought Eddie was dead, my mother was definitely dead, and Neil Clifford was on the run."

107

"Eddie and I moved back into my grandmother's house. She was a wonderful woman, and she did everything she could to help us, but obviously, there was no way to cure this. Meanwhile, Neil Clifford got himself involved in a drug deal that went bad in Los Angeles eight months later and ended up with an axe straight through the middle of his head. Top down. Small price to pay for what he did to Mother in my estimation. I promised Eddie I would take care of him, that I would spend every waking moment with him that summer if I had to. My mother's younger brother Roy's girlfriend kicked him out, so he moved back in too. Roy is a funny, larger-than-life sort of guy, and I thought having him around would be so good for my brother. But Eddie didn't care what any of us did. He preferred to sit on my grandmother's couch in front of the little black-and-white television or sometimes play with the neighbor's two-year-old daughter. He hated going to the mall or the beach.

"Then one day he shocked me by telling me he would like to someday find our father's family. This was a day I had successfully dragged him to an outdoor concert with some of my friends. He was obviously way too young to be there, but I needed this child out of the house. My grandmother was so concerned about him being cooped up so much. I told him, 'Ed, we never knew Daddy's family. Granny and Uncle Roy never knew them either. I mean, where would we even start?' He never answered, and he never brought it up again. Maybe I should have tried harder to help him. I should have tried harder to help him.

"I worked my way through college while Eddie grew up at my grandmother's. He made everyone very, very proud. He was a straight A student. He excelled in math and science and received a

709

full academic scholarship, which literally made Uncle Roy cry. Then he moved to Nevada and, as far as I am aware, began killing people. He wrote to Uncle Roy two or three times, but Roy always said his letters were brief and to the point, you know, the weather, that he was fine, hope you are too, that sort of thing. He never asked about me, and he never wrote to our grandmother.

"After Eddie was arrested, my grandmother had a series of heart attacks. Three in total, but she didn't die. She had been through so much too, as had Uncle Roy, who had tried his level best to be strong, but I knew at a second's notice, he could have keeled over too. The absolute guilt I felt for letting that child down was so unrelenting that I stopped eating, I couldn't hold much down. Maybe I was punishing myself, I don't know, but I wasn't even hungry.

"Somehow I got through. All my hair fell out, well, most of it anyway, so I shaved the rest. I would go out in public wearing a cheap wig or scarf, or I would forget a head cover altogether. I went to visit Eddie in the county lock-up one time. We were separated by very thick glass. I said to him, I asked him, 'Ed, I don't know what you did, but my god, they got you in here for nine counts of aggravated murder, and that's just the beginning. What on God's green earth have you done? Did you kill people, Eddie?'

"I had not seen my brother in years, but let me tell you, he was no longer a boy. He was a grown man who hadn't shaved and frightened the hell out of me. And he didn't even ask me about my bald head and scarf. He either didn't notice, which seemed impossible, or he didn't care. Then he went on this rant that almost threw me off my chair. That's when he told me that men and women should not be together in any way. He was tangential, and he sounded floridly psychotic. He gave me *his* reasoning as to why men and women should not be together. There were physical reasons, sexual reasons, spiritual reasons. So I asked him if men could be with men, and women could be with women? That's when he told me about the capsules. That we should all be encased in one and either choose to float or roll on wheels. He kept going, and I stopped him, which was the first time in my life I ever had to stop my brother from talking. I told him that whatever was going on in that head of his, it didn't give him the right to kill nine innocent people. Then I asked him if nine was all he killed. That's when he became furious with me and broke free from his craziness for just a second.

"That's when I knew. He asked me to think carefully about what Neil Clifford did to our mother. He asked me what Dad did by drinking himself to death. He told me I was an awful sister because I could not understand and appreciate the capsules. I said, 'Ed, don't even *try* to act crazy. They're going to put you to death for this. And you deserve it.' And I got up, and I left.

"Jeffrey Thomas Stark was in Gretchen's band, and both were my brother's victims. He was in the wrong place at the wrong time, a man having dinner with a woman. Apparently a sin, according to Eddie. He was the first one named in the indictment, and it was evidence from his body that led them to my brother. Eventually, as more victims were tied to my brother, this is where the press somehow got a hold of the fact that I used to call Eddie, Eddie Winkles when he was a small child. And that name stuck like glue. I actually moved to Nevada, and I sat in that courtroom every day. I wanted him put away. He knew right from wrong. He wasn't legally insane, not by a long shot, and we both knew it. So did the prosecutors. It was an absolute press-mongering circus outside the courthouse. Eddie Winkles was no longer my pudgy little brother who lived through the deaths of his beloved parents, who witnessed, who *experienced* horrific violence and needed protection. Eddie may have been mentally ill, but he chose to follow the twisted route of the devil. The one thing I loved more than anything in this world had turned into a monster. Maybe it was in him all along.

"One day after court, I followed Jeffrey Stark's family out into a remote parking lot behind the courthouse. I begged for forgiveness. I told them how sorry I was and that I should have kept a more watchful eye over my brother after our mother was gone. It was my fault. Jeffrey was survived by his parents, a brother, and a sister. They were a beautiful family.

"It was wintertime and later in the afternoon. The sun was low in the sky, and we must have been walking west because the sun was in my eyes, and it was frustrating me. I had so many things to say to

711

them, but they just kept walking with their backs to me. They never turned around. Finally, their attorney stopped and addressed me. He said, 'I'm sorry, Ms. Winkler. The Starks don't blame you for their son's murder, but being the sister of this monster will haunt you for the rest of your life. If I were you, I would change your name.'"

"You never did change your name," I said.

She smiled and shook her head. "Nope. I'm not going to let that little bastard dictate how I conduct my life any more than he already has. I'm Rita Winkler. Rita. Winkler. I didn't kill all those innocent people. Eddie did that. Maybe I could have been a better sister and help chase those demons away. Now I believe I did everything I knew at the time. I saw the same things he did."

"I know, I know you did. At least he's not going anywhere," I said.

"No, Eddie, for all the publicity and the hoopla and *this* and *that*, lawyers were just dying to defend him. He got some hot-shit law firm and avoided the death penalty. He received nine consecutive life sentences, although I believe there are more bodies out there and more suffering families. I only pray that one day they will be found. In the meantime, I will continue to work with families to make sure their loved ones' perpetrators remain behind bars. I have much to build upon."

I nodded and said nothing.

"Look at Barton Withers for instance," she said suddenly. "Eight to twenty-five for murdering Marisa?"

"I was so relieved he didn't make parole," I said.

"I'm sure you were. He could very well have had if he didn't have such a problem spitting."

"What? I heard he was transferred because he was such a model prisoner."

"Oh no. Mr. Fancy-Pants-It-Was-All-an-Accident could have been out of there"—she used her thumb in a backward motion—"if he could have just behaved like a big boy. What would Mommy think?"

"Why didn't Detective Holloway tell me any of this?"

She shrugged. "My best guess would be because he wanted to protect you as much as possible."

"You just did."

"Because I'm trying to show you how easy it is for these people, if you even want to call them that, to slip right back out on the streets again."

"He could have been paroled. He could have gotten the best treatment for his cancer," I mused.

Rita rested her head back on her palms. "And then Ken would have hauled him back in for the murder of Nina Averelle. He may have killed others. Maybe one day we'll find out."

"Yeah," I said quietly. "I've told my story when I had to. But I never felt comfortable. Once to the cops and the DDA. I know they never really believed me. Once to a really nice and helpful social worker, of course my psychiatrist. I threw out bits and pieces to counselors and groups when I was in the hospital only because I *had* to, or I probably would have delayed my discharge. But it was funny, it helped me most talking with the other patients."

"I understand you don't want to talk about it. A lot of times *I* don't want to talk about being the sister of Eddie Winkles, but unfortunately, we are unique people. Alice, we have been put on this earth to help others get through their own horror, and we can do this. We have been cursed and blessed at the same time. Cursed because we lost the people we loved in the most brutal and unfair ways, right in front of our very eyes. Even Eddie was taken from me. He took himself from me. We're cursed with guilt and regret. I never know which one of those is the right word. But we are also blessed because, speaking for myself, anger and passion have driven me to do positive things with my life—to write, help good families, great people, and work for those out there who have hurt just as much as you and I have. And like us, *they* never had a chance to come up for parole."

Passion, revenge, passion, revenge. I didn't even know there was a real difference between the two, just like Rita Winkler had a hard time differentiating between guilt and regret. Were they all interchangeable? Running away because the monster directed me to while he was killing my sister was the greatest regret of my life. I was guilty in my mind for what I thought was doing the wrong thing. And then one day, an old broken-down man with severe depression said it best. "It's pie in the sky thinkin' that a little girl's gonna think clearly enough to find the biggest, sharpest knife in the drawer and plunge it into the big guy's back deep enough to kill him. Ain't gonna happen. Things in real life ain't the way they are in the movies. I can attest to that."

"You can tell your story, or if you don't want to talk about the order of events, you can talk about your beautiful sister and what she meant to you, how friends and family members grieved so differently."

She was so tapped into me that it was eerie. It had been a couple of times now throughout our conversation that I felt as if I had known her for a long time. I briefly thought about telling her about Reza and his experiences, and then I quickly decided not to. Something in my head told me that it would be very wrong, and it nagged at me. It nagged me a lot.

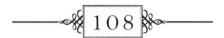

108

"I love you!" I was almost hollering as the phone line crackled and fizzed like an old record.

"I love you too!" he hollered back and hung up.

Lately, I always felt as though I said "I love you" first. Maybe I said it too much, and maybe it sounded desperate and insecure to him. I decided that should change.

Reza's flight would be landing in New York at 1:36 p.m., and after about a half hour or so wait, he would be landing in Wellton at 3:12 p.m. When I checked the flight schedule, it said his plane would be arriving a little earlier. I was so excited to see him again. He had sent me a letter telling me how much he missed me and that he had taken some breathtaking photographs. Although I was glad to receive his letter and phone call, it was difficult being away from him for so long. It would be one of those things I would have to put up with being married to him. On the other hand, I supposed I could always travel with him. I wondered how that would work out.

I was a bundle of frayed nerves the entire morning. I couldn't even eat. Why was I feeling so insecure? At the height of my anxiety, I mistook the time to the airport and arrived too early. Reza had asked me to meet him at the curb so as not to inconvenience myself. I decided to park the car and meet him at the gate. I walked through the automatic sliding glass doors into the small international airport and walked through the terminal toward the gate.

The plane wasn't there. I had about another twenty minutes. I bought a diet soda and a magazine and sat and waited as I continued to look out the window, watching for Reza's plane to taxi in. My stomach fizzled with anticipation and excitement. Then there was a shift in the group of people around me, and a small child ran past. I had become engrossed in the magazine article I was reading, trying to occupy my mind as much as possible. When I looked up, the plane was firmly attached and Reza was near.

I got up and stood back by a garbage can. I didn't want to be that desperate, lovesick woman who jumped on her man, attacking him with an all-four-limbs hug regardless of who was watching.

Passengers continued to shuffle and file through the open door, and then I saw him alone, just for half a second it seemed, only enough time for me to breathe in, for my lips to part, to notice that his shirt was blue. And then I saw her. Kinsey Forman reaching down for something and then looking up at him, her eyes as bright and sparkly as perfect diamonds, her face beaming with light, her smile the one that should have been mine. He put his arm around her and pulled her into his chest and kissed her: one, two, three seconds. He pulled away so slowly.

I felt as though I couldn't get certain things from him, yet I didn't know what those things were, and now, it was all playing out. That minute, right in front of me. It *was* real, even though it was still like a dream. He didn't see me. They didn't look around, nor did they keep it a secret.

Hamburg. He had a "layover" in Hamburg. He most certainly did. No wonder he insisted that I pick him up at the curb.

I started to walk. I blinked hard. A woman looked at me. I smiled absentmindedly. I threw out my empty soda can and magazine, and then I began to walk faster and faster. I did everything I could not to cry. I picked up speed, and a jog turned into a sprint, and I ran all the way back to my car. As soon as my tired head fell on my steering wheel in the darkened parking garage, I realized that I lost a love from my life, and it will be a love loss that again will be so much different than the others. This love, after it's gone, lives. I would still physically see Reza, and I would still love Reza. He was the one I gave my soul to, and he betrayed me, and now he was gone. He might as well be dead. But he was not dead. He was very much alive, and although he had departed, he still lived.

* * * * *

I sat in the chair in my bedroom. It was raining, and I watched from my window. God was crying, but it wasn't for me. Miranda was upstairs playing some kind of unusual music. I was happy the volume was fairly low. It had been almost three hours, and the phone hadn't rung. Maybe he hadn't thought of me. Maybe he hadn't thought of the smallest thing, like picking him up at the airport. He was probably screwing Kinsey Forman right about then anyway. My bed was made perfect and tight, and I actually arranged my three throw pillows. I changed the sheets.

"Why didn't you come get me?" There he was standing about ten feet to the side of me.

I surprised myself at how composed I was. I gave myself a few seconds to breathe before I began. "I *did* come to pick you up at the airport—"

"I was at the curb," he interrupted. He was angry. He was impatient. "I waited for you."

"Why didn't you just get a ride home with Kinsey Forman?" I didn't move.

He winced as if a mosquito were flying toward his eye. "What?"

"I was there, Reza. I was early. I came to the gate. I saw the two of you kiss."

His mouth dropped open as his once olive skin tone turned a grayish white. It even looked like blood drained from his hair. Reza's shine was gone.

"What's the matter? Don't have anything to say for yourself?" Right then and there, I knew it was over.

"Alice—"

"Alice what?"

"Look—"

"My grandmother was right about you," I spat. "She never trusted you. Never."

"Ah, your grandmother—your whole fucking family."

I shrugged. "My whole fucking family. Well." I could feel my heart beginning to race. "At least you got to meet *each and every* one of them. I don't even know if you really have this great big wonderful

717

family that you always go on and on about. We *were* supposed to get married!"

"Oh, I sure have. Even the deceased. What about the dead sister you can't forget about? You care more about her than you do about me."

"That is not true. And I will *never* forget about her. No more than you will forget about Estera. Or have you already forgotten about her, you insensitive ass?"

"Frank's funeral—we spent the entire day mourning as if it were an assassination of a president. He was middle-aged. He had a heart attack. It happens. It's life. Then we have to go through boxes of your sister's shit that have been lying around for over a decade!"

My hands flew to my mouth. All his encouragement. Everything he said. He lied about everything.

"You can't handle life, Alice. I'm up to my asshole in your depression and drama—"

I laughed, and he stared at me like I was crazier than he thought. "You know, Reza. I'm not going to argue with you over families and sisters and whatever my mental health is, you know why? Because these are your excuses for fucking other women when you are an engaged man. I'm just glad I know this now instead of after we got married."

His entire body started to melt. I sat back down in my chair. I was finished with this.

"Alice, I'm so sorry." He knelt down in front of me and tried to put his hands on my face.

"No!" I pushed him away.

"We were thrown together in the middle of the savanna on this research project," he whined.

"How *dare* you lie to me like this? You are nothing but a liar and a cheat."

He was kneeling before me now, his head nearly in my lap. I kept pushing him away.

"Alice, I love you. She means nothing to me," he explained.

"Really? Then why were you kissing her? Did you say the same thing to her about me?"

"Of course not!"

Finally I had had enough. I hated him. I could no longer stand him touching me and hanging all over. I hated his smell, his shaving foam, his shampoo, his soap, the feel of his skin, all of it. "You're only acting this way because you got caught. You make me sick!" I yelled as I walked out into the kitchen. "I will not tolerate your sleeping with other women. My father did it to my mother, and—"

"You hate your mother."

"I hate you more."

He stared at me in disbelief.

"Now, get whatever shit is yours out of here, and please don't call me again. And here." I touched him one last time by placing my engagement ring in his palm.

But he wouldn't leave. He walked over to where I stood and touched my shoulder.

I became enraged. "Don't you get it, Reza? I don't want you here. I don't love you anymore."

He jumped back at that declaration. "You cannot turn off feelings of love just like that." He snapped his fingers.

"You did, Reza. Just like that. Or maybe I'm thinking you never had those feelings for me to begin with."

"How can you be so unforgiving, Alice? I'm so, so sorry."

"I don't want to talk about this anymore."

"Jesus forgave."

"Right. And look what happened to him." I could see that my anger was getting the best of me.

"Oh, Alice. This is not you."

"Go. Go now!"

"Alice?" Miranda's face slowly appeared around the doorjamb. "What on earth?"

I was relieved to see rescue.

Reza was exasperated. "Oh, for the love of God! Miranda, for the first time in your pointless life, will you please mind your own damned business?"

"Don't talk to her like that. She's been a good friend to me, and she is a resident of this house. You are neither. Now. For the hundredth time, leave, or this time I'm calling the police."

He backed away, hands up, and he started to walk out. "Yes, Alice, I forgot the cops are at your beck and call."

Miranda looked at him and then back at me in amazement.

"That would be correct," I quipped.

When I heard him drive off, I collapsed on the floor. All the shock and anger I had stored up inside me throughout the day accumulated into sheets of tears that spilled onto Miranda's shoulder. She held me tight on the old linoleum floor.

"What did he do?" she asked. "Cheat on you?"

"How did you know? Could you hear us arguing?"

"No, it wasn't that. I could just see the guilt all over his face."

109

"Rita."

"Alice? Hi."

"Hey. I wanted to let you know that I would like to speak at the initiative dinner."

"Oh—oh, *great!* Wonderful, wonderful, Alice. That's great. Thank you. What made you decide?"

"Don't even ask."

She chuckled. "One of those pesky situations. I understand."

I called Detective Holloway to tell him the same thing. He was so happy, I thought I heard tears in his voice at one point during our conversation. "You're not crying, are you?"

"No, no," he insisted. "I get some kind of allergy to grass this time of year, I think I told you that."

Allergy to grass. What a crock.

Reza continued to call nonstop. I was happy that my days were so full with tasks that I didn't have time to think about him or deal with him until the one day he finally came into the office. He informed me that Dr. Stephens would be moving up to northern Minnesota to work on a research project with some gray wolves and that he, Reza, would be taking over as executive director of the New Wellton Zoo and Conservation Center. Apparently, Kinsey Forman was stepping down from that position and leaving too.

This gave me pause to think. I went to Jean and told her that it would be brutally uncomfortable to work with Reza as a client since the breakup of our engagement. She couldn't have been more supportive since she had plans of her own, and I had more or less given her an opportunity to discuss them with me. Leah McGillis would be moving to Australia to be closer to her elderly parents who relocated to Sydney about ten years prior, and she would be doing some consulting work. Collins & McGillis, Inc. was being acquired by a huge firm, and Jean planned on moving to Florida to set up another small firm. She and Leah would be giving Kathleen, Shirl, and me a hefty severance that would make all of it worthwhile. The New Wellton Zoo could remain with the new firm or find somewhere else. That would be entirely up to Reza, the new executive director.

Kathleen and Denny were talking about marriage and were planning on moving out west. Lots of changes were happening, and I could feel the imaginary strings pulling me in a different direction in life. Everything was happening at once and coming together at the same time, clicking into place. I had good friends, and I would be writing lots of letters. There would be no more living in the past. I had once been punishing myself and making myself suffer for no reason. Marisa never left me and never would. Her spirit, her soul was so powerful that she could do things now that she wasn't capable of doing in life like Holloway said. She was a soul without the body. And I wasn't going to be covered in the dust of others as they moved forward with their lives and dreams. Marisa would not have wanted that. I truly understood that now.

When I pulled open the front door to Boochie's, I saw about twenty-five customers squeezed into the space in front of the counter and the lobster tank. The music was loud, and Aunt Nancy was sitting on the stool in front of the payphone. She looked like she had gained a little weight, but to me, that meant she was feeling a little more relaxed with herself. She craned her neck, and once she realized it was me, her face exploded into a giant grin. I motioned that I would be going around to the back where she met me right away.

"Who's that redheaded kid out front?" There appeared to be a new employee that reminded me of Dr. Paul Keating, the handsome redheaded freckled veterinarian who took care of Shelly all those years ago.

"That's Michael. Rudy hired him part-time. He's only seventeen, and he's such a sweet boy, unlike the other two."

"The other two?" I knew what was coming, and I shouldn't have even bothered to ask.

"Rudy and Scotty, that's who," she said with authority. "I thought Rudy and Frank caused trouble, but no—Rudy and Scotty nearly caused World War *III* in this room the other day." She shook her head in exasperation.

"It couldn't have been *that* bad."

"Damn right it was that bad. Rudy damned near killed me," Scotty called from the other room, obviously overhearing us.

"Oh, come on."

"It's true!"

Dad was running water on the other side of the wall. "Yeah, you would have nearly killed him too. He worked it out the other day that we had grossed sixteen million dollars in one week. One week."

"Now, lemme ask you somethin', Alice. Who wouldn't wanna make sixteen million dollars in one week? He threw his own dad's adding machine at me. He said he's gonna beat me over the head with it," Scotty said with a big grin.

Their arguing turned into the usual eruption of laughter. "He can't add! I leave him with a stack of receipts and a calculator, and he's useless! He tells me the other day we made sixteen million dollars in seven days—"

"That's good, man!" Scotty's giggle was contagious, and he ducked as my father lovingly slapped him on the side of the head.

"If only that were true!" He walked back into the store to keep young Mike from getting jammed up.

Nancy continued to shake her head back and forth. "They are so immature, Alice. They can be so embarrassing." She seemed proud of herself for being the adult in this situation.

I sighed and put my hands around her shoulders. "I know and you know when that's going to change?"

"Never."

"Never."

She rolled her eyes and walked back into the store. When it cleared out, my dad walked back into the office so I could speak to him privately.

"Well, Dad." I lifted my arms and then let them crash onto the side of my body. "I suppose it's a good thing that Scotty can't use an adding machine."

"A good thing?" He was exhausted again, and this time I noticed more gray hairs at the crown of his head and around his ears.

"Sure. Maybe I can take a load off in the office. I need a job."

His face cracked into a big *O*. I couldn't remember the last time he looked this happy.

I put my hands up. "It's not forever, Dad."

He was dancing now. "It doesn't matter. You own the place!" he exclaimed, looking around gleefully. "But what about Collins McGillis?"

"They're in the process of being acquired by a massive corporation out of New York. Both Jean and Leah are leaving, and I'm going to get to that in a minute, but first—I broke off my engagement to Reza."

He looked at me with sorrow in his eyes and pushed a stray hair out of my face. "Oh, honey. I'm so sorry."

Neither of us spoke as we both looked down at the floor for a moment.

"You're a grown woman, so I'm not even going to ask, but Allie, there was *something* about him, and I'm not sure what it was, but I never thought he was good enough for you."

Why did I think he was fibbing just to make me feel better?

"Neither did Frank."

That's not what Frank said in the hospital, but they were obviously trying to spare my feelings.

"He was highly educated and—"

"No." He waved a finger at me. "That's not it. He was too busy trying to be perfect at all times, trying to impress. I think he was sneaky. So did Frank."

"Well, this is just super." I smiled. "The two of you discussing my life. Poor Frank."

"May that old boy rest in peace." He smiled and opened his arms wide. "What else were we supposed to be doin' when you're not around?" He laughed again. "I just want what's best for you. You know that, right? Now. If Reza makes you happy—"

"He doesn't anymore."

"Well, okay. I want you to be happy. That's all. That's my dream now." He put his arms around me and squeezed hard. "Look at my girl, all grown up now. I gotta take some credit for this, don't I?"

"If you must," I said and grinned.

He looked at me with deep brown watery eyes then hugged me close again. "Now tell me something, what are you going to do with Winkles's sister, the crime writer, after your speech? Are you going to travel around the country with her or—"

"No," I said lightly. "She wants me to write a true crime book about my life, Dad, my story of surviving violence and conquering. Surviving. I'm going to write about Marisa and me and how I was able to survive and get through all the damage her murder caused. Because there are people out there who don't survive the damage, like her brother, for example."

He stood back. "Alice, are you serious?"

I nodded.

"Wow. This is something."

"Trouble is I can't string two sentences together. Marisa was really good at that kind of stuff."

He nodded. "Yes, she was."

"Rita will interview me, and we're planning to cowrite it together," I explained quietly. I didn't want anyone else to hear. "And that's for *your ears only* for now, okay?"

He put his hands on his face. "I am so unbelievably proud of you. I don't have words. I don't know what to say. I'm so glad you're gonna be here too, Allie," he whispered.

"Dad—"

"I know, I know. It won't be forever. But who knows, maybe I can *still* get you to change your mind."

We stood there, saying nothing.

Dad was the first to speak. "No matter where you go, Alice, or what you do or where you are, I will love you forever. Very, very much."

"I know you do, Dad. I know you do. I love you too."

* * * * *

When I looked through my closet for something to wear for the Wellton Impact USA Initiative Dinner, I realized that everything I owned were items I bought for work or dates I had gone on with Reza. I would definitely wear them again, just not for this.

It was a hot August afternoon when I went outside and heard Miranda bantering with Chick about something. It sounded funny, so I went to see what it was all about, even though I usually liked to avoid him at all costs.

Miranda was working on her PhD and was an assistant professor in the education department. Neither one of us ever moved from the shithole, as Chick himself called his own property, and had been there since our undergraduate years. I heard her say my name, so I walked over to his pickup to find out what they were talking about.

"Chick's bitching about the twenty-dollar cover to the Crime Impact event." She turned back to him. "That's the *least* you can do is not complain about twenty measly dollars. You're going to be getting all-you-can eat heavy hors d'oeuvres, you cheapskate."

"You were thinking of going?" I asked.

"Of course I was thinking of going. I remember that awful day. You were a brave little girl. That son of a bitch got everything he deserved. I was working at the Hotel St. Clare when that motherfucker got so drunk on a Christmas Eve, he kept pressing buttons in the elevator and got stuck. We had to dig him out."

"What a loser," Miranda said.

"I thought he got stuck in the shaft."

"Now that would have really sucked for him. He would have been dead twenty years ago," he said with a laugh. "Seventy-one, seventy-two. It was in the paper. Everything he did in those days made the paper."

"I only had a few tickets I gave to my dad, and—"

"Hey, I'll be there. Looking forward to hearing you speak. And don't listen to your friend here. As usual, she's taking everything out of context." He took off his shirt, exposing many of his tattoos and causing Miranda to make an *ick* sound. He laughed and walked toward a car that pulled up in front of the house.

"God, those tattoos are hideous. What was he thinking?" she said.

"Probably wasn't. Hey, do you want to go dress shopping with me? I need something new for the event. No, let me restate that. I want something new for the event."

We walked back toward the house. Miranda was beaming. She loved going shopping for clothing, shoes, and jewelry when she wasn't in her hippie phase. "There's a new boutique in Harbins owned by the same—"

"First of all, I'm not a size 6, and secondly, I don't have three hundred dollars to throw around."

She looked at me the way my aunt did when I was a teenager, just before she would examine my face for blackheads. "You don't have to be a size 6, and if there is anyone who can find a bargain, it is I. Oh, you know what? We should take Candace along so you can go and play with the dog first."

The mother I never had. Do I always give the impression of being a dependent adolescent? Though I was always happy to see Arturo, sweet guy was getting older. Like all of us.

I talked to myself over and over about Marisa, our relationship as I saw it, her murder, and the effect it had on my life and what I saw from those around me, the part of her ashes I kept for years and then finally dispersed along with Shelly's. That was a secret only Reza and I knew. When Reza heard about Crime Impact USA and my speaking, he called just like I knew he would. I told him I would prefer if he did not show up to the event. He promised me he would not but wished me all the best and went on and on a little too long about it. I was polite even though it was excruciating. Somehow I thought that telling him to go straight to hell would jinx my speech. But I had no control over him or anyone else. There was nothing that could stop him from buying a ticket just to piss me off. But I had so many positive things going on in my busy life, I couldn't and wouldn't worry about him anymore.

The Wellton Civic Center Auditorium was named after none other than Barton Withers I. The only thing that did was turbocharge me to the point where I felt as if I could run a marathon. As I peeked out, however, I listened to Rita's powerful words and crushing lead up to what used to be one of the most prominent names in the community. I saw her—Mary Jo then Danny sitting right next to her. How did she get the news all the way out in Colorado Springs? Probably from her frustrated elderly parents or even Helena.

There goes that lunatic Alice again twisting the truth about our poor son, my poor daddy who died such a horrible death. In prison! He never meant to hurt anyone. Please. Nina Averelle's discovered body blew that excuse right to hell.

Remembering the "if you can see them, they can see you" rule, I just peeked with one eye from the back. I noticed a woman next to Mary Jo on the other side. She was very pretty and looked a lot like Marisa. Her eyes were a huge bluish green, her hair was bright purple with blue streaks framing her face, and she had a sparkly piercing in her nose. I realized suddenly it was Kay Schuester, Mary Jo's niece and Lil's daughter. She dressed my and Marisa's hair all those years ago in Northrington. The Withers wanted to send her to medical school, but she moved to New York City to become a hairdresser instead, blemishing the family name and becoming disowned.

Everyone showed up. Aubrey, Aubrey's mother, Walter, and Walter's mother, who flew up from Florida, were all sitting together. Candace and Miranda sat next to Walter. Dad was flanked by Scotty and Tommy and Aunt Nancy on the other side. Once again, I felt as though I needed to have a discussion with my aunt prior to an important event. I mentioned to her that the police, Rita, some others, and I would be covering some violent and unpleasant topics, and if she needed to excuse herself, she could take a long walk down the comfy carpeted corridor. Once again she put her hands on my face and said, "Alice. Your dad told me the same thing, but it sounded so much better when you told me. Thanks for trying to save my life." She kissed me on both cheeks. I took that to mean she would be attending, and she would be fine.

Jean Collins and her husband came, Shirl was there with an older gentlemen, Kathleen and Denny were there, Leah McGillis brought a date. I recognized some people from my college years and a bunch of Dad's customers. Bunic and Bunica sat up front. The three people who didn't show up were my mother, who had apparently moved to London with some new rich guy with an *Esq.* next to his name, my little sister Helena, and Reza. I was grateful. The three who were there were Shelly, Frank, and of course, Marisa. And knowing her, she probably wondered if I would be nervous and trip over my tongue like the chicken that I was.

Not tonight, Marisa. Not tonight. This one is for you.

As the sound of applause filled the air, Rita spotted me. "Not nervous, are you?"

"No, surprisingly not at all. And you sounded wonderful, if that's even the right word. Not a dry eye out there."

"Well, that happens. But these emotions motivate people to get the right things done," she said. "You have important work to do. I'm so glad you're here, Alice. Good luck."

I nodded. "Me too. Thank you."

Detective Holloway talked about Wellton, its crime rate, again how most murders are committed by people one knows, that fateful day. Two girls. Alice and Marisa. He told the audience an officer found me under my bed, terrified, and he talked about how far I had come over the years without giving away anything I would address in my question and answer.

"Ladies and gentlemen," he began, "without keeping you waiting any further, may I have the honor and privilege of introducing Wellton's Alice Buchner."

About the Author

Andrea Landy was born and raised in Syracuse, New York. She received her degree in psychology from Alfred University and also studied creative writing, French horn, and classical piano. Shortly after finishing college, Andrea worked extensively in mental health including vocational rehabilitation, chemical dependency, and activity and group therapies. She was a prolific traveler and had lived in both Europe and the United Kingdom for a time. She had written newsletters for several different organizations and had also compiled a collection of poetry.

Eager to see America, Andrea got her commercial driver's license and spent two and a half years in an 18-wheeler, exploring the lower forty-eight states and documenting her journeys. Andrea currently lives with her husband of over thirty years, a dog, two cats, and a parrot.

Milton Keynes UK
Ingram Content Group UK Ltd.
UKHW011033250424
441751UK00001B/59